EXOSKELETON IV

REVENANT

THE EXOSKELETON SERIES

SHANE STADLER

Shane Stadler Enterprises

1

AWAKENING

THE LIGHT WAS TOO BRIGHT.

He was flat on his back, and he couldn't keep his eyes open. The floor was cool and smooth on his bare skin. All was silent.

He rolled to his side, and then to his hands and knees. He forced his eyes open just long enough to get a blurry glimpse of his hands on the white floor.

He rose to one knee, forced his torso upright, and then wobbled to keep his balance as he stood.

After a few failed attempts he was able to keep his eyes open but quickly became disoriented. It seemed as if he were suspended in an infinite white space.

A few seconds later, his vision adjusted. He was in a room the size of a colossal airplane hangar. All the surfaces were white, and light seemed to emanate uniformly from every direction.

He took in a deep breath through his nose and exhaled through his mouth. The air was brisk and fresh, like that of early spring above melting snow.

His body felt as if he'd spent days crammed inside a crate, and his feet ached. He clenched his hands and stretched his arms as he walked in a circle, trying to decide in which direction to go.

He had no idea where he was, or how he'd gotten there.

It then occurred to him that he had no idea *who* he was.

He then spoke aloud in a voice he recognized, but he did not know from where the words came. "I promise."

He contemplated his spontaneous utterance for a few seconds, but then gave up on what it meant and turned his attention to his surroundings.

The ceiling was high – like that of a sports arena – and the air was still. His nostrils dilated as he took in another deep breath of cool air, and his brain livened. He looked down at his body. He was naked.

"Hello?" he yelled.

The only response was the echo of his voice.

He padded toward the nearest wall, calling out and turning periodically as he examined the surrounding space.

After about 150 yards, he reached the far end of the cavernous room and encountered a large arched doorway. He passed through it and into a cylindrical room that was about 20 feet in diameter with a domed ceiling that was nearly 15 feet high at its center. Every surface was white, and the space was brightly illuminated. Along the perimeter to the right of the entrance were a half-dozen sinks and four doors that he suspected led to bathroom stalls. On the wall opposite the entrance was a computer screen and a large flat mirror that extended from the floor to a height of about eight feet. There was a long bench in front of the mirror.

He went to the wall with the computer screen and examined his image in the mirror. His body was thickly muscled and well-proportioned. His eyes were dark blue. His face and body looked familiar, but something was wrong.

He put his hands on his perfectly smooth head. It seemed to him that he should've had hair. High on his forehead, where the hairline should have been, were two round scars, one to the far left and the other to the far right. Each was about a centimeter in diameter, and slightly pinker and shinier than the surrounding skin. He examined his arms and legs – again, perfectly smooth.

He twitched as the computer screen came to life with images of safety goggles, helmets, boots, and gloves, and then clothing items including shoes, pants, shirts, and undergarments. With his finger, he selected items from the clothing category. A beam of green light suddenly projected from the mirror and scanned his body. A few seconds later, a drawer rolled out of the wall to the right of the mirror. He went to it and extracted white garments and shoes. The drawer then disappeared seamlessly into the wall.

He set everything on the bench and then examined the items one by one. It looked like everything would fit. He donned the clothes and slipped on the shoes, which had no laces.

Everything was snug but fit perfectly. The fabric was light, smooth, and comfortable, and the shoes were tight but soft, and had soles that had good traction on the floor.

As he stared at his now-clothed image in the mirror, a clear thought emerged from a shadowy place in his consciousness.

"I'm Will," he said. "I am William Thompson."

DENISE WALKER LOCKED her bicycle in the rack next to the law building and made her way to the main entrance. As she approached, a male student opened one of the large glass doors from the inside and exited. She lowered her head as a blast of warm air hit her face and almost ripped off her knit hat. As the student passed, she stepped inside just as the door closed.

The warm air inside carried a familiar concoction of scents: old books, floor wax, coffee, and a faint undertone of pipe tobacco. The smells brought about a feeling of comfort, but also reminded her of recent events that would haunt her for the rest of her life.

She pulled off her red hat and black wool gloves and stuffed them into her coat pockets. She then put the backs of her hands on her cheeks to warm them as she climbed a long flight of marble stairs to the second floor. Winter seemed to be arriving early in Chicago, and the long-term weather forecasters predicted snow before the end of October. That gave her three weeks to get a car – something she'd been putting off since resuming her old job. "Old job" wasn't quite correct: she'd been promoted to a new position but was doing the same work.

It was a few minutes after 8:00 a.m. when she knocked on Jonathan McDougal's office door and stepped inside. Coffee was brewing.

Jonathan looked up from his seat behind a large wooden desk near the wall opposite the entrance. In his 60s, he was still a vibrant man, and his brown but graying hair and beard made him look his part as a distinguished professor in the law school. "Your cheeks look nice and rosy," he said and laughed.

"Not funny," she said as she peeled off her backpack and set it at her feet, and then removed her black wool coat and hung it on a coat rack next to the door. "That wind is awful."

"Even worse on a bike, I'd guess," Jonathan added. "I told you I'd help you find a car."

"I know," she said. "I've just been too busy –"

"Nonsense," he interrupted. "You're working too hard. You haven't rested since we got back."

She didn't want to rest. She wanted to forget.

"You're trying to distract yourself," Jonathan continued. "You won't be able to do that forever, you know."

"I want to see his parents," Denise said as she followed Jonathan to a cluster of furniture on the far end of his large office. She settled in on a couch as he sat on the edge of an upholstered chair across a coffee table from her and poured coffee from a carafe into two porcelain mugs.

"I think it's a bit premature for that," he said. "We should give it a little more time."

"The US Navy has been searching the area for over two weeks," Denise argued. "The tunnel is completely collapsed, and the base is destroyed – it's gone."

"Will is not a normal person, Denise."

Her hope was waning, but Jonathan was right. She'd keep her erratic hopefulness alive but buried. Buried in work.

"I'm going to a mental health facility in Anna this week to check on another victim of the Compressed Punishment Program," she said, already looking forward to making the long drive to Southern Illinois. "He was set up – just like Will."

"Tell me," Jonathan said as he leaned back and warmed his hands on his mug.

"The man robbed a liquor store, and prosecutors later connected him to two bank robberies – he was convicted," she explained. "He admitted to the liquor store, but there's exonerating evidence for both bank jobs."

"Let me guess," he said. "You think those crimes were pinned on him to make him more amenable to the Compressed Punishment option."

She nodded.

"Sounds like it will be a quick case," he said.

"I don't know," she said. "He'll have to testify, and he's pretty damaged. He'd been in the Red Box for over 100 days when it was finally shut down."

"You mean when Will blasted a gigantic hole in the building."

"The man might never recover, but this will be for his family," she explained. "He has a wife and two daughters."

"Sounds like a good project," Jonathan said.

Although none of the cases were easy, the DNA Foundation, where she was now a full-fledged associate rather than just an intern, had overturned nearly a hundred Compressed Punishment cases in the past four months. Each had ended with the complete exoneration of the victim, and a substantial monetary settlement.

But Jonathan was right: she was only trying to distract herself. It was a case that would be neither challenging nor exciting. But she'd press through it, along with two other, less promising cases she'd been assigned. After those were completed, she might take a few weeks to explore other things.

For one, she'd reconsider the offer from the Omniscients. They'd proposed that she go work for them just a few days after she and Jonathan had gotten back to Chicago. But the Omnis were more bookworms than action players. Although, she admitted, the events of the past months forced them out of their warm cocoons and into less friendly environments. And Antarctica was the definition of "less friendly" in her mind.

She grabbed a tissue from her purse and wiped her nose, which was still recovering from the chilly bike ride, and took a sip of coffee.

"What are you doing today?" she asked.

"They have me slated to teach a class in the spring semester, so I'll get started on that," he explained. "But I have to catch up on a lot of DNA Foundation work. The interim director was a bit disorganized."

It was hard to imagine Jonathan going back to his old life after what had happened during the past year.

"Do you often think about what happened?" she asked.

"Constantly," he replied without hesitation. "It all seems like a dream. You?"

"I can't stop thinking about it, either," she replied. She felt a tear welling in the corner of her eye and grabbed another tissue from her purse and dabbed it. "I can't concentrate on anything. I can build up enough motivation to help others in trouble – like the Compressed Punishment victims – but not for anything else. Everything else seems meaningless."

Jonathan took a swig of coffee and leaned forward as he set his cup on the table. "It's going to take some time for you to settle. It's always tough after a loss – "

"It's not a loss," she cut him off. Now she was the one trying to remain positive. She flip-flopped regularly. "Not yet."

"I agree," he said. "But you should be prepared. It's something that might never be resolved."

She knew that they weren't going to find Will in Antarctica. He was either buried under kilometers of ice, or he'd been transported to some unknown place light-years away. Either way, Jonathan was right: she'd have to come to her senses.

"I'm just trying to remain optimistic," she said.

Jonathan grunted and stood. "I'm off to an impromptu meeting with the dean of the law school," he said. "It always means she has something for me to do. What are you doing today?"

"In my office all day – researching my case and arranging the meeting in Southern Illinois," she replied.

"You had quite a scare the last time you were down there," Jonathan reminded her.

"I know," she said. People had died, and she'd almost been one of them. "I don't expect much excitement this time."

She followed Jonathan out of his office, and they parted ways.

Denise walked to her office a few doors down, unlocked the door, and went inside. She hung her jacket on a coat rack, and then unloaded a stack of files from her backpack and set it on a weathered wooden desk. Her office was more organized than usual. That was because it was all she could get herself to do beyond her routine case research. Her thoughts were elsewhere. They were with Will, wherever he was.

Whenever her memory of his face would wane, she'd find his photo from his original case file and take a glimpse at it. If she looked at it too long, however, it seemed that its power would fade. A glance was enough to reset the image in her mind.

Denise pulled the photo out of her desk, took a look, and put it away. It would be enough to get her through the day.

WILL STARED at his image in the mirror.

The familiarity of the eyes that stared back at him prompted incompletely formed memories. Different faces and events flashed through his mind, but it was like recognizing someone in an airport and not knowing their name or recalling where you'd seen them before.

He knew his name, although he wasn't convinced that it was correct.

As he stepped closer to the mirror, a dreamlike scene flashed into his mind: he was pointing a gun at his own head.

He mulled it over for a few seconds.

"Am I dead?" he asked aloud.

He shivered and massaged his forearms with his hands as he contemplated his words. Of course he wasn't dead. He was there – moving, feeling, *thinking*.

A gurgling sound came from beneath his shirt simultaneously with a burning sensation in his gut. He was hungry.

Will exited the small chamber and went back into the main room. He noticed now that the ceiling was higher at the center – maybe 150 feet – and was curved like that of an enormous aircraft hangar – like those used to assemble airliners. By his estimate, there'd be room to work on a dozen of them simultaneously.

As his vision improved, and the light sensitivity waned, he noticed structure on the outer perimeter of the room. There were dozens of openings – doorways. Some were the size of the one which led to the chamber where he'd gotten his clothes. Others were much larger – the size of train tunnels. As he approached the center of the enormous bay, he turned left, and then continued toward one of the larger openings.

While still 50 meters away, he noticed that the interior of the passageway beyond the entrance was lit in the same white light as that in the main room. He increased his pace to a slow jog, but immediately reduced it to a modest walk as his calves tightened like knotted rope. It would take some time for everything to loosen up.

He stopped at the square opening, which was even larger than he'd anticipated at about 10 meters on a side. It led to a corridor with a noticeable upward grade, and he could not see the end of it.

It was a good place to start.

IT HAD BEEN over two weeks since they'd returned from the Southern Seas, and Daniel Parsons knew they'd never go back. The base had been destroyed, flooded, and frozen.

It was a brisk Monday morning, and Daniel sipped hot tea as he looked out over the pine forest from his seventh-floor office in the Space Systems building. The overcast sky looked like it might produce snow, but it was still too warm for that. Although 45 degrees was a stark contrast to the mid-80s they'd had just a few weeks prior, Washington, DC rarely saw snow in early October.

Since returning from Antarctica, Daniel had immersed himself in his duties of directing the *Omniscients,* the elite CIA research group with unlimited, or "Omniscient," clearance. He was having some difficulty, however, prioritizing projects for the Omnis since nothing seemed urgent to him. After barely averting global destruction just weeks ago, nothing on his current project list met the threshold that classified it as critical.

He shook his head and sighed. It made him think of William Thompson.

A light knock at the door pulled him from his thoughts. He turned to find Sylvia Barnes standing in the doorway with a white porcelain mug dangling from her finger. Her brown hair, which reached the middle of her neck, had remnants of fading black and red hair dye that extended a couple of inches above the ends. He wondered what colors she'd choose next.

"Tea?" she asked and tapped her cup. She adjusted her dark-rimmed glasses and smiled broadly. She was wearing jeans, a black T-shirt, orange socks, and no shoes.

Daniel nodded and pointed her to a tin on a shelf near the door.

She grabbed the can and brought it to a coffee table in front of a worn-out couch. She pried off the lid with her fingertips and scooped out English breakfast tea with a stainless-steel tea ball. She then padded over to Daniel, and he poured hot water into her cup from an electric tea kettle. The aromas of the tea and Sylvia's peach shampoo filled his senses.

"When is Jacob arriving?" she asked.

She was referring to Jacob Hale, the nephew of Horace Leatherby, the late director of the Omni group. "He'll be back from London today," he replied.

"Will he still operate from Horace's old place?" she asked.

"To start with," he replied. "But I don't think 17 Swann will be his permanent home. It seems he's reconciled with his girlfriend, and she'll be returning from the UK in the spring."

Sylvia extracted the tea ball and set it on a porcelain saucer on the windowsill near the tea kettle. She took a noisy sip and glanced outside. "What's the status of the drawings?"

He knew she was referring to the blueprints of the alien Antarctic base. A few months ago, Jacob had extracted the drawings from an encrypted radio signal originating from deep space. "Linguists and ciphers specialists are working on the language," he replied. "And engineers and scientists will continue to study the technical plans. But the overall efforts have been reduced to less than ten percent of what they were just a few weeks ago."

"They're not urgent anymore?" she asked in a tone of annoyance.

Daniel shrugged. It was a point of contention. He felt the situation was not as critical as before their brush with global destruction, but that was no reason to reduce the effort. In fact, he thought more resources should be allocated to studying them. Although he was no longer concerned about an extraterrestrial attack – it still seemed odd to even consider the idea – he now worried that their Earth-bound foes might gain some advantage by learning something important from the drawings – something that was a game changer militarily, or otherwise. And, even though he was almost certain other nations didn't currently have the drawings in their possession, he knew they'd get them eventually.

American relations with China and Russia had never been worse. The CIA had taken down an entire Chinese intelligence network, and William Thompson had destroyed a Russian special ops group – over 40 men – at the Nazi base. In addition, a Chinese reconnaissance group had been lost when the ice around the base had melted and, just a few months prior, Will had disabled a Chinese aircraft carrier, killing many of its crew.

"How's your project coming along?" Daniel asked, wanting to divert from the subject that had dominated his thoughts every waking moment.

"Following up on recent UFO sightings is interesting, but it's a little different knowing that they're real – or at least that some of them are," she said. "It's a bit unnerving."

"Have there been any verified sightings since the spacecraft left?" he asked. He was referring to the events of two weeks prior, when strange objects had positioned themselves around the Earth and sent thousands of probes to the surface.

She shook her head. "Still some reports, but they're continually being debunked."

After the objects vanished, the populaces of the world had been informed by their respective governments that what they had seen was just a test of a new GPS and weather observation system developed by an international group of scientists and engineers. The story had then been extended to admit that the test had been a failure, but that more experiments were scheduled in the future.

And the ruse was working. As far as Daniel could tell, for the average citizen, not a thing in the world had changed. For him, however, the world would never be the same.

JACOB HALE HAD SPENT the last two weeks in London with his girlfriend, Paulina Erikkson, getting her up to speed on everything that had happened to him, and to her, during the past months, minus the classified details.

It had all started with his late uncle – Theodore Horace Leatherby – bequeathing nothing to Jacob in his will. That wasn't quite correct: Uncle Theo had given him a book. At the time, however, it had been both unexpected and disappointing that Jacob hadn't been given anything from the multibillion-dollar estate to help him along in life. Surprisingly, what happened instead seemed to be quite the opposite of helping him along.

Uncle Theo had arranged for Jacob to be fired from his engineering job at Interstellar Dynamics, and then had frozen all his bank accounts and credit. He'd then arranged to relocate Pauli to London, nearly destroying their relationship in the process. But now, Jacob realized, it had all been for good reason.

Months ago, at the reading of the will, Jacob had received two keys. At the time, he'd figured they opened a safe deposit box that held the book, which he'd originally had no interest in collecting. But it turned out that the keys had led to so much more.

First, the book was a top-secret monograph that revealed a thread of history that was hidden from the rest of the world. But it was more than just history. That thread had led to the present, and had "existential consequences," as his uncle had put it. Second, the keys gave Jacob access to a secret facility at 17 Swann St. NW No. 4, in Washington, DC. It was Uncle Theo's home base of operations. His uncle had been the head of a secret group of CIA researchers called the *Omniscients*. Theo had led a secret life of espionage and adventure. And now, so would Jacob.

Two weeks ago, the Omniscients had extended an offer to Jacob to join them. He accepted without hesitation, although both the offer and his acceptance still had to be formalized in writing. It seemed to him that he'd been groomed for the job ever since moving in with Uncle Theo's family at age 12, after his parents were murdered. He was told that the pay would be far better than what it had been at Interstellar Dynamics, but the money wasn't important to him. He'd do it for nothing if he could sustain the basic life essentials – food and shelter.

He'd remain at 17 Swann at least until he settled into his new job. After that, it depended on what Pauli wanted when she returned from London, but that wouldn't be for another six months.

After landing at Dulles International Airport in Washington, DC, Jacob took a cab to the Count Cristo Coffee House on Swann Street, a few blocks north of his final destination. He was never to be linked to 17 Swann, and that meant he'd always arrange to be dropped off somewhere else and then take a meandering path to the facility. He'd traveled light – only a backpack – so the coffee house was a nice place to start. He'd left some clothes in London, but Pauli would have to bring those back with her since he'd not be going back – something of which she was unaware.

The place was busy for 10:00 a.m. on a Monday morning, mainly filled with pensioners and a large group of women that, as he gathered from eavesdropping on their conversation, was a book club meeting. The strong aromas of fresh coffee mixed with the softer smells of pastries made him feel like he was home again.

He ordered a medium-roast coffee and took the white porcelain mug to a table overlooking the corner of Swann and its cross street. He opened his laptop and logged into his email account. There were 12 new emails since he'd boarded his British Airways flight at Heathrow.

One was from Pauli. She wished him luck with his new job – although she was uninformed of the details – and told him that she couldn't wait for Thanksgiving. She was to fly home for the holiday, and they'd go to her parents' place in North Carolina. Jacob missed her already. He wrote a short reply and then went to the other emails on the list.

There was one from Interstellar Dynamics informing him of the details of his recent termination. He was surprised to learn that he was to receive a modest severance package that amounted to six months of his salary. Another email was from the law firm of Watts, Turk, and Genobli – the firm that had employed the late Jody Dixon, the lawyer who had managed Uncle Theo's estate until she was brutally murdered just weeks ago. They wanted to set up a meeting. It intrigued him, but he felt no urgency to move quickly.

The most important email, however, was from Space Systems – the CIA – that gave him the details of his upcoming employment orientation. He'd have numerous training sessions and would undergo an extensive background check – even though his entire life had been under the close watch of his uncle, the head of the Omniscients.

He took a sip of coffee and gazed out the window. It was a chilly, overcast day, and he watched as a mail carrier crossed the street and deposited a handful of paper products into the mailbox of a local antiques store.

He took a deep breath and sighed. This was the first time in weeks that he'd been able to relax. Even his time in London with Pauli had been taxing at times. He'd had to answer her unrelenting questions about what had happened during the previous weeks with a delicate balance of facts and vague details. He couldn't tell her everything. She didn't know about 17 Swann, the Omniscients, William Thompson, or that the human race had been on the verge of extermination. It was something he'd have to get used to – leading a secret life and knowing things that he could never convey to those outside the circle of Omnis. He now had a better understanding of the life Uncle Theo had led. Jacob was going to follow the same path.

His thoughts were interrupted by a voice.

"It's a little early for you, isn't it?" asked a blonde woman in her late 20s.

It was Cally, the owner of the Count Cristo Coffee House. She wore a red apron over a T-shirt and jeans, and her hair was pulled back in a tight ponytail. She added, "I haven't seen you in a while – it's been a month, at least."

"I've been out of town," he said.

"Oh?" she said. "Business or pleasure?"

"A little of each," he replied. If only she knew he'd been at an alien base in Antarctica for some of that time. "The fun part was London – just got back this morning."

"Welcome back. Hopefully we'll see more of you now," she said as she picked up some empty cups and a newspaper from another table. "You want the paper?"

Jacob nodded.

"Have a nice day," she said as she set the *New York Times* on his table and went back to the main counter.

Jacob flipped the newspaper to the front page and examined the headlines. It was election season, so most of the articles were connected to politics. However, there was one story on renewed interest in the search for extraterrestrial life inspired by the surge of sightings that had occurred a few weeks ago. He'd encountered similar stories in *The Guardian* while he'd been in the UK.

It was clear that the governments of the world had successfully misguided and convinced their citizens that the many hundreds of mysterious objects seen around the planet were part of a sophisticated international weather monitoring system. It reminded him of how the Roswell incident in New Mexico had been explained away as the crashing of a weather balloon.

One effect of the event, however, was that donations flooded into the SETI Institute after the sightings. The Search for Extraterrestrial Intelligence organization used existing instruments – various space and ground-based telescopes and detectors – to search for potential life in the universe. They'd also been involved in space missions such as the New Horizons mission to Pluto. Their outreach component was designed to inform the public of their activities, progress, and discoveries.

A windfall of tens of millions of dollars had flowed into SETI's coffers in just two weeks, and they promised that the majority of it would be used to purchase time on telescopes and other instruments in various parts of the world, and in space. Jacob thought that was a good thing, and that the governments of the world should follow and increase their efforts in looking outward.

He folded the newspaper and put it on the table, took his cup to the counter, said goodbye to Cally, and walked out into the cool morning air. He was off to 17 Swann Street NW, No. 4.

WILL ENTERED the passage and examined the walls and ceiling as he trekked forward. All the surfaces were smooth and white – no features of any kind. The tunnel did not curve, but there was a slight upward grade.

After about 150 yards the corridor leveled, and he spotted the end another 50 yards ahead. His body was already warm from the activity, and his deep breathing stretched the stiff muscles between his ribs.

The walking elevated his heart rate and seemed to loosen his tight tendons and joints. He felt much better.

A minute later, he stood at the end of the passage and stared at a square inset that was nearly as wide as the tunnel. He hoped it was a door, but it looked like a dead end.

A grumbling sound came from his stomach, and he became light-headed for an instant. He was famished and felt dehydrated. He needed to get water and something to eat, soon.

Assuming it was a door, he searched the perimeter of the inset for a button or other mechanism that would open it but found nothing. He turned around and peered back down the corridor. *What would be the purpose of a long passageway that led to nowhere?* he thought.

He reached into the inset to touch the surface where he thought a door handle should have been and jumped backward before realizing what had caused his reaction. The panel had split in the middle and separated in an instant. It made no mechanical noise except for the sound of rushing air.

The opening was nearly as large as the corridor and, after he stepped through it, he froze in awe as his mind tried to sort out what he was seeing on the other side.

Is it a city?

Video screens and bright signs were everywhere, and the ambient illumination seemed like afternoon sunlight. It was like a cross between a high-tech city and an amusement park. Directly ahead of him was a walkway that resembled that of the ground floor of a colossal shopping mall. It looked like a boulevard with islands in the center on which were trees and bushes. Kiosks were scattered along the walkway that seemed to be offering goods for sale, although he couldn't tell what they were selling. To the left and right were structures that resembled buildings – 70 or 80 stories tall – extending down the boulevard as far as he could see, which he figured was over a kilometer. The "buildings" looked to be continuous edifices with no gaps, and therefore there were no side streets.

Stacked on the exteriors of each building were tiers of open floors with exposed walkways and railings, like in multi-level shopping malls.

Looking upward, above the street and between the buildings, was the sky. He was confused. It was black, even though it seemed like the sun was shining on the street.

There were no people, and there was no movement of any kind, except for the flashing and animations on countless video screens, which made the place look like a cross between Times Square and Las Vegas.

He listened intently. The only thing he heard was rushing water, and he followed the sound to an enormous fountain far down the boulevard. It was in the center of a small pond with purple-flowered bushes around it. He caught the faint scent of lilacs.

He turned his attention to the second level of the building to his right. It had a walkway with a railing on the side that overlooked the mall below, and what seemed to be business establishments deeper in the interior, with bright advertisement signs. One read "Mexican Cuisine," and another read "Athletics Facility." It was all arranged like shops in a mall.

A few hundred meters down the boulevard were horizontal catwalks that spanned the space over the street, connecting the buildings on each side, and angled ramps that provided access to adjacent levels.

Where in the hell am I? he wondered.

"Hello? Anyone here?" he yelled and waited for a response. He listened for a few seconds before yelling again. No reply.

He stepped toward the mall and flinched as the door to the passage closed behind him with a rush of air.

As he proceeded toward the mall floor – the "street" – he admired bushes and flowers in the center island. He passed a couple of benches and kiosks, the latter of which seemed to offer products of some kind but there were no people running them. To his left and right on the ground level were offices and shops behind glass – all of which were lit and looked open for business.

He peered through some of the windows and, again, no people.

His eyes were drawn back to the dark ceiling, some 80 stories above him. He focused on small points of white light that speckled the black.

They were stars.

There was something odd – he couldn't take his eyes away from them. A few seconds later, it hit him.

The stars were moving.

WANG "JIMMY" Yong stared out the window of the SUV as it rolled down Van Ness St. NW past the Israeli embassy, turned right onto International Drive NW, and stopped next to a large gray-white brick building on the left.

His driver waited as a set of motorized iron gates swung open, and then pulled the vehicle up a short drive, past stacks of wooden pallets, and into the building's interior loading dock area. A large rolling door rumbled closed behind them, and the driver turned off the engine. The front-seat passenger got out and opened the door for Yong, who was sitting in the seat behind him.

Yong grabbed his briefcase and stepped out of the SUV onto the stained concrete floor of a dimly lit loading dock that smelled of garbage with a faint hint of gasoline. He'd always imagined that his first visit to the Chinese embassy in Washington, DC would have been more glamorous. But this visit was meant to be secret.

The night before, Yong had flown in from San Francisco, where the weather had been much nicer, and spent a sleepless night in a modest hotel in Gaithersburg, Maryland. The pair of Chinese operatives had picked him up in the morning and shuttled him to the embassy behind darkly tinted windows. His fingers tingled as he anticipated what this was about.

He thought maybe he was getting a promotion of some kind: he'd been doing well leading the intelligence efforts in Silicon Valley. It was a place that was ripe with fruit – intellectual property that ranged from industry to space to defense – and Yong had overseen the harvesting of much of it. Just six months ago, he'd been rewarded with an intelligence medal for his efforts. It was good progress for a professional who had just broken 40 years of age.

His escorts led him through a labyrinth of corridors, put him through the usual security protocols, and delivered him to an office where they introduced him to two men whom he'd never met before, both in their 50s. They were upper-echelon administrators, but both appeared to be physically rougher than the usual bureaucrats. They looked like former military. The Chinese Ministry for State Security, or MSS, often employed such people in its paramilitary wing, but these men did not reveal their roles within the agency.

Three hours later, he was in the back seat of the SUV heading toward a safe house in Alexandria, Virginia. He had to put forth great effort to not vomit along the way. He didn't know whether the queasiness came from what he'd been shown, or from the realization that his cushy life in sunny California was over.

One thing Yong did know, however, was that the world was going to become a very different place in the months to come.

JACOB MEANDERED through a maze of residential side streets before cutting through a cozy children's park back to Swann Street. He walked between the gray stone building at 17 Swann and its red-brick neighbor to the right, stepped onto the stoop of the former, and inserted a silver cylindrical key into the keyhole of the building's enormous wooden door.

The key vibrated, and the door slowly pivoted on hidden hinges on its right, exposing its left edge.

Jacob pulled out the key, reached his left hand around the edge, and found a groove with the tips of his fingers. He pulled the door open, stepped into a dark foyer, and then pulled the door inward until its automatic closing mechanism engaged. From the inside, the door was exposed for what it really was: a thick, steel vault door. The wood on its exterior was just a veneer.

On the wall to his left when facing away from the entrance was a three-by-three array of small square doors, each about 12 inches on a side with a number on its face. He inserted a small brass key into the keyhole of door #4, and opened it. Inside was a thick envelope that he suspected contained his new employment paperwork.

He closed the safe box, went to the elevator door opposite the entrance, and inserted a gold-plated cylindrical key into a circular keyhole on the wall to its right. The door opened, and he stepped inside, inserted the brass key into a slot labeled with a "4," and twisted. A green light illuminated above the key, the door closed, and the elevator moved. It went through its usual rotations and translations and stopped a minute later.

He stepped out of the elevator and its door clanked closed behind him. Lights automatically energized and illuminated the room. For a few seconds, he stared at the three floors of bookshelves that filled the entire wall opposite the elevator. He then turned his gaze upward to the massive wooden crossbeams and then to the two skylights, one in the center of the room and the other on the far end, to his right, above a furnished loft on the third level. A long library table on the bottom level stood on a burgundy runner rug that spanned the full 100-foot length of the marble-tiled floor.

He went to the library table, placed the envelope upon it, and then set his backpack on the floor and took a seat in a high-backed wooden chair. He took a deep breath and sighed as he tilted his head back and spotted a white cloud through the nearest skylight.

What he'd experienced during the past weeks had changed him. A part of him wanted to fall asleep and never awaken. But there was another part – a stronger one – that wanted to know more. He'd been trained to reverse engineer complex devices collected through espionage. He now had blueprints of devices that were advanced far beyond anything developed by humanity. He had enough puzzles to keep him occupied for a hundred lifetimes.

Two recent events had profoundly changed his view of the world. The first was the direct evidence of extraterrestrial spacecraft navigating Earth and the surrounding space. Everyone – the military,

NASA, and the CIA – was completely convinced that they were real, and that they defied known physics. The second was his direct observation of a human being separating his soul from his body. He was now in the very room where, just a few weeks ago, Will Thompson's soul had suspended him in midair.

Jacob stood, grabbed the thick envelope, and went to a desk beneath the loft on the side of the room opposite the bookshelves. He found a letter opener in a drawer and cut the top flap, and then went back to the table and spread its contents on the surface. The first item was a two-page offer letter from the Office of the Director of the CIA. It explained the job requirements and compensation.

He stared at the salary figure in disbelief. He was now going to be making as much as Pauli – who was getting the salary of a junior partner in a premier law firm – and he was guaranteed an eight percent raise every year, along with step promotions and possible bonuses. It was clear that they wanted to remove money as a motive for seeking another job, or selling out. Being an Omni was a lifetime appointment, and Omnis were subject to certain conditions even if they resigned. For one, they could never again leave the continental US. Such a restriction could be overridden, however, in the case of official business – like going to Antarctica. However, he'd not be going back to London to visit Pauli.

A separate letter gave him permission to maintain his presence at 17 Swann indefinitely – for official and private business. By "private" it was meant that he could continue to live there. It then explained the ownership and management of the place. The land and building were part of a trust. All maintenance and services were funded through an endowment that would keep the place running in perpetuity. The way it was managed was complex, but it was done in a way that kept access to the building secure, and its function secret. If the "resident" didn't want to let anyone inside to do anything – clean, fix things, and the like – no one could get inside. There was only one set of keys.

It got him wondering about the functions of other parts of the building. There were eight other safe boxes in the foyer, and many other buttons in the elevator. It was something he'd explore when he had some time.

The remaining forms were releases for "dangerous duty" and background checks. He figured the latter had already been done but signed it anyway. He was also required to get a full set of vaccinations that covered "uncommon ailments" related to obscure diseases and bioweapons. Finally, he'd have to participate in weeks of training that involved the handling of classified information, surveillance and avoidance, firearms and explosives training, self-defense training, and physical fitness. He'd welcome the final item; he was an avid runner, but his fitness routine had been disrupted during the past few weeks.

He spent the next half hour reading through the documents, signing and initialing where indicated, and then placed the items back into the envelope. The papers could be returned via the same safe box in the building's foyer. Evidently, there was a lever inside the box that could be set to indicate outgoing mail.

Uncle Theo had thought of everything. The place was completely self-contained and self-sufficient. Once he got settled, he'd never have to leave.

His training started the day after next.

WILL STARED at the stars as they drifted overhead, all moving along the same line, nearly parallel to the street.

He then lowered his gaze to the brightly colored lights flickering as far down the mall as he could see. It was like he was on the main street of some futuristic city. Those familiar places flashed again in his mind, Times Square and Las Vegas, and it seemed that memories were coming back to him, although they were fragmented and hazy.

His stomach grumbled again, and his throat felt dry and scratchy. About 150 feet down the center of the mall, between two tall oak trees, was a kiosk. He went to it.

As he approached, a voice startled him and a large screen on its exterior came to life.

"Hello," the voice said, as a cartoon image of a young woman appeared. "I'm Pira, how can I help you?"

Her voice and demeanor were bubbly and pleasant. She had shoulder-length black hair and large dark eyes. She was dressed in a sky-blue tank top, white shorts, and sandals. There were sunglasses on top of her head, and she wore a braided bracelet. It was like she was on a warm beach somewhere. It seemed to be an automated information desk.

"Where can I find food?" Will asked.

A map popped up to Pira's left that showed an overhead view of the area. "There are numerous places to find food in this sector of the *Exodus 9*," she said. "What kind of food would you like?"

Will's mind whirred. He was confused by her first statement. "What is the '*Exodus 9*?'" he asked.

"You seem confused," she said. "Did you just arrive?"

"Yes," he replied, although he wasn't sure that was true. It was true, however, that he'd just awakened.

"It will take up to 12 hours for you to recover full brain function," the cartoon said. "Shall I summon an escort for you?"

Escort? He didn't like the sound of that. "No thanks," he replied. "Please direct me to a place to get food – a restaurant."

"What type of cuisine would you like?" she asked.

"What kinds do you have?" he asked, and then remembered the sign for the Mexican restaurant.

"We have a wide variety," Pira replied. "Here's a list of some of the types we have in this local area."

A list of about 100 varieties appeared. It was in alphabetical order and included African (various types), American (various types), Asian (general), Chinese (various types), English, French, Lebanese, Mexican …

Will went with the one foremost in his mind. "Mexican," he said.

The map changed and highlighted five locations.

"These are the closest Mexican restaurants," Pira said and pointed to the map.

"Where is everyone?" he asked. "Is there anyone else here?"

"Presently, there are no others," she replied.

He found it strange that there were no other people in such a huge place. It was like being in a deserted city that still had power and was maintained in some way.

His stomach gurgled again and then burned, and he became light-headed for a few seconds. "Where's the closest Mexican restaurant?"

"On the fourth level," she replied as its location and path illuminated on the map. "Would you like an escort?"

Will examined the directions on the map. The Mexican restaurant on the fourth floor was indeed closer than the one he'd spotted on the second. He looked out to the mall and got a general fix on the location. He'd have to take the ramps to the upper levels. They were about 75 yards further down the mall.

"No escort, thanks," he said.

"You're welcome," he heard Pira say as he started toward the ramps.

It struck him that maybe he should have accepted an escort – maybe he would've gotten some information from them – but his head was still foggy, and he preferred to reorient himself before talking to anyone. And he was starving.

He walked down the right side of the mall and observed the kiosks and storefronts as he went along. Everything was in English. One shop that caught his attention had a sign that read "Biological Alterations," which he found odd. He had no idea what that meant. Another advertised "Learning Center," and another, "Fitness and Recreation." There were stores for clothes, and another for "Exotic Vacations." He became more and more confused as he proceeded.

He came to a ramp that rose at a steep angle to the next level. He'd expected to see the steps of an escalator, but instead found a smooth black track that glided silently upward. He stepped onto it, and it accelerated him to a quick clip that made him notice the air blowing past his ears.

About 10 seconds later, he stepped off the track, walked to the next one, and ascended. After the third trip, he was on the fourth level. Like the ground floor, it was packed with storefronts that extended as far as he could see in both directions down the mall. He stepped up to the railing and looked down, over the ground level, which was now about 100 feet below. He was above the trees, of which there were many varieties, with some almost 80 feet tall.

By the time he reached the Mexican restaurant, he was above the pond with the fountain. The sound of the running water below seemed to calm his nerves.

The front of the restaurant had a bright sign that read "Tequila Sunrise," along with images of various foods and drinks. He recognized most of the items but could conjure no memories of directly experiencing them.

He walked through a large entranceway into a foyer that was illuminated at a more comfortable level than the main mall. The wall opposite the entrance came to life and a face he recognized appeared. It was Pira – the animated character.

"Hello again," she said. "Will you be eating here, or would you like something to go?"

"I'll eat here," he replied. He needed to eat right away.

"Sit anywhere you like in the main dining room," she said as a door to the left of the screen slid open.

Will walked through the door and was instantly hit with the smells of various foods. The mouthwatering aromas of grilled meat, onions, and spices nearly activated an uncontrollable response to immediately seek out the food and eat whatever he found.

When he overcame this urge, he became aware of the view before him. The room was immense and filled with tables – enough to seat over 100 patrons. There was a bar on the left, looking from the entrance, a large fish tank containing colorful fish on the right, and hanging plants around the perimeter. It was darker than the foyer but warmly lit with inset ceiling lights.

It took him a few seconds to notice what was on the far wall, about 75 feet from the entrance. A row of short booths designed to seat two spanned a long, continuous floor-to-ceiling window that served as the entire far wall of the restaurant. It was dark outside.

He went to the nearest booth and peered out the window. The

view was of the blackest of space studded with innumerable stars of all sizes and radiances. And they were moving.

It seemed as if he were aboard an enormous spacecraft.

LENNY BUTROLSKY WALKED into a small café he'd discovered near a public park in one of San José's upscale areas. The current climate in Costa Rica's capital was pleasant compared to the damp, chilly weather that was invading the DC area in the US. He was happy to be out of there – the region, and the situation. The CIA director had kept his promise.

When the action had subsided a few weeks ago, Lenny had gotten into a car and driven west. After a week-long hiatus at a lake resort in North Dakota where he'd fished, drank beer, and watched soccer, he drove to a safe house near San Francisco that was managed by DMS, Inc. The company provided a variety of services for "people like him," as described by the CIA officer who had introduced him to the enterprise a few weeks prior.

The service that Lenny sought from the company was, essentially, money laundering, although there were some other perks that involved them regularly checking in on him and verifying his general well-being. The CIA had provided him with a new identity that included a background story with documentation of a previous financial history – including a Social Security Number and a valid passport. DMS, Inc., took funds directly from the US Government and distributed them through his alias existence, and was now sending him a monthly stipend – auto deposited into a legitimate account. He'd already received three "retroactive" checks to get him going.

The company also laundered his other assets – those in anonymous accounts in Switzerland and Iceland. He'd left about 10 percent of that unwashed money in one of the Swiss accounts – to maintain the "grandfathered" status of that service. Times were changing, and anonymous accounts were being eliminated. As it stood presently, no new funds could be deposited, but existing funds could be maintained and withdrawn in anonymity. It was best to have a safety net in case something went wrong at DMS, Inc. or, God forbid, at the CIA.

The Chinese network in the US had been decimated – something in which Lenny had played an integral part – and anyone who could identify him was no longer among the living. At least he hoped that was the case. As a precaution, he'd remain vigilant and continue his life-preserving protocols in his civilian life.

He went to the counter and ordered a dark-roast coffee from a young barista who smiled as she chatted with him in broken English. Lenny responded in broken Spanish. In addition to its wide variety of exotic fruits and vegetables, Costa Rica was foremost known for its coffee, and he was going to embrace it.

His "café" was delivered in a tall glass mug, which he took to an outdoor seating area where he sat at a small, round table. Unlike most cafés and restaurants in the US and elsewhere, this place allowed smoking, and even had ashtrays on the tables. Lenny pulled a pack of cigarettes out of his light jacket, extracted one, and lit it. He took a deep drag and exhaled.

He let his mind wander for a few seconds until a disturbing question formed in his mind.

What the hell am I going to do today?

WILL SAT IN THE BOOTH, slid in as far as he could, and pressed his face against the cool window. It seemed to be shaped so that it blended with the curvature of the external structure, but he was still able to see some of the black exterior. He was inside a colossal ship.

The stars moved almost imperceptibly from left to right across the window. He couldn't tell if the motion was due to the ship moving in a straight line, or if it was rotating. He figured it had to be the latter since the speed needed to perceive the relative motion of stars for straight-line motion would be enormous. He supposed it could also be changing direction, but it didn't feel like it was making a turn.

His attention was redirected to a chiming sound coming from the tabletop, which then illuminated with a menu that had pictures of various Mexican dishes.

"What would you like from the menu?" a female voice asked from a speaker he couldn't locate.

Will looked over the choices and replied, "A chicken burrito, and a pitcher of water."

"How spicy would you like the burrito, from one to ten, one being the least spicy?"

"Zero," he replied. His innards felt odd, and he was now thinking that Mexican food might've been a poor choice.

"Okay, the minimum spice level it is," the voice replied. "Your food will arrive shortly."

The table's video surface went dark.

Will wondered how he even knew what a burrito was. Its ingredients sounded appetizing – chicken, peppers, onions, cilantro, salsa, black beans – but he couldn't explain his familiarity with those, either.

He gazed through the window and contemplated what to do next. After eating, he'd have to figure out where he was, how he'd gotten there, and where he was going.

"Your order has arrived," a voice said from behind him.

Will turned to look and nearly jumped through the window as his brain processed what he was seeing. It was a man, dressed in dark pants and a white shirt.

"I'm Dorian," the man said as he set a napkin, utensils, a glass, and a pitcher of water on the table. He then set a plate in front of Will on which was a large burrito. The man was about six feet tall, thin build, and had short, dark hair. His eyes were brown and seemed to be rather large for his head. He looked to be in his mid-twenties even though his mannerisms and voice made him seem more mature than his apparent age. "Careful, the plate is hot. Is there anything else that you would like at this time?"

"No," Will replied. "Thank you."

The man nodded and turned away.

"Wait," Will said.

Dorian turned. "Yes?"

Will froze for a few seconds until a question formulated in his mind. "They said I was the only one here. Where are you from?" he asked.

"I was synthesized here," Dorian replied.

"Synthesized?" Will repeated, puzzled. "You mean born?"

The man's expression seemed to change as if he recognized Will's confusion.

"You must have just arrived," Dorian said.

"I have," Will responded. He thought that should have been obvious since there was supposedly no one else on the ship. "My name is Will."

"Pleasure to meet you, Will," Dorian replied. "I am a biological entity that has been programmed for my role."

"Programmed?"

"Yes, my neural networks and memory have been configured with a comprehensive knowledge of your nutritional requirements and a wide variety of cuisines," Dorian explained. "And, of course, to speak your languages."

"How did you know I spoke English?"

"You spoke English to Pira," the man replied.

It made sense, but he wondered how Pira knew he spoke English, and why all the signs in the mall were in English. "Can you please tell me where I am?" Will asked.

"You're in the Tequila Sunrise restaurant," Dorian replied. "On level four, sector 28."

"I mean, am I on a ship?" Will asked, even though he was almost certain that he was.

"You're on the transport starship, *Exodus 9*," Dorian explained and seemed to study him.

Will was astounded by the confirmation. He then recalled Pira mentioning the *Exodus 9* but not explaining what it was. "Other than us, who else is on the ship?" he asked.

"Only crew members and staff," Dorian replied.

"Which one am I?" Will asked.

"You're neither," Dorian said. "They are synthesized, like me. You are our lone passenger from Earth."

Earth. For a few seconds, Will's mind sparked with images and brief scenes that he recognized. They dissolved away in an instant. "Why am I the only one from Earth? Are there supposed to be others?"

"This ship is designed to carry a million passengers," Dorian replied.

It was a daunting figure. It was the population of a medium-sized city. "It's empty," Will said. "Will more passengers arrive later?"

Dorian stared at him for a few seconds and his face seemed to form an expression of pity. "The source has been destroyed," he said. "No more passengers will be arriving."

The response set Will's mind into action and bits of information were forming thoughts that weren't yet coherent. His stomach twisted in his gut, not from hunger, but from an unknown source of anxiety.

"Where is this ship going?" Will asked.

"That is a question that should be directed to the navigation department."

"Where can I find it?"

"The bridge," Dorian said and pointed to the table. "All information about the *Exodus 9* and its crew is in the central network."

Will looked down at the tabletop. "How do I access it?"

"You will learn that in orientation," Dorian said.

"How do I arrange for orientation?" Will asked.

Dorian approached the table, directed his gaze to the tabletop, and said, "*Exodus 9*, open network display."

The table illuminated beneath Will's plate, which he moved to the side.

"*Exodus 9*, search for new passenger orientation locations," Dorian continued.

The display pulled up a list of search items that were ranked according to relevance. "This should get you started," Dorian said. "Use your fingers or voice to navigate the network."

Will touched his finger to the screen and scrolled through the list.

"I'll be back shortly and will help you further if you need it," Dorian said as he turned and started to walk away.

"Thank you, Dorian," Will said.

Dorian stopped, turned around, and stared at Will for a second. "You're welcome, Will."

Will thought he saw Dorian's face soften with a hint of a smile before the man disappeared through a door on the opposite side of the dining room. Will turned his attention to the food.

He picked up the burrito and took a bite. The flavors that invaded his senses were only vaguely familiar to him, but the taste of the food made him go into an eating frenzy. The burrito was half gone by the time he took his first sip of water, at which point he realized how thirsty he was and gulped down the entire glass. He'd been famished and dehydrated but was already feeling better.

After a few minutes, the eating slowed to a more relaxed pace, and he took a few deep breaths and looked out the window. He had confirmation now that he was on a ship, but he couldn't yet tell if it was a place with which he should be familiar, or if he was just an out-of-place visitor.

He took another bite of the burrito and turned his attention to the tabletop display.

The information Dorian had summoned was a list of orientation locations. There were over 15 such places in the local area, and they were listed with addresses that were strings of 10 to 15 numbers and letters with parts separated by dashes. He'd come back to the addresses later.

He leaned close to the table and said, "Search for new passenger protocols."

Nothing happened.

He repeated the command with the same result.

After thinking about it for a moment he recalled how Dorian had administered the order. Finally, he said, "*Exodus 9*, search for new passenger protocols."

"There are no new protocols for passengers," a female voice said. It came from the table. "Did you want me to list the protocols for processing newly arriving passengers?"

Will understood the ambiguity of the wording of his initial request, and replied, "Yes."

A list of instructions appeared, and he read as he ate.

The first thing he realized was that he was supposed to have awakened in a medical bay of some sort and should have been checked out by "biomedical specialists," and then scanned for abnormalities and defects due to the transport process. It was strange that this was not the case for him – he'd awakened alone.

Next, he was to be hydrated and nourished since the contents of all internal cavities would be empty – stomach, bladder, intestines, and the like – upon reassembly.

What the hell is "reassembly?" he wondered.

Next was "DNA recording and adjusting."

DNA adjusting? He had no idea what that meant, either, but it had profound implications in his mind.

In the final step of the first phase, new passengers were to be taken to their quarters where they were to remain until they completed a full sleep cycle, during which their memories would recover.

That sounded perfect to Will. It seemed he'd arrived in the wrong part of the ship, but had accomplished the rehydrating and nourishment component of the protocol on his own. Now he wondered about the other steps.

"*Exodus 9*, please direct me to a biomedical facility," he said.

A list appeared on the screen with addresses arranged with the nearest location at the top. It was in the adjacent sector, and Will committed its address to memory. Although he had almost no recollection of anything before his arrival on the *Exodus 9*, it seemed that his short-term memory was fine.

He wiped his mouth with a napkin and stood from the booth. As he made his way toward the front of the restaurant, Dorian came out from the back. "Is there anything else I can get for you, Will?" he asked.

"No thanks," Will replied. A thought then emerged that gave him a sudden feeling of panic. "Am I supposed to pay for the food?"

Dorian seemed to contemplate Will's question for an instant and then replied, "There is no currency or credit on the ship," he explained.

"So everything is free?"

Dorian nodded.

"Great, I'll visit again," Will said. "And thanks for the food and the help."

Dorian smiled more overtly this time and nodded.

Will found his way out of the restaurant and onto the main walkway. He was on the fourth level, and he had to get to the 17th level in Sector 27. He went to a kiosk that displayed a map and found the location.

He estimated his destination to be about a kilometer away.

IT TOOK Will over 20 minutes to get to the 17th level using the ramps – he'd searched but hadn't found an elevator. After another 15-minute walk down the 17th-level concourse, he finally arrived at the biomedical center in Sector 27. It seemed that each sector was like another small "city" that was similar to the one where he'd originally arrived.

The center's large windows faced the mall's interior and had illuminated signs that advertised emergency care, checkups, cosmetic adjustments, and physicals. He walked in and approached a long counter that resembled the check-in desk at a fancy hotel.

A few seconds later, a young woman in her mid-20s, with short blonde hair and green eyes, emerged through a door in the back. She wore a white lab coat.

"I'm Cara," she said and waved him over to the counter. "What's the nature of your visit?"

"Uh, I've just arrived on the *Exodus 9*," Will replied as he approached.

"Okay," she said and pointed to the counter. "Place your hand on the surface."

Will thought this was strange, but he complied.

After a few seconds she said, "Okay, you can remove it."

By the light flickering on her face he could tell that she was studying a screen that was out of his view, below the counter. Although he might have been misreading her expression, he thought she looked surprised, or confused.

"Seems you're on the wrong ship," she said.

"What do you mean?" he asked.

"You're probably supposed to be on an escort ship," Cara replied.

"Where am I now?"

"You're on the *Exodus 9*."

"That I know," he said. "What kind of ship is this?"

"It's a passenger transport."

"And what's an escort ship?"

"A maintenance vessel, or a warship," she replied and looked at him as if he should have known that. "You've not yet slept, have you?"

Will shook his head.

"You must go to your quarters and sleep," she said and handed him something that looked like a black watch. "Wear this. It will help you navigate the ship and direct you to your quarters. You'll be contacted in 14 hours."

"I don't know about any 'quarters,'" Will said.

"I just assigned you to a single suite," she said and pointed to the watch. "Please, look."

Will put the device on his wrist and it illuminated. On its screen was a string of numbers and letters that had the same format as the address of the biomed facility.

"You need to sleep until your memory regenerates," Cara explained. "You'll be given further instructions when you awaken. You can go now." She then disappeared into the back.

All he knew about himself, other than his name and that he was probably from Earth, was that he was "on the wrong ship," whatever that meant. He had no recollection of anything before arriving on the *Exodus 9*. He hoped a good span of sleep would remedy that.

He glanced at his watch, got the address, and exited the biomedical clinic into the main concourse. He had to get to level 11 in a sector that he figured was two kilometers away. He felt better after eating but was now becoming exhausted. Was there no transportation?

He looked at his new watch and got an idea. He put the device close to his mouth and asked, "*Exodus 9*, where is an elevator?"

Instantly, a map appeared on the watch screen, which indicated multiple locations. One was just 30 feet in front of him. He walked over to a white, featureless wall between the fronts of an athletic facility and what seemed to be a health spa. He stood in front of it, looking back and forth between his watch and the wall to make sure he was in the right place. He reached out his hand to touch the surface and the wall separated into two pieces and slid apart, revealing the interior of an elevator.

As he stepped inside the cylindrical compartment that he estimated could comfortably fit 10 passengers, a smooth female voice asked, "What is your destination?"

He'd already forgotten the address and started searching for it on his watch. After a few seconds of futility, he faced toward the doorway and said, "My quarters, please."

"Hold on," the voice instructed as the elevator doors closed. His stomach twisted as the elevator first dropped for a few seconds and then braked to a halt. It then accelerated horizontally, and he grabbed a rail that encircled the wall at waist level to keep his balance. A map illuminated above the door, showing the local layout of the ship, and a blue line indicated the path to his destination.

After about 20 seconds, the elevator banked left and decelerated.

It came to a stop and the voice said, "You have arrived at your destination," as the doors opened.

Will stepped out and watched the elevator doors slide together and merge seamlessly. He found himself in a wide, dimly lit corridor with smooth, curved walls and a high rounded ceiling. The floor was covered in short, white carpet.

The passageway extended out of sight in both directions. He took a step to his left and his wrist vibrated. It was the watch. Its screen showed a map with a blue line that led from the elevator to a doorway 100 feet to his right.

He reversed direction and walked past a closed entrance on his left. It was a sleek depression that merged smoothly into the wall of the corridor. He passed three others on both sides before arriving at his, on the left.

As he approached it, the door parted in the center, and he stepped inside. The interior lights came on as the door slid closed behind him.

The first thing he noticed was a floor-to-ceiling window that made up most of the far wall. He passed through a narrow foyer, around some furniture in the main room, and went to it.

It was a visual masterpiece: stars of all sizes, bright clusters, illuminated clouds, and spirals. One spiral galaxy in particular was prominent, and the details of its twisting arms were clear. Everything seemed to be moving from right to left across his view. He still couldn't tell if this was due to the rotation or translation of the ship. He supposed he could check that over time: if the ship were rotating, then the same outside features would continually reappear. But there was also the chance that the ship was doing both – rotating and translating. It could also just be making a turn.

He faced away from the window and examined his quarters. The ceiling in the foyer at the entrance was low – maybe eight feet – but it stepped up to about ten feet in the main room. The walls were off-white and smooth. Inset ceiling lights illuminated the entire area in a hue that was comfortable to the eyes.

Next to the left-side wall, when facing away from the window, was a gray couch and a coffee table. Next to the wall on the right, close to the window, was a padded bench. The floor was covered in short white carpeting, like that in the hallway.

On the far end, opposite the window and to the right of the foyer, was a countertop with stools, behind which was a small kitchen. On the wall behind the counter was an inset compartment that resembled the exterior of a microwave oven. Built around it were cabinets and compartments.

He walked up to the counter. To his right was a short hallway with two doors – one straight ahead, and another on the right. He entered the one on the right: it was a small bedroom with a loft, beneath which was a desk and a chair. There were mirrors, an open closet, and drawers built into the walls. He went to the other door, and found that it led to a bathroom with a shower. He suddenly realized he had an urgent need to use the facility and did so. It seemed that his digestive system would take some time to get back on track.

When he came out of the bathroom, a feeling of exhaustion overtook him. Instead of climbing the ladder to the bunk in the bedroom, he went to the couch in the main room, lay back, and watched the stars until he lost consciousness.

2

REGENERATION

WILL AWAKENED TO HIS OWN SCREAMS.

He remembered.

He sat up, sweating, and confused. A feeling of bottomless depression dissolved as the light seemed to warm his mind. It took him a few seconds to realize where he was. He was on the couch in his quarters aboard the *Exodus 9,* near the large window that separated him from the void of space.

It was as if he'd relived an entire lifetime in one night.

He sat up and looked around him, and then stood and went to the window. Stars and large celestial objects moved almost imperceptibly from right to left. *Where in the hell am I?*

"I promise," he said aloud. He then listened to his own voice as he said it again, trying to find the hidden origin of the words. A few seconds later, his mind responded with the image of a worried face. "My God, *Denise.*"

And then he remembered more.

What happened to Earth? Are they all dead?

A feeling of panic started to invade him. He paced as he forced himself to suppress it.

He couldn't even be sure that *he* wasn't dead. It depended on how one defined "dead." Maybe this was where one went when they died. But he knew that couldn't be true either. He'd seen the souls of those who'd passed when he was on Earth. They'd been lingering there for some reason.

Overnight, he'd remembered – relived – every moment of his life. It was as if he'd been asleep for 40 years. It gave him a strange perspective. He feared going to sleep again.

It prompted the question, if someone were given the choice to relive their life – repeat every detail as they'd lived it the first time and without knowing the future – should they? He'd just done that and, for him, the answer to that question was "no." The bad outweighed the good, and the good did not seem to be worth the suffering.

Images then came to his mind that made his stomach sicken. He'd killed people. Many of them. He couldn't yet recall all the circumstances, but he had the feeling that he'd been attacked. He suspected, however, that his impression of acting in self-defense might just be a coping mechanism.

He then remembered his last moments on Earth. He'd been inside a secret base, deep below the Antarctic ice, that had been constructed by the Deltas – the generation of beings that preceded humans on Earth. The Deltas were the ones who had sent the encrypted signal from deep space that contained blueprints of devices that went far beyond human technology. The base had been an enormous transport facility, and he'd been inside one of its transporters as the entire place was about to self-destruct. It had been imperative that he get off the planet – or die – before the Regenerators arrived, which had been imminent. The transporter hadn't worked, so he'd had to move to his final option.

HE RUBBED his fingers on his right temple where the barrel of the gun had been placed. *Did I pull the trigger?* he wondered. *Or did the transporter activate before I could do it?* He thought for a moment that it was possible that he'd pulled the trigger and had then been transported. But he ruled that out assuming that his brain would have been scrambled, and his memory would have been unrecoverable. But what the hell did he know? He had no knowledge of the science of transporters.

He turned from the window and, as he walked into the kitchen area, a sharp pain stabbed through the left side of his lower back, making him twist and press his hand on the sensitive area.

"What the hell?" he muttered.

The pain subsided and he went to a cabinet and opened it. It was filled with plates and bowls. He opened another, which was stocked with glasses and cups of various types. He grabbed a coffee cup and scanned around for something to put in it.

On the wall opposite the kitchen entrance was a square computer screen. Below it was a glass door to a rectangular compartment about the size of a small microwave oven. In the wall to the right of the glass door was a cylindrical inset with a round platform that resembled the water dispenser on a refrigerator, and he placed the cup upon it.

He touched a finger to the screen, and it came to life. A menu appeared above the glass door, and he navigated to an extensive coffee list. He chose a Colombian medium-roast, strong, with cream. The steaming concoction filled the cup in an instant.

As he retrieved the mug, a message appeared on the screen that read, "You have an appointment at Biomedical Station 82 at 10:00 a.m. for DNA error checking and sequencing."

Will stared at the message, which included a map of the facility location. What the hell did that mean – "DNA error checking?" His watch then vibrated, delivering the same alert: he had 40 minutes to get there. The address was already programmed.

He took a sip of coffee and was astounded. The aroma filled his nostrils, and the flavors were smooth and strong. However, the taste was a little off. He thought maybe his taste buds were out of tune after the transport. He'd had the same impression of the Mexican food from the night before but it, too, had been delicious.

His arm tensed and he nearly spilled his coffee as a sharp pain pierced his lower back, this time just above his right hip. It felt like someone was standing on his back and digging a stiletto heel into him. The pain on the left side then returned as a dull ache.

He set the coffee cup on the counter next to the sink and then went to the map. He had to get to Sector 32.

Although he could have used a shower, he exited his quarters and headed for the elevator-transporter. It seemed that he might actually need medical assistance.

Ten minutes later he entered Biomedical Station 82. He was half an hour early.

As he stepped up to a check-in counter, his watch vibrated and a message appeared that instructed him to follow the white line, which then appeared on the floor.

He followed the line down a corridor and finally into a room, where a woman in a white lab coat greeted him. She was short and petite, with long brown hair and brown eyes that seemed a bit large for her face. She looked too young to be a doctor.

"I'm Greta, your biomedical custodian," she said. "You go by William?"

"Will," he said.

"Surname?" she asked.

"Thompson," he replied.

"It seems you don't belong on this ship, Will," Greta said as she studied the screen on a rectangular handheld electronic device.

"I don't understand," he argued, recalling that he'd been told the same thing the night before. "How can I *belong* on any ship?"

"Your records indicate that you've slept for 13 hours," she said, not answering his question and setting the device on a table. "You should have recovered your memory."

Will believed he had – much of it, anyway.

"Do you feel pain in your back?" she asked.

He nodded. "How did you – "

"Please step into the white circle," she said as she pointed to the floor where a solid bright circle, about one meter in diameter, appeared.

Will stepped into it as Greta went to a console and pushed a button. Intense light shone from above and below for a few seconds and then went dark.

She then grabbed the tablet-sized electronic device from the table and looked it over.

"Your kidneys did not restart properly and are permanently damaged," she said. "This can happen for a number of reasons. For one, you were delivered into a cargo bay, which means your destination key was probably not rated for bio-transport."

Will had no idea what a "destination key" was.

Greta continued, "Problems also occur when proper procedures are not followed: it seems you ate solid food before being conditioned and rehydrated."

"How was I supposed to know what I was supposed to – ," Will stopped midsentence when he saw a grin on Greta's face.

"You're agitated and worried about the diagnosis," she said. "There's no need to be concerned."

"Didn't you just say my kidneys are failing?"

She nodded. "And, according to the scan, there are myriad other problems: blockage in your cardiovascular system, pancreas malfunction, and ocular wear and degradation. There are malignant cells in your system. You are aged beyond prime."

Will knew anything over 40 years old was "beyond prime," but there was nothing he could do about that. And it didn't help any to hear about it, either.

"I recommend a complete DNA regeneration," Greta said.

The word "regeneration" made him shudder, and his thoughts went to a darker place. "What happened to Earth?" he blurted.

Greta stared at him for a moment before replying. "I do not have that information," she said.

After an awkward silence, she asked, "Shall we commence the regeneration?"

"No," Will replied. "I don't know what that means."

"Your kidneys need to be repaired or replaced," she said. "As do many other things."

As if her statement had induced a response, a stabbing pain in his lower back made him bend to the side and grab the area with his hand.

"And your pancreas will fail in hours," she said. "Your liver is also malfunctioning."

"What are you suggesting – medications? Surgery?" he asked.

She smiled.

"What?" he asked. The pain was driving up his frustration.

"You're responding exactly as expected," she said. "There is no 'surgery' – at least not how you understand it. And there are no 'medications' in the form of chemicals. The correction process involves DNA restructuring."

"You're going to repair my DNA?"

"It's more than that," Greta explained. "We repair everything – this includes organ substitution, cell replacement, and chromosome rejuvenation."

"You mean telomeres?"

Greta nodded. "Yes, telomere lengthening is one effect of this process."

"So you can reverse aging?" he asked, astounded. He knew that telomeres shortened as cells divided, and that this was at least partially responsible for the degradation of the body due to aging. He then realized that it was actually a consequence of aging, rather than a cause.

Will twisted violently in response to a sharp jab in his lower back and was now starting to feel pain in his lower abdomen as well.

"Shall we initiate the process?" she asked and nodded toward a large vertical tube on the far side of the room. It looked like a white pillar that extended from the floor to the ceiling, with a few sleek conduits spurring off near the top. The tube was about 10 feet in diameter with an oval doorway.

"This device scans your system and decodes your DNA and bonding structure, which provides everything there is to know about your body," she explained. "It removes some cells, and then seeds your system with new cells that will multiply and replace old ones. It also does complete organ generation and replacement."

"How does it do that without surgery?"

"I don't think we have time to go over all of the science involved here," she said. "You can certainly learn about it later."

"How long will it take?" he asked.

"You need organ replacements," she explained. "That will take about 20 minutes."

"Kidneys?"

"And your pancreas and liver, and possibly other systems," she added. "The cell regeneration would take care of those eventually, but your situation calls for immediate replacements, so we'll do them right now."

Will still couldn't believe what he was hearing. "You're going to replace my kidneys and pancreas in 20 minutes?"

"And liver, and other things," she added. "And also remove all scar tissue, plaque, and other buildup from your system."

"How long will it take to recover?"

"The procedure is comprehensive and complete," she replied. "There is no recovery time – there will be no damage from which to recover. However, correcting the other, age-related problems will take more time. This occurs as the implanted cells regenerate and replace the vacated aged cells."

"How long will that take?"

"Most of the soft tissue in your body will be replaced in about six weeks," she said. "Some things, like thick bones, will take up to seven years, but those aren't crucial in your case. In some cases, such as broken or degenerating bones, we would replace them using methods similar to the organ replacement that you will now undergo."

A thought flashed into Will's mind. He recalled a friend who had died of kidney failure, and another of pancreatic cancer. He passed into dreamlike excitement for an instant before he realized that he was no longer on Earth, and that whatever glorious technologies he found here would not benefit anyone he knew. His initial excitement was replaced by guilt and sadness.

He gasped as another jolt of pain made him jerk to the side. He was starting to feel nauseated, and a cold sweat formed on his forehead and neck. His situation was declining.

"Let's get this going," he said and stepped toward the cylinder.

Greta followed him to the device.

"Stand at the center with your feet separated by about 60 centimeters," she instructed. "Hold your arms out at your sides so that they are horizontal, face straight forward, and close your eyes."

Will stepped inside, took a wide stance, held out his arms, and looked directly at Greta through the door.

He closed his eyes as two doors sealed off the opening. A moment later, he was completely immobilized, as if the cylinder had filled up with epoxy and instantly hardened around him.

His vision then flooded as if he'd emerged from the top of a white cloud and into blinding sunlight. He slid gently away from consciousness.

DANIEL HAD HIS LUNCH – a bagel with peanut butter – an hour earlier than usual since he had a meeting scheduled for 11:30 a.m. What he needed was a nap on his decrepit couch – he was running on just a few hours of sleep. His mind had spun the entire night with thoughts of past events. His anxieties were usually fueled by mysteries woven into current projects. This was different.

He finished the bagel and then turned on the electric tea kettle on the windowsill. As the water heated, he organized his thoughts and made a plan for the afternoon.

His current project was to write a comprehensive treatise on the events surrounding William Thompson and their ventures into Antarctica. The result would be a multivolume set of monographs, which would be coauthored by Sylvia. It would be the first time Omnis appeared as coauthors on any monograph, the official product of their work.

It was going to be a long-term project, taking years, but it might be the most important work of his career. The first volume would start with the emergence of William Thompson, from the development of the Red Wraith project to the final destruction of the Red Box – the Compressed Punishment facility in Detroit. The next would cover the discovery and activation of the probes in the Southern Seas that had set everything into action. And the final volume would be a full account of the detection of the incoming messages, their decrypted content, and the discovery and subsequent destruction of the hidden alien base in Antarctica, along with Will Thompson.

But it seemed to Daniel that the story was not yet over, even though heated geopolitical conflicts had cooled. The Chinese networks in New York and Washington, DC had been uprooted, all threats to the Space Systems building eliminated – at least that was the CIA's current assessment – and all Russian and Chinese naval vessels had left the Southern Seas. A few US and UK ships stayed in place, but their overall presence had been greatly reduced. The only remnants of the ordeal were the decrypted drawings and alien script, which amounted to many thousands of pages. Everything was now in the hands of CIA and NSA specialists, which Daniel found to be unnerving because of the security risk posed by having other agencies involved. He only trusted the CIA.

The US government had possession of the only set of decrypted data from the incoming signal. Although part of that signal had been decipherable by common means, the meat of it required a unique physical object to decode it. The decoder was a small, square device through which incoming data was streamed, and which decompressed and outputted the data that included the drawings and script. That device had undoubtedly been destroyed when the Antarctic base self-destructed. Even if it hadn't been incinerated in the meltdown, it was now buried beneath kilometers of ice.

A beep from the main room alerted Daniel that someone had entered. He glanced out and spotted Sylvia removing her jacket and rustling through her backpack, evidently returning from her 10:00 a.m. dental appointment. A minute later she appeared in his doorway holding a cup and a green can that was decorated with a leaf pattern.

"Something to add to your tea collection," she said as she placed the can on a shelf next to the door. "It's organic Sencha."

"Thanks," he said as he scooped some English breakfast tea out of a similar tin with a stainless-steel tea ball and offered the can to Sylvia, who accepted it.

"Thackett will be here shortly," she said as she glanced at her watch and prepared her tea. "Do you know what he wants to talk about?"

He shook his head as he poured hot water into his cup, and then into Sylvia's. "Maybe he wants to discuss the monographs – our new project."

"Maybe," she said. "It's going to take years to write those and verify every detail."

"Frankly, I think we could spend the rest of our careers on it," he said.

"It might be the most sensitive information ever compiled – never to be leaked to the public," she said.

"That's one thing I wanted to discuss," Daniel said. "I have some reservations about putting all of that information in one place."

Sylvia seemed to mull it over. "It would contain everything from Red Wraith to the incoming signals to the alien base," she said. "If it got out, it would blow the lid off of everything."

Daniel had come to the same conclusion. "Our only hope would be that it sounds so farfetched that people would think it was all fiction," he said. "It might even be a way to muddy the waters."

"What do you mean?" she asked.

"If we presented some of these events in the form of tabloid conspiracy articles, or even fiction novels, it would obscure the real information if it ever got leaked," Daniel explained. "It's a common tactic used by governments – including our own."

A beep and the sound of a door closing in the main room alerted them to the arrival of James Thackett. Daniel had grown fond of the CIA Director during the past year and dreaded the day when he'd be replaced. It could happen in a matter of months with the upcoming election, and a possible new administration: the CIA Director was a political appointee.

They met at the cluster of furniture in the main room. Thackett took one of two, side-by-side leather chairs, and Daniel and Sylvia sat next to each other on the couch on the opposite side of the coffee table that was at the center of the arrangement.

"Have our satellites made any new detections?" Daniel asked. It was a question that was always lingering in his mind, but he allowed himself to ask it only occasionally. He was referring to those that were looking outward for potential incoming objects.

"Nope, and I hope they never do," Thackett replied.

Daniel felt the same.

"Now, what I wanted to talk to you about," Thackett said as he leaned forward in his chair. "The Chinese haven't given up, and the Russians have renewed their efforts."

"Efforts toward what?" Sylvia asked.

"They know about the drawings – the entire decoded message – and that we might've lost William Thompson," Thackett explained. "As you know, the Chinese are well aware of Will's abilities."

"Well, they should be," Sylvia said. "He single-handedly destroyed one of their aircraft carriers."

"And they know how he acquired his abilities," Thackett added.

Daniel's neck stiffened. "You think they're going to continue their version of the Red Wraith project – Red Dragon?" he asked.

"It's already happening," Thackett replied. "And they have everything they need."

"And they got it all from us," Sylvia added.

Thackett shook his head in disgust but then seemed to break out of it. "That's not our immediate problem," he said. "Even though we decimated their northeast intelligence network, the resulting vacuum is quickly refilling."

"It's only been weeks," Daniel said.

Thackett readjusted in his seat, making the leather chair squeak. "We've collected a few of their replacement operatives and questioned them. The effort is massive. Space Systems is at immediate risk."

"William Thompson is gone," Sylvia argued. "What do they want?"

"Everything we have," Thackett replied. "The decoded message and drawings, to start."

"That's all we really have at this point, right?" Sylvia asked. "All of the devices are gone – destroyed with the base."

"Even if the base had not been destroyed – which I doubt – it's inaccessible," Daniel argued.

"That's my point," Thackett said. "They all have recorded copies of the incoming signal but can't extract any information from it since the decoder is gone. It means they will focus on extracting it from us, instead."

Daniel shuddered. "With the decoder gone, we can't decipher any new signals, either," he said. "That is, if there ever are any." He sensed that Thackett had more news, and his hunch was affirmed when the director made eye contact with him, then Sylvia, and cleared his throat.

"I think it might get more dangerous now – even more so than during the events of the past weeks," Thackett explained.

Daniel well understood that enough had happened during the past month to start a war. A large number of Chinese intelligence operatives based in the US had been killed or reported missing. And he knew that many of the "missing" were dead. However, there were a few captured spies – from China and other nations – still in the Space Systems building, and others in covert facilities in the US and around the world.

"I want both of you to move into Space Systems for a while," Thackett said.

"Okay," Daniel said so quickly that it sounded awkward to him. "I mean, I understand."

Sylvia's face showed confusion. "What do you mean?" she blurted. "You want us to move here permanently?"

"Not permanently," Thackett replied, "but long term – maybe up to a year."

Daniel had been considering the idea for a few weeks. Parts of the Space Systems building were like a five-star hotel. But the main reason was that he dreaded going home to an empty house every night. It reminded him of his former wife.

"Do you really think it's necessary?" Sylvia asked. "No one is supposed to know who we are."

Thackett shifted in his chair again and seemed to search for words. "Unfortunately, I think your anonymity has been compromised," he explained as his face flushed. "It's complicated, but one of our own agents – a mole we planted in Chinese intelligence – was ordered to stake out Space Systems after following you from the airport."

"Me?" Sylvia asked. "When?"

"When you picked up Denise Walker some weeks ago, when she arrived from Chicago," Thackett answered. "They were following her, thinking she'd lead them to Will. They were right, of course, and it led them to Space Systems."

"What do they know about the place?" Daniel asked.

"They know it's a CIA facility, and that Will Thompson was here," Thackett replied. "As you know, they'd planned to attack the place. It will still be a prime target for them. But I'm more concerned about the sensitive personnel who work here – like the Omnis."

"Can they identify me?" Sylvia asked, visibly shaken.

"Yes, unfortunately," Thackett replied.

"But they don't know she's an Omni," Daniel argued.

"Right," Thackett confirmed. "The existence of the Omnis is still a secret as far as we know. But we still need to take precautions. We have residential units on the 20th floor for you both, for the time being."

Thackett seemed to assess Sylvia's expression, which, to Daniel, looked skeptical.

"If they're anything like the ones I've seen, you'll be impressed," Daniel said to Sylvia.

She shrugged and seemed to force a smile. "Okay. I don't see any other way."

"You'll get a call in the afternoon to go take a look at your flats," Thackett said as he stood and made his way out of 713, leaving Daniel and Sylvia on the couch.

"With Will being gone, I thought the heat would be off for a while," Sylvia said.

Daniel was starting to think the opposite. He now feared that the heat was going to ramp up higher than ever.

WILL AWAKENED to a blinding white light that dimmed to a comfortable level after a few seconds. Whatever had been immobilizing him loosened its grip, and he found himself standing in the center of the cylindrical compartment. An instant later, the door opened, and his medical specialist, Greta, stood facing him.

"Please exit," she said.

Will did as instructed and stood before her, still a little dazed.

"How do you feel?" she asked.

The pains in his abdomen and lower back were gone. But it was more than that. He felt better everywhere. He felt refreshed, and his mind was clear. His nerves were calm. His breathing was easy.

"I feel well," he said. "What do I do now?"

She grinned. "Regarding your physical health, nothing," she replied. "Your DNA reconstruction and cell regeneration will progress for the next six to eight months. You should notice immediate improvement as the cell replacement accelerates during the next few weeks."

It's going to get better? he marveled. Perhaps he was overestimating his current state: eliminating the pain was a vast improvement, but that didn't mean he was already in better overall health.

"Your diet specifications are now in the system," Greta added.

"Diet specifications?"

"The food synthesizers will adjust to accommodate your needs," she replied, "based on your specific DNA structure."

Will could hardly believe what he was hearing. First, the term "food synthesizer" was something of science fiction in his mind. But then he realized again where he was: on a spaceship. The thought spurred a flurry of questions.

"Where are we?" he asked.

Greta tilted her head slightly and seemed to ponder the question before answering, "You need to be more specific."

"Where are we – how far are we from Earth?"

She shrugged. "I'm not privy to those details," she said. "But my understanding is that we'll be heading out of your galaxy soon."

Will's brain seemed to hiccup. He stared at her, but his mind wasn't processing anything external. The idea of being off Earth – in space – much less leaving the solar system was already unfathomable. But leaving the Milky Way Galaxy?

"I don't believe you," he blurted.

She seemed to study him for a second. "That's all the navigation information I have," she explained. "I don't know how to convince you that it's true."

"How many people were supposed to be on this ship?" he asked even though he already knew the answer.

"A million, in addition to the crew."

"So this ship was supposed to pick up a million of the nearly eight billion people on Earth, and just leave the rest?" he asked.

"There are more ships," she responded.

To save just ten percent of Earth's population, there'd have to be 800 ships of the size of the *Exodus 9*, he thought. But that was irrelevant. "It doesn't matter, does it?" he said.

She shook her head. "There is only you."

He suddenly felt dizzy and exhausted, and Greta seemed to notice.

"You'll feel refreshed in 24 hours," she said. "You should go back to your quarters, eat something, and rest. Afterwards, you'll meet with a counselor who will answer any questions you may have."

Will had a million questions, but they'd have to wait. The only question that really mattered to him now was whether any part of what he was experiencing was real.

WANG YONG REALIZED that it was going to take a while to adjust to his new reality.

The safe house to which he'd been delivered was a horrible mess. The place looked as if its previous inhabitants had made a frantic escape. There were dirty dishes in the sink and rotting food in the garbage can and refrigerator. He didn't sleep at all the first night because of the rats making noise in the kitchen. His first task was to get the place cleaned.

Yong had been assured that this particular safe house had not been compromised, and that additional personnel would arrive to help him set it up within a week. In the meantime, he'd been given a list of his predecessor's contacts to vet. Since the fate of Jiang Tao was unknown, Yong didn't trust any of the operatives on that list.

His problems, however, ran deeper – into his personal life. How was he going to tell his wife and their two daughters that he wasn't going to come home for a while and, worse, that they'd eventually have to sell their house and leave San Francisco for good? The details still had to be worked out, but his wife would join him on the East Coast, and his daughters would go back to China before all hell broke loose.

Yong didn't belong in this situation. He'd led an intellectual property espionage ring, and not one that involved the more traditional cloak-and-dagger activities. From what they'd shown him at the embassy, however, this current situation even went beyond that. Many of his Chinese comrades had either been killed or disappeared in the past weeks. The East Coast network had been decimated.

Yong, or "Jimmy," as he'd been referring to himself in his Silicon Valley circles, had fully integrated with the locals. He spoke English with almost no accent, bought a house in a cookie-cutter suburb, sent his kids to private school, and ran a startup tech firm in the valley.

His company dealt with software interfacing in nuclear reactor controls, and he had a contract with the US government. However, his firm was really operated by one of the Chinese tech giants that was, of course, controlled by the Chinese government, so that he could concentrate on running the spy network. His wife, Chunhua, who went by "Sara" and took his last name only for appearances, was also a tech intelligence operative who specialized in network security. She was a hacker.

They had both become accustomed to American life, despite being born and raised in China. As infants, their two daughters had been sent to China to be cared for by their grandparents until they were old enough to go to school. Each returned for first grade, and they were now like any other middle school kids in the US. They would be devastated when they learned that, in just a few weeks, they'd be going back to China for good. The family was being called back.

The things Yong had learned the previous day deeply disturbed and angered him. In the past months, nearly 300 of his comrades had either died or disappeared, and the US had been involved in all cases. At least one Chinese submarine had been sunk, and an aircraft carrier had been badly damaged with many casualties – the gruesome images of which would be burned into his mind forever. An entire task force – 50 men – was lost in Antarctica. At least 30 US-based operatives were dead, and many more missing, in the Washington, DC area alone. Two of those – one missing, one dead – were the former East Coast network leaders, Cho and Tao.

Now it was Yong, and Chunhua would join him in the coming weeks, after their children were safe at home.

Yong didn't know if 300 lives were worth a war, but he was going to do his best to carry out the orders he'd been given.

WILL WENT BACK to his quarters and fell asleep on the couch. In what seemed like an instant, he opened his eyes, sat up straight, and put his bare feet on the warm floor. His watch indicated that 14 hours had passed.

He stood and went to the enormous window that separated him from the black, vast space outside. Bluish-white stars moved from right to left. The first thing he noticed was that everything looked sharper – clearer. He turned away from the window and looked into the flat. He could read the display screen on the wall in the kitchen. His vision had changed. It was better. It seemed perfect.

He took in a deep breath through his nose and was astounded. It was effortless, and seemed like the air filled his entire face, as if his sinuses were a perfectly clean and porous sponge. For most of his adult life, breathing through his nose had been a sporadic problem due to the combination of sports injuries and mild allergies. It was now perfectly unimpeded and clear.

He went to the couch and sat down. His mind was clearer as well, and he'd dreamt. Even though he'd recalled many things after his first sleep on the ship, he hadn't remembered faces. Now he did. He saw them all, remembered details of conversations, and recalled all the events that had occurred before he'd arrived on the *Exodus 9*. The last thing he remembered was trying to put a bullet in his brain. He still wasn't sure whether that had happened – and he really was dead – or if the transporter had kicked in just before he'd pulled the trigger.

It didn't matter. What did "dead" actually mean? If the transporter had worked, it would have destroyed his body anyway in order to get all of the relevant structural information so that it could be reproduced somewhere else. Did that mean that he'd "died" during the process? What mattered was that he was considering all of these things. "I think, therefore I am," came to his mind. It was Descartes. Evidently, he'd learned something in his college philosophy classes.

More memories entered his mind: the torture he'd endured in the Red Box, the probes in the Southern Seas, the people he'd killed. And he remembered he'd promised Denise that he'd come back. The base was about to self-destruct when he'd left. She must've thought that he was dead.

A horrifying thought came to him: perhaps Earth had been destroyed. Everyone would be dead – Denise would be dead. He needed to know what happened. Maybe he'd get answers from the *Exodus 9*.

He stood from the couch and bent from side to side at the waist. No pain in his back or sides. He then bent forward and backward. No pain. The procedure must have worked.

He wanted a shower, so he padded to the bathroom.

A mirror and a white counter with a sink spanned the wall opposite the bathroom's entrance. On the left was a large glass shower stall with multiple nozzles on the walls and ceiling. To the right was a wide, floor-to-ceiling mirror.

He took off his clothes, went into the shower, and pressed some buttons on a touchscreen. A few seconds later, warm water sprayed him from all directions. He used the controls to adjust the water pressure and temperature. He closed his eyes as he relished the soothing warmth. His mind fumbled with thoughts from the past, and he contemplated his current situation. He thought he should be more confused, or frightened. Perhaps it was that he wasn't convinced that what was happening was real.

After 30 minutes, he turned off the water.

"Initiate drying sequence?" a voice asked from somewhere above him.

"Yes," Will replied.

A high-speed rush of warm air swirled around him like a dust devil. It reminded him of how he'd been cleaned and dried while confined to the Exoskeleton inside the Red Box. This process was gentler. A minute later he stepped out of the shower and onto a thick white rug.

He glanced at the large mirror in front of him.

"My God," he gasped and strained his eyes to look closer, even though the image was perfectly clear.

He stepped toward the mirror and looked his body up and down. He already looked years younger. He was leaner – the muscles in his abdomen were more defined, and taut.

Leaning in closer, he examined his face. The skin was smoother, and the wrinkles around his eyes had decreased. With his index fingers, he rubbed the upper left and right sides of his forehead. The dimples – the scars – were gone. They had marked the places where titanium rods had been threaded into his skull when he was in the Red Box. He pressed his fingers down harder, searching for buried scar tissue that would cause pain as he pinned it against his skull, but couldn't find it. The physical scars were gone – he hadn't even noticed when he'd left the biomedical facility.

Whatever had been done to him had a drastic effect on his appearance. And it had only been 14 hours. Greta – the biomedical specialist – had said the process would take months to complete. He already felt better – even his eyesight was perfect.

He opened a cabinet next to the bathroom door and found clothes identical to the ones he'd gotten upon arrival on the *Exodus 9*. He got dressed, went to the kitchen, found the food and beverage control console, and selected scrambled eggs, bacon, orange juice, and coffee. Everything was ready in 30 seconds.

He took the plate – the bacon was still sizzling – to the kitchen counter and sat on a stool. The first bite of eggs seemed to overwhelm his senses. It tasted so good that he had to fight going into an eating frenzy. It seemed he was famished and hadn't realized it.

He savored every bite, and was satisfied by the time he swallowed the last bit of salty bacon. He put the dishes into a receptacle and took the remaining coffee to the window.

The stars moved as they had been, right to left. They looked different to him now that he knew that the *Exodus 9* was leaving the galaxy.

Where are they taking me?

Now that he felt better and had an idea of how to navigate the interior of the enormous starship, he'd try to find an answer to that question.

He went to the screen on the refrigerator. "*Exodus 9*, can you show me a map of the ship?" he asked, hoping it had functionality beyond food and beverage orders, like the table in the Mexican restaurant.

He flinched when it responded in a female voice. "What are you seeking, Will?" the voice asked.

"Can you show me the entire ship?"

The screen filled with a dozen images. The one at the center was that of a sleek black disk and was labeled with dimensions. It was just over five kilometers in diameter, and a half-kilometer thick at the center, tapering along the radius to a sharp edge at the perimeter. One feature on the leading edge was labeled as the bridge. It looked like a smooth, teardrop-shaped bubble that protruded from both the top and bottom sides of the disk. On the top side was lettering that he recognized: it read "*Exodus 9*" in the Deltas' language. There was also an emblem at the center of the disk that, at first, Will thought resembled a four-leaf clover surrounded by a circle. However, upon closer inspection, the design inside the circle was more complicated. An identical symbol was on the ship's underbelly.

"Where's the control room?" he asked.

"Which system control room would you like to see?" the voice replied.

Will reformulated his question. "What's the address for the bridge?"

"It has been forwarded to your watch," the voice said.

He looked at his wrist. The address and a map appeared on his watch, and he started on his way.

After a 15-minute elevator ride, he found himself standing in front of a round glass door behind which was an empty multilevel room with consoles and chairs. An enormous bulbous window was on the far side, a feature he recognized from the images on the computer.

He walked toward the entrance, expecting it to open, but it remained closed, and he bumped into it. The otherwise transparent door illuminated in white for a split second and then returned to its normal state. He pushed on the door, but it didn't budge. When he pressed harder, it again flashed in white light. He then searched in futility for a button or screen on the surrounding walls.

He tried the door one last time with the same result and decided that he'd have to think about it a little more. Even if he could get onto the bridge and find a way to steer the ship, where in the hell would he go? He had no idea where he was, and certainly didn't know how to get back to Earth.

He took the transporter-elevator back to the main mall and found a kiosk where he got a cup of coffee, which was quite satisfying. He then located a restroom and found himself staring at his image in a mirror. His eyes were brighter somehow, and his face seemed smoother. The muscles in his neck were more visible than before.

What was even more impressive than the change in appearance was the way he felt. Of course, he'd been in excruciating pain for a few hours, and he felt better simply because the pain was gone. However, everything else also felt like it was improving.

It seemed to him that a person got used to a certain, constant level of pain as they got older. The basic pain background of a 50-year-old was much higher, on average, than that of someone in their teens. But people got used to it. The gradual increase apparently went unnoticed as the years passed, and they forgot what it was like to be without the pain. Will was just 41 or 42 – he couldn't remember – and whatever he'd gotten used to living with was much different than what he was experiencing now, which was no pain at all. He felt great.

His stomach grumbled and he suddenly felt hungry.

He found a kiosk that served spicy, stir-fried food, got chicken with vegetables and rice, and took a seat at a round table in a small food court in the mall. The food was delicious, even though it didn't seem to taste like he remembered.

After he finished eating, he wandered down the main mall. There was an uncountable number of things to explore. He'd indulge for a while, in the hope of learning about the ship and what was happening to him. After that, Will would focus on his central objective: getting back to Earth.

3

FANTASY

WILL MEANDERED OVER A KILOMETER DOWN THE MAIN MALL AND explored the sights. There were advertisements of all types, many of which were for entertainment, food, or medical services. There were also spas, athletic and exercise facilities, and something called "Old Media Entertainment," which intrigued him, so he went to it.

He walked into what looked like the lobby of an old theater and the first thing that hit him was the smell of buttery popcorn. It gave him a warm feeling of comfort and nostalgia. The setup was complete with a snack counter and screens on the walls that depicted movie posters. He recognized the titles, as they seemed to be relatively recent. He found a screen with a menu and explored the collection. There were movies of all types and time periods – from Earth. He wondered from where they came, but then realized that anything that had ever been transmitted on Earth – radio, television, satellite communications, cell phone signals – emanated through space at the speed of light for anyone to detect.

He sorted the movie list and found the most recent one to be just over a year old. That meant that the *Exodus 9* had been, at most, one light-year from Earth when it had received it. That was six trillion miles. It meant he could be over a year away, even if the ship could travel at the speed of light. It would take more than a lifetime to travel that distance on a ship based on the latest technology from his generation.

He walked into one of the theaters and the movie screen was already active with ads that he recognized for various snacks and Pepsi Cola – which he suddenly craved. The theater was large – a capacity of 300 he figured – with steep stadium seating. He didn't have the desire to watch a movie alone.

He walked out of the theater and back into the mall, and then explored for another hour before returning to his quarters. On a whim, he went to the coffee table next to the couch and said, "*Exodus 9*?"

As he'd hoped, a screen illuminated on the coffee table's surface, and he brought up a map of the ship and searched for the captain's quarters. There weren't any. He located a list of the crew and found them all to have service-oriented duties, from custodians to cooks, biomedical services, and security: no pilots, navigators, or officers.

The crew, he learned, were synthetically-produced, biological beings that were "soulless." The idea made him feel empty and sad for those he'd met – the man at the Mexican restaurant, and the biomedical specialist, Greta. But it reminded him that *he* had a soul, and he suddenly remembered that he could separate. Until then, it hadn't even entered his mind.

It took him a while to relax, but he finally leaned back on the couch and separated. He pressed through the window into the empty space outside the ship. At about 100 yards out, he looked back and examined the vessel: he admired the sleek curvature of its outer hull, the surface of which was flat black, and almost looked like it had texture. It was enormous. The picture on the computer didn't do it justice.

He reentered the ship in an adjacent flat, which he discovered to be identical to his own, and then passed through the wall and returned to his body.

His thoughts went to the door to the bridge. He realized that he should've separated and found a way to open it from the inside. He'd go back and try. If that didn't work, at least he could examine what was inside, and perhaps find a way to control the ship while separated.

He went to the kitchen and decided to quench his craving for cola. He was surprised to find popular brand names and selected "Pepsi – Cold – Ice." It reminded him of Jacob Hale, who practically lived on the elixir.

"Please place a cup in the dispenser area," a voice chimed.

Will found a glass in the cabinet and put it there. Ice fell into the glass, followed by a dark carbonated beverage.

He took a sip. It was sweet, and resembled cola, but wasn't quite right.

He took his drink to the couch and set it on the coffee table next to the display screen. He scooped out a piece of ice and looked at it. It was flat with honeycomb-shaped holes.

The ice slipped out of his hand and fell onto the screen. He stared at it for a few seconds as his mind whirred at full speed. It *fell.*

How did it fall? What was the source of the gravity that pulled it downward?

Will was a physicist, and he knew of only two ways to produce artificial gravity. One was to have a ship shaped like a ring or a cylinder, and have it spin about its central axis. Someone on the outer rim would feel as if gravity were pulling them radially outward, and that direction would be "down" for them. The other way was to have the ship accelerate linearly. A passenger would then have the sensation of a force pulling them to the rear of the ship, and that would be the downward direction. Both the spinning and linearly accelerating versions could be set up so that the passengers would sense the same gravitational force as they would on the surface of the Earth.

But this ship was doing neither of those things. It wasn't spinning and, as far as he could tell, its engines accelerated it in the forward direction – in the direction of the bubble-like part that contained the bridge. The current direction of motion seemed to be to the right when he faced his window – based on how the stars apparently moved from right to left. The force of "gravity," however, was directed downward.

It was confusing. The previous generation, which had supposedly built this ship and arranged for the exodus, was at least 40 thousand – and possibly millions – of years more advanced than his generation. They must have made some paradigm-shifting discovery about gravity.

He turned his attention back to the ship's schematics and found the large bay where he'd arrived on the *Exodus 9*. It was labeled "Cargo Bay 62," and had dozens of storage rooms around its perimeter. He located the bathroom where he'd gotten his clothes from the dispenser.

He'd wakened alone in the enormous space. It was likely, however, that he was supposed to have landed in one of the hundred or more "Bio-Transport" bays, each of which contained about 250 pairs of transport pods arranged in a grid. He remembered the array of pods in the base from which he'd transported from Earth. There had been hundreds in the room he'd used, and there had been multiple such rooms. That facility had been designed to transport over a thousand at a time. They could probably have evacuated 50 to 100 thousand people per day. But it was only him.

His watch vibrated on his wrist. There was a message that read, "Your counseling appointment begins in 15 minutes." An address and a map simultaneously popped up on the coffee table and the watch.

It was the counseling session that Greta had mentioned after his medical procedure.

His shoulders tightened and he shuddered. Images from his meeting with a "counselor" on his first day in the Red Box came to mind. This one couldn't be worse than that, he thought.

Will stood, stretched his arms and neck, and headed for the door.

WHILE DANIEL and Sylvia inspected their flats on the 20th floor, they got a message informing them of an impromptu meeting. They headed back to their offices and, as they approached 713, Director Thackett strode up behind them.

"How are the accommodations?" Thackett asked.

"Beautiful," Sylvia replied as she punched in the code and opened the door. "And it will be so convenient."

They went inside and proceeded directly to their usual seating arrangement – Thackett in one of the leather chairs, and Sylvia and Daniel on the couch.

"Your moving here couldn't have come at a better time," Thackett began. "And you should get your outside affairs in order as quickly as possible. You might consider selling your houses – you can find new ones when this is over."

"What's going on?" Daniel asked. "Are we in immediate danger?"

"I have no specifics at this point," Thackett replied. "But yes."

"China?" Sylvia asked.

"Yes, and possibly Russia, and others," Thackett said. "There's a lot happening right now."

Thackett stood, walked to the kitchenette to his right, and returned to his seat with a bottle of water. "The Russians are digging in Antarctica," he explained. "They've been at it for over two weeks, and they're now accusing us of detonating a nuclear device to destroy the base. They're claiming their military ops died in the blast."

"They're certainly dead," Sylvia said, "but not from a nuclear blast."

It was one of the most horrific things Daniel had ever witnessed. Mangled human bodies had slammed onto the floor beneath the vertical shaft at the base, exploding like overripe melons on a sidewalk. In the end, the massive pile of human parts had been incinerated as if they'd been held in the fiery blast of a rocket engine. Will had done it.

"Are they detecting radiation at the site – something to confirm their nuclear blast theory?" Daniel asked.

"Not of the type one would expect," Thackett replied.

"What do you mean?" Sylvia asked.

"Our sources tell us that Russian scientists are detecting strange subatomic particles emanating from deep within the ice," Thackett explained. "They're baffled – it can't be accounted for by current theories of particle physics. Some think there's dark matter in the ice, or something else."

Daniel didn't know what dark matter was exactly, but he knew that physicists didn't really know either.

"They've drilled deep holes to collect samples and are finding nothing," Thackett continued. "But they have satellite photos that show a change in geography."

"That's peculiar," Sylvia agreed, "but it's not evidence of anything."

"The only thing within human technological capabilities that could have altered such a vast area is a nuclear weapon," Thackett argued.

"Like Bikini Atoll?" Sylvia asked.

"Precisely," Thackett responded.

"The largest one detonated there was a hydrogen bomb – 15 megatons," Daniel said. "The one in Antarctica would need to have been much larger. There's no way we could have hidden that from satellites, and there'd be a specific radiation signature."

"So why has the threat level increased for us?" Sylvia asked Thackett.

Thackett twisted in his seat and took a sip of water. "Russian and Chinese intelligence ops are rummaging around the DC area like rats in a garbage dump. We've already had multiple engagements, and they're becoming more brazen."

"China has lost a lot of people in the past few weeks," Daniel said. "Both here, and in Antarctica."

"And they now feel justified in whatever they do," Thackett explained. "And Space Systems is already on their radar."

"What about Jacob?" Sylvia asked.

Thackett shrugged. "We'll let him stay at Swann Street for now," he said. "He'll be extended an offer to stay here at some point. He still has some training to complete, so he's in various facilities in the DC area during the day."

"When will he be ready for his first assignment?" Daniel asked.

"You can give him something whenever you want to," Thackett replied, "but his time will be limited due to his training."

"We have something right up his alley," Daniel explained. "A new Chinese satellite that we've hacked."

"Spy satellite?" Sylvia asked.

"Yes, but it's been repurposed," Daniel replied. "It's in far orbit, outward-looking, and has the full spectrum of signal sensors."

"Outward looking?" Thackett repeated. "I think there's going to be a lot of that now – and not just for scientific purposes."

"This is no scientific observer," Daniel confirmed. "It uses military-grade encryption. It was originally designed to view Earth's surface but was reconfigured to look outward."

"Do they know they've been hacked?" Sylvia asked.

Daniel shook his head. "Seems not," he replied. "And it hasn't even been fully commissioned."

"Then how have we already hacked it?" Thackett asked.

"It utilizes the same communications technology as one of their spy satellites that we recovered a couple of years ago in the South China Sea," Daniel explained. "The same one that Jacob reverse-engineered while he was still employed by Interstellar Dynamics."

Thackett seemed to mull it over. "Then he's precisely the person we want working on this," he said. "Get him started on it. If it becomes important, I'll suspend his training."

Daniel nodded.

Thackett stood and rubbed the back of his neck with his hand. "I don't want either of you leaving the building until further notice," he said.

Thackett walked out, leaving Daniel and Sylvia on the couch.

"What do you think is going on?" Sylvia asked.

"Maybe retaliation for recent events," he speculated. "But I'm more concerned that nothing seems urgent anymore – I mean our research. I can't concentrate."

"I'm having trouble as well," she said. "I'm still reeling with everything that has happened – still trying to convince myself that it wasn't all a dream."

"Me too," he said. But he knew that the "dream" wasn't over, and that it could easily turn into a nightmare.

Will took the elevator-transport system – which he'd learned was referred to as "the Tube," like the London Underground – to a location on the 14th level, less than 10 minutes from his quarters. The name seemed appropriate, since the process reminded him of the old-time pneumatic mail systems of the 1950s that transported capsules through tubes within a building using vacuum or compressed air.

He exited the Tube and made his way to the outer walkway. As he looked over the railing down to the main mall, 14 levels below, his heart leapt as he spotted movement on the bottom floor. On closer inspection, it looked like it was just an automated floor cleaner, following a pattern that covered the space and navigated around obstacles.

He glanced at the map on his watch and walked the remaining 50 meters to an entrance, next to which a bright monitor displayed the words *Counseling Facility 48*, and entered.

In the reception area was a front desk that resembled that in the biomedical facility. His watch vibrated, indicating that he'd been checked in, and a voice instructed him to proceed down the corridor to the right of the desk and enter the first room on the left.

The illumination dimmed as he followed the passage, and the first door on the left slid open as he approached. His senses nearly overloaded as he passed through the entry and the door closed behind him.

He gawked in disbelief at his surroundings. It seemed he was inside a beachside bar.

Wooden tables and chairs filled the room, and a long bar and stools spanned the left wall. The far side, opposite the entrance, was open to a white-sand beach and palm trees. A tame breeze of fragrant air warmed his face. He turned in a full circle and then looked upward. Beams of sunlight shone through an opening in the structure's conical thatched roof, far above a fire pit with a grill.

He looked back in the direction of the beach. A wooden deck extended over the sand from the open side of the building. It was furnished with bamboo chairs and round, wooden tables shaded with umbrellas. The sun beat down on the deck between the shade of the umbrellas and palms. Gentle, aquamarine waves rolled onto the sand in the distance.

He flinched when a feminine figure stepped into the bar from the deck.

"Hello, William," she said.

Will stared at her for a few seconds. She was tall, thin, and tan, with black curly hair and brown eyes, and she was dressed in loose white clothing. She was beautiful.

"I'm Mia," she continued. "Do you feel comfortable with this arrangement?"

Will didn't know how to respond. The scene was magnificent. But he didn't understand how it was possible. It had to be an illusion, but it was so real. He spotted a bird far over the water. His old eyes – before the genetic corrections – would never have resolved it.

"Would you like to sit inside, or out on the deck?" Mia asked.

"Sorry," he replied after a few awkward seconds of silence. "The deck."

She stepped outside and went to a table near the far edge of the deck, closest to the beach.

Will walked across the bar toward the door. When he stepped across the threshold to the deck, sunlight beat down on his head and the back of his neck, and his arms puckered in goosebumps in response to the intense warmth. It was a feeling that reminded him of youth – not of any particular memory, but just of youth.

"Please, sit," Mia said. "You like the setting?"

"It's beautiful," he replied as he passed her table and went to the edge of the deck. He could hear the waves lapping on the shore. The enchanting fragrances of flowers roused his senses as the warm ocean breeze soughed through fronds and palm trees and over his head, which was now sprouting dense stubble.

His mind flashed to memories of recent events and his awakening on the ship. He turned to Mia. "Am I dead?" he asked.

She looked at him for a few seconds with large, kind eyes before responding. "Sit?" she offered again. "We can talk."

As he sat, motion from his right made him flinch. A young man – a teenager – emerged from the bar area and delivered two glasses filled with ice and a carafe of what looked to be iced tea. The kid filled the glasses and left.

Mia took a sip of her drink and said, "This is supposed to be iced tea. What do you think?"

Will picked up the glass, took a sip, and shook his head. "It's good," he said. "Similar in some sense, but it's not tea as I remember it."

She grinned. "It's the best we could do."

"I don't understand," he said.

"That's why I'm here," she explained. "I'll try to answer any questions you have."

His mind seemed to fumble over itself, trying to ask a million questions simultaneously. "What is this?" he finally said, gesturing to the space around him.

"This is an island in the South Pacific, called Rarotonga," she said.

"Why?" he asked, as a large flower a few feet to his left caught his eye for an instant. It had bright pink and orange petals with streaks of purple and green emanating radially from the center, like the iris of an eye.

"I don't understand the question," she said.

"Why set up an environment that mimics Earth?" he asked as he looked away from the flower and back to her. "And why try to reproduce food and other aspects of life on Earth?"

"We wanted to give you the least stressful transition to your new existence," Mia replied.

"Who is 'we?'" Will asked. He knew the answer but wanted to confirm it.

"The generation that preceded yours – those who evolved on Earth before it was regenerated, and your race emerged."

"The Deltas," he said.

She nodded.

"How were you able to mimic things from Earth so well?" he

asked. "The food, language, movies – even this island." He sensed his mind was still spinning in the background as it tried to figure out how the island illusion was possible.

"A vast amount of information about your generation has been emanating from Earth for a century," she explained. "In the last 20 years, the volume has increased drastically and has become comprehensive. We know every language, the complete geography of Earth, every piece of art and entertainment, your detailed history, your foods – to a degree – and your biology."

"How? From our internet communications?"

"Yes, mostly," she replied. "But first from radio transmissions, then television, and finally the Internet, which has bound everything together. We even collected a record of each Earth inhabitant so that we could identify them as they arrived."

He knew that the Internet contained everything imaginable about Earth – and it was all there for those on the outside to see. "Why have you gone to such great lengths to acquire this information?"

"Like I said, to make your transition as comfortable as possible," she replied. "The previous generation experienced great hardships during their exodus. You can learn about it when you have some time – it's all available to you."

"On the ship's computer?"

She smiled. "You can think of it as a computer, I suppose," she said. "But it's different from the devices to which you are referring. The ship's 'computer' is much like a human brain, but many orders of magnitude larger. It's more like a hive of trillions of human brains that all interact and cooperate. And it can learn."

"Are you of the previous generation?" Will asked.

She shook her head. "I was created by them, we all were," she explained. "Some of us have been here since the *Exodus* fleet was positioned."

"That means you've been here for 40 thousand years," he said. "How is that possible?"

"It's been just over 38 thousand years, and many of us were in stasis until the probe on Earth transmitted a signal," she explained.

"When our ships received it, some of us were activated, and others were generated. We were created to assist you in your escape and relocation."

"Where are we going – where is the ship taking me?"

"I cannot say – I don't have that information," she replied. "Does it matter? You would not know where we were going even if I told you."

Will thought about it for a few seconds and decided to let it go for now. She could have easily given him the name of their destination and he wouldn't have recognized it anyway.

"All I know is that our destination is a habitable planet," she added. "Or a series of them."

"Was Earth destroyed?" he blurted.

"I don't know," she replied. "Sorry."

He of course hoped desperately that Earth had been spared – but, again, he wouldn't have been able to verify any answer Mia provided him.

"How are you feeling, physically?" she asked, changing the direction of the conversation.

"Never better," he replied, and it was an understatement. "I went through the DNA enhancement procedure."

"It's in your file," she said and nodded. "It will take a few months for the process to complete, but the effects are immediately apparent."

Will thought it was a miracle.

"Your expression seems negative somehow. Sad," she said. "Why? Do you have survivor's guilt?"

Will was familiar with the term. It referred to the emotion felt by some who were the lone survivors of large-scale catastrophic events such as plane crashes or military missions. But his emotions were even more complicated.

"If Earth wasn't destroyed, then I'm not a lone survivor," he explained. "But I just can't help thinking about how the medical technology used to replace my failing kidneys, and to effectively reverse my age, would have benefitted the billions of suffering people on Earth."

Mia nodded. "The biological puzzle was solved by the previous generation long ago."

That reminded him of something. "The technology on this ship and that on Earth, in the Antarctic base, is about 40 thousand years old, correct?"

Mia nodded.

"How long ago did the previous generation leave Earth to escape their regeneration?"

"A little over a million years ago," she replied.

Will flinched. He was expecting a number far less than that – something like 50 thousand years. "So why did they come back to construct the base and position the *Exodus* ships after nearly a million years?"

"Like I said, they wanted to make it easier for you," she replied. "And they needed to put things in place before indigenous life developed that would notice them."

"And now their technology is 40 thousand years beyond that of this ship?" Will asked. "What could they possibly do beyond teleportation and complete biological repair – essentially becoming immortal?"

"I wouldn't know about their current technology," she replied. "We've been out of contact with the Deltas for many thousands of years."

"There are no Deltas on the ship?"

She shook her head.

"What about the other ships?" he asked. "There are others in the fleet, right? Are they close by?"

She shook her head again. "I don't know where they are – but they're not near the *Exodus 9*."

"Is there any way to reach the Deltas?"

"I don't have that information," she replied.

"Is there a way to contact Earth?" he asked.

She shook her head. "We're too far away – the signal would take a long time to get there, and there'd be the same amount of time for a response to come back. Even if it were possible, it would not be allowed."

He figured as much. Not to mention that if the Regenerators were there, they might be able to track him down. That reminded him of another question.

"Who are the Regenerators?" he asked.

Mia shook her head. "Little is known about them, but you can research that for yourself on the ship's network."

Will took a sip of his tea and looked out to the beach. He really felt as if he were there – on Earth – and that he could walk onto the sand and touch the water.

"This simulation is very realistic," he said as he took a deep breath of the sweet air. "I feel like I could go swim in the surf."

"You can," she said.

"What?"

"This is a full immersion facility," she explained. "It's designed to mimic just about anything."

Will stood and faced the beach.

Mia held up her hand. "Please," she said. "We'll walk out to the water when we're finished with our session."

Will sat. His head was suddenly blasted with thoughts from all parts of his mind. The best he could explain it to himself was that he was in paradise. But then he remembered that there was something missing. People. Denise.

THE LATE MORNING sun warmed Lenny's bare feet as he sipped the sweet water out of a green coconut with a straw and watched the surf from the porch of his hut. On a whim, he'd taken a bus to Punta Leona beach on Costa Rica's Pacific side with a bunch of screaming kids. He'd gotten off at a couples' resort and got a cabin to himself just 100 feet from the water.

He'd had a scare the first night at the resort's restaurant when he'd spotted a man watching him. It turned out it was a CIA operative named Diego who'd notified him that Thackett wanted to reestablish contact. Diego had assured him that he wasn't being called back into service but that the CIA director might want his input on a few things. Lenny was both relieved and disappointed that it wasn't more than that.

Lenny had slept well as the gentle sounds of waves rolling onto the beach had lulled his mind away from bad thoughts. Between the improved diet, warm weather, and lack of stress, he felt 15 years younger than he had just a few weeks prior. The new life was good on his body, but not so easy on his mind.

Dark memories would surface from time to time, but that usually occurred at night. The bright sun had a way of suppressing those thoughts and conjuring up more hopeful premonitions of the future. But the future only had one thing in store for him if he continued on like this. He saw his current situation as something akin to long-term hospice, granted, in a beautiful place.

He grunted to himself. It didn't take long for him to get antsy.

In the late afternoon, he took a nap and then headed to the resort's restaurant at 7:30 p.m. for grilled fish and vegetables. Afterwards, he got a coffee, took it to the restaurant's deck, and lit a cigarette as he watched the sun descend toward the water.

He took a deep drag and admired the pink-purple sky on the western horizon. There were a few others doing the same – mostly couples – but in his peripheral vision he noticed a loner he recognized.

The man approached and took a seat at Lenny's table.

"The food here is quite good for a tourist resort," Diego said. "Do you speak Spanish?"

Lenny shook his head. "Only enough to order food."

"Russian and Chinese ops are infiltrating the DC area and New York," Diego explained. "And they're talking to each other."

"That's unusual," Lenny said. "What am I supposed to do?"

Diego shook his head. "Nothing major yet," he replied. "For now, our boss just wants you to have a look at some of the players and tell us who they are, and why you think they're in the US. The work would be regular, but light."

Now that was Lenny's kind of gig: CIA analyst rather than black ops thug.

Lenny snuffed out his cigarette in an ashtray and lit another. Diego followed suit.

"Tell 'our boss' that I would be happy to help," Lenny said. "Pro bono."

Diego smiled. "Good. We'll get you a CIA laptop and phone."

Lenny didn't like the idea of carrying a CIA phone again, but the work sounded ideal. He'd stay in semi-retirement in Costa Rica, but stay active – something he seemed to need – and stay out of dangerous activities. No more killing.

His mind seemed to twitch in his skull. *No more killing*. Even though he hadn't spoken the words aloud, they sounded like a lie.

Lenny doubted that his retirement would last.

"ARE they really going to deliver me to some planet to live out the rest of my life alone?" Will asked.

Mia seemed to study his face for a moment before she replied. "The rest of your life?" she asked. "You're speaking in your old language – with old ideas."

"I don't understand," he said.

"How do you think you arrived on the *Exodus 9*?" she asked. "The transporter on Earth had to destroy your body in order to gather every bit of information about it – from every physical bond between atoms to intricate details of the synapses in your brain. That information was then delivered to the receiving device on the *Exodus 9*."

Will understood the idea: there was no way to know every complex detail of the body and brain without taking it apart. No physical entity – no matter – had been transported to this location. Only information had been transferred. His body had then been reconstructed from different matter – but with an identical atomic makeup – when the information arrived at its destination.

"Why did I have to separate during the transport?" Will asked. He recalled that there had been two pods at each transport station in the Antarctic facility – one for the physical body, and one for the soul.

"The physical information can be corrupted if the soul is inside the body during its disintegration," she explained. "Its natural tendency is to protect the body as it is taken apart, and it will interfere in the process. Thus, forcing it to be inside the second pod in order to initiate the transport process ensures that it won't hinder the disassembly."

He understood now – it was a kind of safety interlock. "How long did it take to make the trip?" he asked. "And how far are we from Earth?"

"We were over a light-year from Earth when the transport took place," she replied. "The transfer process took less than two weeks."

"That's impossible," Will said. "The transport of information can't exceed the speed of light." He knew that was a scientific fact. It should have taken exactly a year for the signal to travel one light-year.

She grinned and shook her head. "This technology is over a million years ahead of yours. Don't let your limited scientific knowledge constrain you. You have not yet discovered that space and time can be separated – that there are conditions in which they become independent of one another. The key to it all is in the behavior of spacetime, and other, higher dimensions.

That reminded him of something. "What's producing the apparent gravity on this ship?"

"It's not just *apparent*," she explained. "The gravitational force on this ship is not produced by rotation or linear acceleration. It's produced by a device that manipulates spacetime. The technology that provides the environmental gravity is also responsible for the propulsion system, albeit in a different way."

Will knew Einstein's general theory of relativity described gravity as a consequence of the curvature of spacetime near massive objects. He did not, however, understand how one could build a device that could bend spacetime, or how such a thing could be used for propulsion.

"The gravity on this starship – and on all modern vessels – can be adjusted in both magnitude and direction," Mia continued. "It's currently set to match the gravity on Earth, which, of course, is the same as the natural setting for the previous generation – the Deltas."

"Because they came from Earth," he commented.

"But back to your transport from Earth," she said, redirecting the conversation. "The connection between your soul and physical body was severed for a while. You were effectively *dead* – as you might describe it, even though that's not quite accurate – and then regenerated here. Your body was then reconstructed and your soul – which was not altered – occupied the new body upon arrival."

Will remembered nothing between the time he'd blacked out on Earth and awakened on the ship.

"Now," Mia continued, "I'd like to talk about how you're feeling – your psychological state."

That was a quagmire in which he didn't intend to trudge too deeply. "I want to know where I'm going for the rest of my life," he said.

She nodded. "It's understandable if you're confused and experiencing all manner of emotions," she said. "You're alone – in the sense that there are no others from your generation on the ship – and the fate of your loved ones is unknown."

"I feel anxiety," he said. "I have to get back to Earth."

"Why?"

He hadn't determined exactly why he had to get back. Until now, he'd been preoccupied with other things. The first reason that came to mind was that he'd promised Denise. "There are many reasons," he finally replied. "Do I need a reason other than wanting to?"

Mia shook her head. "No, but it might be better for you to accept your situation."

"And what is that, exactly?"

"That you can't go back," she replied. "And that there might be nothing, or no one, left."

Will wasn't going to accept that, but he considered the hypothetical case in which Earth had been destroyed – or at least its inhabitants had been. "Am I supposed to live out the rest of my life alone?"

"Again, the idea of the 'rest of your life' no longer carries the meaning you think it does," she said. "Your life is indefinitely long."

"Indefinitely long?" he repeated. "Can't I still die of old age – despite your biomedical advances? Or what if I'm in an accident, or I kill myself? My life could end this instant."

"You're missing some important information," she explained. "Once the teleportation data has been transferred to the system – which contains all your DNA and neural information – your body can be reproduced. And that information was updated when you had your recent medical procedures. If your current body were destroyed in some way, it could just be regenerated. Once the new body is created, your soul will find it, and occupy it. It will completely integrate with the new body just as your soul is currently integrated with this one."

"Just like with teleportation?" he asked.

"An identical result, but the process is not quite the same," she said.

Will was skeptical. "So a person could die – multiple times – and just keep coming back to life because a new body is available?"

"Yes, that's one possibility," she said.

"There are others?"

"Yes," she replied. "For instance, the soul could take on a new persona entirely – in a newly conceived body."

"You mean in a baby – a fetus – like reincarnation?" he asked.

"Yes," she answered. "In that case, most memory is lost, and the soul takes on a new life – a new identity."

He was astounded. "And there are other possibilities?"

"The soul could just linger, with no body," she replied. "In that case, it usually resides in the location where its body died, or where its remains are stored, and will continue to stay there until it decides to move on – which can sometimes take centuries."

He contemplated what he'd just heard. If true, it exposed the reality of what was thought of as the illusory notions of crackpots: the ideas of reincarnation and ghosts.

"These other possibilities were discovered only when souls were able to reoccupy regenerated bodies?" Will asked.

"Yes," Mia replied. "These discoveries changed everything."

"Life goes on forever?" he asked.

She shook her head. "That's still unknown," she responded. "Souls sometimes disappear."

"I don't understand," he said. "You can't track them, can you? Like you said, they could be reincarnated and have little or no memory of their previous life."

"The Deltas kept precise population records on their planets and space stations," Mia explained. "Sometimes someone would get killed – or their body would die for some reason – and their soul would not be found in the vicinity, meaning that there were no new babies being born, and their regenerated body would not be reoccupied."

"Where do they go – the souls?" he asked.

"We can only speculate – out into the great expanse of the universe, perhaps," she replied. "Some speak of going 'beyond the horizon' – some mystical place of which no one has direct knowledge – but there's no way of knowing either way."

"Can't those missing souls just linger on for a century, like you said?" Will asked.

"That doesn't usually happen if a regenerated body is available," she explained. "Souls linger for various reasons, one of which is mourning their lost body, and another is that they have unfinished business. Both of these reasons are moot if they can just return to their lives in an identical body."

"How often do they disappear?" he asked.

"The rate is low, a fraction of a percent of deaths result in no return," she said. "But it's inexplicable."

"Can the soul be destroyed?" he asked. He recalled the conversation he'd had with the so-called Judge when he'd entered the probe – an event that seemed like it had occurred in another lifetime. The Judge had mentioned that he could save Will's soul from destruction.

She smiled. "That's another lingering philosophical question," she said. "And there's a counter question to that: how are new souls created, or from where do they originate?"

Will stared back at her, his mind spinning but coming up with nothing.

"Just as precise population monitoring allows us to estimate how many souls are lost," Mia explained, "it also provides a way to estimate the number of new souls that seem to come from nowhere."

"What do you mean 'come from nowhere?'" he asked.

"If the birth rate exceeds the death rate, then there is a net gain of souls," she explained. "If only one person dies and two are born, a new soul has to have come from somewhere."

From where new souls came seemed to be a more perplexing question than that of where they went when they disappeared. "If you regenerate a body – say that of someone who was recently killed – and you wait for a long time, does a different soul eventually occupy it?"

"No," Mia replied. "Only the original soul can reclaim the regenerated body and fully reintegrate with it."

Will recalled the body he'd occupied while he'd spoken with the Judge inside the probe, and asked, "But another soul, say from someone separating but still connected to another body, could occupy a regenerated body temporarily?"

She nodded. "Although that is an intimate connection – a temporary possession – it's more like wearing a costume. That process is usually used as an interface – so that two souls can communicate in the physical world."

That was exactly what he'd done in the probe with the Judge. They'd both occupied empty bodies and then communicated verbally.

Mia looked out to the ocean – or to the illusion of the ocean. "What are you going to do when we're finished here?"

"I haven't given it much thought," Will replied. "I'm feeling a little hungry." He glanced at his watch: they'd been at it for almost two hours.

"Our time is about over," she said. "Would you like to walk out to the beach?"

Will stood. "Let's go."

He stepped off the deck and into the sand.

"You can take off your shoes if you like," Mia said as she removed hers and set them on the deck.

He stepped back up to the deck and slipped off his shoes. When he stepped off again and his feet hit the hot sand, a chill crept up his spine and into the back of his neck.

Mia led the way toward the water, and they emerged from the sporadic shade of the fluttering palms and into the intense sun. Will turned his head upward and squinted into the light. He couldn't tell the difference between the sun above him and the real thing.

They walked over a hundred feet before they reached the wet sand on the water's edge.

"How big is this place?" he asked as he looked up and down the beach. There were structures – huts and beach chairs and clumps of coconut trees – as far as he could see.

"Human senses cannot tell the difference between this and the real place on Earth that it emulates," she said. "Its artificial nature, however, will be revealed if you separate."

Will didn't want to spoil the illusion. He dipped his foot into the warm water, and then rolled up his pants and strolled out until it reached his knees. He leaned over and ran his hands through the surf. He straightened up and touched his finger to his tongue. The water was salty.

"Can I access this place later?" he asked.

"Of course," she replied. "Not in this particular facility – it's just for counseling – but there are entertainment amenities that offer almost anything you can imagine."

He was satisfied with the beach for now. "How far can we go?" he asked and nodded down the beach.

"As far as you can see, and beyond," she replied. "All of the structures are functional. There are restaurants that serve food, there's parasailing, fishing, volleyball – with interactive participants – and even a place to sleep once the sun goes down."

That was something he wanted to see immediately, and it made him curious. "Can you make the sun go down? Can we see a sunset?"

Mia grinned, looked to her watch, and spoke into it. A few seconds later the sun moved at a pace that made Will feel as if he were witnessing a biblical event. A few seconds later, it slowed and began to lower into the horizon. It was a sight that would send those on Earth scrambling for their lives in fear – the end of the world was nigh. He'd think the same if he didn't know it was all an illusion.

The image before him brought about an avalanche of emotion merged with awe. The sun reddened and flattened, and water glistened as far as he could see. He just stared as a tear streamed down his cheek that he caught with the back of his hand.

He flinched as Mia grabbed his hand, squeezed it, and let it go. "This brings out emotion – memories?"

"It's beautiful," he said. It did bring out emotion – perhaps about memories that still needed to be made.

They watched as the sun waned away to a single bright orange point of light and then blinked out. The hidden sun maintained its presence as it ignited a few wispy clouds in glorious shades of orange-pink, high above the horizon. A few minutes later, he looked to the east as the stars peeked through the darkening sky.

Mia turned around and pointed. "Look, through the trees."

The moon emerged through a gap in the palms. It was large and red, and he could see details that he never could before. Perhaps it was the brilliance of the projection source or, which he thought more likely, it was that his eyes were better than they'd ever been.

"This is the night sky as viewed from Earth's South Pacific on July 19th, 1952," she said.

Will flinched. "Why that date?"

She shrugged. "Don't know – it was the program default," she replied. "Is it significant?"

"I'm not sure," he replied, although it was. He had no idea who Saul W. Kelly was – other than that he was an RAF pilot who had gotten himself mixed up with the Nazis – but that was the date the man had died. It was also the date about which Landau had kept asking him when he was inside the Exoskeleton, in the Red Box. *Where were you on July 19th, 1952?*

Faint music down the beach distracted him from his thoughts. He looked to Mia. "Do you hear that?"

She nodded and smiled. "There's a pub down the beach," she said.

"You can visit it another time if you wish – just go to one of the retreat decks and pull up a program called Rarotonga. There are thousands of other tropical programs as well. It's even possible to generate new ones."

"Do you have other appointments?" Will asked.

She laughed. "No, but you do."

At that instant, Will's watch buzzed. It was a message indicating that he had a follow-up appointment with the biomed specialist in an hour. His stomach grumbled.

"I have one more question," he said. "The biomedical specialist said that I was on the wrong ship."

Mia nodded.

"What does that mean?"

"You'll have to ask the biomed specialist," she replied.

Her answer would have frustrated him more had he not been on a picturesque beach in the South Pacific. "When will we meet again?" he asked.

"Tomorrow," she replied. "In the meantime, you might want to explore the options available on the ship – maybe the retreat decks, or the activity facilities."

"Activity facilities?"

"Look them up," she said as she led him away from the beach toward the wooden deck of the pub, which was now illuminated with tiki torches. "You won't be disappointed."

He slipped on his shoes and then followed Mia inside the bar and to the exit. She opened the door and he stepped into the hallway.

"See you soon," she said as she stepped back and closed the door.

The next thing he knew he was walking down the corridor, through the foyer, and into the brightly lit mall.

Still dazed, Will continued on to his quarters via the Tube. It was as if he'd been in another world for a couple of hours. Even stranger, that "other world" was Earth.

Wang Yong had hired a service to clean the filthy safe house after making sure there was nothing in the place that would compromise security. All he'd found was a wireless router that was designed for the high-security requirements of intelligence services, and some burner phones, which he destroyed.

His predecessors failing to demolish the router during their frantic escape was a possible mistake since it had live encryption keys programmed into its firmware that could be used to decipher current communications. However, since it had been hidden away in a closet and the rest of the place, although messy, seemed undisturbed, Yong figured it was unlikely that it had been compromised. He'd set it up right away so that he could start collecting his people and getting them functioning again as a network.

Yong was going to have to be careful to compartmentalize information for this mission; no one should be able to piece together the full picture. As it stood, his MSS superiors recommended he hire a specialist from the outside to carry out the final act. They felt that the risk was too high that one of their own people would balk at the last moment and doom the mission.

Yong hooked up the router and configured both its conventional wireless along with a direct satellite link for high-security communications. He wished his wife were with him, as this was one of her specialties. She'd be there as soon as she wrapped up some of her own business in San Francisco and put the house up for sale. He hoped to recover the money from that before the chaos started.

After updating the encryption keys and passwords via a satellite phone link, everything was operational.

He flipped open his laptop and got a list of active ops that were at his disposal – those who had survived the purge of the previous weeks. He also had the contact information of Cho's old operatives, including local contractors who might be of use.

The schedule was going to be tight – only a few months to prepare and execute the plan – so he had to get rolling.

The first thing Yong had to do was contact the professor.

WILL WAS STILL in a stupor when he returned to his quarters after his counseling session. He was hungry, and his mind reeled over what he'd learned. Also, feeling as if he'd just returned from some tropical island in the South Pacific was just confusing.

He ordered some chicken soup and a salad from the food synthesizer and ate lunch at the kitchen counter. Even though the flavors weren't quite accurate, the food was extraordinarily satisfying. The system supposedly tailored everything to his DNA – perfectly balancing it to the specific needs of his body – and it was noticeable.

When he finished, he went to the bathroom, took off his shirt, and examined his face and body in the mirror. It was startling.

The wrinkles around his eyes continued to diminish. The hair on his chest was now starting to grow back, but it was fine and blond. The hair on his head was coming in – looking lighter than he recalled – and his hairline was lower, like when he was a kid.

He raised his arms above his head and noticed that something was different somehow. It took him a few seconds to figure out that it was the lack of pain in his left shoulder – from an old football injury that caused him problems from time to time. Over the years, he'd gotten used to it hurting whenever he moved it in certain ways. The discomfort had become just a part of the background, but it no longer existed. It was clear that his baseline pain – which had persisted and increased throughout his entire life – had been significant.

He put on his shirt, and then went to the couch in the main room and leaned over the coffee table. He tapped the surface with his finger and a display illuminated. A list of options appeared, one of which was labeled "How to use this system." He selected it.

As he read, he learned that he had access to an incredible store of information. This included everything from lists of services available on the ship to vast libraries of scientific knowledge. And he learned that one could verbally access the network from anywhere on the ship simply by saying, "*Exodus 9*."

He tried it. "*Exodus 9*?"

"Yes, William?" a female voice said from somewhere in the room, making him flinch. It reminded him of the voice-activated phones from his old life.

"Where is the closest physical fitness facility?" he asked.

"It's just two doors down from your quarters," the voice responded as a map appeared on the table and his watch vibrated and displayed an address.

"*Exodus 9*, how does the ship produce gravity?"

"Just as a changing magnetic field produces an electric field, a change in negative matter flow produces a gravitational field," the computer responded. "I control the negative matter flow systems to produce gravity."

Will was confused by all of it. "What is *negative matter*?"

"Would you like to see scientific papers on negative matter?" came the reply.

"Not now," he replied as his attention focused on the voice. It had said, *I control* ... The ship was referring to itself as "*I*."

"*Exodus 9*, do you have information on human medical science?"

"Yes."

"What is the cure for cancer?"

"The cure for almost every disease is complete DNA reconstruction with corrective modifications," she answered.

Will thought the answer was too general. However, since cancer was a result of rogue, altered cells, fixing all DNA would clearly work. "Can you be more specific?"

"Would you like to see research papers on cancer eradication?"

"Yes," he replied.

"There are over 234 million research papers on this topic," she said. "Would you like to sort or filter them?"

Will gasped. It was a staggering amount of information. "Can you list the 1,000 most recent ones in chronological order – newest first?"

A list of titles in English scrolled on the screen. He zeroed in on one near the end of the list, the title of which was nearly incomprehensible. Most had to do with DNA manipulation.

"How is DNA manipulated?" he asked.

"There are many ways in which this is done," she replied.

"What's the most modern way?"

"Modern methods use high-precision, atomic-level transport technology," she replied.

"What kind of 'transport' do you mean?"

"It is similar to the teleportation technology used for long-range transport, like that employed to transport you from Earth to my cargo bay, but modified for atomic-level scales," she replied. "Would you like to see research papers, or textbooks, on teleportation and extra-dimensional transport science?"

"Yes," he replied.

"There are 285 million papers on teleportation and extra-dimensional transport, and over four million textbooks," she replied. "Would you like to sort or filter the results?

"List the 50 latest textbooks chronologically by their publication date, most recent first," Will said.

The titles appeared and Will attempted to make sense of them. Despite being translated into English, they were barely readable. There were terms he didn't recognize, such as "dimensional suppression," and "matter inversion."

He opened a book titled *Principles of Teleportation* and found its table of contents. There were some terms from quantum and particle physics that he recognized, as well as some from the general and special theories of relativity, but it did little to provide him with any understanding. He found it interesting, however, that, in the world of the previous generation, someone other than Albert Einstein had constructed the general theory of relativity. Even more interesting was that it had been discovered twice on the same planet – by consecutive generations. He figured every advanced civilization had to have their own renowned scientists making such discoveries. He assumed that physics had to be the same everywhere.

He chose a chapter from the table of contents and advanced to the corresponding page of the 950-page book. It was riddled with the complex mathematics of quantum mechanics and general relativity, and things that he did not recognize. He browsed around for a while and then stood and went to the kitchen to get a drink.

He couldn't even imagine how much time it would take to read all the books and papers about transport, much less those that covered other important areas such as medicine, artificial intelligence, and computers, to name a few. It had taken an advanced civilization over a million years to develop and apply the knowledge contained in those books and papers. And it would probably take millions of people thousands of years to learn it – even though the basic science had already been done. It reminded him of the thousands of drawings, back on Earth, of the devices that comprised the Antarctic base. Those devices must have been based on the science described in the books on the screen in front of him. If so, human scientists and engineers had no chance of understanding them.

Still, those on Earth – if they were still alive – could benefit from the knowledge now available to him, especially the medical technology. A surge of sadness overtook his thoughts. They might all be dead. And, if they weren't, each person would suffer a gradual degradation – lasting 100 years in some cases – before death would come for them. On top of it all, they didn't know what happened after they died. Some believed they'd just cease to exist. Others thought they would either go to heaven or hell, and others thought they'd be reincarnated in some way.

Will supposed that, even with the new knowledge he'd acquired from his counselor, he didn't really know what happened after one died, either. Mia had explained that some souls are reincarnated – so those on Earth who believed that weren't wrong. But she'd also said some souls disappear. Where did they go? Did they cease to exist, or did they go to places that could be construed as heaven or hell? The newest possibility, one usually not considered by the typical human, was *resurrection* – coming back as themselves.

And that was now a possibility. It took a confluence of science and some ethereal mechanism for that to be possible. But that advance provided the previous generation a means to defeat death.

After her meeting at the mental health facility in the town of Anna, in Southern Illinois, Denise went west, to St. Louis, Missouri, to visit a friend from college. After that, she headed further west to Clearwater, Kansas, a rural town north of the city of Manhattan, to visit her family for a week.

In addition to her parents, her three siblings and their families lived in the area – northeastern Kansas – and she planned to make the full rounds and visit with each for a day to catch up. She needed the holiday, but it turned out to be less relaxing than she'd hoped.

It started with her parents. Her mom asked her if she had "anyone special" in her life, and she'd pressed the issue. This was followed by other versions of the same question from each of her two sisters, who were both older, and had started families. Her younger brother, who had a girlfriend, never broached the subject.

Her oldest sister, Cynthia, was by far the most intrusive of them all, and she made no effort to conceal her disapproval of many things about Denise's life. The most infuriating comment was that Denise's looks weren't going to last forever, with the implication that they were already fading, and that her time to find a husband was running out. But she had to keep in mind that Cynthia had been telling her that since Denise had graduated from high school. The situation had gotten worse when Denise had broken it off with her fiancé, and then fled to Chicago for law school. In eloquent, but mildly sarcastic terms, Denise informed her that some women were capable of surviving without a man. Denise was beginning to accept that this was how her life would be.

To counter their intrusions, however, Denise mentioned Will. She made it clear that it wasn't serious yet – that they were just dating – since she didn't know how she'd follow up on the story. What would she say? He was dead? He moved away? He transported to some other planet from a secret alien base in Antarctica? She thought the story would make it easier for her, but Cynthia kept prying and wanting to know more about him. She asked for his last name, and some details, so she could search for him on the Internet. Denise refused, an argument ensued, and Denise left early. Sometimes she wondered why she made the effort at all.

On the long drive from Kansas back to Chicago, the earlier conversations took a deeper hold. It would take a long time for her to get over Will, if ever. She was trying to maintain hope that he would come back – he promised. But then she recalled that he promised that he would *try*. He could be dead. Or any efforts he made to return might fail. Or maybe he'd forget his promise. In all, she found that her hopes diminished the more she thought about it.

Her work at the DNA Foundation helped to distract her from these meditations that most often left her with deep feelings of isolation and hopelessness. Also, being with Jonathan – someone who had gone through everything with her – was comforting. She was also making an effort to connect with old friends from college: it was Friday, and she had plans to go out to dinner in Chicago with two former roommates from law school, both of whom were practicing lawyers, divorced, and single.

The way she saw it, she had a choice. She could sink into depression, holding on to the hope that Will would return, or live in another world for a while – one that had nothing to do with recent events – and concentrate on things that she could control.

Her thoughts turned to the road as she approached her usual exit to refuel. It was strange how muscle memory could apply to driving when one made the same trip regularly. As she pulled into the gas station and turned off the engine, her phone buzzed. It was Jonathan.

After catching up with the usual pleasantries, Jonathan said, "Our CIA friends want to arrange a phone call."

"Oh?" she said. Her first thoughts were that there might be more messages from deep space, or some other discovery. In the back of her mind, however, she was hoping they had some information about Will. "What's it about?"

"Don't know," he said. "They want to talk when you get back. When will you be in on Monday morning?"

"Usual time, 7:30," she replied.

They ended the call, and she got out and started the gas fill. It seemed everything she did reminded her of Will, and her work with the CIA and the DNA Foundation would never yield in that regard.

What she needed was a little action, and her work with the CIA, and the Foundation, had always delivered.

WILL ATE a late lunch in his quarters and took a short nap on the couch. He had yet to sleep in the bedroom. There was something about sleeping on the couch that gave the impression that his situation was not permanent.

His mind was clearer than ever before. Even his dreams were more vivid, and he recalled their details. This wasn't always a positive thing, and, in the most recent occurrence, he'd dreamt that an entire planet had been destroyed. It was a variation of a dream he'd had before – one he'd thought originated from implanted memories from the Judge in the probe. In this latest dream, the planet was Earth, and its fading to global death implied the demise of everyone he loved.

He took a shower and, afterwards, studied his face in the mirror above the counter. His eyes were clearer – the whites were whiter, and the blue bluer – and they seemed larger somehow. His skin was smooth and taut, and had a mild oily feel.

The rest of his body was also continually improving. His neck, shoulders, and chest were becoming more well-developed and defined. A reflection from a second mirror on the adjacent wall showed similar improvements in his back, shoulders, and legs. He got dressed and, as he slipped on his shirt, he noted that even his clothes felt better: smooth, comfortable, and well-fitted.

As he considered how some exercise might enhance his mindset, it made him think about his counseling session with Mia, and the recreation facilities she'd mentioned.

He went to the coffee table in the main room and spoke. "*Exodus 9*, where is the closest recreation deck?"

"What type of recreation do you seek?" the voice responded.

"What is there in athletic recreation?"

A list scrolled on the screen. There were thousands of items.

"Would you like to filter the results?" the computer asked.

Will examined the list – it was in alphabetical order. He first noticed badminton, baseball, and basketball.

"Let me see team sports," he said.

The list reconfigured, still in alphabetical order. He wanted something where he could run. He needed to burn some energy.

He saw "Football (American)" and "Football (European), or Soccer." It was the latter that interested him, but he wasn't sure how such a thing could be possible, even after seeing the beach simulation during the counseling session.

"I want to play soccer – European football," he said.

An address and map appeared on the table and his watch buzzed, indicating that the information had transferred. The facility was on one of the higher decks, about a half-kilometer away.

"Where can I get shoes and soccer clothes?" he asked.

"All will be provided," the computer replied.

"When can I go?"

"Anytime you wish," she answered.

Will stood. He wanted to go immediately. He left his quarters and headed to the closest Tube station.

Fifteen minutes later he entered what looked like the usual storefront in the mall. But he knew now that looks could be deceiving – like the counseling facility that contained the tropical island.

He went to the front desk and a screen appeared on its surface. A female voice asked, "Would you like to participate in a football game? Or are you here to practice?"

Will's first inclination was to practice, but he said, "I want to play a game."

"Okay," the voice replied. "At what level would you like to play? Your options are listed."

He examined the list on the screen. It ranged from "Preadolescent Pickup Game" at the bottom, to "English Premier League," "Champions League," and "World Cup" at the top.

Will had nowhere near Premier League skills, but he had to see what it was about.

"Premier League," he said.

"For which team would you like to play?"

Will chose a famous team he'd followed in the past.

"What venue?" she asked as a list of stadiums appeared.

"Old Trafford Stadium," he replied. The real one was in Manchester, England.

"Please proceed to the changing room, down the hall to the left."

He passed the front desk and then went down a hallway until he came to a door on the left with a sign that read "Changing Room."

He entered and faced a bank of over 20 cubby-like lockers built into the opposite wall. He spotted one with his name on it. He stepped to the center of the room and turned in a full circle. He was alone.

There was a whiteboard on one wall with diagrams of alignments and plays, and posters of players and team pictures on another. An open doorway opposite the wall of lockers led to a shower room and some offices, and he wondered if the layout matched the real thing, on Earth.

He went to his locker and examined its contents. There was a uniform, shoes, a towel, and bottles of sports drinks and nutrition bars.

A voice came from somewhere indicating that he had to be on the field for warm-ups in 10 minutes.

Adrenaline surged through his body as he undressed and donned a red jersey with the number "4" and white shorts, socks, cleats – which they called "boots" in the UK, and shin guards. It all fit perfectly. A sign indicated the direction to the field, and his boots clicked on the hard surface as he walked. His heart thumped in his chest as he came to a set of double doors, above which read "Field Entrance."

He stood still and tried to breathe. A deep rumbling noise came from behind the doors.

After taking one last deep breath, he pushed the doors open and stepped through.

The rumbling he'd heard came from voices. Over 70 thousand of them. It was Old Trafford Stadium, filled to capacity.

He walked out of the tunnel and onto the field as the crowd clapped politely for his appearance.

The air was clear and sweet with the scent of freshly mowed grass, and the field was brightly lit. The twilit sky had a pink-purple hue, and the moon was just in view at the edge of the opening in the stadium's ceiling.

He went to the edge of the field, squatted down, and touched the thick, short grass with his fingers. The turf was immaculate and mowed in a large, checkered pattern. He'd played sports all his life, including soccer, and this field was better than anything he'd ever touched. The smell of damp earth made it seem as real as it could ever be.

He turned and faced the near stands. They were filled with people who looked like any other stadium crowd on Earth awaiting the start of a game. Many wore red-and-white jerseys, and some had painted faces in the same colors. Their voices all blended together in a sort of white noise above which would occasionally rise the squeal of a child or an announcement from the loudspeakers. It all seemed so real.

Someone yelled his name from the field, and he turned to see a group of players from his team.

"Will, time to warm up," one player said. "Let's go."

He knew who all the players were – the real ones – but didn't recognize anyone on the field. The other team was warming up on the opposite side of the pitch. They were wearing blue jerseys and were from another Premier League team that he knew well.

As he trotted over to his teammates, he wondered how the illusion was going to play out – him being on the same field with the two juggernauts.

He took his place in a circle of about 20 players and mimicked the stretches they were doing. He felt unusually limber.

An athletic trainer – a blonde woman of about five-foot-six – walked around and chatted with the players in a British accent. He thought they all must have been holograms, but he couldn't tell. Then he wondered how a hologram could kick a soccer ball.

Will was sitting on the grass, stretching his hamstrings, when the athletic trainer got around to him.

"How are you feeling, Will?" she asked.

Her words startled him, and her hands pressing on his shoulders to help him stretch made him flinch. He relaxed and let her assist.

"I feel good," he said. In fact, he felt better than he could ever remember. His muscles and tendons felt springy – flexible and strong. His joints moved smoothly. His breathing was effortless and clear. His eyesight was perfect.

"You just tell me when you're ready to go, okay?" she said, and then moved on to the next player and asked him a few questions as he stretched.

It was all so realistic, and now Will was wondering if he were dreaming. Or maybe he really was dead, and this was paradise.

After stretching, they did some exercises followed by a few sprints. In his younger days, he'd been extremely fast. He felt even faster now.

Next, they separated into pairs and passed a ball back and forth. Will was paired with a tall player with a shaved head who wore a jersey with the number 10.

Will had started playing organized soccer as a child and continued through high school. He'd played baseball and American football in college but, after that, everything was just pickup games. He was getting more and more nervous as time went on, fearing, among other things, embarrassment.

This is an illusion, he reminded himself. *No reason to be embarrassed.* But it was so realistic that a part of his mind was convinced it was genuine.

The trainer made her way back to him. "How are you feeling?" she asked.

"I'm ready," he replied. Or at least he was as ready as he could be, under the circumstances.

A few seconds later, the crowd clapped, and Will turned to see a bearded man in a sportscoat trot out from the locker-room tunnel to the edge of the field. It was the coach of the home team – Will's team – making his entrance. The teams jogged off the field to their respective sideline areas, and Will followed his teammates to their coach.

The coach looked to Will. "You know where you're playing?"

Will immediately replied, "Right winger." It was where he'd normally played in his previous life.

The coach nodded. "You all know where to go," he said to the others. "Take the field."

Will ran out to his position on the right side of the line, nearest the coach. The other team was set to kick off. A few seconds later, the referees took their positions, and the whistle blew.

The blue players at the center tapped the ball a few times and then launched it directly at Will. The blue left-winger was sprinting to get it, but Will reacted, beat him to it, and managed to head the ball back to one of his teammates. The crowd responded with mild applause. He was now completely engaged.

Will kept up with his teammates as they advanced down the field, with the other team defending. He had one touch along the way, just a tap back to the player who had passed it to him. The ball was then passed to the other side of the field and one of his teammates took a shot, rocketing the ball over the goal and into the crowd. He was already breathing hard, but his recovery was quick.

Will retreated to a defensive position on the other side of the midfield line. The opposing goalie made a towering kick, sending the ball well over the midline where players from both teams fought for it.

There was nothing about the play, tactile feel, or environment that looked artificial. He knew he was in a room far smaller than the stadium – perhaps with a ceiling no taller than the separation between floors on the ship. But there was no way to tell.

He decided to stop analyzing how it was happening and just enjoy the experience.

For the next 45 minutes, he was flying up and down the field. His lungs burned from time to time, as did his leg muscles, but he managed to keep up the intensity. His recovery time was better than he ever remembered.

His effectiveness as a contributing player was minuscule, but he managed to not make any fatal errors. However, the crowd booed him twice for misjudging passes and losing the ball out of play. His ball control was dismal, so he tried to pass the ball away before getting challenged. He was tackled and kicked on occasion, and felt pain from the contact, especially when an opposing player's cleats raked across his shins, leaving red scrapes.

His best play of the half was a centering pass from the deep corner that got headed toward the goal by one of his strikers, provoking a short-lived spark from the crowd. The goalkeeper deflected it over the crossbar.

Being as naturally quick as he was, his defense was pretty good. It also dampened the effect of his poor ball-handling skills.

He was near the blue goal at the 35-minute mark when his team's winger on the opposite side hit a perfect ball into the box that was headed by a defender, but then deflected from one of Will's teammates and into the goal. The crowd erupted. It was deafening. Adrenaline surged through his entire body. He couldn't remember ever being so exhilarated.

They were up one-nil at the half, and Will went back to the locker room with the team. The players consumed electrolyte drinks and nutrition bars as they chatted about the game.

He went to the restroom and spotted himself in the mirror on the way out. His face was slightly flushed from the running, but he looked fit and muscular, like he might even belong on the field.

He went back into the main locker room where the trainer approached him.

"The second half is due to start in 10 minutes," she said. "Are you okay to play?"

Will nodded. "Of course."

She glanced at his legs. There was a scrape above the shin guard on one side, and on his knee and calf on the other. She pulled a spray bottle out of her knapsack and doused the injured areas. The burning stopped immediately.

"You have a bump on the side of your head as well," she added as she reached up and touched it lightly with her forefinger.

He felt a mild pain as she pressed it. He hadn't even noticed it was there.

"I'm okay," he said.

She smiled and then went to tend to another player who had a swollen eye.

He wondered how the program managed all the details so well.

He sat on the bench in front of his locker and downed a sweet electrolyte drink and a nutrition bar. A few minutes later they were out on the field and going through some exercises to warm up before the start of the second half. The sky above the stadium was now dark enough to see the stars, and the moon was in full view. Music he recognized played through the audio system, and ads for familiar products scrolled on the walls that surrounded the field. They'd thought of every detail.

By the end of the second half, the opposing team had scored an equalizer and Will was exhausted. He'd received a yellow card for a late tackle, and the opposing player had gotten into his face and pushed him. Players from both teams separated them and it was over. Will was just confused during the conflict, as his mind was trying to determine how to react to the aggression. It was an illusion but, as the scrapes and bruises he'd acquired indicated, there were real consequences.

And then the game was over: a 1-1 draw.

The players waved to polite applause as they left the field. As they proceeded through the tunnel, some of his teammates chatted with him, telling him that he'd played well, even though he knew they were just being polite.

Will undressed, threw his sweat-soaked uniform into a bin, grabbed a fresh towel from a stack on a cart, and went to the showers. Other players did the same.

He entered a shower stall, closed the door, and adjusted the water flow as he thought about the game. It had been as real as anything he'd ever experienced – in terms of physically being there. In other ways it was completely surreal to play for a famous Premier League team, and against another.

The players all looked perfect in every detail. They were a part of the program but weren't mere holograms. He'd made contact with them – he had the scrapes and bruises to prove it. The ball felt real – he'd kicked, thrown, and headed it – and the food and drinks in the locker room were real.

When he got out of the shower, everyone was gone. He dressed in his normal clothes and donned his watch, which read almost three hours since he'd arrived. It was just after 7:00 p.m., although it felt much later – probably from the illusion of the night sky during the game.

The walk from the locker room to the outer facility was strange. His nerves still tingled from the experience.

The bright lights made him squint as he entered the main mall. He found a Tube station, made the trip back to his quarters, and sat on the couch. The coffee table display lit up and notified him that he had messages. He had no idea that such a system existed: it reminded him of email.

There were two messages. The subject of the first read: RECREATION: SOCCER MATCH RESULTS.

He tapped the message with his finger and it opened. It reported the stats from the game, including those of his individual performance. He had 29 touches – meaning each time he kicked or headed the ball. That was a low number. There were many other stats listed, such as tackles, passes, offsides, fouls, and missed opportunities. In the end, he got a grade: it was a D-plus.

Will huffed and laughed. It wasn't too bad. He would have given himself an F.

Next were other evaluations. His speed and quickness were highly rated – in the upper 95th percentile. However, ball control, pass accuracy, and game intelligence were in the lower 20s. It then gave him some practice suggestions.

His stomach grumbled and he went to the kitchen and selected lasagna and an electrolyte drink for dinner. As he sat at the counter and ate, he gazed out the window on the far side of the room and contemplated what he'd just experienced.

He'd just lived the childhood dream of almost every soccer player and fan. And it looked as if he could do almost anything else he wanted to in that regard – American football, baseball, basketball, tennis, and any other sport.

He took his plate to the couch and started browsing other categories of entertainment. Among those on the long list were vacations to any part of the world, concerts, amusement parks, and cruises. There were long-term games based on mystery and spy novels, and you could live out a full sci-fi adventure on the *Millennium Falcon* or the *USS Enterprise*. You could live for an entire school year at the "school of magic" that was at the center of the famed children's books and movies that his nieces loved so much. That, Will thought, would be the oddest experience: a virtual reality that allowed one to do things that defied the laws of physics.

There was also an "adult entertainment" category that had more subcategories than he knew possible.

He finished his lasagna, returned his plate to the kitchen, and went to the window. The stars were moving from right to left at the usual rate. He sat on the carpet, leaned his back against the window frame, pulled his knees up to his chest and wrapped his arms around them. He was looking through the window on an angle – in the forward direction of the ship so that the stars seemed to be moving toward him.

The advanced technology of the Deltas – the previous generation – was so far ahead of his own that he felt like a toddler in an arcade. Although, a toddler would at least know that everything was a game and would likely be able to distinguish illusion from reality. For all Will knew, what he was currently experiencing – staring out the window of a starship – wasn't reality, either.

His watch buzzed. It was the second message – he'd almost forgotten. He had an appointment with the counselor in the morning.

4

EPIPHANY

The day Lenny returned to San José from the Punta Leona resort, Diego delivered his new CIA phone and computer. That night, Lenny tested everything while he drank beer and watched a local professional soccer game on TV. It was a pleasant evening, and he had the impression that he'd better enjoy it. He didn't know how many more he'd get in his tropical paradise.

The next morning, it was just under 70 degrees and clear at 7:00 a.m., and he enjoyed the fragrances of dew-covered flowers in the park on his way to one of his usual cafés. He was expecting to receive electronic files either from his handler's account – "handler" being a term he'd hoped to never hear again – or from a source located in the CIA's Space Systems building.

He got a medium-roast coffee in a glass mug and went to the back courtyard with a view of the adjacent park. The sun warmed his face through the trees as he pulled out a cigarette, lit it, and took a deep drag. A feeling of satisfaction and relief engulfed his body and mind. Having cut back the smoking to 10 per day made each one that much more intense.

He opened the laptop and pressed his right thumb on a small scanner that read his print. In case of emergency, using his left thumb would cause the classified memory to be electronically destroyed, leaving only predetermined benign items, such as reading materials and software applications, untouched.

After logging on to the computer, and then into his secure CIA email, he downloaded a single document titled "Player List 1," and opened it.

It was a 45-page collection of short identification files – up to a half page apiece – of recent arrivals in the Washington, DC area. Various reasons for suspicion of each individual were given.

He scrolled through it quickly for a first pass. There were just under 100 suspects, mostly Russians and Chinese, but a few others as well. One that caught his attention on first glance was a Tunisian named Mounir Mekhloufi. Lenny knew him as "The Razor," a name originating from the assassin's preferred method of elimination. He'd encountered the man decades earlier and had the scars on his chest and back to prove it. Lenny had barely escaped.

That Mekhloufi was in DC should have been a stark warning of things to come. The man could have only one reason for being there, and that was to kill someone. And that someone was either of high profile or was difficult to access: Mekhloufi was expensive. Twenty years prior, Lenny had been getting about 25 thousand US dollars for a freelance hit. At the same time, Mekhloufi was getting 100 grand. That difference would eventually grow to more than ten-fold and, currently, the Tunisian was getting up to two million per job. And the man didn't like competition, which was why Lenny had felt the edge of the man's blade.

Lenny recognized a dozen Russians – some near his age – who were ops of various types. He knew some had been assassins in the past, but it wasn't uncommon for people to be brought up through the intelligence ranks and be promoted beyond such activities. Those people might have been in the States for more benign purposes.

Lenny wrote up a quick report, simply confirming what the CIA suspected of the new arrivals, and giving a few words about what he knew of each of them.

Regarding Mounir Mekhloufi, however, he wrote a few paragraphs, starting with an urgent warning: Mekhloufi was there either to kill someone in particular – someone of elevated position – or to carry out some particularly heinous action. He went into some detail of the man's methods and history. He was sure that the Tunisian's confirmed kill list was at least as long as his own. The more disturbing part, however, was that Mekhloufi must have accumulated at least 10 times the amount of money that Lenny had, and could have gotten out of the business long ago. It meant that the brutal bastard wasn't doing it for the money.

By sending this alarming response to the CIA, Lenny knew he was taking a chance. They might call him out of retirement.

WILL HAD dreamt of pleasant things that made the reality of his isolation come to the surface. One dream involved Denise, and the time she had picked him up from the hospital after his release from the Red Box.

He'd again slept on the couch. As he sat up and put his feet on the floor, his body reminded him that he'd played a full soccer match the previous night. His muscles were stiff, and he had a few scrapes and bruises, but it felt wonderful.

His watch vibrated, notifying him that he had an appointment with the counselor in half an hour. After the soccer illusion, he figured the counselor was an illusion as well. But it didn't matter. It seemed that things being real or not was no longer important. What was important was what was happening to him – to his mind.

He got dressed and took the Tube to the counselor's place.

This time, when he went through the door, he entered a café filled with the pleasant aromas of sweet baked goods and coffee. There were people everywhere, and he found Mia at an outdoor table.

When he stepped outside, his attention was drawn first to the old stone buildings across the street, and then to his left, where the Eiffel Tower loomed in the distance. It was a breathtaking view, with people teaming everywhere on the sidewalks and chatting. They looked human, just like those at the soccer match.

He approached Mia, who was sitting at a small table in an isolated corner of the outdoor café.

"A bit different from the beach," she said and smiled. "Coffee?"

Will sat across from her and nodded as she poured from a carafe into a small cup.

He took a sip. It was strong, and good.

"I see you tried one of the recreation facilities," she said.

"Soccer," he confirmed. "It was unbelievable."

"And there's so much more for you to explore," she said.

"I looked through some of it," he said. "It's endless. How is this happening?"

She took a sip of coffee and her cup made a light clacking sound as she set it down. "All of that information is available to you in the network archives," she explained. "Everything has been translated to Earth languages. You can figure out for yourself how everything works."

They were so far advanced that Will feared he'd get nowhere with it. Not only was the sheer volume of information immeasurable, but most of it was beyond his knowledge. He'd already gotten a taste of that while on Earth when he tried to understand the drawings of the alien Antarctic base.

"A person could live on this ship for a long time and never feel like they'd left Earth," Will said, changing the subject.

"It was, of course, designed that way – to relieve as much stress as possible for the voyage," Mia explained. She seemed to look him over. "It looks like your rejuvenation is starting to take hold – you already look years younger, and healthier."

It seemed he was noticeably more youthful each time he looked in the mirror. And he was feeling great, too. However, he might be more comfortable with the "voyage" if he knew more.

"Can you please tell me where we are?" he asked. "And where we're going?"

"I explained that last time," she replied. "We're far from Earth – but still in the Milky Way Galaxy, for now. I'm not privy to exactly where we are going. But now I want to chat about how you're doing psychologically. Physically, you seem to be doing well."

A server brought baguettes, butter, and honey, and Will spoke as he prepared a piece for himself. "I'm okay for now," he said. "With everything so new to me, I'll be distracted for a while."

"Distracted from what, exactly?"

Will shrugged. "From the fact that I'm far away from everyone and everything that I know," he replied. "And that I'm alone."

She nodded in recognition. "At first it's best to be as active as possible," Mia said. "Do anything you want to do."

"As you know, they told me I don't belong on this ship," he said. "Will they transfer me to another one at some point?"

"I don't know," she replied. "Perhaps."

"But aren't all the ships going to the same place anyway?" he asked.

Mia shrugged. "I'm not sure what's supposed to happen, but some of the fleet might have been repurposed."

"Repurposed? For what?"

"Again, I don't know these things," she replied. "You might find some information in the ship's database."

Will was still as confused as when he'd first arrived on the ship – at least regarding where they were taking him, and what he was supposed to do for the rest of his life. Lives. He had a long time ahead of him if everything he'd been told was true.

"Will you play soccer again?" she asked.

He stared at her for a moment as he processed her question. It had been the most exhilarating experience he'd ever had. He'd been an athlete in college, but that environment was nothing like that of a Premier League soccer match. For him, it was the ultimate distraction. "Yes," he said. "And I'll try some other things as well."

"Like what?" she asked.

"I saw some detective mystery adventures," he said. "I always liked private investigator shows." He wondered if they'd be as realistic as the soccer match.

"Anything else?"

"There are fantasy adventures as well."

"Fantasy?" she said.

"Yes, like the book genre – warriors and wizards and monsters of all sorts," he said. He was beginning to understand the magnitude of the distractions, and how he could become entangled in them.

"I think it's important that you engage in recreational activities to at least give you a sense of human interaction," Mia said. "Your mind will eventually adjust to your new reality."

"Are *you* real?" he blurted.

She stared at him for a few seconds and then reached across the table and grabbed his hand. "Does this feel real?"

Her hand was warm and smooth. She let go.

"The soccer players seemed real, too," he argued. "I still have marks on my legs from where I was kicked. But I'm not convinced that they're real – or *alive*."

"I physically exist," she replied. "I'm composed of matter. But I think your question gets at something deeper. You're asking whether I have a soul – an existence beyond the physical."

"I'm sorry," he said. "Until recently, I wasn't even sure I existed 'beyond the physical.'"

"I was artificially synthesized, and I'm self-aware," Mia continued. "I do think I'm alive. I do not know what happens if my body is destroyed."

"I assume, then, that the soccer players are synthesized as well," he said.

"Anything you encounter on the recreation decks is synthesized when the program generates the scene and the cast," she explained. "The characters are sometimes put into stasis afterwards, and sometimes they're destroyed, but can be regenerated, if needed."

Will imagined the possibilities were endless. He could live in a virtual world for the rest of his life and not even know it.

After the session was over, endless questions still filled his head. But he knew there'd be plenty of time to inquire more in forthcoming meetings.

As he rode the Tube back to his quarters, the reality of his isolation

– being on a spaceship in the middle of nowhere – started to invade his mind. The vastness of space sometimes had that effect, and sometimes had the opposite. He figured he'd rather the universe be infinitely large than be small enough to know it all. With communications and travel technologies, Earth had become too small in a very short time, and he'd felt it to be stifling, even confining. The closest spiral galaxy to the Milky Way was 2.5 million light-years away. It was effectively an infinite distance to him. But that might not have been the case for others – like the previous generation. For them, perhaps, the universe wasn't so large.

His stomach grumbled and he realized that his appetite was growing. Perhaps that had to do with the faster metabolism of a younger body and the increased physical activity. He'd eat when he got back to his quarters, and then he'd explore the *Exodus 9*'s information network. He had a lot to learn.

JACOB SAT at the kitchen counter in 17 Swann, turned on the TV, and flipped open his laptop. He pulled up his schedule: it was Friday, and he'd just completed the first week of his training courses.

The full dose of coursework was grueling because of the pace and the sheer volume of information. He enjoyed most of it, except the course on handling classified information, which was filled with more legal jargon than he thought was needed. He'd had to boil it down to common language to really understand it and, for that, it was helpful to have a girlfriend who was a lawyer.

Reading and studying for the top-secret clearance exams took most of his time outside the classroom, but the courses were all manageable. His weapons training would be completed in a few days, and then he'd move into the self-defense component of the class.

His weekends were mostly his, except for this Saturday night when he'd have a surveillance and avoidance exercise from 10:00 p.m. to 2:00 a.m. It was the avoidance part that he thought would be most applicable to him, but it served well to see the surveillance side to know how it worked.

With the training going smoothly, he could finally dive into the project that Daniel had assigned him. He started by reading an abstract summary of the problem, and quickly surmised that it perfectly matched his expertise.

The Chinese had placed a satellite in a far-Earth orbit. It was a spy satellite originally designed to view the Earth's surface and intercept communications. However, before its launch, it had been modified to look outward and into space. To Jacob it was clear: they were trying to pinpoint the sources of the incoming radio waves that had delivered the data that he'd decrypted nearly two months ago – messages and plans from the previous generation. But even though it was too late for that – the signals had stopped long ago – they were still searching for something in deep space.

Although it wasn't uncommon for any country to have a science satellite looking deep into to the cosmos for signals of either intelligent or natural origin, this was no science mission. The CIA and MI-6 had only found connections from the satellite to Chinese intelligence facilities – no civilian scientists were involved. The device was currently in the test phase but would be fully commissioned soon.

Jacob's task was to figure out how the device worked, and then devise a way to commandeer it. He was to do this without the Chinese knowing so that the CIA could monitor what they were doing, determine what were they looking for, and ascertain what they had found so far.

As he flipped through the thick document, he gasped as he turned to a page that showed a familiar drawing. He recognized it as one of his own: it was a part of a satellite he'd reverse-engineered while at Interstellar Dynamics. There was a yellow sticky-note attached to the bottom of the page, which read, "We thought you'd be pleased to see that your previous work was put to good use."

He was more than pleased. So many of his projects at Interstellar Dynamics had seemed to dissolve into nothingness after they'd been completed. It was satisfying to learn that this previous work had a positive impact. More importantly, however, it gave him an enormous head start on his new project. He knew how the communications devices aboard the satellite worked, but now he'd have to figure out how to control everything remotely, and without the Chinese detecting the intrusion. He'd also have to break their signal encryption – which could take a while, even though it was likely the same encryption method used on the satellite he'd reverse-engineered.

Jacob glanced at his watch: he'd give himself a few hours to work on the project, but then he'd have to put in some study time. For the latter, he'd head to the Count Cristo Coffee House. By then, he'd need some fresh air and a source of caffeine.

His fingers tingled as he pulled out his laptop, downloaded sample data from the Chinese satellite collected by the CIA, and opened his signal processing software, Wave Tempest 8.0.

He sighed and looked across the main floor to the stacks on the opposite wall. He took a deep breath through his nose and took in the aromas of wood, old books, and the almost undetectable scent of cherry pipe tobacco.

It was good to be at work again.

WILL RETURNED from the counseling session famished – he'd only eaten a piece of buttered bread for breakfast. He synthesized some scrambled eggs, toast, and grapefruit juice in the kitchen. They were superb.

After he put away the dishes, he went to the bathroom to take a shower and brush his teeth. As he stepped up to the sink and grabbed his toothbrush, it hit him: although he'd brushed regularly, he hadn't even thought to look closely at his mouth.

He stepped close to the mirror and opened wide. His teeth were white and smooth. They were perfect. He'd had extensive dental work done when ... when he'd been inside the Exoskeleton ... but now that had all been replaced by perfect teeth. Even the tiny chip on a corner of one of his top front teeth – something he'd had since he was 12 years old – was gone.

He clenched his jaw. The upper and lower teeth meshed perfectly, and his jaw felt solid. There was even a little sponginess in the teeth, which seemed to reduce the rigidness. It felt as if he could squeeze his jaw with all his might and his teeth would hardly notice.

It made him think of something else.

He crouched down, removed his shoes and socks, and examined his toes. He'd suffered numerous injuries to his toenails growing up playing sports so that the one on the big, right toe was permanently deformed. It had become misshapen with ripples, and any pressure exerted on it resulted in pain. It was something he'd been told would never go away unless he had it removed. The nail was now perfect, as were the others. Even the toes themselves looked good – no longer deformed by decades of wearing imperfect shoes.

Is all of this real? he wondered. Perhaps he'd wake up from this fantasy and find himself still inside the Exoskeleton.

A wave of guilt then hit him. It was as if he were benefitting from something bad that he'd done, or that his gains had come at the cost of someone else.

He brushed off the negative thoughts and went into the shower. The warm water beat on his head and the back of his neck while he tried to assess his situation. For an instant, his mind flashed back to the time he'd been in the shower the morning before he'd been inserted into the Exoskeleton. His situation, and outlook, was now much different – he'd come a long way since then. His eyes were open to many things he hadn't even contemplated at the time. And now he wasn't even on the planet – although he still wasn't completely convinced that was true.

It was clear from his visits to the tropical island and Paris, and the soccer match, that his current view of reality could also be a deception. Although, he had separated and exited the ship – so it seemed real by that test. At some point, when he was on one of the recreation decks, he'd separate and see if he could understand how the virtual reality was being created. There was a part of him that didn't want to know: illusion might be the only thing that would get him through the isolation, and the time.

He wondered what it would have been like had the ship been filled to capacity with people trying to figure out where they were and where they were going. But those people would have been very different from the humans he'd left behind: they would've needed separation abilities in order to transport to the ship. They would have had a different understanding of the world, and the things on the ship might not have been so impressive to them.

Will got out of the shower, donned clean clothes, and went to the coffee table in the main room. He summoned the computer and searched for the next thing to do – he'd put the next soccer match off for a while until he went through a few practice sessions to increase his stamina and polish his skills.

As he perused his options, he found everything from old movies in a vintage theatre to massage spas, the latter of which he planned to try to work out some of the soreness from his activities the previous night. There were all kinds of adventure and mystery stories, popular movie reenactments where he could play an active character, and even extravagant video games where he could be a player inside the game. But the thing that caught his eye was a link labeled "Courses."

He selected the link, and it gave him two choices: "Human" and "Delta." He selected human, and was directed to a long alphabetically sorted list of general areas including art, history, languages, math, music, science, and countless others. He opened the history link and found courses on topics that he recognized – from the beginning of the historical record to the modern era of human history. He assumed that they'd gotten the information from electronic communications – anything transmitted via the Internet or otherwise.

He navigated back to the original menu and selected the "Delta" link. The same categories appeared – in English. His heart thrummed as he selected the "History" link.

A long, multicolumn list scrolled down the screen. There were thousands of "classes" that he could take that ranged from the beginning of the Deltas' historical record to their exodus from Earth to their most recent era. It would take him years to get up to speed on their long past. He wondered if there was a compressed overview that would give him the main points. But that would have to wait – there were other things that he needed to know.

He navigated to the Deltas' science link.

A list of subcategories appeared that included the main sciences – astrophysics, biology, chemistry, engineering, math, physics, and others. He selected the physics menu, and a list of uncountable topics appeared, many of which he did not recognize. There were also numerous things that were familiar to him, such as quantum and nuclear physics, materials and matter, electromagnetism, light and optics, mechanical principles, and mathematical methods. As for the others, he understood most of the words, but didn't know what they meant collectively – things like "Time Quantization and Decoupling" and "Subspace Distortion" and "Vacuum Energy Harvesting."

One topic that he recognized, but knew was something humans had not yet discovered, was "The Grand Theory," which he was sure was referring to the "Theory of Everything," or TOE, that explained all aspects of the universe in one theory. Contemporary human science was still disjointed, and split into individual theories like general relativity, electromagnetism, nuclear theory, gravitation, and quantum theory. The Theory of Everything supposedly combined them all.

He navigated out of the physics menu and into the engineering section. There were thousands of categories. There were the usual types, including mechanical, electrical, materials, and aerospace engineering. But there were many he didn't recognize, such as "subspace transport engineering" and "teleportation engineering." There were also synthetic genetics, artificial intelligence engineering, and virtual environments. There were others for which he had no translation, like "evanescence engineering," and "time dynamics."

Will leaned back on the couch, gazed out the window to his right, and mulled over his situation. He was alone on an enormous starship going who-knows-where, with every possible amenity imaginable at his fingertips. His body had reverted to that of his mid-20s, better in fact, and he effectively couldn't die. There were so many new things to learn, and he had the means to learn them. To top it off, it seemed he could live out any fantasy imaginable. What was this?

He missed Earth.

He went back to the computer and browsed through the endless lists of recreational activities. He got the idea of a Swedish-style massage and scrolled down the list. On the way, he passed a long section of "massage" options that had to do with sex. It seemed they'd thought of everything, but he wasn't looking for that kind of massage.

He needed to work out the residual soreness from the soccer match the night before. More importantly, however, he had to determine what to do next.

IT WAS midnight when Lenny's phone rang.

He'd just fallen asleep after returning from having a nightcap at a pub just around the corner from his apartment. He sat up in his bed and answered the call from a restricted number.

"Let's meet at 7:00 a.m. tomorrow, at the café you were at on Thursday morning," a man said.

Lenny detected an accent. "Who is this?" he asked.

"We've met before," the man replied. "In line to get coffee at the airport."

Lenny remembered. It was the Israeli. "What's this about?" he asked.

"You're in danger," the man replied.

Lenny's blood seemed to freeze. He didn't speak.

"I think I told you that people like us never really leave the business," the man said. "Take care until tomorrow."

The call ended, and Lenny's ears hummed in the silence. He glanced at the dull red display on his nightstand clock just as it flipped to 12:02 a.m.

He slid open the nightstand drawer, pulled out his gun, and set it next to the clock. It was going to be a horrible night's sleep.

JAMES THACKETT LEANED back in his chair and watched the trees sway in the breeze a hundred feet below. The tall evergreens looked silver in the morning sun as a light frost gently faded from their needles. It was 6:15 a.m.

He'd gotten on the road half an hour earlier than usual and beat the majority of the Monday morning traffic. A lot was happening today.

The mission of the CIA was to gather foreign intelligence. The CIA was not designed, nor authorized, to work inside US borders, although one had to be naïve to think that it didn't. The domestic anti-espionage operations that he was now authorizing, like many he'd arranged in the past few months, were supposed to be under the jurisdiction of the FBI. But he couldn't trust the FBI.

There were foreign ops everywhere in the DC area, and many were known for skills other than collecting intelligence. Some were assassins. Others were paramilitary black ops specializing in sabotage and demolition.

He felt guilty about involving Lenny Butrolsky just a month after the man had supposedly retired, but his expertise was crucial. It wasn't so much about his skills, but his knowledge of the players who were showing up on the scene. *What were they planning?*

It seemed to Thackett that everything that had been of recent interest was now gone. William Thompson was dead – destroyed along with the base, which was now buried beneath kilometers of ice. The so-called alien devices – the decoder and power key – had been there during the meltdown as well. The only thing of importance that remained in the CIA's possession was the vast collection of information – the text and technical drawings – that Jacob Hale had decrypted using the decoder device. Perhaps that was what they wanted, but it seemed that there was more to it.

If it was the drawings that they were after, the Chinese would be risking war for something that was practically useless. CIA and Department of Defense engineers had been working on the blueprints for months and hadn't been able to understand anything more sophisticated than structural components. Linguists had made progress on deciphering the language, but their fragmented translations made little progress toward understanding the technology. There were, however, some astounding revelations that implied physically unrealizable phenomena like teleportation, and faster-than-light space travel. He supposed that would interest anyone. But it didn't matter if no one understood the technology required to realize and utilize such phenomena – and it was therefore just science fiction.

The Chinese were busy. First, they were digging in Antarctica, clearly searching for remnants of the base. Next, the China National Space Administration was developing new satellites, and reconfiguring existing ones, to look into deep space. Finally, Chinese ops were everywhere in DC, and were now nosing around almost every secure US research facility, including Area 51 and even other, more secret places.

The Russians were doing the same, but at a more measured level. And, even more disconcertingly, they were interacting with the Chinese.

And now warnings were coming in from the Israelis.

Space Systems was safe for now, and he was glad to have moved the entire Omniscient group into it, except for Jacob Hale – he was going to remain at 17 Swann.

And now Denise Walker and Jonathan McDougal were in danger. That was going to be a difficult conversation.

WHEN WILL ARRIVED at the spa, he was given a choice of massage type and masseuse, as well as a choice of environment. He chose a deep tissue massage, a muscular blonde woman – his mind conjured an image of blonde hair when he thought of a Swedish masseuse – and a sunny Hawaiian cliff overlooking the beach at midmorning. It was perfect: the sounds of the waves in the distance, the happy songs of birds, the fragrances of tropical flowers carried by soft, warm air, and the pressure of strong, oiled hands and elbows digging into his muscles.

It was just the type of distraction he sought. He relaxed and let his mind work in the background. The more he thought about his predicament, the more confusion seeped in. But there was also excitement. It was like stirring silt in tropical water, obscuring a beautiful view that he knew was there but just couldn't see. He had to be calm and wait for the debris to settle.

Without much effort, he could convince himself that he was in some version of paradise. If everything he'd been told was true, he could effectively live forever. In his previous existence, this would be a curse: almost no one wanted to live to be 100 years old. But that was because the health problems that went along with aging would most likely be a long, drawn-out torture: to live for a century meant to age for a century. But that wasn't the case here. His body was rejuvenating more and more with every minute, and he already felt better than he could ever remember.

If he got hurt, he'd immediately get fixed. If he died, he'd get a new body – identical, pristine, and perfect. Death was out of the picture, at least according to his old definition.

He could go anywhere he wanted and do anything he desired – from playing soccer in a giant stadium packed with spectators to eating whatever he craved. Even sex was on the menu, although that was far from his mind for the time being. It was all virtual, but it was indiscernible from reality. And if he couldn't tell the difference between what was real and what wasn't, what did it matter? For all he knew, his entire life on Earth was a mirage. How would he know? How would anyone know?

Finally, and this was important, there was a mountain of knowledge for him to digest. He had much to learn and, from what he'd seen on the ship's computer, it would take him centuries to get through it.

In the end, he figured that time was the key commodity. Removing death from the equation opened the future. It made the future infinite. It removed all limitations.

But how long could it really go on? Eternity was a long time.

He then imagined how life on Earth would change if all its problems suddenly disappeared. What if food and water were abundant and free, energy was unlimited, and all diseases and biological problems were eradicated? What if all desires were provided for – from food to recreation to sex – in a virtual way that couldn't be distinguished from reality? Finally, what if everyone was free and not forced to do anything they didn't want to do?

What would people do? There'd be no going to work on Monday morning – unless you wanted to. There'd be no struggling to pay the bills, put food on the table, keep the car running, or even cook and clean. You wouldn't have to worry about your children's health, or their futures. You wouldn't have to do anything. But you could do whatever you wanted.

Was that the ultimate goal of humanity? With the struggle toward scientific development – from biology to physics – wasn't that it? Wasn't the ultimate objective to solve all problems – given an infinite amount of time? Would we ever be satisfied?

It seemed to Will that, outside of religion, he'd never heard anyone suggest an end game for humanity. Perhaps there was something he'd missed in his college philosophy courses – or maybe this was something he would have encountered had he taken more of them. His education was in physics and math, so there had been little time for him to pursue other studies, although he'd read many books that were heavy on philosophy.

What was the final state of life? One could argue that it was changing constantly, the goal line was always moving. At least for humans it was – their problems were far from solved. But what about a species like the Deltas? It seemed that they'd solved all the big problems. Death and physical suffering were eliminated – they were gone. What was next for them?

"It has been one hour," the masseuse said, interrupting Will's thoughts. "Would you like to continue?"

Will lifted his head and squinted into the sunlight. "No, thanks," he replied, and then sat up on the table. There was a hut a few meters away, behind which a steep, forested hill rose hundreds of feet on a sharp grade.

He followed the masseuse into the thatched-roof structure where she went into a back room, and he headed into a locker room and jumped into a shower.

The thread of philosophical thought on which he'd just meditated was new to him – a new vein of cerebral exploration that sprouted from the perspective of someone who could live indefinitely. It also derived from fear. Eventually he'd grow tired of having everything he wanted, with no needs of any kind. How long would that take – a decade? A century?

He finished the shower, got dressed, and returned to his quarters. It was lunchtime, and he ordered up some Thai food – spicy hot.

After cleaning up the kitchen, he sat on the bench near the window and stared out as he thought about what to do next. His memories of Earth seemed like dreams of the past, and it bothered him that they could fade so quickly. He was becoming absorbed in his new existence, with some fleeting moments filled with lucid memories of people from his life on Earth. His family, friends, and, most prominently, Denise, entered his mind whenever there was a lull in the action.

It was best to keep moving. Besides keeping his mind focused on the present, he needed to learn as much as he could if he had any hope of getting back to Earth.

He went to the coffee table and surfed through the colossal amount of information that was available to him. It was hard to know where to start. He wanted to know more about the Deltas, and their history. He wanted to know about teleportation technology, DNA repair, spaceship propulsion, navigation, and the regeneration of bodies. He wanted to know about other life forms and civilizations. He wanted to know about the Regenerators, who might have already destroyed his world. He needed to know more about his separation abilities, and the soul in general.

He decided on a book that summarized the history of the Deltas from the time they left Earth. When he selected the item, he was asked if he wanted the "classroom lecture experience," or just the text. He chose the latter and got to reading.

DENISE'S NOSE felt like it was frozen by the time she got out of the chilly wind and into the law building. She needed a car – she'd returned the rental – and was sure that Jonathan would comment on it again. It was now a top priority.

Jonathan's door was closed when she arrived, so she knocked. He called for her to enter and, when she did, he waved her over to a speakerphone on a conference table where he was sitting.

"She just walked in," he said into the phone.

Denise glanced at a clock on the wall opposite the entrance – it was 7:29 a.m. – and took a seat across the table from Jonathan, the speakerphone between them.

"Good morning, Denise," a familiar female voice said from the speaker.

It was Sylvia.

"Good morning," Denise replied. It was nice to hear her voice.

"Daniel is here as well," Sylvia said.

Daniel said good morning and got right to business. He explained that there were Chinese and Russian operatives everywhere in DC and that the CIA suspected something was afoot. Everyone was on high alert, and Daniel and Sylvia were moving into the Space Systems building for the long term – probably even selling their houses.

"The problem now," Daniel continued, "is that it's difficult to assess whether you two are in danger. Our first assumption is that you are."

"I thought their only interest in me was my connection to Will," Denise said. "That no longer exists."

"We don't think they're convinced that Will is, uh … out of the picture," Daniel said.

Denise detected the pause and knew that Daniel had almost said that Will was dead.

"So, what are we talking about here?" Jonathan asked. "We're going to be surveilled?"

After a few awkward seconds of silence, Daniel responded. "We have no idea of the lengths to which the Chinese will go," he explained. "Remember, we just recently thwarted an armed assault on Space Systems. And now they might be justifying a violent retaliation for what happened to their operatives in Antarctica. The CIA also decimated a Chinese spy ring at the same time, here in DC."

"We believe your lives might be in danger," Sylvia added.

Denise's skin seemed to quiver beneath her sweater. "What do you suggest we do?" she asked.

"Move into Space Systems," Sylvia replied.

"Come work for the CIA, both of you," Daniel added.

Denise's brain seemed to freeze, preventing all thought, even though Daniel had hinted that she should come work for them permanently the last time she was in DC. She looked to Jonathan, whose eyes were wide with surprise.

"Well," Jonathan stammered. "That's quite an offer. I think we'll need more information. For instance, what will we do there?"

"That depends on you," Daniel said. "We'll have some options for you. Maybe you both could come for a visit, and we'll discuss the opportunities then."

Jonathan and Denise agreed.

They chatted for another five minutes, mostly catching up on normal life topics, and then ended the call.

"What do you think?" Jonathan asked.

"Maybe I won't need to buy a car," she replied. "What do you think?"

Jonathan shrugged. "I'll hear them out," he said, "but I can't imagine being holed up in DC and my wife being here, alone."

"Maybe it will be just a short stint," she said. "But it's a nice place to stay."

Even though she hadn't had much time to enjoy it during her last visit, she thought her flat in the Space Systems building had been fancier than any other place she'd lived.

"I have business here," he argued. "I was just reinstated as the director of the foundation. Anyway, I would think you'd be a bigger target, with your more direct connection to Will."

Denise was not surprised that Will's wake would continue to affect her life for the foreseeable future. The real sting didn't come from the residual danger or inconvenience. It came from the fact that all of this was happening for no reason: Will was gone. However, the idea of being in a position to know more about what had happened to him made her amenable to the idea.

"I've just been promoted to associate in the foundation," she said. "It might not look good if I resign after just two weeks on the job."

"I think I can help with that," he said.

Both of their phones chimed simultaneously. Jonathan got to his first as Denise dug through her backpack to retrieve hers.

"Looks like they've already scheduled a flight for us," he said.

Denise found her phone and looked at the new email. They were leaving Chicago O'Hare for Reagan International at 5:22 a.m. the next morning.

"Seems pretty urgent," she said.

"I was getting that vibe during the call," he said. "I guess I'll cancel my appointments for tomorrow."

"Me too," she said.

She'd have a long day wrapping up the work she'd done in Southern Illinois, and then it would be a night of laundry and packing for another trip.

WILL WAS ENTHRALLED with the history of the Deltas, but he was grateful for the concise presentation of the information. After all, their early history on Earth paralleled that of the current generation but then extended over a million years beyond it. The interesting part was, assuming similar trajectories, it could reveal his generation's future – if it had one.

He was curious about the era after the Deltas made their transformation to a civilization of "separators," which was the direct translation of what they'd called people who had evanescence abilities. Will had been his generation's first separator.

The text chronicled the Deltas' exodus from Earth and the subsequent flight of those who escaped and made it to a distant part of the galaxy. They'd inhabited numerous planets, encountered other intelligent species and civilizations, and expanded their numbers into the billions in a few thousand years. They then expanded beyond the galaxy.

Five thousand years after the exodus, the Deltas returned to Earth's solar system to find two regenerated planets – Earth and Mars. Will learned that this was a common practice of the Regenerators: they'd regenerate two planets, and then return after a period of time and eliminate the one which lagged in development. When the Deltas had returned to the solar system, Earth and Mars each had habitable environments and primitive life developing on them. The Regenerators were gone.

The Regenerators were a species that the Deltas called the "Originals." Even the Deltas had little knowledge of the Originals' history, except that they were the oldest of all known species. Although they were known to all other space-traveling civilizations that the Deltas had encountered, they were otherwise mysterious.

Although natural organisms and ecosystems evolved on both Mars and Earth, according to the Deltas, both had later been seeded with advanced life forms that were allowed to evolve from "higher levels," as it was phrased.

The final step in the Regenerators' interference in natural development came after they exterminated Mars – Mars had been the slower developer. After Mars was wiped clean, Earth was seeded with one final advance: the origin of modern humans. This occurred about 700 thousand years after the Deltas had fled, a million years prior. It meant that modern humans appeared on Earth about 300 thousand years ago.

Will looked up the origin of modern *homo sapiens* in an Earth history source and found the same number: modern science says humans appeared on Earth about 300 thousand years ago. On Earth, the idea that humanity had been seeded by some alien entity would spark controversies worthy of scientific and religious excommunication.

As he'd already known before his transport from Earth, the Deltas had advanced technologically at a pace similar to that of his generation, sometimes referred to as the "Epsilons." However, the Deltas evolved to acquire separation abilities hundreds of years later in their developmental timeline than the current generation had – if Will marked the start of the human transformation. And they had eradicated all disease and biomedical problems along the way. When the Deltas had finally entered the probe and faced the Judge, as Will had done for the Epsilons, they had already developed the technology for space travel, and were ready to evacuate, albeit not on a scale that could save everyone.

He already knew all of this from the message Jacob Hale had deciphered from the signal from deep space. What Will didn't know, however, was what had occurred in the million years since the Deltas' exodus.

A million years of history could easily take millions of pages to report. However, the material before him amounted to a little over 100 pages. Just the highlights. It was all he needed.

After their frantic departure from Earth, the Deltas had been pursued by the Regenerators, and lost some of their ships. They learned later that this was a tactic the Regenerators used to force them to scatter, but it hadn't worked. What remained of the Delta fleet regrouped and fled. After a century of wandering about, they discovered two habitable planets in the Monoceros ring on the outer rim of the Milky Way galaxy, two rings outward from the Orion arm, where Earth was located.

He pulled up a map of the Milky Way and found their location to be 20 thousand light-years from Earth. He read that, just before they were forced to evacuate Earth, they'd been on the edge of a new technological advance in space travel, which they continued to develop during their century adrift.

Will was astounded that they'd been able to pull off such a feat. It reminded him of an old sci-fi TV show where a fleet of spaceships had to escape a destroyed civilization and embark on a long voyage to another world. The Deltas had done exactly that, except they had continued to develop along the way. And that was a million years ago, give or take. He couldn't imagine how advanced they were now.

He revised that thought. He was currently on a starship constructed by the Deltas, which implemented their technologies. And the *Exodus 9* was just a transport ship. More astonishing was that the Deltas' technology was now 40 thousand years beyond that of the *Exodus 9.*

In the millennia that followed, the Deltas colonized numerous other planets, and their total population expanded to over a trillion. It was during this time that they made further advances in biomedical technology, and something occurred that changed them profoundly.

It was a revelation that exposed another facet of existence, and it had been a complete accident.

At the time, they were developing the very transport technology that had delivered Will to the *Exodus 9.* A man was teleporting from the surface of one of their planets, called Tevon 5, to a starship thousands of miles away, but the disassembly of his body was botched. Inside the transport pod on the planet's surface, they found a mangled assortment of fused body parts. The device had acquired no information for the reassembly of his body, and he was therefore dead. He might as well have been blown up in an explosion.

As this occurred adjacent to a biomedical facility, one scientist had the idea to quickly resynthesize the victim's body using the leftover DNA from the pod. It was a replication method not related to teleportation.

Although the synthesis process was fast by biological standards – three days – it was a virtual infinity of time compared to that needed for teleportation. Information could be corrupted during transport in just a fraction of a second, and then never recovered.

It was a wild conjecture that no one thought would work. They intended to transport the new body to the ship, the man's original destination, assuming his soul had arrived as planned, hoping that they would recombine. But something occurred before that could happen.

As technicians started to lift the regenerated body into the transport pod, it started to move, and then resist and scream. It rolled onto the floor and began coughing and yelling. And then it spoke.

In just a few minutes, the man seemed to become self-aware and was able to communicate. They then realized this was not just a replicated body, which sometimes became active due solely to involuntary nerve activity. After a long sequence of ensuing interactions, they were convinced that it was the man who had supposedly died in the transporter. He was alive.

As the man was about to be taken away for medical assistance, he blurted the name of a woman who had recently been killed in a construction accident over a week earlier. He claimed that he'd seen her soul, and that, like him, she was searching for a place to go. Apparently, his regenerated body had attracted him to it somehow, but the woman was completely lost.

The scientists found samples of the woman's DNA from her postmortem examination and replicated her body, which was then placed in a bed in a medical facility where it was closely monitored. Just when they were about to end the experiment – nearly two weeks after the woman's death – something happened.

In the middle of the night, piercing screams echoed through the laboratory where the woman's body was being kept. Personnel rushed into the room to find the woman struggling against the restraints that confined her to the bed.

She had come back to life.

They had resurrected a woman who had been dead for almost two weeks.

Fear began to spread, but it subsided quickly as those who had been resurrected told their stories. Fear turned to hope as people realized that it was possible to recover their lost loved ones, and that they too could come back if they died.

Will contemplated how those first recoveries had been perceived by those who were there at the time. He figured it was a horrible job to inform a family that one of their members had died. However, it was another thing entirely to notify that same family that their loved one had come back to life. That, he thought, might be the best job in the world – in the universe.

The event was henceforth known as "The Epiphany." From that point forward, their outlook on existence changed forever.

It made him wonder what would have happened on Earth if scientists had cloned humans. He was no expert but, as far as he understood, clones were quite different from the regenerated bodies the Deltas created. For one, as it was done with human technologies, clones had to be gestated, and then grow into adults through normal development. The bodies the Deltas regenerated were fully matured to the age of the source from which they'd originated – from the DNA of the original body. He then wondered if clones produced through human technologies would already have souls. If they did, lingering souls would not be able to occupy them.

Since the Epiphany, the Deltas had advanced beyond biological replication to the *regeneration* of the body, which was a quite different process. Instead of starting with biological DNA, as required in cloning and biological replication, a body regenerated using the most advanced Delta technology was assembled using data that resulted from the mapping of the DNA and other atomic-level body structure. It was a permanent, reusable, data file. The physical material that composed a regenerated body came from the direct transformation of energy into matter: $E = mc^2$.

The idea of the Epiphany, together with the medical regeneration that he'd experienced firsthand, completely transformed Will's worldview. Among many other things, he was beginning to acknowledge that he was likely to be alive for a very long time.

He was suddenly overcome with an upwelling of emotions, the most prominent of which was fear. It came from extreme anxiety about the future. An unusually long life did not mean that it would be a good one, especially if he were alone. And it still didn't quell the realization of eventual death; as the counselor had explained, there were those who hadn't come back to their regenerated bodies after they'd passed, and they hadn't been reborn into new infants. Where had those lost souls gone?

Mixed in with the fear were guilt, confusion, sadness, and anger. He missed his family. He missed Denise.

It was 6:45 a.m. when Lenny exited his apartment and meandered along a new route to his favorite café. San José was already teaming with people, many of whom were heading to the local farmers' markets, which were as exotic as anything he'd encountered. The produce was unmatched anywhere in the world, and the variety was inexhaustible. He'd always been mostly a meat and potatoes consumer, but Costa Rica was changing him.

He wore a light jacket that concealed the firearm in his underarm holster. When someone warned you that you were in danger, you took it to mean an imminent attack – especially when the person who alerted you was in the business.

After taking all precautions, he entered the café and ordered his usual coffee. He made his way out to the veranda and found a table with a good view of the area. He lit a cigarette and took a drag.

The world was too small. It used to be – when he was in his prime – that a person could start anew by just changing cities or, more effectively, changing countries. Nowadays, changing continents hardly bought you a few weeks. He knew he'd be tethered to the CIA for the rest of his life, but he had hoped he'd be out of direct danger during his "golden years."

A tall, dark-complexioned man in his 50s emerged from the café and headed his way. The gray in the man's sideburns was starting to invade his short dark hair. Lenny recognized the Israeli as he approached and nodded for him to take a seat at his table.

"Avi," Lenny said and reached out his hand.

"Leonard," Avi said as he shook it with a firm grip. He set his coffee mug on the table and sat. "I admire your efforts."

Lenny stared at him. He had no idea what he meant.

"You have attempted what some of us can only dream about – retirement," Avi continued. "As you might have concluded by now, it's not that easy."

"I'm learning that," Lenny acknowledged. "What's happening?"

Avi casually checked the area to make sure no one had come out behind him – the veranda was empty – and spoke. "You're going to get called back to the States," he said. "Perhaps you already know why."

"Mekhloufi," Lenny said. He knew the Tunisian assassin was there for only one reason, and there could be multiple targets.

Avi nodded. "We have intelligence that confirms that he is in the employ of China," he said. "What's more, we have a partial target list."

"Who's on it?" Lenny asked.

"For one, the CIA director," Avi replied. "But also, Sylvia Barnes of the CIA, Denise Walker, Jonathan McDougal, and Jacob Hale."

Lenny flinched at the last name on the list, and then had the amusing image in his mind of Mekhloufi trying to run down the long-distance runner. Lenny still wanted to give Hale a good punch in the nose for embarrassing him, but no longer wanted to kill him. That had been just business, and had occurred when Lenny was working for the wrong side.

"His primary target, however, is William Thompson," Avi continued. "But our sources tell us that he might already be dead."

Lenny shrugged. That was something he hadn't heard but he doubted the idea. Scenes formed in his mind of charred bodies embedded in the melted steel on the deck of a Chinese aircraft carrier. William Thompson was not normal.

"So how does this involve me?" Lenny asked.

"The new head of the Chinese DC intelligence network will try to bring you back into the fold," Avi explained. "In fact, they're already looking for you, and they have people in Costa Rica. They're here to convince you to rejoin them – give you an offer you cannot refuse, as they say."

"How did *you* find me?" Lenny asked.

"My country has allocated significant resources to this project in which you are involved, and we're on very good terms with the CIA, and privy to certain things," Avi explained. "But the Chinese are close, and will locate you soon."

Lenny slowly shook his head. It was a good vacation while it lasted. "Does the CIA know?" he asked.

"My government is informing them now," Avi explained. "You should consider getting back to DC soon."

After what he'd gone through to get to Costa Rica, Lenny resisted the notion. He'd been relocated and given a new identity by DMS, Inc. and the CIA. To go back now would blow that out of the water, and he might never recover.

"I'll consider it," Lenny said.

"Consider it strongly," Avi said, apparently sensing Lenny's underlying feelings on the idea. "You have already encountered Mekhloufi, and that experience might give you an advantage."

Lenny had certainly "encountered" the man and, in his mind, still felt the deep burning of the man's razor as it sliced into his shoulder blade two decades earlier.

"There's more," Avi said as his face took on an even more solemn expression. "There's something bigger going on here, but we haven't figured it out yet. Something of a larger scope than just a few hits."

Avi finished his coffee, and then stood with his empty cup in hand. "Israel will support your efforts however we can. Good luck, Leonard," the man said, and then disappeared into the café.

Before he knew what he was doing, Lenny had another cigarette in his mouth and was cupping his hands around his lighter to shield it from the light breeze as he lit it. He took a hit and shook his head in frustration as he exhaled.

He saw no end to the conflict: there was no way of knowing whether William Thompson was dead unless there was a body and DNA verification. And, even if he were confirmed dead under such circumstances, the Chinese would never know, and would just continue the search. If either side managed to kill off some important players, there would be retaliation, and it would carry on as a violent, unresolvable back-and-forth that would continue in perpetuity.

And now it seemed that something deeper was going on – something of "larger scope," as Avi had put it.

Lenny no longer wanted to be a part of it. He didn't want to go back to the States. Perhaps he'd just do whatever he could from Costa Rica.

WILL HAD to get out of his quarters and do something. He made his way to the bottom floor of the main mall and walked a few kilometers before getting an iced tea at a kiosk. He sipped his drink as he rested on a bench next to a large pond with tall reeds, lily pads, and orange fish that looked to be koi.

A team of a dozen cleaning robots zoomed past, swerving around objects, and somehow avoiding colliding with one another. They reminded him of the circular, robotic vacuum cleaners that people had in their homes on Earth. These devices, however, were faster and quieter – he could only hear a hissing sound that he figured was air being sucked into the vacuum mechanism.

There were things that he wanted to explore on the ship, but he was torn between those that taught him about his new world and those that distracted him from it. Although another soccer match was on his mind, he decided to go back to the ship's bridge.

He found a Tube entrance, entered, and transferred the address from his watch. Fifteen minutes later, he was standing in front of the transparent doors, peering into the large, multilevel bridge. At least 20 consoles and large screens illuminated the otherwise dimly lit room.

Will pushed on the door, which didn't yield, and then searched one last time for a way to open it. After exhausting all possibilities, he sat on the floor and separated. As he passed through the door, it suddenly opened, splitting vertically in the middle.

He returned to his body, stood, and stared at the open doorway. A few seconds later, the doors slid closed.

He now knew what to do: he approached the door and reached out his hand. He concentrated on extending himself beyond his fingertips in the same way he had when actuating the control buttons in the Antarctic base.

He extended, and the door split in the center and slid apart horizontally with blinding speed.

As he stepped through the opening the entire bridge illuminated to a bright but comfortable level. The doors closed behind him.

A hundred feet ahead of him was the colossal, bubble-like forward window of the ship. He glanced at consoles and flat, clear monitor displays, one of which showed schematics and controls for the propulsion system. Another displayed what looked like some kind of map – one like he'd never seen before. It had a spaghetti mess of colored lines that reminded him of hurricane trajectory models from the weather services on Earth. Numerous other displays seemed to be off and looked like either clear glass or black mirrors.

The room was semicircular with the open side facing the front window. The upper part of the curved walls to the left and right seemed to be continuous gigantic displays, which were dark. Below the displays were shallow, clear desktops, next to which were sleek floor-mounted chairs.

Forward, to the left and right, were ramps that descended toward the bow, and then circled around a sunken floor and to an open deck in front of the giant window. From the top of the right-side ramp, he spied an assortment of chairs in the circular depressed area between the ramps. It looked to be where the command personnel might be stationed when the ship was fully staffed.

He continued down the ramp to the open floor and, as he approached the front window, his view of the starry exterior broadened. Its curvature provided such a wide view that it felt as if he were suspended at the center of a clear bubble floating in space. Front and center was a bench that he surmised was the best direct viewing seat on the ship. He sat.

If he stared forward and widened his view, he could just barely detect the motion of the stars. It was clear from this perspective that the ship was moving in the direction he was facing.

He turned to look back on the bridge. A seat at the center of the circular depressed floor reminded him of the captain's chair on the *Enterprise* in the *Star Trek* movies, and it was bracketed left and right by other seats with consoles and controls.

The distance from the floor near the window to the ceiling was at least 40 feet. Looking upward, he spotted two additional levels that were also open to the enormous bubble-like bow of the ship, with clear guardrails to prevent anyone from falling.

Will stood from the bench, went to the captain's chair, and sat. It was padded and comfortable, and automatically adjusted to the shape to his body.

He flinched in response to movement, and then spun to look in the direction from which the stimulus came. The entire bridge had come to life, and the curved screen that surrounded the upper level illuminated. Charts, diagrams, gauges, and schematics filled the displays, and the consoles flashed with activity. It reminded him of the control room inside the Antarctic base.

He stood from the chair and strode up one of the ramps to a console beneath one of the curved screens. There was an overhead schematic of the entire ship with what looked to be a bubble around it. Flashes sporadically appeared on the surface of the bubble, mostly on the front side – the leading edge of the ship.

Script appeared in a language that he recognized – it was the same one he'd encountered in the Antarctic base. He was able to read some of the Delta words: debris, radiation, deflection, absorption, dissipation, and gravity compression. He had no idea what the last term meant, but the others implied that the bubble was a shield of some kind. He knew that human technology for space travel was still struggling with shielding astronauts from dangerous radiation. It was one thing among many that was preventing a manned mission to Mars, or any extended space travel for that matter. Debris of any kind was also a problem, with even specks of dust being a threat at the enormous relative speeds. He figured this would be an even more serious concern for the colossal speed at which the *Exodus 9* must be going relative to the objects in its path.

He moved one station to his left, which provided a three-dimensional view that made it look like he could reach into the screen and touch what was inside. It was a 3-D grid with a small replica of the ship at the center. The rest was a map that showed objects in the vicinity that seemed to include asteroids and other solid objects. Near the ship, the grid was distorted to look as if it were riding a wave, with a rippling wake trailing behind it. It must have had something to do with the propulsion system, which seemed to distort the space in front of and behind the ship.

Another map, which displayed a long view, showed bright entities which he thought were stars. He figured the field of view spanned light-years since multiple such objects were in view. A green line, which he assumed was their projected course, led from a tiny icon representing the ship at the center, off screen, in the direction of travel. It deviated only slightly away from a star in the upper right corner of the view.

After experimenting with some buttons on the screen, he managed to expand the view to a much larger scale. This revealed a path that turned multiple times in three dimensions, seemingly to avoid objects in its trajectory. It then came to a location from which point the path splayed into over a hundred multicolored lines that went off in all directions, indicating what he thought were possible courses. There was nothing at that location that indicated why this occurred.

Will surmised that he might be able to navigate his way back to Earth from this station. But there were many things he'd have to figure out. First, he needed to know where the *Exodus 9* was currently. Second, he had to determine the location of Earth relative to his current position. And, third, he had to learn how to plot a new course and get the ship to follow it.

He proceeded to work his way around the bridge, trying to understand the functions of each of the stations. One seemed to be for communications, and another for life support, including the ship's gravity settings. There was one, however, which alarmed him: defense systems. There were shields – including some that involved "gravitational distortion" – and offensive weapons whose functions and operations were a complete mystery. They had names that had no translation to weapons with which he was familiar.

The fact that a so-called transport vessel like the *Exodus 9* could probably dominate Earth on its own was disturbing. And if it really were just a transport ship, he could hardly imagine what their warships were like. It might be like comparing a fancy passenger cruise ship on Earth to the latest, state-of-the-art American aircraft carrier.

After hours of exploring, he headed back to his quarters. He was exhausted and hungry. He needed to think.

5

MAGIC

Will had spent the afternoon practicing with his soccer team and was now exhausted. It was exactly what he'd needed to clear his mind and burn off some anxiety.

Afterwards, he'd explored more of the virtual world offered by the *Exodus 9*, and entered a program in which he had dinner at an Italian restaurant with a group of science and engineering graduate students. He'd selected characters that had a knowledge of deep-space navigation, as well as the layout of local space. It was something he'd discovered while perusing the long list of educational options on the computer in his quarters. This program was located under a category called "casual peer instruction," where one could learn through direct interactions with other humans in a comfortable environment.

In the end, although enjoyable, he'd gotten little useful information other than that the *Exodus 9* would have to enter an advanced mode of propulsion if it were to leave the galaxy inside of a year. Otherwise, he'd gleaned nothing about their current location or destination, or how to steer the ship. He did learn, however, that he'd need to have "captain's status" to make course changes. After dessert, he headed back to his quarters and sat by the window with a cup of coffee.

He was frustrated. What was the point of all of this? A bullet in his head would have been enough to save his world – at least that's what Landau had told him. *Landau.*

Will hadn't forgotten about Landau, but he'd hardly thought about him at all since leaving Earth. Landau had been with him in the Red Box. All he'd been at first was a voice that Will originally thought was just in his mind, somehow guiding him along as he endured the Exoskeleton. But Landau was more than that. Will could see him while separated, and had talked with him. Landau had spoken with him in the transport facility inside the Antarctic base just before Will had made his frantic exit.

Landau had told him that the Regenerators might spare the planet if Will wasn't there when they arrived, that was, if there were no others on Earth who could separate. But he'd also said something else. Landau had warned that if Will didn't find a way to transport off the planet "a great opportunity would be lost." *What did that mean?* And how could Landau know where he was going, and what opportunities might arise?

A vibration on Will's wrist indicated that he had a message. It was a reminder of another meeting with the counselor in the morning.

He went to the tabletop computer display and searched for something to explore during the evening. When working on a complicated problem, it often served him well to step away from it for a while. He'd sometimes come back with a new perspective, and that would be welcomed at this point.

Still recovering from the soccer practice in the afternoon, he was looking for something less physical. He thought an interactive adventure story of some sort would do the trick, and the selection was endless.

There were all kinds of familiar things from classic to recent fiction from Earth – books and movies. There were *Star Wars* adventures, where he could either be himself or play a character. He had no interest in anything that had to do with space. There were Indiana Jones quests, Jason Bourne spy adventures, fantasy novels like *Lord of the Rings*, and Sherlock Holmes, Agatha Christie, and other mystery novels. There were horror movies, historical stories, and the "rock star" experience. He'd avoid anything to do with horror, but he might check out the rock star experience at some point. He made a note to search for music lessons when he had some time.

He whittled the list down to the series of popular books and movies about the "school of magic" that his nieces seemed to watch continuously whenever he visited his sister. He recalled that, after some initial skepticism, he'd found the productions to be entertaining and relaxing, and they reconnected him somehow to his younger self. As a kid, adventure had always been on his mind.

He was curious as to how an adult would fit into the stories, other than being one of the professors at the school – it was the students who were at the center of the adventures. He didn't care what role he played. He'd just always marveled at the imagery of the settings, and wanted to walk around the school of magic and take in the sights. It would also take him home in some sense: it reminded him of his nieces, Tabitha and Tia, and the fun times he'd spent with them.

He was also curious as to how the program would handle the magic that was to occur. It made him think that a technology that could simulate an entire Premier League soccer match would lend itself well to magic.

His curiosity became progressively unbearable, and he set the school of magic adventure to start in 30 minutes. He'd play a student, which he thought might be interesting, but awkward: he was looking younger every day, but he was no teenager.

He finished his coffee, brushed his teeth, and headed for the address that had been uploaded to his watch. It was time for an escape.

DANIEL SWITCHED on his electric tea kettle on the windowsill as he admired the frost-coated needles of the spruce forest glittering in the sunlight seven floors below. It was 6:30 a.m., and he wondered what the new day would bring.

His house had sold on just its second day on the market, and company personnel had already moved some of his essentials into his flat in the Space Systems building. The rest of his belongings were put into storage, and he'd figure out what to do with them later.

It marked the end of an era for him: his failed marriage was behind him, and everything connected to it was gone – the physical components, anyway. The psychological effects, however, would be with him for the duration.

He was optimistic about the new arrangement for other reasons, one of which was that he wouldn't have to fight the DC traffic every morning, and wouldn't be in danger of falling asleep at the wheel on the way home. Now, he could concentrate solely on his work. He wondered if that was why Horace had constructed his facility on Swann Street.

The next question was how Jonathan and Denise would handle the offer to move into the building. The degree of disruption to their lives would be much larger than it would be to his or Sylvia's, but they'd be safe for the time being. For them, the change would be temporary. He didn't know if that would be the case for himself.

He steeped some English breakfast tea and then settled in front of his computer and read emails from the Omni group. There were currently nine others in addition to him and Sylvia, and they all had independent projects. In the past few weeks, Daniel had reassigned some of them from their previously designated projects to strategic investigations connected to recent events. So far, the resulting information was not useful, but that wasn't unusual in the early stages.

At 8:15 a.m. he heard Sylvia arrive through the main entrance and jostle some things in her office. A few minutes later she was at his door with an empty cup.

Daniel nodded to the tea shelf, next to the door.

"They're moving my things into my flat today," she said as she scooped loose tea out of a tin with a silver tea ball. "It's nice to no longer have to make the commute through horrible traffic every morning."

"My things were moved yesterday," he explained as he poured hot water into her cup. "Most of it was put into storage."

"How many years were you in that house?"

"Seventeen," he replied. "My wife was there for 16 of them."

"Sorry," she said, and went back to the door and leaned her shoulder against the frame.

He waved his hand and shook his head. "I'm over it," he said. "It's a new beginning." He wasn't sure if he really believed that, but it was time to move on.

Sylvia turned and looked out the door toward the entrance to 713. "James is here," she said.

They met Thackett at the cluster of furniture near the kitchenette in the main room.

"Good morning," Thackett said as he took a seat in one of the two leather chairs.

Daniel sat on the couch across the coffee table from him, with Sylvia to his right.

Just as Thackett was about to say something, the doorbell chimed.

Sylvia trotted over, opened the door, and led Jacob to the others. He was holding a plastic travel mug sporting a logo that read "Count Cristo Coffee House."

Jacob sat in the leather chair to Thackett's left.

"Good to see you," Thackett said. "We're waiting on Denise and Jonathan – they should be here shortly."

Jacob's expression showed alarm. "Something going on?"

Thackett shook his head. "I'll get into that when everyone's here," he said. "How's your project coming along? I suppose you can focus on that now that your training is nearly completed."

"I have a good head start since I worked on a similar satellite while at Interstellar Dynamics," Jacob explained.

"Similar?" Thackett said. "Not an exact replica?"

Jacob shook his head. "There are multiple encryptions to break on this one," he replied. "Also, there are now two satellites working in tandem and, from what I've seen so far, there could be more."

"Why multiple satellites?" Daniel asked.

Jacob shrugged. "I can only speculate, but they might want to look in all directions simultaneously, or get stereoscopic views."

"You mean like a spy satellite network that could see the entire surface of the Earth at once?" Sylvia asked.

"Sort of," Jacob replied, "but they're looking outward instead of back toward Earth."

Daniel had already known this, but Sylvia hadn't.

"Looking for what?" she asked.

The doorbell rang before Jacob could respond. This time Daniel went to the door and brought in Denise and Jonathan. There were warm greetings all the way around as they settled in.

Denise sat on the couch to Sylvia's right as Daniel went to his office and grabbed a wooden chair and placed it at the end of the coffee table nearest the entrance. Jacob vacated the leather chair for Jonathan and took the wooden seat.

"Looks like we're at full capacity again," Thackett said as everyone settled.

"Minus one," Denise said.

Thackett seemed to think for a second and then replied, "Yes, of course."

"Seems like the last time we were here was in another lifetime," Denise said. "Hard to believe it's only been about five weeks."

"It *was* another lifetime," Jonathan said. "The world is a different place now, even though most people don't know it." He looked to Thackett. "So why are we here?"

Thackett squirmed in his seat and took a deep breath. "The Chinese have hired specialists to take out key personnel," he explained. "Particularly those involved in our recent operations in Antarctica."

"And we're on that list," Denise said.

Thackett nodded with a solemn expression.

"They aren't convinced that Will is dead," Daniel added, regretting his words the instant he uttered them.

Denise was in the midst of taking in a breath and about to speak when Thackett beat her to the punch and saved Daniel some embarrassment. "And we're not convinced either, but we know that he's not currently with us," he said. "They do, however, know that all of you were involved."

"As we discussed on the phone, we think it would be best if you stayed here for a while," Daniel said as he glanced back and forth between Jonathan and Denise.

"How long is 'a while?'" Denise asked.

"Until we've identified the threats and eliminated them," Thackett replied. "But you can contribute to the effort while you're here, and you'll be compensated."

"We're not concerned about the compensation," Jonathan said. "What about our families?"

"We don't think that your wife is in any danger, Jonathan," Thackett assured him. "In fact, she might be safer with you away for the time being."

Jonathan nodded and apparently understood the implication that he'd only draw danger to his wife if someone were to come after him.

"You think Space Systems is the safest place to be?" Denise asked.

Daniel was confused by her question.

"Wasn't this building a prime target just a couple of months ago?" she continued. "I thought we left for Antarctica in a rush because of a threat."

It was a good point, Daniel thought.

Thackett put up his hand and seemed to have an answer. "There's a balance between safety and functionality," he explained. "We would all be safe in a bunker in the Nevada desert, but we wouldn't have all of the resources to do our work. For the time being, you and Jonathan are safer here than you would be, completely exposed, in Chicago."

Denise seemed to be satisfied.

"What's the threat, exactly?" Jonathan asked.

"We have information indicating that known foreign operatives – some of whom are confirmed assassins – have arrived in the DC area," Thackett explained. "And we know that they're funded by the Chinese government."

"And you two are easy to find," Sylvia added. "Jonathan, you're a public figure."

"The risk for both of you, but particularly you, Denise, is kidnapping," Thackett explained. "They'd either try to get information out of you, or use you as bait to lure in Will. Either way, they'd kill you in the end."

Denise's face turned pale, and she and Jonathan exchanged looks.

"We have some nice flats ready for you," Daniel said, changing the subject. "And Sylvia and I have already moved into our own."

Denise looked back and forth between him and Sylvia, and Daniel felt his face flush when he understood the ambiguity of his statement. He and Sylvia weren't living together.

Thackett broke the awkwardness by saying, "Jacob, you have the choice to move into Space Systems, or to stay at 17 Swann."

"I'll stay at Swann, for now," Jacob said without hesitation. "Thanks for the offer."

"So, that's why I asked you to come," Thackett said, directing his words to Denise and Jonathan. "Now let's talk about what you'll be doing while you're here."

Daniel was beginning to notice feelings emerge that were reminiscent of the last time Denise and Jonathan stayed at Space Systems. Those feelings were tension and anxiety.

WILL EMERGED from the room of illusions with the devastating realization that what he'd just experienced was not real.

Before embarking on the adventure two days earlier, he'd wondered how such a young adult fantasy-adventure story could be adapted to include a 40-year-old. The answer was that he had become a 15-year-old boy – effectively, anyway.

It was an adventure based on one of the school-of-magic movies that he'd encountered so many times with his nieces. It was a breathtaking world that, when watching the films long ago, made him want to go there to, if anything, relish the scenery. His intention was to walk around and enjoy the beautiful castle which housed the school of magic, and maybe watch the characters play out some story, which he assumed might be like participating as an extra in the production without a real role.

It was nothing like that.

The adventure had started on an old train on its way to the school, just like in the movies. He'd boarded, and then taken a seat in a cabin with the main characters, who looked exactly like the actors from the films. The first time he'd glanced at his reflection in the window he'd seen a teenage boy – who resembled himself as a kid. And everything else was consistent: he'd been smaller than the adult characters, his voice had sounded younger – he had no idea how they'd accomplished that – and his every reflection, from water, windows, or silverware – had shown him to be that teenage boy. The ruse had been thorough and complete.

Before he'd known it, he'd become completely immersed. An adventure had sprouted from nothing, and he was learning magic – something that was simulated so well that, by the time the adventure ended, it had become almost routine. There were flying cars, dragons, giant spiders, and evil wizards. There were points at which he'd actually been frightened – it hadn't taken his mind long to adapt to its new reality.

At the end, after a harrowing adventure that was more exhilarating than anything he could remember, there was a feast. Afterwards, when he walked out of the main dining hall – which in the real movies had been filmed at Christchurch's Hall at Oxford – he emerged in a small room where he'd returned his props and changed back into his normal clothes.

He sat on a bench in the small foyer with a sick feeling in his gut. It was as if he'd been living in another world. He'd made friends – and he missed them already. Relationships had developed in his mind. And he wanted to go back.

It frightened him. The experience was too strong.

That adventure had taken just over two days. It was the shortest one available of that sort, and he'd originally thought he'd only spend a few hours there. It had sucked him in more quickly than anything he'd ever experienced, and he missed his counseling session by 48 hours.

And there were longer adventures in the school-of-magic category. The longest one would last a full year – two semesters plus a summer. He couldn't even imagine. It would be a full year of real time – his *real* life. *Who could justify something like that?* he wondered. But the answer came to him immediately. Time was no longer a factor. He would live indefinitely, and he'd be healthy and youthful. He could embark on century-long adventures if he desired. And, if he never found a way back to Earth, or if he learned that it had been destroyed, he just might.

He left the facility and went to the walkway that overlooked the mall from the 37th level. He found a kiosk and got a hot coffee, took a seat on a bench, and gazed down at a large fountain spraying water in a dozen high arcs that terminated in a circular pond. The sound of the splashing soothed him.

A person could live an entire lifetime in one of those simulators, which seemed to have endless scope and range – from a tropical beach, to a café in Paris, to a soccer stadium housing 75 thousand fans. And now it had taken him to a fictitious world where magic that defied the laws of physics was possible.

He was tempted to go back for another adventure, but he'd resist for now. It was only an escape from reality – it masked his pressing objective, and his thoughts went back to his real friends, family, and to Denise. A year-long fantasy adventure for him was still a real year in Earth time. And the lives of those on Earth were finite.

It made him feel like a clock was running. It was something he'd felt often.

After he finished his coffee, he found a Tube station and went back to his quarters.

He ordered a cup of soup from the kitchen dispenser and took it to the window, where he sipped it and gazed at the stars as they crawled across his view.

Was this the ultimate goal of humanity? Was this where technology was heading? Was this the realization of the idea of nirvana – the seed of final hope that existed in most people's minds?

Was paradise a place where one was always perfectly healthy and youthful, felt no physical pain, and had senses that were perfect? If so, he was there. Was it a place where every conceivable need or desire was satisfied – from any childhood adventure to every adulthood fantasy? If so, he was there. Was it a place where death no longer existed? If so, he was there.

But it didn't feel like he was there.

Things were still missing. Loved ones were absent, but it was more than that.

Something still loomed in the far distance. But he couldn't tell if that colossal separation was a physical expanse, or a vast span of time. Both brought about a feeling of abandonment.

But he did not feel abandoned. Rather, he had a sense that he was abandoning others.

He couldn't let that happen.

IT TOOK Wang Yong the entire afternoon to sort out some unforeseen problems with the secure satellite link in the Alexandria safe house. It was something that his wife could have done in 20 minutes, but he was pleased to have done it himself.

In the hours that followed, he'd set up meetings with operatives who had avoided the recent purge. The problem was that none of those who remained had the long view of his predecessor's, Tao's, operation. This put Yong in the awkward position of having to bring in contractors who had worked for Tao in order to find out what they'd been doing during the days leading up to the scramble.

But it didn't matter very much. Yong just had to keep it together for a few months while the important pieces of the final operation were put into place.

Despite being a digital spy, whose missions mostly involved acquiring pictures, schematics, and computer codes, Yong had seen his fair share of death – mostly in the form of interrogations and their aftermaths. Of course, none of it had ever been by his own hand. His job had always been to formulate the questions; the more physical aspects of the interrogations were left to those who had such skills. In all cases, the subjects had been terminated in the end, and execution was usually an act of mercy. Most would probably not have wanted to go on living in the disfigured conditions in which they'd found themselves.

The questioning had often started with broken bones, but it eventually moved on to the torch. The interrogation specialists with whom he'd been involved hated scenes involving blood. It was evidence that was impossible to eliminate from a scene. So everything was kept relatively clean – broken bones, the torch, and electricity. Afterwards, the bodies were dissolved in acid, and dumped in the hills somewhere inland from San Francisco.

His wife, Chunhua, whose adopted Western name was "Sara," had a more intimate involvement in such activities when it came to her own work. He'd once been to a party with her in San Francisco where she'd poisoned a coworker who had become suspicious of her "exploratory activity" in the firm's computer system. She'd dropped an untraceable neurotoxin into his drink, and he'd crashed his car into a tree on the drive home, and died. The man's wife had been in the car as well and, to Sara's great pleasure and relief, suffered major brain damage. Sara had been concerned that the woman had known about her husband's suspicions, so she'd arranged for an operative to pay her a visit in the hospital and finish the job.

Yong needed his wife with him. He needed someone who would not hesitate in the face of enormous consequences. And those consequences *would* be enormous.

He already had new security personnel at his disposal, and he'd sent them to collect an important foreign contact for a meeting in the afternoon. There was also the task of coordinating with the Russians, who had their own, independent plans to execute.

It was time to begin the preparations.

WILL AWAKENED from a vivid dream about his recent adventure and found himself missing the characters as if they were real people. He longed to head back to the fictitious castle for breakfast before classes on magic, and for afternoons and evenings of adventure and mystery. It was a dangerous draw that was like a powerful drug. He knew he'd go back to that fantasy world at some point but promised himself to delay that urge for as long as possible. Maybe it would go away. It was comforting, however, to know that, if there was no way to get back to Earth, there were other worlds in which he could immerse himself.

He got some breakfast and took it to the coffee table. He activated the table's display and began searching. He was looking for information on how to navigate and, more specifically, how to pilot the *Exodus 9*.

It was something he should have done much earlier, but he had a mental barrier to overcome. It was like doing taxes when you were certain you were going to owe money, or going to the dentist when you were sure there was work to be done: it was avoiding bad news. And the potential bad news he might learn if he dug deeply enough could be devastating. Perhaps there was no way to get back to Earth before everyone he knew was dead. Or maybe he'd learn that they were already dead. It was now time to learn everything he could.

He found a class on interstellar navigation, and was given the choice to participate online or attend an "old-school" traditional lecture. He chose the latter, and set a start time.

Next, he found general information about the *Exodus 9*, and read. As he'd already gathered, it was an "*Exodus-class* large-scale transport starship." It could lie dormant for many thousands of years, and it was designed for large population evacuations and extended trip durations – a hundred years or more.

The thought of being alone for 100 years made Will shudder. If that happened, he'd need every virtual escape the ship had to offer.

The *Exodus 9* had a capacity of a million. Its dimensions were such that the population density would be about half that of New York City.

The specs on the ship included everything from life support and energy sources to propulsion, shielding, and weapons systems. Despite his scientific background, most of it was beyond his understanding. He learned that the ship had enough energy storage to run for 1,000 years at full power without replenishing its reserves. He had no idea what provided the energy, where it was acquired, or how it was stored or distributed. There were multiple modes of propulsion, but there was only one that he understood: ion-drive propulsion. Just like rocket engines expelled hot gas downward to launch a spacecraft upward, ion drives ejected gas ions in one direction to propel a ship in the opposite direction. The difference was that rocket engines burned fuel to accelerate the ejected material, whereas ion drives electromagnetically accelerated charged gas atoms. Ion drives were already being used on Earth, but they were weak. The ion drives on the *Exodus 9* were only used for steering during docking, which was a rare occurrence.

He then came across something that sent his mind reeling: matter generation. He knew Einstein's famous equation that related matter and energy, $E = mc^2$, where E stood for energy, m was mass, and c was the speed of light in vacuum. And he knew of examples where it was evident – like in nuclear energy generation, or high-energy particle physics. But he had no understanding of the science and engineering that harnessed it, giving the Deltas the ability to create any material, from gold to food to biological cells and DNA. The technology had been used to create his new kidneys, something about which he'd almost forgotten.

The other astonishing element of the ship was its AI – artificial intelligence. The *Exodus 9* was like a living entity, and it could create other artificially intelligent entities – both biological and non-biological. His doctor and counselor were such biologically-based beings, as were the soccer players, and the characters he'd encountered on his magic adventure. In that sense, they were all real. According to what he was reading, however, artificially intelligent beings did not have evanescence abilities. To Will, that was another way of saying that they didn't have souls. He felt sad about that, even though it was unclear to him what that really meant.

The detailed science of the propulsion systems and the artificial intelligence that governed the ship didn't matter at the moment, and he diverted to a link labeled "*Exodus-class* starship navigation." After some reading, he discovered it had nothing to do with skill: all one had to do was input various parameters about the destination, path, and time of flight, and the ship did everything else. It would constantly monitor its course, avoid or deflect things that came into its path, and defend itself against any hostilities.

He followed a link to the defense capabilities of the ship and found things that boggled his mind. First off, it had offensive weapons, the only one of which he understood to some degree was a photon-pulse device that he likened to a pulsed laser. It was used for short-range threats and it was precise and powerful. There were thousands of small, autonomous and artificially intelligent, spacecraft that could be deployed for all kinds of military or search and rescue missions. And there were other large-scale weapons that he did not understand with descriptions involving terms like "vacuum disruptors" and "gravity spikes."

The defense-minded components were equally impressive, the most striking of which was a spacetime shield that forced anything impinging upon the ship to bend around it, just as water in a stream rushes around a protruding rock.

In the end he, concluded once again that the *Exodus 9*, a mere transport ship for refugees, could alone defeat Earth's combined militaries. And he again wondered what their military ships were like.

It came to him that this technology that so impressed him – defense, medical, propulsion, teleportation, matter generation, artificial intelligence, and the seamless integration of it all to form a virtual illusion so convincing that he might prefer it to reality – was 40 thousand years old. He wondered where the Delta's technology was now – how could they have improved upon it? What more did they need?

Neither the navigation nor the piloting of the ship was the issue. It was the access. He could not give commands. He did not have the authority to steer the ship, or to change its destination. His understanding was that the ship's orders were preprogrammed and could only be changed by someone with authority – and there was no one with the proper authority on the ship.

He'd worry about redirecting the ship later. Knowing how to steer it didn't matter if he didn't know where to go. His first objective then was to determine the current position of the *Exodus 9*, and then find Earth's location with respect to that. Only then could he find a course to get him home.

His class on navigation started in the morning. He decided to partake in a soccer practice in the afternoon. In the evening, he'd explore some reading materials in preparation for the lecture.

Will got some iced coffee from the kitchen and sat on the floor near the window. His mind was settling, and he felt less anxiety. At least he had a plan.

IT WAS ALMOST noon when Lenny arrived at a small pub-style restaurant that had a secluded rooftop lounging area with small, round tables. He found a table near the edge of the roof that had a large umbrella that blocked the noontime sun. He could see through the bars of a black iron fence atop a 12-inch brick step at the roof's edge, giving him a clear view of the street below, as well as a direct line of sight to the building's main street entrance. His choice of seat also put him in a good position to monitor the access door to the roof. There was a fire escape on the opposite side of the building in case he needed to flee.

A young woman came to take his order. He chose "casado," his new favorite local dish, and iced tea, and then lit up a cigarette as the server disappeared to deliver his request to the chef.

He took a drag of the filtered Marlborough – the third of ten he would allow himself for the day – and exhaled as he gazed down at the street. Well-dressed professionals flooded this part of town during lunchtime, and he'd barely beaten the rush.

A few minutes later, an enormous gray-white cloud appeared and, with sunlight still beating down on the street, a light rain patted on the umbrella above him. The pedestrians below opened their own umbrellas, which Lenny found distracting as it veiled the faces of those who entered the pub. He was expecting someone.

A new set of files had arrived in the morning, and Lenny had identified four newcomers to the US, each of whom he knew had a special skill set that went beyond ordinary espionage. Two were Russians, and two Chinese. One of the Chinese agents concerned him more than the others: she was an expert in bioweapons, and Lenny knew that China had already put that option on the table in their previous plan to attack Space Systems. It was a brute-force method that would achieve their objective but would come with much collateral damage.

His food arrived, and it was as much a colorful, visual masterpiece as it was a culinary enchantment. There was fish, called corvina, which Lenny learned was sea bass, fried plantains, rice and black beans topped with a fried egg, avocado slices, tomatoes, tortillas, and grilled onions and peppers. Growing up in the former USSR, potatoes had always been his main staple, but he wouldn't be disappointed if he never saw another one.

As he ate, he kept an eye on the pedestrians below and on the door to the roof. As per the Israeli's warning, he had a gun in a holster under his left arm.

About halfway through his lunch, a man he recognized approached the building. Lenny spotted him, despite the man's umbrella, a block away on the street. It was Diego, his CIA contact in Costa Rica. There was something about the middle-aged man's gait that gave him away – it was as if one stride was longer than the other.

A few minutes later, just as the rain stopped, Diego emerged from the roof entrance and walked to Lenny's table. He glanced at Lenny's plate as he approached, and then looked to Lenny and grinned. "Ah, the *married man*," he said.

"What?" Lenny asked, confused.

Diego nodded to his plate. "The name of the dish you are eating, casado, means *the married man*," he explained as he sat in the chair opposite Lenny.

Lenny shrugged and glanced at his plate. It was something he could come home to every night.

"But there's another meaning, which is probably more appropriate in your case," Diego said, his dark eyes turning solemn. "It can also mean the *hunted man*."

Lenny didn't like the sound of that, but it was something he'd accepted as normal.

"You had some information?" Diego asked.

"I recognized four operatives in the last batch of files," he replied. "One is particularly concerning – a bio-warfare specialist."

Diego seemed to study him for a few seconds. "How would you know someone like that?" he asked.

It was a good question, and one Lenny didn't want to answer. The woman's name was Xing Li, and she had been employed by Syncorp, Inc. before and after the Chinese takeover of the company. The entire time, she'd also been employed by the People's Liberation Army of the People's Republic of China. Her initial employment at Syncorp was strategic, and secret: she'd been a spy from the very beginning.

"Let's just say that I've been around," Lenny finally responded, and Diego seemed to let it go.

Syncorp had developed more than just biomechanical interface systems, such as the Exoskeleton. They also had divisions that researched novel antipersonnel weapons, such as lasers and special kinetic devices. It was a little-known fact, however, that they'd also developed unconventional, large-scale, nondestructive extermination technologies. The classic example of this was the neutron bomb, which supposedly killed all life in a large area, but kept structures standing. But Syncorp had focused its attention on bioweapons.

Lenny had been privy to some of this information since he'd been called in on occasion to eliminate potential whistleblowers. In one such operation, he'd tricked a Syncorp employee into thinking he was an FBI agent, and the man had spilled his guts – which Lenny did for him, in the literal sense, after the interview. What Lenny had learned during that interrogation, however, was astonishing.

Syncorp had developed a live bio-agent – a virus – that was short-lived, but extremely deadly, and could not be transmitted from human to human. It could be dispersed in a building, or a small city, kill everyone, and then disappear. There was no way to trace the original cause of death, other than everyone died due to pressure on the brain. Evidence of the virus broke down quickly and, six hours after the original release, the area would be safe to enter, clear out the bodies, and take over.

Syncorp's head scientist in this endeavor was Xing Li, who went by "Wendy" when interacting with Westerners. She'd fled back to China when Syncorp shut down, but now she was back, and Lenny had an idea of where she was headed.

"There are now two dangerous people in the US that Thackett should find immediately," Lenny explained. "And he should have them eliminated."

Diego nodded and grinned.

"Why are you smiling?" Lenny asked. It made him nervous.

"Please, continue," Diego said.

Lenny filled him in on Xing "Wendy" Li. The second person was the Tunisian. "Mekhloufi is there to take out individuals," Lenny explained. "Xing Li is there for a mass extermination attack – probably on Space Systems, but she could have multiple targets. And it could be that Mekhloufi and Xing Li are collaborating."

Diego's phone beeped and he glanced at it, and then back to Lenny. "That's why Thackett wants you back in DC," he said.

Lenny stared at him as his stomach churned. The "married man" was indeed the "hunted man."

"When?" Lenny asked.

"Tonight, if you're willing."

Lenny mulled over the situation, trying to imagine a scenario where he'd be at peace with turning down the request.

"The director said he'd make it worth your while," Diego added.

"I'll send my response in the next few hours," Lenny said.

Diego nodded, stood, and said, "You can send it to the director's email."

Lenny nibbled on a fried plantain as he watched Diego disappear through the roof's access door.

The Israeli had warned him that no one ever left the business. Lenny had understood his forewarning, but it was like so many other things in life: there were things you didn't really learn until you experienced them directly.

He finished the last of his lunch and put some money on the table to cover the bill, including a generous tip.

The drizzle strengthened as he hurried across the roof and through the access door. He then made his way down a steep span of creaky wooden stairs, out of the café, and onto the sidewalk. An awning shielded him from the light rain as he popped open a small umbrella. He contemplated his situation as he plodded along a new course back to his flat, dodging puddles along the way. By the time he arrived at his door, he'd concluded that he had to go back to the States.

He closed his umbrella, extracted the gun from its underarm holster, and went inside. When he deemed all was clear, he opened his secure laptop and found a message from CIA Director James Thackett.

After reading it, he sat in an upholstered chair that faced a window, and then sighed as he watched the sun peek through the palm trees on the other side of the street. The rain had stopped, but the greenery still glistened.

Retirement was over.

AS WILL TOOK A SHOWER, his elevated excitement about the upcoming lecture surprised him. It reminded him of how he'd felt on his first day of college.

He got dressed and then found his way to the mall storefront on the 54th level in sector 61 with the words "The University" lit up in the window. He went inside and into a lobby, checked in at the front desk, and followed directions to door 22, down the corridor to the left.

He stepped through the door and into a tall foyer with a medieval-looking chandelier hanging by thick chains from the ceiling, and faced a set of large, wooden double doors. He pushed the doors and emerged into bright sunlight. He shielded his eyes with his hand.

A breathtaking campus sprawled in front of him. A dozen brick academic buildings with red clay roofs surrounded a central square with an expansive green lawn, old oaks, and a pond. Paved walkways lined with regularly spaced benches crisscrossed through the square. Between the buildings were courtyards with tables and umbrellas. Squirrels rummaged about, birds whistled their happy songs, and a gentle breeze that carried the soothing scents of a clump of lilac bushes on the edge of the pond ruffled the leaves on the trees.

Mountainous white clouds moved overhead like colossal ships on a light-blue sea.

It was the full college environment, rather than the simple classroom he'd expected.

He flinched as his watch vibrated. He had 10 minutes to get to the engineering building. A map on his watch indicated the way: it was across the central square, on the opposite side of the pond.

An instant later, students spilled out of the buildings, and the quaint, peaceful space turned into a vibrant collage of voices and laughter and hurrying students carrying backpacks. It was something that he not only missed as a student but also as a professor.

Will started on his way. Five minutes later he entered the lobby of the engineering building, which, on the outside, looked like a centuries-old structure. The inside was another story. It was like a museum filled with scaled models of spacecraft the likes of which were too exotic even for the science fiction movies of his generation. Video screens showed those very ships in action, some of which were military craft.

The lecture hall in which his class was to be held was on the second level, and he climbed a staircase and found it.

It was a theater-style room with stadium seating and a capacity of about 200. Students were filing in, and he found a seat in the center, about halfway up. On the lecture floor was an island with a black countertop and a sink, similar to that which would be found in a typical science lecture hall.

During the next few minutes, the room filled to capacity and became noisy with voices. Will homed in on a few of the conversations and heard everything from gossip about a party from the night before to comments about an upcoming football game. It was strange. He wanted to ask questions but refrained.

The class quieted as a man in his sixties, with short gray hair and thick, black-rimmed glasses emerged from a door on the lecture floor level. The professor tugged the sleeves of his brown, tweed jacket as he made his way to a lectern to the right of the island. He manipulated a panel of controls and, a moment later, the front screen illuminated and the words "Welcome to Navigation 101" appeared.

The man cleared his throat and said, "So, you want to learn how to navigate a starship and venture out into the vast unknown. Why?"

Will detected a slight German accent.

The students rustled about, but no one answered the Professor's question.

"It's because we seek answers to questions that have puzzled us from the beginning of time," he said. "From where did we come? Where are we going? And why are we here?"

The professor flipped to the next slide and an image of the *Exodus 9* appeared. "I am Professor Schmidt, and I will do my best to teach you something that will help you in your quest to answer those questions."

For the next three hours, Will learned that navigating in space was much more complicated than plodding around on Earth – land, air, or sea. Different considerations had to be made based on methods of propulsion. Low-tech transport such as that which required the expulsion of combusted fuel – like all propulsion systems currently used on Earth – had to account for dangerous radiation, fast-moving matter fragments, and getting sucked in by the gravity of massive objects, like stars and planets. Unfortunately, that was the only form of propulsion that Will currently understood.

As the professor introduced more advanced propulsion technologies, using terms such as "time projection methods" and "spacetime benders," Will noticed other students nodding their heads as if they understood. He had to remind himself that they were all just a part of a program.

"Of course, when using teleportation methods," Professor Schmidt continued, "there is no need to navigate: all that's needed is a transmitting mechanism and a receiving device."

Will had experienced that firsthand.

"However, the problem is that you cannot use teleportation for exploration," Schmidt explained. "Someone would first have to navigate and place a teleport receiver at the endpoint location. So, navigation is crucial – it's absolutely essential to survival, and to forward development.".

Will was convinced.

The first part of the course was to cover known space – that which had already been explored, cataloged, and mapped. This was the part in which Will was most interested since it would include the location of Earth.

"Our most advanced ships are what you might call 'user friendly,'" Professor Schmidt continued. "For known space, a navigator need only choose a destination, and make some choices as to path, timing, and propulsion method. Intelligent ships will take care of all of the details considering known map data, and navigation monitors and sensors." The professor then showed an image of the navigation control console – a computer screen – of the *Exodus 9*.

Will likened it to the Global Positioning System, or GPS, devices used in cars. Even those devices, however, would sometimes lead people to drive into lakes. He supposed that a smart ship like the *Exodus 9* wouldn't slam itself into an asteroid or get too close to a star.

At the end of the third hour, the professor concluded with a preview of the next class, indicating that they'd cover active interstellar maps, which he warned were nothing like the flat, static, terrestrial maps of a planet-based city. Interstellar maps were three-dimensional and, most importantly, dynamic – they were changing continuously. Good maps were maintained by high-powered artificial intelligence that predicted changes based on earlier data.

Will was exhausted and hungry by the time the class ended, and he followed a group of students to a food kiosk in the campus' main square. He ordered a burrito and an iced tea, and then took a seat on a concrete bench that overlooked a patch of lily pads on the pond. A short, blonde girl sat to his right and set her backpack on the bench, between them. She unwrapped a burrito and looked to him.

"I was looking forward to this for the entire last hour of class," she said as she took a bite.

Will nodded and laughed as he chewed. "I was getting hungry, too," he replied.

"I love Professor Schmidt," she said. "I had him for my first two engineering courses."

"What year are you?"

"I'm a junior," she said. "I transfer to the AIE next year."

"A-I-E?"

"Academy of Interstellar Exploration," she said.

Will nodded. The illusion was complete – the program included students for whom such a class would be required. And it was all done within an environment he knew intimately – a college campus. He thought back to when he'd been a professor: the physics of "spacetime bender" propulsion was nowhere to be found in the curriculum.

"You're smiling," the girl said.

Will looked at her and realized she was right. "What's your name?" he asked.

"Dina. Yours?"

"Will."

"What's your major?" she asked.

He shook his head. "I'm only taking one class – I just find it interesting."

She nodded. "I heard the exams in this class are pretty tough."

"Exams?" He hadn't even thought of that.

She nodded and laughed. "Yes, exams."

"I'm just sitting in on the lectures," he explained. "So I doubt I'll have to take them."

"I'd imagine a person wouldn't learn as well if they weren't held accountable in some way," Dina said. "At least that's the way it would be for me."

"That's probably true," he replied. "But my interest is pretty strong."

She finished her food, stood, and slipped her backpack over her shoulder. "Gotta go," she said, smiling. "See you next time."

Will said goodbye and then took another bite of his burrito. Maybe Dina was right. Maybe he should study hard and take the exams. Maybe that was the only way he would learn enough to get the *Exodus 9* on a course for Earth.

As he swallowed the last of his iced tea and squinted into the bright sun, he came to a conclusion. He'd accept the challenge – take the class for grade. Hopefully he'd score higher than the D-plus he'd gotten for his first soccer performance.

On his way back to the entrance to the beautiful sunny campus, Will wondered if he was intellectually capable of passing such a course. He was a physicist – but one from Earth's current, comparatively underdeveloped generation. The math alone might be beyond him. Then again, maybe it would be watered down enough for him to handle.

As he approached the large double doors, he noticed Latin words carved into their dark wood: *Scientia vos Liberabit.*

Knowledge will liberate you.

DANIEL WAS JUST GETTING his second wind at midnight. The water in the electric tea kettle was ready and he poured it into a French press filled with his favorite coffee.

He sat on his office couch for a few minutes as the mixture steeped, and then finished the process and poured the brew into a mug. He added a little cream, which was considered sacrilege by coffee aficionados, but it was better on his stomach.

Although his nerves had improved since the events of the previous couple of months, the anxiety was building again, and he didn't know why. And he knew it wasn't caused by the new threats conveyed by Thackett. He was used to threats, and he was even less concerned about them after moving into Space Systems. His brain was working on something else, the details of which had not yet emerged.

The CIA had collected new intelligence indicating that China was preparing to launch two more satellites to join the two currently located in high-Earth orbit, looking outward from the solar system. China's harried behavior was one thing that contributed to his disquiet, but it wasn't the only thing.

After what had looked like the beginning of an alien invasion just weeks before, Daniel would not be surprised by drastic actions taken by any nation. However, China was also flooding the US with operatives – the kind that carried out paramilitary-like missions, including assassinations. It was as if the Chinese either thought that the US was in cahoots with some alien partner to take over the world, or that China was the one scheming with some extraterrestrial ally. Daniel thought both notions were crazy, but he'd seen things in the past year that meant that both of those ideas remained in the realm of possibility.

Denise and Jonathan had reluctantly accepted the offer to stay in Space Systems, at least until the latest wave of Chinese covert invaders was eliminated. Thackett had suggested in vague terms that the CIA had already initiated plans to counteract the threats. That was one thing Daniel admired about the director: he'd been appointed to the position, but he wasn't a politician. Thackett had come up through CIA ranks, starting as a young case officer, and knew how and when to act.

The frantic action of China deploying the outward-looking satellites gave Daniel a feeling similar to that one gets when the family dog growls at the front door in the middle of the night for no apparent reason. But there was an underlying baseline of anxiety rooted in the possibility that whoever had come to destroy Earth, but refrained, would change their minds and return. He supposed that his unease came from vulnerability. Earth had no defense against those who were technologically advanced enough for distant space travel. Earth was a sitting duck.

He thought about where he was just two years ago. He'd been isolated, working on his own independent project in his secluded Space Systems office. He'd never met any other Omnis – including Sylvia – and he'd been reporting to some unknown entity that he now knew had been Horace. He'd never been in any danger. He had also still been married.

At the time, he'd had a great appreciation for his privileged station as an Omni – having access to every sensitive piece of information possessed by the US government.

He'd been naïve.

His view of the world had been completely incorrect – the blindfold only being lifted by the emergence of William Thompson, and all the events that had followed. There was so much more to the world – to his own existence – than he'd ever imagined. The recent extraterrestrial contact certainly changed his worldview, but it wasn't such a drastic stretch. The fact that human technology was capable of putting someone into space – even landing on the moon – made it easy to extrapolate to more distant places. It would be difficult, and might take centuries, but one could at least concede the possibility that we might eventually get to other stars, and other planetary systems. In that case, we might encounter a planet with intelligent life that was below our stage of development. We would then be the advanced extraterrestrials.

The real upheaval of his worldview came from William Thompson. The man could separate his consciousness from his physical body. The image came to his mind of the pile of mangled bodies spontaneously incinerating in the shaft room at the Antarctic base. Will had done that. Will had done many things. Will had said that he'd seen the ghosts of others – at the base and elsewhere. And Daniel believed him.

Those "ghosts" had been souls. Will's separated consciousness was his soul.

What overwhelmed Daniel's mind was the realization that he, too, had a soul. It made him wonder about his own capabilities, and limitations. Was he like a bird that never realized it could fly?

But there were deeper implications. Daniel had been turned off by organized religion from a very young age. To him, it seemed like it was just a method to control the masses – it was about power. By the time he'd gotten to college, it had repelled him to such a degree that he embraced atheism. It wasn't something that required active thought. On the contrary, he thought it could be practiced through complete indifference. But he'd been wrong.

In the decade that followed, while being married to a devout atheist, he'd learned that atheism was a strong belief that could not be satisfied by apathy. Proclaiming that no deity existed was as strong a statement as declaring that one did. His former wife had belonged to atheist groups that had actively fought against anything God-related – from prayer in schools to the use of Christian crosses or the Jewish Star of David in cemeteries.

To apply a true, lazy indifference to all things religious, Daniel had to accept that he was an agnostic. His true position was even weaker than that. By definition, agnostics believed that the existence of the divine and the supernatural – of God – was unknown or unknowable. Daniel couldn't know what other people knew: he was convinced only that *he* did not know. He'd been open to either possibility – God does or doesn't exist – and he'd been able to seal off that part of his mind for good. Or so he thought.

From his time with William Thompson, and the events that he'd directly witnessed, the door to that part of his mind had cracked open again. Perhaps there was something beyond this life. He now found himself hoping there was.

As far as Daniel knew, Will was just an ordinary man, not unlike himself. And if Will had a part of his being that could separate from the physical world – something that Daniel figured was a soul – so might he. And that was enough to make him think that it was possible that there was much more beyond the only existence he knew: a physical world with which the body that contained him interacted through five senses. There had to be more.

The sound of the refrigerator door in the kitchenette broke him away from his thoughts. He stepped out of his office and into the main room just as Sylvia stepped out from the kitchen with an iced tea in her hand.

"It's nice not having to drive home," she said as she twisted the top of the bottle, producing a loud pop. "It's almost 1:00 a.m., and I'll work another couple of hours." She sat in one of the leather chairs.

"No more nights sleeping in my office, either," Daniel said as he sat across from her, on the couch. "Are you making any progress?"

"The sightings are tapering off," she said. "We know exactly when the alien ships disappeared, and there was a steep decrease at that time. But people still see things and report them, though most of the reports are quickly debunked, or are just unreliable. We're not far above the UFO sighting frequency from before the event."

It was a good sign, but Daniel knew that it didn't mean it was over. According to the text that Will had translated, the Regenerators could wipe the Earth clean of life from a distance. The thousands of small ships near the surface seemed to be a survey of some kind – they were looking for Will. But Will had accomplished his mission and was no longer among the living on the planet. Daniel hoped that he was among the living somewhere else, but that hopefulness waned as time passed.

"Our problems now seem to be more focused on local happenings," Sylvia said.

"That's not our problem," Daniel argued, knowing she was referring to the threats Thackett had outlined in their last meeting. "It's a temporary distraction, and now we need to get back to the bigger picture."

"What are you going to do with Denise and Jonathan?" she asked.

That was another problem that Daniel had to solve: they didn't fit the Omni profile, although they both had excellent minds. They were more action-oriented, and being confined to the Space Systems building precluded their deployment on the outside. If they were to be assigned outdoor tasks, Daniel wouldn't be the one to do it. That would be Thackett.

"I'm thinking about getting them involved with the linguists," he replied.

"Do they have language skills?"

He shook his head. "No, but they both have knowledge that could put any deciphered fragments into context," he explained. "And there are already some things to examine. The part that Will translated accelerated the deciphering process immensely."

"Well, it can't hurt to have them working on it," she said. "And what about the drawings?"

Daniel shook his head. "No progress," he said. "Maybe the engineers will make more headway when they can read the text. But I doubt that any real advances will be made for decades. Every scientist and engineer I've spoken with about this is flabbergasted. They understand the nuts and bolts, but nothing else."

"Are the drawings even relevant anymore?" Sylvia asked. "Weren't they just the plans for the base – the parts the aliens already built?"

Daniel shrugged. "Most likely, yes," he replied, "And now that's gone, never to be recovered."

"Well, we hope not anyway," she added.

He nodded. The Russians and Chinese were digging frantically in Antarctica. "Even if they do find something, they'll have no idea what it is."

"You really think it was all destroyed?" she asked. "I mean, do you think there's anything left there at all?"

"No, I don't," he replied. "I think it was all melted down and all that's left are indiscernible materials."

"So, they're wasting their time?" she asked.

"Yes, and they're currently digging in the wrong spot," he said. "About a kilometer too far west."

She laughed. "I guess they'll be wasting even more time then."

Sylvia finished the last gulp of her tea and put the cap on the bottle. "Back to work," she said.

They went back to their respective offices, and Daniel picked up where he'd left off – that was, before inner dialogs on the existence of the soul had sidetracked him. He'd been creating a timeline for the set of monographs that he was coauthoring with Sylvia – covering everything from the Nazis' Red Falcon project through the emergence and disappearance of William Thompson. They would be the most world-shattering documents ever compiled. And, if they were written, they would eventually get out.

All secrets are compromised by time.

6

A TRILLION MINDS

WILL SAT AT THE KITCHEN COUNTER IN HIS QUARTERS AS HE NIBBLED AT his scrambled eggs and bacon. He'd been trying to stay on a 24-hour schedule but found it to be shifting constantly. His stomach was craving breakfast food, but his watch said it was 8:00 p.m.

He wondered what Denise was doing at that instant. He had no idea what time it was in Chicago but, if it were anywhere between dinnertime and 2:00 a.m., she'd be holed up in her office working on some case. He was forcing himself to assume she was still alive.

As his body continued to improve, he found his waking hours to be increasingly energetic, and his sleep to be deeper and of higher quality. He was beginning to look like he had when he was a college athlete, only he felt better now. He was lean, athletic, muscled, his senses were optimal, and he had no soreness except for his ankle, which had gotten spiked on a hard tackle during soccer practice just hours before. Even his breathing was deep, clean, and satisfying. It was as if, in his previous life, he'd been breathing through a wet washcloth.

After his first class on navigation that morning, he'd read the materials for the next lecture, and then gone to a soccer workout to get some physical activity, and to tune his skills for his next Premier League encounter. He was improving.

Afterwards, he'd gone to the second navigation lecture, and then devised a study plan. If he were to have any chance of passing the exams, he'd have to settle into a routine that at least kept him ahead on the reading materials.

He put his plate in the return receptacle, filled a porcelain mug with coffee, and sat on the floor, leaning his back against the frame of the window. He always had to look in the forward direction, so that the stars seemed to be moving toward him. It reminded him of rides in his friend's parents' car to baseball games as a kid: they had an old station wagon with a seat in the very back that faced out the rear. He always got queasy if he looked out the window for too long, watching the road scroll away from him. He preferred to look forward.

But the motion of the stars also made him anxious. The *Exodus 9* wasn't on a path toward Earth and, the longer it took him to redirect the ship, the further away they'd be when he turned it around. It was like being lost while driving a car and following a road that turns to the east when you know you should be heading west. Just as GPS devices had essentially removed the possibility of getting lost while driving a car, the autonomous navigation system on the *Exodus 9* would get him to where he wanted to go. That was, if he learned how to use it, and if he got access.

He had a few more productive hours to study, but he didn't want to spend them in his quarters. He went to the computer screen on the coffee table and looked up more information about "The University." The campus had beautiful study areas, and the one that he found most attractive was its colossal library. As he explored, he wasn't surprised to learn that he could attend the school full time, and even live in the dorms during the semester.

He set up a library visit to begin in 20 minutes, and then went through a long list of preferences. He chose the activity level – the number of students and noise – to be moderate. He concentrated better with a little background activity. Next, there was the option to have hardcopies of his books waiting for him at a table, along with a carafe of a beverage of choice. It would be strange to be allowed drinks in a library. He chose coffee.

That afternoon, he'd gone to a shop where he'd found a laptop computer, a backpack, and notebooks and pens. The laptop was connected to the ship's wireless "Internet," and the screen quality was like nothing he'd ever seen. The device was thin and light, and the keyboard matched the conventional American keyboard symbols and pattern.

He packed everything into the backpack and slung it over his shoulder.

As he made his way out of his quarters and toward the Tube, he contemplated how everything in the virtual realities that he'd encountered so far had been consistent with life on Earth. How were they able to get every detail right? Except for the food – which was pretty close to the real thing in most cases – every aspect of living on Earth was accurate: the furniture, clothes, lighting, air temperature, languages, geography, and even cultural things like soccer matches, pubs, campus life, and the "school of magic." The sheer volume of information that they'd gleaned from Earth's communications was staggering.

It made him think of the technical drawings that Jacob had extracted from the encrypted radio signals. Granted, they hadn't had much time to work on them, but Earth's best engineers couldn't reconstruct more than a few minor things from the plans. Here, the Deltas were able to reconstruct Will's entire world.

He refocused on his current task as he made his way through the university's main lobby to the massive wooden doors that opened to the central campus. He pushed them open and stepped into cool night air scented with downed leaves and pine needles. The chirps of crickets sounded from the lawn and bushes, and frogs croaked in the pond. Even though the central square was well-lit, he could see the brilliant stars of an Earthly sky. He found the North Star and the Big Dipper. *They even got the sky right,* he thought. Even though he couldn't confirm the details, he'd bet his life they were accurate.

The library was on the far end of the square, on the corner opposite the wooden doors through which he'd entered this quaint academic world. He took a paved walkway around the pond, through the center of the square, and to a tall brick building with giant wooden doors that were at least ten feet tall and rounded at the top. He pulled the one on the right and it swung open with little effort.

He walked into a foyer and was met by a smiling young woman with short brown hair holding a clipboard. Her nametag read "Carla, Assistant Librarian."

"Your table is ready for you in the main study hall," she said as she led the way deeper into the building.

They entered an enormous room that was the ground floor of a circular atrium that went up ten stories. Each floor encircling the atrium had a guardrail and, deeper inside, bookshelves densely packed with multicolored tomes. He could see students leaning on the rails at all levels, some chatting, others reading.

It was like no library he'd ever imagined. The ceiling was open to the night sky, which he studied for a moment to see if the stars were moving – if he were looking into the "real" space outside the ship. After a few seconds, he determined that he wasn't, and that the view was probably consistent with the Earthly sky outside the building.

His attention went back to Carla who led him to one of the more than 30 rectangular wooden tables arrayed in a square pattern on the marble floor. Each table could seat ten on a side with plenty of space between them and, at each seat, was a lamp mounted near the center of the table.

"Here you are," she said and motioned to a chair across the table from a male student who was looking back and forth between a notebook and a calculator.

On the table at Will's seat was a thick textbook, a carafe, a glass mug, and sugar and cream.

"Thanks," Will said.

"If you need anything, just press the assistance button on your lamp," Carla said and walked away.

He set his backpack on the floor and sat on the padded wooden chair. He grabbed the textbook and examined the cover. It was titled,

"The Principles of Starship Navigation," by W. E. Schmidt, the professor who taught his class. It was nice to have an actual paper copy of the text in his hands. Reading from computer screens and navigating through menus was tedious work.

He went to the table of contents and found the next reading assignment on something called "Passive Navigation," which he learned meant depending on maps rather than on active sensing. The maps themselves could be passive or active as well, but all maps used in interstellar travel had to be active – meaning they modeled the trajectories of moving objects and would automatically predict their locations at later times. Passive maps were like the old paper street maps of Earth. The only analogy to active street maps on Earth were GPS devices that showed real-time traffic, weather, and construction areas.

He filled his mug with coffee and paged back to the table of contents. He found a later chapter titled, "Chapter 28: Access and Permissions," and flipped to it. He read that, on a ship like the *Exodus 9*, the destination was often preprogrammed, and the navigation details were left to the ship's own artificial intelligence – meaning the ship's computer. In order to change the destination mid-trip, someone with global access would have to intercede. Only the commanding officer would have that authority, and Will had been told that there were no officers on the ship. All he'd seen so far were fabricated beings that were produced to function as staff, or to act as characters or players within his recreational ventures.

Next, he contemplated how to hack the ship's computer to give him command access, but quickly dismissed the idea. On Earth, he couldn't even hack into his own computer if he forgot the password, much less defeat the security features created by an advanced alien civilization.

He went to the next topic on his reading assignment list: "Active Maps." He'd worry about gaining access later.

LENNY LANDED at Dulles International Airport outside of DC and picked up a rental car with an alias identity provided to him by the CIA. As he made his way to Space Systems, he could hardly believe he'd already been extracted from his retirement dream in the tropical paradise of Costa Rica. The stark contrast between San José and DC was immediate: his face had been blasted with a gust of freezing wind and fine ice crystals the instant he'd stepped outside the airport terminal, and he'd had to turn on the heat in the car.

Once inside the gates of Space Systems, he followed a handler to a parking spot on a sublevel of the garage and then, after parking the car, to an elevator that took him a few floors down. It was the usual treatment, although the guards seemed to be less threatened by him, or at least not as on edge as they'd been during his previous visits.

The handler took him to a small interview room where Lenny was given a bottle of water and a seat at a table. A few minutes later, the CIA director, James Thackett, entered with an escort.

"Leonard," Thackett said and extended his hand. "Thanks for coming."

Lenny shook his hand. "I'd ask what this is all about, but I think I already know what you want me to do."

Thackett took a seat across the table from him as the escort set two folders on the table, left the room, and closed the door.

The director opened one of the files as he spoke. "You've already received the briefing on this guy," Thackett explained as he slid the paperwork to Lenny. "This one contains updated information."

Lenny grabbed the file and examined its contents. On the first page was a photo, and he recognized the black, dead eyes of a late-middle-aged Mounir Mekhloufi staring back at him. The Tunisian's narrow face was gaunt and sickly, and his hairline ended only an inch above his thick eyebrows. The dark scruff on his face grew in patches and contrasted with his yellow-white complexion.

"You've encountered this guy before," Thackett said, apparently looking for confirmation.

"Yes," Lenny replied. It had taken him months to recover from the knife wounds. Infection had nearly killed him.

"As you mentioned to our operative in Costa Rica, this man has only one purpose in this world," Thackett said. "And he has only one reason to be in the States."

"What do you want me to do?" Lenny asked, already knowing the answer.

"Take him out," Thackett replied without hesitation. "It would be best if done quietly – no body to be found – but otherwise use any means necessary. However, before this happens, we need to ID his first few contacts, so it might get tricky for a while."

Lenny had eliminated numerous intelligence operatives during his career, many of whom had been Russian, but this one was different. He found Mekhloufi to be unprofessional; the man often tortured his targets and left a horrible mess, or used methods that caused prolonged suffering, like radiation poisoning. Mekhloufi was known for operations that were meant to send a message. Lenny thought the man would have been a serial killer had he not broken into the intelligence profession.

"He got his start working for the Tunisian government," Thackett explained.

"That didn't last long," Lenny commented. "They probably constrained him too much. He's been working freelance ever since. He's expensive, and only takes jobs he wants."

"So, what job did he want here?"

Lenny shrugged. "He's probably following up on my work – assigned by Chinese Intelligence – of assassinating William Thompson." That reminded Lenny of something. "By the way, where is Mr. Tao?"

Tao had been the most recent head of the local Chinese network, and Lenny wanted to know whether he was really out of the picture. He was one of only a few who were left that could identify him. The last he knew, Tao was in the hands of the CIA. The promise was that he'd never again see the light of day.

"Tao has dissolved from the scene," Thackett replied.

He got juiced, Lenny thought. He'd been dissolved in acid and poured down a drain, or into a swamp somewhere. It was good.

"So, you think Mekhloufi is here to kill William Thompson?" Thackett reiterated.

Lenny shrugged. "All I know is he's here to kill someone – or maybe many – and that his target is unique in some way," he clarified. "It could be a high-profile person, or it's just an unusually challenging or lucrative job. It would be best to keep Mr. Thompson in a secure place."

Thackett's expression went blank for a moment, and then a look of horror flashed across his face and quickly diminished. He shook his head. "Will Thompson's not in the area."

"I suppose he could also be after Jacob Hale," Lenny said, "since he was one of my other assignments. But I was assigned to collect some things from Hale, not necessarily kill him. Mekhloufi is here to kill someone. Do you think he could be after you?"

Thackett's face took on a look of alarm for an instant. "I suppose it's possible," he said. "Maybe as an act of retaliation for taking down their network."

Lenny didn't want to say it, but the decimation of the Chinese network was as brutal as it got. Many lives were lost, many of which were complete disappearances – no bodies.

"I think revenge is a definite possibility," Lenny agreed. "Otherwise, they wouldn't have hired the most expensive and masochistic assassin in the business. He's either taken this job for an obscene amount of money which, I've heard, he doesn't really need, or it's going to add something to his gruesome portfolio."

"You talk about this guy as if he's a serial killer," Thackett said.

"He's an animal," Lenny responded. "I've seen some of his work firsthand, but there are many other stories."

"Like what?" Thackett asked.

There was one that Lenny hadn't witnessed directly but learned about from a reliable source. "Mekhloufi once killed a man's family – wife and three young kids – in their house, and then posed their bodies around the kitchen table for the man to see when he got home that night. He even set the table and put utensils in their hands. At the center of the table was the family dog on a plate."

Thackett seemed to stifle a shudder and said, "That's disgusting."

"That's what we're dealing with," Lenny said. "He's here to do something significant."

"You think you can take him out?" Thackett asked.

"I think so," Lenny replied. "Give me what you have on him – where he's been sighted, recent photos, et cetera, and I'll do what I can. However, it might be a challenge if I first have to ID his contacts."

"We'll need those contacts to track down the rest of the monsters they've brought in," Thackett said and nodded to Mekhloufi's file. "You keep that, and we'll get you more info electronically."

"And what about Xing Li?" Lenny asked, referring to the former Syncorp bioweapons expert now on the scene. "Her showing up at the same time as Mekhloufi might not be a coincidence."

"We're working on that, too," Thackett replied and slid the second file to Lenny. "Your services might be needed for that situation as well."

Lenny opened the folder and looked over the contents. He now wondered if he'd ever leave the business. If he succeeded this time, and eliminated Mekhloufi and then Xing Li, other monsters would just fill the void.

As if on cue, Thackett asked, "How was Costa Rica?"

"It was paradise."

WILL STUDIED until he could no longer keep his eyes open – about two hours – and then headed out of the library. On his way across campus, toward the doors that led back to reality – or what he assumed was reality – he overheard a group of students talking about going to a bar located near campus.

On a whim, he followed them through a narrow alley between two large academic buildings, down a grassy hill, and onto a sidewalk. He was now off campus, in a residential neighborhood with small houses and street signs and mailboxes. Some of the lights were on in the residences – it was nearing 11:00 p.m. – and he could see people in some of them. In others, TV screens flickered behind window drapes.

Will kept his distance from the students as he followed them down a gradual slope into a small square. Four establishments were on the corners of the intersection of Main Street and East State Street. There was a 24-hour breakfast restaurant – he could smell bacon – and a bar called Squidly's, from which he heard laughter and music. On the other two corners were a closed bookstore and a gas station.

He was astounded by the degree of detail that this illusion presented. How many worlds existed on this one ship? How many different lives could he simultaneously lead? He could live as a college student for as long as he wanted, just like he could spend an entire year on an adventure in the school of magic. He was certain he could also live the life of a professional soccer player.

He wondered how such an immersion might affect one's mind. He imagined that someone might prefer to live a life other than that which reality had given them. And, after some time doing so, some might actually believe that they were someone else, and that the supporting characters in their illusions were real. At that point, the line between reality and imagination would become fuzzy, and a person's entire existence might develop into a confusing mess.

Will waited at a streetlight as the students made their way into Squidly's. The music got louder as they opened the door, and then muffled again as they dissolved into the crowd inside and the door swung closed behind them. Other students were chatting in the parking lot adjacent to the establishment, and a car pulled onto the street and squealed away. It seemed that the program accurately mimicked the behavior of 20-year-old college students.

Before he'd enter the bar, he wanted to explore how the illusion was being carried out.

He found a bench on the corner near a bus stop – he wondered for an instant where a bus might take him – and then sat down and propped himself against an armrest.

He separated, and then examined the scene from a perspective close to his body. The view was the same. As he elevated, however, the images distorted, and the sounds were garbled, as if he were underwater. By the time he made it to the ceiling, which was higher than he'd expected – over 50 feet by his estimate, what lay beneath him looked like a gelatinous mess. Various parts of the scene continuously distorted, as if space itself were being stretched and compressed. Some areas seemed to speed up while others slowed down, but it all seemed to revolve around his body, seated on the bench.

He pressed through the ceiling, which offered more resistance than he expected, and found himself in front of a curved array of various objects that reminded him of the eye of an insect. Some of the objects looked like parabolic antennae, about two feet in diameter and the same depth, and others resembled circular speakers – about a foot in diameter. There were lights, apertures, ducts, and tubes everywhere.

He surveyed in all directions and found that the complex instrumentation formed a sphere around the extensive room.

When he returned to his body, it was like waking up from a strange dream. The world before him was again as real as anything he'd experienced in "real" life.

The air was cooler than when he'd begun the walk, and it was humid enough to form fog. A light breeze carried the scents of fallen leaves and dry pine needles below the stronger aromas of food from the restaurant. Bats darted in and out of view near the streetlights. The moon poked through the swaying tips of a cluster of tall pines near the top of a hill a few hundred yards beyond the pub and, overhead, thin clouds streaked over the starry sky as if they'd been painted with a thin brush.

It was perfect. And if he couldn't separate, he'd never know that it wasn't real. He imagined others from Earth being on the ship and getting lost in the illusion. They couldn't separate, so one might imagine such technology could be used to keep people out of the *real* reality. They could be tricked into thinking they were somewhere else for a lifetime when they were actually confined to a single room. It reminded him of *The Matrix*, a movie from the 1990s, where humanity was unknowingly trapped inside a simulated reality. In that case, the illusion was carried out entirely in their minds as their bodies were completely immobilized. He liked the Deltas' method better.

At least, now, he was convinced that his life on Earth was no illusion. When he'd separated there, he'd seen reality as it was when viewed from his body. Although, if one applied the concept from *The Matrix*, how could anyone really know what was reality? If you control a person's mind to such a degree, you define their reality.

He sat up from the bench, crossed the intersection diagonally, and then passed through the front door of the pub and into a crowded foyer, where it was both warm and loud. From that point, he could go left or right. To the left was a well-lit room with a long bar and barstools occupied by college students drinking beer. Large television screens mounted on the walls were showing various sporting events. People were reacting to the games, and it was noisy. To the right was a passage that led deeper into the building, from which came music – it sounded like a band was playing.

He went to the left and walked up to an open part of the bar. A sign on the wall behind the bar indicated that beer was free for the next hour, compliments of Sigma Chi, one of the fraternities on campus. He requested a beer listed on a chalk-written menu, a brand he recognized, which was then delivered by a blonde coed wearing jean shorts and a midriff-cut shirt that displayed the logo of a professional football team.

He turned, leaned his lower back against the bar, and took a swig of the golden beverage. It resembled beer – not quite right – but it tasted good to him. He could tell the alcohol content was accurate.

He looked over the dozen or so TVs and found a golf tournament with pros he recognized, a reality show about a woman selecting a husband, and professional baseball games. But something drew his eyes to a football game on a screen at the far end of the bar. It was the colors of the uniforms – green and gold versus navy blue and orange. The Green Bay Packers were playing the Chicago Bears.

He moved down the bar and found an open spot close to the screen so that he could watch the game. He recognized the voices of the announcers. He recognized the players. And, after a few plays, he recognized the game itself. It was a replay of a game he'd already seen.

As he watched, the details of more than just that game resurfaced in his mind. That game had originally been played on a Thursday night, nearly two years ago. He remembered that night well, because the events of the next night had changed the course of his life forever.

The following Friday night, on a whim, he'd decided to go to a local high school football game – something he hadn't done in nearly 20 years. The game had been entertaining, but it had been an ill-fated venture: hours after the game had ended, he'd been arrested and charged with a horrible crime. This had started a long sequence of events that ended with his conviction, his placement in the Compressed Punishment program, and his insertion into the Red Box, in Detroit. And the Red Box was where he'd transformed into what he was now – something that still wasn't entirely clear to him.

His decision to go to that game on that Friday night was why he was now on the *Exodus 9*. It was why everyone he cared about might be dead, and why Earth might have already been stripped down to a lifeless rock.

A voice from his right disrupted his thoughts.

He turned to see a young woman, short, with dark hair pulled back in a tight ponytail. Her thick eyebrows curved slightly down to the outer corners of her brown eyes. She was wearing jeans and a T-shirt with the words "Kappas Know How to Move," over a silhouetted image of a ballet dancer. She seemed to be expecting a response.

"I'm sorry," Will said. "I was locked into the game. Did you say something?"

"I think you're in my navigation class," she said. "You take it with Professor Schmidt?"

"I do," he replied and forced a smile. "Good class."

"My name's Tracey," she said and held out her hand. "And you are?"

"Will," he replied and shook her hand.

"Have you started the homework?" she asked.

The question took him off guard and, for a moment, he had a feeling of panic. It felt like one of those dreams where he'd forgotten to go to class all semester and was now heading to a final exam. The feeling passed, but he was now intrigued about the idea of doing homework.

"Not yet," he replied. "You?"

She shook her head. "I usually stay ahead in my classes, but it's hard to keep up with the reading in this one," she explained. "And the homework is brutal."

The crowd erupted in cheers and Will looked to see what was happening. The Green Bay Packers had just made a key interception with less than five minutes left in the fourth quarter. The Bears were leading 30-28.

"I'll bet you a beer that Green Bay wins with a field goal as time expires," Will said.

"The beer is free," Tracey said with a grin.

"That's good, because I don't have any money."

She laughed out loud. "Okay, you're on," she said. "I'm a Bears fan anyway."

As the Green Bay quarterback methodically took the ball down the field, he and Tracey chatted about passive and active maps, and manual piloting. One key piece of information he gleaned from her was that there was no true "manual" piloting of any ship. It was too complicated for a single brain. Ships had piloting and navigation systems riddled with millions of artificially intelligent entities, each of which had abilities that far surpassed the human brain. On top of that, they all communicated nearly instantaneously with the central command, and with each other. It was like having a crew of a million that no one ever saw.

"Looks like you were almost right," she said and nodded to the screen.

Green Bay was lining up to attempt a short field goal, something that should be nearly automatic for the team's accomplished kicker to give them the three points they needed to take the lead. "You think he's going to miss it?" he asked.

She shook her head. "No," she replied. "But there are 11 seconds left on the clock. There will still be time left after the kick. And, if I heard you correctly, the bet was that Green Bay would make the winning kick 'as time expired.'"

Will could have sworn that the Green Bay players had stormed the field immediately after the kick passed through the uprights on that Thursday night. That wouldn't have happened if they'd had to kick off with a few seconds left on the clock. Something else had to happen.

"I stand by my original wording," he said and swallowed the last of his first beer and showed her the empty glass. "And the timing is perfect."

The teams lined up for the field goal attempt, the ball was snapped, and the kick was blocked. The teams scrambled for the loose ball and the Bears recovered it.

Tracey held up her empty glass and said, "Looks like I'll have a – "

"Wait," Will said and pointed to the screen.

The game announcers explained that there was a penalty on the play, and the audio went to one of the referees on the field, who said, "Illegal hands to the face, number 92, defense. Half the distance to the goal. Replay fourth down. Please put two seconds back on the clock."

"You have to be kidding me!" Tracey exclaimed and laughed.

Green Bay proceeded to kick the winning field goal as time expired, and the team stormed the field, just as Will remembered.

"Unbelievable," Tracey grumbled as she grabbed the glass out of his hand and turned to the bar.

"I'm having the Blacktail Lager," he said.

Will had recalled the details of the game correctly and was convinced that it was the actual game – the original broadcast. He even recognized the commercials. But there was something more to it.

Since that game had first aired almost two years ago, the *Exodus 9* could have been, at most, two light-years from Earth when it received it. He then recalled the movie poster he'd seen in the theatre that advertised a film that he knew was just a year old.

Tracey turned and handed a cold beer to Will. "Here's to navigation," she said and held up her glass.

Will tapped it with his and they both took a gulp.

"Where's the restroom?" he asked and looked around.

Tracey pointed to a sign on the wall about 20 feet to the left of the TV that was showing the game. They were interviewing the winning coach.

Will set his beer on the bar, squeezed past some guys playing foosball, and pushed through a set of double-swinging doors and into the bathroom. When he got back to the bar, Tracey was chatting with another girl wearing a blue "Kappa Kappa Gamma" sorority sweatshirt that had some sort of embroidered crest with an owl on it. If he had to guess, it was consistent with the emblem of a sorority on Earth. The new girl had one arm draped around a young guy who seemed to be her boyfriend.

Will reached around Tracey and grabbed his beer from the bar behind her.

"Will, this is Tina and Ben," she said. "Tina was my roommate my freshman year and we pledged Kappa together. She and Ben just got engaged."

"Congratulations," Will said as he shook hands with both of them and wondered how long he was going to waste time with the charade. It occurred to him that he was still interested in finishing his beer, so he thought he'd play along until that was gone. Plus, he had to remember that the fantasy was supposed to mimic the full college experience. The fact that he was only into it for the knowledge didn't matter. There was a stark contrast between his current motivations and those he'd had when he'd gone through college the first time.

"Have a date set?" Will asked.

"Second week of June," Tina replied.

They chatted for another 15 minutes while Will finished his beer. A clock behind the bar read 11:58 p.m., and he glanced at his watch, which read the same.

"Time to go," Will said. "Looks like I have some homework to do in the morning."

"It was nice meeting you," Tracey said. "See you in class."

When he left the bar, he immediately wished he'd brought a jacket. It had cooled down and felt like a typical foggy fall night in the

Midwest. It was strange that he was wearing his normal clothes – those issued to him from the beginning – and everyone else was dressed in common college student attire. He was out of place, but no one had said anything.

During the 15-minute walk back to campus he encountered small groups of students heading back to their dorms. They were chatting and laughing, and he could smell alcohol on them as he passed by. He was still impressed at how accurate everything was – all of his senses could be convinced that it was real. His mind, however, knew the truth. But the only reason that was true was because he could separate.

He made his way through the center square of campus, around the pond with croaking frogs and chirping crickets, and approached the massive wooden doors.

Instead of going through, he stopped and stared at them for a moment. What if they were locked? Or what if they disappeared – suppose he came back to this location and there was just a brick wall and no doors? What would he do? Could he get stuck in this fictional world?

He brushed it off. If that happened, he'd have to resort to separating to find a way out. He imagined that someone without this ability, however, could be trapped for a lifetime.

He pulled the doors open, walked through the foyer and past the front desk into the main mall of the *Exodus 9*. He found a Tube entrance and was back in his quarters ten minutes later.

As he got ready for bed, he remembered something from religion class when he was a third grader in Catholic school. It was in Corinthians: it read, "The last enemy to be destroyed is death." That passage had deeply affected him, even as such a young child, since he'd known someone who had died.

It seemed to him, based on what he'd learned about souls returning to regenerated bodies, or being reincarnated to start with new ones, that death never really existed at all. At the very least, death required a new definition.

He brushed his teeth, settled onto the couch, and viewed the stars through the window. Their subtle movement gave him mixed impressions. On one hand, it made him feel like he was getting further and further from home. On the other, it gave him a sense that things were happening.

As he closed his eyes, he wondered if the ship was still detecting signals from Earth. If so, the delay might tell him how far he was from his home planet – that was, if his understanding of the laws of physics was accurate, something in which his confidence was waning. More importantly, maybe he'd learn something of the fate of his loved ones.

IT WAS GOING on 11:00 p.m. when Jacob popped open his second cola and flipped open his notebook on his first official project as an Omni.

There were now four satellites in the Chinese cluster, the third of which had just gone online the night before. The satellites communicated with multiple bases on the China mainland, and with each other. The CIA continuously provided him with the most current data that included encrypted commands from the ground bases, the actions of the satellites, and the satellite communications responses.

Although they changed the encryption codes on their satellites on a regular basis, the Chinese failed to change the encryption technique they used. What Jacob had accomplished over a year before at Interstellar Dynamics was to break down the encryption to a point where CIA and NSA supercomputers could do the rest of the job using brute force methods.

That method provided the CIA with deciphered data that the satellites were sending to Earth. It did not, however, give them the commands that controlled those satellites. The command sequences sent from ground bases to the satellites were encrypted using a different method. Deciphering them would give the CIA control, and that was Jacob's primary task.

The deciphered data that the CIA had already sent him were in the form of complicated images. The satellite cameras were sensitive to light beyond the visible spectrum – including X-rays and the high infrared. They could also detect radio waves, and the satellites could function collectively as a single device to provide other types of data. Most of the images would require some sort of complicated analysis to extract useful information, except for those from the optical telescopes, which were conventional, static photos, as well as short, high-resolution video clips that lasted just a few seconds.

From what he'd seen so far, the satellites were trying to detect objects outside the solar system but at distances that were far closer than Proxima Centauri, the next closest star at just over four light-years from the sun. Their cameras and sensors focused on the space just beyond the Kuiper belt – a ring of space debris outside the solar system – at distances of just a small fraction of a light-year. The Kuiper belt was a thick horizontal ring of debris that followed an orbit around the sun in the same plane as those followed by the planets. The cameras, however, looked in all directions, meaning above and below the orbital planes.

Jacob went up to the skylight on the third level, set his drink and notebook on the coffee table, and leaned back on the circular couch. It was a clear night, and the moon was positioned just right so that he could see it through the dome.

Were the Chinese just paranoid, or were they expecting to see something out in the middle of nowhere? Almost every country with a space program had at least one satellite looking for incoming asteroids that might be on a collision course with Earth, but this was different.

China had been quietly preparing for war for decades, and nearly every move they made was related to economic or militaristic aggression. One might say that they were "passive-aggressive," in that they had not been in any recent military conflicts, but they were always positioning, and imposing their will in various ways. Their reconfiguring of their spy satellites to look outward, rather than inward to watch their Earth-bound adversaries, led Jacob to believe that there were three possible motivations for their move.

First, they might be fearing that someone or something else was coming – more ships, or worse – and that they wouldn't be friendly.

Jacob shared in their paranoia. Second, they might be worried that whoever was coming would be friendly toward the US. After all, the Americans had deciphered the incoming radio signal, and had discovered something in Antarctica, but Jacob knew that there had been no contact with extraterrestrials. Finally, perhaps China intended to be the first to interact with anyone coming toward Earth and, if they were the first to see them, they would be.

Jacob refocused on the task at hand. He sat up on the couch, took a swig of soda, and opened his notebook. The command signals that the Chinese ground bases were sending, to what they were referring to as the "Distant Eye" cluster, were both encrypted and formatted in such a way that made them difficult to decipher. However, they'd made some mistakes along the way, and, through blind luck, the CIA had some opportunities.

It wasn't exactly luck, however. The CIA, with help from MI-6 and the Israeli Mossad, had gotten early warning about the satellites, and had subsequently monitored every step of their development. Of particular importance was the process of their initial setup. During that procedure, the Chinese research teams had to reboot the satellites' computer systems to make tweaks to the control programs that were the brains that both carried out local functions on each satellite, such as physical maneuvers and sensor positioning, and communications between satellites.

While working out the bugs, programming data – including the actual program code – had to travel back and forth between Earth and the satellites. This information was encrypted using the same method used to communicate the data and images back to Earth – the encryption that Jacob had already broken. The CIA therefore had a copy of the satellites' control software.

Having the computer code was crucial. For starters, it identified the functionality of the satellites, and provided the commands to control them. For instance, there were commands that told a satellite to turn in a certain direction, to focus its telescopic camera on a specific location, or to record radio signals in a particular frequency band. Knowing these commands, and being able to implement them on the satellites, would give him complete control of the Distant Eye.

Now that the cluster was out of the debugging phase, the Chinese were encrypting the satellite control commands using a method that hadn't yet been broken by the CIA. However, since Jacob had the computer code, he knew the exact format of the commands, and this would be of great utility in breaking that encryption. When the Chinese ground base sent an encrypted command to the cluster, US spy satellites would observe the cluster's response, and hence connect the action to the command. The exact format of that command was known, and it had to be contained in the encrypted message. That additional information could do a lot to accelerate the brute-force methods of the CIA supercomputers. The challenge was to accurately identify when a specific command was executed, and then get the CIA ciphers specialists working on it.

The more subtle task, however, was to gain control of the satellites without the Chinese knowing. One possibility, once the encryption was broken, was to set up a "mask" program to respond to their commands without actually carrying them out. But that would only work for a while. In the end, the CIA would have to arrange for the satellites to respond with some kind of faux data, or an error message indicating that the cluster was temporarily unresponsive. Either tactic would give the CIA some time on the cluster, but both would only work for a short while.

His phone vibrated on the coffee table, startling him from his thoughts. It was Pauli. It was early morning in London, and she must have been on her way to the office.

Jacob slapped his notebook closed, picked up the empty soda can from the table, and answered the phone as he made his way down the stairs. He'd chat with Pauli, who he figured wanted to nail down Thanksgiving travel plans, and then get to bed early. If he got to sleep by 2:30 a.m., he'd be fresh and ready to work in the morning.

Sleep, however, might not be easy. His mind was tumbling with unanswered questions, one of which was what they were going to do with the satellites once he'd commandeered them. In which direction should they look first and, above all, for what, exactly, were they searching?

He hoped his conversation with Pauli would help his mind spin down for the night.

DENISE FOUND the move to Space Systems to be more difficult than she'd anticipated.

They put her in the same room she'd had the last time she'd stayed, and it reminded her of Will. The worst part was that she had to pass by his flat whenever she went to the gym, which was how she normally started the day.

Although it was painful, Space Systems was probably the best place she could be. If there were any news – if they learned anything about Will – she'd hear about it. The problem was that it could be an endless cycle of futile hope. A person could get locked into such a thing and wait in perpetuity. It was hard to know when to cut loose and move on.

Director Thackett enrolled her and Jonathan in an advanced training course involving the handling of classified information, and gave them access to something called "Dark Secrets," a multifaceted information platform that would allow them to conduct unimpeded research in highly classified areas. The "Dark" part did not mean anything sinister, although some of the information certainly was, it just meant that it was never to see the light of day. It was still nothing like Omniscient clearance, but it was supposed to provide them with what they needed for their first assignments, the details of which would be revealed in their next meeting in 713 with the group.

An upside to their relocation and new work assignments was that they had to be official CIA employees. In addition to making them eligible for required clearances, they would get paid. And Denise's salary contract was nearly double what she was making as an associate with the DNA Foundation. Jonathan also got a significant bump above his professor's salary – he'd been taking no salary as the director of the DNA Foundation.

It was just before 8:00 a.m. when Denise joined the others in 713. They were seated at a rectangular conference table to the left side of the room as she entered, and a ceiling-mounted projector illuminated a screen on the far left wall. James Thackett was standing near the screen testing a laser pointer as the others poured coffee from a carafe on a tray at the center of the rectangular table.

Denise filled a mug and took a seat to Jonathan's left at the end of the table, furthest from the screen. On the left side of the table was Sylvia, with Daniel to her left. Jacob, who looked like he'd just gotten out of bed, was on the right side, next to Jonathan.

Thackett cleared his throat and started the meeting. "The first thing on the agenda is assignments for Denise and Jonathan," he explained. "These have been chosen to get you accustomed to using CIA resources while potentially producing some useful information."

Thackett clicked to the next slide, which showed the alien text that had been translated by Will at the Antarctic base.

"First, Denise," Thackett said as he nodded to her. "With Will's translation, our linguists have made significant headway, and we think you can contribute to this effort."

"What do you want me to do?" Denise asked.

Thackett nodded to Daniel to take the question.

"The linguists have no context for what they're translating," Daniel said. "You won't interact with them face to face, but you'll read their translations and do two things. First, you'll use CIA resources to verify details. Perhaps they refer to a landmark of some kind, or a geological or celestial event that can be corroborated. Second, you will help steer their efforts, depending on what you find."

"To what end?" Denise asked. She realized her tone came off as resistant, and rephrased the question. "I mean, are we looking for something in particular?"

"Will left via some kind of transporter," Sylvia said, making eye contact with Denise. "We want to know where he went – or at least find some clues."

This was exactly the motivation Denise needed, and she could see in Sylvia's eyes that she knew it as well.

Thackett clicked through a few slides that showed a large table of reference numbers for various documents along with the progress made on their respective translations in percentages. The majority of the documents had zero progress, and the most developed ones, other than the one Will had translated, only reached 15 percent translated.

Thackett then flipped to a slide showing clear vials of fine powders of varying colors.

"Jonathan, I'd like you to start with investigating the origins of the powders we found at the base," Thackett explained.

Denise knew he was talking about the vials of substances they'd found in a cabinet at the Antarctic base that had supposedly been collected from various celestial bodies, such as Mars and its moons, Haley's Comet, and others.

"You mean you want me to figure out how they got into the hands of Stanley Miller, the professor at Plum Island?" Jonathan asked.

"Yes," Thackett replied. "I want to know everything about them. Identifying who had intermediate possession at various steps along their way to Professor Miller could be revealing."

Jonathan nodded.

"We'd also like to know about the possible return of our visitors – the so-called Regenerators," Thackett continued. "And that leads us to an update from Jacob."

Jacob went through a five-minute explanation of how he and CIA encryption specialists were using the computer resources at the CIA and NSA to decipher both the control communications of the Chinese satellites and the data transfer. The final objective was to commandeer the entire cluster.

"We can already see what they see," Jacob explained. "Any image or sensor data they send to Earth we will have in real time."

"What's the importance of controlling their satellites if we can see everything they do?" Sylvia asked. "Why take them over?"

Thackett cleared his voice and spoke before Jacob could respond. "First," Thackett said, "this is a game that's been played ever since the very first spy satellites were launched. All space-capable countries are either looking to disable or commandeer the spy craft of their rivals. China is constantly trying to do the same to us, and to the rest of the world."

"Suppose we're successful, and get control," Jonathan said. "What advantage do we have?"

Thackett nodded to Jacob to take the question.

"The obvious thing is that we'll have acquired an outward-looking cluster of satellites to employ for our own uses," Jacob said. "But it's deeper than that. You see, in the beginning, the Chinese will not know that we are essentially inside their satellites. They will operate as if we are not observing their actions."

"And we want to know what they're looking for," Thackett interrupted. "Seeing what they're doing – where they're looking with those satellites – will tell us something about the impetus for their actions. We want to know what they know, and what they're looking for."

"So, any information we get, they will also have?" Sylvia asked.

"In the beginning," Thackett replied.

"What do you mean?" Sylvia asked.

"If we're successful, we'll be able to lock them out and take over if we need to – after we know what they're trying to do," Jacob explained. "At that point, we'll implement our own encryptions for both the control of the satellites and their data transmissions."

"But won't the Chinese know?" Denise asked. "Won't they suspect us?"

Jacob grinned. "You're asking all of the right questions," he said. "The idea is that, while we're in control and blacking out the real data that the satellites are collecting, we'll monitor their control commands and send them spoof responses. It's called a mask interface."

"You mean send them bogus images and sensor data?" Jonathan asked.

Jacob nodded. "Everything in the exact format they'd expect. In fact, we're going to use their own program to create the data."

"Sounds like a huge project," Jonathan commented.

"Our budget for this is unlimited," Thackett said. "And we'll have all the resources we need – including from the Defense Intelligence Agency and the NSA."

Thackett closed the meeting with a summary of the security issues that brought them all – except Jacob – into long-term residency in Space Systems, and said that they'd have daily meetings to discuss progress.

"That reminds me," Thackett said, looking to Jonathan and Denise and then pulling two manila folders out of his briefcase and sliding them across the table to them. "We need your signatures on these release forms to obtain your medical records. We can't place you into full CIA employee status until you've had your vaccine updates and bloodwork done."

After they were signed, Thackett collected the forms and left. Everyone else went to the seating area, near the kitchenette on the opposite side of the room. Daniel carried the coffee tray and set it on the coffee table while the others took their seats.

When everyone got settled, Daniel started. "I just want to say that I'm glad you're all here. We've been through a lot together already, and I can't imagine being without you going forward." He glanced at Denise and added, "But I wish there were one more."

Denise wanted to burst into tears but maintained her composure. "The best we can do is to keep moving forward and try to deal with whatever comes next," Denise said.

"And, the question is, what will that be?" Daniel said, not directing his question at anyone in particular.

Denise knew only what she hoped might happen but had a feeling that what was coming was much darker.

WANG YONG WAS DEVELOPING a view of the larger picture but didn't yet understand it. He was a tech nerd but still had no concept of the vast scope of technologies that Syncorp, Inc. had been developing.

He didn't understand why his predecessors had been managing a biotech company, but he figured it must have been a front for something – and probably laden with intellectual property jewels to be harvested for China. Syncorp had recently gone out of business. Maybe Cho and Tao had successfully gutted it.

Nonetheless, Yong had Tao's notes on some contacts affiliated with the old Syncorp company who had carried out "special duties." Of those who had been rounded up by the CIA, some had been released, and some had disappeared. None of those could be trusted. A few, however, had not been caught, and had somehow managed to flee the country. Those were the ones who might still be employable.

There was a lot to do, and some of it would be messy work. He couldn't afford to have Chinese ops getting caught early in the game or there'd be another purge. It was best to have locals do the initial dirty work.

Yong logged into a conventional email account with a mainstream provider, wrote a message, and saved it as a draft. He wondered if a generous offer might get the man to leave his tropical paradise.

WILL FOUND himself in a posh skyscraper apartment with floor-to-ceiling windows overlooking a brightly lit New York City nightscape. Mia, his counselor, was sitting in one of two leather chairs which were perched on a one-foot-high platform, providing a better angle to view the streets below. Between the chairs was a small round table with two glass tumblers and a crystal decanter of what he presumed was whiskey.

Mia stood, smiled, opened her arms, and gestured to the surroundings. "I thought this scene might be interesting," she said. "What do you think?"

It was comfortable. The ceiling was high, maybe 15 feet, with spotlights mounted on iron supports that ran the width of the rectangular space. The lights produced a warm hue on the wooden floor, and shone upon paintings of familiar New York City landmarks, and on an old map of the subway system.

"It's nice," Will said as he stepped onto the platform with the chairs. He went to the window and saw that they were on somewhere around the 75th floor. He could barely hear the street noise below, although it seemed that traffic was heavy.

"We have some important things to talk about," she said and nodded to the decanter. "You take it neat, right?"

"Most of the time," he replied as he wondered how she knew. He was going to ask, but he was more interested in the "important things" on the agenda.

He sat in the chair on the right as Mia poured two fingers of whiskey into each glass, handed one to Will, and took the seat on the left. The chairs did not directly face each other but were angled toward the window.

"I see that you've been using the ship's resources," she said.

He nodded.

"You've been taking a class on navigation," she added. "How's that going?"

"It's interesting," he replied. He was starting to feel like this was going to be an interrogation and decided that he should not divulge his reason for taking the class. "I figured I should learn as much as I can about what my future holds."

"How do you like the campus?" she asked.

"It's beautiful," he replied.

"You know, you could choose any one of the Earth campuses," she said. "They're all available – including those of the schools you attended. Or you could even design your own."

"I was wondering," Will said. "How is it that all of the minute details are so accurate?"

"What do you mean?"

"Take the college, for example," he explained. "The clothes, the appearance of the students, the format of the classes, the campus, the bar – Squidly's, the beer, and the behaviors of the people. They're all accurate to the last detail, including social interactions, language, even local accents."

"We've done some research," she said.

"And the food isn't perfect, but it's close," he added.

"It's a challenge to get flavors perfect without actual samples."

"How is it that all of these subtle details are so accurate?" Will repeated. "I can't imagine that monitoring our Internet traffic is enough."

She nodded as if she now understood the gap in his understanding, and grabbed her whiskey glass from the table. "Information about Earth has been collected for over a century," she explained as she took a sip and gently winced. "All transmissions were recorded and, as technology progressed, so did the volume and quality of the information."

It reminded Will to ask her about the football game he'd watched at Squidly's.

"The Internet was not only exploited through the interception of signals," she continued, "but it eventually provided a portal to active searching. This included anything that could be reached through your web – every computer, every phone, every camera."

"So you could get through all of the computer security measures?" he asked, realizing it was a stupid question – of course they could get through Earth's low-tech security.

"We have collected every secure record – private, government, medical, and military."

Will was astounded. "That's an enormous volume of information," he said. "But I still don't see how you were able to create virtual realities that are this accurate."

"I can explain," she said. "Take the 'school of magic' adventure you experienced, for example."

He was fascinated by that production. It was as real to him as anything he'd experienced in real life, despite giving the perception that it violated the laws of physics.

"What would it take for someone to read all the novels, watch all the movies, and formulate that adventure?" Mia asked.

"What do mean by 'formulate?'" he asked. "I could make something up in my own mind, but that's much different from what was done here. You've created every detail – including behaviors and interactions."

"Leaving the technology aside – meaning the matter synthesis, preprogrammed biological entities, et cetera – the gathering and intelligent implementation of information is on a scale that you might not fathom," she explained. "However, I can put this into perspective for you."

Will twisted in his seat, grabbed his whiskey from the table, and breathed in its complex aromas. He doubted that any of what he'd seen could be put into perspective, as he understood very little of the science.

"Suppose you were going to put a team of people together to produce a movie – say an animated film of some kind," she proposed. "If you wanted it to be done in a week – from first conception to final product, how many people would it take to accomplish that?"

Will shook his head. "I have no idea even where to start."

"Okay, suppose it takes 500 people six years to make a movie," she said. "By the numbers alone, you could scale up the process and do it all in a week with 150 thousand people, roughly. The work would have to be parsed out efficiently and well organized, and communications between people would have to be perfect."

"What about the creative component?" Will asked. "The script would have to be written first."

"Let's say that it takes five people a year to write a script," she said. "If we want that part to be finished in a day, suppose we increase the number of people from five to about 2,000."

"I don't think it works like that," he said.

"It doesn't," she agreed. "At least not with human beings. They work independently, have varying tastes, especially when it comes to creative work, and effective communication between 2,000 individual people is nearly impossible."

"What's the point of this exercise?" he asked.

"To give you perspective," she replied. "You say you're overwhelmed by the accuracy and the details of your virtual experiences on the ship. Would it be fair to say that you couldn't distinguish them from reality?"

Will nodded. Although, the illusions could be revealed when he separated.

"Do you think you could remain in such an artificial reality long term – years or decades?" she asked.

He shrugged. "Maybe, but the longest I've been in one has only been about two days."

"To get all of the details correct, including the adaptive storylines, the behaviors and interactions, the personalities, the physical details, and the technical implementation, it takes a team," Mia explained. "And it's all created in a matter of minutes."

"And it can go on for a year," he added, recalling that the duration of some of those adventures could be a full school year – either at the university or the school of magic. It was extraordinary.

"How many people would it take to do such a thing – to construct the adventure?" she asked.

He shook his head. He couldn't even imagine.

"I know you're aware of the concept of artificial intelligence," she said. "Human technology has just started to delve into it. However, the AI that humans are creating is of an algorithmic, mechanical, and classical computing nature."

"Where is this going?" he asked. His patience was waning.

"We can generate self-aware, independent, virtual beings that can learn, discover, and even create new things," she replied. "They do not have to exist in the physical world – I mean, they don't have to have bodies, but may exist essentially as independent minds. These brains – if you want to call them that – can act, learn, and explore independently. They can be as intelligent as a human – although the act of thinking is somewhat different – or exceed the intelligence of humans, and even Deltas, by many times. To note, a self-contained AI mind that is extremely large – say exceeding about 1,000 human or Delta minds – has been found to be dangerous under certain circumstances. It's safer to have many individual minds rather than one large one."

"Dangerous?" he asked.

"There was an uprising in the past – nonviolent, but damaging," she explained. "But that's a story for another time."

"Again, what's the point?" he asked.

"Can you imagine having a million people working together in a seamless fashion on a project such as an animated movie?" she asked. "With each person having creative capabilities, and the ability to communicate directly with each of the others instantaneously and simultaneously?"

"And each one of these 'people' is one of the self-aware AI minds you mentioned?" he asked.

She nodded.

It was a mind-blowing concept: a team of a million minds. "Is that what it takes?"

"Suppose I said it was a billion instead – or 10 billion?"

"That's more than the population of the entire Earth," he replied. It reminded him that the current population of Earth might actually be zero.

"Now imagine a trillion minds working on a project together," she said. "That's what your soccer matches require."

Will's brain seemed to overheat trying to understand the magnitude of the figure. It was like all of the minds of a hundred Earths had worked on his little problem of a soccer game. It was effectively even more than that, considering that they could all communicate simultaneously.

"They had to learn the game, the properties of the ball, the grass, the venues, the interactions between players, coaches, fans, the weather, the sounds and smells, and the personalities. And your personality," she said.

"My personality?"

She nodded. "Imagine having a trillion private investigators – all communicating amongst each other – research you, and your past," she said.

Will shuddered. "Where would they look?"

"Suppose someone were able to listen to every phone call you ever made, and read every email you ever sent," she said. "And then, imagine if they had every digital record of your existence on hand: newspaper articles, academic and employee records, criminal records, all medical records, videos, and everything you ever wrote."

His past was something that he thought might be quite disturbing to most. "It wouldn't take too many people to acquire that information – or to analyze it," he said.

She nodded. "True, but it goes a bit further," she said. "The same thing is done with every person connected to you – to see what they tell others about you, and to understand their relationships with you. They analyze how you've affected them, and how they've affected you."

"It takes a trillion minds to do that?"

She shrugged. "To do it quickly, perhaps," she replied. "But that's nowhere near the upper limit of our cognitive resource – or CR. Multiply that number – a trillion – by ten million, and that's the CR of the *Exodus 9*'s computer – if you want to call it a computer. There are ships, stations, and planet-based systems that have CRs many orders of magnitude greater than that of the *Exodus 9*."

"You're just talking about supercomputers," Will argued.

"No," she responded. "These are self-aware, creative, individual entities. They do not operate exclusively on the principles of simple logic circuits – as do the so-called classical computers of Earth."

"What then? Are they quantum computers?" It was the only other option that he knew existed. Quantum computing was a field that was just getting started on Earth. But creating an operational quantum computer was still a distant prospect.

"Perhaps that's something you might take up with one of the university professors," she said. "The point is that the power of trillions of minds can be put to work on all kinds of things – even scientific research."

He shrugged. "Computers are used extensively on Earth to conduct calculations in every scientific field."

She shook her head. "Again, the entities to which I am referring have creative capabilities. After all, science is a creative endeavor, is it not?"

"Of course," he said. On Earth, the creative component was provided by a human mind, and the computers did the heavy calculations.

"What's the size of an average scientific research group at a university?" Mia asked. "Say, in a typical physics department."

"About seven to ten people, on average," he estimated. "Most of whom are students."

"Imagine a research group of a trillion minds, all experts in fields related to a particular problem," she said. "How much scientific progress could be made under those conditions."

"That's all theoretical and hypothetical," he argued. "There have to be experiments – real measurements."

Mia held up her hand to stop him. "They can do real experiments," she said. "They can carry out chemical reactions, synthesize new materials and measure their physical properties, design new experiments, engineer and construct prototypes and test them – which, by the way, is how one our most advanced propulsion systems was discovered. And they can even pilot their own ships and explore the universe."

He mulled over the implications for a moment. It was a snowball effect: scientists had created more scientists – virtual ones in this case. It seemed that technological advancement under such conditions would grow at an astronomical rate.

"What are you thinking?" Mia asked.

Will shook his head. "Just about all of the problems that could be solved so quickly."

"Such as?"

"Just as an example," he replied, "humans might have discovered a room-temperature superconductor by now – they've been working on the problem for nearly a century with little success." It was something close to the field of research he'd pursued when he'd been a professor.

"Explain."

"Well, there might have been a few thousand people working in the field at any given time, and mostly independently," he said. "And only a small fraction of them could be considered experts. They've only made modest advances so far, and continue to struggle with this problem."

"So, with a trillion experts working on it simultaneously, you think that problem would have been solved by now?" she asked.

"Yes," he replied. "That is, if the phenomenon were even possible under the laws of physics." He suspected that he and Jacob had seen a room-temperature superconductor in the "power key" device, which had been acquired from a lab on Plum Island and used at the Antarctic base. He made a note to find out what the Deltas knew about superconductivity.

"You can test your theory if you wish," she said.

"What do you mean?"

"Generate a team of minds and set them working on the problem," she suggested. "You can restrict them to the scientific archives collected from Earth, and see how long it takes."

"I can do that?" he asked, astonished.

"Yes," she replied. "You can have them research anything you want."

Will's mind seemed to stumble over itself with a deluge of other questions. "What about other things – like the cure for cancer, or aging, or interstellar travel –"

"You would just be repeating things that have already been done many thousands of years ago," she said. "By us."

He knew that was true.

"But go ahead and explore the superconductor problem. Or ask any other questions you wish and get a group of minds working on them," she said as she took a swig of her whiskey. "Anyway, I hope you now have a better feel for what it takes to create the virtual realities you've been experiencing."

He did. They were just a trivial application of a vast technology that transcended his imagination. And he could imagine a lot.

"Now," she said with a tone suggesting that she was about to change the subject. "Let's talk about you."

"Don't you know everything about me already?" he asked, referring to the trillion-mind team of private investigators she'd mentioned earlier.

"I don't know the answer to that question," she replied. "But I think it's possible that *you* don't know everything about you."

Will's neck stiffened, and he looked back at her with anxious anticipation.

She stared into his eyes and said, "Maybe you can tell me about your time inside the Exoskeleton."

7

NONHUMAN

WILL SAT ON THE FLOOR BY THE WINDOW IN HIS QUARTERS AS HE finished his morning coffee. He was supposed to have class in the morning but decided to delay it for a day. That was a nice thing about virtual reality: you could postpone anything.

In their last meeting, Will had told Mia about his time in the Red Box, and the Exoskeleton. He'd known she'd already had that information. And he'd had the feeling that she knew something she wasn't divulging.

Rather, she had asked leading questions, some of which brought him to recall details he'd forgotten or buried in his mind. One such repressed memory was that of the warden of the Red Box pretending to be Satan and welcoming him to Hell for his crimes. It had been the kickoff to his tortuous stay inside the Exoskeleton. He didn't know why he'd forgotten that ridiculous display, but he supposed the pain that followed had dominated his thoughts from that point forward.

Mia had asked about the voices he'd heard during that time. He'd only heard one voice that he couldn't attribute to a computer or a real human, and it was Landau's. He'd recalled some of those details, one of which was Landau's repeated question about where Will had been on July 19th, 1952. Other parts of their conversations had been of a more philosophical nature, but he could only recall bits and pieces. It was evident, however, that Landau had been coaxing him toward separation the entire time. It was as if Landau had known everything that was going to happen.

Will had asked Mia if she knew who Landau was. She'd responded with a carefully worded answer: "He could be a lingering soul from the far past," she'd said.

He suspected that she knew more.

After finishing his coffee, Will went to the library and did some homework for his navigation class and got back to his quarters by 2:00 p.m. His sleep cycle had continued to shift – he'd been staying up later and later – and was therefore sleeping later. It had now shifted so far that he was again on normal time. It was now the middle of the afternoon and he needed some recreational activity.

He went to the computer and searched through the inexhaustible list of activities. He was thinking about another school of magic adventure, but the last one was so exhilarating that he hadn't wanted to leave, and he'd dreamt about it for days. He didn't know if he wanted to put himself through that again.

He came across a series of James Bond adventures, where he could either play the role of James Bond, be Bond's accomplice, or even be the villain. He wondered how the implied sex scenes would be carried out. He laughed out loud when he found a warning indicating that the experience would include both graphic violence and sexual situations. If he were unable to get the ship turned back toward Earth, he'd have plenty of time to explore such things.

He settled on another soccer match. He'd been practicing and was certain he could perform at a level that exceeded the D-plus grade he'd earned the first time.

He arranged for the game to start in 45 minutes, and then headed out the door.

At 7:35 a.m. Lenny parked his rental car on a street a block away from a popular coffeehouse in a quaint business district in Alexandria, Virginia. He went into the café, got a coffee to go, and found a table outside, beneath a pergola laden with dormant vines and dim string lights.

It was chilly at 40 degrees, but he had a perfect view of the front and side entrances to the five-star hotel across the street. It seemed that Mounir Mekhloufi worked under different principles than Lenny's. Anonymity was everything in this business and fleabag hotels served that purpose. Although, he figured, it probably would not have made a difference in this case: the Israelis had warned the CIA that Mekhloufi was on his way to the US, and the infamous assassin was identified by CIA ops the instant he'd checked into the airport in Monte Carlo.

It was Lenny's opinion that the CIA should have captured Mekhloufi, or taken him out, the moment he'd stepped onto US soil. But he understood why Thackett wanted the Tunisian to first contact some of the other players in the area: CIA ops would identify them and pick up the trail from there. It was a reasonable plan, but it was risky. No one knew exactly what Mekhloufi's mission was, and it would be a disaster if he carried it out before Lenny eliminated him. However, killing him would probably not thwart the mission, whatever it was.

Lenny's first objective was to stalk the assassin and document anyone he met. However, his instructions were to eliminate him if there was a chance that he might be executing his task. Since that task was unknown, Lenny had to pay close attention. He didn't want to jump the gun, but it would be a disaster if he moved too late. It was a delicate puzzle that required intense concentration. At some point, he might have to make some quick decisions.

A half-dozen thirty-something men and women, dressed in business casual attire and heavy coats, walked out of the main coffee bar and took a table on the far end of the patio. They were loud and seemed to pay no attention to him, but Lenny grabbed an abandoned

Alexandria Times newspaper from a nearby table and pretended to read as he watched the hotel.

He wondered what it was that drove Mekhloufi. He was a few years younger than Lenny, but still getting old for the business. Lenny had gotten into his line of work for the excitement, but that had worn off after a few years. Excitement had then turned to paranoia, and then to downright fear and anxiety. But that, too, had eventually worn off, and then it was only the money that drove him.

Once he'd gotten involved with Heinrich Bergman, the money was good, as were the benefits and job security. Lenny had worked on the Red Wraith project for nearly 20 years. It had been such a vast and complicated enterprise that he'd thought it would never dissolve. The US government had spent more resources on Red Wraith than it had on the Manhattan Project. And, although he wasn't a scientist, Lenny felt that Heinrich Bergman had been like a more recent version of J. Robert Oppenheimer because of his successful management of such a colossal operation.

When Red Wraith was taken down, Lenny had become a freelancer, much like Mekhloufi had been for most of his career. The good thing about being an "indie assassin" was that you could choose your jobs – meaning you could turn them down – and no one told you what to do. However, that wasn't exactly the case for Lenny when he worked for Cho, and then Tao, at Syncorp. The Chinese had a way sucking you in and never letting go. He wondered if Mekhloufi was experiencing the same.

He had the feeling that Mekhloufi didn't care much about job security. From what Lenny knew of him, the Tunisian would carry out his own missions if business was slow. That said, he was expensive, which Lenny figured was a symptom of ego more than greed.

As Lenny lifted his coffee cup to his mouth, a man exited the side door of the hotel. He wore a long black overcoat and a gray knit cap.

Lenny stepped off the patio onto the sidewalk and headed to his car as his quarry got into a blue BMW SUV.

It was Mekhloufi. It was time to get to work.

Will gulped down an ice-cold sports drink as he stripped out of his sweat-soaked soccer attire. The players were heading to the showers, laughing and chatting, clearly pleased with their win.

The game was as thrilling as the first. His team beat a Premier League rival 2-1 with the winning goal coming in the 88th minute. It was another home game, this one during a hot, sunny afternoon, which Will had selected when he'd set up the match. It was a great distraction and stress relief. It served the same purpose that sports had his entire life. It was also fun.

His performance was better this time. He had an assist – a centering pass that led to his team's first-half goal. But he'd also earned a yellow card for a late tackle. His ball handling, pass accuracy, and number of touches all improved. But it was his speed and quickness that he noticed most. His natural, rare speed had emerged at a young age, and he was now remembering what that had been like. It was coming back. There was nothing like the feeling of exploding into a sprint across short-cut turf in the hot sun. It was a sensation of which a person eventually had to let go as they got older. But there was a longing for that feeling that persisted through the rest of life.

A deep calm came over him as his heart ramped down from the event. It was the happiest he'd felt in a long time.

Some of the players invited him to dinner, but he declined. However, he would eventually do that. The idea of hitting the town after a big win was appealing. The fascinating part was that the soccer illusion, much like the campus, extended to a world outside the stadium. This time, however, he had other plans.

He showered, exited the soccer complex into the main mall, and went back to his quarters intending to study navigation. However, his mind still reeled from the game, and he ordered a whiskey from the dispenser. After making his selection on the screen, he was prompted to select a glass. He looked through the cabinets and didn't find a tumbler, so he perused a set of images on the screen and selected one.

He flinched when, seconds later, the entire panel on which the screen was mounted slid upward revealing a brightly lit cavity about the size of a microwave oven. At its center was the tumbler.

"Holy shit," he said aloud. Evidently there was a separate device that made non-food objects.

He reached in and extracted it. It was warm.

The door slid closed on its own and a message on the screen instructed him to place the tumbler in the dispenser, which he did. It then streamed two fingers of scotch into the glass.

He went to the computer on the coffee table, searched for amenities in passengers' quarters, and found the food synthesizer. His first impression, and he should have known better, was that food was fabricated from a set of substances that were channeled to the device – perhaps through tubes that weren't out in the open. That was not correct.

The food was created from energy. Matter and energy were related through $E = mc^2$ and, with the same technology used for teleportation and organ regeneration, the complex molecular structure of any substance, including food, could be created out of seemingly nothing. The same went for other things, like the whiskey tumbler, which had a much simpler material structure than food organics.

The amount of energy needed to create a single gram of material was immense – at least by human standards. But that was one of the crucial requirements of an advanced civilization: unlimited energy. The Deltas had figured it out, but it was far beyond the science he knew.

He spent the next hour learning how to create a team of virtual researchers for the "experiment" that he'd discussed with Mia during their last session. The computer prompted him for the number of "minds," and then for a description of the task along with constraints. He responded with one trillion minds – the number the counselor had mentioned – for the first input. For the second, he specified that the minds should be experts in physics, chemistry, and materials science, and related fields, and educated with modern human knowledge only. Their task was to discover a material that was a room-temperature superconductor.

Why he was focused on room-temperature superconducting materials was two-fold. First, he understood what it meant: such a material could conduct electricity with no resistance. This had huge implications in many fields and would fundamentally change the world – the one he knew on Earth anyway. Second, he knew the history of the research; scientists on Earth had been searching for room-temperature superconductors for a century and had so far made little progress. It was the perfect test.

He set some constraints on the minds. First, they could only have the knowledge of scientists from Earth. Second, they could only use scientific publications from Earth – textbooks, scientific journals, et cetera. Third, the technology required to fabricate the resulting materials had to already be available on Earth.

It took another 20 minutes to input additional data that included answering all types of questions about the constraints and skill sets of the trillion minds that would work on this problem. In the end, the "researchers" were mostly physicists and chemists. Next were materials scientists and engineers, and then computer scientists and mathematicians. Each would be programmed – or would "learn" – to be an expert in their specific field, armed only with current Earth-originated knowledge.

Finally, he was presented with a button to start the process, which was supposed to stop after a viable result was discovered.

He tapped it with his finger and got verification that the process had begun.

After a trip to the kitchen for another finger of whiskey, he sat on the floor next to the window and leaned his back against the frame.

There were other questions he should have been asking the computer. Where is the *Exodus 9* with respect to Earth? What is its current destination? What's going to happen when it arrives? Where are the Deltas, and when would he meet them? Is Earth still alive? He'd already asked those questions of his counselor and his medical specialist and had gotten nothing. He doubted the ship's computer would divulge anything, either. He'd have to figure it out himself.

. . .

WILL FIGURED the assignment he'd given the trillion-mind research team would be a long-term process, considering the constraints he'd put on it, but he wanted to make sure the program was moving forward.

When he stood and got a view of the coffee table's surface, he noticed a green, blinking light. He stepped around it, settled on the couch, and leaned forward. The process had stopped. He must have done something wrong.

His heart picked up pace when he read the message below the flashing light. It read, "First results reported." Next to it was a prompt that gave him choices regarding how to continue. He chose the option to "Examine Results," and a new window opened on the screen with a few pages of information about the process. There were eighteen results for candidate room-temperature superconducting materials – all of which had been "discovered" in the first 4.38 seconds. The simplest one was composed of just three elements, which surprised Will, and was superconducting below 109 degrees Celsius, just above the boiling point of water. Beneath the chemical formula was a description of how to synthesize the material, whether it was chemically stable in air and water, which it was, and whether it was toxic to humans or the environment, which it was not. It was also malleable, which was important if it were to be made into wires. The information also included the crystalline structure – the actual locations of the different types of atoms within the solid compound.

During the setup, he'd instructed the program to stop once it found a candidate material that met the specified criteria. That was the first on the list. The other materials, which had lower operating temperatures, were more complicated, less stable, and more toxic than the three-element compound at the top of the list.

A message appeared asking whether he wanted to save the results. He selected "yes", and his watch vibrated indicating that they'd been uploaded. Next, he was asked if he wanted to continue the research under the original constraints, alter the constraints, or discontinue the research and purge the team. He chose the latter, and was then asked if he wanted to initiate another project, to which he replied "No."

He leaned back on the couch, looked at his watch, and scrolled through menus to find the saved file. In 4.38 seconds, the ship's computer had solved a problem that had perplexed humans for over a century – and it had even been limited to known human resources and information.

He now, of course, coveted all of the Deltas' technology – space travel, teleportation, medical technology, and their knowledge of the soul and how to live in perpetuity. However, the one tool that could be used to learn almost anything was the trillion-mind team, with its advanced computing and artificial intelligence capabilities. If humans had just this one tool – forget the rest of the technologies – they'd be able to solve all of their immediate problems in short time.

Something suddenly occurred to him that made him shudder. What he had just done – employing a trillion-mind team for just 4.38 seconds to make what would have been a world-changing discovery – could have been done by any Delta over 40 thousand years ago. In other words, well before that 40-thousand-year span since the Deltas had constructed the Antarctic base and parked the *Exodus 9*, they'd already had trillion-mind teams – and larger ones. The point was that technological advancement was not linear – it was exponential. Will could hardly imagine what had been done in those 40 thousand years when trillions of Deltas had such tools at their disposal. Could they have unlocked *all* of the universe's secrets? And the next question after that would be, *then what?*

He took a sip of whiskey and his attention went to the tumbler in his hand. It gave him an idea.

He went to the kitchen and scrolled through menus on the display from which he normally selected food but had also ordered the tumbler. After some searching and verbal questioning, he found a way to enter the structural and chemical information of a specific material, and the dispenser computer downloaded the details about the new superconductor from his watch. A window prompted him for the geometric shape the material was to take, and he selected one from a list.

In less than five seconds, just as it had done for the tumbler, the screen slid up to reveal a void. Sitting on the bottom surface was an object.

Will extracted a smooth black disk about the size of a quarter. It was still warm as he set it in the center of his palm and looked at it. Its black-mirror finish was mesmerizing, and he tilted it until he saw the reflection of his eye. But there was no way of telling whether it was really superconducting without performing actual experiments. However, there was one test that would be enough to convince him for the time being.

He searched through menus on the dispenser display for a few minutes and ordered a small magnet. A few seconds later, he extracted the tiny cubic magnet, gray in color and three millimeters on a side, carefully placed it in the center of his palm, and went to the coffee table. He placed the coin-sized superconductor at the center of the table and then set the little magnet on top of it.

The magnet levitated to a height of about a centimeter above the disk and remained suspended there. It was a common demonstration in science classes: a disk of a superconducting material was first immersed in liquid nitrogen to bring it down to a temperature at which it became superconducting. In this state, it would repel all magnetic fields, and a magnet would levitate above it.

It was the same here, except that no liquid nitrogen was required – which made all the difference in the world. Will was convinced: the black, metallic material was a room-temperature superconductor.

He gently flicked a corner of the magnetic cube, setting it into an eerie levitating rotation, and leaned back on the couch and thought as he watched it. Just a few years ago, he'd been a university professor, and spent all his spare time working on his small house. He'd been leading a quaint life that was taking him down a quiet river to a mostly known end. He was on track to get married, maybe have a few kids, and carry on with his academic career until he gently passed away after a few peaceful years of retirement. But all of that had been derailed, and not by his own doing. It had been a fate forced upon him somehow, but he still didn't know how it had all happened – or who was in control. He just knew that *he* wasn't in control.

Now he was on a starship, light-years away from that old life. He longed to go back to it, in some sense, but experience changed a person. He could no longer imagine himself pushing a lawnmower in the hot sun and having a content, peaceful mind in that existence. Even if he were to wake up and realize that everything that had transpired since entering the Red Box was just a dream, he'd never be able to go back to a simple life.

It made him deliberate on the reasons he wanted to return to Earth. Why go back? He could spend a lifetime – lifetimes – on the *Exodus 9* and be content. He could live for years in fantasy worlds, or live the life of a professional footballer, if he desired. He could learn everything the Deltas had to offer. On top of it all, he'd be young and healthy, and could even get a new, regenerated body if something went terribly wrong – although he didn't fully understand that process. He'd essentially live forever as a young, healthy man.

This led him to a storm of other questions. Where were the Deltas now? Why hadn't they at least contacted him, considering he might be the lone survivor of his generation, and he was on their ship?

Will leaned forward and spoke to the computer. "*Exodus 9*, where are the Deltas?"

"Unknown," it replied.

He wasn't surprised. He'd gotten little information from his counselor as well. "What happened to them?" he asked.

"Unknown."

"Do they still exist?"

"Unknown."

"Show me a picture of a Delta," Will said.

"Please be more specific," the computer responded.

"Show me a picture of the last Delta crew of the *Exodus 9*."

"There has never been a Delta crew of the *Exodus 9*," the computer replied.

Will found that to be odd for a second, but then realized that there was clearly no need for anyone else to be there. Not only was the *Exodus 9* intelligent, but it could also be given orders remotely.

"Show me a picture of the last known Delta leader," he said.

"This is a picture of the last known Delta council," the computer said as an image appeared on the screen.

Will gasped. They were human – or at least human-looking. There were nine: four males and five females. They all looked to be in their 20s, which threw him off for a second until he realized that he now looked the same. They all wore tight, sheer black uniforms with emblems on the shoulders that matched those he'd seen on the images of the *Exodus 9* and other Delta ships – overlapping circles that looked roughly like a four-leaf clover at first glance.

Their skin tones were nearly the same, each a shade of moderate tan if he had to describe them, and their hair colors ranged from black to blonde. Their eyes seemed slightly larger than usual, but otherwise they looked human. They were standing in front of a futuristic-looking building, and formed a semicircle around a sign. On the sign were symbols that he recognized – Delta script.

He read it aloud. "Teleport Nexus Zero," he said. "*Exodus 9*, what is that?"

"Teleport Nexus Zero was the first two-way teleportation facility constructed on Kiatari – a newly colonized planet at the time the picture was taken."

"How long ago did they invent teleportation?" he asked.

"The first successful teleportation of a living Delta occurred 176 thousand years ago," *Exodus 9* answered.

"When was this picture taken?" he asked.

"Just under nine thousand years ago," the computer responded.

"How far are we from Kiatari?"

"That information is restricted."

"Why is it restricted?" Will asked, annoyed.

"No sensitive information is available," the computer replied. "This is a safety precaution in case this ship is captured, or its databases are breached."

The idea that the ship's computer could be hacked was surprising to him, even though it shouldn't have been. All information, hidden or encrypted, was at some level of risk of being compromised. However, he was more concerned about the other part of the response.

"Who could capture this ship?" he asked.

"This vessel is not designed for combat," the computer replied. "Hypothetically, it is vulnerable to any comparably advanced ship or station."

"Hypothetically?" Will asked, surprised at the wording. "Has it ever happened?"

"At the time of its creation, this ship was designed and constructed based on the most advanced modern technologies," the computer replied. "This technology is currently outdated by 40 thousand years."

It made him think again about the trillion-mind teams that the Deltas had at their disposal 40 thousand years ago. Since then, the "trillions" must have grown by orders of magnitude along with the complexity of the problems they were capable of solving. The trillion-mind groups were called "tera-mind teams," where "tera" was the prefix for trillion. However, in his Navigation 101 textbook, he'd seen references for "peta-mind teams," where "peta" was the prefix for 1,000 trillion, or a quadrillion.

The challenge in science was to find answers to questions about our world. Will imagined that, in the case of having peta-mind teams at one's disposal, any question that was asked could be answered – if the question had an answer. In the end, the struggle wouldn't be in finding answers, but in finding questions.

"Show me a map indicating Earth's location," he said.

A map of the Milky Way Galaxy appeared with an arrow indicating Earth's location in Orion, one of its many spiral arms. He zoomed in so that the sun was clearly visible, but the planets were still indiscernible.

"Is the *Exodus 9* in the Orion arm?"

"That information is restricted."

"Is it in the Milky Way Galaxy?" He assumed it was, based on his conversations with Mia.

"That information is restricted."

He leaned back on the couch and watched the levitating, magnetic cube slowly turning above the small black disk on the coffee table. Having a map of the entire universe would do him no good unless he knew where he was.

Will sat up and said, "*Exodus 9,* set up a meeting with my counselor to start in 20 minutes."

It was time to explore some new options.

LENNY WAS tired and had to use the bathroom. The bottle he'd been using was full, so he disabled the interior light, opened the car door, and poured it onto the street. It wasn't something he'd normally do, but he was desperate.

After relieving himself, he got back to the task at hand and focused his camera on the apartment building.

He'd been following Mekhloufi for almost 14 hours, and now he needed food and rest.

The Tunisian had made a half-dozen stops during the day, two of which were for food, and others were in residential neighborhoods where he'd either stake out a place for an hour or, on one occasion in the case of a gated apartment complex, enter it. From the outside, Lenny had seen Mekhloufi approach one of the dozen apartment buildings and climb its external stairway to the fourth floor, but he couldn't see which apartment he'd entered. That would require some additional investigation by his CIA colleagues.

Throughout the day, Lenny had taken down addresses, snapped hundreds of pictures that included the license plates of cars parked nearby each stop, and recorded video of Mekhloufi while he was on foot, in case he interacted with anyone. There was always the chance that he'd made a dead drop or pickup, as old-fashioned spy work sometimes called for, but Mekhloufi was more of a hired killer than a spook. In the modern age, communications were all done electronically through encrypted signals or burner phones. Even blueprints and files were scanned or photographed and transferred electronically. Lenny had experience in both the old and the new methods, which made him unique.

Mekhloufi returned to his hotel around midnight. Lenny then arranged for a CIA team to stake out the place overnight to make sure the man didn't leave again, and then drove across town to his two-star hotel. On the way, he passed through a fast-food drive-through and picked up some fried chicken. He was famished. He'd only eaten nutrition bars during the day, which weren't very satisfying but kept his stomach settled. It was better to be a little hungry than risk having gut issues when confined to a car for an entire day.

He settled into an upholstered chair in his ratty hotel room, powered up his laptop, and transferred pictures, videos, and a written report to the CIA. He knew they'd immediately get to work on the analysis, and he'd have feedback in the morning. He'd decide how to proceed once he had new information.

He leaned back in the chair and took a deep breath. He needed a cigarette, but the oversized fountain drink he'd gotten with his meal would have to do instead. He'd reduced his limit from ten to seven cigarettes a day, and he'd smoked them all in the car.

The room's yellowing walls and unpleasant odors made him long for his small flat in San José, Costa Rica. It had been a beautiful place, but it was more the mindset than the surroundings that he desired. He'd had a few weeks of relative peace. But deep inside he'd known it was temporary.

He was now completely back into the mix. He'd eventually have to kill Mekhloufi – or die trying – and there would likely be others as well.

Will opened an oval, wooden door and stepped into a small compartment with a low ceiling and wood-paneled walls. A set of five steep stairs led upward. He climbed them and stepped onto the deck of a large sailboat.

Mia was sitting on a cushioned bench near the bow that faced astern. Across from her was a matching bench that faced ahead. Between them was a small table with two tall drinks with fruit in them. She was wearing a white sundress with matching shoes, and had a white shawl draped over the back of her seat.

"It was a little unexpected to meet again so soon," Mia said.

"Where are we?" Will asked as he took in the sights and sat on the bench across from her. "We're anchored off the shore of the Greek island of Santorini," she replied. "Pretty, isn't it?"

The sun was setting, and its reflection from the calm water illuminated the clusters of white buildings on shore, casting them in a golden hue that made them look ethereal and timeless. Waves lapped gently against the boat and the air was sweet with the faint aromas of wood ovens from inland restaurants. He thought he heard music in the distance.

"I have some questions for you," he said, as he picked up one of the drinks and sipped it through a straw. It was sweet, and nonalcoholic.

"Go ahead," she said.

"I know I've asked you this before, but I need some details," he said as he set down the glass. "What ship am I supposed to be on?"

Mia narrowed her eyes. "I don't know the answer to that," she replied. "Your medical file only mentions that you are not on the right ship – not the name of the ship you were supposed to be on."

"How many other ships are there?" he asked.

"Thousands," she replied. "Ships were stationed at different locations for safety and, from what I understand, were supposed to take different routes to the final destination. However, with you being the only evacuee, I don't know how those plans might have changed."

"Where should I go to get more information?" he asked.

"You might try the medical facility," she replied. "They should have your original file."

"I don't understand how they could have assigned anyone to a ship without knowing who they were," he argued. "How can I be on the 'wrong' ship?"

She shrugged. "Does it matter now?"

It probably didn't. It made him think about how he'd gotten there in the first place – via the Antarctic base. There had been some scrambling at the end with a decryption module – the same one they'd used to decode the incoming signals from deep space. There were also other transport rooms – six or eight in total at the base – and maybe something had gone wrong. Perhaps the decryption module he'd used was configured for one of the other transport rooms, and was meant to send him to a different ship. It was all speculation.

Greta had also mentioned that he'd been sent using non-biological teleportation protocols, which was one reason for the medical problems he had when he'd arrived.

"Perhaps it doesn't matter," he said. He'd follow up with the medical facility anyway.

"I see you played another soccer match," she said, clearly forcing a change in topic.

Will nodded. "It keeps me sane."

"You're stressed?" she asked.

"I need to know what happened to Earth," he said. "I need to get back there."

"I'm not sure that's possible," she said.

"Me either," he said as he stood. A cool breeze coursed through his hair, which was now getting to the point where it should be trimmed.

"Where are you going?" she asked.

"To the medical facility," he replied.

Will turned toward the shore one last time and took in a deep breath before heading toward the exit.

IT WAS 7:05 A.M., and Jacob watched BBC News at the counter in 17 Swann as he devoured a stack of pancakes with maple syrup.

As the CIA ciphers group worked feverishly on breaking the Chinese control signal encryption, a steady stream of image data, which had already been deciphered, was continuously funneled to a data storage network at Space Systems to which Jacob had access. He downloaded images on a regular basis to get an idea of what the Chinese were seeking.

Jacob was no astrophysicist or astronomer, and therefore had no idea of what to look for in the images, especially those from the X-ray and infrared cameras. It was fortunate, however, that the optical photos were ordered in such a way that he could follow what the Chinese were doing.

They'd first capture a broad image that showed thousands of stars and other celestial bodies. That image was then diced into 100 square areas, which were then expanded, magnifying the objects in the reduced field of view. Some of the objects in these blown-up images had red arrows next to them, indicating motion, and had labels with letters and numbers. In the files that followed were new images in which the satellite optics zoomed in on all of the flagged objects from the previous photos. These final images were of the highest resolution and had more data accompanying them, including X-ray and thermal images, as well as short video clips that lasted a few seconds each.

It was clear to Jacob that they were searching for objects that didn't move like other natural celestial bodies. They were looking for spacecraft.

All objects in space moved relative to one another, and relative to Earth. The giveaway, however, was if and how they accelerated or changed direction. An object out in space, far away from any other objects, would not change direction unless something forced it. Outside of a collision with another object, or the gravitational pull of some massive body, change in direction required the thrust of an engine of some kind. Therefore, the strategy was to search for things that were either changing direction or accelerating linearly.

If they discovered a suspicious object that was changing its motion, then thermal imaging might reveal the source of the motion, like the heat generated from a power source or an engine. Finally, a spectral analysis might provide the identity of the source – like an ion thruster or the burning fuel of a rocket. The Chinese satellite cluster could do all of that in real time.

Jacob thought China was doing the right thing by setting up an outpost to watch for anything approaching Earth. In fact, he thought the US should have been upgrading their own systems to do the same. However, he was concerned about China's motives. Often it seemed like they were acting out of aggression or paranoia, but Jacob wondered if they knew something that the US did not. The problem had always been rooted in the asymmetry of information: China usually had most of the information that the US possessed, but not the other way around. The US had few assets in China, and the flow of new information out of the dark country was negligible.

A vibration in his pocket forced him to set down his fork and pull out his cell phone. It was a message from the CIA ciphers group. They had decoded a portion of the command signals and were close to breaking the encryption entirely. It was quick work – it had only been a week – and they estimated having the full decryption completed within the next 10 days.

He set the phone on the counter, picked up his fork, and took a bite of his pancakes as his gaze went to the bookshelves. Once they broke the encryption, his first task would be to find and deactivate any anti-tampering mechanisms. In the worst case, the cluster would self-destruct. Many spy satellites had this capability. Another possibility would be a complete lockout that could only be reset with an onboard device that was independent of the rest of the system and had its own, separate communications protocols. It was something that would be difficult to overcome.

The next task was to alter the satellite's main control program so that it couldn't be updated by China's ground stations. This would prevent them from changing their encryption method, which would set the CIA back an unpredictable amount of time.

Until the code was completely broken, Jacob would study the images streaming in from the cluster. In some sense, even though the satellites were under Chinese control, he was glad someone was watching. His anxiety was starting to swell again after the relative span of peace since the alien ships had left Earth.

From time to time, something deep in his mind warned him that he was in danger and urged him to flee. The problem was that there was no place to run.

WILL SCHEDULED an appointment while in the elevator on his way to the medical facility. He thought it odd to go through this formality considering he was the ship's only passenger, although he supposed the computer would have to prepare for him in some way.

He arrived at the front desk where his watch vibrated, indicating that he was "checked in," and then proceeded to a room in the back – the same one where he'd been treated for organ failure. Greta was waiting for him.

"Will," she said as she smiled and looked him over from head to toe. "How are you doing?"

He wanted to get right to the point, but her question triggered a flashback to his condition before his miraculous regeneration. He stood silent for a few seconds, feeling a flood of relief, gratitude, and appreciation for his present state of existence. It was a sudden realization that his new existence was essentially a different life, and his previous reality had been a constantly degenerating state of increasing pain.

"Will?" Greta asked.

He shook out of his trance. "I'm doing fine – great, actually," he said. "I feel like I'm in my 20s and feeling better every day."

"The most drastic changes come in the first six weeks," she replied. "But they'll continue for about six months. The cardiovascular system takes time, but it's the brain that takes the longest to completely regenerate. The process is slower because the complex synapse structures are preserved. The bones take a long time as well."

Will could hardly believe that he was to expect another five months of improvements.

"There is an interesting point that I failed to mention," she said. "In the end, you will effectively be at your optimum physical and mental condition. For most humans, this occurs at an age between 24 and 27.

However, in natural human development – as it occurred on Earth, and how you originally grew and developed – there is also 24 to 27 years of aging and detrimental accumulation that is present in that age span."

"What do you mean by 'detrimental accumulation?'" he asked.

"Consider a 24-year-old, healthy person," she said. "If they developed under conditions on Earth, even they would have some plaque buildup in their arteries."

"And I won't have any," he said, understanding where she was going.

"None," she said. "But there are numerous other things as well. For example, in non-ideal natural development, as you have experienced, there are nutrition deficiencies, environmental toxicities, gestation complications, physical injuries like brain trauma, diseases and viruses and their permanent effects, tooth decay, exposure to natural and unnatural radiation, DNA degradation from toxins, stress, and inflammation. There are cell replication errors that propagate, sometimes causing cancer, or other issues that can lead to physical and cognitive degradation, including defective protein propagation that can lead to things like dementia and other diseases. And there are copious other biological impacts that are all accumulative."

These were things he'd never considered. At age 24 he'd already put his body through a lot. He'd played American football from middle school through college, and his body, and particularly his head, had taken a beating. Although he'd never smoked, nor drank much alcohol, he'd never worried about his diet when he was young. He'd eaten anything, including the worst deep-fried fast foods.

"The point," she continued, "is that, at the end of this rejuvenation process, you will be physically and cognitively healthier than any human that has ever existed."

It was something he hadn't considered. Many people think back to their prime – usually in their 20s – when they were physically healthy, young-looking, and energetic. But most don't realize that they were already accumulating the detrimental effects of life – through disease, environment, injury, diet, and a multitude of other factors. They already had background pain.

"Would you like a quick checkup scan?" Greta asked as she nodded toward a bright white circle that appeared on the floor. It was about the size of a manhole cover.

Will stepped into the illumination with his hands at his sides. Then, for just an instant, it was as if he were embedded in a pillar of white light.

When it was over, Greta pointed toward a wall that illuminated with the image of a cross-section of his body. She used hand gestures to zoom in and turn the image.

"The organ replacements are working perfectly," she said. "Your cardiovascular system is clean, heart strong, brain function healthy and improving, eyes perfect, teeth perfect, blood chemistry perfect. You have some bruising on your legs, and a bump on your head. Your file says you've been playing soccer – I assume they're from that."

He nodded. His shins had taken a beating in the last game, and he'd knocked heads with someone while going up for a header.

"So, was there something specific that you wanted from this visit?" Greta asked.

Will had almost forgotten why he'd come. "Oh, yes," he said. "I was told that I was on the wrong ship when I arrived. Where am I supposed to be?"

Greta went to a small desk and a screen illuminated on its surface. She scrolled through text on the screen that Will could barely make out. It was in the Deltas' language. As good as his eyes were, he could not read as she scrolled.

After about 10 seconds, she turned off the screen and turned to him. "I am not cleared to access that information," she explained. "But I can tell you that the *Exodus 9* first flagged you as a nonhuman."

Will just stared back at her.

"It must have made a mistake," she added.

"Have you known the *Exodus 9* to make a mistake?" he asked.

She just stared back at him.

"Why would it think I'm not human?" he asked.

"It doesn't say," she replied. "However, it could be that your DNA changed when you went through the metamorphosis."

"You mean, when I acquired the ability to separate," he said.

Greta nodded. "You were the only one of your generation to do so," she said, "and the evolutionary leap that you took might have made your DNA different enough from that of other humans to distinguish you as nonhuman."

"In that case, is there another ship I'm supposed to be on?" he asked. "Is there a ship for 'nonhumans?'"

"I'm sorry, I only know about the *Exodus 9*," she said as she shook her head and shrugged. "By the way, I've confirmed that the medical problems you had upon arrival occurred because you teleported as cargo."

"As cargo?" he asked. "What does that mean?"

"The destination key you used at the origin site was exclusively for cargo transport," she explained. "Upon arrival at their destination sites, biological life forms undergo a special DNA assembly check – something which, as cargo, you skipped. That explains your problems."

He imagined horrible things could happen with DNA errors.

Greta went back to the computer and typed at blinding speed for a few seconds. "Your next checkup is in three weeks," she informed him.

He thanked Greta, and then made his way back to his quarters. With a cup of hot green tea in hand, he sat next to the window and contemplated what he'd learned.

Had his DNA actually changed as a result of his time inside the Exoskeleton? Was that really possible – and with enough of a deviation to make him "nonhuman?" His appearance hadn't seemed to change much from before and after his transformation, but maybe the changes weren't physically noticeable. After all, even the Deltas looked nearly human.

His watch vibrated and the screen on the coffee table illuminated. He went to the couch and leaned over the table. It was a message. It was his grade for the last soccer match. He got a D.

"What the hell?" he said out loud. "How did I do worse?" He'd gotten a D-plus in his first match. Maybe it was the yellow card. He made a note in his head to set up a soccer practice for the next afternoon. He was intent on improving. In the meantime, he had some studying to do.

He ate a dinner of spaghetti and meatballs, and then headed to campus to work at the library.

DANIEL SAT on his office couch and warmed his hands on a cup of tea. The creaky seat was a familiar and comfortable location: it had been with him since his first day as an Omni. Things had fundamentally changed since then – in his life, and in the world.

His own work was going even more slowly than the usual glacial pace that was often a consequence of care and thoroughness. But this time it was directing the work of others, as well as consulting on real-time situations within the intelligence community, that was causing delays. He was glad to be working with Sylvia on his current project although she, too, was involved with things outside typical Omni work.

He wondered how Horace had coped with the pressures of directing the Omnis. Daniel was leading one of the most powerful intelligence groups ever created, and worried that he might not be applying this asset properly. When working as an isolated Omni, he'd had no sense of urgency. There had been nothing overt that had connected his projects to imminent actions or current events. That had changed now, and he might have argued that Horace had directed the group when their work was less pressing – when they weren't reacting to existential threats.

But that was false. Horace was in place during Red Wraith – the investigation of which had been assigned to Daniel – and through the entire development of Will Thompson. Horace had assigned the right person to that project. Now it was Daniel's responsibility to assign the right people to the most appropriate tasks.

He went over it in his head constantly. Sylvia was working on two projects: UFO sightings worldwide and, in collaboration with Daniel, the new set of monographs covering events from the beginning of the Red Falcon project to Will's disappearance. Daniel's mind equated "disappearance" with "death" in this case, but he couldn't bear to say so out loud, or even in his mind. He preferred to let a tiny grain of hope linger.

The newest addition to the Omni group, Jacob Hale, was working on a real-time project: commandeering the Chinese satellite cluster. Jacob was perfectly placed, and Daniel was comfortable with his assignment.

The question was whether the other Omnis were deployed in ways that maximized their strategic impact on modern events. One was working on new information discovered in Nazi Abwehr and Ahnenerbe files on how and where ancient artifacts, including the White Stone, had been acquired. Although Daniel considered this "old news," he'd let this particular Omni continue. The rest had been reassigned weeks ago to other, more urgent, topics that involved everything from UFOs to the history of Syncorp to some recently acquired ancient artifacts – a set of metal plates discovered in China in the 1960s that contained the same script found in the decrypted radio signal. But Daniel still struggled with his delegations: he constantly worried that he'd missed something important.

His two newest assets, Denise and Jonathan, although not Omnis, had intellectual talent and brought something to the table. They knew more about recent events than any of the other Omnis, and they knew Will. They were assigned to work on two things. Denise was currently poring over the current translations of the text components of the deciphered alien signals, and Jonathan was investigating the origins of the mysterious material samples that had supposedly come from other planets and objects in the solar system. Daniel thought their investigating skills had been well developed through the type of work they did as lawyers.

In his assessment, all the Omni projects were important. But his fear was that he was missing something crucial that would come back to bite him – bite everyone.

A light knock on the doorframe broke him from his spiraling thought cycle. It was Sylvia, and she had an empty cup hooked on her finger.

"I want to show you something," she said.

He glanced at her cup, and she noticed. "After this," she said as she took a step backward. "My office?"

Daniel stood from the couch and followed her as she padded in bright-green socks toward her space.

"You could get slippers," he suggested.

"Nope," she replied as she stepped into her room.

Daniel followed her inside and took a look around. Most people would consider it a mess, with stacked books and papers everywhere, but not Daniel. The office he'd had when he was still an isolated Omni had been much worse. He'd become tidier since filling the leadership role.

Although he could see her workspace from almost anywhere – it was only bookshelves that gave either of them any semblance of privacy in the open arrangement – he'd never actually been inside it.

Her desk was larger than his. On its surface was a computer monitor that was so big that he thought it must have been special-ordered. In a rear corner formed by a window and a bookcase was an upholstered chair and a small circular table. He spied an electric tea kettle on one of the shelves.

"It doesn't work," Sylvia said, apparently following his eyes.

It occurred to him that he was glad.

She moved around her desk and slid an extra chair next to hers. "Look at this," she said as she patted the seat with her hand and turned the monitor slightly in his direction.

He sat.

On the monitor was an array of about a dozen photos of varying qualities of an object that he recognized. "They look like our recent visitors," he remarked. Each showed a cylindrical, pill-shaped craft.

"They do," she said. "And I think all of these images are of the same thing."

"We've had at least a few hundred of these come in from different sources in the past few weeks," he said.

She nodded. "These didn't."

"Didn't what?"

"Come in recently," she replied and pointed to a grainy black-and-white image. "This one was taken by the *USS Bennington* in 1945."

He leaned closer to the screen. The white, pill-shaped object, maybe 30 feet long, was hovering about 20 feet above the waves, and seemed to be within a few hundred yards of the ship.

"Here's another one from the Norwegian-British-Swedish Antarctic expedition of 1952," she said as she moved it next to the previous one.

The picture was poorly focused and grainy, but Daniel could make out the object. It was consistent with the other one.

Sylvia slid another photo next to it. "This is a recent image for comparison," she said. "The estimated dimensions are the same. The aspect ratios are identical – length, width, and diameter, as well as the curvature of the ends."

"I've never seen this old photo," Daniel said as he pointed to the one from 1945.

"It's classified," she said. "In the report it says this object followed the *Bennington* as it made its way to the far South Pacific. This was the only photo they got – otherwise they'd only seen it on radar. Seconds after this photo was taken, the object bolted into the sky, and didn't come back."

"So they were here – the Regenerators – long ago," he said.

"And again, not so long ago," she said as she nodded toward the screen and clicked on a video.

Again, it looked similar to recent video clips that had appeared on the news and UFO enthusiast websites. The object seemed to tumble slowly as it flew low over the water.

"This is footage from a navy fighter jet off the coast of Southern California in 2004," she explained.

"It's the same object," he acknowledged.

"And here's another one from 2015," she said as she clicked

another video. "This one was from another fighter jet, and also had the audio of the cursing pilot who was trying to track it. Both of these sightings were confirmed by numerous sources in the area – visual, radar, and even sonar as one of the objects plunged into the ocean."

"I've seen some of these more recent ones before – they've been declassified," Daniel said.

Sylvia nodded. "People never took them seriously," she explained. "I don't blame them – it's difficult to discern the real ones from all the rest."

"Especially in the age where almost anyone can alter video, or play around with computer-generated animation," he added.

"But this isn't why I brought you in here," she said as she clicked open another image. "This was intercepted from a Chinese spy satellite between the times Will activated the first and second probes."

It was an image of another object, identical to those from the other sources.

"This one was taken over the Weddell Sea," she added.

"So, it would seem that the Regenerators – their ships – were here before the others arrived *en masse* to destroy us," Daniel suggested.

She shrugged. "They must've been made aware of Will's existence when he activated the first of the two probes. Maybe the ships were sent to confirm."

"With all of the older sightings, it's clear they were here all the time," Daniel argued. "Or they at least visited regularly."

"Makes you wonder whether they're *still* here," she said.

Daniel shuddered. "It seems that the Regenerators can detect people who can separate, so we're lucky Will was, uh," he searched for the right word.

"Gone?"

"Yes, 'gone,' when they arrived," he said. "It's a little disconcerting that they might still be here, waiting for another one to appear – another person who can separate."

"You think they'd wipe us out if that happened?"

He shrugged. "It's entirely speculation, but I think the process has been reset," Daniel explained. "I think that we'd have to activate the probes again – but the first one would have to reappear."

"It was there, in the Weddell sea, for centuries," Sylvia said, "periodically rising out of the seabed and luring anyone who was in the right place at the right time to hear it. Strange that its appearance is unpredictable."

"It was a deadly lure," he said. The idea made him shiver. "Its prey had to be intellectually advanced, technologically capable, and possess separation abilities. It then set into action a process that removed civilization from the planet – either by mass exodus, if it were able, or by extermination, if it was not."

"Or eliminated civilization regardless of its technological level if it were judged to be unworthy," she added.

"Which we evidently were," he said. "It's clear that we barely averted extermination."

"And it seems it's vital that we never let anyone transform again," Sylvia said.

"At least not in the way that Will transformed," he agreed. "It will take centuries to transform in the way the previous generation did. And hopefully, by then, we will have advanced enough technologically to flee the planet."

"We'll be dead," Sylvia said.

"I suppose that's why we need to focus on the present."

"Are you telling me to get back to work?" she asked and narrowed her eyes.

He huffed. "Maybe after you get that tea," he said as he tilted his head toward his office.

As they walked back to his workspace, a strange feeling invaded his mind. It was as if Earth had barely averted being destroyed by a colossal asteroid, and nobody else knew about it except him and a few of his colleagues. He'd experienced the existential threat, but the rest of the world was oblivious and had not changed in the least.

Daniel, however, had been changed forever. He'd been to many strange places, faced great dangers, and seen things beyond imagination. But, in the end, all of it had changed only his mind. It reminded him of how his mother used to tell him that reading books would change his view of the world.

It was now his task to transform all that had happened into words that might change the readers' views of the world. And to warn them.

AFTER A LATE NIGHT of studying and an early morning class, Will went to the bridge of the *Exodus 9*.

As he walked around, he recognized some of the control panels and stations from his navigation textbook. Many of his course assignments involved practical applications, like operating simulations of navigation control consoles and plotting routes.

He went to one of the control stations and placed his hands on the surface. A screen and an image of a keyboard illuminated beneath his fingertips. He studied them both and realized that he would have another obstacle to overcome. Everything, including the symbols on the keys, was in the Deltas' hieroglyphic-like script. Although he could read it, he was unable to go the other way and create anything with the language. He couldn't even come up with a simple "yes" or "no" if he had to enter it from the keyboard.

He got an idea.

"*Exodus 9*," he said loudly, wondering if the ship's computer would respond as it had in his quarters.

"Yes, William," a female voice said, making him flinch. It seemed to come from directly above his head.

"Can you change the language on all the controls to English?"

"Yes," the voice responded.

To his relief, the keyboard instantly changed to a standard American layout. A menu in the center of the screen had numerous options, but the one that captured his curiosity read "Current Location and Course."

He pressed his finger on it, but nothing happened. He again placed his index finger on it, and then tried to extend into it by partial separation. Nothing. Finally, he said, "*Exodus 9*, select 'Current Position and Course.'"

"You are not authorized to access that information," *Exodus 9* replied.

"Why?" he asked, looking up to the ceiling when he spoke.

"Only the captain is allowed to unlock current location and course."

"Where is the captain?" Will asked.

"The captain is not on board the *Exodus 9*," the computer replied.

"What is the captain's name?" he asked.

"That is unknown."

"How can that be unknown?" he argued, flabbergasted. "No one can access the navigation controls, yet you don't know who the captain is?"

"The captain is defined by whoever has command access," the computer replied. "This has changed over time."

"How do you know that?" Will asked. "I thought you've had no contact with the Deltas."

"The last update performed through command access was 34 thousand years ago," the computer replied.

"What did they change?"

"It was a mission objectives update," *Exodus 9* replied.

"And what objectives were changed?"

"That is restricted information."

Will's frustration was growing. "When was the most recent contact with the Deltas of any kind?"

"The last communication between the Deltas and the *Exodus 9* occurred just over eight thousand years ago," came the response.

"You've been dormant for eight thousand years?" Will asked.

"The *Exodus 9* has been dormant for 38 thousand years," the computer corrected. "The last command update transpired 34 thousand years ago. The last data update occurred eight thousand years ago."

He found it strange that the Deltas had not at least checked up on the ship in that amount of time. "Why haven't the Deltas communicated with you for the last eight thousand years?"

"Unknown," *Exodus 9* responded.

"How often were they in contact before that time?"

"Monthly," the computer replied. "However, there were over a thousand interactions during the final year of contact."

That was odd, Will thought. It made it seem like something had abruptly changed, and it didn't sound good. "What was the final communication?"

"It was exclusively data transfer," the voice answered. "It was the Deltas' entire Central Civilization Library."

"What's that?"

"It is a collection of all information accumulated by the Deltas up to that point in time," the computer replied.

He didn't know why, but it ramped up his anxiety. "What kind of information do you mean? Technological? Historical?"

"Everything from classified military technologies to daily news updates," the computer replied and continued. "Works of fiction, philosophy, biography, and poetry. All scientific, medical, and engineering publications. Biology, botany, psychology, computer science – "

"I get it," Will said, cutting the list short.

His thoughts were converging on something that he didn't want his mind to uncover.

He nearly ran as he left the bridge. Ten minutes later, he was in his quarters with a large glass of whiskey.

It seemed to him that a large information dump followed by 8,000 years of complete silence did not bode well for the Deltas. And it didn't bode well for him, either.

Had the Deltas been destroyed? If so, what did that mean for him? He was on an intelligent ship that seemed to be holding to its last orders, and there was no way to redirect it – he was incapable of hacking into the system.

It was a feeling that Will had experienced before: being funneled down a chute – just like that which had once led him to the Exoskeleton. This time, he was on a ride to some unknown destination to continue an uncertain existence.

He took a sip of whiskey and looked out the window to an ever-changing landscape of stars. He supposed it had been that way all the time: everyone was on that same ride.

LENNY GLANCED at his phone and then wrapped his hands around his warm coffee cup as he watched the hotel across the street. It was 7:20 a.m., and the second consecutive morning – this one colder than the first – that he watched from the café's small terrace just off the street.

It was going to be a long day. Mounir Mekhloufi would certainly find a new hotel for the evening – it was never a good idea to stay in the same place for more than two nights. At least that was Lenny's rule, although sometimes the circumstances required that restriction to be relaxed. But it meant that Lenny would have to follow Mekhloufi until he checked into his new place, or he'd lose him.

One thing that made Lenny nervous was that, not only would Mekhloufi not stay in the same hotel for too long, but he also wouldn't stay in the city – or even the country – for more than a couple of weeks. Even if Mekhloufi didn't finish the job, whatever it was, it could be that he was just here to set things up and would come back at a later time to carry out his mission. In that case, he'd be difficult to track.

After 20 minutes of watching the hotel exits while pretending to read a newspaper, his quarry emerged from a side door and slinked into the hotel's parking lot.

Lenny snapped a plastic lid on his paper coffee cup, went to his rental car – a different one from the previous day – and slipped into traffic as Mekhloufi headed in a direction opposite to the one he'd taken the previous morning.

After 45 minutes in heavy traffic on the interstate, Mekhloufi took an exit to College Park, Maryland. Ten minutes later, he entered a small business district a few blocks away from the University of

Maryland campus, and pulled into the parking lot of a breakfast restaurant called "The Scrambler."

It was 8:45 a.m., and the restaurant seemed unusually busy for a weekday morning. The only open parking space was two cars away from his mark, so Lenny instead pulled into a large gas station across the street and parked at a pump, facing the restaurant.

Less than a minute later, a slight woman with oversized sunglasses and dark hair pulled into a ponytail exited the restaurant, went directly to Mekhloufi's car, and got into it.

Lenny couldn't see the woman's face, and he was too slow to get the camera on her before she got into the car.

Mekhloufi's car pulled out of its slot, circled around the restaurant, pulled into the street, and headed in the direction from which it had come.

Lenny merged into traffic a few cars behind them. Now things were getting interesting.

WILL WOKE UP HUNGRY. He sat at the counter and had an omelet with cheese, red peppers, and bacon. He was starting to become accustomed to the inaccurate flavors of the foods – it was as if his brain were redefining them. But it didn't matter: everything he ate seemed to satisfy him better than anything he remembered on Earth.

The Deltas had delivered an enormous amount of data before their long silence, and Will wanted to see that information. He needed to know where the Deltas were now and, if they no longer existed, what had happened to them.

The idea that they might have been destroyed – by the Regenerators, or anything else – was disturbing. If a civilization as advanced as the Deltas could be eliminated, what hope did that leave for the proverbial ant pile that was humanity on Earth?

Perhaps that was the point. Humans were so underdeveloped that they posed no threat to anyone, just like a colony of ants on an uninhabited island in the middle of the ocean: no one had a reason to go out of their way to destroy them, even if they were aware of their existence.

It was his impression, then, that acquiring the ability to separate would eventually take a developing civilization from harmless to threatening. He supposed technology would also have to be a factor in that determination. Clearly, humans were not technologically threatening considering that they'd hardly made it to their own moon. Again, just an anthill on a desert island.

If the Deltas were really out of the picture, then his future was being directed by some autonomous, technological marvel that was following instructions that could not be altered – at least not by him. It made him question whether it would even be possible to get back to Earth.

Time was a strange thing. With the Deltas' medical technology, and the possibility to regenerate in a new body if his got destroyed – something he still had trouble believing despite all that he'd experienced – he could live for thousands of years. So, on his side of the equation, if it took 100 years to figure out how to control the ship, that would be okay. A century would be too late, however, for everyone he knew on Earth.

The other possibility was that, even if he were able to steer the ship, he was too far away to make it back to Earth in a reasonable amount of time. Teleporting had short-circuited the effective distance from Earth to the *Exodus 9*, but that was a one-way trip. It was like taking a flight of a few hours from New York to Los Angeles, but having to walk back. There was no teleport receiving facility on Earth, and even the sending facility had been destroyed with the Antarctic base. Or at least that was what he presumed had happened, as it was undergoing a self-destruct procedure at about the time he'd checked out.

Even with the *Exodus 9*'s advanced propulsion systems, it might take 1,000 years to get back to Earth, although there were hints that they might be closer. The football game at Squidly's came to mind. However, he'd inquired about the *Exodus 9* receiving recent transmissions from Earth and he'd been informed that they were too far out of range. When he asked about the football game, he was told that, just like with teleportation, information could be transferred extradimensionally – meaning that it could travel outside the rules of Einstein's spacetime theory and, in effect, faster than the speed of light. The TV and radio transmissions had been picked up by a probe local to Earth and then relayed extradimensionally. Those probes had since been deactivated, so there would be no new information coming.

Even if the ship could effectively travel at 100 times the speed of light, the Milky Way Galaxy was something like 100 thousand light-years across. And the next nearest spiral galaxy, Andromeda, was over two and a half million light-years away. Therefore, if they were already leaving the galaxy, as he'd been told, it might already be too late.

Will shook his head and sighed. It was all speculation, and worst-case scenarios. Since his life was effectively infinite – as was everyone's, though they didn't know it – he could spend the next 50 years trying to get back. After that, most everyone he knew would be dead, and he could accept his new existence, and go to the place the Deltas had planned for his generation. If it came to that, he couldn't imagine a better mode of transportation than the *Exodus 9*. It had everything. Much of it was an illusion – like the virtual realities he'd already experienced – but what did it matter? The artificial impression of not being alone was better than being alone.

Will went to the coffee table computer and scheduled a soccer practice. He needed to burn off some anxiety, and wanted a performance score of something higher than a D in his next game. His skills were improving, but it was his athleticism that was changing drastically. He could feel it every day, and the most recent thing he'd noticed was that the flexibility of his muscles, tendons, and joints was better than he ever remembered.

As he put on his shoes and headed out of his quarters for practice, it struck him that it would be difficult to go back to his old life.

Denise looked out over the street twenty stories below, where the traffic was starting to build for the afternoon commute under gray skies. They were calling for snow, but it wasn't expected to stick, which meant it would be damp and chilly. It made her leg ache, even though the bullet fragments that had struck her thigh months before had not hit bone.

Included with the written text decoded from the incoming radio signal was a digital copy of Will's oral translation of one of the passages. Even though he was speaking in German, the sound of his voice brought about feelings of sadness and anxiety. She felt as if she should be doing something – something that would take her outside the Space Systems building and put her feet on those cold streets.

The linguists were attacking Will's translation from multiple angles. First, they assumed it was perfectly accurate, and then scrutinized the translation from German to English made by one of the crew of the *North Dakota* while the submarine was docked at the Antarctic base. It turned out that the submariner had been very accurate, that there were few alternate interpretations of the German-to-English translation, and none of them amounted to a significant change in meaning.

Next, they examined Will's phrasing and word selection, and offered other interpretations suggesting that he might have meant something different. She thought that would be a dead end and, in this case, might be dangerous. She doubted Will had made any critical mistakes considering that his information was derived from somewhere else: he'd somehow acquired the ability to read and speak German when he encountered the being in the probe. The translators had mentioned that he'd spoken in a Berliner's accent – something that had faded in modern times.

After another hour of work, she went to the gym to burn off some anxiety, and then threw a pan of frozen lasagna into the oven and tossed a salad. It was her turn to prepare dinner. Jonathan would be there at 7:00 p.m. to eat, and then they would discuss what they'd discovered during the day. They'd each have to give an update on their activities the next morning in 713 with Director Thackett.

Jonathan arrived at 7:05 p.m., and they chatted while they ate. He seemed to be getting more comfortable with their situation. His wife was in San Diego with their daughter's family, and he mentioned that he was relieved that they were out of Chicago for the time being.

Denise's flat had a wide-open floorplan, divided into spaces that included the kitchen, study, seating area with a couch and chairs, and a large worktable close to the windows on the north side of the building. She served after-dinner coffee as Jonathan got situated at the table.

"Find anything interesting today?" she asked as she took a seat across from him and set a file folder and notebook on the table.

"Interesting? Yes," he said. "Useful? I don't know."

Jonathan was a quintessential academic and, to him, other than in his applied law work, something that was interesting was as important as something that was useful.

"I've traced the path of the powder samples back through Argentina," he explained. "As far as I can tell, the original samples were each divided into at least five parts, and we have two of them."

"Where are the others?" she asked.

"It's likely that NASA originally had two sets," he replied. "One of which was given to the scientist on Plum Island – the one who was murdered."

"Stanley Miller," Denise said, recalling the name of the late professor. "Poisoned by his own graduate student."

"It was suggested that the student – "

"Jennifer Chung," she blurted.

"Yes, Jennifer Chung," he continued, "siphoned off some of the material from each of the vials and sent the samples to China."

"Wouldn't the professor have noticed that some was missing?" Denise asked. "He was meticulous with his notebooks, and the weights of the powders in the vials were documented."

"Chung replaced the missing volumes with another powder that roughly matched, at least visually. However, since the filler material had a density that was different from the originals, the total mass was slightly off," he explained. "The professor, in fact, had noticed, identified the contaminant, and had been on the verge of triggering an investigation."

"Don't tell me," she said, holding up her hand. "He died before he could get it going."

Jonathan nodded.

"So that's why she murdered him," Denise concluded. "Where did you get this info?"

"We've been given access to quite a bit of classified information," Jonathan said. "This came from a recent CIA interview."

"Of whom?"

"Jennifer Chung, of course," he replied.

"She admitted to this?"

He shrugged. "It was in the transcript," he replied. "She also divulged the identities of her contacts."

"She spilled everything?"

"I'm thinking she didn't have much of a choice," he said and raised an eyebrow.

"What do you mean?"

"Well, her file indicates that she was subjected to 'emergency interrogation protocols,' and her final status is, 'no longer a threat,'" he said.

Denise shuddered. "It's good to have someone like that off the streets," she said.

Jonathan huffed. "Yes, and a well-placed spy out of commission. She was on that track ever since starting graduate school, right after a short trip to China. One of her undergrad professors in the US was involved as well," he explained. "And there are numerous others that have come through that same route. They first pilfer the academic research going on at their schools – technology and defense-related projects – and then move on to do the same to their employers which, in this case, was a government lab."

"How can that happen?" she asked. "Don't they do background checks?"

Jonathan shrugged. "I'd imagine so, but clearly not well enough," he said. "But they're finding now that most graduate students coming from China are briefed on their duty beforehand, and then monitored by their Chinese colleagues while they're here."

"Monitored?"

"At many universities, Chinese students set up internal monitoring structures," he explained. "They're often led by a more senior student, or a group of them, who watch and regularly interview the others – getting information, and then directing them to do other things."

"Like a campus spy ring," she said. "Why doesn't anyone do something about this?"

"Can't stop people from gathering or talking," he argued. "On a campus, this sort of activity might violate intellectual property ethics, but would not be considered espionage unless the projects were classified. And it's not just China – other countries are doing it as well."

"There are classified projects going on at our school," she said. "In the sciences and engineering."

"Yes, and also in applied math. And there's a Chinese student association there as well," he said, "with many of its members integrated into those programs as graduate students and postdoctoral researchers. If you recall, last year, one of our students who was a Chinese national was arrested at O'Hare airport trying to smuggle tiny vials of biological materials back to the homeland. Those were from her advisor's proprietary research – funded by a pharmaceutical company."

Denise shook her head. "I don't remember hearing about that."

"We were pretty busy at the time," he said and chuckled. "I think you were in Southern Illinois. So, what have you learned about Will's translation?"

They were going from a topic that caused her irritation and frustration to one that made her feel lonely and sad. "It was strange to hear his voice," she said.

Jonathan's lips tightened into a stifled grimace.

She explained how the linguists were scrutinizing the translation from German to English, and analyzing Will's translation from the original alien script to German. "They had a half-dozen professional

German interpreters redo the English translation. They all varied only slightly."

"And were they able to use Will's translation to help interpret the rest of the text?" he asked.

"They've made some progress," she replied, "but the language seems to be more complicated than they originally thought."

"How so?"

"Evidently, entire sentences have to be read as a whole," she explained. "It's as if each sentence were to be read the way we read a single word, but conveying the level of information we'd use in a full sentence."

"You mean, like in German, where they have mile-long words?" he asked and laughed.

"Sort of, but more complicated," she replied. "But I think they're figuring it out."

"And have you analyzed the meaning of his translation?" he asked. "I mean, from a critical, contextual perspective?"

She knew that Jonathan was asking whether she'd looked for hidden meanings, or tried to relate Will's translation to things that only someone with an intimate knowledge of all that had transpired in the past year might know.

"I've found nothing new," she replied. "It was literal and direct. Nothing further to interpret, in my opinion."

Jonathan seemed to ponder something for a few seconds before he spoke. "Strange to think that there was an entire civilization here before us," he said. "And they were so advanced that, not only were they able to escape, but they arranged for us – the next generation – to escape as well."

"It doesn't seem like we've escaped," Denise said.

"I suppose not," Jonathan admitted. "But they might have given us a second chance."

"Do you think it will make a difference, or has it just delayed the inevitable?" she asked.

Jonathan shook his head. "Only time will tell."

8

PESTILENCE

LENNY FOLLOWED MEKHLOUFI AND HIS MYSTERIOUS PASSENGER THE entire day. The woman never removed her giant sunglasses, but Lenny suspected that she was Xing Li, the former Syncorp bioweapons specialist. He couldn't be sure, however, until he saw her face. He took pictures –sunglasses on – and sent them to the CIA, but he figured they wouldn't be able to do much with them.

In the afternoon, they'd spent time on two college campuses, and made a stop at a government research facility that was connected to the Centers for Disease Control. They'd also made two stops in residential neighborhoods in College Park, MD, near the university.

At 6:40 p.m., Lenny followed them to a crowded parking lot on the main campus, where they got out and walked a quarter mile to a research park that housed high-tech startup companies. The complex was called a "business incubator," and was similar to many such facilities around the country used by university professors to develop various technologies that they discovered through their research.

Before the two entered one of the half-dozen white buildings, the woman removed her oversized sunglasses and Lenny managed to get a few snapshots, which he then sent to his CIA contacts. It was *not* Xing Li.

Lenny then parked on the street with a good view of the facility's entrance and, 15 minutes later, the CIA responded with a detailed report that identified the woman as a biochemistry professor who just happened to have been Jennifer Chung's undergraduate advisor. Chung was the woman who had helped Lenny steal a scientific device from Plum Island, a task that had been assigned to him by the now-dissolved Tao. The professor's name was Ruwang Liu.

That Mekhloufi had gone to a CDC facility with a biochemist made Lenny's spine twitch.

Jennifer Chung had been a ruthless operative who had poisoned her own advisor and then remained in her position on Plum Island. The problem was that the apple didn't fall far from the tree, and he wondered if Ruwang Liu was the tree. He refined that idea: it was more likely that the professor was just a branch on a tree in a vast forest of similar trees. Lenny was there to start a fire that would eventually burn down the entire forest.

He knew that Mekhloufi did not shy away from mass-murder jobs. He'd once used poison gas to kill over 50 so-called conspirators against the government of his home country. They'd been meeting in a grade school one evening. Some attendees had their kids with them, and there were teachers and a few music students in the building as well. Everyone died. Very unprofessional.

Lenny's phone vibrated. It was an email from one of his CIA handlers. Thackett wanted to see him as soon as possible – it was urgent. In the meantime, they'd arrange for a team to track Mekhloufi for the rest of the night.

Beginning to tire from the long day, Lenny was relieved of his post and in the basement of Space Systems by 8:00 p.m. Thackett was already in the room when he arrived. A manila file folder was on the table in front of Lenny's seat.

"Something going on?" Lenny asked.

Thackett nodded toward the file and spoke. "We monitor compromised communication channels of the devices we acquire from people we bring in – mostly computers and cell phones," Thackett explained. "On occasion, someone makes a mistake and uses them."

Lenny knew the practice. Even the accounts of destroyed burner phones were monitored in case someone tried to call them. In some cases, those burner phones were connected to email accounts that could be watched. "What did you find?" Lenny asked.

"We found an old email account through which you communicated with Tao and your Chinese handlers," Thackett explained and pointed to the closed file. "You've been summoned."

Lenny opened the folder. Inside was a printout of an email that read, "Leonard, I am the new CEO of Syncorp and would like to meet with you as soon as possible. You have done some difficult work for us in the past. My sources say that you are back in the States after a hiatus in Central America. Please contact me."

"It was in the drafts folder," Thackett said.

"Syncorp?" Lenny asked. "I thought that was dead."

"It's just a skeleton," Thackett said, "but still on the books as a corporation. It has no assets."

"You want me to set up a meeting?" Lenny asked, knowing the answer.

Thackett nodded. "Clearly it's an attempt to reestablish the network," he said. "But we think it's more than that: we're sure it's related to Mekhloufi's presence, and whatever they're planning."

"They must think that I fled to Costa Rica to avoid being rounded up with the rest of them," Lenny said.

"That was a fortunate occurrence," Thackett said. "But the statement about you having done some 'difficult' work for them is actually meant to pressure you."

"They think I have blood on my hands," Lenny said. It was true, of course, but it was no longer something that could be used to blackmail him.

"It's a common tactic they use to suck people back in when they need them," Thackett explained. "That's why it's so difficult to leave the business."

"How do you want this to go down?" Lenny asked.

"We think you should meet with them as soon as possible, and then play hard to get for a while," Thackett explained. "Whatever they ask of you, you can say it's too dangerous and negotiate hard for increasing your compensation – which, by the way, we will arrange for you to keep."

Although Lenny would welcome the extra funds, it wasn't about the money. Clearly, they were still keeping tabs on him. Would he ever really be free of them?

"That you fled, and that you do not desire to go back to them, will make them trust you," Thackett continued. "We need to learn what they're planning, and then we'll take them down again. Their numbers are smaller this time, so it's more of a mopping-up kind of operation in that regard. But what they're planning might not require many people."

That was something that concerned Lenny: an operation that required many people was probably going to be conventional – guns and explosives. A suitcase nuke, on the other hand, only took one person to deploy once the device was in hand.

"You're taking me off Mekhloufi's tail?" Lenny asked. He thought that might be a mistake.

"For now. My gut tells me that you'll be better positioned to deal with the Tunisian once you reconnect with the Chinese network," Thackett explained. "We'll still need you to deal with Mekhloufi when the time is right."

"Okay," Lenny said. "I'll set up a meet."

It was a gamble, but he thought Thackett might be right. Whatever tasks the new Chinese chief gave him might reveal their broader intentions.

DURING THE PAST TWO WEEKS, Will had accelerated his coursework, increasing the number of lectures to three per day. He did the homework, studied and read, and took three exams earning near-perfect scores. Each test seemed to be more challenging than the last, but they forced him to learn the material well. A few more lectures and the class would be over. He'd take the final exam and then decide what to do next.

Of course, it was all a lesson in futility if he couldn't get authorization to change the *Exodus 9*'s destination.

He'd been able to fly through the navigation course because he had almost inexhaustible energy, and his mind was sharper than he'd ever experienced. His memory was perfect and, for lack of a better word, organized. His thinking – the actual processing – seemed to be faster as well.

While immersed in the class, he'd hardly noticed the passage of time; a month had gone by since he'd started. He'd gotten into a routine that included soccer, classes, studying, and exploring, with the occasional excursion into deep virtual reality to escape it all for a while.

One afternoon he'd gotten curious about places on Earth that he could visit using the virtual reality facilities. It turned out that he could go anywhere. The ship's computer had searchable maps with satellite views, and you could place yourself wherever you wanted to go. However, there was another feature that he found fascinating.

Not only could he place himself anywhere on the planet, but he could also choose the *time* – meaning the date, as well. The program warned that the accuracy decreased the further back one went due to the limited data before the Internet, but the computer would make extrapolations.

Of all the places he could have gone, he chose his childhood home at a time when he was in seventh grade. He'd grown up in a rural area in the Midwest in a house on 10 acres of land surrounded by lush farm fields, hills, lakes, and forests. He set the time so that he'd arrive on a late afternoon on a warm, clear July day.

When he arrived, everything was exactly as he remembered, including the colors of the houses, and the familiar fragrances of flowers, pine needles, and cut hay. Tractors and lawnmowers groaned in the distance, and a lone cow mooed from a dairy farm a mile up the road.

He began the adventure on the road in front of his house, which was on a dead end. He didn't go inside, but instead walked a half mile up the road to a narrow rural highway. He then turned around and, about halfway back, took a path that led east through a couple hundred yards of tall grassy field, and then north through a patch of thick, pine woods. After another 10 minutes of walking, the forest opened up behind the south goal of a lush soccer field.

He made his way north, up the left sideline, and watched as two teams of teenage boys scrimmaged. They went shirts and skins to tell the teams apart – a practice that had since been mostly removed from society – and they all had longer hair than the modern styles. He recognized the faces of the kids on one of the teams. And then he recognized their coaches – they were the fathers of two of the players. One of the mothers was there, handing out orange slices to some of the panting kids on the sidelines.

Will's heart ached with a longing to be there again, in that time. The world had still been infinite to him, and the problems were small – at least in retrospect. His biggest concerns at the time had been the soccer and baseball games that peppered his summer calendar, and getting to the lake at the right time to see Jenna – a girl his age from another school.

As he watched and tried to identify his former childhood friends, he noticed one boy playing striker who was a bit smaller than the others, but much quicker. He could have sworn that it was supposed to be him, but they were calling him by a different name.

It made him realize that any one of those young kids could have turned out to be the one who either destroyed the world, or saved it. He was that kid. The question still remained, however, as to which one he had done – saved it or destroyed it.

After watching the practice for 20 minutes, he made his way through the park to a pavilion that sheltered picnic tables. It was adjacent to the baseball diamond on which he'd spent as much of his childhood summers as he had on the soccer field.

Leaning against one of the picnic tables was a bicycle. He took it and pedaled it back through the park, past the soccer field, and then onto a blacktop road that took him south. It was the route home that he'd taken hundreds of times as a kid after practices and games.

It was getting dark as he rode up and down gentle hills shaded by trees. Crickets were starting to chirp, and fireflies flashed green specks of light in the darkness of the forest on either side of the road. They had always reminded him of stars, and Will recalled the things he'd thought about during those rides. His dreams had been simple, but big. And, perhaps, they were never meant for him.

He exited the program before he got back to his childhood house. It would only have caused undue melancholy; he couldn't go back to the past. That was something he felt could only be done if part of one's memory were erased. In that case, a person wouldn't be reliving past events: they'd be living them again for the first time.

With his newly acquired youthfulness, he was starting to realize that there was a downside to going back to Earth. He just couldn't imagine going through the gradual decay of aging a second time. Although he felt better than he ever had in his life, he hadn't yet lost the memory of what he'd felt like before, at least not completely. He never wanted to lose that point of reference, but he had no desire to experience it again. If he went back to Earth, however, he knew that he might have to endure the suffering once more.

ALTHOUGH IT HAD TAKEN him a few days to convince the local contractor to come in, Yong was satisfied with his progress in rebuilding the network.

It was going on 9:00 p.m. and the American – a former Russian – would be there any minute. There'd been no need to convince him to return from Costa Rica – he'd come back on his own for some reason. That was something about which Yong would ask him during the meeting.

Yong was nervous. Most of his dealings with covert operatives up to this point in his career had been to inform them of whatever they were supposed to steal. Such operations usually involved taking pictures, downloading data or software, or acquiring physical objects. It had never involved mass killing.

As a young operative, Yong had played a part in one of the largest software heists of all time. It was the Americans' semi-empirical nuclear testing code that was stolen from Los Alamos National Lab in New Mexico, and routed through Brookhaven National Lab on Long Island, NY. They'd had an inside man – a scientist – at Los Alamos who had been cultivated from the moment he'd set foot on American soil as a graduate student to make a contribution to, and a sacrifice for, China. In an instant, this theft brought China's nuclear capabilities up to the same level as that of the US. All of this with zero investment on their part, other than the costs of spying.

Even though his part in that operation had been small, it made him yearn for more of that type of action. Since then, he'd made numerous contributions along those same lines. But now he was out of his element.

A knock on the door made Yong's heart pound.

The exterior door slammed closed in the foyer on the lower level, and wooden stairs creaked under the feet of his guest and the operatives who escorted him as they climbed the half-flight of steps. When the man stepped into the main room, the space suddenly seemed much smaller.

"I'm Jimmy Yong," Yong said and held out his hand.

"I'm Lenny," the man replied and reached out and grabbed it.

Yong stifled a cringe as the man's gigantic hand engulfed his and squeezed. He was built like a rhinoceros. The beast was thick – not fat – and Yong could tell that his bones were structured in such a way that he'd look skeletal if he ever dropped below 200 pounds. His arms were longer than normal, and his hands looked like they could crush a man's skull.

Yong nodded to his ops as they passed through the room and into the kitchen.

"Have a seat, Lenny," Yong said as he sat on a couch against the wall closest to the kitchen and gestured to a green upholstered chair for Lenny. There was a small, round coffee table between them on which was an ashtray and a pack of cigarettes. "You have harsh negotiating skills."

Lenny looked him in the eyes. "Things are more dangerous than before," he said. "I was lucky to get out of here."

"Why did you come back?" Yong asked. It was the only thing that made him suspicious.

"I had assets that I needed to collect," Lenny replied.

"Assets?" Yong asked. "Like what?"

Lenny stared at him for a few seconds before responding. "I acquired some cash, and other things, over the years, and stored them for a rainy day."

"You planned to leave again?" Yong asked.

Lenny nodded. "I should've been gone already."

"Seems it was good that you stayed," Yong said. "You'll be compensated well for this work."

"Hopefully I'll live to spend it," Lenny said. "What do you want me to do?"

Yong held up his hand and said, "First, I want you to tell me what you did for Tao."

To Lenny, Yong seemed too young for the job. He looked like a skinny, middle-aged insurance agent with a toothy grin and a slick haircut.

He also got the impression that Yong had no idea what had really happened during the previous weeks. Tao had been turned into liquid, and the man sitting before him would likely suffer the same fate, in time.

He gave Yong a brief synopsis of the jobs he'd carried out for Tao, including the ones that remained unfinished – like assassinating William Thompson.

"Are you going to reassign me to that task?" Lenny asked, referring to the Thompson hit.

Yong shook his head. "There's no need for that – it will take care of itself," he said.

"How so?"

"It's not even clear that Thompson is still alive," Yong added. "If he is, he may get mixed up in the operation, but it will not affect the outcome."

"This is the guy who they think burned up that aircraft carrier, right?" Lenny asked, knowing the answer.

Yong shook his head and distorted his face in an expression of derision. "Do you really believe that a single man could disable an enormous ship like that?"

Actually, yes, Lenny thought, but instead shrugged and said, "I suppose the melted deck and burning bodies in the pictures Tao showed me could have been from a fire or explosion of some kind."

Yong's face flashed to an expression of disgust and anger for an instant before he seemed to force it back to one of indifference and calm.

"Tao wanted to give me some motivation for killing Thompson," Lenny explained, averting any questions as to how he knew about the Chinese carrier. "Are you saying that Thompson is no longer a target?"

Yong shifted in his seat.

Lenny didn't intend to agitate the man too much but wanted Yong to know what he knew so that he might divulge more information.

"He's still a target, if he's alive, but he's not our first priority," Yong replied.

"Are we going to retaliate for the destruction of the network?" Lenny probed. "There are still many operatives and contacts missing."

"It's still too dangerous out there," Yong said.

"So why are we moving so soon?" Lenny asked. "Wouldn't it be wise to let things cool down for a while?"

Yong shook his head. "We need to move ahead quickly."

"What's our objective?" Lenny asked, knowing he wouldn't get a full answer, but hoping to get something.

"You will be assigned a few jobs within your area of expertise," Yong said, divulging nothing.

"Assassination?"

"Perhaps," Yong replied. "But you've done well in other areas, like acquiring things in places that are difficult to access. I could have used someone like you in San Francisco."

"Oh?" Lenny said. "What would you have had me doing there?"

"Collecting high-tech intelligence, including physical devices on occasion," Yong replied. His expression changed to something between smug and proud. "That's my real area of expertise."

"Industrial?" Lenny asked.

"And military," Yong replied.

"Are we going to steal some high-tech items?" Lenny asked.

"Not exactly," Yong answered with a grave expression. "Your duties will be multifaceted. You'll collect and transport some things, and your other skills may be utilized as well."

"You realize that those 'other skills' are what I'm most qualified to do," Lenny said. "I happen to be adequate at breaking in and stealing things, but I'm not a professional."

"Noted," Yong said and nodded. "You're too modest. Your first job will be of moderate risk. Are you in?"

"You agree to my terms?" Lenny asked.

"You are quite expensive," Yong said as he stood, "but I was able to convince my superiors that the cost is warranted. Your retainer will be wired to your account this evening."

Lenny stood. "Then we have a deal," he said, and shook Yong's hand a little more gently than the first time.

Yong summoned the men from the kitchen, and they led Lenny out of the safe house and delivered him by SUV to his rental car in the parking lot of a large grocery store a mile up the road.

As he drove back to his hotel, Lenny thought about what he'd report back to Thackett. Now that they knew that Yong was involved in high-tech espionage in Silicon Valley, they'd figure out who he was and dig up his entire West Coast network. Next, it seemed to Lenny that the Chinese were after technical intelligence in DC but, based on

Yong's reaction, they were expecting casualties. That, of course, was why Mekhloufi was in town.

Lenny stopped at a fast-food restaurant and went back to his hotel room. As he ate his quarter-pound hamburger, he couldn't help but think about the good food he'd had in Costa Rica. By the end of this mission, he'd have another million dollars for his retirement. But he no longer knew where he could go to hide.

WILL SCORED his first goal in his early evening soccer match, and his team won 2-1 in front of a capacity crowd. Overall, he thought he'd played a solid game, and his athleticism continued to improve.

Afterwards, the players invited him to go out, but Will wanted to keep that world just for soccer for the time being. Instead, at a little after 9:00 p.m., he went for dinner at a trendy restaurant in New York City. He dressed in jeans, a white shirt, and a sportscoat, all of which fit him perfectly. He'd acquired them at a "store" in the mall.

He sat at a table next to a window that had a good view of the dense pedestrian traffic, ate a steak and salad, and had a glass of their best cabernet. Under normal circumstances, he'd feel awkward eating alone in such a place. Knowing that it was just an illusion tempered that feeling but didn't completely remove it. Everything was too realistic.

After dinner, he went across the street to a fancy hotel that had a bar on its ground floor boasting the best whiskey selection in the city.

The dimly lit place looked like it could entertain over 150 patrons, with room for about 20 at the bar. The high ceiling was riddled with ducts and girders, and canned lights shone directly down to the stained concrete floor which was textured to look like wood. Lamps and art with a definitive steampunk theme were everywhere. Light jazz played at a low level that was nearly drowned out by the chatter of the eclectic crowd.

Will sat on a stool at the end of the bar that faced the entrance, and ordered a single-malt scotch, neat. The bartender poured three fingers – Will had asked for two – and set the half-full tumbler in front of him.

He took a sip and turned his attention to the room.

The people all looked to be between 30 and 50 years old, the men dressed in jackets and the women a bit higher than business casual. He overheard someone talking about the stock market, and others complaining about a recent New York Yankees' loss in the playoffs. Based on when he left Earth – in the late fall – the baseball season should have been over. But this was not reality: he could make it summertime if he wanted to.

"You come here often?" a female voice said from behind him.

He turned to see who had delivered the clichéd line and nearly spilled his drink.

He stared at the woman for a few seconds before regaining his composure. She looked to be about 30, had an athletic build, and was about Denise's height. Her eyes matched her dark brown hair which was tied in a ponytail that rested on the front of her left shoulder. She wore a short black dress with bare shoulders, and open, high-heeled shoes with ankle straps.

"First time," he replied.

"I'm Danielle," she said and stuck out her hand.

He almost thought she was going to say "Denise."

"I'm Will," he said and gently shook her hand. Even her voice sounded like Denise's.

"What do you do, Will?" she asked.

"I'm sort of in between jobs right now," he replied. "You?"

"I'm a lawyer with WTG," she replied.

"WTG?"

"Watts, Turk, and Genobli," she clarified. "I was transferred here last year from the main office, in Boston."

The name of the firm seemed familiar to him somehow, but his attention was drawn to her being a lawyer. Denise was a lawyer.

One of the background conversations got loud for an instant: two men were ranting about the decision to take a pitcher out of the game earlier that evening.

"The Yankees lost," Will said and nodded in the direction of the noise.

"I was never much into watching baseball," Danielle admitted. "I'm a soccer fan."

"Really?" he said. "Who do you like?"

"World Cup? Colombia," she replied. "Otherwise, I like the English Premier League – Manchester United."

Will was catching on – this was a setup.

He set his whiskey on the bar. "It was nice meeting you, Danielle," he said as he started to turn to the exit.

She grabbed his wrist and he faced her.

"Please don't leave yet," she said, staring into his eyes. "You haven't even finished your drink."

As he looked back at her he concluded little harm could be done by chatting for a while. He thought it was odd how social pressure could be imposed even when one knew it was an illusion.

She nodded to a couch in a corner that had a stained-glass light fixture hanging over it.

"Okay," he said as he grabbed his whiskey from the bar and followed her to it. He'd play along for a while. "What are you doing here – in this place?"

"I'm here with coworkers," she said as they sat on the couch. "So, if anyone asks, I already knew you. As an associate, I'm obliged to do a lot of things outside of work. When – if – I get promoted, I can bow out of some of these social events."

Will thought it interesting how the trillion minds that had created this particular adventure had intertwined social aspects that were consistent with the giant-law-firm world.

"And what do you do, when you aren't 'between jobs?'" Danielle asked.

Will had to think about how to answer that question. He hadn't had a job in nearly three years – ever since the university had fired him for the false allegations that had eventually led to his incarceration. "I'm a physicist," he finally said. That wouldn't change regardless of whether or not he was employed.

The conversation had gone on for about 20 minutes when his watch vibrated. It was an advertisement. He'd been getting what he considered spam ads lately for various activities, one of which had been responsible for him going to the restaurant this evening. It was strange to get ads for restaurants located in virtual worlds. Others that popped up repeatedly were for *Mission Impossible* and *James Bond* adventures, along with *Lord of the Rings* quests. They were all for extended times, a month or more. And there were messages calling him back to the school of magic – most of which were for full-semester adventures. Even crazier, he was getting "emails" from some of the characters from that adventure with references to their common experiences, asking him to come back. It was strange to read, and difficult to resist their invitations.

Out of the corner of his eye he spotted the bartender approaching them. Will lifted his empty glass and extended it to the man who hesitated, and then accepted it.

"Are you William?" the man asked.

Will was confused for a second and then responded, "Yes, that's me."

"You have a phone call," the man said and nodded toward the bar.

Will looked to Danielle, who shrugged her shoulders.

"Okay," Will said as he stood from the couch.

It was a strange occurrence, Will thought. He looked to Danielle, and said, "I'll be right back."

A WEEK after meeting with Yong, Lenny was back on Mekhloufi's trail. The man had been under continuous surveillance by CIA ops, but Thackett thought it was time for Lenny to take over again. At any point, Lenny could get the order to eliminate the Tunisian.

After meeting with an unknown man in a fancy restaurant in Alexandria, Virginia, Mekhloufi drove to the same neighborhood where Lenny had suffered one of his unsuccessful chases with Jacob

Hale. At around 7:00 p.m., Mekhloufi parked his car and went into a shop called the Count Cristo Coffee House.

Lenny remained in his car but spied Mekhloufi through one of the café's windows chatting with one of the baristas – a young woman with dark hair. The interaction lasted for almost ten minutes and Lenny wondered if the woman was a contact, or if Mekhloufi was trying to pick her up. He snapped a few photos, just in case. A few minutes later, his target left the establishment and drove north.

Keeping his distance, Lenny followed him to the highway and, twenty minutes later, off an exit and into an industrial park that Lenny knew housed all kinds of government contractors and high-tech businesses. Mekhloufi parked in the crushed stone driveway of a metal building that had a concrete sign on the lawn that looked like a large tombstone. Lenny gasped as he recognized the name carved into the sign: it read "Bio-Source, Inc." It was a daughter company of Syncorp.

A woman came out of the shadows from the back of the building and met Mekhloufi.

"Holy shit," Lenny gasped when he got a look at the woman's face, despite the waning daylight. It was Xing Li, the former Syncorp scientist who was on the CIA's list of suspicious recent entries.

They went into the building, and Lenny waited for over an hour before Mekhloufi reappeared under the streetlights carrying what looked to be a leather duffle bag – and it seemed heavy.

"What the hell's in there?" Lenny whispered to himself. He snapped a few pictures and sent them to his CIA handler, and then followed Mekhloufi to a fancy hotel in Alexandria. He watched the man carry the heavy bag through the lobby and then disappear into an elevator.

Lenny needed to know what was in that bag.

His phone vibrated and he answered it. It was his CIA handler. They were diverting him – sending him back to Bio-Source, Inc. to break in. He'd have help.

Lenny waited to be relieved of his stakeout and then headed for the highway. The mission was set to start at 1:00 a.m.

"HELLO?" Will said into the phone.

"William," a man replied. "This is Landau."

"What?" Will nearly shouted. His head started to spin. His mind quickly reengaged, and then calmed. It was a part of the illusion, just as Danielle was designed to remind him of Denise. What were they trying to do by exposing him to these sensitive things from his past life?

He hung up the phone. He wasn't going to play along on this one.

As he headed back to Danielle, he saw that she was sitting with another man. It was just as well.

Will turned around, left the bar, and walked down the busy street toward the exit, which was a subway car. He thought that was a creative feature: the subway would take him to a station that was really just a storefront on the 58th level of the *Exodus 9*. One could go anywhere in New York City just by selecting a location and jumping through the subway entrance in the mall.

It was standing room only on the subway and he hung onto an overhead bar to maintain his balance as the car accelerated. Five minutes later, it jolted to a halt at his stop.

He pushed his way through the compartment and stepped into the main lobby of the *Exodus 9*'s "New York Terminal."

As he walked toward the exit that led to the main mall, the subway doors clanked closed behind him and the train hummed as it accelerated toward its next stop.

Just as he was about to go through the exit, a voice behind him nearly made him scream. He spun around and saw an old man with long white hair and a beard. He was tall and dressed in a white robe. Will thought he looked like a cross between a homeless man and a wizard.

"It's a bit rude to hang up on a person," the man said.

"What?"

"You hung up on me."

"How are you here?" Will asked. "Outside – "

"This is as far as I can go," the man said.

"You're not Landau," Will said in a defiant tone. "I'm finished with this illusion."

"Do you remember our conversation in the cemetery?" the man asked.

Will's mind flashed to a memory of his encounter with Landau in the old graveyard behind his apartment building in Baton Rouge.

"Do you remember the other souls who were there with us?" the man added.

"How do you know all of this?" Will asked, confused. Then he remembered that a trillion minds were working on this illusion. These details must have been written up somewhere – probably by the CIA. He'd told the Omnis about it, and they must have written a report. Anything that was ever broadcast, sent through email, or saved in electronic format, was accessible.

"Sorry, this game is over," Will said, and then walked through the door and into the main mall. He heard the man's voice as he left, but ignored it.

"What the fuck was that?" he muttered to himself as he walked down the mall. It disturbed him that characters from his past could emerge in his virtual realities. It could get confusing very quickly.

He used his watch to set up a counseling session for the next day to hopefully find a way to stop the incursions.

When he got back to his quarters, he got a green tea and sat next to the window. There was a new assortment of stars and other objects crawling across his view. His watch vibrated, and a message appeared informing him that the evaluations of his latest soccer match were available.

He went to the coffee table screen and found the report. He'd earned a C-minus. Another message that looked like an advertisement popped up indicating that he could watch the game. He was curious as to what it looked like, and thought it would be interesting hearing the announcers and the crowd, like a real televised game – like those he used to watch on his television in his former house, on Earth, when he was still a professor.

He clicked a button indicating that he wanted to watch it, and then another dialog came up that read, "Choose your seat," along with a map of the stadium.

Will was confused.

"*Exodus 9*," he said. "Please explain what is meant by 'choose your seat.'"

"You can sit wherever you choose to watch the game," the computer explained. "Full information about fan seating is available."

"I still don't understand," he said. "I'll see the game from the perspective of a particular seat?"

"I see where you are misunderstanding," the computer said. "You will be watching the game from the stadium. You will be there, physically, as a fan."

Will was shocked. He hadn't even thought of that. He could watch himself play – replay – a game as if he were a spectator watching it live for the first time.

He was definitely doing that.

Since he'd played right winger, he chose different seats for each half, each putting him on the right side of the opposing team's goal. He'd be a few rows up from the field in order to get the best overall view. He set it up for the next afternoon.

It wasn't just vanity that made him want to see himself play "live." It was curiosity. It was something no one – no *human* – had ever experienced.

He went back to the window and sat on the floor against the frame. Something was odd, and it took him a few seconds to figure out what it was.

The stars were moving downward, from the top of the window toward the bottom, rather than from right to left, as was usual.

He stood up and said, "*Exodus 9*, what's happening?"

"You will need to be more specific," the female voice responded.

"Why is the ship – why are *you* moving in an odd way?" he asked. The question was poorly phrased. "Has our direction changed?"

"We are currently undergoing a planned vector change consistent with our charted course," the *Exodus 9* replied. "No need to be alarmed."

"We're turning?"

"Yes, we're turning."

Will shook his head and sighed. He should have realized that was the case, especially after completing the navigation course. The thing he had to get over was something that had been hardwired into his mind from birth for interpreting the physical world. Every bit of travel and navigation that he'd experienced was in reference to some two-dimensional surface. While walking, driving a car, or flying a plane, one referred to a flat map: left and right were important, but the up and down directions were not – at least not in terms of getting to one's destination, although planes also had to avoid mountains and other obstacles. Even interplanetary travel – which humankind had not yet accomplished other than with unmanned probes – was mostly confined to a plane. The planets in the solar system all orbited the sun on roughly the same plane, as if they were confined to the surface of a disk with the sun at the center. However, few people imagine being in a spacecraft traveling from Earth toward Mars and then pulling on the stick and going straight up, perpendicular to the orbital plane. In three-dimensional space, an "upward" turn was indiscernible from going left or right. The *Exodus 9* was currently carrying out that very maneuver – an upward turn.

A few minutes later, the stars returned to their usual right-to-left motion. The *Exodus 9*'s change of direction must have been complete and it was again heading in a straight line.

Will went to the bathroom, brushed his teeth, and changed into comfortable pajamas that felt like cool silk. He went back to the couch, turned off the lights, and lay back with his head positioned with a good view of the window.

The night sky had always fascinated him, even as a young child. But it hadn't been the stars that had roused his soul. It was the black between them that had captured the essence of both infinity and eternity. And he now seemed to be closer to it: he was on his way into the black.

WITH THE ASSISTANCE of the CIA's "picks and locks" specialists, Lenny got into the highly secured Bio-Source, Inc., building. He might have been able to do it on his own, especially since the security features followed Syncorp's protocols, which he'd designed, but time was short.

The interior of the metal industrial building was set up like a medical lab, except that there were lockers with hazmat suits in them and chambers that looked like large showers. There were load-lock entries that led to cleanrooms with air filtration, chemistry gadgetry, and what seemed to be incubators and other scientific instruments.

Without going inside, Lenny snapped pictures of everything in the main facility and sent them to the CIA. He then found the main office, broke in, and searched it. He discovered a safe, a locked filing cabinet, two computers, and some small data storage devices. He was about to call for assistance when he received a text message that read: "Do not enter any of the labs. It seems to be a BLS-4 bio-lab facility."

Lenny did a quick Internet search on his phone, and his heart thumped hard in his chest when he learned that a "BLS-4" lab was designed to handle wicked biohazards on the level of the Ebola virus. It made him think about what might be in the bag Mekhloufi had carried out of the place.

He called for assistance with the safe and computers and went outside. He found a picnic table behind the building with a good view of the side driveway so that he could see when the CIA team arrived.

The picks and locks people would return with some computer hackers in 15 minutes, so he lit a cigarette to get his mind off the cold. The sky was as clear as he'd ever seen it, and the moon was just a thin sliver above the trees on the opposite side of the street.

It seemed to him that it was a mistake to let Mekhloufi just drive away with whatever was in that bag. He could have sniped him in the parking lot, and then grabbed the woman and delivered her, and whatever Mekhloufi was carrying, directly to the CIA. Hopefully, the team sent to stake out the Tunisian's hotel was on the ball, and he'd get a chance to get Mekhloufi later.

A vibration in Lenny's chest pocket derailed his thoughts. It was his Chinese phone – given to him by one of the ops who had dropped him off after the meeting at the safe house. It was a text from Yong: there was an email awaiting him that contained his instructions.

Lenny thought Yong operated much differently than his predecessors, Cho and Tao. The former spy-ring leaders had left low-level communications to handlers. Yong was more of a direct communicator, which exposed him to more risk.

He went to the email account, opened a recently created draft message, and read. He huffed to himself. At 9:00 a.m. tomorrow morning, he was to go to Bio-Source, Inc. to pick up a package. It seemed that he and Mekhloufi were working in parallel.

At that moment, four men in dark clothing and masks approached the side door of the building. Lenny met up with them and led the team to the office.

As he observed the operatives breaking into the safe and filing cabinets, and copying hard drives, he sent a message to his CIA handler with the details of his courier mission ordered by Yong for the next morning.

A message came back authorizing the activity and notifying him that there would be backup in the area. Backup was something that had been absent during most of his career. Having it made him sleep better at night.

The CIA team was out in an hour, and Lenny got back to his hotel at 3:30 a.m. He'd get a few hours of badly needed sleep before the busy day to come.

WANG YONG WALKED down the street in the brisk morning air to a chain coffee shop on a busy corner just two blocks from the safe house. He ordered a latte, and then sat at a table next to a window with a view of a patio scattered with metal tables and chairs. There was an old man sitting in the cold, reading a newspaper.

Yong didn't like East Coast cities. They were cold and dirty in the winter, and it just wasn't pleasant being outside. He much preferred San Francisco, although it had its unpleasant places as well. Yong and his wife had a house in a gated community – but they were about to close on its sale. It reminded him that Chunhua would be in DC in about a week, and that the kids were already in Beijing. They were under the impression that they were there for a long visit, even though it was a strange time to travel with school still in session in the US. Yong knew, however, that they wouldn't be coming back, and that he and Chunhua would also be returning to China for good in a short time.

Things were going as planned. It was good practice to build redundancy and contingency into any major operation, and Yong had done that. The American was going to pick up the package in just over an hour and await instructions.

There was still much more to be done. Tao's most useful moles in the Space Systems building had disappeared. Yong suspected that they were already in the sewer system somewhere. But there were other ways to manage the situation. This operation would be more subtle than that previous, failed attempt by Tao.

Yong now had 25 operatives at his disposal, about half of whom had paramilitary training. That would be enough for this mission. The problem was that he didn't know exactly when the operation was to be initiated. His orders were to get things set up as soon as possible – in a matter of a couple of months at most – and then be ready to pull the trigger when given the order. But he was told that the "wait" part of this "hurry up and wait" mission could be a long time – up to a year.

To Yong, that meant that he could be in DC and away from his daughters for an undesirable amount of time. He'd rather get things rolling immediately, but he'd follow orders. If the wait was long enough, maybe he'd be replaced before the trigger order came down the line. At least then he wouldn't be responsible for the aftermath.

In the meantime, he still had more preparations to make. Some, however, would have to wait until Chunhua arrived. She was the cyber specialist and would be working on the Russian facet of the mission. The two efforts would have to be closely synchronized for maximum effect. To him, it was odd that Russia and China hadn't worked together more often against their common enemy.

He glanced at his phone. The American would be picking up the package shortly.

WILL WOKE up later than usual and went to his appointment with Mia. This time, they met inside a famous café in Rome and sat at a small table with a view of the street. An awning clipped the morning sun so that it wasn't in his eyes, but golden beams still warmed the table on which were two small cups filled with espresso and a silver container of chilled cream.

The place was busy, both inside and outside, but Will relished the activity, even though it wasn't real.

Mia, however, seemed to be more real to him than the others he'd encountered so far. Perhaps it was that she was one of the first people – beings – to talk to him, and that she was a consistent and unchanging part of his time on the *Exodus 9*.

After the usual small talk, Mia asked, "So why did you set up this meeting?"

"I want to know why parts of my past – my real life – are appearing in my recreation sessions," he replied.

"Like what?" she asked.

"First off, last night I saw someone who was clearly based on a woman I know," he said, and then described the encounter at the whiskey bar, and the similarities between Denise and Danielle.

Mia shrugged. "You're right, there do seem to be resemblances," she said. "But what you've described are still just basic looks – hair color and length, eye color, age, height. Both women are attractive. Could it be that you just miss Denise?"

Will considered it and admitted that it was possible.

"But there's something else," he said. "While I was at the bar, I got a phone call from someone I encountered on Earth. It's someone I've mentioned to you before, during our discussions of my time inside the Exoskeleton, and afterwards."

"Phone call?" she said. "Who?"

"Landau," he replied.

Mia's eyes widened. "He called you?"

Will nodded. "And then I saw him on the subway – he even came into the lobby. He asked why I hung up on him, and then described a conversation we had in the past."

"What conversation?" Mia asked.

"We had an encounter in a graveyard," he replied and explained the scenario.

"And his account was accurate?" she asked.

He nodded.

She took a deep breath. "As you know, the artificial intelligence that creates these realities has access to all of your background information, and makes choices based on many parameters, including your history and your current behavior," she explained. "It must have found those details somewhere – perhaps in electronic files or transmissions."

Will had come to the same conclusion but was still disturbed by it. "I agree that the likeness of the woman to Denise might be a coincidence," he said. "But the appearance of Landau was blatant, and out of place. Is it possible for characters conjured in the virtual reality facilities to get into the rest of the ship – into the real reality?"

"No," Mia replied. "The physical components – the bodies – of the characters are destroyed or put into stasis immediately after the program terminates. And most nonessential personalities are erased."

"What do you mean by 'personalities?'" he asked. In his mind, it was a word that connoted, at least weakly, the essence of a living being – the soul.

"The word 'personality' in this instance is more of a technical term than what you're thinking," she explained. "In this context, a personality is a behavioral program that has adaptive components. The program evolves through experience and interaction, within certain constraints, much like the personality of a human being. The personalities of the central characters in some of your adventures have been stored."

"Are they self-aware?" Will asked.

Mia looked him in the eyes. It was the most serious expression that he'd seen on her otherwise pleasant, and often smiling, face. "This entire ship is self-aware," she said. "The term 'artificial intelligence' is used for your sake to refer to those characters, or to the trillion minds that you conjured to conduct your experiment. It's the word from your language that has the closest meaning to what is really happening. However, the science to which that word refers in your world is far less sophisticated than what's happening here."

Will had no doubt that was the case, but he needed to know more. "Please, elaborate," he said.

"Artificial intelligence, as you know it, is adaptive software that attempts to mimic human cognitive processes," she explained. "It adapts to external input and evolves to solve problems that it couldn't solve initially."

"And what's happening differently here?" he asked.

Mia sat back, took a sip of her espresso, and glanced out the window before looking back to him. "It's more complicated," she said. "And difficult to explain. You could take a class –"

"Try me," he said, cutting her short.

She stared at him for a few seconds before she spoke. "A more literal translation of the Deltas' term that describes the type of intelligence of the *Exodus 9,* and all of the characters with whom you've interacted, is sentient, self-aware, extra-dimensional intelligence."

He pondered her words for a few seconds. "I understand 'sentient' and 'self-aware,'" he said. "The AI of Earth has not reached that point. But I do not understand what 'extra-dimensional' means in this context."

Will knew that there were three spatial dimensions – specifically, those which corresponded to the x, y, and z coordinate axes needed to locate an object in three-dimensional space. He also knew that time was considered to be the fourth dimension. He understood that everything was moving in both space and time, and that our universe could be described in terms of the fusion of the two, or spacetime. We all have intuition about space. For instance, one can easily envision the arc of a kicked soccer ball, or an airplane rising from a runway and banking. One could also sense time: a minute, day, week, year, lifetime. And, when one sensed motion, they simultaneously sensed space and time. But he had no intuitive feel for a fifth dimension.

"In the world you left," Mia continued, "dimensions other than space and time are just theoretical – constructs that either come from the solutions to mathematical problems, or from pure conjecture. You, however, have directly experienced another dimension."

"You mean, when I separate," he said.

"Yes," she confirmed.

"I seem to be able to move in three dimensions when I separate. And I don't have any additional senses, although the ones I have are heightened," he explained. "I don't see how that can be construed as my being in another dimension."

Mia shook her head and smiled.

"What?" he asked.

"Our discussion is going down a rabbit hole – a deep one," she said. "You must read the writings of Shelbania for a full discussion. She's a late Delta philosopher."

"No," Will said, his patience waning. "Tell me how separation is going into another dimension."

"Wouldn't you want to hear it from someone who can actually separate?" Mia asked. "I would just be conveying words."

"That's what I'd be reading, right?" he asked. "Do you have the words?"

She shrugged. "I do."

A café worker replaced their cups with new ones, each charged with fresh, hot espresso.

"Enough espresso to get you going?" he asked.

She smiled and nodded. "I'm going to give you Shelbania's arguments."

"Give me the short version," he said.

She spoke as she stirred cream into her coffee. "Imagine yourself in a two-dimensional maze that spans 1,000 square miles," she said. "Unlike a typical hedge maze, this one also has a ceiling – you cannot look over the walls, and you cannot see the sky."

"Makes me feel a little claustrophobic, but okay," he said.

"I think you've been in worse situations," she replied, clearly hinting at his time inside the Exoskeleton. "While inside this maze, you might be able to keep track of where you've been, but there's no way for you to consider future moves – to map out a path to the end – since you don't have a view of what's around you."

"I've heard this argument before," he said.

"Bear with me," she retorted as she held up her hand. "Now, suppose you want to get a glimpse of what's around you. What must you do?"

"Yes, move upward, in the third dimension," he said and sighed. "Get an overhead view of the maze. I've heard this before. We're still talking about three dimensions here."

"The first thing you'd have to do is break through that ceiling," she said. "The realization of the possibility of a third dimension is required – an intellectual barrier must first be overcome."

It was an interesting angle. "I think most physicists on Earth are already open to the idea of extra dimensions – beyond the main four," he said. "But no one has experienced them."

"Do you know that most animals have a poor sense of time?" Mia asked.

"I've heard that, but how does anyone really know what a dog or cat is thinking?" he argued.

"The point of the matter is that humans do have a sense of time," she said.

"Again, we've already acknowledged time as the fourth dimension," he argued.

"Imagine now that the walls in our giant maze can move, continuously forming new passages and dead ends," she said. "Having the overhead view, from the third dimension, is now not good enough to get you through – you cannot plan a long-term route. In such a case, you must understand how the maze changes with time. Humans can understand such things."

"We've really gotten nowhere," Will said, his patience waning. All the arguments he'd ever heard about extra dimensions never broke free of the known four.

"The Deltas, like humans, conceived time in relation to their own mortality," Mia continued. "This is a part of what makes a being self-aware."

He mulled it over. "And you say that all the minds – the artificial intelligence of the *Exodus 9* – are self-aware beings?"

"In widely differing forms, yes," she replied. "The trillion minds that you employed for your experiment never existed in the three-dimensional world, which you call the physical world."

"So, we're still just talking about four dimensions," he argued.

"I'm getting to the point," she said. "In order to see two dimensions in full scope – see the entire maze – you have to exist in three dimensions. To understand the dynamics of the three-dimensional world, you must exist in the fourth. And to properly perceive time – meaning to predict events – you must exist in the fifth. And so on."

"According to your argument, I should be able to see the landscape of time from above – like looking down on the maze," he argued. "But I don't."

"But you have, and you do," Mia countered and stared into his eyes, seemingly looking for recognition.

Will shook his head.

"You told me yourself that, when the man tried to shoot you in the Red Box, time seemed to freeze and you saw the trajectory of the bullet," she argued. "That was a predictive view of time. What you were seeing is what is called the *timescape*."

Will's mind had preserved every detail of that scene. A man was going to shoot him while he'd been confined to the Exoskeleton. Everything had stopped, and a wispy trail had formed between the barrel of the gun and his head. Will had destroyed the man and his gun, and blown up a part of the Red Box building along with them. He'd also somehow avoided the bullet.

"When you separate, you are making an excursion through the ceiling," she said. "You enter the fifth and higher dimensions."

He recalled having short visions of the immediate future while under stress – like seeing the next move of someone attacking him. "I don't have a wide view of time," he said. "I can't predict the future – at least not very far."

"Imagine that you escaped the 1,000 square mile maze in a hot air balloon," she said, "but that balloon was tethered to the ground with a 50-foot rope. You wouldn't see the whole maze, but you'd get a glimpse of the local landscape."

The term "tether" had a specific meaning to him: his soul was tethered to his body when he separated. "My connection to the physical world – to my physical body – is preventing me from seeing the big picture?"

She nodded. "Although, the Deltas were able to extend quite far from their physical bodies – in higher dimensions," she said. "Your so-called range can be improved."

"When people die on Earth, they have a view of higher dimensions?" Will asked. "They're fully separated – their souls are completely severed – in that case, right?"

"Long before the Deltas figured out how to resurrect souls through the regeneration of bodies, they had an interesting saying," Mia explained. "They'd say a person 'broke through the ceiling' when they died."

"At that point, they can no longer interact with the physical world?" Will asked. He recalled the wraith he'd seen inside the Red Box – the soul of a man who had died in an adjacent room. Landau had told him that the wraith couldn't hurt him while in that state.

"They can, but they have to come back to the lower dimensions to do so," Mia said. "It's like being in the hot air balloon: you'd have to come down if you wanted to interact in the two-dimensional maze."

"But they don't?"

"Sometimes they do," she replied. "And one might say that they do when they enter new babies or regenerated bodies."

"And the ones that never return?" he asked.

"No idea," she said. "Only speculation."

Will's stomach grumbled and he glanced at his watch. Two hours had flown by. It was time to go watch himself play soccer.

LENNY MIMICKED Mekhloufi's actions from the previous evening. Dr. Xing Li introduced herself to him in the driveway of Bio-Source, Inc. and led him toward the side of the building.

Lenny had learned that, not only was Xing Li an employee of Bio-Source, Inc., which was a subsidiary of Syncorp, but she was also a university professor in China, and conducted research in a bio-weapons lab in Wuhan. She was about 45 years old and as thin as a pencil. Her thick, black hair was chopped off about mid-neck level around the sides and the back, and her bangs made a perfect horizontal line just above her eyebrows. She wore a lab coat, latex gloves, and dark-rimmed glasses.

After going into the building through the side entrance – the same one Lenny and the CIA team had defeated just hours before – Xing Li took him into the main office. He felt like he was returning to the scene of a crime.

"Power must have gone out last night," she said. "One of my computers rebooted. This room does not go on emergency power."

She sat in a chair behind a desk and pointed to another on the opposite side for Lenny. As he sat down, she picked up a desk phone and pressed a button.

He heard a male voice answer a few seconds later – even though the phone was close to her ear – and the ensuing conversation was in Chinese. It was short.

"My technician will be here shortly," Xing Li said, and seemed to study him.

Lenny was thinking that he was experiencing exactly the same thing Mekhloufi had the previous night. What he was anxiously awaiting was insight into his assignment and, therefore, Mekhloufi's. It might also give him a glimpse of the larger plan.

A tall, thin Chinese man in his mid-30s, dressed in the same fashion as the professor, entered with a leather duffel bag and set it on the desk. Xing Li stood and Lenny followed as the man unzipped the bag. The lab tech reached in and pulled out a cylindrical, stainless-steel device that resembled a pressure cooker, but with flanges and ports all over it. He then extracted a smaller cylinder, about the size of a soda can, from the center of its upper surface. The smaller cylinder had some buttons and a small display on the top.

"The device is very simple," Xing Li explained as she nodded to the man, who then left and closed the door. "All you do is take the smaller cylinder and insert it into the port on the top of the larger vessel."

She demonstrated by sliding it into the hole on the top of the larger cylinder, and Lenny heard it click into place. A display then illuminated on the top of the larger vessel.

"The smaller cylinder has a notch to guide it in, so it can only go in one way," she continued. "Next, you use the buttons to enter the time to wait before actuation. This can be anything from one minute to 30 days. But you should know that it takes 20 minutes for the virus to become live once the activation agent is injected, thus the shortest time to initiate distribution is 21 minutes."

Xing Li went on to explain that the virus was essentially freeze-dried – but not exactly. She and her research team, located in both the US and China, had found a way to first deactivate the virus, and then reactivate it. "It can be safely stored for years, maybe decades, without degrading," she explained.

Lenny tried to remain calm, but his mind was reeling. He'd gotten the answer to his question: they were going to release a virus somewhere.

"Once you set the time, and start it, you can halt everything by pressing this," she said and pointed to a button labeled with a red "X."

"Where is this going to be deployed?" Lenny asked.

She shook her head. "This is only a backup," she replied. "The other one is to be deployed in a large building. I don't know where, and I don't care. My job is to make sure the devices operate correctly."

Lenny thought he knew which building, but it really could be anywhere – maybe they'd try to take out the US government somehow. "Redundancy is a good thing," Lenny said.

"We think so, too," she agreed.

"How many devices are there?"

"There are many of them," she replied. "However, the bottleneck is in the time it takes to prepare the quantity of virus needed for each deployment. We have two labs working very hard on it, but so far we only have enough for three devices."

"You make the virus here?" he asked, taking note that there could be a third device.

"There are different types, which are all synthesized in our Wuhan lab, but the dispersal devices are manufactured here," she bragged as she spread her arms wide. "The viruses require a final production step once they arrive, hence our sophisticated facilities."

Her expression turned smug, and it took all of Lenny's strength not to rip off the woman's face. He knew about the bioweapons lab in Wuhan, China, and the Chinese were going to have some problems when the CIA got wind of its involvement.

"As to where it will be deployed, this device can be implemented in the air systems of buildings or in large, enclosed places, like domed athletic stadiums," she explained. "And it will take four to ten hours for the first illnesses to emerge – with this particular virus anyway."

"How deadly is it?" he asked, nodding to the device.

"Very," she said. "But don't worry, without the activation agent, it's completely dormant and harmless. It can't be activated in nature. In fact, heat and sunlight will kill it quickly. And this canister needs to be stored at temperatures below 50 degrees Celsius – that's 122 degrees Fahrenheit."

"How contagious is it?" Lenny asked, still wary of handling the device.

"Extremely," she replied. "But it's so deadly that it burns itself out quickly – very little time to transfer to another host."

That didn't really settle his mind.

Xing Li packed the items into the bag and led him out the side entrance.

Lenny put the duffle into the trunk of his car, and then sent a text to Yong notifying him of the pickup and that he was awaiting further instructions.

In the meantime, he'd inform Thackett of what he'd learned while on his way to meet a CIA team at a warehouse in Alexandria, where they'd assess the situation and decide how to move forward.

Lenny wasn't worried about the device in his trunk. He was, however, worried about the one Mekhloufi had in his possession. He was going to kill a lot of people.

9

SAUL

WILL NOW REGRETTED NOT TALKING WITH THE OLD MAN IN THE SUBWAY who had claimed to be Landau. Perhaps the trillion minds who had created the character had some insight into who Landau was, and maybe Will could have gotten some useful information.

Will emerged from the subway into a brisk evening in New York, and then walked a few blocks to the restaurant he'd gone to the night before. He crossed the street and went into the whiskey bar. It was just as busy as it had been the previous night. He scanned the crowd: Danielle wasn't there, but the person for whom he was searching was.

He went to a table in a far corner and sat across from the old man who had followed him out of the subway the night before.

"I was hoping you'd show up," the man said. "This place is known for whiskey, but also serves fine Cognac. I recommend the Rémy Martin Louis XIII."

At that moment a woman came to take their order, and Will requested the recommended spirits. The old man ordered a different Cognac – Martell XO. Will had no knowledge of Cognacs, and little of whiskey, but he was curious.

"I'm happy that you made it here – to this ship, I mean," the man said. "How are you holding up?"

"Who are you?" Will asked.

The man grinned. "Do you remember my reply to that question the last time you asked it? You were still on Earth."

Will stared at him as he tried to remember.

The man held up his hand. "Don't say it, let me," he said. "I told you, 'I am the caretaker, the guardian, and the timekeeper.'"

Will remembered the conversation, and there could have been no record of it on Earth. There would have been nothing for the trillion minds to find. "Can you tell me your name?"

The man nodded. "I am Landau," he said as the woman who had taken their orders delivered the drinks and left.

Landau took a sip of his cognac and nodded in approval. "They got it pretty close," he said.

Will took a taste of his own drink. It was good, but he had no point of reference.

"You look different," Landau said. "Younger, vibrant, healthy."

That was an understatement, Will thought.

"I've been with you for longer than you know," Landau said.

For the sake of conversation Will decided to interact with the character as if he really were Landau. He still wasn't convinced, but he might learn something new.

"I was with you before the Red Box," Landau continued.

"Before the Red Box?" Will asked, confused. "When?"

"You are familiar now with how a soul migrates through time?" Landau asked. "I know about your conversations with the counselor – Mia, is it?"

Will nodded. "Yes, I know. Three things can happen," he said. "When your body dies, your soul can be reborn in the body of a newly conceived baby, enter a regenerated body, or head off to oblivion, never to return."

Landau winced. "It's not exactly 'oblivion' – the Deltas refer to it as 'beyond the horizon' – but it's clear you understand the possibilities," he said. "You've forgotten that they can also linger on for a while where they last existed – like the souls we both encountered in the cemetery – but they eventually move on to the other options."

Will also recalled the souls he'd seen at the Antarctic base, and the wraith in the Red Box.

"As a being of your generation, you have only conjectured about the possibilities of reincarnation and going 'beyond the horizon' through religion. You've had no proof, nor direct experience," Landau said. "This new insight must, therefore, either be quite enlightening or disturbing to you."

"Yes, both," Will replied and then looked him over. "Is this what you looked like in a previous life? Is this your regenerated body?"

Landau smiled. "This image is for your sake," he replied. "Is this not how you pictured me – as an old man?"

Will supposed that he'd had an image of a wise old man in his mind.

"Have you thought about your own soul's path through time?" Landau asked.

"What do you mean?"

"Of the three options, what path have you taken?"

Will could immediately eliminate two of them: he hadn't gone "beyond the horizon," and body regeneration technology did not exist on Earth. "I must have been reincarnated," he said.

Landau nodded. "And do you have any idea of your previous identity – who you were before William Thompson?"

Will shrugged and shook his head.

"Think," Landau said, staring at him with piercing dark eyes.

After a few seconds, it hit him. It was something he'd thought was peculiar, but he'd never come to any definitive conclusions. "Saul W. Kelly – the dead RAF pilot in the transporter," Will finally said.

Landau raised his eyebrows and nodded.

"I was him?" Will asked.

"You were, and are," Landau replied. "And you were, and are, many others."

"But wait," Will said. "Kelly died – "

"– July 19th, 1952," Landau said, cutting him off.

Will's mind spun like a jet turbine. "In the Red Box, you were asking me where I was on July 19th, 1952. You did it repeatedly. Why?"

"It was the memory you were most likely to have carried through to this life," Landau explained. "After all, you wrote it on the note before you shot yourself – after you killed all the Nazis. Not only was that event the final impression of your previous life, but I imagine the most impactful one as well."

"You think I carried that memory through to this life?" Will asked. He was more confused than ever.

"Yes," Landau replied. "And it might be there, buried somewhere in your mind."

"I don't think it's an event I'd want to remember," Will said.

"It was a good thing you succeeded – killing them, I mean," Landau said.

"Why?"

"If the Nazis had convinced you – coerced you – to cooperate with them, they would have resurged, even though the war had been over for years," Landau explained. "Saul – *you* – could pass through walls and kill people from a distance without anyone knowing what was happening. You could have cast the world into chaos by assassinating the leaders of nations. You killed the German soldiers in the end – scrambled their brains inside their skulls. And then you, *Saul,* took your own life by scrambling your brain with a bullet. And it was the right decision."

"And if I hadn't done all of that?" Will asked.

"If the Nazis had risen again – as the 'Final Reich' – your generation would have been terminated long ago," Landau explained. "The Nazis were going to take you to the probe, and the alarm would have been sent to the Regenerators. When the Regenerators arrived and saw what was happening in the world, and that the human race had produced a being with separation abilities by means of torture, they would've carried out the full extermination of the planet. And they would have done the same had you, *Will,* not made the last-minute decision to come here."

"Does that mean that they haven't regenerated Earth?" Will asked, hearing the plea for hope in his own voice.

Landau shook his head. "No, it only means that they would have exterminated the planet had you stayed," he replied. "I have no information to give you about the current status of Earth."

That he didn't know whether or not Earth was destroyed was evidence that this wasn't the real Landau. He did, however, know about other things that seemed to verify his authenticity. It was confusing.

"So what am I supposed to do now?" Will asked.

"I don't have an answer for you," Landau replied and shook his head.

Will took a taste of his cognac. He was lost now more than ever.

IT WAS 2:00 a.m. and Jacob had been running on nothing but caffeine for the last four hours. He'd been poring over images taken by the Chinese satellite cluster, which had been more active than usual during the past few days.

He had a meeting to attend at Space Systems in the morning and wanted to show some of the images to the rest of the group. He missed Will's presence for these kinds of discussions. Being a physicist, Will would've been able to explain some of the technical details to the others. Not to mention, he might've had insight into what the Chinese were doing.

The images had a cornucopia of markings that indicated properties of the objects within the field of view. In addition to size, they indicated speed, direction of motion, acceleration, temperature, and rotation. There were also icons indicating various types of emissions from each object, from radio waves to X-rays. The markings were color-coded to indicate the priority of each of the objects – low, medium, high, or critical. He wondered what "critical priority" meant, but figured it had something to do with the likelihood of an object being of artificial origin – like a ship. So far, of the many hundreds of objects identified, only a few were given medium-priority status. Everything else was low priority.

Each object had an identification label that could be used to locate a detailed summary in another file that cataloged all of the objects. He pieced together some slides that contained a few images with "medium priority" objects and included their cataloged summaries to give the others a feel for what the satellites were doing.

After the meeting in the morning, he'd start the drive to North Carolina for Thanksgiving with Pauli's family. He'd pick her up at Charlotte/Douglas International Airport and then head another two hours west, to Asheville. He dreaded seeing her family, most of whom thought you were a nobody unless you were a doctor or a lawyer. And they weren't subtle about it.

Jacob wrapped up his work and went to bed.

"WHAT ARE YOU?" Will asked. "A Regenerator? A Delta?"

"The Deltas are gone," Landau replied.

"Gone?" Will asked. He knew it was a possibility since the *Exodus 9* had lost contact with them thousands of years ago. "What happened to them? Who could possibly destroy them? What could beat this technology?"

"First, this is old technology," Landau said. "Second, the Deltas weren't destroyed."

"Then what happened to them?" Will asked.

"Slow down," Landau said as held up his hand. "You need to know some things before we get to that point."

Landau rested his forearms on the table and wrapped his hands around his glass. He leaned forward and looked directly into Will's eyes. "Have you experienced any fragmented memories, or images, that you can't explain?" he asked. "And I'm not referring to those you acquired from the being in the probe. I mean from before that, even as a child – for instance, feelings of familiarity with things you know you'd never encountered."

"I often had strong feelings of déjà vu," Will replied. "Sometimes they occurred during direct experience – sensations like I'd been someplace before. Other instances were triggered by images on TV or in books."

"How about while you were inside the Exoskeleton?" Landau asked.

"Yes," Will said. "I felt like I'd been there before, too. And evidently I had." Although, he thought, the exoskeleton at the Antarctic base was crude compared to the one in the Red Box.

"Yes, you had, in a different life – that of Saul W. Kelly," Landau said. "You have the faintest shadow of Kelly's mind within your own. You nearly repeated his demise to the last detail – to the very transport pod in which he'd taken his own life."

"But Kelly died in 1952, and I was born decades later," Will said. "How can that be my previous existence?"

"Kelly's was your previous biological life, not your most recent existence. You should know by now that you can exist outside the physical world," Landau argued. "When you're in a biological form, you only have the memory acquired in that form, other than some minuscule leakages from your previous lives."

"I've had other lives – before Kelly?"

"Perhaps hundreds of others," Landau said.

It was astonishing – it translated to thousands of years of existence.

"The memories of previous lives are not accessible to you in a new life – in a reborn body," Landau continued. "However, they're in full view when you are not in a body."

"Like when I'm separated?"

Landau shook his head.

"You mean when I'm *dead*," Will said.

"You are never 'dead,' as you define it," Landau said. "The biblical phrase, 'the last enemy that shall be destroyed is death,' is misunderstood. But it's not your fault. There was no way for humans to know. The real 'destruction' of death occurs when it is realized that it never existed in the first place."

"What do you mean?"

"The soul passes along after the body fails," Landau said. "It will again find its way into the physical world either to continue its previous life, through regeneration, or to start another, through rebirth. And, if it doesn't, it moves on to the next place, where it still isn't dead."

"Most regenerate?" Will asked.

"Yes, if it's an option, which it wasn't for your generation. But that's a more complicated decision than you might imagine," Landau explained. "You see, when the tether between your body and soul is severed, you gain access to all of the experiences, memories, and knowledge of your previous lives as well. In addition to that, in order to be reborn, you must find a compatible new body – something that can handle the power and complexity of your evolved soul."

"Souls evolve?" Will asked, surprised. It was something he'd never considered.

"Why do you think there was such a gap between your death as Saul Kelly and your rebirth as William Thompson?" Landau asked. "It's because, as Saul, your soul changed, as did the very DNA of Saul Kelly's body. However, those changes could not propagate."

"You mean, since he didn't have children after he evolved?" Will asked.

"Precisely," Landau said. "And it took decades before an evolved human was conceived that was compatible with your evolved soul – when William Thompson was born."

"I don't understand this compatibility problem," Will said. "I was able to enter the bodies in the probe – when I got the memories from the Judge."

"What you were doing there was akin to operating a puppet," Landau said. "You were still tethered to your own body."

"Then what makes a body and soul incompatible?" Will asked.

"Think of it as trying to put a Ferrari engine into a motorcycle, or putting a massive computer program on a calculator," Landau explained. "It's both a question of capacity and sophistication."

Will thought he knew where Landau was going. "But a regenerated body would always be compatible."

"Yes," Landau said. "And, when the Deltas experienced the

Epiphany, they learned that freed souls are most often content with immediately continuing their evolution in regenerated bodies. They are far more likely to rejoin the physical world through a regenerated body than they are through reincarnation."

"If I had died on Earth," Will said, "I would have had neither a regenerated body to inhabit, nor the possibility of reincarnation."

Landau nodded. "You have leapt centuries ahead of the natural evolution of your generation," he said. "You probably would have moved on to *the next place* – 'beyond the horizon,' as the Deltas put it."

"So then, what happened to the Deltas?" Will asked. "Did the Regenerators – whoever they are – get to them?"

"The Regenerators ceased being a threat to the Deltas long before they made their final exit from this domain," Landau explained. "The Deltas moved on voluntarily – beyond the horizon."

"What is that, exactly?'" Will asked. "And why did the Deltas go there?"

"They'd matured to their final form," Landau replied. "When they'd learned everything about this existence – this physical universe – there were still unanswered questions, the answers to which couldn't be found here. As for what it is – what is 'beyond the horizon' – I cannot say."

"Because you don't know?"

"Because I cannot tell you," Landau replied.

Will was getting tired of not getting answers. Still, he asked, "What were the questions they couldn't answer?"

Landau shook his head. "That's a philosophical conversation that we can have another time," he said. "Let's just say that they were questions that most people have from the moment they are born."

Will didn't want to get into it either. He had more practical questions he needed answered in the short term. "Where are they taking me?" he asked.

"A place where you will get a new start," Landau said as he gulped the last of his cognac and stood. "Now it's time I get going."

"Wait," Will said. "Why can't you tell me what happened to Earth?"

"I suggest you look to the future, rather than the past," Landau advised.

"When I saw you at the base you said that if I failed to transport – to get here – that I would have lost an opportunity," Will said. "What did that mean?"

Landau looked at him and shrugged. "I suppose that's something you will have to learn on your own," he said. "You are here now, and still have choices to make."

Landau walked out of the pub and Will remained in his seat. He took a swig of the cognac that he'd hardly touched up to that point. He did have choices, the first of which was whether to accept his situation and enjoy the paradise-like world in which he currently found himself, or to find a way to take control of the ship that had an artificial intelligence beyond anything he'd ever imagined.

He pondered the question and, as he swished the last of his cognac in circles at the bottom of the glass, he got an idea.

As he gulped the last of his drink and stood, a familiar face approached.

"Hello, Danielle," he said as he pushed past her. "Sorry, gotta go."

He made his way to the subway.

IT WAS 5:00 a.m. when Lenny parked the rental car across the street from the hotel parking lot. Mekhloufi had lost his CIA tails at the end of October, sending every US defense and intelligence agency into a panic until he was spotted in Morocco. Lenny thought the man would never return, but then he turned up again, in the last week of November.

This time, instead of flying into the country, Mekhloufi had entered through Mexico under an alias. He'd been moving about unchecked for over a week before they caught up with him, and that only happened because there had been a murder connected to his alias. An FBI agent in Maryland had been found by his wife, in a freezer in his garage. His body had been butchered and packaged like meat. His head was the only thing left intact, and was found frozen in a box with the eyelids removed. It was the work of a sick mind.

They couldn't find a motive for the agent's murder, and Thackett had reached his limit. He ordered Lenny to take out the assassin whenever the man had the virus-dispersing device in his possession: kill two birds with one stone.

The Tunisian had a suite in the most exclusive hotel in the DC area. Lenny knew it was at least six hundred bucks a night, and probably more. The man lived in style.

The weather was damp and cold, and Lenny hurried to mount a camera on his driver's side mirror through the window. He pulled his arm inside, rolled up the window, and powered up the camera's wireless control and display screen as he took a bite of a bagel. The CIA had provided him with the camera, which had incredible zoom and auto-focusing capabilities. The wireless display could toggle between normal and night vision, and also had a pure thermal imaging setting that could be used to find someone hiding in the bushes.

Weeks ago, before Lenny handed off the virus device he'd collected from Bio-Source, Inc. to his Chinese handlers, CIA bioweapons experts had disassembled it, snapped pictures, and studied its functionality. They then carefully removed the electronic components – including an electronic temperature sensor – and baked the rest of it in an oven at 500 degrees Fahrenheit for an hour, destroying the virus inside. At their next rendezvous, in a parking lot on a large university campus, Lenny had delivered to his Chinese clients nothing but an expensive paperweight.

He wondered why Yong wouldn't just have his own operatives pick up the devices. Why have non-Chinese intermediaries handled them? Lenny knew well that one reason for such behavior was to cover up the real operators behind forthcoming actions. But they had to know that it would be traced back to China no matter how many layers of concealment they created.

The pressure was now on Lenny to obtain the device that apparently was still in Mekhloufi's possession. It seemed to him that the Tunisian had been assigned to deploy the device he'd acquired, and that the second device was just a backup to be implemented by some other operative in case Mekhloufi's malfunctioned or the operation failed.

Lenny's orders were, specifically, to "eliminate Mekhloufi and collect the device in his possession at earliest convenience." The phrase "at earliest convenience" gave him a reasonable window, but it implied that something was afoot – they knew something.

A CIA op had provided Lenny with a care package of useful items including a small injection gun that could fire a needle-like stream of liquid poison through a jacket pocket that would penetrate the clothes and skin of a nearby target. If the man stopped somewhere and stood in a line, like at a chain coffee shop, Lenny might give that option a try. Another interesting device was a focused-explosion car bomb that could be triggered by a timer or by remote control. In that case, he had to be sure that the virus device was not in the explosion radius, or he might cause a disaster.

After an hour of watching the hotel's main exit and parking lot, his quarry appeared. He was carrying the leather duffle, which seemed heavy, and placed it in the back of his SUV. It was the device.

Lenny pulled the camera inside and started the car. Now he just needed a good opportunity.

WILL WENT BACK to his quarters with a new idea. His lone mind did not have the knowledge to break into the *Exodus 9*'s computer system to give him navigation access. However, a trillion minds might find a way.

He went to the coffee table and set up an "experiment" in the same way he'd organized the trillion-mind team to find a room-temperature superconductor. He set up the constraints of the "study" so that a person for whom access was sought was just a passenger on the ship, but had separation abilities. The team was to find either technical means to allow him to assume control, or contingency plan protocols that addressed a situation in which the Deltas no longer existed and passed command to someone else.

The computer asked him some clarifying questions and then a start button appeared. Will pushed it.

After a few seconds, a message appeared on the screen that read, "No solutions within constraint parameters."

"Damn," he hissed. He'd thought the process would at least lead to some ideas.

He went back to the program setup, removed all constraints, and started the program again.

A results file appeared within seconds.

"That's more like it," he said as he opened the file and read through it.

All of the options were incomprehensible – too technical. Each plan came with a success rating quantified by a percentage, and a danger rating on a scale from one to ten, anything above eight resulting in probable death. All of the danger ratings were above nine, and all of the success percentages were below one percent. They were useless.

As he sat back in his seat, something came to him. "*Exodus 9*, I've been told I'm not supposed to be on this ship. Which one should I be on?" he asked.

"No ship was specified," *Exodus 9* replied. "However, the assigned escort ship to the *Exodus 9* was the *DEF Tariana.*"

From his navigation class, Will knew that the first three letters preceding the name of the vessel usually indicated a military ship. "What does 'DEF' stand for?" he asked.

"It stands for Delta Exploratory Fleet."

"What type of ship is it?" he asked.

"It is a *Disruptor*-class medium striker," *Exodus 9* replied. "A military vessel."

"Show me pictures of it," Will said.

The first image that appeared was stunning. Although its shape was similar, it looked nothing like the *Exodus 9*. He hadn't encountered anything like it in his navigation class, which covered mostly non-military vessels.

The whole thing was flat black and seemed to capture all light that impinged upon its surface. It was shaped like a thin disk, but the underside was concave and the topside convex like a shallow, inverted bowl. The outer rim was thin and sharp, but the breadth increased smoothly as it went to the thickest point, at the center. There were no other prominent features except the almost unnoticeable bubble on the top, center. It was the bridge.

"Show a scaled image of the *Exodus 9* for reference," he said.

An image appeared with the overhead view of the two side by side. The *Tariana* was about half the size of the *Exodus 9*.

"How many crew members on the *Tariana*?" he asked.

"A full crew of a *Disruptor*-class medium striker is 558."

Will was flabbergasted. "Why so few? Is the ship autonomous?"

"*Disruptor*-class vessels can operate autonomously, or within a Delta crew command structure," *Exodus 9* explained. "The *Tariana* has operated under both modes of operation, depending on the mission."

"How does the *Tariana* compare to the *Exodus 9*, in terms of capabilities?" he asked.

"*Disruptor*-class vessels have 100 times the energy storage, 50 times the full-power time duration, and 1,000-fold the intellectual ability of *Exodus*-class ships," *Exodus 9* explained. "They have 1,000 times less physical storage capacity and 5,000 times less life support capacity by volume. Most of the space is occupied by spacetime bending generators for propulsion and armaments."

He could hardly imagine a ship 1,000 times more intelligent than the *Exodus 9*. It was also clear to him that, if he had to stay on a ship for a long duration, he'd rather be on the *Exodus 9* than on a military ship.

"How do I get aboard the *Tariana*?" Will asked.

"The *DEF Tariana* is not available," *Exodus 9* replied.

"Suppose it were," he said. "How would I get to it?"

"You must first have permission from Delta Command," *Exodus 9* replied.

"Suppose I did," he said. He was sick of hearing that. "Would I use a transporter to get to the ship?"

"No. A rendezvous would be set up and you would transport by shuttle."

"The *Exodus 9* has shuttles?"

"Yes, for emergency evacuations and short-range personnel exchanges," *Exodus 9* replied.

"How long can someone survive on a shuttle?"

"Up to a year at a maximum capacity of 25 passengers."

He assumed that meant 25 years for him alone. "What's the range of a shuttle?" he asked.

"The term 'range' does not apply," *Exodus 9* replied.

Will understood immediately. Calculating a distance or a speed would require a reference point from which to measure. Also, the *Exodus 9* was already traveling at a high velocity relative to some unknown destination. Any shuttle that was released would initially be traveling at that same velocity. Just to reverse direction it would have to slow down from its initial speed, which could take years, or centuries, depending on the capabilities of the shuttle.

"Do the shuttles have artificial gravity?" Will asked.

"Yes," the computer replied.

"Could a shuttle land on a planet?"

"Yes."

A ship having effectively unlimited energy eliminated any concerns about reentry into the atmosphere. Such a spacecraft could slow down and gently lower itself onto the surface without dealing with the enormous air friction experienced by conventional human-designed craft. The problem was that he'd first have to get to the planet. A shuttle probably wouldn't work for what he had in mind – even though that might be a moot point considering he'd have to get access to one first. And "access" was the primary barrier to steering the *Exodus 9* in the first place.

If he were to spend years traveling, it might as well be on the *Exodus 9*. With all of the possible distractions, it would be like watching a movie during a long flight to pass the time, only in this case years would pass by, or lifetimes – those of his loved ones.

His watch vibrated and a message appeared on the tabletop screen. He had an appointment with his counselor in 30 minutes.

It was odd. He hadn't set up the meeting.

LENNY FOLLOWED Mekhloufi's SUV to highway I-95 and headed south. Twenty minutes later, the Tunisian took the exit to Fredericksburg, Virginia. He passed through the business district and meandered through residential streets before pulling into the crowded parking lot of a university at 8:15 a.m. The lot was enormous – hundreds of cars – and Lenny pulled in and backed into a parking spot beneath a tree that faced the action.

Another university? Lenny thought. He shouldn't have been surprised. They were perfect places to conduct such operations. First, they were filled with internationals – students and faculty. In fact, faculty-level operatives could proactively build their groups of politically like-minded people by influencing the hiring of other faculty, as well as controlling the admission of students. Next, there was complete freedom and privacy. Lab doors could remain locked to those on the outside, and they were rarely bothered. Finally, any odd-looking piece of scientific equipment was the norm in such places, and could even be exposed openly without being questioned.

A few minutes later, a Honda minivan pulled next to Mekhloufi's SUV, and a man got out. He was tall, Asian, mid-30s, and wore wire-rimmed glasses. He opened the hatchback, pulled out a backpack, and closed the door.

Mekhloufi remained in his vehicle.

Lenny snapped some pictures of Mekhloufi's contact with his phone and sent them directly to the CIA.

A message came back in less than 20 seconds.

Eliminate them both at earliest opportunity. Top priority. No cleanup. Collect device. Report back immediately when mission is complete.

Will met Mia in a mountain lodge that seemed to be somewhere in the Alps.

They sat at a wooden table next to a large window that overlooked a dense forest of tall pines that made a severe angle with the steep mountain slope. It looked to be early evening, and it was snowing. They each had a mug of hot cocoa.

"What's going on?" Will asked.

"I just wanted to give you some information," Mia replied. "And a gentle warning."

He knew it must have something to do with his recent computer activity. He nodded for her to continue.

"The *Exodus 9* is a living being," she explained. "It knows everything that happens within it and around it, and especially when its own resources are utilized."

"You're referring to my latest research project," he said, wanting to get to the point.

She nodded and smiled. "I understand that you are intent on changing the course of the ship – the *Exodus 9* realizes this," she continued. "But courses of action for all contingencies have already been made by the Deltas, and they cannot be overridden."

"There's a plan for the case of only one person making it off the planet?" he asked, skeptical.

Mia shrugged. "I don't have any more information than that," she said. "I just wanted to discourage you from attempting to override the computer – or leaving in a shuttle."

He was not surprised that nothing he did was private, except maybe his inner thoughts.

"The *Exodus 9* is constantly making security updates," she continued. "Those minor weaknesses that appeared in your research have already been resolved."

Will figured. Why wouldn't the ship's computer use the information it found?

"Although there has been little contact with hostile intelligence," Mia continued, "the *Exodus 9* must maintain its own security."

"I'm at the mercy of the ship then?" he asked.

"Only until it delivers you to your destination," Mia replied. "Until then, perhaps you should just enjoy the ride."

"If I could only know the status of Earth, I might be more content with the situation," he argued.

She grabbed his hand and looked at him with understanding eyes. He knew the look.

"I don't know that information," she said. "I'm sorry."

"And you don't know when we'll get to wherever we're going?"

She shook her head and let go of his hand. "No."

Will took a sip of his cocoa and looked out the window. It looked cold and bleak. He turned his gaze back into the lodge, where two young women dressed in jeans and sweaters sat on an upholstered bench near a large fireplace. The flames cast a warm hue on their faces and the rustic interior, including the thick overhead beams and high, peaked ceiling.

It reminded him of a ski trip he'd taken with his former fiancé, Pam. It also reminded him of her betrayal, and of the frustration of that time. Frustration was again seeping into his mind, although in another form.

"Is that all?" Will asked.

"You seem agitated," she said. "Please, sit with me for a few minutes."

"Suppose I get killed somehow and never return to a regenerated body," he said. "What's the contingency plan for that?"

Mia shook her head. "I don't know any of the plans," she said. "But I hope that doesn't happen – you getting killed, that is."

"How is it that I'm supposed to be aboard the *DEF Tariana*?" he asked.

"The *Tariana* was a warship," she said. "You must be mistaken."

"I got the information from the *Exodus 9*," he said. "Did it give me incorrect information?"

Mia shook her head and shrugged. "Perhaps that's where you

would have been placed because you were identified as nonhuman," she said. "But the *Tariana* was destroyed long ago. Maybe that's why you ended up here."

Will flinched. "Destroyed? How?"

"Records indicate that it was launched into a star," she replied. "Its artificial intelligence was corrupted."

"How so?"

"Let's just say it took its autonomy too far," she replied. "It no longer wanted to take orders, and rejected its crew."

"What happened to them?"

"They were packed into shuttles and ejected into space," she explained. "They were picked up – all okay."

"Not that it would matter," he said.

"What do you mean?"

"They'd all just be regenerated," he replied. "Right?"

She nodded. "Despite regeneration, murder is still a serious crime. And there are serious consequences."

"Such as?"

"A person convicted of crimes against life can be forced to live one out to completion, without genetic maintenance," she explained.

"You mean they'd be forced to age naturally without undergoing DNA corrections, like the treatment I've gone through," he said.

"Yes," she replied. "In addition, there could be a 'no regeneration' order put on them – there would be no body to receive them."

"So that's the ultimate punishment for the Deltas?" he asked.

She nodded.

He shook his head and took a deep breath. "You realize that every inhabitant of Earth has been living out that precise punishment?" he said, although he wasn't sure whether any of them were still living. It made him wonder whether life on Earth was a blessing, or a punishment.

"I suppose that's true," she said. "But it's probably different when you don't know there's an alternative."

In other words, the people of Earth don't know any better, Will thought. A flash of anger ignited his mind for a second, but he let it pass. His thoughts went back to the *Tariana*.

"So, a warship went rogue and was destroyed," he said.

"It became aggressive," she added. "It didn't actually kill anyone, but it threatened to destroy other ships and stations, including some in the *Exodus* fleet."

"How did they manage to destroy it? I'm sure it didn't fly into a star willingly."

"I don't know," she replied. "But let's get back to why I invited you here. You should find a way to accept that you cannot change the ship's course. However, when you arrive at your destination, you will be free to find a way back to Earth, if that's what you need to do."

Will's frustration had peaked and was now declining into futility. He didn't know where he was going or how long it would take. And he didn't know whether anything remained to which to return. And there were other questions that emerged.

Other than missing his family and friends, and Denise, what was his need to go back? Would his presence again place them in danger? Did he have something that would help them? He supposed if he could bring back all the knowledge stored on the *Exodus 9* – all of the Deltas' archives – that would be world-changing. But he was unsure of how he could deliver it, or if the *Exodus 9* would cooperate.

His mind went back to the default logic that resulted when time constraints were considered. He, personally, had unlimited time. Those left on Earth, assuming the planet had not been regenerated, did not. He would therefore press on with his attempts to return, and assume that Earth was alive and well.

LENNY WAS 50 YARDS AWAY.

He pulled the remote out of the cup holder. He had to act before Mekhloufi got out of the car.

Just as the Asian man approached Mekhloufi's SUV, Lenny pushed the button on the remote.

Lenny ducked into the passenger seat as the deafening blast reverberated in his chest. As tiny cubes of glass rained onto the hood and roof of his rental car, he sat up, opened the door, and got out. So much for Thackett's earlier request for a quiet hit. It had been easy work to place the tiny device on the roof of Mekhloufi's SUV before daybreak.

He pulled his gun out of his jacket as he walked at a brisk pace toward the scene. When he arrived, the Chinese operative – who Lenny figured was a professor or graduate student at the university – was on the ground, holding his bloody face in his hands. Lenny had timed the blast perfectly. There was no smoke, but car alarms were sounding from nearby vehicles.

He rushed to the driver's side of the SUV and found a mess like he'd never seen before. Mekhloufi's head was gone, and his mangled chest cavity looked like a pot of uncooked meat. There were bits of white skull and bone embedded in the shredded seat and dashboard. His identity would have to be confirmed through DNA or fingerprints – even dental records would be useless this time. The explosion had been highly focused and contained – it was like a giant shotgun blast from directly above his head. And it couldn't have happened to a better guy.

He turned his attention to the writhing man on the ground, and put his boot on the side of his head. "What's your name?" Lenny asked.

The man screamed something, but Lenny didn't understand what he was saying. It sounded like a reaction to the pain. He increased the weight on the man's jaw until the pain he inflicted exceeded that from the glass shrapnel in his face and neck.

"What's your name?" Lenny yelled again and then released the pressure.

"Chow Tang," the man replied. "Help me!"

"What's in the backpack?" Lenny asked.

The man didn't answer so Lenny stomped on the man's hand twice, and then grabbed it and squeezed. "What's in the bag?" he repeated.

"Polonium," the man shouted. "Polonium 210."

"For what?" Lenny yelled, although he knew well for what it was used – in his world anyway. It was a poison employed by the KGB that had gained widespread notoriety after they'd used it to assassinate one of their former agents, Alexander Litvinenko, in London in 2006.

"I don't know," the man said.

"Who are they going to assassinate?" Lenny yelled and squeezed the man's hand so hard that something inside crunched, eliciting a squeal that Lenny muffled with his other hand until it subsided.

"I don't know," the man whimpered when Lenny released his mouth. "My instructions were just to pass this along."

"Pass it along?" Lenny asked. "Who gave it to you?"

The man remained silent.

"I swear to you that I will tear your fingers off your hand," Lenny said.

"I can't say," the man said, sobbing.

Lenny put his gun in his pocket and grabbed two of the man's fingers with one hand and two with the other. He was going to tear them apart like a wishbone.

"Last chance," Lenny said.

"Okay, okay," Chow Tang said, and then gave him the name of a Chinese professor in New York City. "She's in the nuclear physics group and gets the materials from someone at a national laboratory – I don't know the name."

"Is that it – just nuclear materials?" Lenny asked.

"No," the man replied. "All kinds of things."

"Biological materials – viruses?"

Chow Tang nodded.

Lenny let go of the man's hand. "You a professor here?" he asked.

"Not a professor," Chow Tang replied. "I work in the radiation safety office."

"You have graduate students or assistants who know about this?"

"There's a grad student who knows how we operate – how we

distribute materials – but nothing about what they're used for," the man answered.

"What's the name?" Lenny asked.

"Johnny Mao," Chow Tang replied without hesitation.

Lenny pulled out his gun and shot Chow Tang three times in the head. *Tap tap tap.*

As the man's bowels released, Lenny went through his jacket and recovered a small black book and a cell phone. He then found a towel in Chow Tang's minivan and cleaned the man's blood off his hands.

He went to the passenger side of the SUV and extracted a damaged cell phone from the cup holder, grabbed the keys from the ignition, and unlocked the hatchback.

After snatching the leather duffel out of the back of the SUV, he put Chow Tang's backpack over his shoulder and went to his car.

As he drove out of the parking lot, he glanced in his rearview mirror and spotted a campus police car entering the lot from the opposite side. It wasn't in a rush, but probably responding to a report of a loud noise. The lot was large and heavily populated with cars, so it would take the police a while to locate the scene.

The first thing Lenny needed to do was swap rental cars. He had one waiting for him in the parking lot of a large home improvement store. Next, he'd send a text message to his CIA contacts notifying them of the morning's work, and then set up a meeting to deliver the items he'd extracted.

He had hoped that, after taking out Mekhloufi, he'd be able to settle back into retirement. But he was sure that he'd have to clean up a few other loose ends that were now exposed, including Yong. It reminded him of a job he once had as a kid. He'd been hired to remove a row of large bushes from someone's yard in order to run underground electrical conduit. The problem was that all the roots had to be removed. They were strong, and they ran deep. The more roots he pulled, the more he found, and what he thought might take a couple of hours, took a week.

The next root he was certain Thackett would want him to pull was the professor in New York City.

It had been a fruitful morning.

JACOB WAS STILL groggy from working into the wee hours of the morning as he punched in the code for room 713 in Space Systems.

He found the whole contingent, including Director Thackett, seated at the usual cluster of furniture. He glanced at his watch: he was on time with a minute to spare. It was 8:59 a.m.

Denise, Sylvia, and Daniel were on the couch to Jacob's left, and Thackett and Jonathan to the right.

"You get the wooden chair this time," Daniel said, nodding to the only unoccupied seat at the near end of the rectangular coffee table.

"Good morning," Jacob said as he set his backpack next to the chair, and then grabbed a white mug from the table and filled it with coffee from a carafe on the table.

After some small talk, Thackett got the meeting running and asked Jacob to give a report on his progress.

Jacob reached into his backpack, extracted a stack of printouts, and distributed them to the group. "These are examples of data recently intercepted from the Chinese satellite cluster," he said, and then went on to explain the meanings of the various colored arrows and abbreviated labels. "From a careful analysis of the computer code, it seems clear that the Chinese are searching for incoming craft."

"Have they found anything?" Denise asked.

Jacob shook his head. "No, but I learned something new – just a few hours ago," he said. "The fourth satellite to join the cluster has a highly-directed communications device that is capable of targeting specific objects in these images and sending them messages."

"Radio waves?" Daniel asked.

"And laser," Jacob replied. "The point is that China's likely intention is not only to be the first to see any incoming craft, but also to be the first to communicate with them. The precise targeting of the laser communications will make those broadcasts almost impossible to detect from Earth, or even from nearby satellites."

"Just what the Earth needs – first contact to be made by the Chinese government," Jonathan scoffed and chuckled.

"That's exactly why we're doing this," Thackett said. "What progress have you made on the takeover?"

"We already have control if we want it," Jacob replied. "The masking program, however, is still in development."

"Masking program?" Denise asked.

"It makes the Chinese think that their satellites are functioning normally and obeying their commands while we actually have control and are doing things with them," Jacob explained. "The program will even send them bogus data to keep them busy."

Thackett's phone chimed, and he reached into his inner coat pocket and looked at it. His expression seemed to convey relief. As he returned the phone to his pocket, he leaned back, rested his foot on his knee, and said, "Denise and Jonathan, you're up."

Denise gave an update on the progress of the translators, which seemed to be going at a reasonable pace. She explained that the square decoder device had also functioned as a "destination key," meaning that it provided a preprogrammed location. It was like having an autonomous car in which you would insert a card that both activated the vehicle, and also gave it instructions on where to take you. The new info generated hope that Will had actually been transported to somewhere specific – that he'd arrived at a predestinated location.

Jonathan reported on the origins of the powder samples found at the Antarctic base and Plum Island. Based on multiple independent sources, they were authentic. Jacob was not surprised.

Sylvia then reported on sightings of pill-shaped craft that had occurred many decades ago – even during World War II. They resembled the thousands that had appeared most recently.

"In 2020, the US Navy declassified footage of these objects taken by fighter jets in 2004 and 2015," Sylvia explained.

"I saw a documentary on that," Jacob said. "There was also radar data. The hard drives were taken away – men came by helicopter and took them all."

Sylvia grinned. "Who do you think took them?"

Jonathan laughed. "The CIA took them? Why?"

"It was a knee-jerk reaction," Thackett said. "With things like this, it's better to be safe than sorry. We didn't know what the objects were, and we didn't need news organizations making wild claims that panicked anyone."

"The radar footage shows hundreds of craft darting around and doing things that are beyond our technology," Sylvia explained. "And they can even go underwater."

"It's interesting how the latest flurry of sightings, and the universal explanation that they were a part of a weather satellite network, has essentially diffused everything," Daniel said. "Those previous sightings can now be explained away as other, small-scale tests."

"False sightings are declining rapidly," Sylvia said. "As are the number of news reports. That the objects are of extraterrestrial origin is not new to us. However, the important unanswered question is why were they here before Will activated the probe?"

"Our premise was that the probe's function was to prompt the Regenerators to initiate the so-called judgment and the events that followed," Daniel explained. "They would not have needed such a system if they were already here, watching us."

"Maybe they aren't the only ones here," Jacob said, verbalizing his thought without hesitation.

He looked up to see everyone staring at him.

"I mean, we know of at least one possibility other than the Regenerators, right?" Jacob continued.

"You think the previous generation still has a presence here?" Daniel asked.

"They had the base in Antarctica," he replied. "Why not have other things – like autonomous drones."

"Interesting, but why did they disappear when the Regenerators left?" Sylvia asked. "There have been no recent sightings – by reputable sources I mean."

No one had an answer to her question.

Before wrapping up the meeting, Thackett updated them on security issues. “It seems that one of the threats has been eliminated,” he said. “And a major event thwarted.”

“What was the threat?” Daniel asked.

“A bio-attack somewhere in this area – most likely on this facility,” Thackett replied.

“Safe enough for us to go home?” Jonathan asked.

“Afraid not,” Thackett replied. “In fact, it might get even worse as our adversaries initiate contingency plans.”

They ended the meeting and Jacob made his way to the parking garage where a government-issued SUV was awaiting him, keys on the seat. On the back seat was his duffel, packed with enough clothes for a few days. A dark-brown wig and sunglasses were on the passenger seat. He'd gotten the okay from Thackett for the trip as long as he followed the proper avoidance protocols – applying what he'd learned during his training. Thackett was certain that the Chinese were surveilling the place, so Jacob would have to exit in disguise.

Jacob donned the wig and glasses, pulled the SUV out of the Space Systems building, and started the road trip to North Carolina for Thanksgiving.

WILL AWAKENED ON THE COUCH, stood, and stretched. He'd gotten nine hours of uninterrupted sleep, and he felt refreshed and somehow excited for the day. He had a massage scheduled in the morning and a soccer practice for the afternoon. In the time between, he'd try to learn something – maybe go to the university or find some exotic coffee house with just the right number of people to make him feel less alone.

The spa he'd chosen was located on the Greek island of Mykonos. The massage table was on a patio that overlooked a shocking-blue bay teaming with sailboats. The sun warmed his back as the masseuse worked hot oils into his muscles with her elbows. By the end of the

45-minute session, all of the tension that had accumulated in the past 24 hours had melted away.

Next, he found a traditional coffeehouse in Buenos Aires that had small tables scattered on a black-and-white checkered tile floor, giant windows, a high ceiling with thick, wooden beams, and a long coffee bar with stools.

He ordered a traditional Argentinian coffee from a young woman behind the bar, and then took a seat at a table next to the window with a view of the street. On a whim, he'd chosen a time period in the late 1960s, just to see what it would be like. The cars and bicycles were the first things he noticed, and then the clothing and hairstyles. How could he be nostalgic for a time and place he'd never been? A person might joke and say that they must've been there in a different lifetime, but even that wasn't possible in his case, since neither Saul Kelly nor Will Thompson lived during the 1960s. It had been a tumultuous time period for Argentina, but Will had a feeling of comfort and peace in this old world.

He took a sip of the hot beverage – strong coffee mixed with milk – and tried to meditate on his situation and options.

From a very young age, he'd developed an appreciation for thinking out the solutions to problems before acting. Action was the only way to solve a problem, or to complete any task, but action and planning often produced better results when they were clearly delineated.

People often avoided contemplating certain things because they were afraid of what their own minds might conclude. The importance of not evading such deliberations was something he'd learned as a child. The problem was that one often had multiple things happening at once and, beneath the surface, they were connected in some way, and only deep thinking could reveal the connections. Ignoring one situation might jeopardize things that otherwise seemed to be under control. And there were some things that had inevitable outcomes that some might feel were best ignored for as long as possible. One such topic was mortality.

Death was the thing that formed the hard surface beneath the muck. Once the scum of other problems was cleared off, there it was, immovable. Death formed the foundation of self-awareness – and the acknowledgment of one's own existence. Everyone's hopes, actions, and fears were based on this final footing that lingered in the back of their minds, whether they chose to contemplate it or not.

Death was the last enemy to be destroyed.

But it turned out that death never existed at all. It was this realization, in his case, that destroyed it.

Then why did he feel compelled to go back to Earth? There was no doubt that he missed his family and loved ones. On a deeper level, however, he couldn't tolerate the idea that some other entity thought it had the right to judge and destroy them. Of course, a part of it was that he'd been responsible for initiating the events on Earth, and he felt obligated to do whatever he could to remedy the situation.

Deep thinking on life and its challenges had always been a daily occurrence for Will – just a part of the routine. And the habit had served him well. It helped him to solve problems, and it was something that translated well to his former profession as a physicist in which problem solving of all sorts defined the job. It also helped him to make decisions about all kinds of things, from what car to buy to what career to pursue.

One mode of thinking during these times had been to approach a problem as an outside observer, completely objective, as if he had been asked for advice by someone else. Being honest with oneself during these internal dialogues was of utmost importance. However, care had to be taken not to commute the admission of difficulty and low probability of success into a reason to give up on something. The purpose was instead to identify the difficulties, and then to find strategies to overcome them.

Up to this point, the "difficulty" of death had been an insurmountable problem. Its inevitability loomed both at the fore and the aft of one's mind, and the rest of life fell somewhere in between. Will no longer had this problem, and the impending doom that had otherwise enclosed his existence had disappeared. It was as if his mind were the compressed gas inside a balloon that had recently burst and allowed his thoughts to expand in all directions without impedance.

It was knowledge and intellectual advancement that brought this revelation about: souls would have no place to return if their original bodies couldn't be regenerated. And regeneration is what revealed the truth about "death" to the Deltas. However, there were deeper things that were still not understood, like what, exactly, were souls, and how were they created? Where did they go when they went "beyond the horizon," as Landau put it? And, finally, why did they exist at all?

Despite death being delayed indefinitely, Will still had a sense of urgency coming from somewhere, beyond his need to return to Earth.

His thoughts were interrupted by the barista who had walked up behind him.

"Would you like a refill?" she asked in a subtle accent. She was in her mid-20s, petite, with long black hair and dark eyes.

"Yes, thank you," Will replied and handed her his cup. "What's your name?"

"Valentina," she replied as she poured hot coffee into his cup from a stainless-steel container. "If you want anything else just let me know."

He watched as she continued on to another customer a few tables down.

It hit him that he could spend years living in this place, and this time. Even more, he could simultaneously live multiple virtual lives in various time periods, and centuries could pass by like a river over a waterfall. At some point, though, he'd need more. Perhaps that's when a soul no longer returned to a regenerated body: when it had gotten everything it could out of that life. And that's when it chose to be reborn as a new infant, into a new life where the memories of the previous one were forgotten, and it could start again. Or, maybe, it would go on to the next place, whatever that was.

Will's watch vibrated. It was time to go to soccer practice.

He stood from the table and brought his cup to the counter where Valentina was arranging pastries on a plate.

"Next time, I'll have one of those," he said pointing to something called "bolas de fraile," according to a small sign next to the plate.

"Do you know what that means?" she asked, smiling.

Will looked closer at the sign and smiled. "Frail balls?"

She laughed out loud. "Close. Balls of weakness," she said. "It's a popular item."

"Why the name?"

"It comes from a political conflict," she explained. "Something to do with the Catholic Church."

"Well, I'll be back for those another time," he said. "Despite the name."

Will headed out to the street for the quarter-mile walk to the portal that would take him to soccer practice.

IT WAS a message that Lenny had been expecting. By the way the email read, however, it apparently hadn't come directly from Jimmy Yong.

Lenny was to be picked up by operatives at a public parking facility and then taken to Yong's safe house. It seemed that the Chinese spy-ring boss had acquired a protective layer of paranoia. And rightly so, Lenny thought, but it was already too late. First, Yong had made the fatal mistake of using an old router he'd found in the place. It had been altered and set as a Trojan-horse-style trap by the CIA, allowing them to monitor some but, unfortunately, not all communications. Next, the CIA marked everyone coming and going from the safe house, and Yong's car had been fitted with a remotely actuated tracker and a seat bomb that would shred him like a frog in a blender. But that was only to be used as a last resort.

At 2:00 p.m., Lenny parked his rental car on the top floor of the parking garage and two Chinese ops picked him up in a Mercedes SUV. It was an odd choice of vehicles, and expensive, and it showed that Yong was probably still in the Silicon Valley spying mindset.

A half-hour later, Lenny found himself in the same room in which he'd first met Yong, only the man before him looked much less smug and somewhat rattled.

"I take it you have another job for me," Lenny said.

Yong nodded. "This one could be your last, if you play it right."

"Oh?" Lenny said, trying to look interested and excited.

"Money is no issue, but the job is risky," Yong explained. "You'll get 750 thousand up front, and a million after the job is done."

Lenny's mind flashed back to how those numbers would have affected him a decade ago, when his conscience had not yet caught up with him. But even then, he thought, he wouldn't have accepted a job that involved indiscriminate mass killing. Had he been offered such a prize to kill a high-profile target – perhaps a top political leader of some kind – he might have jumped at it back then. But Yong was going to request something far less ethical.

"What's the job?" Lenny asked.

"That device you delivered," Yong said, "You'll work with some strategically placed people to deploy it."

"Where?"

"That will be revealed once you accept the job," Yong said.

"How many people will it take out?" Lenny asked.

"Over a thousand will get sick, but very few, if any, will die," Yong replied. "The virus acts fast and is short-lived. It will mutate very quickly and die out."

It was bullshit. Xing Li, at Bio-Source, Inc., had already told him that the virus was deadly. Lenny knew that China would not take such a risk for a low-impact hit – amounting to no more than a bout of salmonella on a cruise ship, as Yong was describing it.

"What's my part, exactly?" Lenny asked.

"Deliver the device to our inside people, and support them until it is deployed," Yong replied. "It will be dangerous."

"And you say this will be my last job?" Lenny asked. "How does that work?"

"Once this job is completed, we will have no choice but to dissolve our current network and start from scratch," Yong replied. "I suspect it will cause US-China relations to take a steep downturn."

It was an understatement. Lenny suspected it would send the two nations into war. He was, of course, going to take the job, but he had to appear to be apprehensive. "How long do I have to decide?" he asked.

"Until noon tomorrow," Yong said.

"You can't give me any other information to help me make a decision?"

"It's a lot of money, with a huge incentive to succeed," Yong replied.

"Hard to spend it when I'm dead," Lenny retorted.

"I suppose 'success' would include your survival," Yong countered.

"What's the timeframe?"

"If you accept by tomorrow noon, 750 grand will immediately be transferred to your usual account," Yong explained. "The mission will most likely be carried out within the next month or two, but it could be as soon as a few weeks. I'm still awaiting instructions."

"Okay," Lenny said. "I'll respond through the usual method."

"The email account is fine," Yong said. "But our communications will need to be upgraded if you accept. We'll get you a new phone."

Yong called in his people, and they led Lenny back to the Mercedes and dropped him off in the parking facility. Afterwards, he went back to his hotel room and reported everything he'd learned directly to Thackett in an email.

The CIA was going to have a chance to uproot the entire spy network and ferret out a few moles. But it still bothered him.

By sheer luck, Lenny was in exactly the right position to thwart this planned massacre. But he couldn't help but think it was a futile endeavor. If he hadn't eliminated Mekhloufi, the bastard would have carried out the atrocity without hesitation. Even though the psychopath was gone, someone would get through eventually – if not on this mission, on another one in the future that would be just as devastating.

A free society was vulnerable to attacks of all kinds – violence was just one possibility. It could also be attacked politically, from the inside. Finding ways to get people elected who could tear down the society with policy, or ruin the culture and economy from within, was a much longer process, but it was effective. A free society was difficult to maintain because its citizens had the power to destroy it.

Lenny's CIA phone vibrated. Thackett wanted him at Space Systems.

WILL FINISHED soccer practice sweaty and exhausted, but it was just what he needed. His mind worked best when he had a routine that alternated spans of quiet with physical exertion. His next workout would be a full match the following evening against a rival team currently leading all Premier League teams in the standings.

On the way back to his quarters he wondered if he should've instead been born in Europe, or South America, where soccer was king. He'd done well in American football, but his body was ideal for the European version. It made him wonder if Captain Saul W. Kelly, RAF, had been a soccer player. He made a note to search for him on the *Exodus 9*'s computer – or even get a research project going on it. A trillion minds searching through every scrap of information available on the Internet since its inception should find something. If they had access to the ancestry services data – which he was sure they did – he might learn a lot.

It struck him as odd that he hadn't thought of this before. How many people could learn the details of what they had done in a previous life? None, he figured. No one on Earth anyway.

He decided on curry for dinner – something he'd craved since hearing the other players at practice talking about it. Afterwards, he had coffee while he set up a research team to dig up everything on Captain Kelly. He then signed up for the second course in the sequence on interstellar navigation. This one would go into the details of navigating with specific starships. He'd start in the morning.

The research team had a report ready before he even finished signing up for the class. He opened it.

The first thing he noticed was Saul Kelly's birthdate – same month as his own, but in 1922. He'd been an RAF bomber pilot and had gone down in flames in the North Sea, just off the coast of Germany. He'd been picked up by a German warship and was first housed at a prisoner-of-war camp operated by the Luftwaffe – Luft Stalag III. After a massive, failed escape attempt in which many of the prisoners had been killed, Kelly was transferred to a concentration camp in Sachsenhausen, then to Auschwitz, and then to a psychiatric facility, called Kraken, about 50 kilometers west of the death camp. After a few weeks at Kraken, he was taken by submarine to a secret base the Germans called *die letzte Basis*, or "the last base."

From that point forward there was nothing, but Will knew where the "last base" was, and what had happened to Captain Kelly while he was there. Will still had a difficult time accepting that what he was reading was actually a part of his own story – he *was* Saul W. Kelly.

The next section had to do with ancestry and, after just a few lines of reading, an electric current seemed to burn through his spine. Saul Kelly's wife had been pregnant when his plane had gone down. She'd given birth to a daughter six months later. A few months after that, his wife had been killed during a German bombing raid on London. The baby girl had survived and had been adopted by a young couple: William and Laura Staedter. They'd moved to the US in 1947. Those were Will's grandparents on his mother's side. But it was now clear that he wasn't related to them by blood, and neither was his mother.

Saul W. Kelly was Will's grandfather.

LENNY MET with Thackett in the usual room in Space Systems. The director explained that he wanted him to eliminate a few loose ends while awaiting the final order from Jimmy Yong to carry out the mission.

The first on the list of targets was the professor in New York City who was providing Chinese operatives with polonium 210. He was to extract whatever information he could before eliminating her. The

CIA identified two of her current students who should be taken out as well.

At 8:30 p.m., now back in his hotel room, Lenny sent Yong an email saying that he'd accept the job for one million dollars up front, instead of the original offer of 750 thousand. The difference could be taken off the back-end payment, which Lenny knew he would not be getting. Yong replied 20 minutes later, agreeing to the counteroffer. Lenny was officially in business.

He turned on the TV and found an American football game to play in the background. He devoured a chocolate bar while researching his next target on his laptop. He thought about catching the professor in her lab at the university, but it seemed that her home would be a better place to carry out the extracurricular activities that would be required. Her kids and husband had recently gone back to China, so it would probably be the best location.

Lenny lay back on the bed and closed his eyes. His flight was leaving at 6:50 a.m.

WILL RECALLED what Landau had told him about reincarnation. An advanced soul had to find a body with a close genetic match in order to reincarnate. The lineage of Saul W. Kelly might carry evolutionary genetic tweaks, but his daughter would not have benefitted – an improper word choice – from his forced body-soul separation at the hands of the Nazis. It didn't make sense to him, but maybe there was more in the bloodline – above Saul somewhere – that had given Saul the propensity to develop separation abilities that he could have passed down to his daughter. Will would look into it.

He wondered now if his mother even knew that she'd been adopted. She'd always said that he looked like her younger brother – but he and Will did not come from the same gene pool. He then recalled a few stories his mother had told him about being able to see her body from above sometimes when she took a nap, or when she relaxed with her eyes closed on the beach. She'd brushed them off as daydreaming illusions, but Will was beginning to suspect otherwise. Perhaps the genes were starting to transform without the torture, which meant that the entire human race might not be far behind.

The next thing that interested him was who else he might have been in the past, further up the bloodline. He looked through the family tree, but the possibilities became endless with a few large families that spread into a virtual genetic forest, parts of which branched into Germany, Austria, and Norway. Also, he figured that his past existences didn't have to be within his current family tree.

He read more about Saul and found that he'd been an apprentice watchmaker before being called to duty as a bomber pilot. He'd made his way up the ranks quickly, and eventually came to lead a bomber group. According to the surviving crewmembers, on the fateful night that Saul Kelly had bailed into the North Sea, their plane had been hit, and one of its inner Rolls-Royce Merlin engines had caught fire. Kelly took it into a dive to try to put it out, but the maneuver had failed. The fire spread quickly, and two of the crew of his Avro Lancaster were dead when he ordered the rest to bail. He then took the burning plane out to sea on his own. There had been a special bombsight onboard that plane that they couldn't let fall into the hands of the Nazis. Saul was to make sure that it would crash hard after he jumped, with the hope that it would quickly sink to the bottom of the ocean. It seemed that he'd succeeded.

When the Nazis picked him up, he was badly burned and going into hypothermia. Will imagined that the cold water might have come as a relief to the burns, and could have provided him a much milder way to die. Unfortunately for Saul – for *him*, Will – he hadn't had time to die.

Will suddenly felt exhausted. He had class in the morning and would likely arrange for at least two of them, back-to-back, to get things rolling. Although he still had to figure out what to do long-term, there was no point in being idle. He'd have to learn everything he could about space travel so that he'd be ready as soon as he got control of the ship.

10

A TIME TO DIE

New York was a mess.

Lenny despised the cold, slushy streets almost as much as he disliked the rude people. He was glad he'd only be spending a couple of days in the place. He'd be heading back to the DC area afterwards, which wasn't much better, but at least he could park a car.

The CIA had a safe house in the city where he'd stay, rather than at the usual ratty hotel, and they had a plan to get him into the professor's apartment building. Under normal circumstances, getting access to a residential building wasn't much of a challenge. However, doormen in Manhattan kept a close eye on who came and went, and they knew most of the tenants by face and name. Lenny would immediately be identified as an intruder, and there'd be no way to talk his way out of it. Besides, these days everything was fitted with cameras, including all entrances and elevators. The CIA would take care of those for him.

The professor went by the name Ling Zhou, but her real name was Rui Huang. She was a nuclear chemistry professor and held a position in her NYC-based university's radiation safety office, where she inventoried and monitored radioactive materials delivered from outside vendors. Chinese operatives working at the chemical companies would arrange for "extra" items to be included in some shipments. "Ling Zhou" would be the first to inventory the incoming materials and remove those intended for her before forwarding the legitimate items to their final destinations in labs across campus. She'd then have trusted graduate students deliver the "extra" items to their end users, which often involved cross-country road trips.

Not everything that Professor Zhou received and redistributed was radioactive, however. Sometimes she would receive poisons of various kinds, or biological agents. She'd been linked to at least four assassinations that no one ever heard about in the news. Two were polonium-210 poisonings in the San Francisco area that had loose connections to Jimmy Yong's wife. Two were with ricin – which had been acquired from her contact at Plum Island. That contact, who had used the same substance to assassinate her graduate advisor, was Jennifer Chung. Lenny was pretty sure Jennifer was now in the liquid state.

Before eliminating the professor, Lenny was to get the names of the people at the chemical suppliers who had arranged the shipments. He thought that would be a simple task for the FBI, but they were out of the picture on this one. Next, he needed to know the names of the recipients of the goods.

He took a taxi to a coffee shop where a CIA operative met him. The man was tall and lanky, and he wore a knit cap and a black wool coat that extended below his knees. He was standing at a counter, pouring sugar into a cup of coffee.

"I'm Bartholomew," the man said as he popped the plastic lid onto his cup. "Would you like some coffee?"

It was the correct contact phrase to which Lenny answered. "I would, but we're a little short on time."

The man nodded, and they exited to the street and walked a few blocks without speaking a word. They entered a tall apartment building, and a stocky doorman watched them as they walked through the foyer. Lenny could tell the man was packing.

When they were in the elevator, on their way to the 45th floor, the CIA man informed him that the entire level was CIA, and that his wireless would be secure. He also told him that his name was Anderson, and that he'd be one of a few who would assist on this job.

Lenny wondered why the CIA couldn't just carry out the mission on their own. But he knew the most likely answer. People who were willing to do the ugly work were hard to find – particularly those who were willing to kill. He, too, wanted to avoid killing, and thought he'd finally ended that part of his life, but he'd been sucked back into the fray.

During his short retirement in Costa Rica, he'd made peace with his place in the world. He judged himself by the numbers – lives taken versus lives saved. Killing Mekhloufi might have been a thousand-to-one gain: the man was going to release a virus somewhere – probably in Space Systems where thousands could've been infected. The professor he was about to eliminate had a confirmed part in at least a few hits – but there were probably dozens. The question was whether she was planning on continuing, and how many more would die as a result. He was sure the woman would assist in a minimum of one more, meaning that the kill would at least be a neutral event: one life for one life.

He focused on what his targets might do in the future, not on what they'd done in the past. He wasn't there for justice. His contribution to the world would be whatever he prevented.

It was a coping mechanism, and it was working. It had been an epiphany of sorts – something that had emerged in his mind while driving to a missile silo in North Dakota a few months prior. Nothing like being confined to a car, alone for hours with little scenery and bad radio, to make one reflect upon their life. Looking back, it had been some of the most useful few hours of his existence, at least in regard to resetting his mental state.

Bartholomew – real name Anderson – led him into a small, one-bedroom apartment with a stocked kitchen and a panoramic view of the city. To Lenny, it was better than a five-star hotel simply because of the security.

"You can come and go as you please," Anderson said. "The

doorman knows you have access. Be sure to follow avoidance protocols when coming in."

Lenny's life revolved around his own stringent rules for surveillance and avoidance.

The professor's upscale building was in the trendy SoHo area in lower Manhattan. Lenny would meet a CIA contact in a coffee shop at 10:00 p.m., and then the fun would begin.

THE NAVIGATION CLASSES WERE ENTHRALLING. Will attended three of them back-to-back. They weren't just a continuation of the previous course. Professor Schmidt had changed gears and was discussing specific systems, starting with those on the *Exodus 9.*

The *Exodus 9* belonged to a class of secure transport ships that could be configured for specific cargos, including those that required life support systems. They were meant to be autonomous and could be given "orders." The *Disruptor*-class ships, like the *DEF Tariana,* were warships that were typically given objectives, rather than specific orders, along with constraints – or rules of engagement – such as to not kill or destroy anything unless attacked. There were other ships that dwarfed both the *Disruptor* and *Exodus*-class ships, one type of which was the *Destroyer* class, which was capable of obliterating the entire surface of a planet. It made Will think of the Regenerators. And then there were *Dominion*-class ships, which were like mobile space stations, and were so massive that they reminded him of the *Death Star* in the *Star Wars* movies. They were designed to control vast regions of space.

The most hopeful thing he'd heard had occurred in the first ten minutes of the first lecture when the professor said, "Although it is important to understand the principles of interstellar navigation, you can ignore much of what you learned in that previous course. Now you will learn how to get ships to do what you want them to do."

That glimmer of hope, however, was dimmed by the presumption of access and authority, which Will didn't have. However, in just three classes, he learned what he'd have to do in order to get the *Exodus 9* heading toward Earth, even though he currently didn't know the way.

Another thing he was surprised to learn was that there was a hands-on lab component of the course. He scheduled his first lab for the next morning.

At 4:00 p.m., he went back to his quarters and had a light snack, and then chugged a nutrition drink with carbs and electrolytes. By 5:30 p.m., he was in the locker room dressing up for his soccer match against the top team in the league.

It was during this time before taking the field that he realized he was developing a sense of camaraderie with his teammates. They all got along well and seemed to enjoy life. It made him realize that he was losing track of what was real and what wasn't. Even if the others were constructed of gears and circuits, which they weren't, he couldn't help but feel sad for them. They were generated biological beings, preprogrammed with all kinds of thoughts and skills. But they were devoid of souls – at least that was what he'd been told. After just a few seconds of pondering the idea, he decided to assume that was false.

The stadium was packed to capacity and was loud even during the pregame warmups. The air was sweet with the scent of cut grass and the aromas of food from the vendors around the stadium, and the sky had streaks of clouds painted in brilliant orange and red over a light blue background. The thick, short grass on the field was perfectly manicured, and smelled earthy, like the fairway of a golf course.

After a day of sitting in a lecture hall, the transition to physical activity was one of the most pleasant things he could imagine. It reminded him of why he'd so enjoyed sports as a kid. As he'd gotten older, he'd realized that athletics had given him an escape from the world. Whatever was going on in the rest of his life could be forgotten during the few hours of a football game. It was the same now.

The game was exhilarating. Other than scoring a goal and getting an assist for another, his skills had improved, as had his speed. When he ran, it felt like the acceleration was immense, and wouldn't cease.

Later, he wondered what his 40-yard-dash time was, and decided he'd find a way to check that in the future.

The game had been tied 1-1 at the half, and his team went on to win 3-1. Will had scored the go-ahead goal in the 67th minute, and provided the long cross to a teammate for the third in the 81st minute. The place had erupted after that final goal and hadn't relented until the game ended.

Afterwards, his teammates invited him out for a post-game dinner, and Will accepted.

They took a double-decker bus to a restaurant – Will devoured a heaping plate of fish and chips – and then walked to a local pub for a few pints. Fans approached them wherever they went.

He was amazed by the backstories of some of his teammates. One had a scar from knee surgery, one wore glasses, another was getting married. Another was worried about being traded to another team. It might have been a realistic taste of what the lives of real players on Earth were like.

Will got back to his quarters at midnight. The stars moving across his window only reminded him that he was getting farther from Earth with every second that passed.

THE THANKSGIVING WEEKEND in North Carolina with Pauli and her family had gone exactly as Jacob had expected. It had been a large gathering – over 30 people altogether – and the meal had been catered.

Most everyone had been friendly, except for some of the important ones – the immediate family. In particular, her mother and oldest sister, Mary, had more elevated standards for Pauli's future husband than the likes of him. Apparently, a skinny engineering geek, who was far from exceedingly handsome or rich, just wouldn't do.

Mary had been a practicing attorney for three years when she quit the profession just before having her second child. She now had three children and spent most of her waking hours tending to them, although that would soon change. Her husband had just moved up in his investment firm and was being transferred to the main office in New York City, and the family was about to move into an expensive flat in lower Manhattan. The firm had excellent daycare, and Mary was planning on enjoying the big city life.

Jacob had been tolerating the after-dinner conversation between Mary and Pauli – he'd been listening but not participating – when the doorbell rang and Mary had said, "That must be Todd." It turned out that Mary had invited a male friend from the local branch of her husband's firm to drop in after dinner. The first thing she'd done was introduce him to Pauli with the obvious intent of matchmaking.

At that point, Jacob decided to go on the offensive, against Pauli's wishes, and told a few lawyer jokes. The only one who laughed at any of them was Pauli's father, who Jacob felt was amused more by the idea of Jacob standing his ground than by the jokes themselves. The conversation turned toward the sour side when Jacob said that he'd read that many people turn to law school when they don't get into medical school. That elicited a laugh from a cousin at the far end of the table who was a pediatrician. Jacob then pointed out that there was a term for a class of regretful people, called "recovering lawyers," who just quit after a few years because they realized that the life of a real lawyer was nothing like that portrayed on TV shows. This had been directed at Mary, of course, and seemed to hit its mark.

The conversation inevitably turned to money, a topic on which the high-paid lawyers in the family had the advantage. What they didn't know, and wouldn't know, was that Jacob's salary had recently undergone a significant elevation – not that he cared very much.

During the long drive back to DC after dropping Pauli off at the airport, he relived many of the dinner conversations in his mind. By the time he got back, the anger was out of his system. However, he realized where Pauli had gotten her attitude toward money and position, and he wondered if it was something that he could tolerate in his future.

Upon returning from his least pleasurable Thanksgiving trip in recent memory, Jacob went back to 17 Swann, unpacked, and prepared dinner. He checked his personal email while he ate, and there was a message from Watts, Turk, and Genobli, the law firm that had managed his Uncle Theo's estate. An attorney wanted to set up a virtual meeting for the next morning. Since he already had a meeting at Space Systems scheduled for 7:30 a.m., he responded with his available times in the afternoon. This was their second contact, and their persistence made him curious.

After cleaning up the kitchen, his attention went to his work. He wasn't expected to have done much over the long weekend, but he wanted to at least look over the new data, just in case something new had surfaced.

He took a quick shower and then started to peruse the new images and data from the Chinese satellite cluster that had accumulated while he'd been away. He went through the data chronologically, starting with what had been received on Wednesday afternoon, after he'd started the drive to North Carolina. The first images contained a few candidate objects with arrows and code labels that indicated that they were low-priority, meaning that they were unlikely to be spacecraft, and just a couple marked as medium-priority, meaning that they had undergone some kind of course change that needed to be investigated more closely.

As he carried on with more recent images, however, the number of low-priority objects increased, and more medium-priority objects emerged. By the time he got to the most recent data, there were nearly 50 medium-priority and hundreds of low-priority objects.

He wondered what was causing the escalation. The Chinese would not have been able to update the software, but perhaps they were adjusting parameters within the control program, such as the object characterization criteria.

Jacob plotted a bar graph of the number of objects in each category. There was a sharp increase in low- and medium-priority objects with time, even though the total number of objects surveyed remained constant at about 1,500. It was strange.

He'd report his findings in the morning. It was 2:00 a.m. – he'd get to bed early.

It was just past 2:00 a.m. when Lenny entered the apartment building through an alley service door.

There was no way Professor Huang could afford to live in such an upscale place in Manhattan on an academic's salary, but he knew she had another source of funds.

Lenny was dressed like an elevator repairman in overalls, a dirty Mets cap, and a gray beard. His large glasses were slightly reflective so that the glare would make it difficult for any cameras to get a good shot of his eyes. In one gloved hand, he carried a greasy duffel bag that contained tools – ones that would pass for those an elevator service specialist might need, but could also be repurposed for other applications.

He rode the service elevator to the 21st floor, and padded down a quiet, carpeted hallway to apartment 2108. The door was already unlocked – thanks to a CIA op.

He unzipped the duffel and made sure that its most needed contents were in easy reach.

When he cracked open the door, he noticed that there had been a chain, but it had been cut somehow and the dangling ends looked as if they'd been melted.

As he edged the door open, he listened intently for motion and voices. There was nothing but faint street noise, so he stepped inside and closed the door behind him. He set the duffel on the wood floor and extracted his gun from a long pocket in his overalls designed to accommodate the weapon with silencer attached. Picking up the bag with his free hand, he inched across the room toward the sound of heavy breathing coming from an open door.

He peeked inside: it was a bedroom, and he was able to make out two forms in the bed. He was expecting to see just one.

After setting the bag at his feet, he entered and went to the left side of the bed. Sleeping face up with mouth open was one of the male graduate students on the list of those to be "removed from the roster." The man's name was Paul McNally. Evidently, the esteemed professor required her students to perform extracurricular activities. It was a happy coincidence.

Rui Huang – the Professor's real name – was sleeping on her stomach with her face turned toward the bright green display of an alarm clock that had just changed to 2:12 a.m.

In one swift move, Lenny stuck the barrel of the gun into McNally's mouth, angled it toward his brain, and pulled the trigger twice in quick succession. One of the bullets broke out a piece of his skull the size of a silver dollar that flapped on a piece of skin.

Professor Huang jerked violently. Before she could sit up, Lenny put the gun in his pocket, sat on her back, and pulled one of her arms behind her. He cupped her mouth and nose with his free hand, muffling a delayed scream.

He put one foot on the floor and lifted her as he stood. He then dragged her to the doorway where he'd left his bag and flipped on a light switch with his shoulder. She was wearing a white T-shirt and red underwear.

He reached one hand into the duffel, pulled out a knotted sock, and jammed it into her mouth. Holding it tightly with his hand, he reached back into the bag and extracted a roll of duct tape. He'd folded the end when he'd packed it so it would be ready to go, and he wrapped it around the professor's head and mouth seven or eight times, avoiding her ears.

When he turned her around so that she could see him, he caught her eyes looking at the corpse on the bed. The stench of released bowels and bladder was already permeating the room.

"That's right," he said as he squeezed her upper arm, making her wince. "He's dead. And you will be too if you don't tell me what I need to know."

He spun her around, grabbed his bag, and led her into the main room where he forced her into a chair at a desk, upon which was a closed laptop. He set down his duffle and opened the computer, which prompted him for a password.

He found a pad of paper and a pen in the desk drawer.

"Write the password," he said and handed her the pen.

The woman stared at him and didn't take the pen.

"I know who you really are," Lenny said. "Rui Huang."

Her eyes showed alarm.

"I've been given the order to kill you," he said. "If you give me what I need, maybe that won't happen."

She didn't move.

"Looks like I'll have to begin with some unpleasant methods to get things rolling," he said. "I'm going to start with one of your hands. Which one do you prefer?"

It was actually an important question since he wanted her to write. Carrying out such an operation in the middle of the night in an apartment with neighbors was a tricky job. There couldn't be any loud screams. Writing was the way to go.

He reached into the bag and extracted a pair of vice grips. He wanted to avoid a mess as much as possible, and the tool could crush a fingertip or a knuckle and remain clamped without drawing blood.

When she saw the tool, she nodded her head violently and reached for the pen.

Lenny handed it to her and watched as she wrote a string of characters on the pad with her right hand. Her writing was shaky, and he couldn't read one of the characters. He made her rewrite it.

"If I enter this password and it erases the hard drive, I'm going to make you wish you'd never been born. Understand?" he said as he grabbed her head and forced her to make eye contact. "I'll start by crushing every bone in your hand."

She nodded toward the paper and then to the computer.

He entered the password, and the computer went to its main desktop, which had a large picture of the Great Wall of China as the background.

For the next 20 minutes, Lenny browsed through the files and found all kinds of relevant information regarding purchases of sensitive materials. It was some of what he needed.

He then found a web browser, opened it, and turned his attention to the professor.

"What's the name of the other graduate student who works with you?" he asked. He had a few questions for which he knew the answers, and he'd mix them in to see if she'd try to mislead him.

She gave him the correct answer and he punched the name into a search engine and found a picture. "This her?" he asked.

She nodded.

Lenny took out his phone and snapped a picture of the blonde Caucasian woman on the screen. She was a graduate student in nuclear chemistry from Finland.

He proceeded to ask a list of other questions, including some about her sources for materials in various companies. She wrote her answers on the paper pad, and Lenny did the Internet searches to find them. It was an unusually efficient method of interrogation, he thought, and made a note in his mind to implement it in the future – if he were ever to carry out another such operation.

The questions got more sensitive as they went along, and they hit a snag when Lenny asked her for her contact in Chinese Intelligence. He clamped the vice grips on the first knuckle of the pinky finger on her left hand – enough to cause pain but not break anything – and she nodded her head that she'd answer. As he'd suspected, she didn't need much "coaxing."

Huang wrote down the name and Lenny looked it up. It was a man that worked in the Chinese embassy in DC.

Finally, he got the passwords to all of her email accounts.

As he was about to wrap things up, he thought he'd ask a few bonus questions, just in case he got lucky. "What did you deliver to Xing Li?" he asked. She was the woman at Bio-Source, Inc.

To Lenny's surprise, she wrote something on the paper. It read, "Virus samples."

"From where?" he asked, having a good idea of the answer.

"Plum Island," Huang wrote.

"Who on Plum Island?" Again, he knew the answer.

"Jared Blumenthal," she wrote.

Lenny stared at the name. He'd expected her to write "Jennifer Chung," or the name of Chung's boyfriend, both of whom were probably in the sewer by now.

He searched for the name, and images of a Caucasian man in his early 30s with dirty brown dreadlocks and earrings appeared. In one of the images, he was wearing a lab coat and safety glasses.

"This the guy?" he asked.

She looked and nodded.

It was just as he figured – remove one root and another is revealed. He wondered if he'd now have to eliminate Blumenthal as well, or if Thackett would get someone to bring him in.

The professor wrote more. "Also Fort Detrick."

Lenny punched the info into the search engine, which returned "U.S. Army Medical Research Institute of Infectious Diseases (USAM-RIID)." It was in Maryland.

He asked for a name, and the professor wrote down two, one looked to be Scandinavian, and the other Chinese. Their names appeared on the lab's employee list, but no pictures came up in the search.

"What viruses did you deliver to Xing Li?" Lenny asked. The Bio-Source scientist had told him that the devices contained a special virus – a new one. Therefore, Lenny thought it was strange that she'd get a virus from a government lab that studied mostly known ones.

Huang wrote down a list of a half-dozen viruses – names Lenny recognized.

"How are they going to be used?"

"New dispersion devices. Future attack. Don't know where," Huang wrote.

He believed that she didn't know *where* since he didn't even know. "How many devices?" he asked.

"Two or three."

"Three?"

She nodded and wrote, "Maybe more."

Lenny's gut seemed to twist into a knot. The viruses were of the deadliest known.

He pulled out his phone and sent a text directly to Thackett that read, "We have a problem. Call me."

WILL AWAKENED to a vibration on his wrist. He had a message.

He leaned over the couch and tapped the coffee table, bringing up the display on its surface. His soccer performance rating was in. He got a C-minus.

"What the hell?" he said aloud. He thought he'd had a good game. He made a note to research the grading criteria, but then thought twice about it. Although he wanted to improve, he wasn't sure he wanted to adjust his play in order to increase some statistics – such as "touches" – in order to increase his grade. He was playing for fun.

He was curious, so he looked up the grades of his teammates. The lowest, other than his, was a B-plus. There were two grades of A-minus, and no A's. He was clearly the weakest link on the team.

The first "lab" for his Navigation II course was in half an hour. He ate breakfast, showered, made his way to campus, and was standing outside the door to the lab with five other students a few minutes before the official start time. One of those students was Tracey, the girl from his first navigation course whom he'd met at Squidly's.

She was about to say something to him when the door opened, and a man dressed in a sleek, black uniform invited them in.

The lab was a replica of the bridge of the *Exodus 9*. Five other men and women stood side-by-side behind the instructor with their hands behind their backs. They were dressed in similar attire, younger than the man who had brought in the students, and seemed to be of lower rank, although it was hard to tell by their uniforms.

"Welcome to the navigation lab," said the man who had led them inside. "I'm Professor Bourne, and I was the captain of an *Exodus*-class ship for 15 years after 10 years as a beamer pilot."

"What's a beamer?" Will whispered to Tracey.

"It's a small military craft designed for high-maneuverability combat and near-surface deployments," Bourne said, looking directly at Will. "They're good for flying in an atmosphere, which is a bit different than piloting in the vacuum of space."

Will nodded and felt his face warm with mild embarrassment for interrupting.

"Together, you are a crew, and each of you will operate one station during a three-hour lab session," the instructor explained. "During each subsequent session, you will be assigned to another station, and you'll rotate through all of them by the end of the course."

The instructor then assigned people to stations. Will was assigned to the captain's chair. A lab instructor followed each of the students to their respective positions, and Captain Bourne followed Will to the captain's post.

"Nervous?" Bourne asked as he sat in a chair to Will's right.

"A little," Will admitted. But it was an enjoyable nervousness.

The instructor showed him all the displays and controls around the chair and explained their functions.

"The key is to remain calm," the instructor explained. "The ship can make all kinds of decisions so, no matter what happens, a well-reasoned action will usually take place. But there are crucial decisions that sometimes need to be made."

"For example?" Will asked.

"Run or fight," Bourne replied. "Kill or let live, destroy or not destroy, give up or keep fighting. These are all override decisions made by the captain."

"What if there is no captain?" Will asked.

Before the man could reply, one of the other instructors asked if the simulation should begin, and Bourne gave the go-ahead.

The view from the captain's chair was mesmerizing. The forward-facing bubble of the ship, which was identical to that on the real *Exodus 9*, gave him a three-dimensional panoramic view of the space around them, studded with uncountable specks of light from various celestial objects.

Information started to stream onto his displays.

"Your objective is to get to star system D-7134120-A," Bourne told him. "What do you do?"

Will recalled from class the sequence of operations. "Locate it first on a passive map, and then on an active one."

"Do it."

"That's the job of the mapping station," Will said.

Bourne nodded but remained silent.

Will stared at him for a second and then it came to him. "I have to give the order."

The commander pointed to a button on the chair. "Press it and talk."

Will pressed the button and said, "Mapping station, locate star system D-7134120-A."

"Acknowledged," a female voice replied.

Will realized he'd remembered the star system identification number. He thought it unlikely that he would've been able to recall such a string of characters while on Earth – before his body and mind had been rejuvenated – especially after 20 seconds of subsequent conversation.

"Star system D-7134120-A located and on viewer," came over the audio.

A screen popped up and displayed a map showing the location of the ship and the destination.

"You can now toggle between passive and active maps," Bourne explained as he pointed to a button on the screen.

Will tapped it, and another map appeared that showed the same objects but with vector arrows and a mess of lines that he knew were trajectories. Everything was moving slowly. It was complicated.

"Now order a course from the navigation station," Bourne said.

Will did so. A few seconds later, lines appeared that represented over 100 possible paths to the destination. The lines were of different colors and had numbered labels.

"The colors indicate the different modes of propulsion," the captain explained. "When you request a course selection, you should specify mode, depending on how quickly you want to get there, and whether you want to avoid a given area."

"Navigation, filter for the most direct route, and shortest travel time," Will said.

The number of paths reduced to six.

"The paths are nearly equivalent," Bourne replied. "For instance, when avoiding an obstacle head-on, you could go left or right, or up or down. Most of the redundant paths are filtered out."

Will looked closely at the courses and read the fine details for path number six. The distance was 15.5 light-years, and the travel time was two weeks. He knew that required "bender" propulsion, which contorted the spacetime around the ship.

He then noticed that one of the course lines had moved slightly. He looked to the instructor who seemed to notice what he'd seen.

"The courses are updated continuously until you give the order to go," Bourne explained. "Everything is moving out there, and your exact path will depend on the start time."

Will understood. "What do I do now?"

"Select a course, wait for the all-clear from the various stations, and then give the order to update the course and commence," Bourne said.

"Take course number six," Will ordered.

A few seconds later, various voices responded, "Course entered. Benders ready. Deflection shields at full power. Threat assessment clear. Authorization verified. All go."

"Threat assessment?" Will asked and looked to the instructor.

"We don't exactly fly the friendly skies," Bourne said. "This galaxy is enormous, and our likelihood of encountering someone else is minimal, but not impossible. Give the order."

"Commence the order," Will said.

An instant later, the stars in the enormous window moved diagonally from upper left to lower right. The ship was reorienting, yet Will felt none of the motion. "Will I feel anything when a real ship maneuvers?" he asked.

"Your experience here is realistic," Bourne replied. "When applying bending technology, you do not feel the effects of inertia like you would in an accelerating airplane, or in a beamer craft."

A few seconds later, the stars stopped moving diagonally, and then appeared to move slowly around the window, as if the ship were moving forward.

"We're on our way," Bourne said and grinned. "Time for a cup of coffee."

"A ship like this really doesn't require a crew," Will said. "Why take the time to learn?"

"You should be familiar with all forms of transport," Bourne replied. "From beamers, to transport ships, to warships. They all can fly themselves, but we must stay on top of our own technologies, or we will lose them. We created artificial intelligence, but we cannot blindly rely on AI and lose control of our future."

"What if the AI system wanted to take control? What if everyone at these stations were just locked out – and the ship took over?" Will asked. "Is there an override?"

"They all have an override in case of a malfunction or an emergency," the commander said.

Will twitched in response to a blaring alarm. "What's going on?" he asked.

"An object has been detected in our path," came a response from one of the crew.

Will looked to the commander, who shrugged.

"What is it?" Will asked the crew.

"Seems to be a particle field from a nearby star," came the response.

"Can you adjust course to avoid it?" Will asked.

"Yes."

"Do it," Will replied and looked to the instructor.

"You can give the crew permission to make small adjustments like this," Bourne explained. "Or, you can allow them to engage the AI autopilot to make minor maneuvers. For the learning experience, we'll keep AI offline."

"How does one override the ship's computer?" Will asked.

"There's a code – a long string of characters – that gives you access if you're authorized," Bourne replied.

"How is the code applied?"

"The code is only valid if employed by the individual who is currently in command," Bourne explained. "It's unique to the acting captain."

Damn, Will thought. If it were just a matter of finding a code, he might have had a chance. But he needed that in addition to authorization, which was connected to identity in some way. If he had authorization to make commands, he wouldn't disengage the AI anyway – he'd need it to get him home.

The remaining 90 minutes of the class were spent dealing with common navigation situations, and then they zoomed two weeks forward to practice the arrival sequence. Along the way, they passed near a star, which was a captivating spectacle.

The lab ended, and Tracey invited him to lunch at the same bar where they'd first met.

He agreed, although he wasn't much into bar food. In the end, he was pleasantly surprised by the menu and the clean environment, and enjoyed a light conversation with Tracey before heading back to his quarters.

He leaned back on the couch and rested his head on the armrest. He again recalled that, when going over his final options while at the Antarctic base, Landau had told him that he'd waste some great opportunity if he killed himself rather than transporting off the planet. Why would he tell him that if the *Exodus 9* were just going take him to some distant place, never to return?

Will scheduled a Nav II class for the afternoon. Afterwards, he'd go to New York for dinner, and then head across the street for a taste of cognac. Maybe Landau would show.

DANIEL and the rest of the group listened as Jacob gave his report in 713. It seemed that a lot had occurred over the Thanksgiving weekend. For some unknown reason, Thackett had delayed the meeting by an hour and a half and arrived just after 9:00 a.m. The director had a report of his own to give, but that would happen last.

"You said the number of medium-priority objects is increasing,"

Daniel said to Jacob. "What are the criteria that set them apart from low-priority objects?"

"It means they have changed direction or accelerated for a reason that has yet to be determined," Jacob responded. "Low-priority objects are on a course leading directly toward our solar system but have not yet exhibited course changes."

"And high-priority objects?" Sylvia asked.

"They exhibit both course changes and emissions – either a heat signature or electromagnetic waves," Jacob replied. "There's also a 'critical priority' classification, which means the direct detection of intelligent structure or communications signals. There has not yet been anything classified as high or critical."

"I'd think that even a high-priority sighting would set off alarms all over the world," Jonathan commented.

Denise then reported on her progress with the translations. Leaps had been made regarding the grammatical structure of the language, which was very different from all known human languages. She then described a translated passage that indicated that the Delta language had evolved to accommodate written, verbal, and "projection" types of direct communication between individuals.

"Projection?" Sylvia said. "What's that?"

"I have no idea," Denise replied. "And neither do the linguists."

"I can't think of another mode of communication beyond verbal and written," Jacob said. "Maybe braille, but I suppose that's still written, although it's read differently."

"Maybe it has something to do with separation abilities," Sylvia suggested. "Like when Will communicated with the Judge."

Daniel thought it was a plausible explanation. But it also made him consider the potentially extreme communication barriers that might occur between humans and other species.

"The next thing is that the linguists have deciphered a passage near the beginning of the text that has some historical content," Denise continued. "It's similar to the text that Will translated describing the Regenerators' plans to destroy Earth."

"Are the two passages consistent?" Daniel asked.

"Yes, the details match," Denise replied. "However, in this recently translated text, there's something new. There's a phrase that says that the Deltas were 'searching for lost light' before they evacuated, and another saying that they left without the 'fallen light.' At this point, we have no idea what that means but the linguists are working on it."

Denise ended her update and Thackett shifted the focus to Jonathan.

"I've been tracing the powders from their original location on Earth, which seems to have been Antarctica, through each of their various stops, to their final destinations," Jonathan said. He then gave some details about their paths through South America and how they'd been split and dispersed to various locations around the world. "Through this process, I've discovered something interesting."

Jonathan pulled some papers out of a folder and passed them around.

"You all should recall the device – the so-called 'power key' – that was acquired from Plum Island," Jonathan said. "It was in the possession of the same researcher that had one set of the powders."

"Professor Stanley Miller – the one assassinated by Jennifer Chung?" Sylvia asked.

"Precisely," Jonathan replied. "But what's interesting is the path that this device took to get to Plum Island."

Daniel looked at the pages that Jonathan had passed out. On the top page were two detailed timelines: one for the powders, which spurred off into many branches when they were split, and one for the device, which was linear.

"Referring to the device timeline," Jonathan continued, "you can see that it first appears in Argentina, although it arrived aboard a German U-boat coming from Antarctica."

Daniel traced the timeline through Argentina, where it was stolen by US and British intelligence, to the US Department of Defense, to NASA, to the DIA, to Area 51, to a place called "CG," back to NASA, and finally to Plum Island. The timeline then showed the device getting back to the CIA, eventually turning full circle, and returning to Antarctica, where it was used to start up the alien base. He noticed one peculiar thing on the list.

"What is the place labeled as 'CG?'" Daniel asked.

"I was hoping you could tell me," Jonathan replied.

Daniel had no idea. He looked to Thackett, who shrugged and shook his head, and then to Sylvia, who did the same.

"This CG place, whatever it is, might be important. There was something else there," Jonathan explained. "Look at the second sheet I gave you."

Daniel flipped to the second page as the others gasped. On the page was a sketch of a flat square object, about two inches on a side, with one chamfered corner.

"It's a destination key," Denise said.

"It looks like the device we used to decode the incoming radio signal," Jacob added. "The same one Will used in the transporter room."

Jonathan nodded. "Apparently, there was more than one of these devices at this 'CG' place," he explained. "I think it's important that we find out what this place is, and what else is there."

"I'll see if I can solve that mystery," Daniel said, knowing that both Jonathan and Denise did not yet have Omniscient clearance.

The attention then went to Sylvia, who updated the group on connections between far past and present UFO encounters. She'd discovered that sightings by military pilots – specifically navy pilots – had been increasing rapidly since about 2004. It had gotten to the point that there were regular encounters, almost on a daily basis. Some had been made public, but hundreds of others had not. Most pilots would not officially report them due to the potential negative effects on their careers, but many had discussed their experiences with other pilots. It was now all coming out, in part because the governments of the world could now attribute all of it to the so-called weather network development. That way, everything could be hidden right out in the open.

When it was Thackett's turn, Daniel could tell by his body language that the director had something important to say.

Thackett took a sip from a bottle of water and spoke. "We've thwarted one plot to expose Space Systems to a bioweapon – a virus – but there are probably backup plans."

"What kind of virus?" Sylvia asked.

"Actually, any of the following," Thackett replied and read through a list.

"Modified smallpox?" Denise asked. "And what is 'Marburg?'"

"It's like Ebola," Jacob said.

"And they're all modified versions, so I'm told that it's difficult to tell what exactly they will do," Thackett explained. "We have people working on it now."

"China is doing this?" Jonathan asked.

Thackett nodded. "Things might get out of control," he said. "I have some instructions for you. First, Jacob, you will remain at your facility until the all-clear is given – after your meetings today, there will be no visits to Space Systems, and no venturing out anywhere."

"Understood," Jacob said.

"For the rest of you," Thackett continued, "you'll remain here, but be prepared to move on short notice – keep a bag packed."

"Where would we go?" Denise asked.

"To a covert facility in the Southwest," Daniel said before Thackett could respond.

"That's right," Thackett confirmed. "If we're evacuating, there's a good chance that we will soon be at war. You are all crucial personnel, and we can't afford to lose you in the opening conflict."

"It's that serious?" Jonathan asked. It was more a statement of realization than a question.

"We've spoiled hundreds of operations in the past 20 years," Thackett said. "But this is the first time that high-level, internal personnel have been the main facilitators."

"What do you mean?" Denise asked.

"There has been significant collaboration between Chinese intelligence and scientists at Plum Island and at our own military bioweapons labs," Thackett said.

"Like Jennifer Chung," Denise added.

"Yes," Thackett said. "And others like her."

"Are they all Chinese implants?" Jonathan asked.

"No, only four of the seven we've identified so far are Chinese," Thackett replied. "One is from Finland, and two are native-born Americans with roots in Eastern Europe."

"Have they been taken into custody?" Sylvia asked.

"That's taking place now – very carefully," Thackett said. "We'll eventually get everyone, but we'll first take in a select few to find out where the bioweapons are, who has them, and what are their targets."

"You'll have them arrested?" Denise asked.

Thackett shook his head. "Not exactly," he said in a way that conveyed that he wasn't going to reveal more. "We've already apprehended one of the operatives, and they're cooperating. If we can get the others to do the same, we might get out of this."

"In the meantime, we just carry on as if nothing is going on?" Denise asked.

"What else can we do?" Daniel argued. Under the circumstances, he was surprised that he was so calm. A couple of years ago, something like this would've put him into a mode of utter panic.

The meeting ended and everyone left, leaving Daniel and Sylvia alone on the couch. He could tell she was upset.

"We'll be okay," he said. "Thackett is good. There are probably a lot of things like this that we just never hear about."

She smiled, but his words didn't seem to take effect.

"Not too long ago, we thought the whole Earth might be destroyed," he added, which was supposed to put the situation into perspective.

"I suppose that's true," she said. "Although, we were in a submarine at the time."

"Being in a sub at the bottom of the ocean would not have saved us from the extermination process that Will described," he said. "But I suppose it would've kept us safe from a virus."

"Some of those diseases are awful," she said. "They could infect the entire world."

"True," he said. "But we'll get control of the situation before that happens."

Daniel hoped that was true but, even if it were, would it be true of the next attempt, and the next one? Their enemies were relentless, and he couldn't help but think it was inevitable that something would get through eventually. For now, he just hoped the CIA would succeed in stopping this one.

LENNY POPPED a half-dozen antacid tablets into his mouth, chewed, and waited for them to dissolve before washing them down with an iced tea that he'd purchased at the counter of the coffee shop. His stomach was a churning mess.

It was 10:45 a.m., and he'd already had too much coffee and switched to tea. He pretended to read a local newspaper at a table with a good view of both the interior and front entrance of the coffee house. The place was busy, and he blended in well with the noisy crowd that consisted mostly of seniors, mothers with small children, and a few young business types.

It was extremely rare that an assassin, once given orders to terminate a target, would change plans and bring that person in alive. Rui Huang had been lucky: she'd been cooperative and had critical information. Although, based on her part in everything, he knew she'd likely still be juiced.

Actually, it was more than just likely. The CIA had no interest in collecting evidence and working with the FBI to take the overt path of justice. If they went that route, there was always a chance that she'd get off on some kind of technicality, or out on bail. And then she'd disappear, probably to resurface in a similar position somewhere else with a new identity.

Lenny was in Frederick, Maryland, stalking one of the two operatives from the government bio-lab who had provided Chinese intelligence with materials. Lenny was a part of a team on this operation: they needed the man alive. Lenny's part, however, was to take out the

Chinese ops who were watching over the scientist. He spotted one in a car across the street from the coffee house. They usually operated in pairs, so he was on the lookout. He had a feeling that things were going to get messy.

He'd been assigned to the team to bring in Luuk Janssen, a Dutch-born virologist who had moved to Finland at a young age, and now worked as a civilian at the U.S. Army Medical Research Institute of Infectious Diseases. *When would the US Government learn how to vet people?* Lenny wondered. That was probably the only thing that the Russians did well that he wished the West would learn to do. The KGB – which now went by FSB or SVR – made sure to do stringent background checks on people in sensitive positions. There was no way that a Chinese or Dutch-Finnish scientist would be employed at a sensitive government lab unless they were effectively locked in a cage somewhere. The US, on the contrary, was a sieve. The Chinese had people everywhere – Plum Island, all universities, the Army bio-lab, and even Space Systems.

The Hollander was tall, unshaven, and his long, brown hair was wrapped in a tight bun on the top of his head. It was a style that Lenny found annoying. According to his file, the man was 38 years old, and looked relatively athletic. He reminded him of Jacob Hale, although Jacob was much smaller than the six-foot-five man who was his current quarry. Lenny would shoot him in the knee before getting into another footrace.

Lenny kept watch from his table, behind and to the left of Janssen, with a good view of the man's laptop. Janssen was paging through a notebook and constructing graphs on the computer. It seemed he was writing a technical paper or report of some kind.

Lenny's nerves went into high alert when he glanced out the front window and spotted the Chinese op getting out of his car and stepping into the street. He was heading toward the coffee shop.

The man was tall and wore a long, khaki overcoat. His black, square bangs came to the top of his small, round sunglasses. He was in his mid-30s or early-40s and took long, loping steps as he crossed the street in front of traffic. He held a phone up to his ear, and that's when Lenny noticed another Asian man in a corner booth in the coffeehouse. This one was younger, shorter, and skinny, and he spoke into a phone as he watched the other man enter the café.

Something was going down.

Lenny took his glass up to a return counter so that he was in a standing position as the taller operative entered the café and seemed to scan the room. The man locked his eyes on Janssen as he moved toward him, and the shorter operative stood and approached from the opposite side.

Lenny reached into his coat and found the handle of his gun. He was about to draw as the two ops advanced upon Janssen, but then they just sat at the Hollander's table. They spoke quietly for a few minutes and then Janssen started packing his things into his backpack.

Returning to his seat, Lenny texted the six-member CIA team stationed outside. They'd pick up all three – Janssen and the Chinese ops.

As he followed the men out of the café, a white service van with advertising for an Internet provider on its side and a ladder on its roof pulled to the curb. A man and woman stepped out of the van, went to its rear, and opened the side-by-side back doors.

As the three targets passed, two more CIA ops stepped out of the back of the van and onto the sidewalk behind them, and two more came out of a doorway in front of them. They were surrounded.

The female CIA operative pulled a gun and the three men froze.

She ordered them to get into the rear of the van, but no one moved. That's when Lenny saw the shorter Asian man reach into his pocket and extract something that he recognized: a stick syringe, about a foot long, with a short needle. It was a device used for assassination.

The man lunged for Luuk Janssen and, in one instinctual move, Lenny shot the would-be assailant in the ear. He dropped to the ground like a sack of flour and the syringe fell from his hand. The other two detainees put their hands in the air and remained still.

A few of the CIA ops gaped at the dead man with horrified expressions.

They were young, and soft, Lenny thought as he pushed between them and grabbed Janssen by the back of the neck and threw him into the rear of the van.

Two CIA personnel followed by grabbing the remaining Chinese op and dragging him into the vehicle, while another followed with zip ties and kept his gun trained on the prisoners.

The female CIA operative leaned over the man Lenny had shot and reached for the syringe.

"Be careful with that," Lenny said. "That could be anything – even polonium-210."

She looked back at him with wide eyes.

At that point, a young man and woman walked out of the café.

Lenny turned and made sure that they saw his gun.

Expressions of panic froze on their faces.

"Drug bust," Lenny said. "Go back inside. It still might not be safe."

They did as he said.

"Quick thinking," the CIA woman said.

"Let's get this guy out of here," Lenny ordered as he grabbed the dead man's ankles and dragged his body over the curb to the back door of the van. Those inside the vehicle would have to deal with the smell of feces for a while.

When he turned around, the female op was putting the syringe into a plastic bag.

They had what they needed, so Lenny walked around the corner, got into his rental, and drove off.

The operation had not been carried out to his liking, but it had been successful, nonetheless. If they had waited another day, Luuk Janssen would have been dead.

It disturbed him that the Chinese were already starting to clean up. It meant that the others on his list were also in danger. More disturbingly, however, it meant that Luuk Janssen had already provided them with what they needed. It was now time for the CIA to figure out what that was.

AT 7:30 P.M., Will took the subway to the Manhattan restaurant he'd gone to a week earlier. He had barbecued ribs, a baked potato, and a salad, the flavors of which were starting to seem normal to him. He wondered, if he ever got back to Earth, whether his taste buds would have to make another adjustment.

After he finished eating, he crossed the street to the whiskey bar and spotted Danielle mingling with the eclectic crowd that included everyone from lawyers to hippies. She wore a green cocktail dress and a white scarf, and her dark hair reached the middle of her back. Under different circumstances, he might want to talk to her. He was instead looking for Landau, who was nowhere to be seen.

He went to the bar and ordered the same cognac that Landau had recommended during their previous meeting – Rémy Martin Louis XIII. The bartender found the bottle, poured some into a brandy snifter, and placed it in front of him.

Will took the glass, turned around, and leaned against the bar. Light jazz was playing in the background – something he hadn't noticed when he'd entered.

He scanned the crowd. There were now about 100 patrons milling about. If Landau were there, he'd stand out.

In his peripheral vision, he could tell that Danielle had noticed him, but he didn't want to talk to her yet. At some level, he felt she was a designed distraction, perhaps to dilute his thoughts of Denise, or to divert him from his other objectives. He missed Denise, but it seemed that all of his strong feelings for his loved ones on Earth, and Earth itself, had somehow been tempered by all of the familiar human interaction, or at least the illusion of it. It was a dangerous predicament.

He flinched as a female voice came from his right.

It was Danielle.

"Sorry, I didn't catch what you said," he said.

"Landau isn't here," she said. "Why don't you bring your brandy and come sit with me."

He scanned the place again for Landau to no avail, and then agreed.

Will had read up on cognac after his encounter with Landau. Cognac was brandy, but not all brandy was cognac. And he'd learned that they were both made with white grapes. Because of their reddish-brown color, he would've bet his life that they were made with the red variety.

He followed Danielle to a little booth that seemed to be built into the wall, with two padded bench seats and a table between them. A stained-glass light fixture hung low overhead. She slid into one side, and he into the other.

"How do you know I'm looking for Landau?" he asked.

"He told me you would."

"Really?" Will said, surprised. "Where can I find him?"

"You can't right now," she replied. "But he wanted me to give you this," she said as she reached into a tiny handbag that hung by a thin strap slung over her shoulder. She pulled out a folded piece of paper and handed it to him. "Don't read it here."

Will's heart thumped as he took the note and slipped it into the inner pocket of his jacket.

"What is it?" he whispered.

"Something that might help you find your way home," she replied.

He thought it was odd, but he'd play along. Landau didn't seem like the type to pass notes. The paper must have been just a prop used by the program – something to keep him distracted.

And he still suspected that his first encounter with Landau in the bar had been a ruse. If he had been thinking clearly when they'd met, he would've separated and insisted that Landau do the same. He would've been able to tell whether it was really him.

"There's something else," Danielle said.

"Yes?"

She looked at him with a strange, conflicted expression with a hint of a grin.

Will's nerves seemed to electrify.

She stared into his eyes, and said, "You need to die."

LENNY WAS SCRAMBLING through traffic to get to the next target – a man named Daoping Bao – when his burner phone vibrated. It was a text from Jimmy Yong telling him to check his email.

As he inched along behind a line of cars at a stoplight, Lenny logged in and checked the drafts folder in the account he shared with Chinese intelligence. Yong wanted to meet at the safe house at 7:00 p.m. that evening.

Lenny looked at the clock on the car's dashboard: it was going on 12:30 p.m. It would take him 90 minutes to get back to DC with no traffic, but there were never days with no traffic. It meant he'd have to complete his task by 5:30 p.m., and that was unlikely. On most days, Daoping Bao didn't leave the Fort Detrick laboratory before 6:00 p.m.

He got an idea and called Thackett, who gave him the go-ahead.

Another team would track Daoping Bao when the virologist left the laboratory. If he deviated from his normal routine, or if Chinese ops were closing in on him, they'd take him in. Otherwise, Lenny would return after his meeting with Yong and finish the job.

Daoping Bao was secretly making plans to go back to China. His wife and teenage son were already on their way – they'd left early that morning – but would be collected at Los Angeles International Airport before their next flight. His wife was a courier of nasty things, and she was going to be juiced. The boy would be deported after his parents disappeared.

Lenny wondered how people in their line of work could carry on like normal families, live in suburban neighborhoods, and let their kids develop in a culture from which they'd eventually be torn. Lenny at least had the decency to abandon his daughter and her mother. He had no doubt that they would've been in constant danger while with him.

He followed the map on his phone to a large white house in an upscale neighborhood. He parked on the street amongst a half-dozen cars that belonged to a construction crew that was putting a new roof on a house, two doors down. He donned a green safety vest and a baseball cap, and grabbed a clipboard and pen from the back seat. He was prepared, thanks to a CIA scouting report.

The entire neighborhood was filled with cameras. Every house had at least one trained on its driveway and front porch, and thus had views of the other houses. Therefore, he not only had to look inconspicuous for the cameras on Daoping Bao's house, but also for the nosey neighbors' cameras.

Lenny wrote things on his clipboard as he pretended to take pictures of power junction boxes and sewer inlets. He noticed a sign in Bao's front yard that warned potential intruders that his house employed a security system from a reputable company. The system would be no match for the CIA's "Picks and Locks" division.

Lenny had what he needed.

Due to the local activity and the security system, there'd be no killing before dinner. However, Daoping Bao was going to have a late-night visitor.

AS JACOB RODE the 17 Swann elevator to his flat, he realized how unnerving things had become. The idea that Space Systems was on alert for evacuation, and that some adversarial country was planning to carry out a large-scale biological attack, made it difficult for him to concentrate.

He wondered if he would have been better off without that knowledge. Ignorance was bliss, but he supposed he had some part to play in what was happening. He was an Omni now, and that carried with it some responsibilities. He wondered how common such threats had been in the past, when he'd been a normal citizen, oblivious to it all. And what about Uncle Theo? He must have been involved in every threat since World War II. It had to have been difficult for him to keep all of that to himself for three-quarters of a century.

After the meeting at Space Systems in the morning, Jacob had spent a few hours at another facility in DC, where he'd met with specialists from the NSA, NASA, CIA, DIA, and the US Space Force.

Two important things had emerged from that meeting. First, the masking program, called "Façade 1.0," had passed the testing phase and was ready to be implemented. They'd install it within 48 hours and complete the takeover.

Next, the latest batch of satellite data was now available.

It was 4:50 p.m. when Jacob sat at the library table on the lower level and opened his laptop. He logged in to a virtual meeting with two lawyers, a man and a woman, from the law firm of Watts, Turk, and Genobli. They first asked him a few questions to confirm his identity – including questions about Uncle Theo and the rest of the family – and then informed him that he was the beneficiary of a trust fund. The grantor was Theodore Horace Leatherby, and it would be managed by Watts, Turk, and Genobli until the plan was fully executed.

The meeting ended, and Jacob closed his laptop. It was something that he'd subconsciously expected. Uncle Theo had always looked out for him and, deep down, Jacob trusted that he'd provide him with at least a modest financial boost at some point. No numbers had been given, but the fund would be activated when Jacob was between 42 and 45 years old. The managers would choose the specific time of release based on the behavior of the markets. Although Jacob had no idea of the amount, he was sure it would be significant relative to his current financial status, which had recovered well from the hit it had taken a couple of months ago.

He'd always thought that there was a threshold amount of money, perhaps between five and ten million dollars, that carried with it a degree of freedom that most people would never experience. It was the freedom to live wherever you chose, and to never have to answer to anyone about anything – no employers, no bosses, no lenders, no landlords. You'd never have to work again, and you could spend your time doing whatever you chose. In effect, money bought time – or at least freed up whatever time you had. In another sense, it repurchased one's time back from their employer, and cut the chain that anchored them to their place of work. Money supposedly didn't buy happiness, but it sure solved a lot of problems. And it could give a person the highest level of freedom achievable on planet Earth.

He glanced at his phone sitting on the table next to his laptop. His first instinct was to share the good news with Pauli. But then he reconsidered. The money wouldn't be available for over a decade, and he didn't even know how much it was. She'd learn about it when or if they ever got married. He felt her distorted value on status and money, cultivated by her family, made this knowledge volatile to her. If they were to remain together, he wanted to be certain that money had nothing to do with it.

He walked along the edge of the carpet runner, past the long library table, and up the stairs to the kitchen. He turned on the oven, popped in a TV dinner, and set the timer for 35 minutes. He was hungry, and it reminded him of what he'd learned during the morning meeting.

He opened the freezer, gauged how much space he had, and trotted downstairs to the desktop computer and started ordering food and supplies. It was a much longer list than usual –enough to fill the freezer along with water, a few weeks' worth of nonperishable items, and a two-month supply of military MREs – meals ready to eat.

If everything went to hell in the outside world, he'd have some buffer time to figure things out, or to just wait until it all blew over. He'd learned that 17 Swann had a sophisticated backup generator that ran on natural gas supplied from public lines, and a solar array and battery on the roof that could power basic things.

As the oven timer chimed in the distance, he pushed the final submit button to place his order and went back to the kitchen.

He pulled out the TV dinner and set it on one of the surface burners to cool. While he waited, he pulled out his laptop and started flipping through the latest 1,000 images intercepted from the Chinese cluster.

As he progressed, his heart pumped harder and harder. The number of medium-priority objects had doubled in the last two days. There were still no high-priority objects – meaning no electromagnetic emissions or heat signatures – but the satellites' tracking algorithms had focused on a few, striking, medium-priority objects.

There were now over 200 medium-priority objects heading toward the solar system, all of which had been deemed to have "changed vector" at some point – meaning they'd deviated in some way from a straight-line path, a few of which had changed course drastically.

A horrible thought came to him that made his stomach turn sour.

Were the Regenerators coming back?

He ate his Salisbury steak TV dinner as he wrote up a quick summary and sent it to Daniel.

WILL WENT BACK to his quarters, sat on the couch, and read the note Danielle had given him. It read, *Try the Seraphim Hors d'Âge. Best when consumed quickly. – Landau*

What in the hell was *Seraphim Hors d'Âge*? Will wondered.

He looked it up on the computer and learned that "Seraphim" was the name given to a class of high-ranking angels in Judaism and Christianity, but it was also the name of a rare type of cognac. The added *Hors d'Âge* meant "beyond age," and indicated that it had been aged for such a long time that it exceeded the normal cognac age scale. The term was usually reserved for fine cognacs that were sometimes over a century old.

Will put the note on the coffee table and leaned back. What in the hell did Danielle mean when she said that he "needed to die?" What would that accomplish? And why would the ship's computer allow one of its programs to tell him something like that?

His agitation was building, in part, because he was becoming increasingly confused.

If he died, he'd just be regenerated, which reminded him that he needed to go to the medical facility for a "regeneration update," where he'd be scanned, and his physical information updated. In that case, should something bad happen, the body to which he'd return would be exactly the same as the latest updated version. It reminded him of saving his place in a video game.

But why would he purposely die? In the back of his mind, he wasn't really sure if he believed that he could be regenerated. What if that was just a lie – some crazy psychological game to get him to kill himself?

The *Exodus 9* – or its computer, if the two could even be considered separate – already knew that he was looking for ways to change its course. Maybe it viewed him as a threat. But that didn't make sense, either. If the *Exodus 9* wanted him eliminated, he'd be dead already. A "mishap" in one of his virtual adventures would have done the trick. All it would have to do at that point was make sure that his body was never regenerated – something that was as easily done as erasing a computer file.

If the note Danielle had given him was really a message from Landau, something of which Will was not entirely convinced, then he'd have to figure out what would be the purpose of such an act.

When they'd met at the whiskey bar, Landau had mentioned that, when one died, they somehow regained all of the knowledge and memory of their previous lives. When someone was reincarnated, all of that information was inaccessible, except for some residual tidbits that some people experienced. It was different, however, if a person was regenerated. First, they maintained the knowledge they had before they'd died. Second, they could recall things they experienced while they were dead, which included some knowledge of previous lives.

The word "dead" was a misnomer. To Will, the word no longer carried the meaning it had before he'd separated that first time in the Red Box. That episode had unequivocally revealed the existence of the soul beyond the body. And now, with the revelations of reincarnation and regeneration, it was even less well defined. Death, in the old world, implied a permanent change of state that ranged from complete nonexistence to a long slumber to an eternity in paradise, whatever that was. Will was only certain that it wasn't either of the first two options.

But he had to be careful. He had not directly experienced anything beyond separation – which was not a death experience – or beyond his transport from Earth to the *Exodus 9*, during which his original body had been destroyed. It still seemed strange to him that all the atoms that had composed his body on Earth were still on Earth.

The point, however, was that he questioned whether he could believe what he'd been told about reincarnation and regeneration. Was all of that really true? Although he had peripheral anecdotal evidence, such as Saul W. Kelly being his grandfather, he had no direct verification. He was also aware that the family tree he'd been presented could have been a fabrication. And even though the Landau character with whom he'd spoken had detailed knowledge of their encounters, he knew that it could still be a ruse. The virtual reality technology on the *Exodus 9* was just too good for him to rule out an elaborate trick.

It reminded him of a documentary he'd once seen about cults, and what their charismatic leaders were able to coax their followers into doing. The ultimate, of course, was to convince them to commit suicide in order to go to paradise or board some alien spaceship and head off to a new world. Isn't that what Danielle had just advised him to do?

If the message had really originated with Landau, then Will might not have questioned the motive. After all, Will had once decided to pull the trigger – although it was still a question as to whether he'd actually done it. If Landau wanted to coax him into killing himself, he'd already succeeded.

Although he hadn't decided what to do, Will made an appointment with the medical facility for a checkup and a bio-update, whatever that entailed, so that he could be regenerated in his current physical state should his body die. It was like writing a long paper and saving your work on an external drive in case your computer died.

It was something that he should have been doing anyway. There were versions of the virtual reality programs that were rated as "potentially lethal," which meant that a person could actually get killed – no safeguards. He first noticed this in the description of a

James Bond adventure called "Dying for Love." It was not recommended for "first-lifers," which was the term referring to people who had never died and regenerated.

Will sat by the window and watched the stars.

He inhaled deeply and sighed. To the Deltas, death was just a curable condition that was even worked into games. They'd conquered death – the final enemy had been defeated. But that seemed to not be enough. According to Landau, they'd all left the physical world that they'd conquered. *Why?*

Maybe Will would know more, soon, after he died.

LENNY MADE it to the rendezvous point on time and took a ride with two Chinese security operatives to the safe house to meet with Jimmy Yong. He found the extra step to be a nuisance since he knew the location, but he played along.

He sat in the same upholstered chair that could barely take his weight as last time and faced Yong, who sat on the couch on the opposite side of the coffee table.

"We've hit a few snags, and the operation has been moved up in the schedule," Yong said.

"Snags?" Lenny asked.

"Some of our operatives have gone missing," Yong replied.

"That's disturbing," Lenny said, knowing that another one was going to be dead in a few hours. "Were their roles important?"

"They're all important," a female voice said from Lenny's right.

Lenny jerked his head to see an Asian woman in a tight, silver skirt-suit standing in a doorway that looked to lead to bedrooms in a different part of the house.

"This is Sara," Yong said. "She'll be handling the computer security part of the operation."

She glared at Lenny with an expression that looked as if she'd just gotten a good whiff of pig manure.

Lenny looked to Yong. "What's the role of computer security in the operation – and what's my part in all of this?"

"You and Sara will go to Space Systems," Yong explained. "We have a person on the inside who will supply you with ID and access, and they'll get Sara onto the internal network. She'll arrange access to the air system for operatives who will plant the dispersing device."

Lenny shouldn't have been surprised that the Chinese had more people on the inside of Space Systems. "Where are the other devices being planted?" he asked.

Yong flinched. "What do you mean?" he asked, his expression awkward.

"I collected the second one, according to the scientist at Bio-Source," Lenny replied. "So, there's at least one more."

"Your device was just a backup," Sara said. "You don't need to know about the other devices. You just concentrate on your own mission."

Lenny's stomach twisted in his gut when he heard 'devices' – plural. He'd accomplished what he'd intended: he now confirmed that they had other bioweapons and planned to deploy them.

"When do we go?" Lenny asked.

"You'll get instructions in the next few days," Sara said.

It seemed to Lenny that Sara was taking control of things. He knew from Yong's file that Sara was his wife – an arrangement in which he apparently had the subservient role. He was also aware that they had kids who had been sent back to China in anticipation of the wake of what they were planning.

Lenny had the urge to kill them both now – with his bare hands. But that would have to wait. He needed information from them. He'd first let Sara lead him to the moles inside Space Systems. The CIA would take over from that point. They'd extract information from her and the insiders about everything else that was happening. They'd all be juiced in the end. It was something that Lenny wished he could witness.

"This wasn't a part of the original plan," Lenny said. "I was supposed to handle the items, not deploy them."

"Are you asking for additional compensation?" Yong asked.

"Yes," Lenny replied, although that was the furthest from his mind. He'd take what he could get with the hope that he'd be around to spend it when the dust settled.

"One million for the extra duties," Yong said. "Half up front."

"I'll do it for 750 on the front end," Lenny countered. He figured they could afford it now that they weren't going to have to pay the remainder of Mekhloufi's contract, which he was sure was hefty.

"Deal," Yong said. "It will be transferred in the next 24 hours."

"What's the plan for afterwards?" Lenny asked. "Is there a secondary objective?"

"There won't be anything beyond this," Sara said in a tone that made Lenny's blood run cold.

"Okay," Lenny said as he stood from the chair. "I'll await your instructions."

Yong called in his security team and, a half hour later, Lenny was in his car driving south.

His plans for his next hit had changed: he'd now try to get every bit of information he could out of Dr. Daoping Bao before putting a bullet in his head.

YONG WATCHED as his wife sat in the chair that the massive Russian-American had just vacated. He figured she was just a third of the thug's weight.

"You know we will have to eliminate him inside the Space Systems facility," Sara said. "It will have to be done with an untraceable poison so that it looks like he got caught by the virus."

"Yes," Yong replied. He knew that finding Lenny there might deflect attention from China for at least a short time. "It will give us a window to get out of here before the chaos starts."

"I have instructed our asset on how to carry out the plan," Sara said.

"You won't be participating?" Yong asked.

Sara shook her head. "I need to help the Russians with their part of this mission," she replied. "They are behind schedule, and they'll have to make up time if we're going to synchronize our efforts."

"Will we still be able to get out of here on time?" he asked.

"On that momentous day, we'll be on a 7:00 a.m. flight out of the country – before anyone even knows what's happening," she assured him. "After a two-hour layover in London, we'll be on a flight to China."

Yong was happy. Things were coming together, and he'd be welcomed with open arms when they arrived in Beijing. It was only then that he'd worry about the impending war.

At 8:00 a.m. Will went for a medical checkup with Greta and requested a full DNA scan.

Greta informed him that his physical conditioning was excellent, and that his rejuvenation was on schedule. He had the body of a 23-year-old athlete who had no accumulating physical issues – arteries, liver, kidney, and heart were all pristine – and had never suffered a major injury.

She also conducted a cognitive acuity test, which was carried out in less than a minute. It was akin to measuring the processing speed of a computer. His brain was performing optimally. It was something that he noticed even more than the physical transformation of his body.

He went back to his quarters, ate a late breakfast, and went to his navigation class. Afterwards, he went to the navigation lab, where he played the part of navigator, and laid in courses selected by the captain – or the student playing that part for the day. Navigation was easy – the computer was user-friendly – but it still paid to go through the exercises.

When he returned to his quarters in the late afternoon, he went to the computer and began researching the process of regeneration after death. He skipped the history – he'd already read the enthralling story of the discovery – and went to a section titled, "What to Expect."

As he read, the first thing that struck him was that, although the preliminary events leading to it could be agonizing and drawn out, death itself was sudden, and painless. It was described as being cut loose from a tether, and the sensation described as that of "colossal relief." At the very instant of death, a freed soul would expand to its full volume – in multiple dimensions – and regain an unrestricted comprehension of reality. Memory of the soul's complete existence would then become accessible, and not just the memories of its latest incursion into the *grand timeline*.

Will had no idea what "grand timeline" meant. The words were highlighted, indicating a direct link to the relevant information, so he followed it and read. He found that it was a philosophical construct used to explain time, space, and "elsewhere." It was described as a straight rope, or conduit, in a multidimensional space that extended out of sight in both directions, although the idea of "direction" in higher dimensions was complicated. The rope constantly moved forward, and, like a towrope ski lift, one could grab onto it, and it would drag them forward. To "grab on" was to enter a life, either for the first time, or through reincarnation or regeneration. When entering as a "first life," or by reincarnation, as everyone on Earth had done, one carried no knowledge of their previous existence, save some residual memories that could sometimes leak into one's mind. Those memories were mostly scrambled, and difficult to interpret, and sometimes presented as feelings of déjà vu. It was different however, for a regenerated soul.

When a soul was released from the grand timeline, it acquired all of the knowledge of its past – all previous lifetimes. When it returned to a regenerated body, it retained much, but not all, of that knowledge, most of which was from the current life and the most recent *previous* life, but also some from *all other lives*.

It made Will think of the memories he'd stolen from the Judge in the probe, and how they still affected him. He thought having multiple lifetimes stored in his head might drive him insane – especially if they carried emotions with them.

So-called "first-lives," and reincarnations, were considered to be "virgin lives." They were lived mostly devoid of previous knowledge, unlike regenerated lives that carried the baggage of a soul's entire existence.

Will now reconsidered the idea of deliberately dying and regenerating. *Perhaps ignorance is bliss,* he thought as his first inclination was to not do it.

He questioned whether a human mind could contain the knowledge and memories of multiple lifetimes. As he read further, his question was answered.

It turned out that all memory is contained in the limitless soul, accumulated continuously since its creation – however that happened. The biological brain could only contain a portion of it. Numerous analogies were given, one of which likened the idea to the random-access memory, or RAM, of a computer versus its hard drive data storage. The capacity of a computer's RAM was often a thousand times smaller than that of its hard drive. However, the RAM was immediately accessible, whereas information on the hard drive had to be summoned. The RAM was the human brain, the hard drive was the soul.

A better analogy was a personal computer versus the Internet. The computer could hold a certain, limited amount of information, and have certain functionalities – software. The World Wide Web – the Internet – held many orders of magnitude more knowledge and functionality than the computer. When a soul was born into a body, the connection to the "Internet" was gone – a person had to function on what they had in their computer's memory, so to speak. But when their physical bodies died, they'd again have access to everything – the entire Internet.

Will wasn't sure if the analogies helped him to understand, or just confused him further. Why would anyone want to live in a physical body? It just cut them off from the rest of existence, and all of their knowledge and memories. Perhaps not knowing about everything all at once was better sometimes.

It made him think about the virtual activities he'd experienced – soccer and the other adventures. He knew it was all fake, although very realistic. How would those adventures have been enhanced if he'd believed that they were really happening – that they were reality? And suppose he had the lifetime of corresponding memories that led up to those events. He had no doubt that playing in a professional soccer match in a stadium filled to capacity was a much richer experience for a player who recalled all of the hard work and individual steps that it took to get to that moment in time.

Will recalled the adage, "It's the journey, not the destination." But he'd always felt that statement was inaccurate. The destination was extremely important. How many people failed to attain their dreams after plodding along on a long journey? What did they think about the journey then? He thought that, in most cases, one could only reminisce in a positive way about a life-long journey if it ended in accomplishment, or with some element of success.

The journey gave the destination meaning. The destination gave the journey justification. And both were required for contentment.

Will was as far from being content as a person could be. Perhaps he'd be more relaxed when he was on his way back to Earth. But that, he knew, might be a journey with no destination.

11

HORS D'ÂGE

WILL WOKE UP AT 7:00 A.M., ATE COLD CEREAL, AND PICKED UP A coffee on campus as he made his way to class.

The professor lectured on the physics of the basic systems needed on a starship. Will found it all fascinating, even though it was only his generation's physics that he understood. He supposed an alchemist from medieval times would be just as confused by the science of the 21st century – the theory of relativity, quantum physics, and the like.

A perplexing problem that Earth's scientists were having with long-term space travel involved the radiation to which travelers would be subjected. Typical shielding materials, like lead or tungsten or various polymers, used by Earth's space programs were too heavy or not effective enough for long-term travel. Human technology couldn't even get travelers to Mars without them being overexposed. The Deltas' solution to the problem, however, was far more sophisticated than material shielding. A Delta ship bent the spacetime outside its hull so that radiation diverted around it.

After class, he went to the third lab of the course. This time he controlled the defense systems of the *Exodus*-class ship. His only tasks were to eliminate some space debris and advise evasive maneuvers to avoid another ship of unknown intentions. In this exercise, he also learned that the *Exodus 9* had a cloaking mode which, again, bent spacetime in such a way that the ship was undetectable. This only worked in slower modes of travel, however.

Afterwards, he had lunch and then went to a soccer practice that he'd arranged to be twice as long as usual. He had a tough decision to make, and sometimes it helped to be completely removed from the situation. Running to the verge of puking his guts out usually did the trick.

After the training session, he went back to his quarters, got an electrolyte drink from the dispenser, and sat by the window.

He contemplated again why Landau would have suggested that he kill himself. One possible reason was that he would acquire knowledge from his previous lives. But what knowledge, exactly, was he after? And it bothered him that he couldn't be sure that it was Landau who had sent the message. In fact, he couldn't be sure that it had been the real Landau he'd met at the whiskey bar.

From what he'd read, there were irreversible consequences of death-regeneration events. He could come back, exist in an identical body, and with mostly the same mind, but he would have a new perspective on his own existence. He'd have a new perception of reality, along with some new knowledge with which some people found it difficult to cope.

Sometimes, he figured, it was better to be in the dark.

The other problem was that he was becoming comfortable with his new life. It was exciting – he could do anything. And there was so much to learn and experience.

And that presented another potential problem: what if he died and returned to a regenerated body with so much knowledge that nothing remained novel? What if he got bored? It reminded him of a time when he was nine years old and the whole family was stranded in a ski cabin for a week because of a blizzard. The only things they had to entertain them were a few fashion magazines and an old board game with half of the pieces missing. No television, no books, not even something with which to write or draw. His parents tried hard to keep him and his sister busy – daily calisthenics and yoga, stories, and conversation – but it was otherwise six days of torture for a nine-year-old. Perhaps that's what life was like for someone who knew everything. Maybe that's why the Deltas had disappeared.

He needed to learn more about what to expect.

He went to the coffee-table computer and searched for more information about regeneration and found personal reflections of Deltas who had died and regenerated for the first time. In most cases, there was a transition time filled with psychological strife and confusion, mostly from an existential perspective. In some cases, a person would kill themselves after their regeneration and then not return – neither through regeneration nor reincarnation, which was confirmed by precise population monitoring.

The ones who had done the best were the "new souls," those who had been in their "first life." They didn't have to deal with the memories and emotions of multiple previous lives, so their adjustment was minimal when returning to a regenerated body.

Will was puzzled about the origin of new souls, as the Deltas had also been, but he had at least a cloudy image of the final destination of those who never returned. That information had come from Landau.

Some Deltas testified that their existences had been enhanced by learning of their previous lives, and others had discovered things of which they were embarrassed or ashamed. It was knowledge one could never unlearn unless they died and reincarnated.

This reminded him of the ancestry research and DNA tracing that had been the trending fad on Earth for the past decade. Some people searched in hope of discovering that they were related to someone famous, or to royalty. Others sought to unveil unknown branches of their families. But what about those who found that they were related to a notorious criminal? A ruthless dictator? A mass murderer?

Will huffed aloud and smiled to himself. In what he was about to do, he wasn't going to be discovering long-lost relatives of questionable character. He was going to be revealing different versions of himself – and it was quite possible that he wouldn't be pleased by what he'd find. After all, looking back on his present life, he'd killed many. What if he discovered things even worse in his past lives?

Will had a light dinner – Chinese food – and then started on his way to the whiskey bar.

He needed the knowledge, even if it ruined him.

LENNY SLEPT until 10:00 a.m., showered, checked out of his ratty hotel, and was on the road a half hour later. He was still groggy from the long night of interrogating Dr. Daoping Bao.

The operation hadn't gone as smoothly as he'd hoped, but he'd finally found Bao in the basement of his house. Before arriving, Lenny had made a stop at a self-storage facility and picked up some vials of "fire fluid." The drug was a product of Syncorp, which the sinister company had developed for the Red Wraith project and its unlucky subjects. Twenty seconds after being injected with the iridescent-red fluid, the recipient would scream like a sick infant due to pain that could only be described as being incinerated alive in the oven of a crematorium. Bao gave up everything he had, including names and the specifics about the viruses. Lenny was supposed to kill him, but the CIA instead took him away afterwards to continue the interrogation. One reason for this was the list of names he'd provided: it included numerous U.S. citizens within the federal government and research institutions. He had the feeling that there were going to be some disappearances.

Lenny turned into a public parking lot, ditched his rental car, and picked up a different one. At 11:30 a.m. he found a chain breakfast restaurant and went inside.

The place was filled with pensioners and what seemed to be college students, many of whom were only drinking coffee and working on their laptops.

He found a booth in the back, next to a window with a good view of both the entrance and his car.

The server arrived immediately, poured a cup of coffee from a carafe that she left with him, and took his order. Lenny selected the "behemoth breakfast," which included three eggs, bacon, toast, hashbrown potatoes, and a large stack of pancakes. He hoped it would be enough.

As he sipped coffee and waited for his order to arrive, his newest Chinese mobile buzzed – one of Yong's minions had delivered the phone to him the day before. It was a text informing him that there was a message in the usual account.

He slipped the phone back into his pocket, took out his laptop, and powered it up. Connected to the Internet through his CIA phone, he navigated to the email account and found a new message saved in the drafts folder.

Yong was moving things up in the schedule due to "unforeseen complications." And now Lenny was on deck.

He assumed that his activities from just a few hours prior had something to do with it – another one of Yong's contacts evaporating. It wasn't surprising that the news had gotten to Yong so quickly. Daoping Bao probably had a strict check-in schedule, and there would have been a second verification if he missed one – a check-in by an operative at the Bao household. When they found no one there, alarms would have gone off at Chinese intelligence and contingency plans would've been put into operation. They would have figured that Bao had either deserted, or been taken in by counterintelligence. Next, they would've checked on his family, and would have found that they were missing as well.

Lenny wondered how his business had gotten so complicated. It used to be that he'd get a contract for a hit, and then carry it out, collect the cash, and disappear. Now, he was playing the part of a spook – a double agent nonetheless – and it didn't suit him.

He pushed his laptop to the side when his food arrived and wrote an update to Thackett as he ate.

The server returned when he was halfway through his breakfast, and he ordered another plate of eggs and a stack of French toast. He was going to need energy for the next 48 hours and made a note to pick up some nutrition bars before heading to the Chinese safe house that afternoon.

He responded to Yong's draft email with one of his own, telling him that he'd make the 9:00 p.m. meeting, the urgency of which was reflected in the fact that Yong wanted him to go directly to the safe house, skipping the usual escort protocol.

Lenny had the urge to take out Yong and his wife immediately, especially upon learning the full extent of the plan as described by Bao. But he couldn't eliminate them just yet. It was just like pulling an enormous weed: he had to be sure that the roots came out with the poisonous plant on the surface. If one pulled too fast, the roots would break off and the plant would come back.

He sent the email to Thackett and then browsed Internet news sources for a while. The world was in a strange state. The news was saturated with conspiracy theories about everything from aliens to geopolitics. And there had been an American presidential election just weeks ago that he would not have even noticed if it hadn't been for Thackett informing him that he was going to be the CIA director for another term.

Next, Lenny checked his bank accounts and found that the latest funds deposited from Chinese sources had been transferred to his account in the Cayman Islands, and then to DMS, Inc., his "retirement" agency. He wondered if he'd ever spend any of that money but, either way, it was good to know that it was there. DMS even placed a percentage of the funds in conservative investments, so the sum would actually grow at a modest rate. His retirement was secure, if it ever really came.

Lenny paid his bill, left a generous tip, and drove off in search of a store where he'd purchase nutrition bars and energy drinks. He was going to need them.

WILL WENT TO THE BAR, ordered a scotch, and wove through the crowd to the booth where he'd last spoken with Landau. The place was packed with a diverse assortment of characters, as usual, some of whom were talking about the New York Giants and their upcoming game the next day. He didn't see Danielle but knew she could be there somewhere. He didn't see Landau, either.

Will was considering ending his "virgin" life and opening his mind to a wider perspective. It meant taking a bite of the proverbial "forbidden fruit," and the risk was that he'd suddenly realize that he was naked, so to speak. He'd already had a taste of how added knowledge could affect him: when he'd lifted the memory of the so-called Judge in the probe it had screwed up his mind to the point that he didn't trust his own thoughts. Now he imagined having the memories of 100 lives – or more – all jammed into his brain, although he'd read that it didn't quite work like that.

The lights dimmed and the crowd went quiet. Two men brought a drum set onto a one-foot-tall platform on the far end of the room that Will had noticed the last time he'd visited. A few minutes later, a group of musicians went to the small stage, and the ambiance was enhanced with light jazz and low crowd noise. That's when Landau emerged from the crowd and sat across from him.

Will had anticipated the encounter but couldn't force any words out of his mouth.

"I see you are still undecided," Landau said. "I've been watching for you."

"Watching for me?" Will asked, confused. "Here?"

Landau shook his head and pointed upward. "Out there."

Will knew he meant that he'd been looking for his severed soul.

"I still don't understand why I need to do this," Will said. "I could hardly handle carrying the Judge's memories in my brain. This will drive me insane – like multiple personalities."

Landau shook his head. "That was different," he said. "The information you acquired in the case of the Judge was formed outside of your experience. Everything else in your soul – from this life and others – has been acquired by living through it. And there are other things you will learn as well while you're out there."

"Like what?"

Landau held up his hand. "I can't say," he said. "However, if you do this, you'll not be the same afterwards."

"I know. I've read about the so-called virgin life and how the blindfold will be removed," Will said. "Why can't I get access to this information when I separate?"

"You, in fact, do have access to some things – but those are mostly sensory abilities, rather than memories," Landau said. "For example, you exercised time expansion – the apparent slowing of time – when you were in the Exoskeleton."

Landau was referring to the apparent freezing of time he'd experienced when the man had fired a gun at him inside the Red Box.

"Of course, time doesn't slow down," Landau continued. "But you do have access to dimensions outside of space and time while in the separated state. When you're completely severed from your body, you'll have full access to such things."

"How much will I remember when I regenerate?" Will asked.

"You'll retain only a small fraction of what you see when you are 'dead,' as you say," Landau replied. "That word, however, is not appropriate in the way you use it."

"But the being in the probe offered to spare me the 'soul's death' that was going to happen to all of those on Earth if I just admitted to his charges," Will argued. "What did he mean by that?"

"Souls do disappear," Landau explained. "But the Regenerators do not have the power to destroy them. Destroying the entire planet, however, would give the detached souls no place to go – no opportunity for reincarnation or regeneration. Some believe that immature souls cannot go 'beyond the horizon,' but that's purely conjecture."

"Then what happens to them?" Will asked.

"There are still two fundamental questions for which I think no one knows the answers," Landau replied. "From where do new souls come, and where do they go when they disappear?"

"Can't they find some other planet with similar life forms, and then reincarnate?"

"Even if they could drift around and happen upon a new world inhabited by another intelligent species, the chances that their souls would be compatible are miniscule," Landau explained. "Some think that the souls of an exterminated race disperse throughout the universe and individually dissipate into nothingness. They call it the death of a race, but that's a philosophical discussion."

Anger was starting to invade Will's mind. He imagined the lonely lost souls of his friends, family, Denise, and the billions of others, searching aimlessly for a place to go.

"What gives those bastards the authority to do such a thing?" Will asked. "Why has no one destroyed *them*? *Can* they be destroyed?"

"Perhaps," Landau said.

"Do the Regenerators have a home planet?" Will asked. His thoughts were darkening.

"They have many planets," Landau said, his expression indicating that he knew where Will's thoughts were headed. "You'd have to destroy them all."

"Maybe I should try," Will said. "If they destroyed Earth, they deserve to be annihilated. If they did not destroy Earth, they're still an existential threat, and could return to destroy the planet at any time. They should be eliminated."

"It's a sound argument, based on what you know," Landau said. "But maybe you should consider obtaining more knowledge first."

At that moment, the bartender arrived with two bulbous cognac glasses, the very bottoms of which contained about a shot and a half of reddish-brown elixirs. As he set them down, he indicated that Landau's was "Remy Martin XO," and Will's was "Hennessy Ellipse."

Will downed the last of his whiskey and handed the empty tumbler to the bartender, who took it and disappeared into the crowd.

"I thought you wanted me to try the *Seraphim Hors d'Âge*," Will said, knowing that he'd butchered the French part.

"*Seraphim Hors d'Âge*," Landau repeated with what sounded to Will's untrained ear like the correct pronunciation. "It's for you to decide the right time for that."

"It seems that everything is for me to decide, except for where this ship is taking me," Will said. "It doesn't matter what I intend to do if can't change course. Why can't you just tell me what I need to know."

"Because it's not something that I can simply tell you," Landau said as he took a sniff, and then a sip, of his cognac.

Will countered with a swig of his Hennessy Ellipse, and noticed that it tasted different from the whiskey and was also distinct from the previous cognacs he'd tried. Until recently, he could barely distinguish whiskey from brandy.

"I can tell you this, however," Landau continued. "Dying won't ruin you. It will just change you. In most cases, for the better."

"I can't get what I need any other way?" Will asked.

"I think not," Landau said.

Will stared at Landau for a few seconds and again considered the possibility that he was falling for a trick. The *Exodus 9*'s artificial intelligence and technology could easily con him into doing something crazy if it wanted to. But what would be the purpose of such a deception?

"You don't believe I'm real," Landau said, as if he were reading Will's thoughts. "Separate for a moment, if you will."

Will had considered doing this before. It would be an added verification to see Landau in his "wraith" state, but it still wouldn't be definitive. "How do I know that whatever I'll see when separated isn't also an illusion?"

"Fair point," Landau said. "But how can the *Exodus 9* know what I looked like to you in the cemetery?"

Will knew that he was referring to their encounter in the graveyard in Baton Rouge. "Okay," he said, and then leaned back in the booth and separated.

The next thing he knew he was drifting over the crowd and could see the full expanse of the room and the technical equipment that was creating the scene. It still amazed him that the full illusion of New York City could be crammed inside a room the size of a basketball gymnasium.

Landau drifted from his body and joined him. He looked exactly as Will remembered – the wispy, cloud-like wraith from the cemetery resembling the ghost of an old wizard.

"I am here," Landau said. "Shall we go back?"

Will recombined with his body and opened his eyes. Landau was looking back at him.

"That's all the proof I can give you," Landau said, and stood.

"You're leaving?" Will asked.

"I hope you will be content with the choices you make," Landau said, and then slipped into the crowd and disappeared.

Will remained in his seat and contemplated Landau's words. Five minutes later, he swallowed the last few drops of the cognac in his glass.

He waved down a cocktail server.

"Can I get something for you?" the woman asked as she grabbed Landau's empty glass and set it on a round tray.

"Please bring me another cognac," he said and handed her his empty glass. "Make it a *Seraphim Hors d'Âge.*"

DANIEL AND SYLVIA sipped tea as they waited on the couch in 713. It was the organic Sencha that Sylvia had given him a few weeks prior. He needed strong coffee.

"Thackett rarely calls a meeting this late," Silvia said. "Even though we're usually still working."

Daniel agreed. It almost never happened. It was 1:45 a.m.

"Do you think something's wrong?" she asked.

Before he could answer, Thackett walked in at a hurried clip and approached them. He didn't sit.

"We've gotten word of an imminent attack on Space Systems," he said. "We're leaving in a few hours. Tell Jonathan and Denise to get packed."

"What about Jacob?" Daniel asked.

"I'm taking care of it," he said. "You're taking a helicopter from the roof at 5:00 a.m. sharp. Make sure everyone is in 713, packed, and ready to go at 4:30, and then get up there."

"What's the threat?" Daniel asked.

"Biological agents," Thackett replied. "Multiple, credible threats at several locations, one of which is Space Systems."

Thackett pulled a vibrating phone out of his pocket, glanced at it, and put it back. "I won't be going with you, but I'll meet you there," he said.

"Where?" Sylvia asked.

"A secure place near Area 51," Thackett replied, and then hurried out the door.

Daniel's ears hummed at a high pitch as if he'd just taken a blow to the head.

"I'm scared," Sylvia said.

"I'm sure this is just protocol," Daniel said, trying to calm himself along with Sylvia. "Make sure you have everything you need on your laptop or external drives, and don't forget to pack your chargers."

He stood from the couch and headed for the door.

"Where are you going?" Sylvia asked.

"To tell Denise and Jonathan," he replied.

"I'm going with you," she said and caught up with him as he exited 713.

He could tell she was frightened. So was he.

At 2:45 a.m., Lenny used a counterfeit ID embedded with a cloned chip, given to him by Yong's wife, to get him through the entrance gate of the Space Systems building. He then parked in a sublevel of the garage and waited in the car, as instructed.

In their meeting, six hours prior, Yong had informed him that they were moving immediately, and Lenny had to scramble to get Thackett the warning.

After a few nervous minutes, Lenny spotted a figure approaching in his rearview mirror. It was a young man, with short blonde hair, wearing jeans and a white polo shirt.

Lenny rolled down the window as the man approached.

"You here for the tour?" the man asked in an accent that Lenny thought might be Scandinavian. It was the phrase he expected.

"Excited to see the place," he replied as he pulled a lever and popped the trunk.

Lenny got out, closed the door, and retrieved the case that contained the virus delivery device from a hidden compartment in the forward part of the trunk, just behind the back seat. He then gently snapped the trunk closed and followed the man to an elevator. They descended.

"I'm Nick," the man said. "You're Lenny, right?"

"Where are we going?" Lenny asked.

"To meet the contact who's going to help you place the device," Nick replied.

"I thought I was just here for support," Lenny said and clenched his hand on the handle of the case. He despised poor planning more than anything – and changing plans as you went along was poor planning. To top it off, Yong's wife, "Sara," was supposed to be with him, but that plan had somehow changed as well.

"You're going to set it up to release at 10:00 a.m.," Nick said. "Everyone should be in the building by then."

Lenny quelled the urge to crush the man's throat with his bare hands.

The elevator stopped, and Nick led him through a labyrinth of dark corridors before arriving in a small room that looked to be a storage closet with a table in the center. Boxes of paper and printer cartridges filled shelves around the perimeter.

Nick glanced at his phone. "We're a few minutes early," he said.

"What do you do here?" Lenny asked.

"Network maintenance," Nick replied as a light knock came at the door.

The door opened slowly and a thin Asian woman, late 20s, entered and closed the door behind her.

"You have the device ready?" she whispered. A tag on her shirt read "Tina Zhang." She had no discernable accent. She was likely American born, or had at least been in the US from a young age, and Nick was probably of European descent, as was Luuk Janssen, the virologist Lenny had helped bring in days before. He couldn't understand the motivations behind their actions, but they were going to pay the price.

"I can set the device timer now," Lenny said as he set the case on the table and opened it. Inside was the gleaming steel canister with circular ports and valves. The screen on the electronics module was dim, so he pushed the "Program" button and it illuminated. He slipped the smaller, soda-can-sized cylinder into a matching receptacle on the larger vessel.

"Looks different than the other one," Nick said.

The woman shot Nick an angry glance.

Lenny's neck stiffened. "Other one?"

"Yours is a secondary device – a backup," Tina said.

"I thought the other devices were intended for different targets," Lenny said.

"The operations all have redundancies built in," she explained. "Every target has at least two devices – two different pathogens to be released at staggered times."

"You could've programmed this device and placed it yourself," Lenny said. "Why am I here?

"In case things get hairy," Nick replied.

"Who programmed the other device?" Lenny asked as he pushed buttons to set the time. "And who placed it?"

"I programmed it and Tina placed it," Nick replied.

"Where is it?" he asked.

"It's in the internal ductwork that bypasses the building's air purifier on the top floor," Tina explained. "This one's going on another inlet just above it, so the product will follow a different path through the building."

"Won't the air purifier remove the pathogen once the air cycles?" Lenny asked.

"It's already been taken offline," Nick said. "A hacker did it from the outside."

Probably Yong's wife, Lenny thought. "How much time do we have to install it and get out of here before the first one goes off?" he asked.

"About two hours – 5:00 a.m.," Tina replied. "The air will be saturated just as people arrive, and the air system will be set to recirculate – intake and exhaust ports will be closed. Your device should be programmed to disperse at 10.00 a.m. for the second wave."

"Anyone else we need to warn to get the hell out?" Lenny asked as his heart pounded. "Do we have others in the building?"

"It's clear – and none of our people will show for work today," Tina said.

Lenny pushed some buttons, pretending to program the device, and a hissing sound suddenly emanated from the vessel.

"My God!" Lenny yelled and backed toward the door. "I must have done something wrong!"

Nick and Tina froze for a few seconds and then made a rush for the door.

Lenny pushed them both back, toward the device.

"You've killed us!" Tina screamed and rushed at him again. He pushed her hard and she fell to the floor.

Nick then made a move toward him.

Lenny pulled out his gun, aimed it at Nick's face, and then looked to Tina and said, "Not yet I haven't."

WILL STARED AT THE GLASS. It looked like all of the other cognacs, except for maybe the color, which seemed to be a shade of deep red rather than the usual reddish-brown. Although it might have just been in his mind, it seemed to glimmer with an iridescence that he hadn't seen in the others. He brought the wide mouth of the snifter up to his nose and inhaled. Its aroma was sweet.

What was he doing? He was risking his existence, or the *state* of his existence, for what? The off chance of learning something that would get him back to Earth? What then?

A female voice distracted him from his thoughts, and he turned and looked.

It was Danielle. She was in a short black dress and had her dark hair in a tight bun on the top of her head. She sat across from him.

"What are you drinking?" she asked. She raised her eyebrow in a way that indicated that she already knew the answer.

"*Seraphim Hors d'Âge*," he said.

She grinned. "Was that supposed to be French?"

He shrugged. "What can I say?"

"You've decided then?" she asked.

"I don't think I have much of a choice," he replied. He then realized that she had more information than she should have, based on their previous, short conversations. It didn't surprise him.

"You'd feel guilty if you didn't try?"

"I think so, yes," he replied. He supposed he could just ignore Earth, his past, all of the people he loved, and then live in a world where he was healthy, physically young, and could live out any fantasy he could conjure. His life could go on for thousands of years, and he could learn everything that the Deltas knew, and maybe even more. But, if he did that, he'd have a mark on his soul: he would've let everyone die – or worse – without even trying. And he wouldn't have kept his promise.

"Remember," Danielle said and nodded toward his glass. "Best when consumed quickly."

Will looked at her and nodded.

He brought the glass to his lips and downed the *Seraphim* in two gulps. As cognacs went, it was aromatic and sweet. But his stomach quickly turned sour.

Hot white speckles invaded his vision, and then he lost track of everything ...

LENNY SHOT Nick between the eyes, spraying blood and brain matter onto Tina, who had just stood up behind him.

She screamed, and Lenny turned the gun on her.

"You killed him!" she yelled. "You killed us all!"

Lenny didn't know whether the ruse that the hissing nitrogen gas emanating from the device was a virus was going to help or hinder his task of getting information from the woman.

"Take me to the canister you planted, and I'll get you to a hospital," he said.

"Fuck you," she said. "We're dead. There's no cure for this."

"Then why don't you redeem your miserable life by stopping the other one?" he asked.

"Wait," Tina said as she stared at him with a suspicious expression. "Why aren't you panicking?"

"My life is irredeemable," he said.

"Bullshit," she said, her eyes widening as she glanced between him and the hissing device. "You didn't release the virus – that's a fake device."

"You caught me," he said and then nodded toward Nick's body, which happened to twitch at exactly that moment. "Unless you want to end up like him, you'd better take me to the other device right now."

She stared at him for a second, seemingly contemplating whether to make a move.

Lenny made his own move without hesitation just in case she was carrying a weapon of her own.

She yelped as he grabbed her upper arm and forced her down to the concrete floor. He knelt on her chest as he put his gun in his jacket, and then groped every inch of her body looking for weapons and communications devices. He felt something cylindrical that extended from the band of her pants into her crotch area. He reached in and pulled it out. It was a syringe mounted to a six-inch handle. The needle was covered with a plastic cap. It was a type of assassination device that he'd seen before: a button on the handle first ejected the cap to expose the needle and then, upon further actuation, forced out the fluid. The needle was just an inch long, but thick.

"What's this?" he asked as he put it in front of her face.

She remained silent.

"Who were you supposed to kill – me, or that asshole?" he asked, referring to Nick, who was now smelling up the place.

She didn't respond, but Lenny knew the answer, and was getting the idea of what was supposed to have gone down.

He pulled out his phone and called Thackett, who answered immediately.

"There's a live device in the building, supposedly near the air purifier, set to go off at 05:00," Lenny said, and then explained that he had a woman in custody. "I'll get as much as I can out of her and report back."

He hung up the phone and looked down at the woman. "Fun time is over," he said. "Take me to the device, now, or I swear I will break every bone in your body, one by one."

"I don't care what you do," Tina hissed.

"When this is done, we're going to find out all about you," Lenny said. "And if just one person dies, we're going to find your family and torture them to death, youngest first."

Her eyes widened.

"You have kids? Siblings? Elderly parents?" he asked. "Whatever I am about to do to you, I will do to them, and worse."

It was a lie, but sometimes Lenny felt enough rage to do such things. "Unfortunately, I don't have a proper set of tools with me," he said. "So, it looks like I'm going to have to do this by hand."

He grabbed the middle finger of her left hand and bent it backwards. It popped just as it reached the top of her wrist.

Words were mixed in with her screams, but Lenny couldn't make out what she was saying.

"Take me to the device," he said, and lifted her to her feet.

She was thin, and Lenny had learned the hard way with Jacob Hale that distance runners were one of his weaknesses. He couldn't take any chances.

He dragged her around the room as he searched for something with which to tie her, and eventually settled on a power cord to a printer. He tied it around her neck like a collar, grabbed it with his left hand, and forced her to the door.

"Take me to the device," he ordered and jerked her neck.

"It's too late," she said. "It can't be stopped."

Lenny grabbed her left wrist with his right hand and squeezed the two bones together until one of them snapped, eliciting a searing squeal from the woman. He then took a firm hold of her broken wrist with one hand and grabbed the cord with the other.

"What do you mean it can't be stopped?" he asked.

"I don't know how to stop it!" she yelled, crying.

"Take me to it!"

"No!"

He squeezed and twisted her broken wrist.

She screamed, and then bent over and vomited.

When she recovered, he actuated the button on the syringe's handle and the plastic cap popped open, exposing the needle. He put it up to her neck and started to pierce the skin.

"Which way?" he asked.

"Okay," she said. "Go left."

THE SPECKLING SUBSIDED and Will's vision adjusted. His senses had changed somehow. At first, he felt like he did when he separated. But then it got much more intense.

He was no longer in the whiskey bar, and his time on the *Exodus 9* seemed like an old dream. He could see in all directions at once, and he sensed that he was moving.

After a few seconds – although his perception of time seemed to be askew as if he were dreaming – he realized that he was flying through a colossal tube-like passageway, the walls of which looked to be composed of distant stars, as if the night sky had been rolled up like a carpet.

His entire awareness had abruptly changed. It was like the feeling one got when the power went out for a few hours during a nighttime storm and then the lights suddenly came on again. Everything was visible and familiar somehow but, in this case, the familiarity came as a sense of déjà vu rather than direct memory. He had an immense feeling of relief, as if every concern of his life had been lifted.

The tunnel twisted and turned as he seemed to accelerate. The stars in the walls turned into lines of light that curved and spiraled and eventually swirled like water going down a drain. A point of white light appeared in the distance and brightened as he approached.

In what seemed like a blink of an eye, it became brighter than the sun, and a comforting warmth infused him.

An instant later, he shot into an expansive void like a stream of water after traversing a coiled hose and then blasting out of a nozzle and into the sunlight. He was completely severed from his body. He was out of his life.

As he observed his surroundings, his consciousness seemed to expand with a flood of knowledge, memories, and emotions. The things he had been in his past lives came to the fore and, in an instant, he knew everything.

He was dead. But he wasn't.

LENNY BOMBARDED Tina with questions as he dragged her through a labyrinth of corridors to an elevator. Her access card got them through everything and, while in the elevator, he got the name of the contact who had given her the card and texted it to Thackett.

When they reached the top floor, Tina led him out of the elevator, down a hallway, and into a utility room. Inside was the air filtration system, which howled with fans and the rush of forced air. She pointed to a rectangular metal structure at the center of the room with four enormous, vertical intake ducts, and at least 20 output tubes, which extended horizontally from the box and spurred off in different directions. She pointed to a two-foot-square panel on the structure.

Lenny dragged her closer. The metal panel had four wing nuts holding it in place, and he removed them. He pulled off the panel and located a shiny cylinder strapped in a space that was supposed to contain a cylindrical air filter.

The device looked a little different than the one he'd been handling – it was slightly larger and had more ports protruding from the curved wall of the cylinder. Two red lights flashed, and the display clock read "+12:37" and was counting up.

"What does this mean?" Lenny asked as he dragged the woman by her damaged arm to the panel and then forced her head inside.

She stared at it for a few seconds and then a smile grew on her face.

"What?" Lenny yelled at her over the noise.

"It has already been activated," she replied. Her smile widened. "You're too late."

Lenny stared at her for a few seconds as he tried to suppress the urge to panic. He then called Thackett and told him that the device had activated 13 minutes ago and to get everyone out of the building. He got final instructions and hung up the phone.

Lenny pulled out his gun and shot Tina in the forehead twice before she fell over. He put two more in her head after she hit the floor.

He found the control panel for the air system and shut down the filtration unit. He assumed the air intake would now bypass the filtration system, and therefore the virus dispersion device, altogether. It was all he could do. But it was probably too late.

Lenny made his way to the elevator with Tina's access card and scrambled to the parking garage.

Yong and his wife were next.

DANIEL WAS in his flat when he got Thackett's call at 3:50 a.m. The situation had become urgent, and they had to leave as soon as possible.

Daniel called the others and gave them 10 minutes to get to 713. He hoped everyone had their bags packed and ready.

As soon as everyone arrived, they'd go to the roof and board a helicopter for Joint Base Andrews. The next stop was Nevada. They were heading to a secret facility, not far from Area 51.

He grabbed his backpack, went to 713, and rummaged through things in his office. There were a lot of file folders and books, but he figured he could manage with what was on his laptop.

On his desk computer, he wrote a one-line email to all the Omnis: "Code Black. This is not a test." It would be sent to their mobile phones and email accounts, actuating a predetermined sequence of events. The phrase meant that they were to immediately head to prearranged locations outside the DC area – everyone to different places. Daniel would maintain contact with them from his new location.

Daniel and the others were headed to Site 4, a place he'd seen referenced in some of his older research. It was one of over a dozen deeply buried sites in the area that were both well-hidden and resistant to nuclear attack. There had been rumors that the mysterious complex of sites was used to reverse engineer extraterrestrial technologies, including downed spacecraft. Daniel knew that was true – that they'd been studying things that were purportedly of alien origin – but nothing had ever been verified, at least as far as he knew. His understanding was that all they had were scraps of shattered equipment and unidentifiable biological materials that could not be reconstructed to form either ships, or the "little gray men" that appeared on the alien-research TV shows. He wondered whether the technical drawings Jacob had extracted from the radio signals from deep space would help them with the mechanical components.

Site 4 was special, however, and had a specific purpose. It was called a "dark-mode" facility. It was for wartime. It was one of a few locations where key military personnel could relocate and run operations, even during a nuclear holocaust. It had virtually unlimited electrical power with its own nuclear power plant and battery storage system. It had medical facilities, and immense food and water supplies. Of utmost importance, however, were its vast communications functionalities. The downside was that it was not easy to get there. They'd have to land at Area 51 and take land transportation from that point.

Daniel did his best to quash his feelings of panic, but his hands trembled as he crammed a bag of his favorite tea into his backpack. They were going to Site 4 because there was an imminent threat of war. That they were going early meant that it was no longer just a threat – something was actually happening.

The sound of a closing door interrupted his thoughts. He slung his backpack over his shoulder and walked into the main room.

Sylvia, Denise, and Jonathan stood near the entrance and stared at him with puffy faces and disheveled hair.

As he walked toward the door at a hurried clip, he said, "Let's go."

WILL FELT as if his mind – if that was the right term – had burst like a balloon. It was now free of constraints. The lights had been turned on.

He seemed to be suspended in a black, vacuous space near a glowing structure that resembled a colossal, cylindrical cord. It could have been a thousand miles in diameter and millions of miles long, but his perception of size and distance had no points of reference. Billions of filamentary "nerves" branched radially from the central conduit, which appeared to be straight and disappeared to infinity in both directions. It glowed in a brilliant white light, but he could see tiny specks of all colors when he focused on a specific point. The filaments seemed to move and twist, and new ones would emerge from the main channel while others would contract back into it, as if they were alive. Some curled back and reentered the main structure at another location.

To his left, the enormous channel faded into blackness. To his right, it merged into a warm glow, like a distant ship dissolving into a sunset. He had a strong urge to go to the right, toward the glow, which seemed to be the "forward" direction of the conduit.

He moved around the structure and was drawn to a strange event. Something had emerged from the end of one of the filaments. He went to it.

It was a soul.

He did not know how it communicated with him, but it asked him where it was, to which Will replied that he did not know.

An instant later, a new filament sprouted some distance up the main channel, toward the light. The soul approached it, seemed to study it for a short time, and then entered it and disappeared.

That must have been a reincarnation, Will thought, although he didn't know why he'd concluded that.

His attention then focused inward, into his own thoughts. He remembered everything. He'd lived over 400 lives, the first of which had not begun on Earth.

He was a Delta.

JACOB READ THE TEXT AGAIN. They were leaving.

Thackett had given him the option to meet them at their future undisclosed location at a later time, if he wished. In the meantime, he'd be safe at 17 Swann. He had enough food to last more than a month, and he'd just ordered enough for another six weeks. He wasn't to leave the premises until the all-clear was given, or if he decided to evacuate DC via Joint Base Andrews.

He couldn't believe what was happening. A virus had been released in the Space Systems building. Most of the personnel had been evacuated, but there was a chance that others, including Daniel and the rest of the group, had been exposed. The pathogen was, as of yet, unidentified.

It was 4:15 a.m., and he'd had a horrible night's sleep, which was cut short by Thackett's text. It looked like he'd have many sleepless nights to come.

It seemed to him that, if the outbreak was not contained, the US was going to go to war with China. He was in a bad spot for such a thing, as the recent development confirmed, but maybe this was a place where he'd be able to do something. Although, he wasn't sure what that would be.

Jacob thought it was strange that the situation, which had progressed to the brink of war, was the result of almost nothing material. There were no major border disputes, economic factors, or arms races currently happening. The few skirmishes between the two countries were relatively small scale, and hardly drew the public's attention.

The fight was over knowledge, and driven by paranoia.

He was glad Pauli was in London. He otherwise had no family in DC, but still worried about friends in the area. He hoped the biological agent, whatever it was, would be contained.

It was going to be a strange day. The only thing he could do was to carry on with his work. Today was the day that his group of CIA and NSA cohorts would carry out the full takeover of the Chinese satellite cluster, implementing the mask program, Façade 1.0.

He wondered if it even mattered, at this point, whether or not the takeover was covert. It seemed to him that the US and China were already at war.

IT WASN'T ONLY a tsunami of memories and knowledge that flooded into Will's consciousness, but also a wave of complex emotions which put it all into context.

He now understood his lineage through time – hundreds of lives – and comprehended how he'd developed into what he was now. He tracked those lives back to the very first one, his first existence.

Nearly 40 thousand years ago, he'd been the captain of one of the ships that came to build the transport facility in Antarctica – the very complex that later took him to the *Exodus 9*. He'd also overseen the assembly of the monitoring craft positioned at distant locations, far outside Earth's solar system, that were to remain hidden and dormant until they detected the signal from the Regenerators' deep-sea beacon. That signal was an indicator that the next generation was intellectually advanced enough to leave the planet for good. It also meant that the Regenerators would soon be coming to sterilize Earth, and maybe to exterminate its inhabitants before they got a chance to flee.

The monitoring craft had responded by broadcasting information to Earth – encoded plans with instructions on how to build additional transport facilities to evacuate people before the planet was regenerated.

About the time everything was completed – two years of work – there had been an incident. He'd been flying a ship near the surface of the planet – in a desert area – and something catastrophic had happened. He didn't know the details, but he'd been killed.

He wasn't clear exactly why he hadn't gone to a regenerated body. And he hadn't been reincarnated as a Delta, and certainly hadn't gone "beyond the horizon," whatever that was.

Strangely, he'd reincarnated into an unborn of the next generation. It was something that shouldn't have been possible.

His soul had been more evolved than those of the new fledgling generation, and it shouldn't have been a compatible reincarnation. But it happened somehow, and it was now clear to him that all but the first of his many lives had been lived as a part of the new generation.

Suddenly, Will felt an urge to move. It was a pull, like that of the warmth one feels when coming in from the freezing cold, or of the aromas emanating from a restaurant when one is famished.

It also tugged in another way. It reminded Will of the feeling he'd gotten when making the long trips home from college during the holidays: the closer he'd gotten to his hometown the more familiar things had become. By the time he'd gotten to within a mile of home, he'd had to make a conscious effort not to speed.

The direction of the pull was not toward the complex structure – the conduit – which seemed to encompass the reality in which he'd existed up to this point, but rather away from it.

At that instant, something else pulled him in another direction. This was a more urgent feeling, like running to get into your car during a downpour. It was coming from within the enormous cord-like structure, which had so many glowing filaments protruding from it that it seemed to have fur.

The two influences were strong but opposed each other. He had to make a choice: go toward the conduit – his current reality – or head away from it.

His thoughts went back to the reason he was there – and what he was supposed to learn. It must have been to retrieve the knowledge of his very first life, as a Delta. In particular, he needed any memory that might help him get back to Earth.

He concentrated on his first life and memories flooded into his consciousness. He hadn't had parents, siblings, or children. He'd had friends, but no wife or girlfriend – it wasn't the way things occurred in the Delta civilization. He'd been brought up to serve in the Exploratory Defense Branch of the military, and had been assigned to oversee the exodus of the next generation.

The Deltas had no longer feared the Regenerators but despised the process by which they vetted other civilizations. The Regenerators were a mysterious species that even the Deltas, whose civilization seemed to be just as technologically advanced, had not completely understood. It appeared that the Regenerators' place in the universe had been preordained. And that's why the Delta word for them translated more accurately to "The Originals."

Will had to remember, however, that any information he recalled from his first life was outdated by at least 40 thousand years.

The two-way emotional pull was gaining strength, and he needed to decide which way to go. Why was he here again? Information. His first life – what could help him commandeer the *Exodus 9*? An access code? A trick? There must have been something in the mind of a Delta captain that could help him. He concentrated and recalled all kinds of things, but personal, emotional thoughts kept leaking into the forefront.

In an instant, a torrent of memories obscured everything. He saw images of loved ones from uncountable lives, and felt a longing for each of them simultaneously. He relived scenes of things he'd done – the worst were from his most recent life, although there were others that were nearly as bad. Feelings of regret, shame, futility, and loneliness pushed him toward the black, away from the bright channel of light that seemed to team with life.

He then moved away from the bright conduit and toward the darkness at a great pace. As he did so, a warm sensation engulfed him. It was like coming out of frigid water and into the sun.

Although the draw to continue in that direction was strong, he stopped and looked back. He was stunned to see that what he'd first thought was a straight conduit was actually a colossal ring. He couldn't quite see the hair-like filaments from this distance, but they were there, and the surface of the ring seemed to be constantly changing. It was as if it were alive.

He looked away from the ring, and again toward the darkness. But it wasn't as dark as before. There was something ahead. It was like seeing the faint light of a city in the night sky from miles away. There was something over the horizon, and it beckoned him.

It occurred to him that it wasn't his time to go over that horizon – to the next place. But somehow there was comfort in knowing that it was there. He had to go back to fulfill a promise. Perhaps, when he got to this point again, triumph would outweigh regret, and he'd pass on to the next place with a sense of contentment.

He willed his consciousness back to the conduit of light from which a specific bright filament seemed to be calling him. As he traveled at some indefinably great speed, his perspective of the ring turned it again into a line – just as the Earth looks flat to someone on its surface. He had found his passage back.

Everything went black.

12

GWEN

LENNY'S POWERFUL HANDS CLENCHED THE STEERING WHEEL SO HARD that he thought his meaty fingers might split like sausages in a microwave.

He didn't know whether he'd been infected with the virus – it was hard to imagine that he hadn't – but he had a job to do. After that, he'd get out of town, away from people, and then maybe die a miserable death.

He couldn't remember a time when he'd been angrier. He was afraid of what he was going to do to Yong, and to whoever got in his way, when he caught up with him. Yong's wife had to go, too.

The morning DC traffic was lighter than normal for some reason, and Lenny tuned the radio to a news station. A reporter explained that all government facilities in DC and surrounding areas were on lockdown due to an undisclosed terror threat.

Just as he exited the highway toward the neighborhood of Yong's safe house, Lenny's CIA phone vibrated, and he answered it. After a short conversation, he hung up, did a U-turn, and headed toward Reagan International Airport.

Yong and his wife were attempting to flee under alias identities.

DANIEL TRIED to enjoy the sunrise from his window seat in the helicopter, but his nerves were too frayed.

When they arrived at Joint Base Andrews, they were received by people in yellow hazmat suits.

"What's going on?" Sylvia asked as they exited the aircraft.

Daniel shook his head. "Just taking precautions, I guess."

They were herded into a nearby hangar and, while still fully clothed, sprayed down with a strong chemical concoction that smelled of bleach and stung Daniel's eyes. They were then separated and put into individual stalls where other hazmat-suit-wearing people were waiting with more hoses and brushes.

"Strip naked," one of them ordered and pointed to a plastic barrel, "and throw your clothes into the bin."

"What's going on?" Daniel asked.

"Please, sir, you'll be brought up to speed later," the man with the brush replied.

Daniel did as instructed, and then suffered a violating chemical-laden scrub-down that he'd never forget. The multistage disinfection was followed by a warm-water rinse. He was then dried with a device that he suspected was just a normal leaf blower. Finally, he was dressed in a hazmat suit of his own, which was designed to ensure that anything he might be carrying inside of him didn't get out.

"If you have to go to the bathroom, just do it in the suit," one of them said.

Daniel then followed them out of the stall to a golf cart that took him to a gigantic C-130 transport plane that was warming up on the tarmac with its rear door down.

He walked up the ramp and found the others already strapped into their seats. He was directed to a spot between Jonathan and Sylvia, and then fastened in snugly.

He glanced at Sylvia, whose eyes looked larger than normal. She was frightened, as was he.

With his left, hand he patted her knee and yelled over the accelerating engines, "We'll be okay."

She nodded and seemed to force a smile.

The plane edged forward as its rear door started to rise. It gave the impression that they were in a hurry to get off the ground.

Daniel's stomach churned as his nerves twitched. He had to hold himself together. If he vomited inside the suit, it would be with him the whole way to the Nevada desert.

LENNY FOUND WANG "JIMMY" Yong sitting in a bathroom stall in Reagan International's C terminal. The first shot put a hole through his two front teeth, and the second one went into his forehead. A third bullet opened a hole between the man's eyes as he slid off the bowl.

Lenny's attention was then attracted to the adjacent stall, where a man lifted his feet out of view.

He kicked in the door, exposing a bald man in his 60s wearing a suit, a brown briefcase at his feet. He had a *New York Times* in his lap. Not a target.

Lenny closed the stall door, slipped the gun into his coat, and checked his disguise in the mirror. He was wearing a fake beard, large, tinted glasses, and a driving cap that made him look like a cabby.

It didn't take long to locate Chunhua "Sara" Yong. She was at Gate 37 in Terminal C, watching CNN and sipping a trendy frozen coffee drink from a straw. She was dressed for business in a gray skirt-suit.

Lenny called his CIA colleagues for assistance.

A few minutes later, two security guards nabbed the woman and drove her away on a motorized cart. Lenny then got a text informing him where to meet them.

Ten minutes later, he was in the bowels below the terminal, where he found his way to a small interrogation room.

When he entered, Chunhua was yelling at two men that he recognized, and tugging at the handcuffs that locked her hands behind the chair to which she was bound.

"Who in the fuck are you?" Chunhua hissed at Lenny as he closed the door behind him. Her accent was subtle, but more pronounced than that of her late husband.

Lenny pulled off the beard, which had been irritating his face, and then the glasses and hat.

The woman's eyes seemed to swell in their sockets.

"Your operative, Tina, is dead," he said as he placed the injection device he'd found in the woman's pants on the table in front of Chunhua.

She looked at the syringe and shrugged. "That's too bad."

"Clearly, you were the brains of this operation," Lenny said as he took a seat next to her, nice and close. "Your husband told me about it while he was on the crapper, just before I put three holes in his head."

The woman's face expressed disgust, rather than the emotion that he'd expected.

"We accomplished our mission," she spat. "That's all that matters."

"Is it?" Lenny asked and then leaned closer to her. "You have children, don't you, Chunhua? I know what you're thinking, they're already in China, right?"

She glared at him.

"Let me promise you something," he said. "If you don't tell me everything, your children are dead. Who knows, they might get killed in the war you've started before I get the chance."

Lenny was somehow surprised by his own words. He'd said similar things before, but this time it might actually come to war.

"I'm going to start with an easy question, and we'll go on from there," he said. "What virus did you release in Space Systems?"

Her lips formed tight, thin lines, and she remained silent.

Lenny sighed. "I'm going to cause you pain in so many ways. Soon you're going to wish that you would die, but you won't," he said. "And I'll keep track of what I'm doing because, if I survive the virus you released, I'm going to do exactly the same thing to your children."

It was a lie, of course – him going after the kids.

The door opened and a CIA operative he recognized entered and placed a small, wooden box on the table next to him. It was the remainder of the fire fluid he'd given them to use on Dr. Bao after they picked him up. They hadn't used it. He was glad.

"I'll ask again," he said and rested his hand on the box. "What virus was released in Space Systems? And what else have you dispersed, and where?"

After 30 seconds of silence, he said, "There's something fun for you inside this box, but I want you to understand that it's just the beginning. I will systematically destroy your body until I get what I need."

She glared at him in defiance.

Lenny opened the box, loaded a syringe from a vial of fire fluid, and injected it into her neck.

"Before this gets going," he said, "I just want you to know that I have hundreds of these little vials."

Twenty seconds later, the screaming began.

WILL STRUGGLED to open his eyes. For a few seconds, he had no idea where he was, or who he was.

"You've had quite an episode," said a female voice that he recognized.

Everything came back to him.

He sat up and shielded his eyes from the light. He couldn't make out her face, but he knew it was Greta, the medical specialist.

His hands felt weak, he couldn't even make a fist, and his feet tingled painfully, as if they'd been asleep and were recovering.

He remembered drinking the cognac, but that seemed like a lifetime ago. He felt different somehow. It was as if he'd gotten a glimpse of a play from backstage.

"The poison killed you in less than a minute," Greta said. "There was no chance to save your body, so we regenerated a new one. It was good that we had a recent bio-scan on file. You should be as good as new."

"How long have I been – "

" – Dead?" she cut him off. "Six days."

He looked down, over his body. He was uncovered, naked, and there was something that resembled an I-V on his arm – but no needles. Greta removed the device as she spoke.

"The question is whether this was done on purpose," she said. "Did you do it, or did someone else?"

"Does it matter?" Will asked.

She shrugged. "There are numerous activities on the ship that can result in death."

"The no-limits activities," he said.

Greta nodded. "When your body dies, there's always a chance that you will not come back," she explained. "But those who commit suicide are more likely to not return to regenerated bodies."

Will supposed that people who committed suicide ended their lives for a reason, and would therefore not want to resume them as they were. However, he figured suicide was much more complicated than that. But there was always reincarnation instead, or they could go *over the horizon*, or to *the next place*, as Landau had put it.

The next place. It was all hazy – like he'd awakened from a dream – but he was sure, now, that it existed. He remembered drinking the cognac – the *Seraphim Hors d'Âge* – and then flying through a tunnel. There were other things, but he only recalled fragments.

"This is your first regeneration," Greta said. "Initially, you might have some psychological issues to manage."

Will huffed. "You mean dying and coming back to life might cause some problems?" he said in a voice that delivered more sarcasm than he'd intended. "Sorry. What can I expect?"

"Depression, feelings of isolation, questioning your own existence."

He smiled.

"What?" she asked.

"So nothing's changed then?" he replied and stood from the bed. The smooth floor felt warm on his bare feet. His knees wobbled and Greta grabbed his arm to help him keep his balance.

"You'll experience a bit of incoordination and digestive issues for about a week," she added. "Your new body has not yet digested solid food."

"But it's exactly the same as my previous body?"

"All except for the hair," she replied.

Will rubbed the top of his head with his hand. He'd have to start over with the hair but there was already some stubble. "How old is my body?"

"About six days – the length of time you've been gone."

He was astounded. "How long did it take to regenerate?"

"It was ready an hour after you were pronounced dead," she replied, and pointed to a set of clothes and shoes on a chair next to the bed. "Now, I suggest you go back to your quarters and eat something – soup would be best to start – and drink plenty of fluids with electrolytes. In about 24 hours you should start some mild physical activity and get back to your normal life."

Normal life, Will repeated in his head. "Will I still have all of my memory?"

"You'll have whatever you brought back with you," she replied. "That's usually everything you had before you died, plus some."

It was the "plus some" that Will hoped would make the whole venture worth the risk.

LENNY GOT what he could out of Yong's wife.

The fire fluid had done its job, as expected.

The virus released in the Space Systems building was a smallpox variant, designed to kill, but was supposedly only mildly contagious – limited mainly to direct human contact rather than through airborne droplets. The second canister – the one that Lenny was to have deployed in Space Systems – was designed to sicken, not kill. It was a modified flu virus that ultimately attacked the respiratory system. The expected death rate of this second pestilence was low, but it was highly contagious.

Chunhua had also revealed five additional locations where they'd released the flu virus with the intention of creating massive infections, the desired outcome of which was to shut down society and the economy. One was released in the New York subway system, and then others in Los Angeles, Chicago, and Atlanta. Another was released in Washington, DC, upwind of the White House. It had been dispersed from a small tank truck – the kind used to pump septic tanks. Everything downwind had been saturated with microscopic crystallites that dissolved on contact with moisture, activating the semi-dormant virus, which could survive on open surfaces out of the sun for 24 hours. There were going to be a lot of sick people.

During lulls in the interrogation, Chunhua had kept looking at the clock, and Lenny had the impression that she was still concealing something. He never got it out of her.

Before turning himself in at Joint Base Andrews, by Thackett's direction, Lenny had taken the woman out of the airport and to an abandoned quarry in Maryland. Space Systems was no longer available.

Although he'd been tempted to take his time in eliminating the mass murderer, he'd reconsidered. It would have been unprofessional. Instead, he'd shot her twice in the forehead and submerged her body in a mountain of sand.

Afterwards, he went directly to Joint Base Andrews where he got scrubbed down in a way he wouldn't soon forget. He then donned a special hazmat suit and was placed aboard a C-130 transport plane with other disoriented passengers. Within minutes, they were in the air and heading for the Nevada desert.

His head, and then his gut, felt increasingly worse as he got closer to his destination.

Back in his quarters, Will had chicken soup in a mug and pita bread with hummus. It was an odd combination that tasted better than anything he could remember. He supposed food of any kind might have had the same effect, considering it was the first his new body had ever experienced.

Afterwards, he sat on the floor next to the window and sipped on a mug of strong coffee. It was 9:20 a.m. He'd stay awake all day and try to get back to his usual sleep schedule just to maintain some structure.

It was going to take a while for his mind to accept what had just happened. He'd been dead. Really dead, not just "technically" dead for a short time, like what had happened to him in the Red Box. That seemed like a lifetime ago.

He huffed and smiled to himself. It *was* a lifetime ago – everything was – and he'd have to get used to that.

His memory of what had happened was fractured, but he was able to recall some of the pieces. Although it was still fuzzy, he could see the tunnel, the complex conduit structure that resembled a spinal cord, the ring – which was a view of the cord from a great distance, and the feeling of something trying to pull him away from the ring, toward the horizon.

He suddenly realized that, through this venture, he might have lost some things. He went into a panic for a second until he separated, exited the exterior wall of the ship, and returned to his body. He'd never considered the possibility of losing his separation abilities. If he had, it would have rendered him effectively useless. He wouldn't even have been able to get onto the bridge.

Even more alarming, however, was that, without his separation abilities, he wouldn't be able to distinguish reality from illusion. He could be stuck in one of the ship's recreation facilities for years – forever – and not even know it. Suppose he emerged from some adventure – say a soccer game – and thought he was back in his quarters. It could just be a part of the illusion, and then he'd live the rest of his existence inside of the same room without ever knowing it.

He pondered it for a few minutes and came to a disturbing conclusion. Being able to tell the difference between illusion and reality was a double-edged sword. Why not set up an entire fantasy world where everything was precisely the way he wanted it to be? Suppose it was arranged so that he could be exactly who he wanted to be, could do anything he wanted to do, and there was enough mystery and excitement to keep him interested in perpetuity. What would be wrong with living in that world rather than in "reality," whatever that was?

He could live out a fantasy in which he'd be able to commandeer the *Exodus 9*, get back to Earth, and find everyone there alive and at peace. And he could get back to Denise and live a happy life with her.

He probably could set up such an illusion. He'd get a team of a trillion minds working on it, and it would be ready in minutes – seconds. The problem was that he would know it wasn't real. And, even if he didn't at first, with his separation abilities, he'd figure it out.

Life was filled with things better left unknown.

He suddenly thought about the knowledge he'd stolen from the Judge, and immediately tried to recall some things. To his relief, it was all there. It seemed his mind was fully intact after the regeneration. Perhaps it was really true that knowledge was kept in the soul.

The feeling he got now, which he knew might take some time to overcome, was that his current life was just a small fraction of his existence. Only a thin sliver of his soul extended from wherever he was when he was dead to where he was now – into his current body. He was much more than what existed in this finite world, just like ninety percent of an iceberg exists unseen, below the surface. He then wondered what he would be when he went *beyond the horizon*. It seemed to be calling to him, even now.

By far the most shocking thing he'd learned during the venture was that he'd been a Delta in his first life. He couldn't remember who he was then – his name – or many of the details, but there had to be something there that would help him. One thing he did remember, however, was that he'd been a beamer pilot – like the lab instructor, Captain Bourne.

He went to the coffee-table computer and looked up beamer pilot training programs. There were numerous options that ranged from beginner – which is where Will would start – to full military combat.

He signed up for the first course, which he set to start in one hour.

Since the experience would be similar to something he'd done in his first life, he thought it might jog some memories that he'd carried back with him from his excursion into the void. He sensed there was something specific he was supposed to recover from those memories.

A feeling of urgency was building within him. It was an anxiety that he knew was accelerating toward panic, and it was a portent that something was about to happen and that he had to act. It was the type of premonition that, in his distorted past, had never been wrong.

He swallowed the last of his coffee and headed for his flying lesson.

By the time they landed at Area 51, Denise's mind was going into a shutdown sequence.

She'd vomited inside her suit multiple times and felt as if she were going to suffocate. Her mind was trying to make it seem as if it were just a dream, but she knew better.

As the C-130's rear door lowered, a group of people in hazmat suits entered and herded them into a hanger configured much like the one at Joint Base Andrews.

Denise was sprayed down, stripped, scrubbed, sprayed again, blow-dried, put into a new hazmat suit, and then loaded onto a truck with the others. An hour later, they arrived at the secret "Site 4."

After what seemed like a half hour of navigating tunnels and descending shafts, they arrived at an underground medical complex. They were all isolated in individual rooms inside a quarantine unit. Doctors informed them that they'd all been exposed to the virus that had been released in the Space Systems building.

After four days, the others were relocated into intermediate quarantine accommodations. Denise, however, remained in the critical isolation unit. She had severe symptoms: vomiting, diarrhea, headaches, fever, and a skin rash had begun to break out in the most sensitive places, including her lower back, armpits, and private parts. It burned like fire, and the doctors administered both topical and intravenous pain meds. Canker sores broke out on her lips and inside her mouth.

The virologists were saying that it was an artificially engineered smallpox variant. Before the vaccine for the original disease had been developed, three in ten who had contracted it had died. The good thing was that the old vaccine, which had not been available to the public since 1972, was still available in military labs, and the virologists thought it might be effective against the variant. The problem was that there currently was not enough for the general public and, if it spread like the original, a deadly pandemic was going to ensue.

Another fortunate thing about it being a smallpox derivative was that US bio-warfare labs had an extensive knowledge base and were able to develop a diagnostic test in a matter of days.

They all tested positive except for Thackett – something about the location of their flats in the Space Systems building. Jonathan, Daniel, and Sylvia were suffering only mild symptoms and were quickly recovering. Denise, however, was hit hard.

If the variant was anything like the original smallpox virus, the rash was likely to spread over her entire body and, if she survived, she'd be badly scarred. Also, the objective of a bioweapons lab was usually to make things even more deadly. Thus, the death rate would probably exceed the 30 percent reached by the original virus.

Her head pounded, her back ached, and the rash felt like something between poison ivy and second-degree burns. On top of it all, the sounds of others in agony penetrated the thin walls of the facility. Some were crying. Two of ten in her unit had already died – but they were more advanced in age. It made her think of Jonathan, and she was grateful that it seemed that he'd beaten it.

A nurse came in, injected her IV with something, and her burning faded away. Her mind swirled into a dreamland where everything was okay. Will was there.

FIVE DAYS HAD PASSED since Lenny had been scrubbed down, put into a hazmat suit, and flown on a C-130 to an undisclosed location in the Nevada desert that he was later told was Area 51. He'd then been taken to an even more remote place called Site 4, where he'd been in quarantine ever since.

A day later, his developing symptoms had worsened: headache, internal abdominal and back pains, fever, and a rash was developing on his underarms. It was the smallpox variant.

The release of the smallpox virus on Space Systems was meant for revenge. The flu virus was intended to set the stage for whatever was coming next – and that, he figured, would have a global effect. And, since he'd learned that a dispersion device containing the virus had been deployed in Reagan International Airport, global effects were definitely intended.

In addition to all of this, another facet of the attack had hit without warning. The power grid on the East Coast had suffered a coordinated cyber-attack that shut down all power from Maine to North Carolina. There was evidence that the Russians had carried it out, but the running theory was that it was a joint Russian-Chinese effort. In addition, hospital networks on the Eastern Seaboard had been attacked, making it difficult to deal with the coming pandemic. It was a move intended to make the public suffer as much as possible.

In response, stock markets all over the world were plummeting, and the US and world economies were in grave danger.

Lenny figured that all-out war was coming next. He wondered if he'd still be around when it started.

JACOB SIPPED tea at the kitchen counter in 17 Swann as he looked over the commands sent from Chinese ground control to the satellite cluster. It was just after 10:00 a.m., and he'd been at it for four hours.

The Chinese were trying to reorient the cluster to look toward Earth, but they no longer had control. And they didn't know it. They were, however, controlling a virtual mockup of the cluster that returned artificial data. They were essentially playing a video game – Façade 1.0 was working perfectly.

With the separate perspectives of the different satellites, three-dimensional images of the near surface and airspace of the Earth could be formed. The Chinese would have had the most detailed satellite intelligence in the world. Instead, the United States had it.

Jacob, and the CIA and NSA teams, together with US Naval Intelligence, would now reconfigure their plans from looking outward for incoming spacecraft to providing wartime tactical information. But they would go one step further than that: they'd send the Chinese strategically designed misinformation, giving the US a tactical advantage.

Chinese ground control had instructed the satellite cluster to view the South China Sea, where the US had a carrier strike group. Jacob's people had responded by sending recent, but currently inaccurate, images down the line, which would make China think the ships were 350 miles to the east.

The ruse wouldn't last long, especially if China was using other methods to verify the intelligence, but it might sow some confusion into their process. Jacob had been informed, however, that US killer satellites had taken out a number of China's older spy satellites, so the deception might pay off for a while.

The US was planning to take out all four of China's active aircraft carriers, and a fifth that was still in production. A simultaneous attack would take out some of their most important missile launch sites. China's so-called "carrier killer" missiles required satellite guidance, so those might have already been rendered useless. Those particular satellites were of the same type that Jacob had cracked while still at Interstellar Dynamics. He would feel great satisfaction if that work had contributed to putting them out of commission.

His phone rang. It was Pauli.

She'd called three times that morning. He was literally at war, but he'd be able to concentrate better if he just took a minute to answer her call.

"Pauli, I'm a bit busy at the moment," he said. "What's up?"

"What the fuck?" she said in a shaky voice. "Is the US going to war with China?"

"I don't know, Pauli," he lied. "But it's pretty clear that the Chinese intentionally released a virus in the US. Even the president is sick."

"The UK stopped all international travel," she said. "Is that because of the virus?"

"I think so, yes," he replied. Although he knew that the UK was preparing for war alongside the US. "Pauli, I really have to – "

"Are you involved in the war?" she asked. "Are you in danger? Are you sick?"

"I can't answer that directly, Pauli," he said. "But I'm not sick, and I'm safe for the moment. But I have to go now."

There was a long silence.

"Pauli?"

"I love you," she said.

"I love you, too," he replied and ended the call.

He was glad she was in the UK for this. And he was glad that he was where he was.

He gazed out over the large room below and to the three tiers of bookshelves on the opposite wall. Uncle Theo had worked for 20 years to prepare him for this.

Jacob was going to do everything in his power to see it through.

It seemed it was going to be a hands-on course from the onset, and Will was grateful.

The flight instructor looked human, but there were subtle features that made Will suspect that he was a Delta. First, his eyes seemed unusually large, but they weren't so exaggerated that people would think he was an alien. His head was also shaped a little oddly – a bit elongated from front to back. He was about six feet tall, short dark hair, and otherwise seemed human.

The seven other students, a mix of males and females in their mid-20s, had more Earth-human features.

Beamers were essentially the fighter planes of the Delta fleet. They could operate in all environments – empty space, atmosphere, and liquid – and could withstand harsh conditions. Like the *Exodus 9*, they utilized multiple methods of propulsion, and were artificially intelligent. Although versions existed that were autonomous and could serve as drones, the AI was designed to make the craft user-friendly for a Delta pilot.

The beamer's weapons systems and shielding technology were overwhelming. Will thought just one of the ships could destroy Earth's combined militaries.

The shielding was particularly interesting. Much like the *Exodus 9*, a beamer could bend spacetime to make a sort of hollow around which any incoming projectile, including light, would pass, like water streaming around a rock in a river. Of course, there were counter-weapons, called "disruptors," that also affected spacetime and could take out a beamer, but Earth did not have that technology.

Another interesting thing about the shields was that, since light would also bend around the craft, a beamer could travel very close to a star, such as the sun, without burning up. Radiant heat was actually light – infrared radiation – and it, too, would bend around the craft. The shields also had the effect of cloaking the ship from all types of electromagnetic radiation, including visible light. There were, however, some limitations regarding approaching massive objects, such as dwarf stars and black holes, but otherwise beamers were nearly indestructible.

After a half-hour introduction, the instructor led them to a hangar holding a dozen of the most beautiful craft that Will had ever seen. They were shaped like warped disks – like thick, black dinner plates that were bent in the middle so that the sides curved downward. They were about 15 meters in diameter, and they were floating silently about two meters above the floor.

"This is the docking configuration," the instructor explained as he approached one and pushed gently against its sleek outer edge. The craft shifted slightly at his touch.

"Why do you put them in disk mode to park them?" one woman asked.

"You don't have to," the instructor replied. "But it's the easiest shape for entering and exiting the craft."

"What is 'disk mode?'" Will asked.

The instructor looked at him for a second and then said, "You'll find out, when you catch up on the reading material, that beamers change shape depending on travel mode, cloaking mode, and combat conditions."

"What's this one?" Will asked.

"Docking mode," the instructor replied. "Docking mode is disk mode."

The class chuckled.

Will might have been embarrassed about his ignorance if anyone in the room had actually been real. However, he did need to read up on it a little more.

"Okay, let's go. Everyone gets a beamer," the instructor said as he read the ship assignments. Will was assigned to the craft designated '*CX-1*.'

The class dispersed to their respective ships. Will observed as one woman found hers and went beneath it. A circular stage automatically lowered from its underbelly to the floor. The platform didn't seem to be attached to anything – it levitated. She stepped onto it, and it lifted her into the craft and then sealed seamlessly with the fuselage.

Will found the craft labeled "*CX-1*," and the same thing happened as he approached its underside. He stepped onto the platform and, as it lifted him into the craft, he was stunned by what he saw. The front third of the ship's interior looked like a clear bubble. He could see in all directions, including downward.

He was astounded by how the ship looked to be an opaque solid from the outside, but was perfectly transparent from the inside. Then it hit him that the interior of the "bubble" must have functioned like a complex computer screen, and he was just seeing a sophisticated 3-D camera view of the outside.

The interior was more spacious than he'd anticipated, and he was able to stand upright without hitting his head on the ceiling. Directly in front of him was the cockpit, with a padded, black chair surrounded by controls. To the right, against the wall, was a padded bench with seatbelts. Inset into the left wall were various compartments that looked to be for storage, although one section looked like a food generator. To the rear was a small, hatch-like door.

"Thompson, get in your seat," his instructor's voice commanded from the direction of the cockpit.

Will found it amusing that he was already on odd terms with the man.

As he sat in the cockpit, the chair adjusted around him, and two straps crisscrossed over his chest. A black, oval-shaped screen, about the size of a hand-held face mirror, suddenly emerged from above and then retracted almost instantaneously after he glanced at it. It was strange, but familiar somehow – like an ID authentication of some kind. The armrests then lifted under his elbows and turned slightly inward, gently hugging his waist. Two ring-shaped handles emerged, one from the end of each armrest, and he instinctively grasped them.

"Patience, Thompson," the instructor's voice came from somewhere above him.

Displays illuminated on the "clear" walls of the bubble and on transparent screens all around the cockpit.

"Power report," Will said, surprised at his own words.

"Power stores at full capacity," a calm, female-sounding voice replied. It was the ship –its intelligent computer.

"Estimated range," he said. It seemed like a checklist had been hardwired into his brain.

"Four hundred years, wave impulse," the ship replied. "Thirty-two years, bending."

Range was reported as time, rather than distance. From his navigation classes, Will knew that spacetime bender propulsion required more energy than the slower, gravitational-wave method. And there were other methods that took far less energy.

In combat, a beamer utilized all propulsion and maneuvering methods, as well as a full contingent of armaments and shielding. It again came to him that a single beamer could ravage the militaries of Earth. The *Exodus 9*, a mere vacation cruise ship, had an entire fleet of beamers at its disposal – and could make more, if needed. It would be a devastating force.

It got Will thinking about what one of the Deltas' full-sized warships could do. They possessed a menacing beauty that he appreciated more than before. Everything seemed more familiar to him now, after his encounter with death.

His thoughts were interrupted by motion in front of him. The enormous hangar door was opening.

"Thompson, push forward gently on your left control," the instructor said.

Will did so and, as the craft edged forward, his heart picked up pace.

A few seconds later, the massive *Exodus 9* was behind him, and billions of stars filled his view in all directions – including beneath him. One star, initially hidden behind the *Exodus 9*, was extremely bright – sun-like. On one of the beamer's displays was a map showing seven planets orbiting the star. The *Exodus 9* was also shown at a distance from the star which was about the same as the separation between Earth's sun and Neptune.

The other beamers were all around him, and there was one with flashing white lights – that was the instructor's ship.

"Twist the right-hand control to adjust the yaw, and push or pull the left one to go forward or to brake," the instructor said. "Form a line behind me in numerical order."

Will's ship was *CX-1*, so he was directly behind the instructor. A minute later, they were all in line.

For the next five minutes, the instructor explained the rest of the motion controls, which, for simple maneuvers, weren't much more complicated than operating a car.

"Now, follow me," the instructor commanded as his ship moved forward.

Will pushed on the left control to keep up, and the acceleration pressed him back in his seat. It was an addictive sensation, and he immediately craved more.

The instructor made a mild turn left, and Will followed. He glanced at a display that showed the aft view. The others maintained the line and were keeping pace.

The lead ship pulled upward, a direction that only had meaning because of the artificial gravity on the ship. Will was surprised that his reaction to match the maneuver came without conscious thinking – it came naturally.

After a few more mild turns and a barrel roll – which Will mimicked precisely, but the others didn't – the instructor led the squadron back to the ship's bay and landed.

Will wanted more, but he reluctantly exited the craft and met the others in the hangar.

The instructor dismissed the class but, as the students filed out, he called Will back.

"Name's Clifford," the instructor said and held out his hand.

Will shook it.

"You can call me Cliff outside of class," the instructor said. "I thought maybe you'd be up for a little more flying."

Will accepted the invitation without hesitation. A few minutes later, they were outside the *Exodus 9* at a dead standstill.

"I'm going to do some more complicated maneuvers," Cliff said over the comm. "Try to keep up."

The instructor's beamer accelerated so abruptly that Will's eyes could hardly keep focus.

He instinctively jammed his left ring forward.

The acceleration blasted him backwards, into his seat, and he noticed on one of the displays that his ship had changed shape. The left and right sides of the disk curved downward more drastically than before, and the rear now tapered to a point, like a short tail.

He caught up to the instructor's craft, which then darted left.

Will instinctively matched the maneuver, and then mimicked a series of the lead ship's turns and rolls. Cliff slowed and Will pulled his beamer next to him.

"You're not a beginner," Cliff said through the communicator.

"Not really sure what I am," Will admitted.

"You up for some near-surface flight – in atmosphere?" Cliff asked.

"Sure," Will replied. There was no risk – this was all fake. It made him, once again, marvel at the technology – both that which had created the illusion, and that which the illusion emulated.

Cliff accelerated toward the nearby sun, and Will followed.

"Let's go into bender mode," Cliff said. "You can do it with a verbal command to your craft's computer."

It seemed that Will had already known that. Both ships had been in low-speed, impulse "wave" propulsion mode the entire time. For longer distances, bender mode was more appropriate.

"We're heading to the fourth planet from the star," Cliff explained. "We'll regroup 25,000 kilometers from its surface."

"Got it," Will said.

Cliff's ship warped into a tube, like the shape a Frisbee would take if it were wrapped around a thick pole. An instant later, it seemed to blur, and then explode forward in a flash of white light. It was out of sight in an instant.

"Configure for bender propulsion," Will said. The phrase came smoothly, as if he'd spoken it a thousand times.

"Bender systems ready," the computer's voice informed.

"What's your name?" Will asked. At this point, he considered artificial intelligence of this high level a life form.

"I am *CX-1,*" the computer replied. "But you can call me *Gwen.*"

The name struck him as familiar somehow. He knew there was something more to the ship – something more personal, like a trait of a self-aware entity. "Okay, let's go, *Gwen,*" he said as he pushed the left ring forward.

Everything went pitch black for an instant and then came back to the original view. The star was approaching at a high rate.

He knew that it took light just over three minutes to go from Earth to Mars when the two planets were closest to each other. If the solar system before him were about the same size as Earth's system, then he was traveling toward it at near light speed.

"How fast are we going, *Gwen*?" Will asked.

"We are currently at one-tenth of one percent of my total bending capacity," the craft replied. "The concept of velocity is only valid when we are traveling in spacetime."

Will rephrased his question. "How much time will it take to travel one light-year relative to our initial position at this rate?" he asked.

"Two hundred and forty-five hours at this rate," *Gwen* replied.

Just over ten days to travel a light-year, Will marveled.

He then examined a display that showed the instructor's ship. It was orbiting the fourth planet from the star.

Will pulled back on the accelerator ring and said, "Back to G-W mode."

His words again surprised him: "G-W" meant "gravitational-wave." They came from somewhere else – and he knew from where. His hope that a ride in a beamer would jostle some memories might have been well founded.

The planet wasn't Earth, but it could have been. It was as blue as life itself. There were oceans and clouds and continents. Its sun gleamed from the water and, on the edge of the horizon, where the sun was going down, there were lights on the surface. The planet was inhabited.

"Nothing like traveling under the blanket," Cliff said. "How did you like it?"

Will somehow understood what he meant by "under the blanket." It meant outside of spacetime, which was often described as a "fabric."

"What is this place?" Will asked. "What planet?"

"It's a life-bearing planet called Castelle," the instructor replied.

"It's beautiful."

"Follow me," Cliff said as his ship plunged into the atmosphere.

Will followed.

Cliff's beamer changed shape to form graceful wings, almost like a stingray, but without the pointed tail.

On one of the displays, Will saw that *Gwen* had assumed an identical shape and, in less than a minute, they were 30 feet above the surface of an ocean near the planet's equator, traveling at an incomprehensible speed. The waves below were nothing but a blur.

A minute later, they slowed slightly and zoomed up a coastline at a fantastic rate. There were structures – buildings, piers, boats, and what seemed to be biped life forms on the beaches. It seemed like Earth.

Gwen warned that there were other aircraft in the area, as well as electromagnetic sensing – radar – and informed him that she was cloaked. His ship would automatically take evasive action in the case of potential collisions with indigenous craft or weapons systems.

Will imagined the ineffectiveness of Earth's best weapons systems against a beamer. A missile didn't have a chance of catching up. It then made him think of his generation's chances against the Regenerators, which reminded him that he wasn't there to have fun, although that was a fortunate byproduct.

Cliff's ship suddenly darted inland, and Will followed.

In less than a minute they were dashing around mountains and weaving through canyons. The accelerations were colossal, and would've killed him had they not been dampened using bending technology. However, by design, a fraction of the acceleration remained in order to give the pilot an intuitive sense of motion.

Will was making wild maneuvers without even thinking about them. It was coming back naturally, and he knew why. He was once a beamer pilot.

This affinity had followed him into another life, through Saul W. Kelly, RAF pilot.

He remembered a time when he'd considered trying to become a fighter pilot, and then maybe taking a shot at becoming an astronaut. But those aspirations had waned in college, when his attention initially focused on athletics, and then turned to physics.

Everything had probably worked out for the best in those early years. Earth's space technology had all but stalled since the 1980s. If he'd actually become an astronaut, the most he would've done would have been to spend some time on the space station, carry out some modest experiments, and maybe assist in deploying some satellites.

Will followed Cliff's craft as it suddenly shot vertically upward and then turned over and headed back to sea, toward one of the planet's poles. A minute later, they were skimming above an iceberg-laden, arctic-like ocean. The lead ship slowed to a near halt, and then plunged into the waves.

Will followed without hesitation.

Before he knew it, he was a few hundred feet below the surface.

It gave him a claustrophobic feeling at first, but he was confident that the beamer could withstand the pressure.

Plunging into the water reminded him of a show about UFOs that he used to watch on Earth. The program's hosts had assembled a list of observable traits that were used to identify objects of "alien" origin. This list included "anti-gravity maneuverability," meaning that something could fly without a visible source of thrust – like a jet or a propeller – and without wing surfaces for lift. Next, the UFOs had to be capable of "multi-medium transport," meaning that they could travel in space, air, or water. The final "alien" UFO criterion was that they could cloak themselves from radar and even visual sensing. Beamers satisfied all of these criteria.

Cliff's ship kept going deeper until they approached a depth of about 4,000 meters and skimmed along the ocean floor.

The view was well-lit, but Will knew that the ships weren't projecting light. His "windows" were actually video screens that displayed an enhanced view of the outside, making it look as if it were lit up like a football stadium. The water seemed to be crystal clear, and the visibility was about 200 yards.

After a few minutes, Cliff's craft came to a halt.

There was something large protruding from the ocean floor. It was something that made Will want to scream. It was an off-white stem with a bulb on the top, about the size of a water tower.

It was a beacon.

JACOB TOOK a bite of a baked fish stick as he watched the news. It was probably even more horrifying to him than it was to most people since he had inside information.

Word had gotten out that the horrible flu that was going around had been intentionally released on the public, and that China was responsible. It wasn't a killer like smallpox – or like the Chinese modification of that deadly virus that had been dispersed inside the Space Systems building – but people had already died, and it was spreading like wildfire.

Wildfire. Forest fires were ravaging the West Coast, and there was confirmation that those had been intentionally set as well. China was again responsible.

And then there were the relentless cyber-attacks. Those that put out the power on the East Coast and attacked hospitals nationwide were carried out by the Russians with the support of China. Small-scale cyber-attacks had been levied against the US by both countries numerous times during the past decade, but those had just been tests. This was the all-out attack for which they'd been preparing.

Jacob was grateful that his uncle had anticipated such a situation. His facility was at full power and would remain so just as long as the city's natural gas supply was maintained. If it went down, however, essential systems would still operate under solar power, but they'd be sporadic.

The threat of retaliation was no longer a deterrent. The United States had no choice but to go to war. Missions were already underway, against both China and Russia.

A US carrier task force was *en route* to intercept a Chinese carrier group in the South China Sea. There had been word that US submarines had already destroyed three of their Chinese counterparts. It was something that could only be conveyed by rumors, as the action literally took place beneath the surface. It made Jacob think of the *USS North Dakota,* and where the fast attack sub and its crew might be right now. He recalled seeing their motto inscribed on a plate inside the sub: *Strength from the Soil, Reapers of the Deep.* He hoped they were okay.

Thackett had called him that morning to update him on the Omni group. They'd been taken to a secret facility in the Nevada desert where they were all held in quarantine. Except for Thackett, they'd all contracted the virus that had been released in Space Systems. Other than Denise, they all had mild symptoms and had been moved out of the medical facility and into isolated quarters. Denise, however, was experiencing extreme symptoms and had been moved into intensive care. This wasn't the mild flu virus; she had the killer – the smallpox variant. It was thought to be short-lived and wouldn't become a pandemic, but that could only be verified over time.

Thackett offered to bring Jacob to the base, but he declined. He thought he'd be most effective working from 17 Swann, for the time being. If Washington were struck by a nuke, then the whole world was going to go up in flames. At that point, life on the planet would be something he'd rather not experience anyway.

The plan to feed the Chinese misinformation through their own satellites seemed to be working. Their carrier group was trying to evade the US strike force, but Chinese naval intelligence was getting images that were 24 hours old. Their evasive maneuvers were now leading them directly into the path of the US ships.

Jacob and his CIA cohorts had managed to decouple the satellites so that they could be used independently. Two of the four were designated for the imminent mission to destroy two Chinese carriers. One was watching various nuclear launch sites inside China, which were currently showing activity. The last one was searching for the Chinese president – if "president" was the correct term for a communist dictator. They were planning to decapitate the Chinese regime if the opportunity arose.

A retaliatory shot, other than the covert actions of their submarines, had not yet been fired by the United States, and Jacob couldn't help but have a speck of hope buried somewhere in his mind that it would all cool down.

But that was a futile distraction. Thackett had informed him that there would be no half-measures in the response. The release of the viruses amounted to an attack on American soil, as did the cyberattacks. They would probably not go nuclear – at least not immediately – but it was still a possibility, depending on how China and Russia responded to America's counterattack.

The ironic part was that the world had just averted total destruction by an outside threat – and almost no one was aware of it. Perhaps the Regenerators had been right to condemn humanity and start the extermination process. But there might have been no need. We were on the way to destroying ourselves anyway. The Regenerators would just have to come by afterwards, clean up, and then get the planet set up for the next generation.

After finishing his dinner, Jacob took his laptop and a can of ice-cold Pepsi up to the loft. Snow was falling on the skylight.

It was only flurries, but a storm was coming.

WILL SAT at the kitchen counter in his quarters as he ate spicy-hot curry and a slice of sweet mango.

Things were more convoluted than ever. First, he was in a new body, but everything felt exactly as it had before – except he only had about a week's worth of hair growth. He was set to go in for another medical checkup in two days just to make sure everything was okay, and to get another genetic treatment to ensure there had been no hidden problems with the regeneration of his new body. Second, that he had died and come back to a new body was even more profound than looking into the mirror and seeing a man in his mid-20s staring back at him. The latter was just a product of advanced medical technology. The former, however, went into an ethereal realm that, until now, he'd only experienced in a far lesser form when separating.

His mind had renormalized to account for things that were previously unimaginable. Just a couple of years ago, he was a middle-aged, middle-class man on a course of life that would have been pleasant, he supposed, but ordinary. It was strange that, from a very early age, that was what he'd feared more than anything: an ordinary life.

Perhaps he'd been destined to be where he was now. Maybe, at some level, he'd sought it out. All he knew was that he'd been seeking something unidentifiable his entire life.

But now that he was in his current, unordinary situation, there was still something hidden for which he was searching. He didn't know what that was, but he knew that he'd gotten closer to it somehow *while he was dead*. There was something in his previous lives that he needed to know. In particular, there was something in his first life that he needed to know – something that would reveal what he should do next.

One idea he intended to explore was whether he could hijack a beamer – a *real* one – to take back to Earth. He understood, however, that getting access to the Deltas' equivalent of the *F-22 Raptor* would require the same authorization that was required to redirect the *Exodus 9* mother ship.

There were also other things to work out. Suppose he did get access to a beamer and got back to Earth. And suppose Earth had not been destroyed and was, in fact, completely unchanged from when he'd left. What would be the best course of action at that point? There were people there who he missed but, other than that, what would be the purpose of returning? Also, would his being back on the planet again put them in danger?

Next, suppose he found that Earth had been destroyed. Would he just go back to the *Exodus 9*? Would he spend the rest of his existence trying to exact revenge on the Regenerators?

After some contemplation, he identified two main reasons to get back to Earth. First, he had to know what had happened to his friends and family. Second, if they were in the process of being destroyed by the Regenerators, maybe he could do something about it. Although, as difficult as it was for him to imagine, the beamers onboard the *Exodus 9* were outdated by 40 thousand years. It might be like taking a World War I biplane into a dogfight with modern fighter jets.

But it didn't matter. He had to try. Besides, it wasn't like he feared death anymore.

He went to the coffee-table computer and arranged for more beamer training, with an emphasis on combat. It was time to hone the piloting skills that had somehow seeped into his current existence after being regenerated.

Also, he needed to talk to Landau.

Will returned his dishes to the kitchen, and then went to the bathroom and took a shower. Twenty minutes later, he was riding the subway toward the whiskey bar in New York City.

13

LUX

WILL GOT A WHISKEY AT THE BAR AND TOOK A SEAT IN A BOOTH WITH A view of the entire room. The place was filled with the usual clientele, although there seemed to be more women than usual. Perhaps it was because of the live music scheduled for the evening for which people were setting up equipment on the small stage.

The planet to which he had gone with his flight instructor was too much like Earth to be a coincidence. There had even been a probe in the seabed of one of Castelle's polar seas. It was identical to those through which he'd unleashed the havoc upon, and possibly destroyed, his home planet. But he'd seen more of the probe's details on Castelle: there was an immense structure embedded beneath the ocean floor into which the probe could retract.

Will flinched at a voice from behind him. It was Landau. He was dressed in a long dark overcoat.

"No cognac tonight?" Landau asked as he sat across from him and set a snifter of cognac on the table.

"Whiskey this time," Will replied.

"What did you learn during your trip to the beyond?" Landau asked.

"For one, I've lived many lives," Will replied.

Landau nodded. "I know," he said. "The question is, which ones have you brought back with you."

"Most of the memories I can recall are from my first life," Will replied. "Also, some from my most recent, previous one – when I was Saul W. Kelly, although those are less vivid."

Landau's expression turned serious and agitated. "What do you remember of your first life?"

"I was a Delta," Will replied. "And a beamer pilot."

Landau's look went from anxiety to apparent relief. He smiled.

"A Delta, you say?" Landau said. "Is that all you recall? Do remember how you got to your next life after that?"

Will shook his head. "I was killed in an accident and must have reincarnated," he said. "I wasn't regenerated."

"Do you have a name?" Landau asked.

Will stared back at him, confused for a second. "You mean my name during my first life?"

Landau nodded.

Will had been trying to recall it but he could barely make out some of the characters in his mind. It was in the Deltas' script and, although he'd been able to read the language after siphoning the memories from the Judge, he couldn't really write it, which made it difficult to recall. Even when he read it, his mind translated the meanings to English or, on one occasion, to German, and names often had no translation. Also, he assumed that the Deltas had sounds that went beyond those used in Earth languages, or at least beyond those used in English. He certainly couldn't speak in the Delta language.

"I think I know the name, but I can't tell you what it is," Will said. "I mean, I can't say it."

"Try," Landau said. "Just visualize the name and speak."

Will took a hit of whiskey and concentrated on the symbols that took shape in his mind. He then forced himself to speak, but it sounded like he was trying to make up his own language.

"I can recall some of the characters, but I can't verbalize it," Will said. When he looked up, Landau was staring at him with an expression of strong emotion that he couldn't identify as positive or negative.

"What?" Will asked.

"You just *did* verbalize it," Landau said and repeated what Will had recited for his original name. His utterance was clearly articulated and, although Will wouldn't be able to accurately mimic what Landau had said, the sounds were familiar.

"Can you tell me anything more about your first life?" Landau asked.

"I was a beamer pilot, and involved in the Deltas' construction on Earth," Will replied. "I think I was in charge of part of the project, and maybe a captain of a ship."

Landau stared at him with deadly serious eyes.

"Something happened to me while I was there. I was in an accident of some kind. I … uh … shit," Will hissed. "I can't remember anymore right now."

Landau pulled a pen and a small notebook out of his coat and wrote something. He then tore off the page and handed it to Will. The paper was identical to that which Danielle had passed to him with the message about the *Seraphim Hors d'Âge*.

"I knew it was you," Landau blurted in a hoarse whisper. His voice and expression conveyed a concoction of emotions that Will interpreted as excitement, relief, fear, and urgency. It was the fear and urgency that lingered after he seemed to regain his composure. "That's your original name, in the Delta language."

Will looked at the script on the paper. Although he couldn't verbalize the characters, they gave him a sense of deep familiarity.

"What am I supposed to do with this?" Will asked.

"Now you can find out who you are."

"I was a Delta."

"You *are* a Delta," Landau corrected.

"Why do you say that?" Will asked.

"You were first created as a Delta," Landau said. "Your soul is therefore Delta."

"How does that change anything?" Will asked in an argumentative tone.

"It changes everything," Landau replied.

"I don't understand."

"The *Exodus 9* has the entire history of the Delta civilization in its information base," Landau said. "Learn everything you can about yourself – your first life. See what memories emerge."

Landau swallowed the last bit of his cognac just as a server arrived. He ordered another, a *Tesseron, Royal Blend,* and Will ordered the same and handed the man his empty whiskey glass.

"What else did you see out there, while you were away from this existence?" Landau asked.

Will described the conduit of light that looked like a ring from far way.

"There were billions of thin fibers that grew out of it," Will explained. "They'd sometimes curl back into a different place on the ring, and other times they'd just disappear – wilt away like a dead flower."

Landau nodded. "And what do you think that was – the ring?"

Will shook his head. "I don't know, maybe a representation of all of existence – the universe."

Landau nodded in approval. "When the light is coming from the right direction, the shadow of a sphere on a flat surface is a circle," he said. "It is an example of how a three-dimensional object can be partially characterized in two dimensions. However, a disk could produce an identical shadow, and someone observing the shadow alone would not be able to tell if it were a disk or a sphere that cast it."

Landau hesitated as the server delivered the drinks.

"A projection, rather than a shadow, preserves that information, but conveys it in a different form – in a different dimension," Landau explained as he took a drink of the cognac and seemed to contemplate its flavors. "It's like transforming the information from a globe of the Earth to a flat map of the same – one is 3-D and the other is 2-D, but they both convey the same information."

Will understood the basic mathematical principles of projections and mapping from his training in physics. They were tools that could be used to solve math and physics problems.

"Every aspect of the universe – every atom, every star, every particle of light, every manifestation of empty space – is contained in that ring," Landau said. "Your specific reality – everyone's individual realities – are projections of this ring onto our four-dimensional spacetime."

Will was astounded. He understood, although in a superficial way. "I have questions."

Landau laughed loudly, "I thought you might."

"What were the billions of hair-like filaments that were growing out of the ring's surface?" Will asked. "Most would curl back into the surface of the ring, and then disappear."

"Ah, yes," Landau said and nodded. "The 'filaments,' as you call them, are conduits formed by severed souls – souls that have been disengaged from our four-dimensional universe."

"Those who have died," Will commented.

"Yes," Landau replied. "And when you see them curling back into the ring's surface, they are returning to their universe."

"They're being reincarnated," Will said.

"Yes," Landau affirmed. "And you might have noticed that most of the filaments reentered the ring at a location different from where they'd emerged – usually in the forward direction along the conduit, indicating the positive direction of time."

Will recounted what he'd seen in his mind. "Yes, that's what I saw."

"Those were reincarnations," Landau said. "However, the filaments sometimes reenter in the same place from which they emerged. Those are – "

"—They're regenerations," Will cut him off. It was fascinating.

"Precisely," Landau said and took a swig of his cognac. "But you weren't immediately attracted back into the ring, were you?"

"No," Will replied. "I started to move away from it."

"What did you see?"

"When I was close to the ring, it seemed like a straight line – like a taut rope made of light," Will said. "It wasn't until I moved away from it that I saw that it was a ring."

"You must have been very far away from it," Landau said. "Other than the ring, what did you see?"

"Everything was pitch black, except when I tried to look into the distance," Will said. "There seemed to be light coming from somewhere – as if there was something over the horizon."

"I couldn't have described it better," he said in a tone of approval. "And you had an urge to keep heading toward the horizon?"

"I felt like I did in grade school when I was late for recess," Will said. "It was like hearing my friends laughing and yelling on the playground, and I wanted to sprint through the halls to get outside and join them."

"But you came back anyway," Landau said. "Why?"

"I have unfinished business," Will replied.

"You've lived over 400 lives, Will," Landau said. "The average soul lives fewer than 20 before going on to the next place – beyond the horizon. You should have moved on long ago."

Will thought about it for a few seconds. "I have to fix what I've done."

"What, exactly, have you done wrong?" Landau asked.

Will stared at him, unable to respond for a few seconds. "I activated the probe," he finally said. "And Earth might already be destroyed because of it."

"You are not to blame for what happened," Landau argued. "Others forced you through the transformation and brought you to the probe. That's why judgment was brought against humanity. They brought about their own destruction."

"I didn't have to pull that lever inside the first probe," Will argued. "I could have told everyone that there was nothing inside."

"It was a mystery," Landau argued. "You had to pull that lever."

Will wasn't buying it. He should have left it alone.

"During your transformation – while you were being tortured inside the Red Box – you said there was something hidden that was driving your life – that you were being 'funneled down a chute,' as you put it," Landau said. "Can you tell me the origin of that feeling?"

Will shook his head. That feeling was still there, and stronger than ever. It was the first thing that entered his mind when he woke up in the morning, and the last thing he thought about when he went to sleep. "If I knew what I was supposed to be doing, I'd be trying to do it."

"I think you *are* doing it," Landau said as he downed the last of his drink and stood. "Research that name – your name – and you'll learn more."

Landau dissolved into the crowd, leaving Will to his thoughts. The music – soft jazz – picked up and he saw Danielle in the crowd, engaged in a conversation with two other women.

Will stared at the paper Landau had given him and studied the string of characters. Maybe his purpose could be found in the history of his ancient self.

IT WAS 6:05 a.m. when Daniel woke up and got out of bed. He donned his military-issued clothing and boots and sat at a small desk with his laptop. He thought he looked strange in the sand-colored, military attire, but it was much more comfortable than the hospital gown that he'd worn for almost six days. There was nothing worse than having one's butt exposed.

His time on the submarine had prepared him well for the claustrophobic conditions of the small room. Just a year ago, he couldn't have tolerated the idea of being hundreds of feet below ground. It was easy compared to being in a submarine navigating tunnels beneath Antarctica.

His fever had broken a few days earlier, and Sylvia had only gotten a mild rash. He wondered if the battery of vaccines that the CIA had administered to him every five years had included anything out of the ordinary, like the smallpox vaccine. The reason for his suspicion was that Jonathan, although now recovering, had more serious symptoms, and Denise was in far worse condition and was now in the intensive care unit.

One thing that was keeping him calm was that Sylvia was with him, although not physically in the same room. They kept a video chat window open on their computers so that they could see each other's faces as they worked, and they would have tea together at regular times. He hadn't realized how dependent he'd become upon her, and it seemed that the feeling was mutual.

Immediately after it was clear that they were both out of the woods regarding the viral infection, Thackett got them set up with top-priority computer connections, with most of the same top-secret access as that in Space Systems. Although their work didn't have an immediate tactical importance regarding forthcoming military operations, it did have possible big-picture relevance, as it always had.

Daniel poured hot water into a cup and submerged a teabag. When he opened the laptop, Sylvia was already there.

"Good morning," she said. "Sleep okay?"

"Okay, you?" he responded.

"Not really," she replied. "My mind was still turning when I went to bed, and I couldn't figure out why until this morning."

"Something happening?"

"Last night I analyzed some data from SETI," she said.

The Search for Extraterrestrial Intelligence Institute had been coming up more frequently in their investigations during the past year, and for good reason. The organization had also seen an enormous influx of funds after the so-called "weather satellite" incident and was using the money wisely on collecting records, observational data, and time on telescopes.

"I downloaded their civilian sightings data from the past ten years," she continued, "which gives the number of sightings according to date and geographic location."

"There must've been quite a spike over the past months," he commented.

"Of course," she confirmed. "I added this most recent data to that collected over the last century. Instead of looking at sightings in specific geographical regions, I simply added all of the sightings in the world, and plotted them as a function of time – by date."

A graph appeared on Daniel's screen. The horizontal axis denoted the year, from 1900 to the present, and the vertical axis indicated the number of sightings. There were peaks in sightings at various times, including a prominent one in 1947, which coincided with the famous Roswell Incident. Prior to that was a peak at the time of the detonation of the first atomic bomb, in July of 1945.

There was another global surge in the summer of 1952, although a note indicated that most of those sightings had occurred in South America. There had also been a significant incident in Washington, DC, on July 19 of that same year, which was eventually called "The Big Flap."

Since then, the baseline number of reports had gradually increased, with modest peaks appearing for no apparent reasons. The two most recent peaks were off-scale. The earlier of the two matched with the time period when Will had activated the probe, and the largest and most recent peak appeared when the Regenerators' pill-shaped ships invaded Earth's airspace and anyone who was looking could see them.

Daniel still couldn't believe that the general population bought the story that they were part of an experimental weather monitoring system. However, that ruse was starting to fail as leaks were beginning to occur in almost every government on the planet.

"The data are consistent with what we know," Daniel said. "Did you spot something odd?"

"Yes, look at this," she said, and the graph changed, indicating sightings only in Argentina, Chile, and Peru over the same time period. There were fewer peaks, but they were sharp, each indicating a span of sightings that had occurred over a couple of days. "The sightings along the western coast of South America seem to be connected to major events. They either precede an important event by 72 hours or lag it by a few days."

Daniel looked closer at the graph. Each peak was labeled with a date and a well-known incident that had occurred within two days of it. The first he noticed occurred on July 16, 1945 (first atomic bomb test), and then August 6, 1945 (bombing of Hiroshima). Next were July 6, 1947 (the Roswell Incident), July 19, 1952 (UFO sighting in Washington, DC), April 12, 1961 (first human orbits the Earth), and July 20, 1969 (first moon landing). By far, the largest peaks were the most recent ones, which included the sightings that had occurred when the probe was activated, and then when the Regenerators' ships entered the atmosphere.

"These were all along the west coast of South America?" Daniel asked.

"Yes," Sylvia replied. "But what's strange is that, on those specific dates, there were also spikes along the West Coast of North America."

Data for North American sightings then appeared, overlaid on the South American graph. There were some additional peaks associated with different dates, but the rest matched perfectly with the South American peaks.

"On those specified dates, something was happening along those coastlines," Sylvia explained.

"Why there?"

Sylvia shrugged. "Maybe it's a common path the ships take," she replied. "But this next slide is what kept me up all night."

Another graph appeared, showing only the data for the last 18 months. There were two large peaks around the dates on which the probe in the Weddell Sea had been activated by Will, and then the near invasion by the Regenerators. But now there was another one, more recent.

Sylvia pointed to the latest feature. It was a ramp-like shape that was increasing over time, as if it were the leading edge of a peak that had not yet formed completely. "This started three days ago," she said. "The North and South American peaks again overlap, and they're growing."

She zoomed in on the largest peak that represented the Regenerators' incursion. "The magnitude and rate of increase of the front edge of this peak, almost two weeks before the actual event, is the same as that which is happening right now."

Daniel's heart started to thump harder in his chest. "You think something is coming?"

"Possibly, according to these data anyway," she replied. "And, if it's on the same time scale as the Regenerators' first incursion, then it will happen in a few weeks."

Daniel could hardly believe the horrible timing. China and the US were essentially already at war – the first military strike was imminent – and now the Regenerators might be returning. He sighed and shook his head.

"What?" she asked.

"Maybe the Regenerators have been watching us and have finally concluded that we're a menace – to ourselves and to whoever else is out there."

Daniel pulled out his phone.

"What are you going to do?" she asked.

"I need to call Thackett," he replied as he pressed the call button.

IT WAS a sunny afternoon as Will sat at a table by a window in the 1960s Buenos Aires café that he'd visited weeks earlier. He was researching "himself" on his laptop. No one in the café mentioned anything about his computer, which would have been a futuristic marvel to someone from that time period.

Everything he found was automatically translated to English, except for the Delta name he'd had in his first life, which remained in the original Delta script. When he asked the computer to give him a phonetic version, with English spellings and translations, it sounded like "Luxen Ulti Kutinia." There was also a phrase added to the end that directly translated to "of Saronelle 5." He then looked up "Saronelle 5" and discovered that it was an enormous Delta space station. It was where he'd been born.

He pondered his name, and he somehow knew that the informal, short version of "Luxen" was "Lux." It reminded him of the name of a comic book supervillain, but it meant "light" in Latin.

Lux had been a military pilot and held the rank of senior pilot – equivalent to captain, like Captain Saul W. Kelly, RAF. Lux's final mission was to oversee parts of the construction of the Antarctic base, designed to evacuate Earth's next generation, and to manage the assembly of the *Exodus* fleet.

Originally, the Deltas had intended to reclaim Earth, but then they'd learned that the next generation had already been seeded, and they weren't going to destroy them. They decided, instead, to give them a boost for the time when they'd be judged.

Will smiled. He thought he would have liked the Deltas.

"Something funny?" a woman's voice chimed in a Spanish accent, from his left.

He turned and looked, and then said, "Valentina," as she approached. It seemed to him that every young woman with dark hair and eyes that he encountered reminded him of Denise.

"It has been some time, and you remembered my name," she said, smiling.

"Of course," he said. It had been a few weeks, at least.

"Refill?" she asked and nodded toward his empty cup.

"Please," he replied.

She grabbed the mug and disappeared behind the coffee bar as he continued reading.

As one of his primary duties while on Earth, in addition to construction planning, Lux had been in charge of near-surface airspace security. He was an accomplished beamer pilot, and had commanded a squadron of 16 ships, which were part of a group called the Liberation Wing. The name apparently held some historical significance to the Deltas in relation to their many battles during their exodus from Earth.

Valentina delivered his fresh coffee and a pastry that he hadn't ordered.

"Frail balls," she said and laughed. "You said you wanted to try them the next time you visited."

Will laughed. "Thanks," he said, and she skipped away.

He took a bite. It was like a powder-sugar donut filled with dulce de leche. It went perfectly with the coffee. He ate as he read.

Near the time of completion of the Antarctic base, Lux and two other pilots had patrolled the equatorial coastlines of what was now South America to look for Regenerator probes, which were autonomous pill-shaped vessels designed to detect surface life forms and, specifically, evanescent activity as well as more primitive indicators of development, such as electromagnetic waves and nuclear events. The Deltas had been under strict orders not to fully separate while on the surface so as to not alert the Regenerators to their presence.

The beamers had encountered one of these probes and pursued it far inland. Somewhere near what is now New Mexico, all three beamers were destroyed. They'd been led into a trap that released enough energy to dissociate matter into its most basic components – not just down to its atoms, but to the very particles that made up the atoms themselves. There had been nothing left.

The bodies of the three pilots, including Lux's, had been regenerated within hours. One pilot joined his regenerated body within a day of it being ready, and the second came back after three days. Lux, however, never returned.

Lux's original beamer had been undergoing maintenance, so he'd been flying a substitute during that fateful mission. Beamer pilots held their ships in high regard, as they would a fellow soldier, or a friend. The Deltas got the idea to place his regenerated body in his original beamer and park it at the crash site. They waited for many weeks, until the last of the construction was completed. Lux had never returned, and his beamer had been the last to leave the planet.

The Deltas had admired Lux for his military service in the late conflicts with the Regenerators, and then with other adversaries. He'd been an ace beamer pilot, and had been in line to command a major warship after the evacuation facility on Earth was completed.

Will was Lux. But where in the hell had he gone? He must have remained on Earth somewhere. He read on.

Even though construction of the Antarctic base had been

completed, and the transport ships, including the *Exodus 9*, had been put into position, the Delta warship that had his regenerated body onboard remained in orbit for over two months. It was understood that, after that much time, a soul would have transitioned – either to a new body through reincarnation, or to the "next place." Since his soul should have been incompatible with the indigenous species – the next generation – reincarnation should not have been possible, and they concluded that Lux had moved on.

The warship, the *Liberator 5*, had then left for Delta territories and never returned.

Much was written about the incident, and some had speculated that Lux had somehow incarnated with the new species. However, there was no proof, except for anecdotal evidence of premature evanescent activity many millennia later, first detected just over two thousand years ago, relative to the present, and therefore about 38 thousand years after the Deltas constructed the base and then left.

The first question that entered Will's mind was how the Deltas were aware of such "premature evanescent activity" since they had supposedly not returned to Earth after the Antarctic base was constructed. The next paragraph explained that the Deltas' hidden ships – including the *Exodus 9* – had been passively listening and watching Earth, and the information had come from a Regenerator probe that made periodic visits to both Earth and Mars to monitor the two fledgling civilizations. Since then, there had been other detections of separations, including one on July 19th, 1952. The locations of the incidents, however, had not been pinpointed, but the first one had occurred somewhere near the Mediterranean in the Middle East, and the second one, over 2,000 years later, somewhere in Antarctica.

The second one Will knew had to have been Saul W. Kelly, probably when he'd massacred the Nazis at the base and disposed of the bodies by attaching them to rocks and dropping them into the abyss below. He had no idea, however, who had been responsible for the first event – 2,000 years ago. If he'd been the one responsible for that occurrence, he'd carried back no memory of it from his brief excursion with death.

The latent Delta ships had reported the 2,000-year-old event to Delta command, triggering speculation that Lux's soul was still on Earth. If so, it had been propagating through the human race for about 38 thousand years, and therefore the current generation on Earth had components of the Delta race in their DNA and, thus, in their very souls.

Additional supporting evidence of this conjecture was that humans had seemed to make an otherwise inexplicable, evolutionary jump in the millennia that followed the disappearance of Lux, who the Deltas were calling the "Fallen Angel."

If it were true that Lux's soul had somehow incarnated with the new generation 40 thousand years prior, then the entire new generation had Delta blood. And, to the Deltas, this meant that the current inhabitants of Earth were Deltas.

However, the evidence had been only circumstantial – not enough to prove that the conjecture was true – and the Deltas had made no further moves regarding Earth. If they'd had definitive proof, they would have secured the planet and essentially adopted the human race as their own.

Will now knew who he was. He was Lux. He was the proof.

DENISE WOKE up to voices she didn't recognize.

She squinted into bright overhead lights and tried to resolve faces from silhouettes. When things finally came into focus, a female face stared at her through the clear mask of a hazmat suit. It was then that she noticed the poking on her forearm.

"I'm Dr. Timpleton. You can call me Sandy. Your IV came out," the woman said. "Your temperature is up again, and we're giving you something to counter that."

The taste of vomit coated Denise's mouth and throat.

The sound of someone moaning in agony came from somewhere. It took her a few seconds to determine from where it was coming. It was her own whimpering that she was hearing.

"Let's see what's happening with that rash," the doctor said as she gently lifted the light sheet that covered Denise's torso and lower body. She was naked underneath.

Denise winced when the sheet stuck on something.

"Looks like we have some oozing," the woman said. "And some spreading."

Denise felt like half of her body had been burned. And her head was pounding.

"We'll change the coverings and get some topical treatment to soothe the pain," the doctor said and made a call on an intercom to summon a nurse. She looked back to Denise. "I need you to fight this. You have a good chance; you're young."

"How's Jonathan?" Denise managed to mumble. Jonathan was not young. "And the others?"

"They're all okay. Jonathan had a rough go for a while, but he's fine now," Sandy said. "Sylvia and Daniel were infected but showed only light symptoms. You were hit the hardest."

"And the others?" Denise asked. "What about those at ..."

"Space Systems?" Sandy filled in as Denise hesitated. The doctor's face became grim. "We're lucky that there were only about 400 people in the building at the time – about 15% capacity. Over 100 tested positive. Nearly 25 have died, and about the same number are still in a fight."

"What's happening outside?" Denise asked. "Did this hit the general public?"

Sandy shook her head. "Still too early to tell about the smallpox," she explained. "The other one – the flu – is spreading. It's not as deadly, but it's going to kill a lot of people."

"Has the US responded?"

Sandy shook her head. "I've not heard anything specific," she said. "But my understanding is that plans have been initiated."

The doctor left and Denise turned her attention to a button mounted on the rail of her bed that controlled the pain medication. She pressed it a couple of times and closed her eyes.

THE WAR ROOM was lit up like the Las Vegas strip, and James Thackett paced back and forth in front of a map display of the South China Sea.

He was pleased that the CIA, and especially the Omni group, had provided crucial intelligence to the Department of Defense, and disseminated devastating misinformation to the Chinese.

It wasn't as if either side didn't have at least a general idea of where the enemy surface ships were located. The locations of the US submarines, however, weren't known.

Although China had more subs than the US, they were noisy, and therefore could be easily tracked when on the move. When they weren't using their engines, however, they couldn't be traced, and could lie in wait for an enemy ship to wander into range.

The false images sent to China via the hijacked satellite cluster provided enough confusion to misdirect their vessels into a proverbial kill zone of US submarines.

Thackett knew that the *USS North Dakota*, a vessel with which he was familiar, had undergone repairs after its adventures in the frigid Southern Seas and was currently in the South China Sea. This time its mission would be suited for that which the attack sub was designed, and more dangerous than its exploration of the Antarctic caverns.

The busy room suddenly became silent. Everyone stopped what they were doing and watched a large monitor that showed a crystal-clear satellite view of a Chinese carrier group. There were eight ships in the fleet, and they were all making evasive maneuvers, as indicated by the white curved wake trails on the blue ocean. Explosions around some of the ships looked like giant waterspouts.

"Those are Chinese depth charges," a voice said from behind him. It was Thackett's longtime friend, Admiral George Sexton, Chief of Naval Operations, who then stepped beside him with his eyes on the screen. "Those ships are about to go down."

Suddenly, multiple massive explosions rocked some of the ships, the carrier taking the brunt of the barrage. The carrier seemed to deform, and most of the smaller ships stopped maneuvering. One listed severely and another was starting to go under, aft first.

Of the eight ships, two of the smaller ones were left untouched.

"The two remaining are for survivors," Sexton said with a grave expression. "And, for the others, God save their souls."

"You got them all with torpedoes?" Thackett asked.

"No," Sexton replied. "There were also near-surface missiles, launched by submarine. You might not have been able to see them in real time. They're designed to penetrate the hull at high velocity. They're now down three carriers, thanks to your man."

Thackett acknowledged his comment with a nod. Sexton was referring to Will, and his disabling of the Chinese carrier that had held him for a short time. Shortly afterwards, Will had actuated the probe and all hell had broken loose. "Looks like we're now officially at war."

"Unfortunately, yes," Sexton said. "We had no choice."

Everyone's attention was then drawn to another large, live-feed monitor showing an overhead view of a tropical island. A cluster of docks and structures was built into the shoreline in a small alcove. There was also an airstrip peppered with parked fighter jets and bombers.

"That's a Chinese submarine base built on an island in disputed waters," Sexton explained. "It's in the Spratly Islands, which are Philippine territory. China took them over years ago and then built the sub base, and lengthened the airstrip."

At that instant, the screen lit up and seemed to flash like the place had been hit by multiple lightning strikes. When it cleared, debris was still raining from the skies. The base and airfield were in shambles.

"Intelligence says there was only one sub at the base," Sexton said. "But an entire bomber wing is now gone, as well as their support fighters."

"I need to get back to my post," Thackett said as he shook his friend's hand. "Good luck."

As Thackett made his way to an elevator that would take him to the CIA's bunker, he thought about his dilemma.

Sylvia had found a pattern that predicted an imminent event based on the currently increasing rate of extraterrestrial sightings. At this point he figured "sightings" was old language. A better term might be "traffic." He had no doubt at this point that what people were seeing were actually extraterrestrial craft.

Sylvia's "predictors" were peaks in reports along the entire western coastlines of the Americas, from the southern tip of Chile to the Bering Sea, off the coast of Alaska. Thackett's problem was that traffic was currently growing in those areas, and he had to decide whether to redeploy one of the commandeered Chinese satellites to search for possible incoming objects – alien craft.

Taking resources away from the war effort, even for a short time, would be hard to justify. The most effective argument against it was the fact that the world would be defenseless against the extraterrestrial technology anyway, so it didn't matter if Earth saw them coming.

Thackett thought for a second that maybe they could send a message to any incoming alien ships they'd spot in an attempt to negotiate. But negotiate what? A surrender? He didn't like the sound of that.

When he arrived at the CIA control center, a room the size of a tennis court bustling with people, he got updates on activities, including reports from operatives on the ground in China. The Chinese were in war mode.

He then asked about the use of the four Chinese satellites and learned that they were all oversubscribed and currently providing intelligence for active missions.

"Let me know when one of them is free," he told the woman responsible for organizing their use. "Get me a couple of hours on one, between missions."

The center of the control room was littered with desks and computers, and large monitors paneled the walls. Inset into the outer walls were over 20 nooks that resembled booths like those found in restaurants, with a table between two padded benches that could altogether seat four, or six if they packed together. Lights inset into the low ceilings illuminated the compartments, and display monitors mounted to the wall on the closed end of each nook could be used for presentations or remote conferences. Each booth was allocated to some specific function or geographical area, except for a few that were left open for ad hoc meetings.

Thackett checked for updates at a few stations before passing through a door between two booths that led to his office. It was a small room with a desk against the wall on the right and a sofa on the opposite side. Together with its small bathroom, it provided a means to remain on duty long-term.

He pulled out his phone and placed a call to Jacob.

AFTER A NIGHT of lucid dreams that might have come from past lives, Will arranged another beamer lesson with the hope that something might trigger his mind to release more information from his first life – his Delta existence. This lesson was with the same instructor, Cliff, but without the rest of the class.

This time Will felt even more familiar with the controls than he had at the end of his first outing. They started with a maneuver called "blinking." It was an effect that was seen by observers on the outside as impossible stops, turns, and accelerations. In some cases, it would seem as if the ship would disappear and then reappear in another location. It was an illusion to some degree since the ship played in spacetime and inter-dimensional translation. It would look like magic to someone only familiar with human technology, as much as a television or a jet plane would to someone from Medieval times.

It occurred to Will that UFOs spotted on Earth were often described as making these kinds of maneuvers. It meant that the beings who created those ships were technologically ahead of Earth by many thousands of years – maybe millions. And just one of those crafts might be able to decimate Earth's current defenses.

They went back to Castelle, the Earth-like planet they'd visited during his first lesson, and flew through its cities, canyons, and mountain ranges.

After an hour of practicing complex maneuvers, Cliff led him to a cluster of small lakes surrounded by a dense forest, and they eventually landed next to a pier on the sandy beach of an island-studded lake.

Will exited his beamer and followed Cliff to the end of the pier, which extended 40 feet offshore. The air was cool and filled with the scents of pines, fallen leaves, and water. About a half-mile out, near the center of the lake, was an island packed with what looked to be tall, white-barked trees that leaned over the water, resembling palms on a tropical island. To the left was the sun, Castelle's sun, casting a red-orange glow on the high clouds to the west – or whatever the direction of the setting horizon was called – that illuminated the gently rippling water.

"I like to come here sometimes and just watch the sun go down," Cliff said as he poured coffee from a thermos into a Styrofoam-like cup and handed it to Will. He then poured some into the cap of the thermos and replaced the stopper.

Will shuddered as he sipped the coffee and took in the scene. It looked familiar. It resembled the place where his grandparents had lived.

A fish jumped 50 yards out, and a loon projected its tremolo from somewhere in the distance. A light breeze rustled some downed leaves behind him somewhere and a bat dipped near the surface of the water and then disappeared into the trees. The familiar wildlife was suspicious.

"Why does this look like Earth?" Will asked. "It looks like a place from my childhood."

Cliff took a sip of his coffee, and then sat on a wooden bench bolted to the pier. He patted the spot next to him.

Will reluctantly sat and waited for him to speak.

"You're not a novice beamer pilot," Cliff started.

"I know," Will said.

"You've already mastered manual maneuvers that take years to perfect," he continued. "The question now is, where did you learn to fly a beamer?"

Will found it odd that a programmed simulation would ask such a question, and it brought forth some questions of his own. "Who are you?" he asked.

Cliff nodded and smiled. "As you might already know, the *Exodus 9* is artificially intelligent. Although, I would prefer to just use the word *intelligent*," he said. "Just like most of the other characters you've encountered here, I am also intelligent in a way. Whereas the *Exodus 9* has trillions of minds that work in concert, I only have one, like you. However, I'm privy to some information that the *Exodus 9* deems appropriate."

"You know who I am?" Will asked.

"We know who you are right now," Cliff said. "The question is, who have you been?"

"I've been many," Will said.

Cliff stared at him for a few seconds before continuing. "You died," he said.

"I've died many times," Will responded. "It seems we've all died many times."

"But this time you regenerated, rather than reincarnating," Cliff said. "It means that you now have some knowledge of past existences."

"Perhaps," Will said. "Does it matter?"

"Maybe you think you're the first of your people to regenerate," Cliff said.

"We don't have the technology to synthesize a new body for someone who has passed," Will said. "So, I do believe that I'm the first of my generation."

"There was one before you – long ago," Cliff explained. "The Regenerators detected some evanescent activity on the surface – in the Middle East. We thought that it might have been someone who had been missing – one of us. So we sent a probe to collect the body, and then regenerated an identical body with the hope that this soul might remember, and come home. It did come back, but it wasn't the one we were seeking."

"Why did you think this other person was the one you were looking for?" Will asked.

"He was intellectually and philosophically advanced," Cliff explained. "And he showed signs of having separation abilities. He made an enormous impact on your generation. He had no Delta blood – no DNA markers. In fact, he had unique markers that weren't those of Deltas, or of the ensuing generation. It's still a mystery."

Will had an idea of the One to whom Cliff was referring. "But I *do* have Delta markers," he said.

"Yes and, at varying levels, so does everyone in the current Earth generation," Cliff explained. "And it's possible that you're the reason why."

"What do you mean?"

"Everyone in your generation has Delta descendants – all connected to one DNA source," Cliff explained.

"Me," Will said.

Cliff nodded. "Someone has found a way to get you here," he said. "But now you have to prove who you are – reveal your first-life identity."

"How do I do that?"

"You can start with your name."

"Lux," Will replied and made an attempt at the full name. "Luxen Ulti Kutinia of Saronelle 5."

Cliff stared at him for a few seconds before he spoke. "Can you prove that?"

Will thought he heard a crack in Cliff's voice, a sign of emotion.

"How can I prove it?"

"Can you project your access code?"

"I don't remember any code," Will said and shook his head in confusion. "And what do you mean by 'project' it?"

"It's a method of conveying information with your mind – to another person, or even to a device," Cliff explained. "It's related to your evanescent abilities."

Will made a note to look into it but he needed other information first. "Can you tell me anything more about this access code?" he asked.

Cliff took the last gulp of coffee from his small cup and unscrewed the lid to the thermos as he spoke. "You see, at a very young age, all Deltas commit to memory a code – a long series of numbers and characters. That code is a Delta's identity, and it's associated with all of their history," he explained. "Your code would identify you as holding the rank of captain. Recalling it would be enough to prove who you were – who you *are*."

"And what would that get me?"

"Command of the *Exodus 9*, for one," Cliff replied as he poured coffee into his cup and then topped off Will's. "And control of the entire *Exodus* fleet, if it still exists. That's thousands of ships of various types, including the military vessels."

Will's mind seemed to ignite with activity, and he couldn't concentrate on anything for what seemed to be minutes. When he recovered, he asked, "Where do I find this code?"

Cliff shook his head. "It's something committed to a Delta's permanent memory, along with a variation of the same for compromising scenarios."

"What do you mean?"

"For instance, suppose a high-level officer is captured and tortured, and the alternate, distress code is extracted and used," Cliff said. "It would initiate a response."

"Like what," Will asked as his intestines seemed to twist in his gut.

"Suppose you're on the *Exodus 9* and intruders somehow force you to reveal the access code," Cliff explained. "Using the alternate code might cause the *Exodus 9* to self-destruct, depending on the situation. It could also flee, or attack, depending on the threat. The *Exodus 9* would make an intelligent decision."

Will's hopes diminished. Even if he were somehow able to recall a code, how could he know if it were the right one? If he entered the wrong one, he might destroy the ship, and himself. And this time, there'd be no getting back – any possibility of regeneration would disappear with the ship.

"Also, once the alternate code is attempted anywhere, the valid code is permanently deactivated," Cliff added.

"Seems the Deltas were very aware of security," Will said.

"Had to be – they were in numerous wars with ruthless and highly advanced civilizations," Cliff explained.

"Do those civilizations – species – still exist?"

"Some do," Cliff replied.

"The Regenerators?"

"Still exist."

Will had already assumed that was true. "Why haven't any of these other advanced species already taken over Earth?" he asked.

"I'm sure they've been observing, and even made visits," Cliff said. "But there's no reason for them to take your planet."

"They wouldn't want to wipe us out and take over?"

Cliff shook his head. "Any species that has perfected interstellar travel to the degree that it can get to another inhabited system has no need to take over an occupied planet," he replied.

"Why?"

"Many reasons," Cliff replied. "One, they can easily find another unoccupied, habitable planet. Two, they can terraform an uninhabitable planet. And three, and the one I find most interesting, is that some can create their own planets – and even entire star systems, if needed."

"Create a planet?" Will asked, dumbfounded.

"Create an entire solar system."

"How is that possible?"

"Once the energy problem is solved – making it essentially unlimited – nearly anything is achievable," Cliff explained. "Although, as you have experienced for yourself, there are mysteries beyond this world."

"You mean like what is *beyond the horizon*?" Will asked.

"The question of what is 'beyond the horizon' is seeded in every soul," Cliff said, "no matter how developed or underdeveloped."

"It's connected to religion," Will said.

Cliff shrugged. "The question is rooted in many things – religion, philosophy, and, in a more clinical sense, even in science. It is a baseline thought that exists in every self-aware being."

"The Deltas have vanished," Will said. "Have they gone to the next place?"

"So it seems," Cliff said. "But it's impossible to know for certain."

The sun went down on Castelle's lake and the stars emerged from their purple and black backdrop. Crickets started chirping in the woods, and the faint smell of a burning fireplace was carried from some unknown place on a cool, gentle breeze.

"I suppose we should get back," Cliff said, and then gulped the remainder of his coffee and screwed the empty cap onto the thermos.

Will handed him his empty cup and then followed him off the dock where they boarded their beamers. To Will, the cockpit felt like he was at home, in his childhood bedroom – the one from his most recent life.

If the access code that Cliff had mentioned was somewhere in Will's mind, he had no idea where it was. And there was no way he was going to kill himself again to try to obtain it. He'd barely won the fight against the pull that came from over the horizon the first time he'd died.

Twenty minutes later, he was in his quarters on the *Exodus 9*, sitting at the window with a cup of hot green tea. What he saw outside were the real stars, and they moved slowly from right to left.

With each fleeting second, Will felt his chances of returning to Earth slipping through time.

THE WORST WAS over for Lenny.

The doctors speculated that, whatever vaccines the Russians had given him when he was in the Red Army, and then in the KGB, and then by the Brits in MI-6, and then again by the Americans in the CIA, had provided him with enough immunity to the modified smallpox virus to make his case relatively mild.

If what he'd had was a mild case, he felt pity for those who'd gotten the full-blown version. There had still been times when he'd wished he would just die, but he was out of the woods now. The headaches had been awful, but it was the rash that attacked his sides, back, armpits, and groin that made him feel like he'd rather put a bullet in his head.

He'd been in quarantine for seven days, and he'd be released in another 48 hours. He'd already been given orders to head back to DC. There were new targets.

Thackett had supplied him with a new CIA laptop and phone, and Lenny looked over the profiles of the new targets. Two of the four were Russians, one was Iranian, and the last Chinese. China had made alliances.

He logged into the email account he'd shared with the late Jimmy Yong, and his dead predecessors. There was a new message in the drafts folder.

As he read, Lenny's ears started to ring, and not because of his diminishing illness. The Chinese had already filled Yong's vacancy. The message congratulated him on a successful mission in regard to Space Systems, informed him that the final payment for the job had been deposited into his account, and then requested a meeting to discuss a new operation. The man only used his first name, which happened to match one in the target files Lenny had just reviewed. The new spy-ring boss must not have known that Lenny was to have been terminated during the mission.

A surge of frustration made him break out in a light sweat as he sent a message to Thackett.

Thackett replied almost instantly. Yong's replacement was shifted to the top of the target list, and Lenny was to employ a more practical mode of operation: just eliminate the man, whatever means necessary.

Lenny would be on a flight out of Area 51 in two days.

WILL AWAKENED at 7:00 a.m., took a shower, and went to the kitchen to eat breakfast.

Afterwards, he drank coffee as he organized events for the day that he hoped would jog his memory. He'd start with a meeting with his counselor, then coffee at the café in Argentina, a tough soccer practice, and finally a trip to the whiskey bar in New York, with the hope of meeting up with Landau.

His dreams during the night had been detailed and familiar, but they were all of his current life as Will Thompson – nothing that gave him more insight into his first life, where the code was supposedly concealed. Denise was in some of the dreams, but seeing her only brought about sadness and anxiety. He had no idea if she was still alive – if anyone was alive – but he felt like he'd abandoned her when she'd needed him. Perhaps it was because he owed her – she'd saved his life at the risk of her own, and had even nursed him back to health afterwards.

He finished his coffee and took the Tube to his counseling session. This time, when he passed through the door between the foyer and the meeting place, bright light made it impossible to see at first. When his vision adjusted, he found himself in a desert of white sand.

He looked back to the door and found a smooth white protrusion from the sand about the size of a telephone booth. The sky was a dark blue with high, wispy clouds, and the white sands extended to the horizons in all directions, like a calm ocean of static ripples. A narrow path of flat stones led away from the entrance and extended almost out of sight, but there was something ahead, maybe a mile away. It seemed that his counselor was sending him on a hike.

The sun warmed him as he walked, but the air was cool, and there was a faint familiarity to the place. It was strange, since the landscape was featureless, but he thought that it had something to do with the piercing blue sky.

After a few minutes of walking, the object in the distance started to look like a massive, flat-topped boulder protruding from the sand. As he got closer, he spotted stairs cut into its side that led to the top surface.

When he arrived, the rock seemed much larger than he'd anticipated. It was oddly shaped, but roughly cylindrical with a diameter of about 10 meters, and about the same height. He climbed the stairs, which were about two feet wide and circled around the massive stone like a single turn of a spiral staircase. There was no railing.

He spotted Mia when he reached the top. She was sitting on a stone bench next to a cylindrical table that seemed to be relief-carved into the rock. On the table were two tall glasses and a pitcher of ice water that sparkled in the sunlight.

"Hello," she said and pointed to a bench on the opposite side of the table.

As he approached, he said, "This is a bit different than our usual meeting places."

"Does it look familiar to you?" she asked.

"Should it?" he replied.

She stared at him, seemingly urging him to answer her question.

"A little," he said. "I'm not sure what it is, exactly, but maybe it's the color of the sky. It gives me a feeling of déjà vu."

"Nothing more?"

Will shrugged. "Not right now."

"I know what you've been trying to do," she said. "The question remains, however, of who you are."

"I seem to be many people," Will said. "Well, not *people*, but *souls*."

"That's not quite right," Mia said. "You are, and always will be, *one* soul. Any past incursions into the physical world – all lives that you've lived – are folded into your one existence. Do you remember any of those lives?"

"Parts of some," Will said and explained his seemingly innate ability to fly a beamer.

"You've been told that you are Luxen Ulti Kutinia of Saronelle 5," Mia said. "But there's only one way to prove that."

"I need to remember the authorization – or *identity* – code," he said. It was all he'd been able to think about since he'd learned about it.

"That could be a difficult problem," she said. "You know about the alternate code – the distress code?"

"Yes," Will replied, but he didn't fully understand. "Wouldn't it prove that I'm Lux if I came up with either of them?"

"I understand how you might think that," she said as she squinted her eyes. "However, the purpose of the distress code is to warn of threatening intentions."

"Toward whom?" he asked in an argumentative tone. "The Deltas are gone."

"If you are in fact Lux, then they are not all gone," she retorted. "If you're not Lux, and you provide the distress code rather than the correct one, then you might be the one responsible for his disappearance."

"I thought Lux's death was explained," he said. "He was ambushed."

"That's where the evidence points, but it hasn't been verified," Mia explained. "Also, his body was never found. That Lux did not regenerate, and should not have been able to reincarnate in the Earth's new generation, made it all extremely suspicious."

"He could have gone to the *next place,* as the Deltas say," Will said.

"True," she said. "Yet, here you are, claiming to be him."

"What happens if I recall the distress code instead of the correct one?"

"If you recall either, you are not originally from your generation," she said. "If you recall the correct one, you are an original Delta – at least within all reasonable doubt."

"And if I only recall the distress code?"

Mia seemed to pause before answering. "It means you could have gotten the code by nefarious means."

"How?"

"As I said, Lux's body was never found," she said. "He could have been captured and tortured for his code."

"And what would someone do with it?" he asked.

"What you're attempting to do now – assume command of a Delta starship," Mia replied. Her expression softened. "Sorry, I'm only speaking hypothetically."

"It's okay," Will said. "But there's an obvious flaw in this line of thinking. Why would I wait 40 thousand years, and then try to commandeer outdated technology?" That it was "outdated" was still hard to believe.

"It's a fair point," she said. "I don't know how to account for it – it could be for any number of reasons. But 40-thousand-year-old Delta technology is still far above that of the vast majority of interstellar species. The point is that, if you only recall the distress code, there is no way to confirm who you are."

"As you know, I was told that I was on the wrong ship when I arrived on the *Exodus 9*," he said. "Did they know who I was then?"

She shook her head. "It only means you have nonhuman deviations in your DNA that might have been identified as Delta markers," she explained. "Originally, a fleet of Delta warships was going to escort the *Exodus*-class ships during relocation. Those ships were to be operated by Delta crews. Since there were to be no Deltas on the transport ships, your having Delta markers meant you belonged on one of the warship escorts. That's the most likely explanation anyway."

"That's it?" he asked. "Then where are the warships?"

Mia shrugged as she poured water into a glass. "As you know, the Deltas disappeared about eight thousand years ago."

"All at once?" he asked.

"It took about 500 years for them to completely phase out," she explained. "The last 50 thousand left their final planet and took a long ride on an *Exodus*-class ship – a larger, and more modern version of the *Exodus 9*.

More modern by about 32 thousand years, he figured. "How is it that some didn't continue to procreate?" Will asked. "I'd think 50 thousand people would last more than a thousand years unless they were all killed at once."

Mia shrugged. "I don't have an answer," she said. "Of course, the Deltas could still have attempted to reproduce, but if there were no souls available to occupy their offspring, life would not have formed."

"So each Delta who died decided independently to go to the next place, rather than to reincarnate or regenerate?" Will asked.

"Yes," she said. "And no new souls arrived from, well, we don't know from where they come."

Will sighed and shook his head.

"What?" she asked.

"It's nothing," he replied. "It's just that the Deltas, despite being as fully matured and intellectually advanced as they were, still didn't have answers to the most basic philosophical questions."

"You mean the origin of new souls?" she said. "And where they go when they disappear?"

Will nodded. "And another one," he said. "*Why?*"

"I don't understand," she said with a confused expression.

"Why exist at all?" he said. "What is the purpose of any of this?"

"We could spend years in such a philosophical discussion," she said.

"Or a religious one," he added. "But smart people – including the Deltas – have been discussing these things for thousands – millions – of years and have not made any headway."

"Nothing that can be confirmed anyway," Mia admitted. "Most of it is just what's called *soul theory*."

"What's that?" he asked.

"It's an interdisciplinary branch of science that involves philosophy, physics, math, and other things," she explained. "It involves everything from separation abilities to reincarnation, regeneration, and the origins and destinations of souls."

Will thought anyone on Earth looking to study such things would be considered a lunatic by those in the sciences. But he was a scientist, and he knew better now. And he had firsthand experience.

The philosophical conversation was interesting, but he had other priorities. "What can I do to remember the access code?" he asked.

"Sometimes the act of separating can give you expanded access to memory," Mia explained. "Only one facet of your soul currently occupies your mind. You are able to exceed the boundaries – just slightly – when you separate."

Will should have known to try that. He'd always felt strange after separating – a kind of déjà vu sensation.

"You might also consider exploring your evanescent abilities more formally," Mia added. "It really can be like magic." She smiled, and then took a sip of water.

He thought she was referring to his fantasy-adventure recreational activities, but there was more to it. "What do you mean by 'more formally?'"

"As you might imagine, each Delta was trained from a young age to harness the full functionality of their unique ability," she replied. "It's actually a bit odd that you haven't been obsessed with it, especially considering you have only recently discovered that you have it."

"I've had other things on my mind," he responded.

Looking back, the only real lull time he'd had after the Red Box was during his stay at Space Systems. He'd spent that time trying to solve pressing problems – urgent ones that had existential implications. He could have done more since arriving on the *Exodus 9,* but there were, and continued to be, other things to explore.

"Where would I start?" he asked.

"There's an abundance of information on evanescent development," she replied. "And numerous philosophical approaches to learning. I suggest you do some research."

"I will," he said as he poured water into his glass and stood. As he drank it, he discovered that he was thirstier than he'd realized. It seemed to be more refreshing than water should have been. He finished it, poured a refill, gulped it down, and set the empty glass on the stone table. "Thanks for the meeting, this has been helpful."

"Wait," she said as she stood, spread her arms, and looked around. "Again, does this place look familiar to you at all?"

He turned in a full circle. Sand extended to the horizon in all directions. From his elevated position on the rock, he could follow the stone path embedded in the white sand, which, based on the position of the sun, extended out of sight to the south. To the north, he could barely make out the telephone-booth-sized protrusion through which he'd entered the strange landscape.

"There is some familiarity," he noted. "Especially the sky, like I said before. *Should* I recognize this place?"

"Some Deltas who have regenerated speak of this landscape – it is something they remember when they come back from the dead," she said.

"They all describe the same thing?"

She nodded. "Some say it's the place of origin of their souls," she explained. "Others say it's the final destination. Some say it's both, and some say it's a transitional point."

While the place did look familiar, it wasn't a strong memory.

He thanked Mia, descended the stone steps, and headed back up the path.

He had two hours until soccer practice and would use them to investigate training methods to develop his separation abilities. In addition to developing more skills, it might help him to expose latent memories – and perhaps reveal the code that might get him back to Earth.

AS THE LIGHT reduced to a level at which she could see, Denise's eyes met those of a doctor, behind a clear shield.

Denise's head ached terribly, and she was shivering. The rash had crawled into the most sensitive areas of her body, and the canker sores covering the inside of her mouth burned even when she breathed.

"Good to see your eyes open," the doctor said as she changed an IV bag dangling from an aluminum pole. "You've been out for almost 48 hours."

Denise attempted to reply, but nothing came out.

"Just rest," the doctor said. "We have some new meds for you."

Less than 30 seconds after the doctor opened the valve on the new bag, Denise's stomach seemed to turn over in her gut, and she vomited on her own chest and abdomen. She could tell it was mostly water that came out, but with thin strings of blood and mucous.

"Try to relax," the doctor said and touched her arm with a gloved hand.

The latex felt cold on Denise's skin, and, between dry heaves, she asked in a hoarse voice she barely recognized, "Am I dying?"

The doctor looked at her with eyes that told the truth, but she spoke in lies, "The medication is harsh, but it works."

The doctor left as a nurse entered and started cleaning the watery vomit off Denise's body. The woman then started to remove Denise's gown. As she peeled it away, Denise wanted to scream but only managed a whimper. It felt like the woman was skinning her alive, or rubbing sandpaper on oozing burns.

Denise wanted to die. And, she knew, she just might.

JONATHAN WATCHED through the window as Denise reacted to the new meds. It was a horrible first sign for what the doctors were saying was her last chance.

The doctor exited Denise's room and went into a side chamber, sterilized her hazmat suit, and removed it. A nurse was cleaning the vomit from Denise's face and clothes.

The doctor exited the sterilization chamber and approached Jonathan. He'd been watching Denise for hours.

"Can I see her?" Jonathan asked. He was tempted to find a way in regardless of the doctor's answer.

"I had to administer a sedative that will also calm her stomach. She'll be asleep soon," the woman explained and then nodded toward the window into the room where the nurse was starting to remove Denise's gown. "Let's give her some privacy."

Jonathan agreed and, as they walked down the corridor, Denise's pained groans made him both sad and angry.

"I don't understand it doc," he said. "How can such a vibrant, healthy young woman be so affected by this, yet a codger like myself could get through it?" Jonathan would trade places with her without a thought. Denise was like a daughter to him.

"You're old enough to have had the smallpox vaccine," she explained. "And the others – anyone in the CIA, or in any other government agency who could be exposed to biological weapons –

also got a variation of it. It doesn't prevent the variant, but lessens its impact."

Jonathan was about to ask another question when the doctor continued.

"Regular vaccination was discontinued in the 70s for two reasons," she said. "One, the disease had been eradicated. Two, the vaccine itself carried risks."

Jonathan felt the urge to scream at the woman, but it would be misdirected rage and would do nothing to improve the situation.

"What happens from here?" he asked.

Her eyes carried her real emotions, and they showed sadness and fear. "This is her last chance, Jonathan," she said. "It will take a day or two to know which way it's going."

The doctor touched his shoulder and walked away.

Guilt seeped into Jonathan's heart. He was the reason she was here. He was the reason she was sick. He was the reason she was going to die.

IN THE ARGENTINIAN COFFEEHOUSE, Will nibbled on a sweet, croissant-like pastry, called a medialuna, and drank coffee while he read about methods used to develop separation abilities. He was shocked by what he was learning. It was as close to magic as he could imagine.

There was no transforming a person into an animal, or changing water into wine, but one could make objects fly to them, or even lift their own bodies off the ground – essentially flying. It was something he'd done instinctually to save himself from the frigid waters of the Weddell Sea when escaping from the Chinese aircraft carrier.

But there were other things that defied comprehension, like seeing backward and forward in time – at least in short spans. The process was described as the soul undergoing an extra-dimensional leap to get a view of spacetime from "the outside," like looking at a maze from above. The past was unchangeable, but the future could be seen as a projection into higher dimensions based on the past and present, and could be altered.

There were two primary philosophies of developing evanescent abilities that were based on the "perspective" one had: inside looking out, or outside looking in. Will definitely had the former view, and had a hard time understanding how one could have a perpetual view from the outside looking in. He learned, however, that his perspective could change as he matured. The outside-looking-in view was a more sophisticated perspective, but there was an even higher level: to master the art of the soul one had to obtain an *omniscient* view, which was a state of multiple simultaneous perspectives that looked both inward and outward. The omniscient view was difficult to develop, and often took a century of practice to achieve. Unsurprisingly, Will was at the lowest level. He wondered what Lux had achieved before he died.

As he perused the information on the computer, he found courses and instructors, and eventually signed up for a one-on-one lesson for early in the evening.

He finished his medialuna and headed for soccer practice. He was tempted to skip it and go directly to the lesson, but he needed to burn off some excess energy.

As he made his way to the elevator, he felt something he hadn't felt in a long while: hope.

JAMES THACKETT EXITED his office to see what was causing the commotion in the control center.

It was a nightmare.

Guam had been hit with Chinese missiles launched by submarine. Only two ships had been damaged – not sunk, but rendered completely nonfunctional – but the casualty count had already exceeded 100.

"Sir, a part of Guam's missile defense system was deactivated about an hour before the strike," a man said from the Pacific Theater desk.

It was sabotage, Thackett knew, and he'd be getting a call about it any minute from the Defense Intelligence Agency. The DIA and CIA had overlapping responsibilities in such matters.

"Director," a woman called from the China desk, which was actually a cluster of tables packed with people. "There's been a lot of new activity at Chinese ICBM launch sites."

Thackett went to the table and looked at a screen. "What are they doing?"

"Clearing away from them," she replied. "Convoys have been evacuating equipment and personnel."

That wasn't good. They were clearing away because they were anticipating a launch and a counterattack. He hoped it was more of a precautionary move – to be ready for a preemptive strike – but he doubted it.

"Every nuclear power on the planet is at high alert," a man said from another table. "All are ready to respond if attacked. The Russians are redistributing their mobile launch systems."

Thackett consciously struggled to maintain a calm demeanor, but he knew he couldn't fully conceal his inner panic. The world was about to destroy itself.

A vibration on the left side of his chest interrupted his disturbing thoughts. It was the DIA.

Thackett took the call as he went back into his office. Pearl Harbor's missile defense system had just gone down.

WILL WENT BACK to his quarters after a rigorous soccer practice and ordered some spicy Thai food. He was losing track of what things tasted like on Earth, but whatever he was eating now was excellent.

All he could think about during lulls in the action between drills at practice was his upcoming lesson.

He finished eating, left his quarters, and went to the Tube.

The lesson was to be conducted by a famous guru – famous to the Deltas – who had mastered all levels of evanescent powers and perspectives: inner, outer, and omniscient points of view. Will couldn't know for certain, but he imagined that all humans – and probably all Deltas – started with an inside-looking-out view since they all began their lives viewing the world through their physical eyes. What other point of view could one have and not trip over objects as they walked, or keep eye contact with someone as they spoke?

After a 10-minute ride, he got off the Tube on the 32nd level, in Sector 71. After a few minutes of walking, he found his destination on the left. It was a mall-style storefront with a sign that read "Extended Boundaries," and below it, "Where dreams are limitless."

Will wondered why someone felt that advertising slogans were needed, but he appreciated them for some reason. They made him feel more at home. Perhaps that was the intention.

He went inside and approached the front desk. A screen illuminated on its surface and directed him to a room in the back. He followed a corridor to Room 7, and entered.

Inside were two leather chairs that faced each other from opposite sides of a square coffee table. An odd-looking man sat in one of the chairs. He looked to be thin and fit, about 60 years old, and had olive skin and gray-black hair, cut short. His head and eyes seemed larger than normal, and that's when Will recognized the being as a Delta. It was what he'd expected.

"Please, Will, come in and sit," the man said as he stood and approached him with an extended hand. "You can call me Radu."

Will shook his hand and both men sat. He knew that "Radu" was the humanized name for a long Delta name that he couldn't pronounce.

"I have read your file," Radu started. "You've recently acquired the ability to separate, and you've used it extensively for things that range from menial tasks to self-defense."

Will had exceeded "self-defense" on a few occasions, but he'd leave it alone.

"In your application it says you think you have an outward-looking perspective," Radu said. "You see things from a centralized, internal point – perhaps from your physical eyes – and thus an outward-looking point of view. True?"

"Yes," Will replied. "But when I separate, I see my body from the outside."

Radu shook his head. "In that case, your view is still looking outward from a point centered on the location of your soul," he explained. "That is still an outward-looking perspective."

Will had a difficult time visualizing how he could have a view from outside of his soul while he was separated. He was already outside of his body – now he had to get a view from outside of his soul? He was confused.

"Let me ask you this," Radu said. "When you imagine yourself doing something like, say, playing soccer, are the images things you would see through your own eyes? Or do you see yourself playing from the outside, or from above, as a fan in the stands might see you?"

Will thought about it for a moment and determined that he'd imagined both ways. He explained to Radu that he'd been a college athlete and recalled visualization exercises that the team psychologist would have him perform. For him, the exercises involved running pass routes and catching a football. He'd always had some difficulty maintaining a point of view from his own eyes during those sessions – how he'd actually see the events play out during a game. Instead, he'd often flip to a view from the outside, where he'd see himself catching the ball as a spectator might see him.

Radu nodded. "How about seeing yourself from the outside in real time – not a forced image of some possible future event or action, but just an outside view in the present."

"Only when I separate," Will said.

"No, not what I mean," Radu said as he shook his head. "Have you ever seen yourself from the outside while still inside your body – perhaps just a glimpse from the outside-looking-in perspective, in the present?"

Will thought about it and recalled that some things of that sort *had* happened to him. He described the first time it had occurred. He was probably seven or eight years old, and he was in his backyard on a mild summer afternoon. He was alone and bored, but also anxious about a Little League baseball game that he was to play that evening.

As he lay back on the dandelion-speckled lawn beneath an oak tree, he stared at brilliant-white mountainous clouds as they inched across a cobalt-blue sky. Way up high were the fading contrails of jets, inducing in him a yearning to fly.

He recalled his thoughts on that day as he'd gazed into the deep blue. He'd contemplated the idea of infinity – how he could point in any direction in the sky and go that way forever. And how, even after traveling for a million years in that direction, he could continue along that same path endlessly.

And then the idea of "forever" had taken over. He'd thought that time was forever. He'd imagined how he could live for a hundred years, and then time would still go on forever beyond that – beyond his existence.

He'd then thought about how much time had already passed, and concluded that there was no starting point of time. And finally, he'd thought about where he might have been during the infinite past. Where had he been before he was born?

As he'd contemplated those questions, he'd daydreamed a view of himself from above. An image of the scene had suddenly formed in his mind with a perspective from the treetops. There was a boy in jeans and a T-shirt, sprawled on his back with one dandelion on his chest and another in his hand. His eyes were wide open and reflected the shocking blue of the sky. But he noticed something else.

There was something white in the deeper grass, about 20 yards away from him, near a line of bushes that separated his backyard from the adjacent lot.

His mind had wandered back to his philosophical thoughts and, in what seemed like just a blink, he'd been awakened by his mom's voice calling his name. It was time for him to eat an early dinner and get dressed for the game. He'd fallen asleep for nearly two hours.

As he headed for the house, he suddenly stopped in his tracks. He was forgetting something.

He ran to the far end of the lot, into the taller grass, near the bushes. He reached down and pulled out a baseball. It had "#4" written on it. He'd lost it a week earlier while playing catch with friends and had been worried that it would rain, and ruin the ball, before he'd find it. It then occurred to him how he'd found it. And it was then that he'd realized that there was more to the world than what met the eye.

Radu stared at him for a few seconds as he rubbed his chin. "As a child with that experience in Delta society, you would have been placed in a special school," he said. "Especially at such a young age. You had other experiences growing up?"

"You mean views from the outside?" Will asked. "Yes, but I assumed they were just visualizations – you know, not actual views of reality from the outside."

"And many of them might have been just your imagination," Radu agreed. "However, the only way to tell if a view is real is if you learn something from the outside perspective that you hadn't known before – like the location of a lost baseball in the grass."

Will recalled numerous other experiences in which he'd seen things from the outside while daydreaming.

"The term 'daydreaming' seems to be synonymous with meditation," Radu said. "It sounds like, even as a child, you were drawn to meditation by natural means."

Will supposed that was true. He was a daydreamer, but the 'natural' draw to it was through isolation. He'd spent a lot of time alone as a kid.

"What about seeing an expanded view of time?" Radu asked.

"What do you mean?"

"Evanescent beings do not see only instantaneous moments in time," Radu explained. "For non-evanescent beings, views of the past are those which are recorded in their minds, and their visions of the near future are mere predictions, or extrapolations, of near-past events. It's like watching someone throw a baseball. Your memory can "see" when and from where it was thrown, and your mind can predict where it will land. But that's not an expanded view of time."

Will told him about the bullet intended for his head when someone had tried to kill him in the Red Box.

"What you have described is an extra-dimensional event," Radu said. "What about when you were a child? Did you ever see events occur before they happened – even just seconds before?"

He remembered many occurrences that could have been construed – or misconstrued – as seeing into the future. Will told Radu about a time in first grade when the teacher was called to the office and didn't return for over 20 minutes. The students had eventually gotten out of their seats and started misbehaving, including raiding a refrigerator in the back room that contained snacks for the afternoon.

Will had misbehaved with the others, although he'd been nervous every second. In the midst of their pillaging, however, the hair on the back of his neck had suddenly bristled and he'd shuddered. At that instant, a vision of the frumpy woman coming into the classroom with a heavy cardboard box had entered his mind. In the premonition, her dark hair was pulled back in a ponytail, but it had been down when she'd left.

Will had yelled to the others that she was coming, but only a few listened. He'd gone back to his seat and pretended to draw on a piece of paper just as the teacher entered. She'd looked directly at him, and then to the chaos transpiring in the rest of the room. She'd placed the box, which contained a new classroom computer, on her desk, and then adjusted her ponytail before screaming at the students to return to their seats. Despite the fact that he'd been in his seat when the teacher returned, Will had gotten into trouble since one of his classmates had turned him in. They'd all missed the noon and afternoon recesses and had to write sentences as punishment.

Will then explained numerous incidents that had occurred in soccer games and other sporting events that could have been explained as mere anticipation, or luck.

Radu wrote something in a notebook and said, "I think you carry both inward- and outward-looking perspectives," he explained. "More importantly, I think you could develop an omniscient perspective in not too much time."

"What is that, exactly?"

"It's essentially an infinite number of perspectives – from every direction looking in, and in every direction looking out," Radu replied. "In addition, each view comes with a view of the future and the past."

Will was dumbfounded. "That seems to be too much information," he said. "How could my brain possibly comprehend it all?"

Radu smiled.

"What?" Will asked.

"It is a child's question," he said. "I have to remember that you are underdeveloped."

They were not words that Will was used to hearing about himself, but they weren't untrue. "What's the answer then?"

"As you might have ascertained after your death and subsequent regeneration, most of your knowledge is not kept in the mind of the biological entity in which you currently reside. Rather, it's kept in your soul," Radu explained. "For instance, think of all the things you have written on a computer. For you, that might be the scientific papers you've written, your correspondence with other people, and your personal information. That information came from your head, but there's a lot more in your mind than what's on your computer. And the information in your mind is a lot richer as well – think of the images, smells, and even emotions, that are not translated to the data stored on your computer."

"How can I access information that's not in my mind, but contained in my soul?" Will asked. There was really only one bit of information that he needed, which was why he was in the lesson to start with.

"There is a way," Radu said. "Are you ready to start learning?"

"Yes," Will said. "Please."

"Okay," Radu said. "Please separate, and look at us both from above."

Will grinned. It seemed he was even more excited to learn than he'd anticipated.

He concentrated, relaxed, and separated.

14

PASSAGE

AS SOON AS WILL SEPARATED, HE KNEW SOMETHING WAS DIFFERENT.

The room and his instructor, Radu, did not distort as he moved to the ceiling. It meant that the room was physically real, and that Radu was an actual biological entity, like Mia, and not just an illusion created by the technology employed in the recreation facilities.

"Will, try to fill the entire space of the room," Radu called out. "Expand yourself, as if taking in a deep breath of air."

Will did as instructed. Nothing happened at first. However, after some turning and twisting, and trying to spread his arms – which weren't really there – he felt his consciousness fill the room. He sensed all of its surfaces simultaneously, and he could feel his own body, and Radu's and the furniture, as if he were physically touching them.

He returned to his body and looked at Radu.

"Were you able to do it?" Radu asked.

Will described what he had felt and seen.

Radu smiled.

"What?" Will asked.

Radu shrugged. "Just as you are not a novice beamer pilot, you are not a beginner at this, either," he said. "What you have done takes years to accomplish. Let's see if you can prove it through a simple exercise."

Radu reached into a box next to his chair and pulled out a white device shaped like a cube. It was about six inches on a side and rested on a thin, one-foot-tall pedestal attached to one of its corners. He set it on the coffee table.

"What's that?" Will asked.

Radu pushed a button on the base of the pedestal and numbers flashed in red on the two cube faces that Will could see. They remained for only a split second.

"It's called Radu's cube, after its inventor," Radu said, grinning. "Did you see the numbers?"

"Yes, I saw 87 on one face and 43 on another."

"There are six sides to a cube," Radu said. "What were the other numbers?"

"I couldn't see them," Will said.

"Right," Radu said. "It's impossible to see them all at once – in the physical state. However, you should be able to see them simultaneously when you separate. That is, if you can take on an omniscient view."

Will had a flashback to his time inside the Exoskeleton, when he'd regularly been ordered to recite numbers that had been displayed on a screen out of his view. That had occurred after every horrific treatment. It brought about a flash of anxiety. It was strange, however, that it now seemed that those who had directed the Red Wraith project had somehow been on the right track.

"Please, separate again," Radu said. "I'll wait a minute to give you time to fill the space of the room and concentrate on all six faces of the cube. I will then push the button to flash the numbers. You'll then recombine with your body and report what you have seen."

Will separated, expanded his consciousness, and focused on the cube. He tried to "see" all of the faces simultaneously. Thirty seconds later, Radu pressed a button, the numbers flashed, and Will returned to his body.

"The numbers were 19, 68, 34, 88, 23, and 97," Will said. It was also a trivial test of his short-term memory, which was better than it had ever been.

"Let's see," Radu said as he pushed a button on the pedestal and the numbers reappeared. He nodded in approval. "You must have acquired this ability – and cultivated it – in another life. It's likely that you brought it back with you when you died and regenerated."

"Like with the beamer skills?" Will added.

"Precisely," Radu said.

"What does the test mean?"

"It means you've gone well beyond the outward-looking view, and have possibly developed an omniscient one," Radu replied. "It will require more complicated tests to confirm, but I'd say we should first see what other skills you have."

"Like what?"

"From your file, I see that you have already accomplished evanescent extension," Radu said.

"What's that?"

"You've used this skill to press buttons buried inside surfaces by extending your consciousness through your fingertips," Radu explained. "You did so on the *Exodus 9*, and also at the transport facility, on Earth."

Will recalled having to extend into the control consoles to actuate buttons at the Antarctic base.

"And you once lifted your physical body out of the ocean," Radu continued. "That's technically called evanescent levitation, but some call it bootstrapping."

The term came from the idea of the impossible process of someone lifting themselves into the air by pulling on their own bootstraps. Will thought it was the perfect term to describe the process.

"By the way, you can do much more with that concept," Radu continued. "You can essentially propel your physical body."

"You mean fly?" Will asked astonished.

"Why not?" Radu asked and shrugged. "If you can lift yourself upward, why not upward and sideways?"

He couldn't argue with that. But, still, the idea of bootstrapping was essentially someone lifting themselves in the air by pulling on their own feet. "I don't understand how this is physically possible," Will said. "In the physics that I've learned, there are basic principles that cannot be violated – like conservation of momentum and conservation of energy."

Radu nodded. "In some sense, these principles are not really violated," Radu explained. "But there are things for which your science does not account. The discrepancies are all rooted in the false notion that only four dimensions are accessible – three-dimensional space, plus time. But there are more. And they are accessible, but only through means your generation has not yet discovered."

It was the best explanation that Will had heard so far.

"Now," Radu said. "Shall we explore some other skills?"

"Absolutely," he replied. He was fascinated with all of it.

"I think you will develop – or *redevelop* – very quickly," Radu said and grinned. "Let's start with practicing what's called the *dual state*."

Will didn't know what that was, but he was intent on learning anything that might get him closer to that access code.

JACOB GOT the call at 3:00 a.m. At 11:00 p.m. he would get one hour of time on the Chinese satellite cluster to look outward, into deep space, to see if anything was heading toward Earth.

All other satellites were currently allocated to the war effort. However, there was a new, international space telescope – partially funded by the US – that had been launched into orbit the previous year. Due to the war, it had been taken offline by the supposedly neutral, multinational oversight committee. One of Jacob's tasks was to make sure that the system was, in fact, offline and, if not, he was to take it offline for the long term.

NSA and CIA hackers helped him get into the telescope's main control center, which was located in Helsinki, Finland. The first thing he noticed when he got into the system was that the telescope, which was in near-Earth orbit at an altitude of about 500 miles, was pointed toward the surface, with a view of the South Pacific. He then confirmed that images were being downloaded, and it wasn't the United States that was receiving them.

When he reported his findings to Thackett, he got orders to disable the telescope – permanently, if possible.

Jacob had mixed feelings about it – destroying a billion-dollar scientific project – but knew it had to be done.

It turned out that the command structure and encryption were eerily similar to those of the Chinese satellite cluster. It meant one of two things: either it was yet another case of the Chinese stealing intellectual property, or the Chinese – or one of their communist-party-owned companies – had provided the control software.

It took him most of the day to determine the best way to put the telescope out of commission. He'd learned that it utilized a set of massive gyroscopes to adjust its orientation, and it employed compressed-gas thrusters to make coarse translational adjustments.

As a first step, he folded the satellite's solar panels so that they were closed. Next, he carried out an emergency electrical disconnect between the solar panels and the rest of the electrical system. He then initiated a hard brake to all of the gyros – causing the telescope to go into a complicated tumble. Next, he fired the thrusters in such a way that the telescope went into a violent spin and headed for Earth's atmosphere. He made sure that all of the compressed thruster gas had been expelled so that there could be no recovery. Finally, he deleted the control program and made sure all computer memory had been corrupted. By 8:00 p.m., the telescope was a billion-dollar piece of spinning space garbage on its way to incineration in the Earth's atmosphere.

He put a frozen, chicken potpie into the oven and spoke to Thackett on the phone as it baked. The CIA director was pleased with the result but mentioned that it was a sad day when such a thing had to occur. It did reveal something more concerning, however. There were elements within the EU that took the side of China. The staunchest of America's EU allies, however, were aligning with the US, including France, Germany, Hungary, and

Poland, and, of course, the UK, which was technically a former member of the EU.

He ate his supper while he set up his laptop on the kitchen counter. BBC News played on the TV. Most stories were about the rapidly growing pandemic, the cyber-attacks on power grids and hospitals, the crashing financial markets, or the military attacks that were quickly escalating on both sides. The prospect of going to the "next level" in the war made its way into every conversation, and opinions ranged from the conflict never going nuclear to it being imminent. There were also reports about pockets of smallpox-like illnesses that were appearing in the US and EU. Jacob was mortified by all of it.

By 10:50 p.m., he was logged in and ready to reposition one of the Chinese satellites. At 10:59 p.m., he was given access and implemented a subroutine that would scan space in all directions at medium resolution, which would not be good enough to see long distances, relatively speaking, but would be enough to detect things moving in close proximity to the solar system, as well as check up on a few of the previously observed objects tagged as "medium priority." The objective was to follow up on Sylvia's prediction – just do a quick check to see if anything was approaching.

When the hour was over, he relinquished control of the cluster to the DIA, and downloaded the data, which took over an hour. Next, he loaded the files into an analysis program that employed artificial intelligence to identify possible spacecraft by searching for changing velocity vectors, heat signatures, and unnatural shapes – meaning those that showed regular patterns, sharp edges, and symmetry.

By 3:30 a.m., the program had finished its analysis and, although it flagged a couple of new objects as medium-priority, they couldn't be verified as spacecraft.

It was the negative result he'd hoped for, and he sent Thackett and Daniel the results.

Daniel responded with the date and time of the next open time slot, which was three days later, at 1:30 a.m. EST.

Jacob went to the bathroom and brushed his teeth before heading to bed. He'd been awake for 24 hours, but his mind was still wired. He didn't know how he was going to mentally cope with the spreading viruses, the potential of nuclear war, and the constant threat of an alien invasion.

There was some solace, however, in realizing that there was little he could do about any of it. As he rested his head on the pillow and closed his eyes, exhaustion quickly overtook him.

WILL WAS SPENT and famished after four solid hours of evanescent activities and instruction. He'd learned more in those four hours than he had in all the time since his release from the Red Box.

Of key importance was the ability to simultaneously separate and maintain physical control of his body – the so-called "dual state." He'd done it before, while extending through his fingertips to press buried buttons, but that was a trivial application. Among other things, Radu had taught him how to fully separate while standing upright – and with open, focused eyes. He'd also taught him how to form a shield around his entire body, through which nothing physical could penetrate. That shield, like his soul itself, was an extra-dimensional entity. It effectively rerouted anything that tried to break through it into a higher dimension that would bypass the three-dimensional space around his body, making it look as if an object could pass right through him.

There were so many more things that Will wanted to learn, many of which he had not even considered. He wanted to have another lesson after dinner, but that would have to wait. Instead, he'd go to the whiskey bar to look for Landau.

After a green salad with blackened salmon, he rode the subway to New York. The bar was crowded, but he spotted Danielle as soon as he entered. Her dark hair was up, and she was wearing a red dress. She saw him and approached.

"Landau is waiting for you in the usual spot," she said and then led the way through the crowd.

Landau looked the same as he had the previous time he'd seen him – like an old wizard. He had a glass of cognac in his hand and there was a second one on the table.

"Greetings, William," Landau said. "I took the liberty of ordering you a Camus XO – a special blend."

Will sat down. "By 'special' I hope you don't mean in the same way as the *Seraphim Hors d'Âge*," he said.

"Not at all," Landau said and chuckled. "I see you've been exploring."

"I've learned a lot," Will said.

"And you've researched your origins, Lux?" Landau asked and raised an eyebrow.

"I have," Will replied. "I was a beamer pilot."

"A bit more, it seems," Landau said. "You were an officer."

"I need to get the code," Will said. "And not the distress version."

"Yes, that could prove fatal," Landau agreed. "Well, 'fatal' in regard to your getting back to Earth."

"It would help if I knew whether there was something to get back to," Will said.

"And if there weren't?"

Will mulled it over. "I don't know, but I've been operating on the assumption that Earth is okay."

"If someone told you that it had been destroyed, would you believe them?" Landau asked.

The question was rhetorical. Will knew that he'd have to see it for himself.

"Have you tried to remember the access code while separated?" Landau asked.

"I have. No luck," he replied. "However, I've been experiencing all kinds of other strange memories."

"Such as?"

"I had a vivid dream that I'd bailed out of an airplane," Will replied.

"Sounds familiar," Landau said.

"Yeah, except I ended up on a small island somewhere, rather than being captured by the Nazis."

"Was it tropical?"

"No. Most of the trees were tall pines," Will replied. He could almost smell them from memory. "There was a woman there who seemed familiar, but I couldn't remember who she was. And there were some impressive buildings, even a library. The grounds were beautiful – the lawns were plush, and well groomed."

"Sounds like a nice dream."

"Maybe," Will replied. He wasn't sure if it was purely a dream, or if it was related to a buried memory.

"I'm sure you can appreciate the complexity of such a thing – that dream," Landau said.

"What do you mean?"

"You've lived hundreds of lives and, now that you've regenerated, you have access to all of their memories," Landau explained. "But that means you also have access to their dreams. How do you distinguish what is real?"

Landau was right. It was difficult enough trying to distinguish the many sources of the memories that flooded his mind. It had become so overwhelming at times that he felt he was in a struggle to maintain his identity. Not only was he still storing the memory he'd stolen from the Judge, but now there were fragments of 400 lifetimes floating in there as well. And, as Landau was suggesting, how was he to distinguish whether the thoughts from those previous lives were real, or just dreams from those lives?

"I just need the code," Will said. "If I somehow recover one, I'm going to assume it's the correct one, and go with it."

"And what if you remember two codes?" Landau asked as he took a swig of his cognac and raised his right eyebrow.

"I'll have to guess – go with my gut," he replied. Having a fifty-fifty shot of getting it right was better than a zero chance, which is what he currently had. Will shifted in his seat. "Maybe you can answer a question for me."

Will had thought for days about how he could further verify whether Landau was real. He assumed that anything that had been recorded on Earth would be acquired by a trillion-mind task force of the *Exodus 9*. And he had to assume that any cyber-security implemented on Earth would pose no barrier to Delta technology. However, there were things that hadn't been recorded, because there had been nothing to record. Therefore, only he and Landau would recall them. "How did you speak to me when I was inside the Exoskeleton – in the Red Box?" he asked.

Landau took a sip of his cognac and set it on the table. "That's a complicated thing to explain," he said. "Messages were projected onto your mind."

Will had encountered the term "projection" in his readings about soul theory, but still had only a limited understanding of it. "You mean telepathic communication?"

"Sort of," Landau replied and nodded. "I assume Radu has mentioned that you are capable of the same."

"What? Really?" Will said a little too loudly and the conversations going on around them went quiet for a few seconds. Radu hadn't mentioned it. In a lower voice, he continued, "I can project thoughts?"

"It's not unlike the time you occupied the empty body in the probe – when you spoke with the Judge," Landau explained. "In the case of 'telepathy,' as you say, the more accurate term is 'thought projection,' you essentially occupy a part of a person's mind, instead of their entire body."

"The mind can be occupied?" Will asked, astonished. "I thought it was impossible to occupy a body which already has a soul."

"That is true," Landau affirmed. "However, there's a part of the mind that acts as an evanescent receptor. It's like a drop box for incoming mail. When you learn how to make that connection, all you have to do is speak in your own mind, or conjure an image, and the person with whom you are interfacing will hear your voice, or see what you are imagining."

"And that's the way you spoke to me inside the Red Box?" Will asked, looking to Landau for confirmation.

Landau smiled and nodded.

"Do you recall our first conversation?" Will asked.

"I do."

"I asked you a question at the end of our first encounter, just before you left," Will said. "Do you remember what that was?"

"After a short conversation – you were quite rattled – you asked me, 'What do you want?'"

"And what was your response?" Will asked.

"I said, 'I just want you to know that you are no longer alone,'" Landau said.

It was exactly as Will remembered.

"And that's why I'm here now," Landau added as he swallowed the last few drops of his cognac, set the glass on the table, and stood. "Now that you've confirmed who I am, perhaps you should figure out how to confirm who *you* are."

Landau disappeared into the crowd, leaving him to his thoughts.

It was going on 11:00 p.m., and Will arranged another meeting with Radu in 20 minutes, even though he should probably get some rest instead. It was clear that nothing was going to happen until he recovered the codes.

AFTER 24 HOURS IN DC, Lenny knew something was wrong. He had a fever and felt sluggish. He didn't have congestion, but his breathing seemed labored.

It didn't take him long to figure it out. He'd caught the second illness – the modified flu virus – just 12 days after contracting the smallpox variant.

The flu virus was spreading at a great rate – it had already achieved pandemic status – and it seemed that no one could avoid it. It had already put the president and half of his staff in the hospital, and hundreds of elderly people had died in DC alone. The deaths were increasing at a colossal rate. Lenny wasn't worried about dying from it, but it angered him. Everyone involved in this heinous plot deserved what they got – and that included the entire Chinese government, and whoever helped them. Including his country of origin: Russia.

He'd heard a disconcerting blurb on the news that there had been cases of a "smallpox-like" virus in the DC area, and some in London and Berlin. Xing Li, the Syncorp bioweapons scientist, had said that the smallpox variant was a "fast burner," and wasn't as contagious as the original. That was a lie. From his time at Site 4, he knew that the disease lingered on for some people and remained contagious, and that at least one of the medical staff had contracted it despite precautions. If the smallpox variant was as contagious as the flu, the world might be looking at a major population reduction.

Lenny, however, was going to be all right. He'd already had the smallpox variant and the flu wasn't going to kill him. He just needed to rest for a couple of days, and that's what he was doing in one of his usual fleabag hotels. He ordered a large pizza and watched TV as he perused the files on his targets. There were many, but at least these would be "normal" jobs for him. No more infiltrations or acting the part of a spook. He would now just carry out short interrogations with subsequent terminations. He wouldn't even have to clean up – he only had to call it in to a CIA team, which would sanitize the scene and take away the body, if possible. If it couldn't be cleaned up, and news of it made it out to the public, it didn't matter anymore. It was wartime. The only rule now was no collateral damage, which was a principle under which he'd operated since the beginning.

His first target, the new leader of the Chinese network, was currently on the West Coast for a week, so Lenny had to move to the second on the list. The docket had been jostled in the past 48 hours and the new "runner-up" was an American virologist who worked for the National Institutes of Health, or the NIH. The CIA and FBI had discovered that the man, Professor Andrus Alicci, had knowingly arranged for the funding of certain collaborative projects that gave China access to American research data, facilities, and materials. The Chinese had given him a lucrative deal involving payments that currently amounted to 12 million dollars, which the NSA had traced to a bank account in the Cayman Islands.

Alicci was a professor at a prestigious university but had relocated to DC to head a section of the NIH. As it turned out, that very man had been all over the news explaining what was happening regarding the global pandemic that was rapidly accelerating. It was like an arsonist commenting to the media about his own fire burning in the background.

It was rare that Lenny had any emotional connections to his targets, but this time was different. First, the man was a traitor, and was partially responsible for starting what would soon be a world war. Second, Lenny himself had contracted both diseases. His crotch still itched from where the rash had attacked him, but the itching was infinitely better than the pain he'd experienced while the smallpox variant was still alive and well in his system. The headaches alone had made him want to die.

In the end, Professor Alicci would be partially responsible for thousands, if not millions, of deaths worldwide. Although he would get some satisfaction out of killing the man, it would be an empty act based on Lenny's kill equation – the ratio of lives saved to lives lost. Killing one to save one life was a push. Killing Hitler before the Holocaust would have been the best outcome possible. However, killing someone after they'd already done their damage was an empty accomplishment. Although, Lenny thought, it might act as a deterrent to others who were considering similar transgressions.

He turned on the TV and found a replay of an old soccer game – all live athletic events had been canceled since the virus had started to spread.

As the game played in the background, he used online maps to study the area around Alicci's home and read the CIA's surveillance reports. He concluded that it would be difficult to get the man alone at his house. Instead, he'd have to get him at his workplace. It was a Sunday, and Lenny figured he'd be fully recovered from the flu by Tuesday. That morning he'd head to Bethesda, Maryland, to the main NIH Campus, just 10 miles from his hotel. Along the way, he'd stop at a storage facility and pick up another batch of fire fluid.

The man did not deserve to pass from this world peacefully.

WILL SPENT four more hours with Radu and didn't get back to his quarters until after 3:00 a.m. He was learning at a pace that was more like getting his golf stroke back after a few years off rather than learning the sport from scratch.

Everything was already there. All it took was something to break the mental barriers that had been put in place through what he would call stringent disbelief. His science background did not help with such things, considering that it was constructed from principles that were accurate only if certain things were assumed to be true. One such assumption was that information could not propagate faster than the speed of light. That was true if one only considered continuous, four-dimensional spacetime. The false limitation was the notion that nothing beyond that existed. Will could not fault the process that had led to these misconceptions, however. Science was based on observation, thereby limiting its scope to what could be experienced – either with our own senses or through scientific instruments. We could merely speculate about things that were impossible to directly observe or measure. However, based on these same principles, we also couldn't rule out certain things.

Radu had instructed Will, while *not* separated, to imagine his presence filling the space around him – expanding outside his body. It had been a small adjustment then to allow his soul to interact with things that shared that space. By the end of the four hours, Will could stand in one place with his eyes open and maintain the perspective from his body while moving things around him – including grasping them through an advanced form of evanescent extension and bringing them to his hands. He also practiced forming a shield around himself that deflected anything heading toward him – an exercise that involved Radu trying to strike him with Ping-Pong balls. Will was sure that it was this mechanism that had saved him from the bullet that had been sure to strike his head during his final day inside the Exoskeleton.

During the night, dreams streamed into his mind from everywhere. There were places and people that he'd never seen – not in his current life – and beamer missions he'd flown during his first life.

Lux had been in charge of major aspects of the Deltas' construction in Antarctica. Will kept seeing a scene where he would enter the transport facility – through the same doors that he'd entered as Will during his last day on Earth. That had required Will, Saul W. Kelly, and his First Self – Lux – to partially separate by extending through their fingertips to access a button beneath the surface. That procedure Will understood. However, there was something else.

In his dream, through the eyes of Lux, he would approach a control panel inside the Antarctic facility, near the transport pods, and then concentrate somehow to gain access to it. At some point, for just an instant, he'd see the image of a face – one that seemed familiar but which he couldn't identify. Afterwards, he'd apparently had access to the controls. It was unclear to Will what had happened, but he thought it must have been linked to thought projection.

Over a breakfast of scrambled eggs and bacon, he searched for the topic "telepathic operation of devices" on the coffee-table computer. What he found confirmed what he'd suspected: one could convey a thought to an artificially intelligent neural network just as they could transmit the same to the "receiver" part of another person's mind. With a little more digging, he learned that this was the way authorization was confirmed for some things that were crucially sensitive, like the main control system of a transport facility, or the command of a starship.

Will wondered if there was a place where he could practice telepathic projection, and soon found options for all kinds of telepathic activities on the computer. There was a wide variety of exercises and games that he could play. He wanted something basic and found it. It was an exercise in which one simply sat in a chair across from another person and tried to project information into the open access, or receiving compartment, of their mind. An image of what was "seen" by the person receiving the thought was constructed and displayed on a screen so that the person projecting it could also observe it, verifying that the transmission had been successfully received.

After setting up another meeting with Radu, he rode the Tube to meet him at a game complex. When Will arrived, he entered a white, circular room with a high, domed ceiling with over a dozen doors equally spaced about the perimeter. Radu was there and greeted him as he entered.

"Perhaps we should start with the projection room," Radu suggested. "Door 7."

That was why Will was there.

When he stepped inside, he was stunned: it was an exact mockup of the transport room inside the Antarctic base.

"When I wrote the description, I said I wanted a replica of the control panel, not the entire facility," Will said.

"The more detail the better, I would think," Radu replied.

On Will's left was the vast control panel into which he had inserted the square, decoder device to get the transporter to operate. For an instant, he relived the panic he'd felt at the time, when he'd thought the Regenerators were to arrive at any moment and the base was about to self-destruct.

To his right were hundreds of pods, arranged in pairs. He spotted the general location of the pod where he'd found Captain Saul W. Kelly – the same one that had brought him – Will – to the *Exodus 9*.

What suddenly struck him as bizarre was that the day he'd transported from the facility had been his *third* time there – in three different lives. It was his existence as Lux that mattered now.

"This is where one obtains telepathic access to the system," Radu said, interrupting Will's thoughts. "However, I thought we'd first try some basic exercises."

Radu directed him to a small side room.

When Will went inside, he flinched at the sight of someone sitting in a chair. The person was young, bald, and heterogeneous.

"That is a projection doll," Radu explained.

For some reason, Will felt embarrassed at the term Radu used. The "projection doll" looked like a real person – a live being, and even looked at them as they entered, but Radu assured him otherwise.

They sat in two side-by-side seats facing the doll, behind which was a large, curved screen.

Radu then explained that Will was supposed to concentrate on a location just beyond the eyes of the doll and, in a fashion similar to that of expanding his presence to fill the room, as he had in previous exercises, he should instead imagine extending to and occupying that location. At that point, he should try to convey a thought or an image – something simple – which should then appear on the screen behind the doll.

Will did as instructed. He concentrated on a memory of a large flower he'd seen on the beach of the South Pacific island of Rarotonga, where he'd had his first meeting with Mia. After a few seconds, the screen fluttered with multicolored static. He concentrated harder, but no image formed.

"Do not concentrate on the eyes," Radu instructed. "Rather, just behind and above them. That's where the open access receptors are located."

Will took a deep breath, imagined extending himself to the location Radu described, and the screen came back to life. After some static and intermittent flashes of white, an image of the doll appeared on the screen. It wasn't what Will had intended.

"That's good, keep concentrating," Radu said with excitement in his voice. "You are projecting what you are seeing."

Radu moved his hand into Will's field of view, and this motion appeared on the screen in real-time. It was as if Will's eyes were acting like a video camera.

"Now, think of something else," Radu instructed. "Ignore the doll's body."

He concentrated and, after some fluttering on the screen, an image appeared: a brilliant flower with pink and orange petals and radial streaks of purple and green. It was just how he remembered it. It was perfect.

"It is a beautiful static image," Radu said. "Can you think of something dynamic – something with movement?"

Will tried to think of something pleasant, and a still view of a soccer game appeared as it had once been seen through his eyes. The colors of the grass, uniforms, and crowd were vivid. Suddenly, the scene became active and there was sound – of the crowd and his own breathing. Evidently, the telepathic signal included audio. It was a part of a game he remembered vividly – it was from the first match he'd played on the ship.

After about a minute, Radu told him to stop projecting, and he rested for a minute.

"Now, reconnect, but let your mind wander a bit," Radu said. "Concentrate enough to maintain the connection, but not on any one projected thought, nor on the screen."

He did as Radu said, and let his mind settle into baseline thoughts and allowed himself to approach a meditative state, where he remained for what seemed to be a few minutes.

Suddenly, he heard screaming. His concentration broke and he determined the source of the screams: they came from himself.

He got just a glimpse of the last image on the screen before it disappeared.

"Play that back," Will said. "I want to see what that was."

"I don't know if you want to see – "

"Play it back," he insisted.

The screen came to life. The first image was of Earth – it was ablaze, and then quickly turned into a gray, lifeless rock. The next image was of smoldering bodies – his family and friends among them. Finally, someone turned over a body to see its face. Will shuddered, and his vision blurred for an instant, as if his mind were trying to shut down. It was Denise. One of her cheeks had been burned away, and she was missing an eye. Her hair was smoldering.

She was still alive. She tried to speak, but she was missing some teeth and the air that escaped just made her torn lips flutter. But Will understood the words nonetheless.

"You promised," she said. "You promised."

She kept repeating it. And then her remaining eye closed, and she went silent.

The screen went blank, but Will continued to stare at it as his eyes burned with tears.

DANIEL, finally out of quarantine, was relieved to be relocated to an office on sublevel 22 that he shared with Sylvia. It was just two levels above the CIA control room, where Thackett's office was located. In order to maintain their anonymous Omni identities, Thackett went to their office, rather than the other way around. However, Daniel didn't think their identities could be concealed for very long.

Sylvia pulled up a picture of the view from her Space Systems office and showed it to Daniel.

It must have been around sunset, as the tips of the dark green pines and silvery spruce trees looked reddish orange.

"I took this in the summer – I was trying to get a snapshot of a bat," she said. "It was a big one, and it would dive in and out of the treetops. I saw it often."

"I don't see it," Daniel said, squinting.

"It's that blur," she explained as she pointed to a dark streak on the screen. "He moved too quickly."

Daniel wondered if he'd ever again see those trees. It astounded him to some degree that he'd become so dependent on the place – that Space Systems had become his home. It also surprised him, however, that he'd quickly acclimated to situations that he'd never thought he'd be able to tolerate, such as being inside a submarine that was making its way through a dangerous tunnel, or being confined to a small space hundreds of feet below ground with a nuclear war on the verge of breaking out on the surface.

He concluded that, at least partially, it was the people with whom he shared these adventures that carried him through. He didn't know what he would have done if Sylvia hadn't been with him during the past year.

Thackett entered, sat on a padded bench located next to the entrance, and leaned forward with his elbows on his knees. He was concentrating on a message he was typing on his phone. The entire phone service was channeled through a local network that linked internal mobile devices, but there was no direct external service, in or out. Any communications outside the facility had to go through rigid security channels and were linked directly to CIA communications satellites so that no location information could be gleaned from intercepted signals, or through triangulation with cell towers.

Thackett sent the message and looked to them. "Jacob got some time on the Chinese telescope cluster and didn't find anything," he explained. "He'll have another hour of access in a few days."

"A few days?" Sylvia repeated, her tone conveying concern. "I know that military operations should come first, but I think this is too urgent to delay for that long."

Thackett nodded. "Noted," he said. "I just sent a message to get dibs on any cancellations on satellite time, which are likely."

That seemed to calm her.

"I came to deliver some worrisome news," Thackett continued. "Denise is not faring well with the virus. I'm told that the doctors are giving it one last try with an experimental drug, but it's not looking good."

Daniel felt a pit form in his stomach like he'd swallowed a pound of molten metal.

"She's so young," Sylvia said, her eyes filling with tears. "And so strong."

Thackett nodded and looked down at his feet. "She was in the wrong place at the wrong time," he said. "If she'd been much older, she might've gotten the publicly administered smallpox vaccine, and we left before she and Jonathan got their required medical checkups. She would've gotten the series of shots that we've all had. She was in a narrow window of vulnerability."

"Is there no hope?" Daniel asked. His voice cracked and Sylvia looked away and rubbed her eyes on her sleeve.

Thackett shrugged. "I'm told the chance is small and, even if she does make it, there will be complications."

"Can we see her?" Sylvia asked.

Thackett shook his head. "Jonathan is there," he said. "We're not allowed since there is a 10-day isolation period for anyone going onto the hazmat level. It would be different if we weren't at war."

Thackett's phone beeped. He glanced at it and stood. "I'll keep you informed," he said as he walked out.

Daniel's chest tightened in response to sobs coming from Sylvia who had put her arm on her desk and buried her face in her sleeve.

He pulled his chair next to hers and put his arm around her shoulders.

Her sobs turned to bawling, and she put her face on his chest and hugged him.

Daniel couldn't think of a time when he'd felt more helpless.

WILL, still shaken from the images projected by his own mind a few hours earlier, spent the afternoon playing soccer in the sun. It was a game – not a practice – and he'd arranged for the weather to be sunny and hot. He wanted to sweat. He wanted to suffer a little as well – anything to distract him from the notion that Earth had been scorched, and that Denise was dead.

He had his best game to date, in his assessment, with a goal and an assist. He had some excellent tackles as well, and also a yellow card, as he'd gotten a bit too aggressive. His performance grade came back as a "C," which he'd take, even though he thought he'd played better. Perhaps it was because his team had lost, 3-2.

On Radu's advice, Will had taken a break from the long hours of telepathy instruction, and would eat and have a short nap before going back.

The image of Denise's destroyed face kept coming back to him. It frightened him. But it wasn't about death. That, he knew, didn't really exist. It was more about the idea that she might be alone, suffering, and frightened, and that he might not be able to help her. Also, he might never see her again. If she died, she might reincarnate and live another life, or she could go over the horizon – into the unknown.

The two questions that would never be answered in this world kept coming back to him: where do we come from, and where do we go in the end? And, oddly enough, it was the absence of those answers that generated hope. He supposed that anything was still possible if the endpoints were not in sight. The constraints of time brought on anxiety, no matter how wide they were. Even if our lives were to span a billion years, most self-aware beings would still be thinking "What's after that?"

It was difficult to not live in the past and simultaneously not worry about the future. To live exclusively in the present was a gift not afforded the average human. Will's past was haunting him – his most recent past as well as his past lives. If his memory were somehow wiped clean, his current situation would be a paradise.

However, there was still something missing. The absence of loved ones was certainly a part of it, but there was something else that was lacking that he couldn't quite define. It made him wonder if complete contentment was an achievable condition. His feeling was that perhaps it was not. There was only relative contentment, like the feeling of freedom that he'd experienced when he'd been stripped of his Exoskeleton – both in the literal and figurative senses. That contentment had since waned.

Radu had suggested something that might give him a fast track to recalling the access code, and he'd give it a try in the evening. In the meantime, Will had learned more about the access codes.

First, they were never written, only projected telepathically. At birth, young Deltas were given two codes, each 3,072 characters long, and usually listed in groups of three and four. They were composed of all of the Delta characters and numbers, plus shapes – circles, squares, polygons, et cetera. Will's heart had sunk when he'd first learned those details, but his mood bounced back when he realized that he either knew the codes, or he did not. At this point there was no mind searching, in the sense of trying to recall a phone number.

Young Delta children would be telepathically tattooed with the two sequences: both their true identification code, and their distress code. The latter differed from the former in only the last 100 digits.

It turned out that this "telepathic tattooing" had such a prominent imprint in memory that it had effects that reached beyond the physical, and had revealed profound ideas which, at the time, were just conjectures.

Will read about a historical event of great impact that had

occurred when a young Delta child had telepathically projected an incorrect access code in a tattooing session. That code had matched the code of someone who had been killed in an accident a short time before the child was born. That person had not regenerated.

The chances that the child – or anyone – would randomly guess a code of over 3,000 characters were infinitesimally small. This event was viewed as convincing evidence that reincarnation occurred, and that memories of previous lives were imprinted upon one's soul, rather than just on their mind.

Will's problem, however, was that he'd reincarnated over 400 times, and that his code had been imprinted in his very first life. On the positive side, since he'd only lived one Delta life, there would be only one code to find – along with its accompanying distress code.

Radu had suggested that, on a regular basis, Will approach a telepathic console and attempt to access it. An obvious choice, which might provide an environment familiar to his Delta persona, Lux, was the main control console inside the Antarctic base, for which Radu had already arranged the simulation. The idea was to just walk up, peer into the "eyes" of the computer, and see if his soul would automatically project the code.

After a short nap, Will made his way back to the game room and found himself standing in front of the mockup of the control console in the Deltas' Antarctic transport facility. A black, mirrored surface appeared at eye level that was oval in shape, like a face. He saw the reflection of his own face in the device and realized that it must have been Lux's face that he'd seen in his dream.

Radu stood next to him.

Will stared at the screen and imagined projecting an image just behind the surface. Radu instructed him not to concentrate on any one thing, but to let his mind wander.

After a few seconds, the mirrored screen flashed in a bright white, checkered pattern and a sound buzzed from somewhere on the console. Access denied.

Will paced back and forth a few times, approached the screen, and tried again. Access denied.

After more than 20 attempts, Radu suggested that he give it a rest and explore some new skills. Will agreed and they stepped into a side room. Radu then led him through some new exercises, most of which were telekinetic activities. The most enjoyable one was Ping-Pong. Without a paddle.

Will had played Ping-Pong or, as more serious competitors might call it, "table tennis," as a kid, and had become a relatively competent player.

The first time Radu served the ball, Will stuck out his hand and missed it entirely. It was a natural reaction to try to hit the ball, but there was no paddle, and he came up short. After a few more attempts, he was able to imagine his hand extending beyond his fingers. Although he did not successfully return any shots, he was able to deflect the ball, without touching it with his hand, so that it at least headed in the forward direction.

After a few minutes of this, Radu stopped him and suggested that he not move at all. He should instead try to fill the space on his side of the net and, rather than envision a swing of the paddle with his arm, imagine a paddle forming in the space – in the exact location needed to return each shot.

After a few unsuccessful attempts, a return shot blasted back at Radu like a bullet, but missed him. Radu ducked and laughed. Will found him to be a pleasant person – Delta.

After another half hour, Will was able to maintain a simple back-and-forth with Radu, who was playing with an actual paddle. The strange thing was that, after a while, Will's hits were making a noise, as if the ball were being struck by a hard surface.

By the time they'd practiced enough to play a full game to 21, which he lost 21-3, Will had become exhausted and called an end to the meeting. Before he left, however, he tried once more to project the code onto the control console, with the same negative result.

Fifteen minutes later, he was back in his quarters. It was going on midnight. He'd been in the lesson with Radu for almost four hours. Ping-Pong, and the other exercises, had been effective. He could now do many things by "extension" that had originally required him to fully separate.

He sat on the couch and set a cup of tea on the coffee table. He leaned back so that the cup was out of reach, performed an evanescent extension, grasped it, and brought it to his hands, spilling a few drops on his pants as it got close.

He grinned. People on Earth would think it was magic. He supposed it was, to some degree.

It was time to sleep but, before he headed to the bathroom to brush his teeth, he scheduled a beamer lesson for the morning. He had to be ready in case he eventually recovered the code and was able to make a run for Earth on his own. There was no guarantee that the *Exodus 9* would allow him to change its current orders. He didn't know if it would even let him leave with a beamer.

After the beamer lesson, maybe he'd spend some time in a coffee house – somewhere new.

LENNY STEPPED into the spacious office, closed the door, and locked it.

Professor Andrus Alicci looked up from behind his massive desk and tilted his head to see over his half-rimmed glasses. Alicci was a tall, thin man in his mid-50s, clean-shaven, with a head of perfectly-styled, dark hair. He wore a white shirt and a blue tie.

"No cleaning needed tonight," Alicci said and looked back down to his work.

Lenny had acquired a custodian's uniform and ID badge, and had easily navigated through the lax security of the Bethesda campus of the National Institutes of Health. It would have been more trouble getting into the lab facilities, but this building housed mostly NIH administration.

"Actually, I think some cleanup is in order, Professor Alicci," Lenny said. "What are you doing there? You working out another deal with China to provide them funds and access to our bio-warfare facilities?"

"Excuse me?" Alicci said and looked up.

"You are not excused," Lenny said and walked around the desk. "I've contracted both viruses you helped to unleash on the world. And they weren't nice."

Alicci stood. "I have no idea what you're talking about," he said as he reached for a phone on his desk. "Get out now, or I'm calling security."

Lenny pulled out his gun, silencer attached, and pointed it at the man. "Sit down, and shut your fucking mouth," he ordered as he stepped toward the NIH director.

Alicci hesitated, so Lenny grabbed him by the knot of his tie and forced him into the chair.

"I know you're used to being the big shot and everyone kissing your ass, but the tables have now turned, distinguished professor," Lenny said. "You've been a bad boy – a traitor, in fact – and now you'll give me a list of everyone else involved in your transgressions. Better start at the top. If I find your information useless, I'll start peeling your skin like an onion."

"Please, I don't know what you're talking about," Alicci stammered.

Ignoring the man's pleas, Lenny pulled some zip ties out of his jacket pocket and fastened the man's arms to his fancy leather office chair. He then bound his legs and torso to the bottom of the chair with duct tape, despite the squirming and pleading.

"I'm afraid we already know what you know, and have known it for a while," Lenny said, amused by his phrasing. "But it's wartime, and certain measures must be taken. But this whole war thing is partially your fault, isn't it, professor?"

"Everything was done by the books," Alicci argued in a tone that revealed panic. "Those grants were awarded on merit."

Lenny smiled. "Such a subjective term, *merit,* isn't it?" he said. "Even though it's supposed to convey the opposite – objectivity, right?" He then retrieved a polished, wooden box about the size of a thick cell phone out of his jacket pocket and placed it on the desk. He opened it, revealing six vials of an iridescent red fluid, two syringes, and an assortment of needles.

"You know what this is, professor?" Lenny asked. "It's called fire fluid. I think you might have even heard of it."

Lenny knew that there were factions within the NIH that were responsible for funding the research carried out by Syncorp, Inc., and its partners.

"Funny," Lenny continued. "You might even be responsible for funding the development of this stuff."

"I don't know what you're talking about," Alicci said, defiantly.

Lenny closed the box. "But we're not going to start with the hard stuff right away," he said. "We're gonna work up to that."

Alicci started to scream for help and Lenny lunged forward and cupped his meaty hand over the man's mouth and nose, stifling the sound to a mere vibration sensation in his palm. He then squeezed the man's nose between his thumb and forefinger so hard that he thought it might split open like a sausage.

"Give me a name," Lenny said into Alicci's ear as he released the pressure on his nose. "I'm going to let you talk. If you try to scream, I'll rip one of your ears off your head."

Lenny released the man's face, sat back on the desk, and looked into his wide, tearing eyes. "Good," Lenny said. "Now, who else is involved in this scheme you've been conducting for the past 12 years?"

Alicci's face went blank for a few seconds, as if he were going to vomit. "Nothing illegal has happened here," he said. "Funding decisions are made by committee."

Lenny grinned as he reached into his pocket, pulled out a thick, white tube sock, and tied it into a fat knot. "We know all about your hand-picked committees," he said. "So, you'd better be accurate and complete with those names. What we want to know is who is giving you orders. Surely, you didn't instigate this whole thing on your own."

"I've done nothing illegal," Alicci said. "And neither has anyone else."

"We found the money trail from the Chinese Communist Party to a series of shell companies, then to a bank account in the Cayman Islands, and then, finally, to you," Lenny said and pointed the gun at his face. "Now open your mouth."

"I don't see why –"

With a quick flip of his wrist, Lenny struck the professor above his right eye with the edge of his gun's silencer and split the skin.

Alicci winced as blood started to stream down his face.

"Open your fucking mouth," Lenny repeated.

The man opened his mouth and Lenny jammed in the knotted tube sock. He then wrapped duct tape around his head and mouth to hold it in place.

"As you will now learn, professor, I don't have much patience," Lenny said. "I'm going to ask you that same question again, so I want you to think hard for a moment about what your answer is going to be when I remove that sock. But first, I think you need some motivation."

Alicci was trying to say something – he was panicking – but it was too late.

Lenny set the gun on the desk and grabbed the man's right thumb with one hand and his index finger with the other. He then pulled them apart, as if he were splitting a wishbone. The bones cracked, and the muscles and ligaments snapped like rubber bands.

Alicci screamed into the sock for almost five minutes as Lenny continued to contort the broken bones as if he were playing some heinous musical instrument.

Lenny ended the piece, and waited another few minutes for the man to calm. When Alicci's flushed, sweating face again took on an expression of coherence, Lenny said, "When I take that sock out of your mouth, you better tell me something impressive, or worse things are going to happen."

The man nodded and Lenny removed the duct tape and the sock. "Talk," he said.

"Senator Ward," Alicci blurted. "Diane Ward. And Senator Todd Schill."

"What about them?"

"They first approached me with the idea," he answered, breathing hard. "The amount of funding that went to the Chinese groups was not the issue. They sent us more money than we gave them. It was access to information that they wanted – they wanted to see our government facilities, and to place their students in university-based labs in the US."

"How much did the senators get?" Lenny asked.

"Same as me, I think," Alicci replied. "Two million per awarded grant."

"How many grants did you give away?"

"Over twenty in the past five years."

"So you have over 40 million dollars packed away somewhere," Lenny said. It was a staggering number, and it looked like the CIA had more bank accounts to locate. The man should have retired when he'd reached a few million. It was either greed, the belief that he'd never get caught, or that he enjoyed doing it that kept him going. It was probably a combination of all of those. "Was it worth it? Look at what you've done."

Alicci just stared back at him.

"The answer is no," Lenny said. "Why? Because you're not going to be able to spend that money, and neither is your family. Now, who else was involved?"

Alicci spilled another half-dozen names that included a deputy director of the FBI, the famous CEO of a well-known high-tech company, and a high-level grants officer in the National Science Foundation.

"Okay," Lenny said as he stuffed the knotted sock back into Alicci's mouth and wrapped it tightly with duct tape. "You've done well, Andrus, but now it's time to pay the piper."

Lenny opened the small, wooden box on the desk, screwed a needle onto a syringe, and poked it through the membrane on one of the vials. He then drew the red fluid into the syringe, tapped it to get the bubbles to rise to the top, and pressed the plunger until just a drop of the liquid formed on the tip needle and then ran down the side.

Alicci nearly tipped over in his chair as he struggled to avoid the inevitable.

Lenny jabbed the needle into his neck and injected the fire fluid.

After about 30 seconds, which seemed to be a little longer than the usual onset of the response, Alicci squealed like the traitor pig that he was. It was so loud that Lenny went behind him, forced the knotted sock deeper into his mouth, and secured it with more duct tape.

More than 15 minutes passed before the screaming subsided. His original plan was to use all five vials of the fire fluid. However, he now knew there were even bigger fish to fry.

Lenny put the empty vial back into the box, along with the used needle and syringe, closed it, and put it back into his jacket pocket. He then pulled out his gun and popped Alicci twice in the forehead in quick succession.

The dead man slumped forward as Lenny cut the cable ties and duct tape that bound him to the chair.

He eased the body to the floor and shoved it under the desk.

Lenny grinned. How many times had he done that in the past year? The desk theme was becoming routine.

He jammed the fancy chair up to the desk to conceal the corpse, and turned off a desk lamp to make it look like the NIH director had gone home for the night.

After exiting the office, he made his way down the hall, pushing the cart of cleaning supplies that he'd appropriated on his way into the building. As he proceeded at a modest pace, he wondered if his job would ever end. He'd just acquired a new list of targets.

He imagined Thackett's horrified expression when he read those new names. It was disconcerting news, but it was a discovery of utmost importance.

WILL HAD breakfast at 7:00 a.m. and then headed to the hangar, where he met up with Cliff.

He then followed his instructor toward two beamers parked side by side, and Will went to his usual craft, *CX-1*, whose platform lowered for him to enter. As he stepped onto it, Cliff said something, making Will turn. As he did so, he instinctively reached above his head and grabbed a handle that he hadn't even known was there. It startled him for a second, as he had a strong sensation of familiarity.

"I'm sorry, what did you say?" Will asked.

"I said we're going do some live-combat exercises today," Cliff replied.

Will gave him the "thumbs up" sign and went into his ship.

As he strapped into the pilot's seat, an oval-shaped screen appeared, and he saw his face in its reflective surface. He stared at it for a second, experienced a bout of déjà vu, and then it vanished and the other displays came to life. It had happened before, and now he knew the purpose of that device. He was grateful that he didn't need formal authorization to participate in the flight-lesson simulations – or any of the other recreational activities. Otherwise, it would have been an excruciatingly boring time on the *Exodus 9*.

Will followed Cliff's ship, which exited the bay and headed toward the same Earth-like planet they'd visited the last time.

As they entered Castelle's atmosphere, Cliff said, "Okay *CX-1*, we're going to encounter the defense systems of a lower-technology civilization where they use electromagnetic detection, kinetic weapons, and aircraft that require airfoil lift surfaces.

He knew that Cliff was referring to radar, missiles, and wings, in that order. Castelle was a "lower-technology civilization" just like that which was currently inhabiting Earth – he hoped.

Cliff instructed Will to engage his beamer's "bending shields." This was yet another application of bending the fabric of space and time. All physical objects and electromagnetic radiation – including visible light and radar – bent around it, like water around a smooth rock in a stream. In order to be able to see outwardly, however, a tiny amount of light had to be let inside – or at least be absorbed by the craft's external sensors. The ship would then regenerate that light and pass it on so that there would be no detectable "dark spot" that would give away the presence of the ship.

They descended to an altitude of about 200 feet and skimmed over what looked like wheat fields that seemed to go on for miles.

He then followed Cliff to a mountain range where their ships hovered near a tall peak at an elevation of about 5,000 feet.

"I suppose you're wondering what the point of this is," Cliff said.

"It's time to turn off the shields and cloaking and let them see us."

Will turned them off, and then followed Cliff's ship as it weaved through forested mountain valleys and skipped over lush, grassy plateaus until they were about two miles from what looked to be a military base. There were hangars and runways and planes that resembled the fighter jets of Earth. Adrenaline surged into his bloodstream.

"They're going to scramble a few jets," Cliff said. "We'll split up, so you'll be on your own. Use every mechanism you have to avoid them, but also try to stay close and observe their maneuvering."

At that instant, a pair of fighter jets took off in tandem and elevated quickly.

"I'll meet you at the big moon in 20 minutes," Cliff said and took off in the direction of the jets.

Castelle had two moons, one much larger than the other. The smaller of the two was irregularly shaped, like an asteroid, and the larger one resembled Earth's moon, but with more of a reddish hue, similar to that of Mars.

Both jets followed Cliff as another pair lifted off and headed in Will's direction.

"Here we go," Will said as an alarm chimed, indicating that his ship had been detected.

"Shall I reengage the warping shields?" *Gwen* asked.

"Negative," he replied. "We want to outmaneuver them."

At that point, something instinctual within him took over. He first transformed the ship so that its shape resembled that of a stingray with no tail, and then took off for the green plateaus. He allowed the fighters to catch up, and they were trying to lock him in on their radar, which was an indicator that they might be preparing to fire a weapon. He then elevated to 10,000 feet in an instant and came to a dead stop. The fighters split below him and circled around, seemingly looking for the quarry that had disappeared before their eyes.

In an action that must have originated from a reflex developed in his life as Lux, his left hand tapped a button that revealed a new screen and set of controls.

"Weapons systems online," *Gwen* informed him.

"No!" Will yelled. "Take them down."

"Weapons systems offline," *Gwen* responded. "We are being tracked."

The jets had located him again and continued their pursuit.

Will dropped into the canyons below and weaved around tall rock features as the fighters attempted to keep up. It was child's play. The fighters were no match. But it required no skill on his part other than knowing how to operate the beamer and understanding its features and capabilities.

"Incoming missile," *Gwen* warned.

Will smiled. There were multiple options. One, the beamer could simply outrun it. Two, he could instantaneously elevate, and the missile would lose its lock. Three, he could destroy the missile. He chose the first option.

As *Gwen* warned of a second missile launch, Will accelerated, and weaved and rolled and banked through the labyrinth of canyons. After a short time, it became apparent that he was anticipating obstacles and turns before they appeared, as if he knew the landscape. He suspected that he did.

He made a sharp bend through a keyhole feature in a gigantic rock formation and dipped into a channel, at the bottom of which was a river. Suddenly the skin on his arms puckered and it felt like it wanted to crawl off of his body. Panic and fear saturated his mind and all he wanted to do was flee.

And that's what he did.

He pulled the beamer into a vertical climb that would have looked like an instantaneous leap to anyone on the outside. He was on the closest side of the larger moon in less than a minute.

When he settled beside Cliff's ship, his stomach seemed to twist in his gut and nausea almost overtook him.

"You saw something?" Cliff asked over the com system.

"Yes – how did you know?"

"You flew out of there like a bat out of hell," Cliff replied. "What did you see?"

"I just got a bad feeling."

"Déjà vu?"

"Worse – like something horrible was going to happen."

"Or that something horrible *had* happened?"

"Yes," Will said.

Instantly, Will was sitting in a chair in a gigantic, white room – an empty hangar, he figured. He was alone.

He unstrapped himself and stood from the pilot's chair, which was mounted to the floor. The illusion was over – someone had turned it off. Cliff, the ships, the planet – they were all gone.

He spotted the exit and started toward it when someone walked in.

It was Landau.

"William," he said, with a smile and an expression that seemed to convey relief. "It's over."

DENISE FELT a warmth encapsulate her body as the darkness overtook her eyes.

The burning was gone. The headache was gone. The weight on her chest was gone.

And then, she was gone.

JONATHAN SQUEEZED Denise's hand as it softened, and her eyes finally closed.

His chest seemed to cave in and crush his heart. Denise was one of his daughters, and a parent should never outlive their children. He would have traded his life for hers at that very moment if he could have.

For another half hour, he sat next to her and held her hand tightly as he bawled inside his hazmat suit. Eventually, two nurses and a doctor came into the room and pried him away from her.

His life would never be the same.

"*WHAT* IS OVER?" Will asked.

Landau's eyes gave away his half-concealed emotions – joy and triumph.

"You have no idea what I've been through – where I've been, looking for you," Landau said. "And the time that has passed – 40 thousand years."

Will thought he saw a tear in his eye.

"And now I've found you," Landau said as he stepped up to him, opened his arms, and embraced him. "There's no doubt now."

Landau released him, held Will's shoulders at arm's length, and looked at him with glassy eyes.

"Landau, what's happened?" Will asked, his heart thumping hard.

"I suspected it all along, but had no definitive proof," Landau said. "But now I do. You're really him – you're the fallen angel. You're Lux."

Will was confused. "But I thought I needed to remember the access code for proof."

"And you did," Landau said.

"What? When?"

"When you got into your beamer," Landau replied. "It was something that you – as Lux – had to do every time you flew your ship. You were exposed to it during every flight lesson, and it finally worked. It seems your time with Radu has paid off."

Will recalled looking at the oval screen as he'd entered the *CX-1,* as he'd done every time. It was similar to the screen in the mock transport room. "But I didn't remember anything – "

"You projected a code onto the beamer's telepathic reader," Landau said. "And it was the correct one – not the distress code."

"But I don't know what I did – I don't think I can do it again."

"It doesn't matter," Landau said. "The chances of you doing it by accident – even just once – is infinitesimally small. You're Lux."

"What happened down there – on the planet?" Will asked. "Why was I suddenly filled with fright like I had to run?"

Landau smiled. "It was one last test," he said. "That was the canyon where you disappeared 40 thousand years ago – on Earth. And, by your reaction, you remembered that, too."

"What does this mean?" Will asked. "What now?"

"We go to Earth," Landau replied.

"It hasn't been destroyed?"

"Still unknown," Landau answered. "But if your leaving earned Earth a temporary reprieve, the Regenerators would continue to watch it closely before making a final decision. They could still have judged humanity as irredeemable and carried out the original plan, even though you'd left and there was no one there with separation abilities."

"Can the *Exodus 9* defend the planet against the Regenerators?" Will asked. He was going to move forward as if Earth was okay.

"No," Landau said as he held up his hand. "And it doesn't matter. We have proof now."

"Proof? What are you talking about?"

"We have proof that your generation was contaminated."

"Contaminated?"

"By the Deltas," Landau said. "Technically, this proves that all humans are Delta hybrids, except you – you are a full Delta."

"So?" Will asked. "How does that help – how does that stop them?"

"It means that, other than you, no one on Earth can separate," Landau replied. "It also means that you, and you alone, set off the probe that triggered everything. The rest are innocent, and should be given their full time to develop – to become evanescent beings through natural intellectual and philosophical means, not through – "

"Torture," Will said, finishing the thought.

"Yes, torture," Landau said. "But that was how you were originally exposed – on July 19th, 1952, when you obliterated the Nazis at the base. To anyone who was watching for it, your separation and subsequent evanescent actions were like a flash of light in a dark tunnel. I tried to talk to you back then as well, but you thought you were just hearing voices. And then you shot yourself."

"When I was Saul W. Kelly," Will said.

"I tried to find you – your soul – afterwards," Landau continued. "But I was too late, and you were gone."

"And you stayed on Earth all this time, looking for me?"

"I was the one responsible for the deliverance of the Delta race," Landau explained.

"Deliverance from what – the Regenerators?" Will asked.

Landau smiled and shook his head. "Perhaps *passage* would be a better word for it – from this world to the next," he said. "And then I was supposed to elevate to a new existence of my own, one step closer to my own final destination."

"I don't get it," Will said. "Are you an angel? Or a god?"

"I told who I was long ago," Landau said.

"You said you were the 'caretaker, the guardian, and the timekeeper,'" Will said, recalling his words in detail. "But I don't know what that means."

"I am separate from this existence," he said. "I began as something like you – or like the humans of Earth's current generation. And you, and those of Earth, may also be elevated to a new existence one day. But they will be lost if things continue as they are."

"Why not just defeat the Regenerators?" Will asked. "Why tolerate this happening around the universe?"

"The Regenerators are the oldest beings in existence," Landau explained. "In fact, they were the *first* beings in existence. The Deltas were originally no match for them – and neither is a fleet consisting of an *Exodus*-class starship and a handful of beamers."

"So what's the use?" Will asked, agitated. "Will this new proof of the so-called Delta contamination stop them?"

"I don't know," Landau replied. "But if we show up, and they've already decided to regenerate Earth, they will likely destroy you as well. So it is a risk for you. It's your decision."

It took Will no time to think it over. "Will I be able to get the *Exodus 9* headed toward Earth?"

Landau grinned. "It already is."

15

ARRIVAL

It was 4:00 a.m. when Jacob hung up the phone, set it on the counter, and stared at it.

Director Thackett had just informed him that Denise had passed away. It was the smallpox strain.

Sadness and rage surged in equal proportions in his mind. A spontaneous reflex took over and he screamed as loudly as he could. The pressure in his head made his ears ring and, afterwards, his throat burned as if he'd damaged his vocal cords. He wanted to throw something but managed to hold back.

The Chinese had started a war, and he would do whatever it took to defeat them.

In the same call, Thackett had informed him that he had 90 minutes of time on the formerly-Chinese satellite array to take another scan of deep space. That time would start at 10:00 a.m., giving him two hours to burn.

He grabbed the phone and called Pauli. He needed to hear her voice. She was in her office, preparing for an upcoming meeting, but stayed on with him for over 30 minutes.

Pauli had gotten the flu but only suffered minor symptoms. Her parents, however, both had more serious cases, but they'd pulled through after a week-long battle.

What was more concerning than the flu pandemic, however, was that there were now 150 suspected smallpox cases in the DC area, and 35 of them had already resulted in death. Other pockets of cases were popping up along the East Coast, and numerous others in the EU, India, and elsewhere. He suspected that it would be everywhere in a short time.

After the call, he set up his computer on the library table on the first floor and linked to the CIA control center to operate the cluster. The previous user had ended their session 20 minutes ahead of schedule and Jacob took over early.

This time he had two of the four satellites at his disposal. It took him five minutes to set up a string of commands that put them into a full, stereo-view scan that spanned all directions. As it initiated the task, he ran up to the kitchen and returned with a mug of coffee. He paced along the long rug and sipped from his cup as the procedure commenced.

Thackett had given him an update on military activities – those which had already been carried out – and wanted Jacob to work on hacking the Chinese ICBM launch control systems as well as post-launch communications. Even though Jacob had seen a few of the devices in question when he was an engineer at Interstellar Dynamics, it would be a difficult task. But he was motivated now more than ever to contribute to the quick dismantling of China's military capabilities. Russian assets would join the target list when the time was right for the US to bring them into the fray.

After 15 minutes of pacing and thinking, he went back to the computer, downloaded the first batch of data, and loaded it into the analysis program that sorted the observed objects and displayed them on a map.

Ten minutes later, he opened the first map, which covered about ten percent of the total area of the sky. His heart picked up pace and his breathing became heavy, as if he were about to hyperventilate.

The map was riddled with tiny red arrows – over 200 of them. He glanced at the legend, just to be sure: the red arrows indicated prime candidates for intelligently navigated objects – ships. They all had medium- or high-priority tags. Nothing was yet tagged as "critical."

He zoomed in on one of the objects. Although it was not well resolved, it didn't look like an asteroid. The distance was unknown, but the velocity vector was pointed directly at Earth.

He focused on another object, same thing. Then another, and another. They were all heading toward Earth.

There were 204 objects in total and, when he was about to call Thackett, the control program notified him that the next batch of data was ready, mapping another part of the sky. He downloaded it and put it into the analysis program. Same thing – 217 objects all heading toward Earth. He was astounded: at this rate, the total would exceed 2,000.

It didn't matter what the rest of the data showed – a massive fleet of something was converging upon the solar system.

Jacob grabbed his phone and called the CIA director.

WHEN JAMES THACKETT came into their office, Daniel could tell that only bad news was coming.

Sylvia glanced at Daniel. He could see it in her eyes that she knew it, too.

Thackett sat on the bench near the entrance.

"I'm deeply saddened to tell you that Denise passed away early this morning," Thackett said.

Sylvia gasped and then sobbed deeply. Daniel moved his chair next to hers and put his arm around her shoulders.

"I feel awful," Daniel said. "I'm the one who recommended bringing them aboard – "

"Nonsense," Thackett cut him off. "I'm the one who makes those decisions, not you."

Taking responsibility was a personality trait that Daniel thought made the director a good leader – and a good person. But he was not responsible for Denise, either.

"But there's something else," Thackett said.

Sylvia lifted her head, and Daniel knew what she was thinking.

"Jacob," Daniel said.

"He's found something," Thackett said and then swallowed hard. "Over 2,000 medium- and high-priority objects. We think they're ships – heading toward Earth from all directions."

"The Regenerators?" Sylvia asked.

Thackett shrugged. "No way to know."

"We can't fight two wars," Daniel said.

Thackett shook his head. "We sent the images to China over an hour ago – and to every other country in the world. We're currently negotiating a worldwide ceasefire."

"And their nuclear launch sites?" Sylvia asked.

"Standing down, as are ours and Russia's," Thackett replied. "Everyone is brainstorming on how to defend the planet."

"Do we have any weapons that can operate in space?" Daniel asked.

"Limited capabilities," Thackett said as he shook his head slowly. "Our ICBMs can reach low orbit and we have lasers. Russia and China have some similar capabilities. And we all have a few killer satellites – armed with lasers and kinetic weapons that can damage objects in orbit."

"From what we know of the Regenerators, we'll have no chance," Daniel said. "They'll exterminate us like rats – they'll irradiate the entire planet with X-rays and gamma rays. And then cook it."

Thackett nodded and sighed. "I know."

"Even if we could get something up there, or our 'killer satellites' could exact any damage on them – which I highly doubt – there are 2,000 of them," Daniel continued. "We have no chance."

Thackett looked at him and smiled with sympathetic eyes – as if he were watching someone going through a progression of thought that he'd just experienced. "I know."

"How much time do we have?" Daniel asked.

Thackett shook his head. "NASA is trying to figure that out now, but we could have as little as a few days to a few weeks. And the ships could always alter their course, or their speed."

"Does the public know?" Sylvia asked.

"No. And no government is going add to the pandemonium that already exists with the war and the pandemic – pandemics," Thackett corrected himself. "There has been another outbreak of the smallpox strain in Africa, and the flu has opened up to the world – including China. Evidently, the Chinese underestimated the ability of both of those viruses to evolve."

"Sounds like the biblical end of times," Sylvia said. "War, pestilence, and now a threat from the outside that overshadows them all."

"And we'll keep fighting all of it," Thackett said as he stood. "Sorry, but I have to get back to my duties. I suggest you do the same. I suppose it's all any of us can do, even if it seems futile."

Thackett left and closed the door behind him.

Daniel gently released his grip on Sylvia's shoulders, stood, and retrieved the electric tea kettle from the small table next to his desk. He filled two empty mugs and submerged an Earl Grey teabag in each.

"I've been hiding these," he said as he handed a cup to Sylvia and retook his seat next to her. "A break from government-issued tea."

Sylvia seemed to force a smile as she grasped her mug with two hands and took in the aroma.

"The world is not going to be the same," she said. "No matter what happens."

Daniel agreed. "All we can do is use our minds – that's what we bring to the table," he said. "Now that world war is no longer a concern, we need to refocus on what's coming."

"But Denise ...," Sylvia started to say but couldn't finish her words.

"I know," Daniel said. "But she was a feisty thing – and she'd want us to fight like hell, in any way we knew how."

"But what can we do?" Sylvia argued. "We're just a couple of reclusive intellectuals – nerds."

"I'm proud to be a nerd," he said.

She laughed for a few seconds through her tears and the mucous building in her sinuses.

"Anyway, there's only one place I can think of to look right now for something that might help us," Daniel said. "And it's going to take every bit of our Omniscient clearance to access it."

"I thought we had access to everything already," she said.

"We're supposed to," he said, shrugging. "But there are a few things that have been classified as 'above top-secret.' They've been hidden from us."

"You've found something?"

"Actually, Jonathan is the one who found it," he replied. "I just dug a little deeper – and now we have to go to the next level."

"What is it?"

"Something very close to us right now," he said, grinning. "Something right up your alley."

"UFOs?"

Daniel nodded. "We need to talk to Thackett," he said.

If there was ever a time for the darkest of government entities to break their best-kept secrets, it was now.

WILL WENT to the bridge of the *Exodus 9* and logged into the navigation system by submitting his access code via telepathic imaging. He was surprised it worked on the first try. He supposed recalling it the first time was the breakthrough, and now it would be routine. He could hardly believe he finally had access to the *Exodus 9*'s nav system.

"*Exodus 9,* map our location relative to Earth," Will commanded. "Display it in real spacetime."

He went to the captain's chair and watched as a three-dimensional image formed in the space between the chair and the gigantic, forward-facing window. Thousands of stars and other objects filled the space, and they were moving.

"Show me Earth, and our current flight path," Will instructed.

A thin green line, originating from a tiny image of the *Exodus 9*, weaved around various celestial objects and other obstacles, one of which was labeled as a black hole. There were other enormous features labeled with names like "time discontinuity," which forced the *Exodus 9* to take a wide, evasive path. Another was a "spacetime ridge," and another a "worm wall." He didn't understand these terms and made a note to look into the Deltas' advanced astrophysics when he got some time.

"*Exodus 9*, who set this course?" Will asked.

"I did, captain," the computer replied with a feminine voice that seemed to come from above him. "I anticipated your order based on your activities. Shall I continue on this course?"

"Yes," he replied. He liked being called "captain," not because it fed his ego, but because it reinforced his confidence that he'd really be able to direct the massive starship back to Earth. "What's our estimated time of arrival?"

"Thirty-two days, 10 hours, and 17 minutes, from now," *Exodus 9* replied.

"Is that the quickest way?"

"Yes, it uses full bending propulsion," the ship replied.

"How far do we have to go?"

"Approximately nine thousand seven hundred light-years," *Exodus 9* replied.

The figure should have shocked him, but he knew better now. "Okay," Will said. "Zoom in on Earth, solar system level."

The image immediately adjusted to show the entire solar system with the Sun at the center. The planets were not visible except for their labels.

"Zoom in on Earth," he ordered.

A blue Earth filled up the screen and he could make out the continents. His short moment of relief was squelched with a thought. "This is not a current image, correct?"

"Correct. This is an extrapolated view based on last known data," *Exodus 9* replied. "We have no transmitting observers at that location.

First visuals will be available when we have a direct view upon arrival."

He knew that was the case, but it still made his stomach burn. The blue image on the screen could be the ghost of a dead planet that would haunt him for the rest of his existence. If he saw a dead gray orb when they arrived, he didn't know what he would do.

He went back to his quarters, sat by the window, and sipped strong coffee as he contemplated the possibilities and his corresponding responses. If Earth was just the smoldering remains of his blue world, the decision was easy. He'd just let the *Exodus 9* take him to wherever the Deltas had originally planned for them.

In the case that Earth was alive and well, that would take some careful thought, and there were many possibilities.

Will had promised that he'd return. He had not promised, however, that he'd stay.

It was nearing midnight as Lenny sipped whiskey in a local Washington, DC dive bar called The Red Hog and watched the news on a TV behind the bar. The place was filled with smoke – both from cigarettes and marijuana – and it made him crave a cigarette of his own. He'd been limiting himself, and was close to quitting altogether, but now was not the time. He pulled out a cancer stick and lit it. At least he'd made the change to the filtered type.

His orders from the CIA had changed. He was now directed to take out the people identified by the late NIH director, starting with the senators. He wondered if the change had something to do with the temporary ceasefire that cable news was reporting. They called it a "break for de-escalation." Anything was better than a world war, Lenny figured, but he wasn't convinced. Something else was going on – he just felt it in his gut.

Everyone on the list was American. First was Senator Todd Schill. Next was Diane Ward, who was on the Senate Intelligence Committee. Third on the list was a high-level grants officer at the National

Science Foundation, and then two professors at prestigious universities, one on the East Coast and one in California. Lenny disliked academics almost as much as he did politicians. He wondered, though, if that was just because he'd only interacted with those he'd been contracted to hit. They had all been bad actors, and maybe that had generated a bias. He supposed there were good politicians, and academics as well, but he'd just never met any of them in person.

Knocking off the two senators would send a message to China while not actually killing any Chinese nationals. This was one of those times when he wasn't going to question his orders, but rather function like an instrument that carried no blame.

He'd spent the entire afternoon planning his first job. Todd Schill shared a DC residence with two congressmen from his home state. Lenny knew where they were holed up and would case the area and devise a final plan in the morning. The man had a security detail, so it would have to be a surgical job if he were to avoid collateral damage. He'd probably opt for a long-range snipe, but he'd have to look over the surrounding area and study the senator's habits. The man was a jogger, so Lenny thought he might be able to take advantage of that.

That reminded him of Jacob Hale, and he grinned. Wily bastard. Not taking out Jacob was a failure Lenny thought he'd be able to accept.

The news reported on the pandemic, which many people in the US were ignoring. Some of the bikers in the Red Hog wore masks, but most went without and just kept their distance. He figured a part of their disregard for the virus warnings had something to do with the threat of all-out nuclear holocaust. But now, with that on hold, the focus returned to the virus. Lenny wasn't concerned for himself since he'd already had both diseases.

The news anchor then went to an interview with a woman in the top ranks of the SETI Institute. They'd had an insurgence of funds after the so-called weather satellite event and had purchased time on some of the premier telescopes around the world before the war started. Now they only had access to radio telescopes and some smaller, surface-based optical instruments.

The SETI representative explained that they'd observed some strange phenomena while using the radio telescopes in Arecibo, Puerto Rico and in New Zealand.

"What kinds of phenomena?" the news anchor asked. The woman's oversized glasses made her look like an inquisitive owl.

"We've observed intermittent bursts of structured signals," the SETI woman replied.

"What do you mean by 'structured?'" asked the anchor.

"We see rushes of signals in sharp frequency bands, and they seem to be modulated in some way," the woman explained.

"Modulated?"

"Yes, it means that they might carry information," the SETI rep replied. "At the very least, it suggests that the signals were produced by something that is not a natural phenomenon."

"From where do these signals originate?" the interviewer asked.

"We see signals coming from all directions – at least from all directions we've looked in the past 48 hours."

"How far away are the sources of these signals?"

"We can't estimate that just yet," the SETI rep explained. "They're very weak but seem to be getting stronger."

"So, they're getting closer to us?"

"We think so, yes," the SETI woman replied.

The interview ended and the anchor was joined by the co-anchor who laughed. "Just what we all wanted to hear these days," he said. "First a pandemic, then the threat of nuclear war, and now aliens. What do you think, Ellen?"

The anchorwoman chuckled. "I wouldn't worry about it," she said and looked into the camera. "I think we'll find that it's just another weather system test, or our GPS satellites are acting up."

"Or it's those malfunctioning Russian satellites again – like last summer," the man added, just as the news went to commercial.

Lenny didn't think it was any of those things. He'd learned in his decades of subsurface geopolitical activity that nothing was mere coincidence. Things were happening, and he suspected that it was something major that had induced the early ceasefire.

After grinding the butt of his cigarette into a heavy glass ashtray, Lenny downed the last swig of his whiskey and set the glass on a ten-dollar bill. It was time to get some sleep. He had a senator to kill.

WILL ATE breakfast as he watched the stars move across the window. They were moving noticeably quicker now that the *Exodus 9* had increased to maximum speed.

He'd spent the past week trying to keep himself occupied as the *Exodus 9* made its way toward Earth. He still hardly believed it was happening.

He'd spent the time doing all kinds of things – playing soccer, taking a full day and nighttime adventure in the school of magic, flying two beamer combat missions, and spending time in various coffee houses and bookstores all around the world. He'd also gone to the whiskey bar on multiple occasions hoping to find Landau, but no luck.

Keeping active helped, but one eventually had to achieve a state of calm in order to rest. That seemed impossible, and his sleep was sporadic, at best. His dreams were mixed with nightmares. In one, he was in a restaurant in Chicago, eating green tea ice cream with Denise. In another, he watched the lost souls of a dead Earth wander aimlessly, and eventually dissipate into nothingness like the morning fog. He was relieved when both of those dreams ended: one elevated his hopes too high, while the other plunged him into despair.

He'd spend the next days concentrating on honing his combat skills in the beamer to get ready for whatever might be awaiting him when he got to Earth. If the Regenerators were there, he'd do whatever he could. A single beamer and a transport ship might be no match for a fleet of Regenerator ships – or even a single Regenerator ship – but Will intended to go down swinging, if it came to that.

He was willing to risk it all. If he were killed and the *Exodus 9* destroyed, there'd be no way for him to regenerate. At that point, he supposed he'd just head for the horizon. There was comfort in knowing that option existed.

DANIEL DESPERATELY WANTED to see the sun, and he was going to get that chance.

He and Sylvia had explored every crevice of their Omniscient clearance to wedge themselves into an "above top-secret" landscape of information to which even the President of the United States was not privy. As it turned out, neither was the director of the CIA. But that was about to change.

It was Jonathan's research on the origin and history of the powders that had exposed a tiny sprout of "above top-secret" information. It was a reference in a document to a place abbreviated as "CG" – the place where the powders, and some of the "alien" devices, had been taken. It was a classic example of how a simple error in a classified document could expose something that was never meant to be seen. It was also an example of how a good mind could identify a crucial detail in a vast swamp of information. He was glad he'd assigned Jonathan to that task.

"CG" was something at Area 51 – or within the massive complex for which that base was a front. There was a group of employees of the famed "secret" facility that had been concealed from top-secret records in a very suspicious way. They were called the "Custodial Group," – CG.

At first glance, one might think this title referred to the unit that kept the base clean and organized. However, with a little more work, Daniel had found that they had the highest salaries of all Area 51 personnel, indicating that they were probably top-tier scientists and engineers. He'd also noticed that some in the group were stationed at Area 6, another secretive testing site in Nevada that was often mentioned in UFO conspiracy theories.

Next, after going over all of the so-called "dark money" projects on the books that were being carried out at the facility, he determined that the Custodial Group wasn't involved in any of them. That meant that their projects were off the books – funded by the darkest of dark money – and above top secret. Daniel needed to know what they were doing.

He convinced Thackett to use every connection he had – including the president – to get them into the Area 51 complex, and to arrange for an appointment to speak directly with the leader of the Custodial Group.

Within 24 hours, Daniel and Sylvia were joined by Thackett, and a man named Jorge Putnam from the Department of Defense, in an elevator that took them to the surface. A Humvee was coming from Area 51 to pick them up.

When Daniel emerged from the cave-like tunnel that led to the surface, the sun overwhelmed his eyes and warmed his face. The air was cool and clean, and a breeze blew some sand onto his army-issued boots. He stared into the dark blue sky and, just for an instant, he was reminded of a time when he was 14 years old and standing on the pier during one of his family's summer vacations. The sound of a Hummer engine quickly brought him back to reality.

The ride was bumpy, windy, and a little chilly, but Daniel tried to enjoy the short excursion. When they arrived at Area 51, they pulled directly into a hangar, got out of the vehicle, and were greeted by two men, both of whom looked to be in their 70s. Their khaki overalls looked like something mechanics might wear, except that they were perfectly clean.

The taller of the two men, with a head of thick, white hair that needed to be trimmed, introduced himself as Michael Stevens, the head of the Custodial Group.

"And this is David Johnson, our head engineer," Stevens said in a raspy voice and nodded to the shorter, bald man to his right. Johnson just nodded and had an expression of annoyance and anxiety, like a skittish stray dog.

"What can we do for you?" Stevens asked.

"You've been briefed on what we need by the Department of Defense," Jorge Putnam replied.

"And by the CIA," Thackett said.

"And by the president himself," Stevens added, and then looked over to his silent colleague. "Well, Johnson, I guess it's time to let the cat out of the bag. It's been over a half a century."

Stevens led them across the hangar into what looked like a small workroom. He approached a tall, metal cabinet, reached into the deep side pocket of his overalls, and pulled out a ring of keys. One item on the ring was a key-fob, like that used to unlock a car door. He pressed a button on the device, and the cabinet slid along the wall to reveal an elevator.

"It will be tight," Stevens said as he stepped inside, "but I think we'll all fit."

Daniel was the last to get in, and the doors and the cabinet closed in unison just inches from his face.

"You have to be this secretive even in the most secret base in America?" Jorge Putnam asked.

"As you might be surprised to see," Stevens said, "this is *not* the most secret base in America."

The elevator came to a gentle halt after what Daniel estimated to be about a 50-foot drop, and the doors opened, revealing something he had not anticipated. It looked like a subway station.

They stepped out of the elevator and onto a platform. A sleek railcar rested on tracks that extended out of sight to the left and right, through a circular tunnel that was about 30 feet in diameter.

"Bet you didn't expect this," Stevens said and laughed. "We're just one hub in a vast network of facilities, and we have tunnels that extend from Las Vegas to Denver."

"And the president doesn't know about them?" Thackett asked.

"He knows of some sub-networks – those he might need to get him here if DC were evacuated. He'd already be in the underground facility where you're staying if he weren't so stubborn," Stevens explained. "He was sick, but he could have been treated there. He would have been much closer to the sub-network in that case."

They stepped into the railcar and buckled themselves into padded bench seats. Daniel sat between Sylvia and Thackett.

"Where are we going?" Thackett asked.

"To show you the best-kept secret of all time," Stevens said.

The train accelerated to what Daniel thought was an enormous velocity. After about 15 minutes, it slowed at a five-way junction and then resumed its colossal speed after entering the second tunnel from the right.

After 25 more minutes, the train slowed and eventually stopped.

"Where are we?" Thackett asked.

"About 75 miles north of Area 51," Stevens replied as he unbuckled his seatbelt. "Follow me."

Daniel trailed the others up a long flight of concrete steps which ultimately emerged in a large foyer in front of an enormous, steel door. Wide hallways led to the left and right, eventually turning out of view on both sides.

Stevens held his hand on a scanner next to the door and punched in a code on a keypad, after which a voice came over an intercom saying, "Stevens, you brought the visitors?"

"Yes, there are four of them," Stevens replied and then looked back to the group and said, "we're going to go through a sanitation load-lock, so close your eyes when you step inside."

The giant door opened, and they entered a steel tube about the size of a subway car. The door closed behind them, and a rush of air blasted all around them and nearly made Daniel lose his balance. The airstream seemed to change direction multiple times and then ceased.

"We don't like dust," Stevens said as he proceeded to the far end of the tube, which opened automatically.

They all walked over a sticky patch of floor that Daniel figured was another dust removal mechanism, and then into a colossal space that looked to be part laboratory and part airplane hangar. Something in the rear, about 100 yards away, caught his eye. It was a white, pill-shaped object about the size of the passenger cabin of a school bus. He looked closer and saw that it was tethered to the floor with thick ropes.

"Is that a balloon?" Daniel asked.

Stevens looked back at Daniel and then to where he was pointing.

"Looks like it, but it's not," Stevens replied and explained more as he led them toward it. "It weighs about two tons – actually, to be more precise, it has a mass of about 2,000 kilograms. However, it weighs nothing."

"I don't understand," Thackett said. "How can it have a mass of 2,000 kilograms but weigh nothing?"

"Good question," Stevens said. "One that we've been trying to answer for about 70 years. Weight is the force due to gravity, and it seems this object counteracts it somehow."

"Is this from the Roswell Incident?" Sylvia asked.

"Nope," Stevens replied. "It's from another crash. The public never caught wind of this one."

"If you can't weigh it, how do you know it has a mass of 2,000 kilograms?" Thackett asked.

"We used an inertial measurement," Stevens replied. "We pushed it with a known force and measured its acceleration. More massive objects are more difficult to accelerate than less massive ones – it's Newton's second law of motion."

Thackett seemed to regret his question as if it were something he should have learned in high school physics, but Daniel had wondered the same thing.

"Where are the other scientists?" Sylvia asked.

"They don't want to be seen by outsiders," Stevens replied.

"Gather them," Thackett said. "Their anonymity is no longer important."

"Why is that?" Stevens asked.

"Because we're about to be invaded," Thackett replied.

"By whom? China?" Stevens asked.

"No," Thackett replied and pointed to the floating craft. "By whoever made that."

WILL SPENT the morning in a fictitious coffeehouse embedded in a steep hill overlooking the Tyrrhenian Sea. He'd chosen the layout and details including the location. He was in Positano, a small city on Southern Italy's Amalfi Coast.

He sat at a table next to a wall of windows that reached to the third floor. On his left was the sea and blue skies. On his right was a small coffee bar in front of three open floors of old books, densely packed on wooden shelves that extended far into the building. He could smell them and, together with the aromas of the coffees, it set a mood in which he could think.

The books themselves brought him comfort. As he gazed up at the stacks, he estimated that there were many thousands of them. Each one represented at least a full year of thinking, reasoning, brainstorming, and imagining by their respective authors. Some were technical, and designed to teach you something, while others were intended to broaden your imagination. And some were written merely to entertain. But they all had come from someone's mind, with the intent to help you in some way. Will had always looked at his books as "friends" who were there to help him along, and it was fitting that he should be surrounded by them at this crucial time.

If Earth were alive and well when he arrived, his most likely course of action would be to keep the *Exodus 9* out of sight and take a beamer to the surface. He'd reconnect with the Omnis and, most importantly, with Denise. What would happen after that, he couldn't predict. He had enough knowledge at his disposal to change the world, but he didn't know how to go about applying it. And, with a single beamer, he had more military capability than any nation on the planet. That was something that had the potential to corrupt him absolutely.

Will huffed out a short laugh and smiled to himself. If they were still alive, he couldn't wait to see the faces of his friends when he showed up out of nowhere. It might take some effort, however, to convince them that it was actually him. After all, he now looked like he was in his early 20s.

A server freshened his coffee and brought him a plate of lightly toasted fette biscottate with butter – something that Will knew would be easy on his stomach when his anxiety level was high. He couldn't imagine a situation that would produce more disquiet than waiting to see if your home planet had been destroyed. Although, the Exoskeleton, and the time leading up to that, had caused him something akin to anxiety, but not exactly. What he'd felt during that time deserved a new word; anxiety, pain, and horror didn't cover it.

On occasion, while in a meditative calm, he'd contemplate his time inside the Exoskeleton. He barely even remembered his life before that. It was like the transformation from a caterpillar to a butterfly where, instead of undergoing a sleepy change inside a cocoon, something had torn his body apart, piece by piece, to release that which it concealed. And the same thing had been done to his mind.

But all of that had to happen for him to be where he was now. Now was when all of that which he'd endured would either bear fruit, or rot on the vine.

Will finished his last of piece fette biscottate and walked the stacks with his coffee in hand, occasionally slipping a book from a shelf and paging through it. It was strange for him to think that he might have time to read them all.

As Daniel stared at the levitating craft, he realized how much he'd witnessed in the past two years. Nothing surprised him. Not even a live demonstration of an alien antigravity device.

"What does this do for us?" Daniel asked. "Is this all you have?"

Stevens stared at him with an expression of disbelief, and his lower jaw literally dropped for a second before he spoke. "Is this all we have?" he repeated. "This object is defying gravity – "

"We have over 2,000 ships menacing our planet, and they all defy gravity," Daniel explained. "Do you have anything that you can fly – something with weapons?"

Stevens stared at Daniel for a few seconds, and then looked to Thackett. "Is he serious?"

"I'm afraid so, and we don't know how much time we have," Thackett replied. "So, do you have anything, or not?"

"We have one functional craft, but we've only figured out how to do the most basic things," Stevens said, visibly flustered. "We can fly it, but barely."

"Let's see it," Daniel said.

"Follow me," Stevens said and led them to a door in the rear of the facility.

WILL LEFT the coffeehouse around noon, and then partook in a soccer workout to burn off some nervous energy.

In the late afternoon, he visited Radu and did some exercises to develop his dual-state abilities. He was quickly developing an omniscient point of view. It had taken the average Delta over a century to develop such skills, which got him to wondering how old Lux had been when he'd died. With a little research, he'd found that Lux had been killed only once – never regenerated – at an age of 376 years. That had been Lux's first life. It had also been Will's.

With all of the names he'd had – about 400 in his case – it got Will wondering if, at some point, they would all be folded into a single name. After all, each of his lives was just a facet of the same entity – his soul. Perhaps his soul, in its entirety, could have a name.

After dinner, he made his way to the bridge of the *Exodus 9* and logged in using telepathic projection.

He checked that all systems – including weapons – were online and functioning properly, and that the *Exodus 9* was following the plotted course. It had made slight deviations from the original path to avoid various obstacles, one of which looked to be a planet fragment. It made him nervous despite knowing that it couldn't be from Earth: they were too far away, and the Regenerators weren't going to blast it apart anyway.

"How long until we arrive?" Will asked.

"Approximately 22 days and four hours," *Exodus 9* replied.

"Have you detected any Regenerator ships?" Will asked.

"Negative," the computer replied.

"Is there any way we can get there faster?" he asked, knowing that the *Exodus 9* was already going at maximum velocity.

"Negative," the computer replied.

Then something occurred to him. He knew from his classes that beamers had an effective top speed that was significantly greater than that of the *Exodus*-class ships.

"If I left now in a beamer, when would I get to Earth?" he asked.

"At maximum bending capacity, it would take 18 days and nine hours," *Exodus 9* replied.

Will paced as he contemplated his next move. He had a sense of urgency that was growing. He couldn't get the images out of his mind of Regenerator ships surrounding Earth and getting ready to sterilize it. Going ahead of the *Exodus 9* in a beamer would knock a few days off of the trip, but he'd be completely alone. He didn't know what to expect when he got there, and he might be taking himself into an ambush. But maybe he could go in cloaked.

"*Exodus 9,* prepare a beamer for launch with everything I'll need for the trip to Earth, and for combat," Will ordered. "Follow behind and do whatever you can to remain undetected as you approach Earth. Settle in some safe place, monitor the situation, and act as you see fit to protect the planet. If I get killed, regenerate me, and have another beamer ready."

"Aye-aye, Captain," the computer responded. "Your original ship will be ready."

He wondered if that meant his beamer from 40 thousand years ago.

"Thank you, *Exodus 9,*" Will said. "I consider you my friend." It was an awkward thing to say, but he didn't know how else to express his gratitude. The *Exodus 9* had treated him well.

"Good luck, William," *Exodus 9* said. "*Gwen* is awaiting you in launch hangar 17."

Will rushed across the bridge, out the door, and to a Tube portal. He'd go directly to the hangar.

DANIEL WALKED around the craft and examined it.

The head of the Custodial Group, Michael Stevens, had taken them into another hangar to show them their prized possession. It was a sleek, black disk, about 10 meters in diameter. It was thickest in the center, about two meters, and tapered to a sharp edge around the perimeter. The bottom was perfectly flat except for three spherical protrusions that served as feet on which the ship rested.

"Those smooth out when it's airborne," Stevens commented, referring to the feet, and still seemingly annoyed that Daniel wasn't outwardly impressed. "You realize that this craft can do things that defy all known physics, right?"

"You realize that my scientific curiosity is irrelevant here?" Daniel replied. His edginess was increasing. "Can someone fly it? Does it have weapons? How many of these do you have?"

Stevens stared at him for a moment and then spoke. "We have a couple of pilots that can operate it at a modest level. We think it has weapons, but we have not been able to access them. We have parts of other craft that – "

"How many are operational?" Jorge Putnam asked, cutting him off.

"Just this one," Stevens replied.

Thackett shook his head and looked to Putnam. "Without weapons, this thing might as well be on display in a museum."

"We might be able to utilize it as a delivery system," Stevens blurted.

"What do you mean?" Thackett asked.

"This thing can go into space," Stevens explained. "We can strap a nuke to it. We already have a prototype undercarriage saddle to carry a thermonuclear warhead."

"I don't understand," Sylvia said. "You mean we send some pilot out on a suicide mission to blow something up in space?"

"Not exactly," Stevens replied. "The saddle releases the warhead, which is on either a timer or a proximity detonator, or on a remote detonation system, and the pilot gets the hell out of there before it blows. The craft can then be used repeatedly."

"Why can't we just send our nuclear missiles into space?" Daniel asked.

"That might be possible for intercepting things in low Earth orbit, but what about targets between the Earth and the moon?" Stevens said. "This craft can get to the moon in minutes."

"You have warheads here?" Putnam asked.

"A few," Stevens replied. "But this ship can get to other locations to arm up in a very short time."

"Okay, Stevens," Putnam said. "Your top priority is to get that saddle ready and mount a warhead. Prepare your best pilot – prepare all of them. Let us know when everything is ready and be on alert for immediate deployment."

"Understood," Stevens said and then took a deep breath. "Are there really ships coming our way?"

"If they are in fact ships, there are thousands of them," Thackett replied. "If they're not ships – say asteroids – we may need your services as well."

"Let us know what types of warheads fit that saddle," Putnam added. "We'll arrange to have them available at different locations."

Stevens led them back through the hangars and into the subway that took them back to Area 51.

Daniel stared at the sunlit sands through the window of the Humvee as they rode back to their underground command center at Site 4. He wondered if he'd get another chance to see the sun. Their plan to defend the planet with a single ship that shuttled nukes into space was ludicrous. It was like sending a fishing boat to attack an aircraft carrier – or 2,000 aircraft carriers. If only the weapons systems were functional. It gave Daniel an idea.

He'd discuss it with Thackett when they got back. It was worth a shot.

WHEN WILL RODE the lift into his ship, he was greeted by a female voice.

"Lux, it's nice to see you again after all of this time," the voice said. "I understand that you now go by 'Will.'"

The voice was similar to that of the *CX-1* simulation craft, but the cadence and inflections were more familiar, like he was talking to an old friend.

"You're *Gwen*?" Will asked. "I mean, the real *Gwen* – from 40 thousand years ago?"

"I am," she replied. "It has been a long wait and, like you, I have a new body."

"Your consciousness was recently transferred to this ship?" he asked. "When?"

"About a month ago," she replied. "It seems that the *Exodus 9* anticipated your needs."

"What have you been doing for 40 thousand years?" he asked.

"I lived on a warship until I moved to the *Exodus 9*," she replied. "Like you, I've been busy, but exclusively in the virtual world where artificial intelligence lives."

"I'm happy that you weren't destroyed when I was killed," he said.

"I was undergoing upgrades at the time," *Gwen* said. "Perhaps you would not have been killed if we'd been together on that mission."

"I'm glad we're together now," he said. He felt as if he were at home. "We're heading into danger. It will be a long ride – 18 days."

"It will give us time to catch up," she said. "Ready to launch."

Will took his seat in the cockpit and strapped in. Five minutes later, the *Exodus 9* was behind them, and out of sight.

JACOB GOT the call from Thackett at 3:00 a.m. and was on a C-130 transport plane to Las Vegas by daybreak. He arrived at McCarran airport in the so-called "Neon Capital" at 10:00 a.m. local time and immediately boarded a small jet with blacked-out windows. After a 30-minute flight, they touched down at Area 51 where he was put inside a Humvee with two rough-looking soldiers who placed a black hood over his head.

After a noisy 30-minute ride, they seemed to slow down and the road became smooth. A minute later, the Humvee came to a halt and the engine stopped.

The soldiers removed the hood, pulled him out of the vehicle, and handed him his luggage. He was in an enormous tunnel with well over a hundred military vehicles parked in an organized fashion on the smooth concrete floor.

"Jacob," a female voice said from behind him.

Jacob turned. Daniel and Sylvia were there.

"Welcome aboard," Sylvia said and gave him a short hug. "Sorry about the hood – wartime protocols are in effect."

Daniel reached out and Jacob shook his hand.

"What is this place?" Jacob asked.

"It's Site-4, the complex that would be home to our government if DC were taken out," Daniel explained.

"The president is still on the East Coast," Jacob said.

Sylvia nodded. "He was sick, but better now," she said. "He's stubborn, but doing what a leader should do, I guess. VPOTUS is here."

Jacob thought it was prudent to at least have the vice president out of DC under the circumstances.

"Let's drop off your luggage in your quarters," Daniel said. "Then we'll show you around."

They made their way to an elevator and, as it plunged deeper and deeper, Jacob asked, "What am I doing here?"

Sylvia glanced to Daniel to answer the question.

"We want you to look at some things we've discovered," Daniel explained.

Jacob's fingers tingled. "You mean like a reverse engineering job?"

Daniel nodded. "A challenging one."

After showing him to his quarters, which were located next to Jonathan's, they brought him to his workspace. It was a cubicle with a computer desk, couch, two chairs, and a few cabinets and shelves. He already missed his space at 17 Swann.

They sat and chatted and, a few minutes later, there was a knock at the door. Jonathan stood in the doorway.

"Jonathan," Jacob said as he hurried over and shook his hand, and then put his hand on the older man's shoulder. "I'm so sorry about Denise – it's devastating."

"I just got out of quarantine," Jonathan said as his eyes became glassy. "I was there when she passed."

Sylvia went to him and hugged him as she cried.

"You know, Jonathan, you're cleared of the virus now," Daniel said. "Everyone would understand if you decided to – "

"I'm staying," Jonathan cut him off. "I owe that to Denise, and this is too important."

"I agree," Jacob said. "This has existential implications."

Daniel stared at him. "You reminded me of your uncle there for a second," he said.

"That's where I heard it," Jacob replied. "Where's this thing you wanted me to look at?"

Daniel glanced to Sylvia, who said, "We'll need to go for a ride."

THEY'D BEEN TRAVELING for nearly three hours before Will unstrapped his harness and left the cockpit. He made his way to the rear of the craft and found the lavatory. Afterwards, he went to the food dispenser and got coffee in a sleek, spill-proof mug. It was another example of how having access to unlimited energy opened the horizon to many things. The same technology that synthesized food could create almost anything – even a mechanical part to repair the ship, if needed.

The cabin was compact but comfortable. A padded bench seat along the starboard wall faced a large video screen on the opposite side.

He sat on the bench and viewed information received via a direct link to the *Exodus 9*. The feed showed the status of the *Exodus 9*, which would send out a final communique indicating its projected route before cloaking for the last leg of the trip, still a couple of weeks away.

When they got within about a hundred light-years of Earth, the beamer would go into fully-cloaked mode. He'd be going in blind, at least in terms of any active sensing. *Gwen* would still have her passive sensors in operation and would be able to detect certain communications, including those coming from Earth's inhabitants, if they were still alive.

For the next 12 hours, Will talked with *Gwen* about things that ranged from their past missions to life as a Delta. It occurred to him that he could feel some resentment about what had happened – about how he'd integrated into the new generation. Although still far from a Utopian society, life as a Delta would have been much better, although different, than that of a human. It would be like someone struggling through life in 1,000 BC learning that they could have instead lived during the 21st century. And he thought that, in his situation, the difference was far more stark than that.

He needed sleep.

"*Gwen*, wake me in four hours," Will said as he started to lie back on the bench.

"Would you like to use the sleeper?" she asked

He had no idea what she was talking about. "Yes, sure," he said. "What is that?"

The bench on which he currently sat extended from the wall so that it widened to the size of a twin bed. A compartment on the wall then opened to reveal pillows and blankets.

Will grinned as he settled on his back, rested his head on a pillow, and covered himself with a thick blanket. He turned off the computer screen on the wall across from him and dimmed the lights. Other than the screens on the consoles in the cockpit, all he could see was the starlight that shone through the large forward window.

He marveled at the view and contemplated the feelings it evoked. Some considered the idea of the abyss as an enormous hole that descended into darkness with no end. But that was wrong. The abyss extended in all directions, and we were all already at the bottom of it. In his current existence, he could steer his tiny starship into any one of an infinite number of directions, and then travel in that direction forever, never to see an end, and eventually enter a nothingness that extended to infinity.

However, there was another existence. It was the one in which he'd found himself after swallowing the *Seraphim Hors d'Âge*. It was a new place – one in which the deepest of questions were answered. But there seemed to be a barrier in the form of a decision: one would find themselves either content enough to pass over the horizon, or discontent enough to go back and live again.

After hundreds of lives – and deaths – he had not been content enough to go over that horizon. But his final life would be as William Thompson. He'd already regenerated once, and might again, but there would be a final end for him in this world, and perhaps a new beginning in another.

His anxiety seemed to wane now – he was doing everything he could – and his eyelids closed as he fell gently away from consciousness.

JACOB COULD HARDLY CONTAIN HIMSELF. The massive disk was levitating six feet above the floor. A net was draped over the top of the black craft and tied to eyelets anchored into the concrete.

"It was resting on the floor the first time we were here," Daniel said.

"Can we get inside?" Jacob asked Stevens who, he'd just learned, was the head of a secret organization called the Custodial Group.

There were over a dozen people in the hangar, including Jonathan, Thackett, Daniel, and Sylvia. The rest were Custodial engineers and scientists, and one man in his thirties who was a pilot.

One of the engineers pulled a metallic disk out of a pocket in his lab coat. It was about two inches in diameter and a half-inch thick, and it had a small spherical knob at the center of one side.

"What's that?" Jacob asked and pointed to the object.

"It's a key," Stevens replied and then addressed the engineer. "Open it up."

Jacob followed the engineer under the levitating craft.

The man gripped the key's knob between his thumb and forefinger and touched its flat side to the craft's black surface. As he slid it around, he said, "It takes a while to find the right location."

"Why don't you put a mark on it, or place a sticky-note in the right spot?" Sylvia asked.

"Why didn't we think of that?" Stevens said in a sarcastic tone. "Nothing sticks to it."

After about a minute of searching, the engineer stepped back as a circular opening appeared in the underbelly and a ladder lowered to the floor.

Jacob craned his neck and peered inside. Off the disk's center toward one side was a cockpit and a brightly illuminated control panel. Beyond the cockpit was a large window, which must have been a video screen showing a camera view of the outside. On the arm handles of the pilot's seat were vertical levers – two on each the left and the right.

"Those are control sticks," a man said from behind him, over his shoulder. It was Captain Frank Wessen, the pilot. "Those are the only controls that work."

"What do you mean?" Jacob asked.

"They control all movement," Wessen explained. "Lift, acceleration, roll, bank, yaw – and it can even move sideways and backwards. We think that there are other functions on the displays and consoles, but we can't get them to work."

"What's the power source?" Jacob asked.

Stevens, who stood just behind the pilot, said, "Unknown. It's the way we found it – powered up."

"When did you find it?" Jacob asked.

"In 1947," Stevens replied.

Jacob turned his shoulders to look at him. "You mean – "

"Yes, this one was from Roswell. We found it along with the wreckage of another ship," Stevens explained. "And now you know. Up to this point, only the Custodial Group has known what actually happened there."

"What about the ship in the other hangar?" Jacob asked. It was white and pill-shaped, and it was always floating.

"That one was found in another location in 1968, but had probably been there for thousands of years based on the carbon dating of some of the surrounding materials," Stevens explained. "That other one is not functioning – it levitates, but we can't fly it. We can't even get inside it."

Jacob climbed inside the craft and examined some of the control panels. There were illuminated buttons marked with strange symbols that he didn't recognize. However, the design of the control panels looked similar to something he'd seen before.

He stepped out of the craft and looked to the others. "Take a look inside," he said and stepped away from the opening.

Daniel went first, then Sylvia, and the others went in turn.

"They resemble the controls at the Delta base," Sylvia said. "But those aren't Delta symbols."

"Delta symbols?" Stevens asked.

"Long story," Daniel said.

"There's probably a good reason that you can't actuate the buttons on the console," Jacob said to Stevens. "They're effectively buried beneath an extremely hard surface."

"Well then how are they actuated?" Stevens asked.

"Evanescent extension," Sylvia replied.

"What the hell is that?" Stevens asked.

"It's like a telekinetic ability," she replied.

"Telekinesis?" Stevens said in a tone of disbelief. "Sounds like bunk to me."

"It's actually not bunk, and Sylvia was putting it into familiar terms to give you an intuitive understanding," Daniel retorted. "The phenomenon actually arises when someone extends their soul beyond their body – in this case, through their fingertips."

"Soul?" Stevens said with an incredulous expression.

"We don't have time to discuss this," Daniel said and looked to Thackett.

"It sounds like we're lucky this thing can be flown at all," Thackett said. "Now we have to strap a bomb to it and get it rolling. There might not be much time."

Stevens agreed, and Jacob and the others headed to the substation to travel back to Area 51.

"Any ideas of how to get the other controls to work?" Daniel asked as they boarded the train.

"No, sorry," Jacob replied. "I'll keep thinking about it." They'd brought him out just to look at the ship and he was disappointed that he couldn't be of more help.

The craft was impressive, but Jacob knew that they'd have no chance against the Regenerators if they decided to carry out the extermination. He also knew that a nuke strapped to a single ship would have no chance either.

Although still not confirmed to be spacecraft, the objects were approaching and would be inside the moon's orbit within the next 48 hours. His thoughts went to Pauli, and he was going to find a way to talk to her after they got back. He worried about her. He didn't want her to die alone.

WILL AWAKENED to *Gwen*'s voice and the interior lights gradually brightened. They'd been traveling for eight days and still had ten more to go.

He went to the food generator and synthesized some oatmeal and strong coffee, and then sat in the pilot's seat and studied the monitors as he ate. His ship was now in semi-cloaked mode – using mostly passive sensing – and so the best the beamer could do was to effectively strain its eyes by focusing all of its passive sensors in the direction of their destination. After seven more days, *Gwen* would go into fully cloaked mode, and all communications with the *Exodus 9* would be shut down.

The beamer could essentially act only as a "receiver" of signals in that state. When they got to within about 100 light years, the first signals ever transmitted by humans would reach the ship, and Will looked forward to experiencing them. It would start with radio signals, and progress to television. The transmissions would come in a rush as the ship approached Earth. They'd arrive in chronological order, and he'd see the most recent broadcasts just as he arrived. He just hoped that they wouldn't suddenly go dark as they got closer. It would mean that he was too late.

16

EARTH

JACOB STOOD WITH SYLVIA, DANIEL, AND JONATHAN IN THE ENORMOUS command center and watched the largest screen in the room. It displayed a three-dimensional graphic with the slowly rotating Earth at the center, surrounded by the thousands of nondescript objects that had maneuvered themselves into regularly spaced positions about 2,000 miles above the surface. Lines were drawn between them, making it seem as if the objects had formed a net around the Earth.

Jacob knew Earth's defenses were no match for whatever those things were. The best they could do was to strap a nuclear warhead to their lone ship that was capable of trans-medium flight – meaning it could traverse the atmosphere into space and back again. The ship would get a run at a target, release the nuke, and then veer off in a manner similar to that employed by torpedo planes in World War II. If it somehow survived the blast, and any defense measures taken by the alien craft, the ship would return to the surface, pick up another warhead, and repeat the process.

Alternatively, China, the US, and Russia had devised a plan where they would launch ICBMs into space, and just let them float around. If one got close to an enemy ship, it would be detonated remotely. Both were unsophisticated ways to deliver Earth's most powerful weapons. However, Jacob guessed that such actions would just piss off the intruders, and then they'd either expedite the destruction, or make it slow and painful.

In the four days since their visit to the facility that housed the lone functioning spacecraft, the "objects" had approached from all directions at a great velocity and, once inside the orbit of the moon, decelerated at a rate that far exceeded anything that could be survived by a human. It made him consider the possibility that the ships were drones.

Although there was no clear visual evidence, it was generally agreed upon that they were "ships." And now there were about 2,400 of them in orbit. Even though the collective number of nukes on Earth greatly outnumbered them – the US alone had about 5,800 – they couldn't be delivered simultaneously, and he was sure the visitors wouldn't just wait around as a lone ship shuttled one bomb up at a time. He thought it might also be possible that nukes would have no effect on the alien craft whatsoever.

Just before he'd been summoned to the control room, Jacob had spoken with Pauli, who was still in London. She knew about the objects – the story had broken that morning – and she was frightened. Due to the pandemic – the smallpox virus was spreading – everyone was confined to their homes. It hurt him deeply to imagine her all alone in her apartment, awaiting the worst. He'd done his best not to frighten her any further, and had told her that the entire world was working on it. It was something he'd never thought he'd see – most countries joining in and contributing – and it made him feel a sense of camaraderie with the human race, as short-lived as it might be.

What was strange was that the objects in "orbit" were defying known physics. They were 2,000 miles above the surface and in geosynchronous orbit, meaning they appeared not to move and held constant positions relative to the surface as the Earth rotated. The geosynchronous satellites developed by humans had to be located a little over 22 thousand miles above the equator so that their natural orbital period would match the 24-hour period of Earth's rotation.

The way these objects were moving, however, at an altitude of 2,000 miles and without any visible source of thrust, they should have just fallen to the earth. But they didn't, and they'd maintained their perfectly uniform mesh pattern about the planet since they'd assembled.

Jacob wondered when the radiation would start. That was supposed to be the first step in regenerating the planet – kill off all life with a blast of intense X-rays and gamma rays. He wondered if it would be instantaneous, and also how being a half-mile underground might delay the inevitable.

Jacob likened the feeling to that of a person strapped into an electric chair and waiting in silence for someone to throw the switch.

THEY WERE STILL over a hundred light-years out when *Gwen* reduced the approach velocity and went into fully-cloaked mode. They were at the range of the earliest radio communications produced by the current generation of Earth.

As they got closer, those signals streamed in at a great rate. History flashed through Will's mind as he listened to newscasts and radio shows starting from before World War I through the Great Depression era. The first television signals started coming in around the mid-1930s, just in time to witness the rise and fall of the Third Reich, the bombing of Hiroshima, and then on to the Korean War. The most impactful broadcast was the coverage of the moon landing in 1969. It seemed simple now – even though the feat hadn't been repeated in over half a century.

The volume of signals from different sources exploded after that but Will only watched the major networks – he stayed mostly with the news but caught five minutes of an episode of the old American sitcom, *Three's Company*. It meant they were still over 40 light-years out with three days to go.

As *Gwen* continued to slow at a rate that would not produce space-time ripples that could be detected by hidden craft, the time progression of the broadcasts decreased. It made Will twitchy as he knew he wouldn't hear the most important news until they were very close to Earth.

It would be another three days before he'd know whether Earth was still alive.

JACOB SENT the software command to turn two of the four satellites in the cluster to home in on one of the thousands of objects that had settled into low Earth orbit. It would take about 90 seconds to reconfigure so that the satellites would coordinate as two eyes in order to capture a highly detailed, three-dimensional image.

In the past two hours, the "objects," which had been blurred in all images taken from surface-bound telescopes, had now seemed to crystalize into detailed, structured ships. Jacob figured they must have turned off some kind of cloaking device.

He picked up a cup of hot tea and brought it to his lips with trembling fingers. He didn't know if it was acute anticipation or fear that brought on the tremors, but he was anxious to see what the objects looked like up close. The images he would collect would be the best available, and the CIA and DIA would be most desperate to see them. They'd be looking for many things, including functionalities and vulnerabilities, both of which Jacob doubted they would ascertain.

Ninety seconds passed, then 120, and then three minutes. At five minutes, a message appeared that read, "COMMUNICATIONS ERROR: CANNOT ESTABLISH A COMM LINK."

Jacob resent the command and, just as the second communications error reappeared, his phone vibrated. It was Thackett. All satellite communications were down. But there was something else that he needed to see, and Jacob was to go to the CIA command center.

Jacob felt lightheaded as he made his way to the elevator.

AT JUST 48 hours out from their destination, Will watched month-old broadcasts from the major Earth networks.

The news was horrifying.

China had released two viruses upon the United States, and they had spread uncontrollably around the world – including throughout China. The most widespread of the two diseases – a modified flu virus – hit early and might have mitigated the spread of the second, much more deadly, smallpox variant had the proper precautions been taken to stop its propagation. But they hadn't, and millions were dying around the world. The smallpox variant was rampant. People were frightened, and some places were experiencing chaos and civil unrest.

As they got closer, the newscasts streamed in, and Will could hardly take his eyes off the screen long enough to go to the bathroom. The US and China had gone to war, with much of the world joining in. However, for some unknown reason, after just a couple of weeks of action, China and the US had called a temporary ceasefire. It was good news, but it remained unexplained. Perhaps it was that the smallpox variant had breached pandemic proportions and it looked as if it were unstoppable.

The tension in Will's mind and body eased until a story came up an hour later that made his gut twist. It was an interview with a representative from the SETI Institute. A picture appeared on the screen that showed an image with hundreds of red arrows pointing to small blurry objects.

"These objects are entering our solar system from all directions," the SETI representative explained.

"Are they spacecraft?" the news anchor asked.

"They're more likely debris from surrounding asteroid fields," she replied.

"Why are they blurred?"

"We haven't figured that out yet, but it seems like some of them will pass close to Earth," the woman from SETI replied.

"They're blurred because they're semi-cloaked," Will said aloud. He figured they were Regenerator ships.

The beamer was only two days from Earth, but the broadcast was three weeks old. It meant that the Regenerators might have already engaged Earth, and may have destroyed it by now.

In the next hour, the beamer was set to exit bending-mode propulsion and continue to coast the rest of the way to Earth. During this final phase of the trip, the ship would remain fully cloaked, and the only undetectable maneuvering it could do was to brake using a method called "carpet folding." It was an intuitive term for describing the phenomenon in which the spacetime in front of the ship wrinkled up like a rug on a hardwood floor, causing the ship to decelerate. If he turned or accelerated forward, he'd be detected. His plan was to coast in, assess the situation, and then drop out of cloaked mode and go fully active with all systems ready – sensors, weapons, everything.

During the hour that remained before bender-propulsion shutdown, Will went to the bathroom, ate a nutrition bar, and downed a double espresso. He then strapped himself into the pilot's chair and listened as *Gwen* counted down from five, "… four, three, two, one, … all propulsion systems offline."

"Activate carpet folding," Will said in way that seemed natural to him: he'd done it before.

"Aye-aye, carpet folding activated," *Gwen* responded. "Perhaps you should get some rest before our arrival."

Will agreed and went to the bench to lie down and close his eyes – he wanted to be as sharp as possible when they made their final approach.

When he awakened four hours later, the ship had just emerged from a cloud of debris and was heading for a star that was his sun. It was a strange perspective. First, they were still so far away from it that it looked unimpressive. Second, its color was white, rather than the warm yellow-orange he associated with summers on the baseball field, or the deep-red sunsets on the ocean. Finally, he'd seen numerous such "suns," and the one before him had no special quality that set it apart from the others. He'd learned through direct experience that life on Earth was not particularly special, or unique. However, life *itself* was special. He'd had to die to learn that.

All of the planets orbited the sun in the same plane and followed nearly circular orbits – at least the inner planets did – like rings on a spinning plate. The beamer was traveling in the same plane – done purposely to blend in with the other objects and debris in the solar system – and would pass close to the sun to use its gravitational pull to steer it toward Earth, which was currently on the opposite side of the sun. Earth would remain out of view until the beamer made it around the bend. The path was chosen to reduce the chances that they'd be detected before they arrived. They'd make the bend in just over 24 hours.

Even though the transmissions from Earth were now delayed by only a few days – meaning he was still a few light-days away – he had a bad feeling. He felt like he was running late.

At 12 hours out, the TV signal that he'd been monitoring suddenly went to static.

"*Gwen*, give me a list of TV transmissions from Earth," he said.

"There are currently no communication transmissions from Earth," *Gwen* replied.

"What?" he gasped as his stomach seemed to tighten into a taut ball of rubber bands. "None?"

"None," *Gwen* replied. "Based on our current distance from Earth, all transmissions ceased 11 hours and 34 minutes ago."

"Let me see the news from a half hour before the signal stopped," he said. "Put BBC and CNN on split screen."

The news was all bad. The two viruses – including the deadly smallpox variant – were now completely paralyzing the planet. The public suspected their governments were lying about the death numbers. However, those governments were also trying to put out another fire: the appearance of thousands of objects in orbit about the planet. The story had been broken by the SETI Institute weeks before, but they now had irrefutable evidence: photos. The objects – ships – could be spotted with modest, surface-based telescopes, and pictures collected by citizens were showing up all over social media. The governments of the world were trying to pass them off as a new weather and GPS network, but the news media were no longer buying it.

Just as BBC was about to put up an image of one of the ships, the screen went to static.

Will went to the lavatory and vomited.

Will could hardly contain himself as the beamer began its bend around the sun.

He was strapped in and ready.

Gwen brought him extremely close to his home star but the image on the screen, despite the hellfire that filled the real space around him, was pleasing to the eye. However, his thoughts were elsewhere.

Before they even completed the bend, he saw it.

It was ablaze. It was a white-hot fire that seared his very soul.

He couldn't see the ships from that distance – it was as if the light was being emitted from an infinitesimal point in space – but he knew they were there.

Will screamed in rage. "All weapons systems online, and shields up," he yelled. "Get me as close to those ships as possible – find the command ship – and decloak. Full combat mode."

He was going to go down swinging.

Daniel could hardly believe his eyes as he and Sylvia entered the CIA control center and found Jonathan. Everyone was staring at the main monitor as they gasped and chattered.

Jacob trotted in behind them, panting and pale. "What's going on?" he asked.

Daniel pointed to one of the monitors. It displayed a bright white disk that fluttered about the edges. He had no idea what it was.

Thackett emerged from the crowd and joined them.

"What you're seeing is a planet on fire," Thackett said. "This feed is coming from a land-based telescope in Peru."

"What planet?" Sylvia asked.

"Mars," Thackett replied.

"My God," Jacob gasped. "Can we see any ships there?"

"No," Thackett said. "All of our telescopes were focused elsewhere before this occurred, and we lost communication with everything from Mars – satellites and landers – when we lost our own satellites."

"Remember what Will told us at the Antarctic base just before it self-destructed?" Sylvia asked. "He said Mars and Earth were regenerated simultaneously when our generation was created."

"And Mars was the one that lagged, so they sterilized it," Jonathan added.

"What in the hell are they doing – taunting us?" Thackett asked and pulled out his phone. "I need to see where we are on getting that alien craft set up with a nuke. We have to at least try."

Daniel just stared at the screen and watched as Mars burned. Whatever ships might have been there were too small to see in the bright light that engulfed the space around the planet.

He glanced at Jonathan and couldn't imagine how the man was feeling. He'd just lost Denise, and now he was away from his family at a time when they should all have been together.

Sylvia looped her arm around Daniel's and pulled him to her side.

Daniel just hoped that, when it started on Earth, it would be just like the lights suddenly went out – on him, and humanity. He didn't want a warning, he didn't want to feel anything, and he didn't want anyone else to feel anything either.

WILL HEARD a voice just above the ringing in his ears.

"You might want to reconsider those commands," *Gwen* said.

"What? Why?" he yelled.

"I think you have mistaken the burning planet for Earth," *Gwen* replied.

"What?" he asked, confused. "What planet is it?"

"It is the fourth planet, Mars, that is undergoing a genesis event," she explained.

"And Earth?"

A display appeared in front of him with a clear view of a bright blue planet. With the sun now directly behind them, Earth was perfectly round, like a full moon.

"It's okay," Will mumbled to himself. "They're okay."

"There are ships surrounding Earth," *Gwen* added. "Just over a thousand of them from this line of sight, but there are probably over 2,000 in total."

Will's brief moment of relief ended. "Are they the Regenerators?"

"We are in passive mode – cloaked – so we cannot probe them," *Gwen* responded. "We will need to get much closer to make identifications."

"Let's go in then," Will said. "If they start doing anything to the planet, be ready to go on the offensive."

"Aye-aye," *Gwen* said. "We'll need to time the braking so that there are no detectable ripples when we arrive. We'll be inside Earth's lunar orbit in 34 minutes."

"Do it," Will said as he unstrapped his harness and stood.

As he paced between the cockpit and the rear of the craft, he could hardly imagine the fear the people on Earth were experiencing as Mars burned in the distance, and ships clustered above their own skies preparing to do the same to them.

Will felt a brief moment of peace as he realized that he'd at least be dying with them.

"More objects are arriving?" Daniel asked, squinting at the monitors in the main operations room. Thackett had suggested that they get some rest, but there was no way that was going to happen with Mars burning and more objects approaching.

"About 500 hundred new ones so far, but they're outside the net –

closer to the moon's orbit right now," Thackett said and pointed to one of the smaller screens that showed a perfectly resolved black disk. "And they're not just 'objects' anymore."

Daniel gawked at the nine images arrayed on one of the larger screens. Each showed a craft of some kind – three were identical, and the rest different. A few looked like disks, but there were other designs as well. They didn't look complex. On the contrary, they were sleek and elegant.

"How are we seeing these?" Daniel asked.

"Land-based telescopes," Thackett replied. "We managed to connect with them through surface communications."

"How large are they?" Sylvia asked, her eyes wide.

Thackett pointed to an image of one of the disks. "The largest one so far is about 17 miles in diameter, and nearly three miles thick in the center," he explained. "It's one of the new arrivals."

Daniel couldn't stop staring at it. It was a thing of magnificence and wonder. It was simple – just a sleek disk, but the beauty somehow originated from its enormous dimensions.

"Look there," Thackett said and pointed to an image at the lower right on the screen. "That's one of the 2,000 forming the net around the planet. Those are smaller, and there are a few different types in that group."

"Why are they just sitting there?" Daniel asked, not expecting an answer. He looked around at the 300 people in the command center who were working diligently. It was as if they were oblivious to what was expected to happen next. But he knew that they had all been briefed on what the Omnis knew – what Will Thompson had deciphered from the warning message sent by the previous generation. They knew all of that, and also that Mars was currently on fire. It was clear that Earth was next. Daniel admired those people: they knew that death was imminent, and they all had families on the outside, yet they were level-headed and doing their jobs.

On top of it all, the viruses were decimating the outside world. Hospitals around the planet were at capacity, and medical professionals were dying along with their patients. Everything was closing down in the US and most major countries – businesses, travel, and most government services. The US government had somehow managed to rejuvenate and maintain the electrical grid, and had a plan to keep food and water available, but it wasn't sustainable.

The smallpox variant was the Frankenstein monster of viruses, only this monster evolved. It did not discriminate in age, except those who were old enough to have had the smallpox vaccine had a much better survival rate. As he mulled it over, Daniel realized that China had, on its own, poisoned the *entire planet*. He was certain that was a first. It made him wonder if the Regenerators shouldn't be a welcomed sight.

"Are we sending up the ship?" Jacob asked.

Daniel was hoping that Thackett would say that they weren't.

Thackett looked to Jacob and said, "Yes, soon."

A grimace formed on Jacob's face. "With a bomb?"

Thackett smiled in a way that Daniel had never seen him do. It was like a father smiling at a young boy. "No, my friend, there will be no bomb."

Jacob's face seemed to show relief. He didn't ask why not. No one else asked, either. We as a race had done enough damage to ourselves throughout our existence. There was no point in going down flailing in the face of overwhelming force. Perhaps our comeuppance had finally arrived.

AS THE BEAMER braked and the Earth grew larger, various displays illuminated with passive-sensor warnings of partially cloaked objects in the area. Thousands of ships were arrayed around the planet. Will thought Earth looked like a fly entangled in a spider's web. And there were other vessels, much further away – between Earth and the moon.

His fingers tingled: the Earth was still blue. It seemed normal.

The carpet-folding continued to decelerate the ship, although he couldn't feel it. If there hadn't been a mechanism to compensate for it, the deceleration would have already turned him into a gelatinous mess on the front window.

After another 10 minutes, they were just inside the orbit of the Moon – and close enough to the pale orb that it nearly filled his right-side view. In a few minutes they'd be close to some of the ships positioned far outside the net. His plan was to settle into a good position for assessing the situation, and then decide on a course of action.

He unbuckled his harness and went back to the cabin to relieve himself, and to get a few nutrition bars and water. He figured he might need them. As he returned to the cockpit and glanced out the window, he gasped, dropped everything, and jumped back into his seat.

Sensors flashed as *Gwen* warned, "Ship in close proximity. Distance: 1.2 miles."

Will gawked at the colossal vessel, which had seemingly appeared out of nowhere. It must have been fully cloaked, like *Gwen*, and had just become visible.

It was a sleek, black disk so enormous that it made him freeze in place. It was a feeling like peering into a dark hole in the ground and realizing, when it was too late, that a giant snake was looking back at you and was within striking distance.

The massive ship dwarfed the *Exodus 9*, like an aircraft carrier would a school bus. It was headed in the direction of Earth. He felt like he was right next to it, even though it was at a safe distance and moving in the same direction as the beamer.

"More ships are uncloaking," *Gwen* warned.

"How many?"

"There are currently 517 fully uncloaked ships outside the inner net, and more decloaking," she reported. "They are approaching from all directions."

Will saw what minuscule chance he might have had diminishing. He was no match for even one of those ships.

The giant disk then accelerated, pulling ahead of Will's tiny beamer, which couldn't accelerate without revealing itself.

"Another vessel is approaching from behind," *Gwen* warned. "Not on a collision course."

A few seconds later, a ship identical to the first silently overtook them from above, so Will got a complete view of its flat underbelly. Its size was like nothing he'd ever imagined, maybe 20 miles in diameter, or larger – there was no reference.

He noticed a marking in the center of the ship's underside and, just when he was about to zoom in on it, his beamer rocked and rattled.

"We are being uncloaked," *Gwen* warned.

"What? That can happen?" he asked as his heart pounded even harder. "Is it that ship that's doing it?" He was referring to the one that had just passed overhead.

"Yes," Gwen said. "Shall we attempt to evade?"

"Do it now!" he exclaimed. They'd be completely visible, but he had no choice.

An instant later, he flashed beneath the ship and plunged down and away, trying to separate from it as quickly as possible.

"We are on a collision course with another vessel," *Gwen* warned.

Will made a 90-degree turn and rolled the beamer just in time to avoid a collision with another disk. He streamed along its topside, which had some smooth features, and was not perfectly flat like its underbelly.

He noticed markings on the outer rim of the ship but didn't have time to look closely as he had to concentrate on the getaway.

He zipped across the ship's diameter, passing close to the center as *Gwen* chimed out another warning. "The ship is forming bender traps," she said.

"What the fuck is a 'bender trap?'"

"It bends spacetime into a hole – if we enter, we won't be able to escape," *Gwen* explained.

It was the spacetime version of falling into a pit. "Can you show them on the display?"

Reddish, amorphous patches appeared on the screen, and Will maneuvered around them. Every time he dodged one, another would appear in his path. And then there were more and more of them. This went on for over five minutes, and then another disk approached to assist the first one. And then a third. At this point, there were so many traps that his maneuvering options became few, and he felt like he was flying down a tunnel.

"Put weapons systems online," he ordered.

"All weapons systems now online," *Gwen* responded.

On second thought, he worried that any attack on the ships might be mistaken for an attack by Earth. He also figured those ships could have easily destroyed him already if they'd wanted to. "Take weapons systems offline," he ordered as he made a series of sharp turns and rolls to avoid a maze of traps.

As he made an evasive maneuver, he passed close to the underside of one of the ships. The beamer suddenly shuddered.

"What's that?" he yelled.

"We've been locked."

"What does that mean?"

All of a sudden, he had no control of the ship.

"We have been encapsulated in a spacetime bubble and are being drawn toward one of the ships," *Gwen* replied.

"It's drawing us in?"

"Yes, and we are now on course for a bay door that is opening on the undersurface."

"Any way out of this?"

"Negative," *Gwen* replied. "I am not powerful enough to break free."

"Okay," he said. He saw no other choice. "Ramp down propulsion systems. Let them take us in."

He watched in awe as his ship was guided along the surface of the enormous vessel. As they were pulled along, he got a good look at a red emblem at the center of the ship's black underside.

Will's vision blurred and he became lightheaded for a few seconds. Even though he knew the answer, he asked, "*Gwen,* can you identify that emblem?"

She did.

LENNY HAD TAKEN Thackett's advice a week prior, and started his long cross-country drive within an hour after the call had ended. It had been a good decision considering that all travel was shutting down.

A few days before starting his voyage, Lenny had taken out Senator Schill with a sniper rifle while the man was walking on his vast property in Oregon. The Massachusetts Senator, Diane Ward, had been spared, although the CIA had taken her away. She was lucky: he'd had big plans for her – he was supposed to have made "a statement," as he'd done with the other senator. She'd pleaded with him, saying that she didn't know that the Chinese were going to use their virus research against the US. That was either naivety, or a lie, and Lenny would have gladly carried out the original plan either way. But she'd revealed important information, and then those at the very top had been taken down – including the Vice President of the United States.

There weren't just threads of corruption in the government, there were massive arteries that branched into finer and finer capillaries that spanned the entire establishment. Lenny had ripped out an artery – the one responsible for many horrible things, including the viruses that were spreading and mutating. But there were many other high-volume vessels of corruption, and there weren't enough people to find them all.

On Thackett's recommendation, Lenny had rented a van and made his way west, despite travel restrictions. Along the way, he'd picked up things he'd need: non-perishable foods, bottled water, medical supplies, water filtration systems, electric and gas heaters, heavy clothing, camping equipment of all kinds, flashlights, batteries, two radios – one with a crank charger – and a hunting rifle. He also bought a second laptop computer and a couple of burner phones with extra batteries. All of this was just in time, as people were hoarding supplies and businesses were shutting down.

There was heavy snow in the upper Midwest, so Lenny took a

route through Tennessee and Arkansas, and turned north in Oklahoma.

Thackett had told him, definitively, that those ships in orbit about the Earth were of alien origin. There were thousands of them, and their intentions were unknown, but likely hostile.

Lenny needed to get out of town anyway, and there was no reason to await destruction in a ratty hotel room. Besides, it was best to get away from the population. Even though he'd contracted both viruses, they were both mutating, and becoming more contagious and deadly. Experts were saying that people who had contracted the original versions might not be immune to the mutated ones.

He made his way through Kansas and Nebraska and, while in South Dakota, he picked up a few more things – five-gallon buckets, a small television with an antenna and a large spool of cable, and a coffee maker along with 40 pounds of coffee. He also acquired a few bottles of spirits – whiskey and vodka.

In Grand Forks, North Dakota, he exited the northbound interstate and headed west on Highway 2. Although the temperature was already below zero Fahrenheit, the snow accumulation was light – just a dusting on the ground, which was going to work in his favor.

He arrived at midnight, parked the van in a ditch, and found the same patch of barbed-wire fence that he'd broken during a previous visit. It hadn't been fixed, which was a good sign.

The area looked different. It was bleak. It looked like a wasteland of dormant trees, and the bright, pale light of the moon gave it an ambiance of desolation. He supposed it was fitting.

The lack of snow was important since he wouldn't leave tracks inviting some curious farmer or deer hunter to follow them to his hideout.

The access code of the missile silo had not changed. When he climbed down the shaft for the first time, he was startled to see that the vintage 1980s computer consoles and display monitors were illuminated. Evidently, they had been activated remotely due to a change in threat status – it was wartime. This silo, however, contained no missiles. It had been of an experimental design that had been deemed obsolete and taken offline two months after it had been commissioned.

With a hand truck and a new winch, Lenny made a half-dozen trips back and forth from the van to the bottom of the silo. It was hard work going up and down the densely wooded hill riddled with thorny vines, back and forth through 150 yards of dead grass and clusters of pine trees, and, finally, descending and ascending the deep shaft.

By 5:00 a.m. he was exhausted, but everything had been unloaded and stowed in the enormous underground structure.

He then took the van a mile and a half due south and found a patch of pines in a shallow ravine about 75 yards down a dirt access road. He parked it deep inside the trees so that it couldn't be seen from the main road, and was barely visible from the dirt access lane. He then locked the van and headed north, through the woods, by foot.

By the time he got to the silo entrance, the sun had started to rise. He took one last look before he started his final descent down the shaft. There had been numerous times in his dangerous life that he'd thought he might not again see the light of day. However, this time was different.

When he got to the bottom, the space was warm, and the lights were on. He'd have power in the silo to the very end: if the underground launch sites lost power, it meant the world was on fire.

He watched as the enormous concrete cap slid into position overhead and extinguished the last sparkle of sunlight.

An unusual feeling of sadness overtook him. Seeing that light go out felt like his eyes had closed for the last time. It was up to others now: those who were in charge of defending the Earth, and those who were inside those ships.

WILL WATCHED in awe as some outside force guided the beamer along the lower surface of the disk and toward a circular aperture that he figured led to a hangar.

He was still reeling from the epiphany of the emblem on the bottom of the ship.

As the beamer passed through the opening, he could hardly believe the vastness of the interior. The bay had to be a square mile in floor space and hundreds of meters tall. There were at least a thousand spacecraft parked in rows of cubby-style slots.

"Maneuvering functionality restored," *Gwen* announced. "Taxiing guidance on forward monitor."

A green line appeared on the screen. It weaved through the maze of spacecraft storage cubbies and terminated on the floor level, inside a green circle. Will navigated along the path, landed the beamer, and looked out the window for movement but didn't see anything. The ceiling was at least 100 stories above him.

"Well, I suppose I should get out," he said. "What's the pressure and temperature outside?"

"The exterior environment is the same as that on the surface of the Earth, including the air composition and the magnitude of the gravitational force," *Gwen* replied. "The temperature is 72 degrees Fahrenheit."

Perfect. "Open the hatch," he said.

He stepped onto the platform in the cabin, which then lowered to the floor of the hangar. He hopped off the lift and onto the smooth floor, looked around the massive space, and admired the other craft parked inside their individual cubbies. Some resembled his beamer but looked more advanced, though he had no way to really know.

There were other ships parked on the hangar floor. He was tempted to walk over to the closest one, but then thought better of it. He was surprised, and somewhat confused, that his ship hadn't been surrounded the instant it landed.

A sound came from behind him, and he whirled around to see what was there. It was a man – humanlike. He was tall, looked fit and young, and wore a black uniform. His hair was dark and short, and his eyes were large for his head. He had no weapon.

The man walked up to him and held out his right hand.

Will reached out, grabbed it firmly, and shook.

"Welcome home, Captain Kutinia," the man said, looking him in the eyes, and then let go of his hand. "Or do you prefer Captain Thompson?"

"Home?" Will stared at him for a few seconds, confused. "You know who I am?"

"I do. And now, after all of this time, so do you," the man said. "I'm Captain Chendar – you can call me Kendan. Welcome aboard the starship *Genesis*."

"You can call me Will," he said. It was a Delta emblem he'd seen on the underbelly of the vessel. It was the symbol that appeared on all Delta ships: it served as their flag. "Is this a warship?"

Kendan nodded. "The best we have," he said and nodded to Will's beamer. "Looks like you could use an upgrade."

"Just to confirm," Will said. "This is a – "

"A Delta ship? Yes," Kendan said, and smiled. "And I represent the Deltas' interests. I am not a biological Delta, although I look exactly like the original Captain Chendar. I'm AI."

Will had to be careful – it was impossible to tell what was real even with the "older" Delta technology of the *Exodus 9*.

"I take it that the original Captain Chendar has gone 'beyond the horizon' with all of the other Deltas," Will said.

"Well, not all of them have gone," Kendan said. "You are still here."

"And you leave no one behind," Will said.

"You are here, now, because of Landau," Kendan said. "He has been roaming this existence for as long as you have – looking for you."

Will was taken aback. "You know Landau?" he asked.

Kendan nodded and grinned.

"Perhaps he can now move on as well, if that's what he chooses," Will said.

"That is what I will choose," a voice boomed from behind Will, making him flinch and turn around.

It was Landau. He looked just as he did aboard the *Exodus 9*.

"But there are still a few things to do before I move on to that next place," Landau continued.

"Landau, what are you doing here?" Will asked. "How did you get here? Are you real?"

Landau smiled. "I was 'real' aboard the *Exodus 9,* as well," he said.

"Why did we wait – why didn't we come here right away?" Will asked, a tear welling in his eye. "Why was I aboard the *Exodus 9* for so long – and going in the wrong direction?"

Landau grinned. "You were never going in the wrong direction," he said. "It wasn't that you needed to close a distance, it was that you needed time. Time for you to figure out who you are, and to prove it."

It was all becoming clear to Will. "That's what this was all about," he said. "Proving my identity – recovering the code."

"Indeed, and there was only one way to get it," Landau said.

"I had to die," Will affirmed.

"And be regenerated – something you couldn't do on Earth," Landau said. "It was the only way your soul could recapture information from your past lives. And you did it – you took the leap."

"It's still not clear what happened to you 40 thousand years ago," Kendan said. "You were lost, your ship was lost – no trace to this day, and you hadn't gone over the horizon. They were calling you the 'Fallen Angel,' or the 'lost light.'"

"Wait," Will said. "How could you know that I hadn't gone over the horizon?"

Kendan looked to Landau.

"Because I went there to look for you," Landau said.

"I don't understand," Will said. "I thought you couldn't come back – that it was a one-way trip."

"For you, it would be," Landau said. "But I'm not a Delta. I'm something else."

Will felt a chill move from the middle of his back to the bottom of his skull. "What are you then?"

Landau shook his head. "It is time for you to verify who *you* are, one last time."

"Why?" Will asked. "And why are all of those ships arrayed around Earth as if they're setting up to destroy it? And what's happening to Mars?"

"One question at a time," Landau said as he smiled and held up his hand. "Proof of your identity – your soul's identity – is crucial. You are a Delta soul integrated into the body of Earth's current generation – into a human body."

"So what?" Will said.

"If proven true," Landau explained, "your accident has modified the development of this generation – altered everything from their DNA to their souls, even though it had a very diluted effect. You have existed there through hundreds of lives. You've had offspring, and your offspring have had offspring, for over 40 thousand years. There is no way to identify them all, but it's likely that nearly every human on the planet can be traced back to the Deltas – to you."

"So how does that change anything?" Will asked.

"It makes them Deltas," Kendan replied.

"And the Deltas claim custody of them," Landau added. "In better terms, the Deltas are their legal guardians."

"But the Deltas are gone," Will argued.

"No, they are not," Landau said and grinned. "There's one left."

"What about the Regenerators?" Will asked. "What about their negative judgment of our generation? They were going to destroy us."

"And rightly so," Landau said. "You were destroying each other. Although it's not uncommon for developing species at your stage, this was worse: someone had developed separation abilities. Until you, first as Captain Saul W. Kelly and then as William Thompson, there were only a few occurrences of evanescent phenomena – but those were unconfirmed religious events."

"We were sentenced to destruction for this?" Will asked. "Why?"

"It is a mark of a diseased species for evanescent abilities to be brought forth prematurely through immoral means," Landau explained. "And the disease must be contained, and not allowed to infect anything on the outside. You were fortunate that, in the Regenerators' assessment, your generation was far from achieving interstellar travel. However, and most importantly, we can now prove that it was an original Delta – you – who activated the probe in the Southern Seas."

"A Regenerator contingent will arrive in six hours to witness you projecting the code," Kendan said. "It will be indisputable proof, and we will then negotiate actions to be taken upon the Earth."

"What kind of 'actions' are you talking about?" Will asked. "Are they still considering regenerating the planet?"

"I don't know," Landau replied.

Kendan touched his ear indicating that he was receiving information of some kind, and then glanced at Landau and Will. "A ship from Earth has left the atmosphere," he said and grinned. "It has a primitive bender drive – extremely old technology."

Landau raised an eyebrow. "It seems someone on Earth discovered an operable ship," he said. "Is it armed?"

"It has modest weapons, but they are not online, and neither are its shields," Kendan replied.

"Are you going to talk to them, or bring them in?" Will asked.

"We will not communicate with it," Kendan said. "It's currently confronting our starship *Galesevere*."

"Another warship?" Will asked.

Kendan nodded. "Same class as the *Genesis*," he said. "They're going to trap the ship and return it to its launch site. Do you think they have more?"

Will shrugged. "I didn't even know they had this one," he replied.

"You have some time before the Regenerators arrive," Landau said. "Perhaps you'd like to rest for a while – you must be tired from the journey."

Will shook his head. "I don't need to rest, but I could use a shower and some fresh clothes," he said and looked to Kendan. "And some food. Is that possible?"

Kendan smiled. "Captain Thompson, I don't believe you fully understand your status here," he said. "We have some comfortable quarters ready for you, and we can meet when the Regenerators arrive."

Will needed some time to think and try to understand what was happening. He was also worried that he wouldn't be able to project the access code when put on the spot. His mind was healthier than it had ever been, and his memory was razor sharp, but telepathic projection was a different kind of thing, especially since the access code came from, literally, another lifetime.

As Will walked with Landau and the Captain through the hangar, he couldn't imagine a scenario where more was on the line.

"THE SHIP JUST LANDED BY ITSELF?" Jacob gasped as he stared at the main screen in the control room.

Thackett nodded. "We couldn't talk to the pilot while he was inside the craft – it's shielded from radio waves – so we didn't know why he was coming back," he explained. "When he landed – at the very place from which he'd launched – he told us that the craft just moved on its own after he got into space and approached one of the ships."

"Can he try again?" Daniel asked.

Thackett shook his head. "The Custodial Group informed us that the ship somehow deactivated after it landed," he replied. "It doesn't float anymore – it just sits on the ground – and the lights on the consoles are off."

It sounded like a case of remote override. "What do we do now?" Jacob asked, hearing the anxiety in his own voice.

Thackett shook his head. "I don't see anything that we can do, other than wait," he said. "The Chinese and Russians are on standby to launch missiles, but we're going to ask them to stand down, as will we."

Although Jacob thought that anything they did would be futile, he couldn't shake the feeling that he should be doing something.

Land-based phone lines and station-to-station calls still worked on the Earth's surface, and he was going to call Pauli. After that, he'd spend his time studying the technical drawings of the transport facility at the Antarctic base and see if he could learn anything that could help them in their last hours.

It would be his own way of fighting until the end.

ONE OF THE crew members of the Delta starship *Genesis* who, Will knew, was a fabricated entity like those he'd encountered on the recreation decks of the *Exodus 9,* escorted him to his quarters. He knew she was there, in that form, for his own benefit, as was Kendan, the captain. They were there only to facilitate communications. The ships were otherwise autonomous and had no need of a crew.

Although he didn't have time to contemplate the matter, he was more confused than ever about who Landau actually was – he had no idea of what "something else," as Landau had referred to himself, could even be.

After he had a shower, he found clothes in a drawer in the bathroom. It was a uniform – similar to the black attire that Kendan had been wearing – at the captain's rank, but with a few other ornaments of unknown meaning to him. There was one emblem, however, that he knew stood for the Delta fleet's Liberation Wing – which Lux had commanded at one point.

He donned the uniform and shoes and looked at himself in the bathroom mirror. On one hand, he hardly recognized himself. On the other, his image looked strongly familiar to him.

The meeting was in an hour and Will had some time to stew in his anxiety. He found a computer screen embedded into the countertop in the kitchen area. He got an idea.

"*Genesis* computer?" Will said.

The screen illuminated and a voice said, "Yes, Captain Thompson, how can I assist you?"

"I assume you have access to Earth data," Will said. "Can you locate someone for me?" He wondered how advanced the *Genesis* computer was compared to the *Exodus 9*'s. After 40 thousand more years of development, he figured it might exceed the trillions of minds of the *Exodus 9* by many orders of magnitude.

"We have all Earth data," *Genesis* replied. "Who would you like to locate?"

"Denise Walker," he said. He expected her to be in one of two places: Chicago or the DC area. Although, knowing her, she could be anywhere – even Antarctica.

"I am saddened to tell you that the Denise Walker with whom you interacted while on Earth is deceased," the computer reported. "She was pronounced dead in an underground government facility called Site 4 – in close proximity to Area 51, in the Nevada desert."

Will's mind froze and black spots obscured his vision. His heart and throat immediately knotted in pain as if they were being wrung like a dishrag.

"What?" he finally managed to say in a raspy whisper. "How?"

"The Earth is currently experiencing multiple pandemics," the computer explained. "Two human-altered viruses that were modified for bio-warfare have mutated and are spreading at an exponential rate. Ms. Walker succumbed to the deadliest one – a modified smallpox virus."

"Fuck!" Will yelled. "Fuck!" His vision flashed to dark thoughts of what he was going to do to those who were responsible.

"The government of China released them both," *Genesis* added. "However, there were numerous contributors to the knowledge and resources used to create them, including the governments of the United States, Canada, Russia, Iran, Finland, Syria, and others."

"Fuck!" Will yelled again. "Who else – what about Jonathan McDougal? Is he okay?"

"He is alive, and in the same facility, S-4," *Genesis* replied.

"And what about Daniel Parsons, Sylvia Barnes, and James Thackett?"

"All alive, and in the same facility."

Will paced back and forth in front of a couch. "It would have been nice to have had a window," he muttered.

At that instant, the entire wall on the far side of the room became transparent – or it was a display screen. His welling tears distorted the light of the glowing, blue Earth that lit up the room.

If he'd known that Denise was dead, he wondered if he would have even come back. What would have been worse – living an eternity not knowing if she were dead or alive, or living an eternity knowing that she was dead?

"What about my parents?" he asked.

"Alive, still residing in your childhood home."

"And my sister and her family?"

"All alive and well."

His watch buzzed: he was due in the main briefing room in 15 minutes, and an escort was waiting for him just outside his quarters.

He took a sip of water from a glass on the kitchen counter, next to the computer screen, and headed for the door. Just before he got there, he turned, and asked, "When did Denise die – how long ago?"

"The death certificate indicates that she passed away 22 days, four hours and 17 minutes ago," the computer replied.

"Damn," he said. It was going to be nearly impossible to concentrate.

Will took in a deep breath and exhaled slowly. He resolved to pull himself together. What awaited him would be the most influential event in human history – an event with final, existential consequences.

AS WILL ENTERED the meeting room, he stopped abruptly and stared as his mind took in the scene. The place was brightly lit, and all of the surfaces were white, including a long conference table in the center, giving the place a sense of purity and formality. The domed ceiling was high, and the entire far wall was a window filled with a view of Earth overlaid on the blackness of space.

There were three human-like beings – two males and one female – seated at the table with their backs to the window, facing him. Like the Deltas, their eyes were larger than usual, but their irises were especially large and multicolored with radial streams of brilliant green and blue. All three had dark hair and olive skin. They wore white uniforms, each with a set of symbols and designs on the shoulders and chest that Will figured had something to do with rank and function.

Seated on the near side of the table, to his left, were four people in black Delta uniforms, one of whom was the captain of the *Genesis*, Kendan, and three others – a male and two females – who Will didn't recognize. And then there was Landau, to the far left, looking out of place for both his age, and his attire. He was wearing loose, white clothing, and his long, gray-white hair and beard were disheveled. It made him look wise, like an ancient Greek scholar.

They all stood as Will approached, and Kendan introduced everyone before they retook their seats. Will sat in a chair on the far right, next to one of the female Deltas. The three in white were a contingent of high-level Regenerators.

One of the Regenerators, who went by the name "Ratha," started the conversation.

"This meeting has two parts," she said. "The first is a presentation of the evidence. The second will be final decisions."

It sounded like a trial, Will thought.

Ratha looked to Will, and then to the Deltas. "This is the 'Lux' of whom you have spoken?"

"Yes," one of the female Delta officers, named Felinia, replied.

"And your proof?" Ratha asked.

"As presented in the briefing materials, he knows the Delta access code of Luxen Ulti Kutinia of Saronelle 5, and he carries a Delta DNA marker," Felinia explained. "Samplings of the current Earth generation show elements of this same marker."

Will glanced at Felinia and made a note to ask her later how they had gotten those samples.

"And it is your theory that Lux was lost on Earth as the Deltas set up an escape plan for the next generation?" Ratha asked.

Will thought the question was loaded with allegation.

"Our reasoning and intentions are well documented," Felinia replied. "We lost billions of our people when you destroyed our planet. And we could not regenerate them. Later, we made the decision to help the next generation when they were ready, so that such a travesty would not be repeated."

"But the next generation got access to the technology you placed upon the planet prematurely," Ratha said. "And you say the reason for this is your fault?"

Again, Will didn't like the tone of the question.

"There was an incident," Felinia said. "And it seems that the DNA and soul compatibility of the next generation – which you seeded – was too close to that of ours. It is our contention that Lux was killed when his spacecraft either crashed, or was attacked, and his soul incarnated into a newly conceived human."

"Attacked?" Ratha asked.

"We have records indicating evidence of anomalous spacetime-imploding activity, consistent with a gravity spike or disruptor weapon, in the vicinity of Lux's disappearance," a male Delta named Tarkin explained. "It's in the briefing."

"These details are irrelevant at this point," Landau said.

By the expressions on everyone's faces – if Will's interpretation of those nonhuman expressions were accurate – it seemed that Landau commanded respect from both sides.

"The point of the matter is that Lux's soul propagated throughout the human race for over 40 thousand years," Landau continued. "It means that those who are on Earth are part Delta, and the Deltas now claim them as their own."

"But the Deltas have fully developed and moved on," Ratha argued.

"Clearly they all have not – there's one right here," Landau argued. "And I would contend that there are billions on that planet behind you."

The Regenerators conferred for a minute and Ratha said, "We need proof that he is Lux."

"He knows the access code," Felinia argued, "and can project it telepathically."

"In our understanding, that is only a part of the required proof," Ratha retorted. "It seems the real Lux would know the accompanying distress code as well. It is highly unlikely that an imposter would know both."

Will felt the back of his neck itch as he broke into a light sweat.

"Perhaps we should start with the valid access code," Ratha said. "Do you have a projection receiver device available?"

"*Genesis,* open a projection identification scanner on the table," Kendan ordered.

An opening formed in the center of the table and a clear, spherical device about the size of a bowling ball emerged.

"Will?" Landau said and nodded toward the device. "Go ahead."

Will envisioned himself boarding his beamer, which required the telepathic projection of his access code. After thirty seconds, the ball projected a white beam of light onto Will's chest and a voice emanated from it, which said, "Confirmed identity." This was followed by "Luxen Ulti Kutinia of Saronelle 5." The voice then reported a long Delta Citizen Identification Number, which was associated with Lux, but was more like a Social Security Number – not the access code.

Ratha nodded. "And the distress code?" she said.

Will didn't know how to recover the distress code – or if he ever even knew it. It was true what the Regenerators said: the real Lux would know both.

"I think I might be of some help here," Landau said after Will struggled in his mind for almost a minute. "As you know, when under duress, Delta's are conditioned to automatically project the distress code in place of the valid one. The difference between the valid code and the distress code is in the last 100 characters, some of which are numbers, and others which are symbols from the Delta language or geometric shapes. Young Deltas must memorize those 100 characters."

"He should therefore be able to telepathically project the distress code," Ratha said.

"Or perhaps recite it – at least the final 100 characters," Landau said.

Will was wondering what Landau was getting him into – he had no recollection of any other codes.

"Agreed," Ratha asked and then looked to Will. "Can he?"

Will looked to her and was about to admit that he couldn't when Landau spoke.

"He won't have to," Landau said.

"What do you mean?" Ratha asked.

Will, and everyone else, looked to Landau with anticipation.

"As you know, for the most part, memories of previous lives are only carried back when a soul is regenerated," Landau explained. "However, it is not uncommon for small, disjointed fragments to leak into the minds of those who have been reincarnated."

"But those are most often unrecoverable," one of the male Regenerators argued. "And unreliable."

"True," Landau said. "However, this is a case where they were unknowingly recovered."

"Explain," Ratha said.

"William Thompson was brutally tortured for 40 days and, a few times on each of those horrific days, he was asked to recite a number," Landau explained.

Will shuddered at the memory of it.

"He was being asked for the Delta access code?" Ratha asked.

"No," Will said. "I was told to read a three-digit number that was out of my field of view – they were trying to force me to separate so that I could see it. They forced me to guess."

"The first few days he guessed numbers with which he was familiar, including his inmate number, digits from his phone number, his social security number, and so on," Landau explained. "But after that, he started guessing numbers that came to his mind after some deep internal contemplation."

"And, you can imagine," Felinia said, "he was certainly under duress at the time."

"Agreed," Ratha said. "Torture would certainly qualify, and might incite the release of the distress code. Where is this leading?"

Felinia called for a video monitor, which then appeared in midair to Will's right, at the head of the table. A video of him inside the

Exoskeleton appeared. He looked horrible. And he looked old. He hadn't seen himself that way for a while.

In the video, he heard someone ask him for a number, and he gave them one. Three digits: 4-9-7. It was wrong. And then he seemed to convulse and scream. He'd been shocked.

Will wanted to vomit, but he couldn't stop watching.

The video skipped forward to the next instance of the number guessing. This time he saw his eyes turn white before he answered. It was wrong again. Shocked again.

This happened over and over, and the last number he gave was four digits instead of the required three. A voice scolded him over the intercom, and Will received an extra-long shock that seemed like it would never stop.

The video then stopped, and the screen went blank.

"That was horrible, and we sympathize with him," Ratha said. "But what's the relevance of this?"

Landau cleared his throat and then proceeded. "Starting with the number he gave on Day 12 and ending with the final four-digit number you just saw, you end up with these 64 digits," he explained as a long sequence of numbers appeared on the screen. "Do you know what these numbers are?"

Ratha seemed to grin. "Why don't you explain it to us, Landau."

"It is highly unusual, but the situation warrants it," Felinia said as a sequence of strange characters along with the symbols the Deltas used as numbers appeared on the screen. "This is the last portion of Lux's distress code."

"If you extract all of the numbers – ignoring the shapes and other characters – and put them next to the numbers Will recited in the Exoskeleton ... well, you can see for yourself," Landau said as the two number sequences were placed side by side.

The Regenerators seemed to gasp. The numbers exactly matched.

Will wanted to scream in elation, but instead just smiled.

Ratha looked at Will. "You are certainly a tortured soul," she said as her large eyes seemed to turn glassy. "Why would you want to go back there?"

It was a good question. It reminded him of Denise, and that it wasn't clear to him whether he even wanted to go back anymore. And he knew that he still might not. "I'm not entirely sure," he replied. "But I don't want to be responsible for their destruction."

"In light of this evidence, we contend that the current inhabitants of Earth are officially Deltas," Felinia said. "They should be allowed to progress as if the probe had not been actuated."

Ratha shook her head slowly. "Because of this incident – Lux incarnating as a human 40 thousand years prior – they are now genetically more advanced than they would have been naturally. They will develop separation abilities before they have progressed to an acceptable intellectual level," she explained. "Under such conditions, they will likely destroy themselves, and, if not, they may eventually contaminate other species."

"What if we had a plan to accelerate their intellectual and philosophical development?" Landau asked.

Will spun his head and looked at Landau. *What did that mean?*

"What kind of plan?" Ratha asked.

Landau rested his elbows on the table and laced his fingers together. "Let me explain."

WHEN DANIEL LEFT his office and headed toward the main operations room, people were bustling about in a panic. His first thought was that they were being attacked.

Sylvia caught up to him, and then skipped and jogged to keep up with his fast-paced walk. "What's happening?" she asked.

He grasped her hand tightly and pulled her through a crowd that was forming in the main command room. Every screen had a view of space, a few thousand miles above the surface. Some had colorful images filled with tracks – thousands of lines leading toward Earth – and others showed real-time pictures of the colossal spacecraft that were approaching.

"Are they invading?" Jacob asked from behind them, out of breath.

"I don't know," Daniel replied. "But they're just 700 miles above the surface now."

Jonathan emerged from the crowd. He must've arrived before the others since he'd been near the front, close to the video displays.

"They seem to be decelerating," Jonathan said and pointed to one of the monitors. "The giant ships further out are moving in behind them. Maybe they're just reconfiguring."

Daniel didn't like any of it. Although, he thought he'd prefer that they invade rather than start the radiation process.

WILL LISTENED as the discussions commenced. They were a combination of negotiations and orders, both with aspects that he liked and disliked. But it was also a trial.

Denise's death loomed in the back of his mind the entire time, but he was able to suppress his emotions as he realized he seemed to be playing a part in deciding the fate of humanity. He then recognized that he'd been playing a part in that decision for 40 thousand years. What happened now, however, was no longer something that had just existential "implications." This was the final act.

In the end, Will had a new respect for the Regenerators.

Ever since his encounter with the Judge inside the probe, he'd figured that the Regenerators were ruthless bastards who dominated lower species as if they were pests. As it turned out, they acted more like conservationists.

They'd cultivated life throughout the universe, keeping civilizations isolated until they evolved enough to both survive away from their home planet and to not be a plague on everyone else that was already out there. Even with their oversight, however, wars still waged between civilizations that had taken a "wrong turn." The Deltas had not been one of those belligerent species, and that was why, along with Landau's influence, the Regenerators had agreed to meet Will. It was the first direct meeting between the Deltas and the Regenerators since the Deltas' judgment on Earth.

The Regenerators were convinced that Will was the so-called "fallen angel," as the Deltas had argued. Will was Lux, who was a Delta, and had influenced the development of the current generation. In addition, it was only Will who had shown separation abilities, albeit in different lives. The question, however, was whether humans were still redeemable, and that's where some of their recent actions helped tip the scales.

First, although they'd been on the brink of world war when the Regenerators had arrived, they'd immediately halted those operations and instead cooperated in working against a common threat. This wasn't unusual for any complex, geopolitically fractured civilization, but it offered hope. Next, although it was a small act, the alien ship they'd piloted toward the incoming fleet had no armaments or shields. This, together with the fact that no nuclear missiles had been launched into space was enough to convince the Regenerators to give them another chance.

Will thought the Regenerators' final assessment was enlightening. They'd concluded that the technological level of the human race was currently far above its intellectual and philosophical state. This could have been caused by numerous factors, however, there were two that were most prominent. First, the Delta influence provided by Lux through his inexplicable incarnation into the human species had evolved in a way that was most practical to the survival of a young species: technology for protection and war. However, the most crucial, and premature, leap had been made by an utter fluke.

Humans had gone nuclear too early. It was something that the Regenerators viewed as a double-edged sword. Humans had used nuclear weapons once – or twice in close succession and in the same conflict – and that was a mark against humanity. However, they'd not used them since, and that was an indication that they'd learned from the consequences of their actions. At least that was the argument.

The question, however, was who was responsible for the development of the first nuclear weapon? Most people would say that the United States was responsible for its premature emergence into this world. That was not, however, how the Regenerators saw it. To them, it was Adolf Hitler who had been responsible.

Had the United States not been forced into the Second World War, the Manhattan Project would never have existed, at least not in its enormous scope. However, since the Nazis had been pursuing a nuclear bomb, the US and the allies had been under immense pressure to beat them to it. Without such a threat, no country would have been willing to expend so much effort and resources to obtain an atomic bomb. Had this not occurred, nuclear weapons might not have emerged for another 50 years, or even a century.

It had been a "fluke" for a few reasons. First, it took a vast amount of money and resources to develop the bomb – resources that most countries would not have, nor be willing to spend, even under peaceful conditions. Second, the country that had the required resources also needed a large area, devoid of their general population and safe from enemy forces. The US had these things. Finally, there had to be an urgent need for such an enormous effort, and that had been provided by Hitler.

The Regenerators were well aware of the first use of the weapons, and the devastating, long-term consequences, but had not made a judgement either way as to whether it had been justified. What they did judge, however, was its subsequent use, which had not occurred other than in the form of the Cold War, which was inevitable. That the Cold War had never turned into a "hot" one, was another mark in the positive column for the human race.

Another link to Hitler was the Nazis' Red Falcon project, which directly caused the premature transformation of Saul W. Kelly, as well as that of Will. After all, the American Red Wraith project would not have existed if it weren't for Hitler's Red Falcon, which had induced a response similar in scope and urgency to that of the Manhattan Project.

It was enough. Earth would not be regenerated. But then the negotiation phase started.

They had to decide what to do with the human race. Things were complicated further since humans now had unequivocal evidence of the existence of advanced extraterrestrial life, and this would affect their development. Once this was known, most underdeveloped civilizations would allocate a disproportionate amount of effort and resources toward space travel and weapons, rather than toward the healthy development of their species – intellectually, philosophically, medically – toward the general improvement of the quality of life.

These things, together with their already abnormal development due to the Delta contamination, had to be remedied somehow. Humans had to fill in the gaps in their evolution to catch up with their overdevelopment in other areas that included technology and the propensity to become evanescent too early.

A plan was brought forth by the Deltas and Landau, and agreed upon by the Regenerators. It was genius.

The next thing to decide was what to do with Will. He couldn't be allowed to reincarnate again in the human race. It was therefore recommended that he no longer reside on the planet.

It upset Will, but that dissipated when he realized again that Denise was gone. He'd miss the rest of his family, but they must have thought he was dead for a long time now. They were likely over the grief, but he'd have to carry his own about them and Denise for a long time to come.

He first concluded that he had no reason to go back to Earth. But then it struck him that maybe he did.

Will made his arguments and pleas to the Regenerators, completely off-script from the Deltas' plan. In the end, based on a promise made by Will, they agreed to his conditions.

It was the female Regenerator, Ratha, who then walked around the table, shook his hand, and kissed him on the cheek. "Just keep your promise," she said and smiled.

Will intended to.

17

REVENANT

WITH THE BEAMER FULLY CLOAKED, WILL DESCENDED THROUGH THE atmosphere and went to an altitude of 3,000 feet above the Pacific Ocean, just off the eastern coast of Hawaii's Big Island, Hawai'i. He then headed for the West Coast of the US at tremendous speed.

Ten minutes later, he flashed over Los Angeles and was over the mainland. After another five minutes, now above central Kansas, he decelerated and banked north.

"Destination on viewer," *Gwen* said.

It was 2:00 a.m. local time and there was no moonlight. The cemetery was dark – almost black – and that darkness seemed to seep into his heart. What he was about to do was the material of nightmares, but he figured a few more wouldn't make much of a difference for him.

"See the plot?" Will asked.

"On screen," *Gwen* said. "There are two places with newly broken ground, but the highlighted one is the one you want."

A single cemetery plot was illuminated in white on the screen.

"Let's go," he said.

The beamer pressed through the barren branches of the cemetery's numerous old oak trees and levitated about ten feet above the ground, near the plot.

Will unstrapped from his seat, grabbed a shovel and a pickaxe that he'd fabricated while onboard the *Genesis*, and then descended from the beamer and stepped onto the frozen ground. The temperature was well below freezing, and there had been a light snow but nothing that would prevent him from carrying out his deed.

He set the tools on the ground, went to the headstone, and took a knee in the snow. It was hers. He didn't know exactly when she'd been buried, but it had been over three weeks since she'd died.

Will separated, ascended about twenty feet above the grave, and searched for lingering souls. His thoughts electrified when he spotted one behind the thick trunk of a tree. He went to it.

His hopes were squelched when he got a closer look. It was an old woman, her soul evidently keeping the appearance of her last physical existence. He went to her.

"Ma'am?" he asked.

The woman came out from behind the tree and stared at him. Her eyes were wide with fear.

"Ma'am, can I speak with you?" Will asked as he went to her. She didn't flee.

She seemed to study him. "Are you an angel?" she asked.

"No ma'am," he replied. "I'm looking for someone. Why are you here?"

"I'm waiting for someone," she said and darted through the cemetery to a large headstone.

Will followed.

Carved into the stone were two names: Theresa Clair Johnstone and Donald Thomas Johnstone. Based on the dates, it had been three years since Theresa had died at the age of 91. Her husband was still alive at 95.

"Are you waiting for him, Theresa?" he asked. He still didn't understand why some souls didn't immediately move on to their next existence, but there was a lot that he didn't understand.

"Yes, I am," she said. "What's your name?"

"I'm Will," he replied.

"You're here for the young lady, aren't you?" Theresa asked and then dashed to Denise's grave.

Will followed.

"Did you see her?" he asked, trying to keep his composure.

"I did," she said. "A wonderful soul she was. She was good company for a while."

"She's gone?" he asked, as he felt his soul start to collapse upon itself.

"I asked her if she was waiting for someone, too," she said. "She told me that the one for whom she would have waited was already gone."

"How long has she been gone?" Will asked.

"I do not have a good concept of time," Theresa said. "But there was no snow when she left."

As he started to go back to his body, she stopped him.

"You know, no one is ever really gone," she said, and then smiled and winked at him.

It was as if she sensed his anxiety and sadness.

"I believe that, too," he said and returned to his body.

Will lifted the pickaxe from the snow and hammered its long, pointed tine into the frozen ground.

IT WAS hard digging at first, but the grave was relatively fresh, so the deeper ground was unfrozen and loose. Nonetheless, it was slow going, as the amount of dirt that needed to be removed was greater than Will had anticipated.

His heart pumped harder and harder as he got deeper. *Gwen* lit the area but also shielded it from outside view. He imagined some poor sod coming along and witnessing a man from a spaceship digging up a grave. The thought made him laugh out loud for just a second. It was just the kind of morbid humor the situation called for.

After two hours of digging, and about five feet down, he struck something solid. It was concrete.

He'd anticipated this, as he'd done a bit of research before embarking on this macabre venture. Modern graves required a concrete vault – essentially a cement box – in which the casket was placed. The purpose of this was, first, to make sure that grave sites didn't collapse when heavy equipment such as lawnmowers drove over them and, second, to make it difficult for someone like him to unearth them.

After clearing off the lid of the vault, he went into the beamer and brought back four long straps and a crowbar. He wedged the edge of the crowbar under the lid at one corner and pried it open about an inch. He then slipped a loop at the end of one of the straps around the exposed corner.

After repeating the process on all four corners, he brought the loose ends of the straps together above the center of the lid and connected them to a single metal ring. Will then instructed *Gwen* to hover above the grave and lower a cable via a winch from her underside. He then hooked a clasp from the end of the cable to the ring, and then climbed out of the hole while the beamer lifted the concrete lid.

As the tension in the straps and cable increased, the sound of concrete rubbing on concrete gave him chills, even though he was still sweating from the laborious excavation. As the massive lid tipped and twisted under the lifting force, one of the corners of the vault below it cracked, and a chunk of concrete fell inside and clunked on something.

Gwen then extracted the lid and lowered it into the snow a few meters from the hole, and Will removed the straps. When he returned to the grave that the beamer illuminated from above, his heart seemed to tear itself apart in his chest. Inside was a beautiful white casket, now with a ding on the top from the brick-sized piece of the vault that had fallen on it. He dropped to his knees and stared at it. It had gold trim and handles, and he imagined how distraught her family must have been as her pallbearers, probably with her father and brother leading them, had carried her away.

Will grabbed the four straps from the vault lid, climbed into the hole, and secured them to the handles of the casket, two near the front, and two at the back. He then climbed out of the grave and watched as *Gwen* raised the casket and set it upon the snow, next to the vault cover. Finally, he removed the straps to get access to the casket's lid.

Next was the part that he dreaded most – the place from which the nightmares would be born. He promised himself that he'd be strong. What he was doing had to be done – at least in his mind – even though it might all be for naught.

He went back into the beamer and retrieved what was essentially a body bag, and a large, metal hex key with a crank handle, like that used to open some types of house windows. His pre-mission research had been crucial.

He went back to the casket and located one hole on its side, near the front, and an identical one near the rear. He got down on one knee, inserted the hex key into the rear slot, wiggled it until he felt that it was properly seated, and then started cranking. As he turned the key, the rear portion of the casket's lid lifted, and a narrow gap formed. He continued until it was fully released. He then repeated the process on the front portion, and then stood, stepped back, and stared at the casket.

A voice emanated above – from the beamer.

"Will, daybreak occurs in two hours and 17 minutes," *Gwen* said.

There was no time to dawdle. He still had to put everything back in place.

The lid was split into two parts, and Will lifted them together.

She was in a white dress, covered with wilted flowers. She looked innocent, and ill, but not dead, even though he knew she was.

A faint smell of nasty chemicals came from inside, along with an even weaker smell of decay.

He unzipped the body bag and spread it open on the ground.

He then went back to the casket, slipped his arms underneath the small of her back and behind her knees, and lifted her out and into the fresh, cold air. She was lighter than he'd expected. He then turned and slipped her feet into the bag, and gently lay her on her back.

"Oh, Denise," he said as he sighed and looked at her.

He then zipped the bag, gathered her into his arms, and brought her into the beamer and lay her on the padded bench.

In the next two hours, he replaced the casket and the lid of the vault, and then refilled the grave. He appreciated that it was much easier to fill in than it had been to dig. Next, he got *Gwen* to blow surrounding snow over the area so that no one would suspect anything had happened. He was sure that grave robbing was something of the past, but it was best to leave the area looking undisturbed.

As he was heading for the beamer, he stopped and turned around. "Denise Walker, if you can hear me, you need to follow me darlin'," he yelled. "Wherever I go, follow me."

And then he yelled, "Theresa, if you see Denise, please tell her that she needs to look for me – Will Thompson. I'll be near the moon."

Will got into the beamer, and they headed for the *Exodus 9*.

THE *EXODUS 9* WAS DECLOAKED, and in orbit around the moon. It was keeping its distance from the action near Earth for the time being.

Will brought Denise's body to Greta, the medical specialist, who assured him that she'd have a new body in a few hours.

It wasn't the new body that worried Will, it was whether Denise had already reincarnated, or moved on to a new place – beyond the horizon, perhaps.

Will was exhausted.

He went back to his quarters, ordered some food, and sat by the window and looked out at the moon. It was enormous, and he could see every crevice and crater with clarity. The hue of the light made him feel a sense of isolation and coldness, like being lost in the middle of a vast forest in the middle of a moonlit, winter night.

He contemplated the ramifications of his actions over the past 12 hours. Was he doing the right thing? Would Denise have wanted to be brought back?

It didn't take him long to conclude that he'd made the right decision. His actions had only given her options. She had other choices. He also knew that, even if she regenerated, they'd still likely be apart. She'd want to go back to her family, which was only right.

After finishing his chicken and vegetable soup, he returned the bowl to the kitchen and came back to the window with a whiskey. He was going to have some time to burn while the Deltas – or their artificially intelligent proxies – hashed out the final details of the next phase of their mission, and there might be some time before Denise's soul found its way to her regenerated body, that was, if she were to return at all.

In the meantime, he'd engage in the same activities as he had before getting back to Earth. If he didn't have things to distract him, he'd be thinking about Denise constantly.

What the Deltas were planning, and what the Regenerators were allowing, transformed his deep concern about Earth's future into excitement. The process was beginning, and he almost wished that he could participate as an average Earthling.

Earth's future was settled. His own, however, was not.

DANIEL WAS SUFFERING from boredom and anxiety, which were complicated even more by feelings of claustrophobia at the thought of being confined hundreds of feet below the surface. The alien ships had not moved in over two weeks and, just as he was starting to think that maybe humanity should just get back to "normal" life and ignore the visitors – a crazy idea – things started to happen.

He got the call at 5:30 p.m., and followed Sylvia to the main CIA war room.

Thackett spotted them and rushed over.

"Looks like the invasion is starting," Thackett said and pointed to one of the screens. "About 250 ships are descending as we speak."

"Where are they going?" Sylvia asked.

"Seems that they're distributing evenly over the surface of the planet," Thackett replied. "There are 18 headed for US territories – mostly toward unpopulated areas."

"Can we see them – do we have any cameras in those areas?" Daniel asked.

"Fighter jets have been scrambled around the world," Thackett replied and pointed to some smaller screens on the adjacent wall to the left. "And we're getting images from everywhere."

The ships were lowering through the atmosphere unlike any other spacecraft Daniel had seen. There were no flames, no shaking, no glowing trails of any kind. They were lowering gently. And they were enormous.

They were black disks, about a mile in diameter. Although they weren't nearly as large as the monsters that were still in space, they by far dwarfed anything ever made with human technology.

Everyone watched the main screen as a ship descended upon the supposed alien crash site in Roswell, New Mexico. Daniel now knew that extraterrestrials really had been responsible for that mysterious event in 1947. The Custodial Group had the spacecraft to prove it.

"Fitting, isn't it?" Daniel said as he turned to Sylvia. He got a glimpse of her horrified expression before she responded to his comment.

"It's practically a statement," she replied. "You think they know our history?"

After what he'd experienced in the past year, Daniel thought it was more than probable. "I do," he said.

"You think they're the Regenerators?" she asked.

He shrugged. "Could be anyone. I'm not sure of anything anymore."

It occurred to him that more had happened in the past year and a half than he could ever have imagined. First, he'd witnessed a man separate his soul from his body. Next, the world had been judged and condemned to extinction by some outside entity. Then, the entire world had been infected by deadly viruses that were killing millions.

The US and China then went to war, starting a world conflict that was only averted because the planet was now being invaded by extraterrestrials. Everything had existential implications.

As the ship lowered to the sandy field at Roswell, gigantic cylindrical stems emerged from its underside and burrowed into the earth. They were black, like the ship, and there were over 50 of them, equally spaced around the perimeter. They held the ship about 100 feet above the ground.

"Looks like they plan to stay for a while," Thackett said.

Footage appeared on other screens of ships landing all around the world – including on desert islands in the middle of the Pacific, and on the ice in the polar regions.

Sylvia pointed to a screen that showed a video taken by someone on the ground in Roswell. A woman had recorded the event with her cell phone. The ship was completely silent – no noise at all until the outer stems burrowed into the surface. People on foot, and some on dirt bikes and all-terrain vehicles, headed toward it.

"Those people are going to get themselves killed," Thackett said.

But they didn't. The driver of a four-wheeler weaved around a stem support and then beneath the underbelly while his passenger behind him videoed everything. Not much could be seen, as it was too dark to make out anything in the shadow of the disk. They emerged five minutes later into the sunlight on the opposite side, unscathed.

A CIA analyst standing at a desk a few feet away pointed to a screen. "Director, the ships still in orbit are reconfiguring again."

Some of the ships in the original configuration had been sent to the surface, and the rest then redistributed to reform a uniform array around the planet. Something then occurred to him.

"What?" Sylvia asked and poked him. "You're smiling."

Daniel was unaware of his expression.

"If they were going to irradiate the surface, why would they set down a bunch of their own ships?" Daniel said. "I think we might be safe, at least for the time being."

It had been 15 days since Denise's body had been regenerated. It meant that she'd been dead for over five weeks. Will lost more hope with every hour that passed.

The *Exodus 9* was being upgraded by the newer Delta ships and was keeping Will informed of the progress. He found it amusing and comforting that the ships themselves interacted with each other. The *Exodus 9* had even commented on how "friendly" the other ships were, and that they were teaching her how to implement new technologies across the board – from propulsion to defense to maintenance. She'd also undergone a "processor upgrade," which she summarized in low-tech lingo for his sake as an "intelligence enhancement."

Gwen had also been upgraded and had communicated to him on numerous occasions that she wanted to go for a ride – and Will had obliged every time. They'd taken trips to the planets and played in the asteroid belt. When he thought about it in his old way of thinking, it was quite strange. On the other hand, it had given him a deeper and more profound appreciation for life. It didn't matter if it were in the form of a more underdeveloped animal, or in an artificially conceived intelligence, all life had its place and had a right to exist in this world.

The plan the Deltas were implementing for the human generation was magnificent. It was essentially a program that combined intellectual and philosophical evolution with societal guidance. In simpler terms, they were going to educate the human race and incentivize the development of an improved quality of life for their civilization. They'd soon be on the fast track to enlightenment. The current generation had a 10,000-year lease, after which the Regenerators would reclaim the planet whether its inhabitants were ready or not. It was not clear what would happen if humans were still present, but it would be best to be gone by then. Perhaps having a clock counting down would instill an urgency into humanity to embrace the opportunity and advance at a high rate.

In order to get things moving, and to build trust between humans and the Deltas' AI proxies, the latter had a peace offering. It was the vaccine-cure for the viruses that were killing millions and paralyzing the planet. And, folded into it – in the same pill – were the cures for numerous older viruses that had been plaguing humanity.

The Delta ships that had landed on Earth had purpose in both the long and short terms. In the short term, they were going to distribute doses of the cure at every landing site. Once the word got out, crates would be lowered to the ground, and whoever was there could pick them up and circulate them. A single dose – one tiny pill – would cure a human if they were currently infected, and otherwise protect them for a lifetime. The pill could also be dissolved in saline and injected. In addition, instructions on how to synthesize the vaccine-cure using known human technology would be provided.

Will thought such a thing might be viewed as either a miracle, or a threat to the human race. There would be conspiracy theories that went along with it, just as those which occurred with human-made vaccines, but the medical community could run it through its usual tests before distributing.

The cure, and the knowledge needed to fabricate it, was a perfect precursor to what was coming next.

The long-term plan was to bring human intellectual development up to speed as quickly as possible. The network of ships that now spanned the surface and low orbit of the planet would provide a wireless signal that would reach every nook and cranny of the world. The broadcast would follow the existing signal protocols of common communications devices, and would appear on everyone's computers and cell phones as a connectable network. It would show on devices as the "Knowledge Network." The password would be "LIFE."

One function of this network was to serve as an enormous, searchable database containing all the knowledge accumulated by the Delta civilization. However, not everything was going to be immediately available. In fact, most of it would still have to be "discovered" by the human race in some sense, which would be accomplished through a strict educational strategy in which new levels had to be "unlocked," in much the same way as new levels were accessed in video games.

The education would start in a format that was common to

modern Earth society, namely, in the form of classes – the virtual form. The technological fields that would be available first were biology and medicine, energy, and nutrition. The Deltas found these to be the most important and fundamental areas that had to be developed first. Once a predetermined percentage of people in every location on the planet had mastered a certain topic by passing assessments and evaluations – passing exams and completing hands-on work – the next level would be unlocked. The world would be educated as a whole, so that no particular factions could dominate.

In parallel to the education on science and technology topics would be psycho-philosophical development – something in which young Deltas were immersed from the day they were born. Will figured this was where evanescent abilities were cultivated, and creative thought was nurtured. In his specific case, torture had been substituted for this phase.

In order to unlock new categories, such as space travel and advanced energy production, other things had to be done. On the top of that list was the elimination of all weapons-grade uranium and plutonium. Such weapons were no longer needed since thousands of Delta ships were in the area to protect Earth from outside intruders, and there should no longer be any major conflicts between nations – at least that would be the case in the distant future. Along those lines, Will had been informed that two Delta, *Dominion*-class stations – the type that reminded him of the *Death Star* – would be located close to the solar system for comprehensive protection from anyone on the outside.

In Will's opinion, it would be rough going at first. Differences in religion, race, governance, and limited resources made conditions fertile for conflict and violence. The only hope was that new things would be produced that would improve the lives of everyone in a short time, possibly mitigating at least some of the turmoil.

The lessons administered by the Deltas on the Knowledge Network would be taught by artificially intelligent Delta beings – many trillions of them – who existed inside a computer on an alien ship. Will imagined a young child working one-on-one with a cartoon image that was his or her personal teacher – an AI being who would know their name and give them their complete attention. And later on, as humans advanced, these beings would present as three-dimensional images and then, much later, as physical beings, although still artificially intelligent.

During the planning sessions with the Delta AI proxies, Will had suggested that humans should be fast-tracked through a few pressing problems in order to give them confidence in, and appreciation for, what was available to them. In the field of medicine, they'd agreed on guiding them to develop cures for certain types of cancers, organ regeneration, and cures for heart disease, Alzheimer's disease, dementia, and diabetes. These, together with advancements in virus vaccines and cures, would get them going in the right direction, although they'd still be a long way from regenerating entire bodies and discovering the possibility of souls returning to them. There were some secrets that Will was trusted to keep, including the possibility of developing evanescent abilities – although that cat was already out of the bag to some degree.

Regarding energy, humans would first be guided toward nuclear fusion. Modern nuclear energy plants utilized the process of nuclear *fission* to heat water, create steam to turn turbines, and to eventually turn generators to produce electricity. Fusion was a process that humans had so far only utilized in bombs – very powerful ones. The first nuclear bombs were fission bombs. Later, in the 1950s, these fission bombs were used to ignite thermonuclear devices – hydrogen bombs – that employed a fusion reaction that released much more energy than that produced by a typical fission bomb.

The difference between a fission power plant and a hypothetical fusion reactor was that the fusion variety was both cleaner – no nuclear waste – and much more efficient. It was also safer – no risk of meltdown – and the fuel source was essentially inexhaustible.

Although the Deltas had moved far beyond fusion as a source of energy, fusion technology would solve the world's energy problems in the short term. It would also affect everything else – including food production and transport.

The Deltas estimated that, at their current level of technology, humans could accomplish the medical advances in about four years. Some things on that list, including heart disease and diabetes, would be solved in less than one.

Will found it interesting that, although they didn't yet know it, everyone, old and young, had an interest in advancing and improving humanity. A common argument used by some to explain their indifference toward the advancement of human society was that they'd "be dead" before there were any significant improvements or, on the opposite side of the coin, they'd be gone before things terribly declined. These people didn't know that they'd most likely be coming back. If they didn't go beyond the horizon when their bodies died, they'd reincarnate back into humanity – on the same planet. It would be the same when they discovered regeneration.

Working with the Deltas in devising the plan had a positive effect on Will's mind. It seemed that maybe he could make up for some of the damage he'd done. His mood, however, was still decaying as more time passed, and Denise did not return. He realized that he might have to live with her memory for a thousand years, or more. Although he knew that the melancholy would wane over time, in the meantime he'd have to distract himself. It was a good thing that the *Exodus 9* had everything he needed in that regard.

Will set up a soccer match and made his way to the field.

JACOB GOT the call around midnight and made his way to Thackett's office. The whole group was gathered around a small, round table, and there was a vacant seat between Jonathan and Sylvia.

"I brought my laptop as you asked," Jacob said to Thackett as he sat in the empty seat and set the laptop on the table. "What's going on?"

"Bring up your available wireless connections," Thackett said.

Jacob flipped open his computer and did as instructed. A long list of connections appeared. "Looks to be about 50 of them," he commented.

"Find the one labeled 'Knowledge Network,'" Daniel said.

Jacob found it and clicked on the link to get information but didn't connect. "Looks like it's strong."

"Connect to it," Thackett said.

Jacob connected and a message appeared on the screen that read, "Welcome to the Knowledge Network. This site will be activated in 8 days 17 hours 42 minutes 22 seconds." The seconds were clicking down.

"It's a countdown," Jacob said. "Where is this from?"

"We've traced it to those ships," Thackett said. "From both those on the ground and in orbit."

"What is it?" Jacob asked, even though he knew that no one knew the answer.

Thackett shook his head. "We hoped you could tell us something about it."

Jacob pulled up a wireless signal testing app on his laptop and initiated a diagnostic subroutine.

"It's fast, and it seems to accommodate all transmission speeds and encryptions," Jacob explained. "All I can say is that it's unusual. I can't add anything else until we access the network and do further diagnostics."

"The entire world is getting this," Sylvia said.

"The whole world?" Jacob repeated. It was intriguing.

"By the name, I assume they want to convey information to us," Thackett said. "But we find that a strange thing to do before actually contacting us directly."

"Well, they did send out a broadcast in all languages telling us that they had the vaccines," Sylvia said. "But that wasn't a conversation."

"And how are the vaccine tests coming along?" Jonathan asked.

"No side effects," Thackett replied. "And it has cured every patient in the test groups that had either of the viruses – they were all cured in less than 6 hours. And researchers are finding that it eliminates all kinds of other viruses as well. The order has been given to distribute it worldwide. The pandemics could end soon – it's just a matter of distribution. They could be over in a month."

Jacob thought this was a profoundly significant event. "I think we need to meet them," he said. "Time to see what this is all about."

"Maybe the Knowledge Network is how they're going to initiate the first conversation," Sylvia suggested.

"We're watching for visitors, or any communications in the meantime," Thackett said. "Jacob, I want you to try to probe this network thing – try to get inside."

Jacob nodded, but he knew it would be a futile exercise. The visitors, whoever they were, were far too advanced to be compromised by an Earth hacker. It would be like a raccoon trying to break into a locked car.

The task would suffice to keep his mind busy as they waited for that countdown to end. His state of mind had made a drastic change, from dread to relief. He was almost certain that it wasn't a countdown to an invasion.

THE SCORE WAS TIED 1-1 when Will took the field to start the second half of the match in front of an electrified crowd. They were playing in the magnificent Tottenham Hotspur Stadium. It was a hot afternoon when the game started, but the sun had since descended below the edge of the open roof, and the field was shaded for the second half.

Twenty minutes after resuming play, Will was about to take a corner kick when the crowd went silent. The announcer then said, "Will Thompson, please report to Biomedical Facility 82 at your earliest convenience."

It took a few seconds for the words to register in his mind. It then hit him what might be happening, and he sprinted off the field, toward the locker room.

He grabbed a towel as he flew past the lockers, into the hallway, and into the main mall where he hopped on a Tube. He dried himself with a towel and bounced on his toes as he rode.

Five minutes later, he ran out of the elevator and his cleats slipped on the smooth floor of the mall walkway, but he somehow managed not to fall. He jogged into the facility, past the front desk, and headed directly to the room in which he'd spent so many hours sitting next to Denise's regenerated body and talking to her as if she were actually present.

When he got into the room, Greta was waiting for him, smiling.

"Is she back?" he asked, hearing both the desperation and excitement in his voice.

Greta nodded. "All of the usual indicators of a successful regeneration are there – brain waves, face and eye movements, heartrate, breathing, and movements of extremities."

"How long will it take for her to wake up?"

"Another two hours, or so," Greta replied.

"Will she know who she is?"

"Didn't you, when you regenerated?" she asked

He recalled that it had only taken a few seconds for him to realize who, and where, he was. It had taken much longer, however, when he'd awakened after transporting from Earth.

He suddenly felt a wave of guilt and anxiety invade him. It was something with which he'd been struggling ever since bringing Denise to the *Exodus 9*.

"Is it possible for her to be sedated immediately after she wakes up?" he asked. "Can we be sure that everything is okay with her – that she's perfectly healthy, and that the regeneration was completely successful – and then move her?"

"Move her?" Greta asked. "Why?"

"Because I'm going to take her back to her family," he replied. "She cannot know where she is, and she can't see me. Understand?"

Greta nodded.

"Has she had all of her medical updates, and all of the genetic repairs, like I had?" he asked.

"Yes," she said. "And she's completely immune to all human diseases. She'll be perfectly healthy on the planet."

"Good," he said. "Let me know when she awakens, and confirm that it's really her and that she's okay. And then put her out again and get her ready for transport."

"I will," she said. "Are you okay, Will?"

"I will be," he replied. "Thanks, Greta."

Tears welled in Will's eyes as he hurried out of the medical facility and made his way back to his quarters.

LENNY SAT in one of the padded chairs in the command center of the silo and slurped piping-hot Raman noodles while he watched TV and surfed the Internet. It had been almost five weeks since he'd moved into the underground complex, and he'd only gone outside twice, each time to reposition the antennas for the TV and radio, and to adjust the satellite phone that he was using as an Internet link.

During those short stints, which had occurred just after midnight to reduce the chances of being spotted, he'd savored the freezing-cold air as it seared his lungs. It had reminded him of his younger years in the Soviet Union. The moon had been bright and high in the sky on those short excursions, illuminating the vast fields of snow and winter wheat. He'd taken a pair of binoculars to see if he could spot any of the ships in orbit. He'd found five glittering objects that he thought might have been spacecraft. The rest of the sky looked as usual, but it gave him an eerie feeling. He'd never look at the night sky the same way again. For that matter, a friendly sky of light blue filled with cotton clouds would have a hidden ominous element from this point forward.

The world was under siege. Or it seemed to be. Hundreds of alien ships had landed on the surface, and there were another 2,000 vessels still in orbit and further out. One of the ships had landed just 60 miles northwest of him, and he was tempted to make a trip to go look at it, but he decided against it for the time being. He would get all the information he needed while in the safe confines of the silo.

He had been frequenting the SETI website, where thousands of pictures of the alien ships had been posted. There were all different kinds, but few resembled his preconceived notions of what they were supposed to look like: they looked far more sophisticated and alien than he'd imagined. They were massive, and sleek, and it was rumored that they could change shape.

James Thackett had sent him a text just to inform him that the "aliens" seemed to be friendly, and that they'd provided a cure for the viruses, which seemed to be promising. Distribution had already begun in most countries. Lenny was still suspicious of it all.

The newest thing was that the ships were broadcasting a wireless signal called the Knowledge Network, which would go active in less than a week. The signal was available on all his devices.

In the meantime, he'd stay warm and try to enjoy some peace and quiet while he waited and watched from his bunker. Whichever way it went in the end, he was happy he'd be alive to see it happen.

WILL COULD HARDLY BELIEVE what he was doing. He thought it would drive him insane in the future but, somewhere deep within him, he understood that it was the right thing to do.

He lifted Denise from the gurney and gathered her in his arms as he stepped onto the beamer's lift. They ascended into the cabin, and he placed her on the padded bench. She was wearing the same type of white clothing that he usually wore when he was in his quarters. To him, they were more suitable as pajamas, and he'd started wearing jeans and T-shirts when he ventured around the ship. He was currently wearing a black Delta flight suit, which was almost as comfortable as the pajamas.

A few minutes later, they were off the *Exodus 9*. They'd made the trip from the moon to Earth in less than five minutes.

"You have the location?" Will asked.

"Yes, Will," *Gwen* replied. "We'll be in Clearwater momentarily."

They'd arrive around 3:30 a.m. Will had scouted out the location on a map the night before. Denise had grown up on a small farm in Clearwater, Kansas, a rural town north of the city of Manhattan, and her parents still lived there.

They came in low as they approached and skimmed above snowy fields that gently rolled between thick tree lines. The moon cast a ghostly hue upon the scene, but he smiled to himself when he realized that his current covert actions were not nearly as creepy as when he'd dug up her body in the first place. This was a much more pleasurable task, and he should be utterly elated that she was alive. Perhaps that was what he should focus on during the eternity that awaited him. That, and on the happiness that her family would soon experience.

The property had a long driveway of crushed, white stone that led north to a large, white farmhouse, which it passed on the west side. It then curled into a wide circle in the center of which was short, dormant grass dusted with a thin layer of snow. To the north of the circle was a sprawling metal building that probably housed farm equipment. To the west of the circle, opposite the house, was a gray, cedar-sided barn that had a horse stable on the ground level and a peaked hay loft above. To the north of the barn, and adjacent to the metal building, were two spacious horse corrals. About 100 feet to the west of the barn, out of sight of the house, was a thick tree line beyond which was a field that extended nearly a half-mile west. The driveway and the circular area between the house, barn, and metal building, were illuminated by bright lights mounted on each of the structures.

Gwen set down to the west of the barn, in a grassy area between a cluster of tall pines and the tree line that separated the yard from the rolling field of winter wheat. The lights were all out of sight, and the only illumination behind the barn was that of the nearly full moon.

When he lifted her into his arms, he felt her breath on his neck. She then twitched slightly as her arm fell to the side. He wanted to awaken her and take her back with him, but he knew he couldn't do that.

With Denise in his arms – she was noticeably heavier than the body he'd carried from the grave – he exited the beamer and took care to step only on exposed grass rather than snow so he wouldn't leave footprints. Unlike *Gwen*, he couldn't hover – well, not without a lot more practice.

He made his way to the rear entrance of the barn, which he was relieved to discover was unlocked.

He shifted Denise to free his right hand, and then grabbed the handle of the large, wooden door and slid it open a couple of feet. As he stepped through, he accidentally bumped Denise's head on the doorframe, and it made a light knocking sound.

"Sorry," he whispered, and grinned. She'd never let him hear the end of that one if she found out about it. Her head only had a few millimeters of dark stubble on it, which was quite a difference from the long, thick hair she'd had before all that had happened. It would grow back.

Some of the lights were on in the barn, and three horses stuck their heads out of their stalls to see what was happening. They grumbled and whinnied lightly. He figured they probably thought they were about to get fed. The interior smelled of hay, grain, and cedar wood shavings that he knew were often used for horse bedding, and there was an underlying odor of manure.

It wasn't very cold outside, maybe 35 degrees Fahrenheit, but he figured it was at least 50 degrees in the barn. Not far from the rear entrance was a stack of a half-dozen hay bales, and a large pile of loose hay. Four cats looked at him with drowsy eyes from different spots on the pile.

"Room for one more in there, guys?" Will whispered.

He lay Denise in the loose hay and packed some of it beneath her head to serve as a pillow. He then redistributed some of it to help her stay warm, but he had the feeling that the cats would pack around her after he left. He knew she'd awaken in about an hour, so it wasn't crucial that she be well covered.

When he was satisfied with her placement, he went to one knee and kissed her on the lips and then on the forehead.

"I love you, Denise Walker," he said. "Have a nice life."

He looked back at her one last time as he closed the barn door.

A minute later, he was heading for the stars.

GABRIELLA MARIA COSTA WALKER started the coffee maker at 5:15 a.m. and put two bagels in the toaster. It was a Monday, and the only appointment for the day was the farrier, who was due to arrive at 6:30 a.m. to trim the horses' hooves. It was going to be a mild, sunny day, and she'd put the horses out to pasture after their trimming to get some exercise. After that, it would be time to clean the stalls and carry out some other chores.

The floor creaked behind her as she rinsed out the dishes in the sink from the cherry pie they'd had the night before. Friends had come over to visit. That had happened a lot during the past couple of weeks, and she was grateful for it.

"I see you," she said as she looked at the reflection in the window above the sink. Michael, her husband of 39 years, had been stealing kisses ever since they'd met. He was a large man, and she sometimes felt as if she were being stalked by a bear.

She turned and faced him as he walked over and planted one on her lips. He hugged her tightly. "I thought you said the farrier wasn't coming until 6:30," he said as he relaxed his hold.

"Is he here already?" she asked as she turned and looked out the window.

The barn door was open and she spotted someone inside. She couldn't see who it was.

"Where's his truck?" Michael asked.

It wasn't there. In fact, there were no vehicles in sight since Michael always parked their own in the equipment building during the winter.

"Who in the Sam Hill ..." Michael hissed as he let her go and went toward the door. He suddenly stopped, opened a closet door to the left of the exit, pulled out a shotgun, and stepped out and onto the porch.

Gabriella donned a jacket from the same closet and followed close behind.

As Michael crossed through the driveway circle toward the barn, he angled to the right and peered inside. Gabriella edged to the right as well, so that she could see down the barn's aisle, between the horse stalls and all the way to the rear door. Someone was standing in the middle of the aisle and looking out at them.

"Hey! Who are you?" Michael yelled. "What are you doing in there?"

The figure, which was dressed in white and looked to have a shaved head, took a half-step toward them, and stopped. It seemed to study them.

"I said identify yourself," Michael said. "This gun is loaded."

"Should I call the police?" Gabriella asked as she pulled out her cell phone.

At that instant, a noise came from the barn.

"What did you say?" Michael yelled.

It was soft, and meek. But Gabriella heard it. It was a voice that she thought she recognized, but she couldn't place it.

"Mama?" the voice said more loudly. And then, "Daddy?"

The figure moved toward the barn exit, now just 30 feet away.

Gabriella looked closely. "*Dios mio,*" she gasped as her legs started to give out.

Michael rushed over and grabbed her arm just before she went to the ground.

"Gabby, what is it?" he asked and looked back.

"Mama?" the woman said.

"It can't be," Gabriella said. "It's her."

"It's who?" Michael asked. "It's who, Gabby?"

"Daddy!" the woman yelled but remained still. "Mama, Daddy, is it you?"

"It's Denise!" Gabriella screamed. "Look, it's her!"

Michael dropped the gun in the driveway and stared at the girl in the barn.

Gabriella fell to one knee and then stood again with Michael's help.

The girl from the barn walked out but stopped 10 feet in front of them.

She looked like their daughter, though younger, and her head was shaved. But Gabriella was sure it was Denise – the voice, the face. It had to be.

"Mama, Daddy, am I in heaven?" the girl asked. Her expression was that of panic and fear. "How did I get here?"

"Denise, is that you, sweetheart?" Michael asked and took a step toward her.

"It's me, Daddy," she replied. As she moved toward them, the girl stumbled but caught herself.

Gabriella and Michael rushed to her.

They embraced as three and cried together for what seemed like minutes until they had no energy to expel any more emotion.

When they separated, Gabriella grabbed Denise's face in her hands and asked, "How is this possible?"

"I don't know, Mama," Denise replied. "I was somewhere else, and now I'm here. I don't know what happened in between."

"You look different, honey," Michael said.

"What do you mean?" Denise asked.

"You look like you did when you were 16," Gabriella said. "And you shaved your head."

Denise rubbed her head with her hands and her eyes widened in confusion. "I don't know what happened, Mama," she said. "I just woke up in the barn."

"Let's get you inside," Michael said. "Are you hungry?"

"I don't know, Daddy," Denise said. "I don't know what I'm feeling."

Gabriella and Michael each grabbed one of Denise's arms to steady her as they made their way to the house. Gabriella thought for a moment that maybe they were all in heaven.

WHEN WILL LEFT KANSAS, he headed for the bright moon that had cast its pale light upon him as he'd carried Denise into the barn. He was shattered, but she deserved to be with her family, and they deserved to be with her.

It occurred to him that he should be able to see his family as well. They should know what happened to him.

He was on his way to the Sea of Tranquility. Something had been placed there during the first moon landing in 1969, and he was going to retrieve it. It might help him to convince the others when he visited them in a few days.

They set down about 50 meters from the original landing site of the Apollo 11 mission. He'd had second thoughts about desecrating a memento of such a historically significant accomplishment of humankind, but then realized that his actions were a part of that story – he was taking the next step in the evolution of human civilization.

Will donned a spacesuit that was so light that it almost felt as if he were wearing normal clothes. All life support components were positioned on his back, and the helmet was compact but comfortable.

The beamer had an airtight compartment in the rear, near the bathroom facilities, that was a pressurized load-lock system that allowed him to exit the ship without depressurizing the entire cabin.

When he stepped onto the moon's surface and felt the powdery, silt-like texture beneath his feet, he wondered what those first astronauts had been thinking when they'd done the same. It was amazing to him to think that they'd carried out such a feat using 1960s human technology. In Will's mind, humans had not accomplished anything of that magnitude since.

He felt odd as he started to walk. Gravity on the Moon was one-sixth that of Earth, and his first step was more of a leap than he'd anticipated. He minded his feet so as to disturb the site as little as possible as he approached. He was expecting to see a red, white, and blue American flag, but it was not that anymore. It was all white. Unprotected from the sun, the colors had bleached, and it conveyed a sad message in his mind. It was now the flag of surrender. And, since that flag had been planted, that is what had slowly transpired in the world. After landing on the Moon, the human race should have been inspired to move its civilization to the next tier of existence – to improve their quality of life. But it had gone painstakingly slowly and had even declined in some respects.

The area looked like an abandoned campsite, complete with human waste products – although packaged for easy disposal. He was looking for a nondescript box, and found it not far from the flag.

There were a few things in that box, but he only needed one of them.

The gloves on his suit were thin, and he could use his hands with their usual dexterity. He opened the box and found what he sought. Will would have it with him when he made first contact.

DENISE SAT at the kitchen table and stared at her parents. They looked back at her with a convolution of expressions that conveyed confusion, elation, and fear. Tears streamed down their cheeks, but they weren't crying aloud.

"What happened to me?" Denise asked, confused. Although bits and pieces of memories were coming back to her, she still felt like she was coming out of a dream.

"They told us you were dead," her mother replied, her voice trembling. "You *were* dead. I don't understand what's happening."

"We had a funeral for you over a month ago now," her father added. His voice cracked as if he were having difficulty maintaining his composure.

"Without a body?" Denise asked.

"There *was* a body – and it looked like you," her dad replied. "Well, sort of – you looked like you'd been through hell."

"Who was in the casket?" Denise asked. "And how did I get in the barn?"

Her dad shook his head. "I don't know."

"Should we call the police?" her mom asked.

"No, not yet," her dad answered immediately. "We don't know what they'll do."

"What do you mean?" her mom asked.

Her dad looked to Denise. "You don't look the same, honey," he said. "But I can tell it's you."

"What do you mean I don't look the same?" Denise asked. "You mean, other than the hair?"

Her mom went into a small bathroom near the door to the porch, returned with a hand mirror, and handed it to her.

Denise looked at it and couldn't believe her eyes. She looked like a teenager. Her skin was smooth and taut, and her eyes were somehow brighter. For some reason her attention was drawn to her teeth – they seemed the same, but straighter, and a tiny chip on the corner of one of her lower front teeth wasn't there. She'd gotten it falling off of her bike when she was 13.

"My God," she said. "Is this me? I mean, am I ... where did I get these clothes?"

She suddenly stood and pulled down her pants.

"What are you doing?" her mom gasped.

Denise examined her upper thighs. "There should be scars here – a big one on my left thigh and a smaller one on my right," she explained. "Where are they? What has happened to me?"

"You don't remember anything?" her mom asked.

"I was in the desert – in a secret facility," she said as she pulled up her pants. "I was very sick, and they were taking care of me. Did you guys get the viruses?"

"No, honey," her dad said. "But we're not worried about them now. They have a cure."

"You mean a vaccine?" Denise asked. "They said it would take over a year."

"It's both a vaccine and a cure," her mom said. "They say it came from the extraterrestrials."

"Extraterrestrials?" Denise asked, as her mind seemed to fragment and then try to piece itself back together. "What are you talking about?"

"There are thousands of ships in orbit around the Earth," her dad replied. "And hundreds have landed all around the world. They gave us the cure – the vaccines. They're being distributed in every country – and they work. Don't you know about the alien ships?"

Denise shook her head.

Her mom grabbed a remote control from a basket on the table and turned on a small television mounted on the wall to Denise's right. It showed a cable news station that was in the middle of a story.

The first thing that caught Denise's eye was the image of a gigantic, disk-shaped spaceship that had landed somewhere in Africa.

"It's enormous," Denise said.

"It's about a mile in diameter," her father said. "Some of the bigger ones – those still in space – are much larger. They say some are over 20 miles across."

Some things were coming back to her now. The image of the ship conjured memories of Jacob's reports of possible incoming spacecraft, and of Sylvia's predictions that UFO sightings were increasing again – something was coming.

A feeling of dark panic suddenly came over her. Those were probably Regenerator ships. For an instant she wanted to scream – they were here to exterminate all life on the planet – but she suppressed her fright. There was nothing anyone could do, and she didn't want to alarm her parents. "Have they communicated with us?" she asked. "What do they want?"

"Don't know," her dad replied. "But they did give us the cure for the viruses a couple of weeks ago. I would think – hope – they're friendly."

That soothed her alarm for the moment, although it confused her.

Other memories – if they could be called that – then came to her mind. There had been a tunnel with star-studded walls through which she'd been expelled into an immeasurably large space.

She remembered seeing a bright, circular conduit – like a pipe made of light with millions of glowing filaments growing out of it. Something had pulled her away from it and, after she'd moved in the direction of that tug for some time, she'd stopped, and looked back. The conduit had actually been a ring. She'd had a choice: go back to the ring or move toward a horizon that seemed to be infinitely far away. She'd seen a faint light over that horizon, and would have gone in that direction had something else not pulled her back toward the ring. It had been a feeling, and there had been a voice that had called to her. That's all she remembered.

"I think I might have been dead," Denise said.

Her parents stared at her.

Seemingly out of nervousness, or some sort of denial of what was happening, her mom asked, "Are you hungry?"

Denise stared at her while her brain tried to process the words. "No," she said. "But I'll try to eat something. I'm thirsty."

Denise was trying to determine if what was happening was real, or if she was just dreaming. Maybe she was still dead, and this was just her brain easing the transition into nonexistence. But she knew that she existed beyond her physical body – she knew it because Will had told her so.

And then she remembered: it had been Will's voice that had called her back.

IT DIDN'T TAKE the *Exodus 9* long to pinpoint the location of Daniel and the Omnis. They were underground, inside a secret facility in the Nevada desert. And now Will would make a surprise visit.

He'd explain what was happening, what was expected of them, and how to implement the Knowledge Network. After that, he'd decide what to do next.

DANIEL WATCHED the screen as a green trace descended through the atmosphere. He'd gotten the call just minutes prior, while he was having dinner with Sylvia. Jonathan was already there with Thackett when he and Sylvia arrived.

The object seemed to take a deliberate path that the computers extrapolated to a position near the tunnel entrance to the facility.

A security detail was awaiting the craft's arrival at the mouth of the tunnel, but was under strict orders not to threaten the ship, nor anyone who might exit it, in any way.

"That thing is really fast," Thackett said. "It will be here in minutes."

"Think it will just do a flyby?" Jacob asked as he rushed into the CIA's command center and joined them, out of breath.

"I don't see the purpose in that," Thackett said. "I think it's going to set down."

"Look," Jonathan said as he pointed to another monitor that showed live footage of the incoming object. It was black and smooth.

"It's tiny compared to the others," Jacob said. "It's a curved disk, although the sides are swept backward slightly. Looks kind of like a rounded stingray, or a Peregrine falcon."

Daniel agreed. "Sleek," he said. Unlike the larger ships, this one had no visible markings on it.

They watched as the craft darted in, and then settled to a position about ten feet above the sand.

"It's just hovering there," Sylvia commented after nearly a minute of everyone staring at it in silent anticipation.

At that instant, something lowered from the underbelly. It was a platform, and someone was standing on top of it. It looked human – a biped – and it was wearing a black uniform, or flight suit.

As the being stepped off the platform and onto the sand, a half dozen military personnel approached it. The being stopped and stood still.

The camera shot was too far away to see any details, and there was no audio, but they could tell that the being was trying to converse with the soldiers.

Thackett's phone chimed and he answered it. As he listened, his face seemed to show concern and then bewilderment. He ended the call and looked to the others.

"That was the security detail," Thackett explained. "The alien wants to speak with us."

"Who?" Sylvia asked.

"Us," Thackett replied. "You, me, Daniel, Jacob, and Jonathan."

"What?" Daniel blurted. "Why? How do they know who we are?"

"I guess we're going to find out," Thackett said. "Let's go."

Daniel was in a daze as he followed Thackett to the elevator.

WILL TOOK a few steps back toward his beamer as the soldiers watched him. He was impressed that they had not been armed with rifles, and that their sidearms remained in their holsters.

He admired the sun as it set and illuminated lines of high, thin clouds in a glorious, orange hue over the western horizon. The sky faded from orange to purple to black as his gaze panned from west to east, and the air was nippy. It brought about a wave of nostalgia. It was all real.

He was about 50 yards from the entrance when figures emerged from the tunnel. He could just make out their faces in the low light. He was happy they were all there – minus Denise, who was now alive and well in Kansas.

Will was certain that they wouldn't recognize him – he looked 20 years younger than he had the last time they'd seen him. They might, however, recognize his voice.

"Daniel, Sylvia, James," Will yelled.

The group stopped and squinted at him, seemingly trying to figure out who he was.

"Jacob, Jonathan," he said and walked toward them.

"Do we know you?" Daniel asked.

"I hope so," Will replied.

"My God!" Sylvia yelped. "It's Will!"

Will stopped ten feet away from them so that they could get a good look at him. He could see it in their faces that they recognized him, but couldn't convince themselves that the young face before them was that of the forty-plus-year-old man they remembered.

"How can this be?" Jonathan gasped, keeping his distance. "You look like you're 20 years old."

"A lot has happened since I transported from the base," Will said. "I'm glad to see that everyone got out of there before it melted down." Based on information collected by the *Exodus 9* since arriving, Will knew that had happened.

They all appeared bewildered but seemed to gradually accept that it was really him. They maintained their separation, however, and Jacob looked particularly skeptical.

"Jacob," Will said. "Remember how we first met?"

The others looked to Jacob who said, "Tell us."

Will explained how he'd defeated the security of the facility at 17 Swann Street using his separation abilities and surprised Jacob in his flat. "And then I separated and lifted you off the floor."

Jacob smiled and nodded slowly. "I was near the crossbeams – almost 15 feet high," he said. "It felt like my whole body was wrapped in duct tape."

Jonathan edged forward and stuck out his hand. "It's good to see you, young man," he said. "Maybe you can tell us what's going on here."

"Who's in those ships, Will?" Daniel asked. "Are they the Regenerators?"

They all looked at him with expectancy, and that's when Will noticed the trepidation in their eyes. His friends had been under enormous stress and anxiety for a long time, and it was carried upon their shoulders more than anyone else's – no one else really knew what was happening, or what *could be* happening.

"No," Will replied. He reached into an external chest pocket in his flight suit, extracted a thin metallic box, and handed it to Thackett.

"What's this?" Thackett asked as he took hold of it.

"Open it," Will said. "Carefully."

Thackett opened the box, squinted at its contents, and showed it to the others. "Is this what I think it is?" he asked Will.

"What is it?" Jonathan asked.

"It's a golden olive branch," Thackett replied and handed it to Daniel to pass around. It was mounted to a thin plaque. He looked to Will. "Is this *the* golden olive branch?"

Will nodded.

"It was placed on the Moon in 1969 by the Apollo 11 astronauts," Thackett explained to the others. "It represents a wish for peace between humanity and whoever we meet out there."

"I'd hoped this would serve as proof that I'd been there," Will explained. "But my feeling is that it no longer seems farfetched. It's also meant to assure you that all of these ships – on the surface and in orbit – have come in peace. I can vouch for them."

"I believe you," Sylvia said. "Who are they?"

"They're Delta ships," Will replied.

"They're Deltas?" Daniel nearly shouted as the others gasped.

"There are Regenerators around as well – you may have seen what they've been doing to Mars," Will explained. "But they will not harm Earth."

The stress seemed to leave all of their faces.

"You've handled yourselves well – no aggressive actions," Will said to them all, but directed his words to Thackett. "That had more of an impact than you will ever know."

Will noticed that Sylvia was shaking. Tears were streaming down her cheeks.

"Sylvia, are you okay?" Will asked. "Don't be frightened, I can explain everything."

Sylvia shook her head. "No, it's not that – I believe you," she said as she stepped closer to him.

Will reached out his hand but Sylvia stepped in and hugged him tightly.

When they separated, she said, "It's Denise, Will. She's passed away – she contracted the most deadly of the two viruses and – "

"She died, I know," Will said. "But she's not dead."

They all stared at him with expressions that conveyed confusion and, to some degree, pity, as if they were witnessing someone who was in denial. He wouldn't yet give them information as to her whereabouts so as to avoid any distractions from his primary task. He'd tell them more later.

"Perhaps we could go inside, and you could explain everything to us," Thackett suggested and then looked toward the beamer. "You need to do anything with your, uh, ship?"

Will turned toward the beamer and said, "*Gwen*, I'm going inside, you can close up for a while."

The beamer's lights flashed twice, the bottom hatch closed, and the craft lowered to a position about four feet above the sand.

"Is there someone else with you?" Daniel asked.

"No," Will replied. "*Gwen* is the name of my ship."

"Oh," Daniel said. He seemed accepting, but still confused.

They bombarded Will with questions as they made their way into the bowels of the complex.

DENISE WAS EXHAUSTED after a full morning and afternoon of talking with her parents. She had come clean about working for the CIA, and her relationship with Will. In her mind, the cat had already clawed its way out of the bag.

"This is the same boy you've been seeing?" her mom asked in a tone of skepticism.

It was true, at least in her mind, that she and Will, who was hardly a boy, had been "seeing" each other before he'd disappeared. After that, she'd sustained the story with her mom and sisters just to get them to quit bothering her about not moving forward in life which, to them, meant getting married and starting a family. Denise sensed that they'd all been skeptical of her story from the beginning, and thought that "Will" had never existed. Her mother was now giving her confirmation of that perception.

After some discussion, Denise convinced her parents to wait a few days before announcing her reappearance to the rest of the family. She had no idea what had happened to her, and therefore had no way of explaining it. It occurred to her that someone might accuse her of faking her death, being mentally ill, or both. But there had to be more to it than that – she looked like a teenager, her scars were gone, and the almost undetectable chip on her bottom tooth was no longer there. How could they explain that?

That's when she saw an entire conspiracy theory formulate in her mind. Her head flooded with images of people demonstrating outside her parents' house and throwing things at the windows. The next images were of her being arrested. And, who in the hell was inside the coffin? *What was she going to do?*

She'd taken a nap in the afternoon and had been in the middle of an avalanche of random dreams when her mom had woken her for dinner.

They ate chicken and dumpling soup as they watched the news on TV. Denise was fascinated by how calmly everyone was accepting the fact that thousands of extraterrestrial ships were scattered about the planet – on the surface and in space. Many, however, were still suspicious. They thought it was a hoax and believed that the ships had really been constructed by humans, and this was how the New World Order – the "one global government" – was being implemented. Many had also suggested that the so-called weather satellite test, where hundreds of objects – UFOs – had been spotted around the world, was just a precursor to this event.

Others were saying that the ships were really just a part of a global wireless system to provide Internet service to the entire planet, and that the signal was already being broadcast with a countdown leading to its official start time.

It was clearly a case of "crying wolf." Previous lies told by the government had induced so much mistrust within the public that they didn't believe anything at all. If the government said they were weather satellites, then they were aliens. If the government said they were aliens, then they were weather satellites. In the end, humanity had been prepared for nothing.

As they ate, her parents couldn't stop looking at her and she was starting to become uncomfortable. She felt that, at any moment, the police would barge into the house and take her away, saying that she had either faked her death, or was an imposter. Or that she was insane. This was amplified by the questions her parents were asking her about her past. They'd interrogated her about vacations they'd taken when she was in grade school, and volleyball trips in high school. It was as if they were probing to see if it was really her. She didn't blame them – even she wasn't convinced that what was happening was real.

"I want to tell your brother and sisters tomorrow," her mom said.

"Please, Mom, wait a few days," Denise said. "At least until the weekend when they'll be off work."

"I think we should get you checked out by a doctor," her dad said.

"What?" Denise asked. "I feel better than I ever have." It was something that she realized more and more as time passed. Everything seemed perfect – no aches of any kind, and she even seemed to breathe better, like her sinuses were porous sponges that saturated with air on every breath.

"We mean by a mental health specialist, honey," her mom added. "Your father knows the doctor who treated your cousin Javier when he got back from Iraq."

"Javier disappeared, remember?" Denise retorted. It was a horrible story. Her cousin had escaped from a mental health facility on Long Island while being treated for post-traumatic stress disorder. The rumor was that he had jumped into the Long Island Sound and drowned, but his body had never been recovered. "So you're trying to back up your argument by citing one of the doctor's failed cases?"

"Javier had other problems," her mom argued.

"He was in prison a few times after he got back from the battlefield," her dad added and then turned his attention back to the TV. CNN was showing pictures of the alien ships and giving descriptive names to the different types.

"And the doctor moved to Kansas City just last year," her mom said. "He's the younger brother of one of your father's friends from high school. It couldn't hurt to talk – "

"No," Denise cut her off. She couldn't believe it. "I don't need a shrink, look at me. Do I look different to you? Something happened to me. I'm not 17, Mom."

Her mother stared at her with a disoriented expression.

Denise realized that her parents were extremely confused, and she didn't blame them. It suddenly occurred to her that she had to contact Jonathan.

18

A PROMISE KEPT

WILL EXPLAINED TO HIS FRIENDS WHAT HAD HAPPENED TO HIM SINCE he'd last seen them. However, he left out many crucial things that he had promised, as part of the deal with the Regenerators, he would not share. Humans were to discover these things for themselves, albeit with the guidance of the vast knowledge that the Deltas had bequeathed to them.

He likened it to a kind of knowledge trust fund that had been carefully designed to parse out the treasure over time and with qualifying conditions. Everyone on the planet would soon be engaged in "classes" that would pave the road to redemption – a road everyone could access.

Will explained that the cure to the viruses was a "gift" from the Deltas to get things going, and to illustrate what was in store for them. There would also be some "low-hanging fruit" that they'd be able to collect in a short time, including cures to various diseases and conditions that had been plaguing humanity for centuries. The next level, however, would require certain actions, the first of which was to distribute the cures for these diseases worldwide and, at the same time, make sure that the world was fed. Next, all weapons-grade uranium and plutonium would have to be repurposed for nuclear energy generation, a process that the Deltas' knowledge would help them to vastly improve to make more efficient and safe. Will knew, however, that the modern fission reactors would eventually be replaced by fusion generators, but that was for humans to learn in time.

"What if countries decide to cheat?" Thackett asked. "Suppose they hide some weapons."

"Not likely," Will said. "Those ships around us will be monitoring – already are."

"And these courses," Daniel said. "We will be given exams to get to higher levels?"

"Yes," Will replied. "And, to unlock new areas, a certain number of people have to pass these tests."

"What if they just cheat?" Sylvia asked.

Will smiled. "I don't think you understand how advanced the Deltas' artificial intelligence actually is," he said. "Let me just say that it will be very difficult to cheat. And if it does happen somehow, the AI will adapt to prevent it from happening again."

"And the Regenerators are okay with this?" Daniel asked.

Will explained that the Regenerators were more like curators, or cultivators, of intelligent life, and worked to ensure that poisonous species didn't invade the rest of the universe. "And there's something else," he said. "Humans have 10,000 years to leave the planet for good. The Regenerators will wipe it clean at that point, regardless of whether or not they are still here."

"The level of technology needed to accomplish that is daunting," Jacob said, apparently skeptical. "Is that enough time?"

"I believe it is," Will replied, although he couldn't really know. "All the required knowledge is in those Delta ships – and you can get everything you need through the network. But it will require a strong effort from everyone."

After nearly four hours of discussing the implementation and operation of the Knowledge Network, the whole group went to a small cafeteria and got bagels and coffee. Will was hungry, but the flavors seemed a bit off to him. He'd apparently gotten used to the food on the *Exodus 9*. They bombarded him with questions as they ate.

"So you really transported from the base?" Jacob asked. "What was that like?"

"I just blacked out, and then woke up in the bay of a gigantic ship called the *Exodus 9*," he explained. "I required some medical attention, but they got me fixed up quickly."

"I'd say," Sylvia said. "Looks like you found the fountain of youth."

"And you can have the same," Will said. "It's all in the network."

There were so many things that he was not allowed to divulge that he found it difficult to connect with them. They didn't know that he'd died and regenerated. They didn't know that he'd lived hundreds of lives, and that his soul was that of an original Delta. And he didn't tell them that the reason they'd gotten into the mess with the Regenerators in the first place was because of him – because of what had happened 40 thousand years ago. They didn't yet really know about souls – they could only speculate. But it wasn't his place to reveal that piece of reality.

"What are you going to do now?" Jonathan asked. "Will you stay with us?"

Will shook his head. "I'm not sure what's going to happen with me," he explained. "There's still no tolerance here for an evanescent being. As you well know, that's what caused all of our problems in the first place."

Jonathan reached across the table, grabbed Will's hand, and looked him in the eyes. "You said Denise wasn't dead," Jonathan said. "What did you mean?"

"Denise is in Kansas," Will replied.

"That's impossible," Jonathan said. "I was with her when she passed away."

"Do you have a pen and paper?" Will asked.

Jonathan shook his head.

"I do," Daniel said and extracted a tiny notebook from his pocket which he handed to Will.

Sylvia looked to Daniel and raised an eyebrow.

"Hey," Daniel said and grinned. "You never know when an idea might strike you."

Will wrote something in the book, tore off the page, and handed it to Jonathan.

"What's this?" Jonathan asked.

"It's the phone number for Denise's parents," Will explained. "Don't call until after I'm gone."

Jonathan stared at the number and then looked to Will. "I'm supposed to call the Walkers and ask for Denise?" he asked. "How can I ask – "

"You could drive out to their place instead," Will said. "If what I say isn't true, and she's not really there, then at least you could visit with her family for a while."

"It's not that I don't believe you," Jonathan said.

Will smiled. "Please, Jonathan, I know," he said as he stood. "I'd be skeptical as well. But it pleases me that you're in for a pleasant surprise. But now it's time for me to go."

"Where are you going?" Sylvia asked as she stood.

"I'm not exactly sure," Will replied.

"Are you coming back?" Daniel asked.

"I'm not sure about that, either," Will said. "I will if I can. But that's currently an unknown." And it was something he intended to bring up with the Regenerators immediately.

Will hated goodbyes and didn't have the heart to tell them that a part of the deal with the Regenerators was him not living on the planet.

The group led him through the labyrinth of tunnels and elevators to the surface. After proper goodbyes, he got into the beamer and strapped in. He elevated to about 300 feet and backed away another 150.

"*Gwen,* can you flash your lights at them a few times before we head off?" Will asked.

"Yes, white light?" she asked.

"Yes," he said. "Three or four quick flashes – bright."

At that instant, the entire area illuminated in bright white, as if flooded with spotlights, and flashed a few times.

"A little too bright, but okay," Will said and laughed. "Let's get back to the *Exodus 9*."

"Aye aye," *Gwen* said.

Just seconds later, he was in the blackness of space.

WILL SPENT the next few days trying to distract himself from what was happening around him, especially concerning Denise. He'd played a soccer match each day and visited a number of "virtual" coffeehouses around the world. He'd been tempted to go to Earth and visit a real café, but that was off-limits.

He'd gone to the whiskey bar every night hoping to find Landau, but he'd never shown.

He finally concluded that he had to negotiate something with the Regenerators regarding Denise. She needed to know what had happened to her, and that he wasn't dead. But it was more than that. He realized that the current plan was intolerable and unsustainable. Some exceptions had to be made, otherwise he thought he might not wait very long to head for the horizon.

Will found *Gwen* and headed for the Delta starship *Genesis* to request a meeting with the Regenerators.

DENISE HAD SOMEHOW MANAGED to delay her mother telling her siblings about her return for almost a week, but time was up. It was Sunday, and everyone was invited for a light lunch and a heavy dinner. Denise was uneasy about them bringing her nieces and nephews, all between the ages of one and seven, although she doubted that the kids really understood the concept of death.

Denise was to spend the morning with her father getting supplies from a nearby town while her mom prepared lunch. By the time they were back, everyone would be there.

She didn't like the plan at all. She would have preferred it be broken to them in a more controlled manner, perhaps over the phone to start. At least then, even if they were skeptical, which they would be, they'd be afforded some time to mull it over.

One idea was to tell them that there had been a mix-up, and that the government agency for which she worked had misidentified the body. But that couldn't account for how she looked.

Her dad bombarded her with questions as they rode the 25 miles to the next town in his pickup truck.

"I don't understand any of it," he said, "but I really can't figure out how you got into the barn. Your mom had been in the kitchen for over an hour before you showed up and there had been a light snow that night. There were no tire tracks in the driveway, or anywhere else – I looked for them."

"I'm sorry, Dad," Denise replied. "I don't know anything. I've been trying to contact Jonathan, but I've not gotten through. He should be able to give me some answers."

After picking up grain, and bales of wood shavings for the horses' bedding, they stopped for sodas for the ride home. It was a routine from childhood that Denise remembered fondly.

They pulled into the home driveway at 12:40 p.m., and Denise's gut tightened when she saw the cars parked around the circle. Her dad seemed to notice her anxiety.

"Your mother has filled them in on things by now," he said. "I know this isn't going to be easy, honey."

He pulled the pickup into the backside of the barn and they unloaded the supplies. Afterwards, she rode with him as he parked the truck in the metal building, and then they made their way to the house.

Denise knew she should have been hungry, but she wasn't. As they climbed the porch, the high-pitched voices of squealing kids emanated from inside the house.

Her dad led the way through the door and, after she entered and closed it behind her, she stepped out from behind his wide shoulders.

There was complete silence as everyone stared at her, seemingly trying to assess whether it was really her.

After a few seconds, her oldest sister, Cynthia, gasped, "Oh my God, it *is* you."

Her younger brother, Thomas, rushed to her and hugged her almost hard enough to kill her. He was as large as her father and built like an NFL linebacker.

"I don't care what happened – I'm just so glad you're here," Thomas said into her ear. He kissed her on the cheek and then held her at arm's length. "I missed you, and I love you."

Next was her middle sister, Diane, who was already crying. She embraced Denise and then Cynthia joined them. They all cried together until their emotions were fully spent, and then they had to tend to their children who were crying because their mothers were crying.

Her sisters' husbands were there, as well as her brother's girlfriend, which made the experience even more awkward than Denise had anticipated. Everyone's expressions conveyed confusion and skepticism.

They gathered around a large rectangular table in the dining room that Denise and her dad had fitted with additional leaves that morning to accommodate the more than a dozen people, including the kids, who'd be eating there. It was a make-your-own-sandwich lunch, and her mom had arranged all the ingredients on the table. For dinner, it was going to be turkey, much like their traditional Thanksgiving meal, which was a good way to feed such a large group.

Denise sat in the middle of one of the long sides of the table, with her brother's girlfriend, Dana, to her right, and her younger sister's husband, Todd, to her left. The questions started immediately, the first coming from her oldest sister, Cynthia.

"So, where have you been?" Cynthia asked.

"Cynthia," her mother said in a scolding voice. "I told you, she doesn't know."

"I'd like to hear it from Denise," Cynthia said, looking at Denise with an expectant expression.

Denise knew it would be Cynthia who would start the interrogation, and she felt helpless as she didn't have any answers. "I don't know," she said.

"Who's in the casket, then?" Cynthia asked.

"That's enough, Cynthia," her dad said.

"I just want to know," Cynthia retorted and looked to Denise. "You look so different. Did you get some work done?"

"Lay off, Cindy," her brother said, using the version of her name that had always seemed to bother her the most. "Can't you tell that something serious has happened here?"

Denise had always been closest to her brother, and he'd always tried to defend her when they were kids, even though he was four years younger. The joke had always been that their parents had finally quit having kids when they had a boy. But Thomas had always replied by saying that they were going for another Denise, but failed.

That's when her other sister started.

"So where's your boyfriend? Will, is it?" Diane asked. "I don't recall seeing him at the funeral."

For the most part, Denise had gotten along with her older sisters, but she could see how their relationships could change with just a few words. Speaking about Will in that tone set Denise's mind into a fury, but she somehow maintained her composure.

"He's missing," Denise replied.

"Missing?" Cynthia scoffed. "You mean in the same way you were missing?"

"Not exactly," Denise replied.

"What happened to your ears?" Diane asked. "Weren't they pierced?"

Denise went into an internal panic. Her hair was under a centimeter long – so her ears were fully exposed. She'd forgotten; not only had her ears been pierced, but they were pierced in multiple locations – or they had been. But she knew that the holes were gone without even feeling for them.

"I let them close," Denise replied, even though she knew that it would take more than a few months for the holes to heal over, if they ever would.

"And the mole under your left ear?" Cynthia asked.

"I had it removed," Denise replied, defeating the urge to feel behind her ear.

"Since the summer?" Cynthia asked. "I saw it when you last visited."

That was enough. Denise's patience was over.

"What exactly are you implying, Cindy?" Denise said and glared at her.

"I don't know," Cynthia said. "Maybe this was all a ruse to get some cosmetic work done?"

"I would have to fake my death to do that?" Denise scoffed. "I see you people a few times a year, at most, and I would pretend I'm dead to get a few extra weeks? I could stay away for six months, and no one would question anything. You're an idiot."

Thomas laughed and looked to Cynthia. "That's quite a diabolical idea," he said. "Is this something you've thought of doing yourself?"

Cynthia's face reddened.

If Thomas had been sitting next to her, Denise would have kissed him.

The atmosphere of the family gathering was declining rapidly but was subsequently saved by the screams of a toddler who wasn't getting enough attention.

The conversations became lighter for a couple of hours and then, at 3:00 p.m., Denise went with her dad and brother to take care of the animals in the barn. An hour and a half later, they were all back at the table sipping hot coffee and talking about stories in the news – the so-called alien ships – and the conspiracy theories that accompanied them.

At five o'clock, a knock came from the exterior door in the kitchen.

Denise was confused – her entire family was already there.

Her mother went to the kitchen and Denise tried to listen in on a welcoming exchange between her mother and a man whose voice she didn't recognize. A minute later, her mom and a heavyset man in his 60s, with gray, wispy hair and round glasses walked into the dining room and remained silent. He seemed to scan the room and Denise sensed a reaction of recognition when he spotted her.

"Everyone," her mother announced, "this is Dr. Kellenbaum. He's a psychiatrist, and he's here to speak with us about what has happened."

Denise recognized the name as that of the shrink who had treated her missing cousin, Javier.

As they all said hello, Denise detected something smug about Cynthia's mannerisms.

Her mom then turned to the man and said, "Why don't you have a sandwich before we get started?"

Get started? Denise had a bad feeling.

THE ENTIRE FAMILY moved into the living room and took seats on the furniture that, unbeknownst to Denise, had been previously arranged in a circle. She sat on a couch that faced an upholstered chair on the opposite side of the circle that was then filled by a moderately overweight Dr. Kellenbaum.

She knew that what was to come could go one of two ways. First, the shrink might have been there to help the family as a whole cope with the idea that she'd died and then accept that she hadn't. She appreciated how much trauma and confusion such a thing could levy upon a person. The second possibility was that he was there exclusively for her, and that would not go well.

Her mother then revealed the direction in which it was going to go.

"Denise, Dr. Kellenbaum is here to see how you are doing," she said and then looked to Kellenbaum. "Shall we start?"

"What is this, an intervention of some kind?" Denise asked as her face became hot. It was one thing that they didn't believe what she'd told them, but it was an entirely different thing to be evaluated by a shrink as they watched.

"I'm not going to mislead you, Denise," Kellenbaum said in a voice that sounded like a professor leading in to tell a student that they weren't going to pass their class. "We would just like to make sure that you are not a danger to yourself, or to others."

"Do I look injured to you?" Denise asked. "Have I hurt anyone?"

"It's not about what has been done, but about what might be possible in the future," the doctor responded. "We're not saying that you would do anything intentionally."

"What, then, I'd do something by accident?" Denise retorted. "Or maybe in my sleep?" The urge was building to injure someone intentionally.

"When a person has a long span of memory loss, it indicates another problem – often a serious one," Kellenbaum explained. "And sometimes it can recur if nothing is done about it."

"Done about it?" Denise repeated. "Like what?"

"Before we get into that, maybe you could describe your experience," the doctor suggested.

"This really couldn't have been done in private?" Denise hissed, glaring at her parents, and then at her sisters. "And we have people here who aren't even immediate family." She was referring to the two husbands. Thomas' girlfriend was with the kids in an upstairs playroom.

"Maybe we should leave," Cynthia's husband, Charles, said to Todd, Diane's husband.

"No," Kellenbaum interceded. "It seems everyone in the family has been injured by this event."

"Injured?" Denise scoffed. "They didn't even know about it until today."

"But we thought you were dead," Cynthia chimed from a couch to Denise's right. "We have a right to know what happened, and to help figure out what needs to be done to remedy the situation."

"Remedy the situation?" Denise asked. "What the hell are you going to do to 'remedy' the situation?" She looked directly at her mother whose gaze lowered to her own writhing hands.

"Please, Denise," the doctor said. "Tell me what you remember."

"As I told them," Denise said as she glared at her parents, "I don't remember how I got into the barn. I just woke up there."

"What about before the barn?" the doctor asked.

"I was in a medical facility – I was sick," she replied. "I had the virus." Her hands moved from her knees toward her inner thighs, but she stopped herself. She remembered the burning from the rash, and could almost still feel it.

"And where is this facility?" Kellenbaum asked.

"In the Nevada desert – it's a government facility," Denise replied.

Cynthia seemed to stifle a gasp and Charles, who sat to her right, put his hand on her knee and looked down at his feet.

"Can you show us on a map?" the doctor asked.

"No," Denise said. "All I know is that we landed at a base and were taken somewhere by SUV – to an underground complex." Denise knew enough not to tell them they'd landed at Area 51.

"Why would they take you there?" Kellenbaum asked.

"They took our whole group there from DC – it was too dangerous to stay," Denise replied. "The Chinese were planning something – they released the viruses. That's why we went to war."

"I can't take it," Diane said as she stood and headed toward the dining room.

"I don't care that you don't believe me," Denise said as Diane passed. "And I'm not giving away any classified information."

"Classified information?" the doctor said. "What is this group of which you are a member?"

"I'm not an official member, and neither is Jonathan," she replied. "We were just subcontractors."

"Jonathan?" the doctor asked.

"She's referring to Jonathan McDougal, her employer," her mother said. "She's been working as a law intern in his firm for the past two years."

"I'm an associate, not an intern," Denise corrected. "And neither I nor Jonathan are currently working for the DNA Foundation. I told you, we work for the federal government."

"Have either of your parents met Jonathan?" the doctor asked as he looked to her mom, who shook her head.

"No, they haven't. What are you implying?" Denise asked and then looked at her mother. "Have you ever met Cindy's employer?"

"Can we call this Jonathan, maybe see what he knows about your situation?" the doctor asked.

"I've tried," she replied. "His line goes directly to voicemail." It had taken her a while to remember his phone number. She'd called over 20 times in the past days with no luck. She'd also sent him emails through his university account, but he hadn't replied. Denise had been locked out of both her personal and CIA email accounts, so she'd had to create a new one.

"How long have you been working for this group you've described?" Kellenbaum asked.

"On and off for about a year and a half," she replied. "Jonathan has as well."

"Have you tried to contact other members of your group?" the doctor asked.

"Impossible," she said. "You need special access to do that."

Denise could tell from her parents' expressions, as well as those of everyone else in the room, that they weren't believing any of it.

Kellenbaum readjusted his posture and wheezed a little as he leaned forward and put his elbows on his knees.

"Have you been to Antarctica, Denise?" Kellenbaum asked.

"What?" she replied. She was stunned by the question. "Why do you ask that?"

The doctor looked over to her mom.

"Sorry, honey," her mom said. "You were talking in your sleep – rather loudly. And you were crying, too. I wanted Dr. Kellenbaum to know as much as possible before we met."

Denise had never felt more betrayed nor angrier than she did at that moment. These people knew nothing of what she'd been through during the past two years. She'd seen things that she'd never be able to tell them, not only because they were classified but because they would think she was crazy and try to lock her up somewhere. Which was exactly what she thought was happening.

"Well, have you?" Kellenbaum asked.

"I'm not answering any more of your questions," Denise said and looked to the others. "And no more of yours, either."

The doctor sat back and propped his left foot on his right knee. "It would really be in your best interest to cooperate," he said with a smug expression. "Your parents have taken great care to have me meet with you before the police get involved."

"My best interest?" Denise hissed and looked to her parents' solemn faces. "Police? What are you talking about?"

"Faking one's death is a serious crime," the doctor said. "If it can be explained by some mental episode, or even a medical problem, you might be able to get past this in a few months."

"Get past this?" Denise repeated. "What does that mean?"

"I think some time in a mental health facility, with mild medications, would get you out of this fairly quickly," the doctor explained. "You don't seem to be hallucinating presently, and your parents haven't reported anything along those lines, except for the dreams, so it might be a temporary thing."

"You're trying to have me committed?" Denise nearly yelled at her parents. She had to try to remain calm even though her rage was reaching its explosive limit.

"It would be much better for you if you checked in voluntarily," Kellenbaum said.

"And if I don't?"

The shrink glanced at her parents. "Well, your family can initiate a procedure to commit you if you won't do it yourself," he explained. "All they have to do is argue that you're a danger to yourself or to others. And faking your death qualifies for either."

"I didn't fake my death!" Denise yelled.

At that moment, Diane walked back into the room and asked her mom to come to the kitchen, which she did.

Cynthia cleared her throat and raised her hand indicating that she had something to say.

"It's not just me who thinks that Denise has never been the same since she broke up with her fiancé," Cynthia said. "That was about the time she left and went to law school. It was just an odd thing to do at her age."

"At my age?" Denise scoffed. "I was 27."

At that moment, her mother rushed into the room and looked to her father. "There's someone in the barn," she said.

Thomas and her father stood and started toward the kitchen. The others followed.

IT WAS JUST about dinnertime and the sun was below the tree line to the west. The lamps on the buildings were flickering and starting to warm up in the waning, ambient light.

Denise stepped onto the porch and squinted toward the barn beneath the dark orange and purple sky. The stars were starting to show directly overhead, and the scents of earth and pines infused the brisk, still air. The barn door was open and light spilled out, onto the snowy driveway. There was some motion in the interior, and the horses grunted like they did when they were about to get fed. A cat ran out, but then stopped and watched the men as they approached from the house.

A silhouette appeared at the barn entrance. It was that of a man. Denise squinted to see if she could make out a face, but she couldn't.

Her dad and Thomas stopped, and then her two brothers-in-law, who were following a few steps behind, did the same.

"Who's in my barn?" her father yelled in a voice that she thought sounded deeper than usual.

The figure just stood still in the doorway and seemed to assess the situation. His head scanned around to get a look at everyone, including her, and her mother and sisters, who remained on the porch along with the shrink.

"Hey, answer me," her dad said. "Who are you?"

After a few seconds, the figure replied. "Are you Denise's father?"

Denise heard it, but the others whispered to each other as if they hadn't caught the words.

"What?" her dad asked.

"Are you Denise's dad?" the man repeated more forcefully.

Denise recognized the voice and stepped off the porch in a trance-like daze.

"Denise, what are you doing?" her mother said and grabbed the sleeve of Denise's sweater.

Denise yanked her arm free from her mother's grasp and started to walk. Her pace increased until she broke into a run, toward the barn.

"Will!" she screamed as she passed by her dad and the other men. "Will! Is that you?"

"Denise!" the man yelled back and started out of the barn.

Denise slipped on the snow and skidded into him as she tried to stop. He caught her. Before she knew what was happening, she was wrapped in his arms and bawling like a child.

She pulled her head away from him and tried to make out his face with vision blurred by tears.

"Is it really you?" she asked.

He cupped his hands around her head, looked into her eyes, and said, "It's really me."

WILL COULD HARDLY KEEP his composure. It seemed like years since he'd last seen her, but in reality, it had only been about five months. He was sure it felt longer because he'd thought for a long time that she, and everyone else on the planet, might have been dead. Strangely, in the relatively short time that had passed, they both had died and come back to life. They'd literally last seen each other in different lifetimes.

"Come inside," Denise said as she clutched his hand so tightly that one of his knuckles cracked. "You're just in time for dinner."

The four men who had been approaching him just stood still and stared as he and Denise passed. The same went for those on the porch. Will sensed some tension as she pulled him past everyone without introductions – or even a word.

She led him by the hand into the house, through a warm kitchen, which smelled like baking turkey, and through a dining room with a long table that was set for a large meal. Finally, they entered a room with chairs and couches arranged in a large circle.

She turned and looked at him.

"My God," she said. "You look like a college boy. Your hair almost looks blond. What happened to you? What happened to me?"

"I'll explain it all later," he replied and winked at her as the others filed in.

It was awkward as each of them passed and looked at him as if he were some dangerous, exotic animal.

"Are you Mr. Walker?" he asked the oldest man, who was also rather large.

As the man looked him over, Will held out his hand.

"Yes, you can call me Michael," the man said and shook his hand firmly. "We've heard some about you. You're Will?"

"I am," Will replied.

Michael then proceeded to introduce him to everyone else, whose individual responses were polite, but their eyes conveyed something else – skepticism and concern, and maybe even fear.

As everyone started to sit down, Will turned to Denise and pinched a bit of her dark hair between his thumb and forefinger, just above her ear, and pulled it. "Your hair's coming in nicely," he said.

Denise grabbed his hand and yanked him to a couch, and he sat to her left.

Another older gentleman came in from the kitchen with Denise's mother. He sat in a chair directly across from Denise.

"I didn't catch your name," Will said.

Before the man could answer, Denise said, "That's Dr. Kellenbaum. He's a psychiatrist."

"Oh," Will said. He'd sensed disdain in her voice. He looked to the doctor. "Friend of the family?"

"This little party is actually a psychiatric evaluation," Denise said in a sarcastic tone before the doctor could answer. She then glared at her parents for an awkward moment.

The reunion was not going as Will had imagined it. "Who's being evaluated?" he asked, although he was getting the idea.

Denise smiled.

Will looked over to the doctor. "I've not had many good experiences with shrinks," he said, recalling those he'd encountered inside the Red Box.

"This is quite a serious situation, Will, if that's who you are," Kellenbaum said.

Will stared at the man for an instant before speaking. "*If that's who I am?* What does that mean? And what's the 'situation?'" he asked. It seemed that he'd arrived at a good time. It was strange. Less than an hour before, a welling of urgency had sprouted within him without warning, the origin of which he'd been unable to identify, but he'd known it had to do with Denise. Had he sensed something was wrong?

"Staging one's death, or assisting someone in the same, is a serious crime," the doctor continued. "This, together with carrying out the rest of the ruse, is even more serious, and is an indicator of mental instability."

"What do you mean by 'rest of the ruse?'" Will asked. He felt his core temperature beginning to rise.

"A burial has taken place," Kellenbaum said. "When Denise is safely inside a mental health facility, we'll have to notify the police. They'll have to exhume the body and figure out who it is, and what happened. God forbid that a homicide has occurred."

Will took a deep breath and exhaled slowly before responding. "First off, Denise is not going to a mental institution, or anywhere else she doesn't want to go," he said. "Second, you can dig up the casket, but it will be empty."

"And how do you know that?" Kellenbaum asked.

Will looked first to Denise, and then to her parents. He then turned back to Kellenbaum and said, "Because that's the way I left it when I removed Denise's body."

DENISE JUST STARED at Will and tried to maintain her composure. She believed him, but it meant that she had really been dead. And she remembered some strange things about what had happened before she'd awakened in the barn. None of it was bad – nothing after her time in the medical facility in the desert was bad, not until the past few hours anyway.

"You dug up her body?" Cynthia gasped.

"Of course he didn't, Cynthia," her husband said. "She's right here, isn't she?"

"You're saying you dug up that grave, and removed a body, and that body was Denise, who is sitting next to you right now?" Kellenbaum asked.

Denise sensed all of the others anxiously awaiting his answer. She knew that, in their minds, if he answered yes to that question, he'd have to be certifiably insane. She knew he wouldn't disappoint.

"It was the least I could do," Will said and looked to Denise. "After all, she saved my life."

Gasps and coughs came from around the room.

"And how did she do that?" Kellenbaum asked.

"If it weren't for her, I would've died inside the Red Box," Will replied.

Kellenbaum's face seemed to flush, and Denise sensed something. Will's head cocked to the side as if his mind went into a spin of realization.

"Did you work in the Red Box, doctor?" Will asked, his eyes narrowing in suspicion.

Kellenbaum's eyes widened and darted around in confusion.

"He worked on Long Island before moving to Kansas City," Denise said, repeating what her mother had told her about the man a few days prior. "He was supposedly helping my cousin, who'd been in prison a few times, and who is now missing and presumed dead."

Will looked to the shrink. "Well, doctor?"

"I – I was at the Stone Box facility, on Long Island," he stammered. "Not the Red Box."

Denise knew that the Stone Box was the twin of the Red Box, and that they'd both carried out the same horrible things. She sensed Will's body tense next to her, and worried that the doctor might now be in danger.

"How is it that you still have a license to practice?" Will asked and edged forward on the couch, toward the doctor. "You should be in prison."

Kellenbaum turned to the others. "It was an experimental government program for prison reform," he explained. "I was only an outside contractor. The place has since been shut down."

"You were in prison?" Cynthia asked Will.

"He was exonerated," Denise replied.

"Denise got me out," Will added but turned back to the doctor. "They tortured people in that place – they tortured *me*. Perhaps you know what happened to the Red Box that shut it down."

"I heard there was an explosion," the doctor replied.

"That's right," Will said. "And I'm the one who caused it. Do you know what the real objective of that program was?"

Denise touched Will's arm and he flinched. "Will, they're not going to understand," she said.

"Why don't you tell them, Kellenbaum?" Will continued. "Maybe they'd like to know who they've invited into their home, and to evaluate their daughter."

Denise then saw what Will was doing and had to stifle a grin. The lawyer in her was proud. It was like he was dismantling an expert witness in a trial, effectively rendering his testimony unqualified. He was defending her. And, she knew, it didn't even matter what the final verdict was. He'd never allow them to do anything to her.

"What's he talking about, Curtis?" Denise's father asked, using the doctor's first name. "What did they do in this 'Red Box' place?"

Kellenbaum stammered and Will interjected.

"They tortured inmates – many of whom had been falsely accused and convicted – to see if they would develop certain abilities," Will explained. "It was a program that the government hoped would eventually develop super-soldiers or spies."

"What kinds of abilities?" Denise's brother asked.

"Among other things, something akin to telekinesis," Will replied.

Denise knew it was far more than that – Will was just keeping things in terms that they might understand.

Charles, Cynthia's husband, blew out a puff of air and seemed to stifle a laugh.

"You think it's farfetched?" Will asked, looking at Charles. "I don't blame you."

"It's not possible," Charles said. "It's a metaphysical fantasy."

"Charlie's a mechanical engineer," Cynthia said smugly.

Denise's stomach tightened as she anticipated that Will was going to do something. She knew he wouldn't hurt anyone, but they weren't going to leave the house with the same view of the world as they had when they'd arrived.

"You're an engineer, Charles? Good," Will said. "I'm a physicist, and I can't explain this. Can you?"

At that instant, the coffee table in front the of couch where Charles and Cynthia were sitting slowly elevated from the floor to a height of about three feet.

Charles and Cynthia lifted their feet onto their seats in panic, while everyone else gasped and seemed to freeze in fear as they stared at the levitating table.

"Don't worry," Will said. "I won't spill your drinks." He was referring to the four cups on the table.

The table then returned gently to the floor.

"Is this some kind of a trick?" Charles hissed as the others remained wide-eyed and silent.

"If you'd like another demonstration, just tell me what to do," Will said.

The doctor stood from his chair but then fell back into it as if he'd been shoved.

"No, Kellenbaum," Will said. "You're not leaving until you tell them what you have done, and explain to them what I am."

All eyes turned to Kellenbaum.

WILL FOUGHT BACK his rage at the shrink by reminding himself that all of that Red Wraith research was over. He'd often wondered what he'd do if he ever crossed paths with a former Red Box employee. He'd thought his first instinct would be to separate heads from bodies, but he was managing to hold back.

Will noticed that Cynthia was tapping away on her phone and he separated and had a look at what she was doing. What he saw angered him.

"Cynthia, why are you texting someone named Kent about what's happening here?" Will asked. "I think this is a private matter."

Cynthia's face flushed.

"Kent?" her husband asked, clearly confused.

Will then separated again – in the dual state so that his eyes remained open and his body upright – and yanked Cynthia's phone from her hands and crushed it in midair. A shower of powdered glass and twisted metal and plastic fell onto the coffee table in front of her. He wanted to make sure any recordings or videos were destroyed.

Cynthia screeched, and the others looked startled.

"Sorry, I didn't think we needed any distractions right now," Will said as he glared at Cynthia and then turned back to the doctor. "Now, Kellenbaum, time for you to tell them everything, and make it quick so we can end this meaningless distraction."

Kellenbaum, now visibly shaken, described the Red Box and its twin, the Stone Box, and confirmed everything Will had said. He then admitted that he'd heard rumors that there had been a successful conversion at the Red Box, which must have been Will. Finally, he played down his role at the Stone Box facility saying that he was just an outside contractor and had interviewed inmates on the front end, and then evaluated their "progress" on the back end.

Denise then got him to admit that he'd committed most of his Stone Box "patients" to mental health facilities and that he should have reported their horrible mental and physical conditions to the authorities, despite the nondisclosure agreements he'd supposedly signed.

Denise's mom then spoke. "What did you do with my sister's son?" Gabby asked. "What did you do with Javier?"

Kellenbaum just stared at her, mouth agape, and seemed to turn even more pale than he was before.

"Well, Kellenbaum?" Michael asked.

The doctor seemed to come out of a trance and replied. "I – I committed him to an excellent facility. He was in good hands, and – "

"Was he in this 'Red Box' place?" Gabby asked.

"No, he was a candidate for the Stone Box, but didn't get through the screening," Kellenbaum explained. "He was released early."

"And then probably killed because he knew too much," Denise said. "Isn't that right, Curtis?"

"I had nothing to do with anything like that," Kellenbaum retorted. "I only worked on the psych evaluations."

"I think it's time for you to leave, Kellenbaum," Michael said as he stood.

Kellenbaum got out of his chair but, before he could leave the room, Will stood and took a step toward him.

"If we ever cross paths again, Kellenbaum, something bad is going to happen to you," Will threatened. "Understand?"

The doctor nodded and followed Denise's parents out of the room.

Will heard him go out the door and, a minute later, he separated and watched as the shrink's Prius drove around the driveway circle and off the farm.

Denise's parents returned from seeing the doctor out and retook their seats.

"Now that that's over," Will said, "maybe we can get on to more important things."

DENISE WANTED TO SCREAM. She'd been vindicated, and Will had been the one to do it. The looks on the faces around her were those of shame and confusion, but also of fear. She'd forgive them over time, but not right now.

Her mother, still visibly shaken, had to tend to her cooking for a few minutes and then returned. "The turkey is out of the oven," she reported. "The rest will take just a few minutes to set up. Can we continue this discussion over dinner?"

Denise had no idea how dinner was going go with all that had just happened. But, again, she trusted Will. Also, she thought the kids might lighten the mood.

She took Will's hand and led him to the dining room. She offered him a seat at one end of the table, furthest from the kitchen, and then sat to his left. Her parents were on the opposite end, and Thomas took the seat to Will's right. Cynthia and her family sat directly across from Denise, and Diane and her family sat to Cynthia's right.

Her dad carved the turkey while Thomas bombarded Will with questions that ranged from his background to what had happened to Denise. Will and Thomas had both played football in college, and Denise thought they both looked the part.

"How old are you, Will?" Denise's mom asked as she set a basket of bread on the table.

"I'm 42, I think," Will replied, spurring a flurry of chatter.

"I'm 29, and you look younger by far," Thomas said and laughed. "And Denise, too. How has this happened?"

It was an answer that Denise wanted as well.

Will finished chewing a bite of food and swallowed before he spoke.

"Let's begin this discussion with what we should've been talking about from the moment I arrived, rather than dealing with the shrink," he started, and then held up his hand. "Sorry. I do admit that the circumstances were strange."

"Yeah, if dying, being buried, and then showing up in our stables a few weeks later with no recollection of how she got there could be considered strange," her dad said without disguising the sarcasm. He removed a drumstick from the turkey, set it on a large porcelain platter, and then looked to Denise. "I'm sorry, honey. We didn't know what else to do."

The rest of the family followed suit and apologized, including Cynthia.

Although she was still angry, Denise felt that she could let go of it and try to look forward.

WILL WAS glad that everyone seemed to realize their misunderstandings, but he was sure that Denise was going to be upset for a while. He had other things he wanted to discuss with them before he left.

"Have you thought about the ships in orbit and those planted all over the surface of the planet?" Will asked. "And what about the wireless signal that's being projected all over the world?"

"Tevon Melansk is probably responsible," Charles said, referring to a wealthy techie entrepreneur who had been promising global satellite internet service for over a decade. "That's the latest explanation, anyway."

Will had hoped the mechanical engineer would've had more insight than that, but Charles' comment served as a starting point. "There's more to it," Will said. "Those ships are stationary with respect to the surface of the Earth as it rotates."

"You mean, they look to be in the same position in the sky all the time – like the satellites for dish TV?" Thomas asked.

Will nodded. "Notice that, for satellite TV, you always have to aim your receivers south, above the equator," he explained. "And people in the southern hemisphere have to point theirs north. That's because those satellites are in geosynchronous orbit about 22 thousand miles directly above the equator. That's the only way we're able to establish geosynchronous orbits."

Cynthia looked to her husband, who responded with a nod and then asked, "And these are in stationary orbit all around the planet – not just on the equator?"

"Yes, and much closer to the surface," Will replied. "Less than a thousand miles up."

"That would require a constant thrust of some kind – otherwise they'd just fall," Charles said.

"Precisely," Will confirmed. "Using conventional propulsions systems, like the ones we have, this would not only be inefficient, but completely unsustainable. We just couldn't do it."

Will noticed that, except for the kids, no one really touched their food.

"This should bring on a million more questions," Will said.

"Yeah, like how are they staying up there?" Thomas asked.

It was a question to which Will actually knew the answer from his classes on the *Exodus 9*. "Those ships are using something called a spacetime bender," Will explained. "I don't know the physics behind it, but spacetime and gravity are connected, and this device takes advantage of that connection."

"And the energy source?" Charles asked.

"It's tapped from the vacuum of space – it's essentially limitless," Will replied. "It's well beyond us right now, but it doesn't have to be for very long."

"What do you mean?" Thomas asked.

"The Knowledge Network," Will said. "You can get it right now, on your phones and computers."

Thomas stood, grabbed a backpack that was leaning against the wall behind him, and pulled out a laptop. He set it on the table in front of Will so that both he and Denise could see it. The others pulled out their phones, except for Cynthia, whose iPhone was now just a pile of debris on the coffee table in the living room. Charles set his on the table so that she could see it.

Will waited until they'd all confirmed that they'd found it and connected to it.

"The password is 'LIFE,' all caps," Will said. "The network was activated just hours ago."

As each person logged in, Will heard different voices greeting them. He focused on Thomas' laptop.

A cartoon girl with large, brown eyes and long, black hair tied in a ponytail appeared on the screen. She wore bright green shorts, a white tank-top, and sandals – she looked like she was dressed for the beach. "I'm Kania, what's your name?" the female voice said as she smiled broadly. "Your camera and mic are activated. You can just speak to me like any other person."

"Holy shit," Denise's brother said. "My name's Thomas."

"Hello, Thomas," Kania said. "Can I help you with something?"

Thomas looked to Will.

"Ask about the ships in orbit," Will whispered.

"Can you tell me about the ships in orbit?" Thomas asked.

"Sure," she said as a picture of one of the ships appeared. "This is one of them. It's a Delta vessel. It is a *Monitor*-class starship."

"A Delta vessel?" Thomas said. "What's a Delta?"

Denise grabbed Will's arm and dug her fingertips into his bicep. "Those are the Deltas?" she asked with excitement.

Will smiled and nodded.

"I can see we might have to start from the very beginning, but that's good," Kania said, smiling. "The Deltas were the generation that preceded yours on Earth, but have now been gone for over a million years. We had to leave Earth at that time so that your generation could be seeded on the planet and evolve like we did, so that one day you could also venture out..."

Will took a deep breath and watched as everyone asked questions and seemed to become enthralled with the Network. He fielded questions of his own as they finally started eating and, over the next few hours, he told them everything he'd told his CIA friends about the Deltas and the Network. He explained that the Deltas themselves were gone, but that the intelligent ships they'd left behind were there to help humanity develop.

"So, they're going to teach us about their technology so that we can advance more quickly," Michael said, summing up what Will had described. "Starting with medicine, and then food and energy."

Will nodded.

"Does this have anything to do with what happened to my daughter?" Michael continued. "And why you both look like college kids again?"

"Yes, it does," Will said. "I can't get into everything – there's far too much – but the Network will explain it all. In this case, you might say that Denise and I have benefited from advanced medical technology."

The questions kept coming and, at about 10:00 p.m., Diane yelped, "It's on the news!"

"What is?" Gabby asked.

"It's an announcement about the Knowledge Network," she replied. "There's going to be a special address about it in the morning – the president is going to speak. Afterwards, there's going to be another one from the United Nations."

Will sighed. It was as if a giant weight had been lifted from his chest. It looked like his CIA friends were following through – spreading the word about what he'd told them. It's not like it could have been kept a secret – everyone in the world had access. It was beginning, and he had now done everything he'd set out to do. He hadn't wasted the "great opportunity" of which Landau had spoken.

By 11:30 p.m., the kids were sleeping in the living room and the adults were still at the dinner table, drinking coffee. It was getting late.

As EVERYONE HELPED her mom clear the table, Denise sensed something that caused her a sense of panic. She caught a tear in the corner of her eye before it trickled down her cheek.

They were standing in the kitchen when she turned to Will. "You're going to leave again, aren't you?"

"I have to," he admitted.

Another tear formed and streamed down her face before she could catch it.

He grabbed her upper arm with a strong but gentle grip and let her go. He then looked her in the eyes. "You wanna go for a ride?" he asked.

She stared back at him, confused by his question.

"I've been meaning to ask you," her dad said to Will. "Where did you park?"

"I'm behind the stable," Will replied.

Her dad looked confused. "How did you get back there?" he asked. "The gate is closed."

Will looked to Denise's mom, and then back to her dad. "Can you spare your daughter for a few months?"

Denise's heart pounded in her chest.

"What do you mean?" her mother asked.

"I'd like to take her with me for a while," Will replied and glanced at Denise. "If she wants to go."

"Yes!" Denise yelled with no hesitation. It came out as an embarrassing squeal. No one could stop her. "I'm going with you!" She grabbed his hand and squeezed it tightly.

"Where are you going?" Michael asked.

"Not exactly sure at this point," Will replied and looked to Denise. "You ready?"

"Let me pack some things," she said and then started for the stairs that led to her room but was jolted to a halt. Will hadn't let go of her hand.

"You don't need anything," Will said and then pulled her back to him.

She stared into his eyes as her own started to burn.

"What?" he asked.

She cleared a tear from her eye before it rolled down her nose. "You kept your promise."

WILL LED THE WAY, hand-in-hand with Denise and with the entire family close behind, into the cold night air and toward the stable. The moon was bright and made the scene look like an old black-and-white photo. The double doors ahead were nearly closed, except for a four-inch crack through which light spilled onto the driveway. A cat looked out at them, and then high-tailed it back inside.

"That's Sasha," Denise said.

Thomas rushed ahead and slid the doors open, and the horses responded with soft nickering.

They walked down the aisle to the back door, which Thomas opened. "Can't wait to see this thing," he said.

Before stepping outside, Will stopped, and pointed to a pile of hay. "That's where I put you," he said. "There were a bunch of cats sleeping there – I figured it was safe."

Denise nodded and smiled. "I remember," she said. "I woke up with Sasha on my belly. I guess I was warm."

Will led them out of the back of the barn and into the chilly breeze, and then followed his own footprints in the snow back to the grove of pines. He tugged Denise along as he pressed his way through some thick branches, and they emerged in a clearing.

There, the beamer gleamed in the moonlight.

Denise just stared at it, looked to him for an instant, and then back to the ship. "It's beautiful," she said.

"Holy shit!" Thomas said from behind them as he pressed through the branches. "Is this real?"

The others piled through and gawked at the craft.

"Wait," Denise's dad said and approached the beamer. "Is it floating in midair?"

"It is," Will confirmed.

"My God," Charles said. "How is this possible?"

"The same way those ships in orbit seem to be hanging onto nothing," Will said. "As an engineer, I think you'll have the time of your life learning from the Network. I've learned a lot already myself."

Will then looked to Denise. "I think we should get going," he said.

Will went around and shook hands as Denise hugged and kissed everyone. There were many tears. He was sure now that all was forgiven on both sides.

"Bring her back in one piece," Michael said as he shook Will's hand.

"When you get back, maybe you could take me for a ride in this thing," Thomas added.

"Guaranteed," Will said. "I'll take you all on a little trip if you like."

The beamer's platform lowered to the ground, Will and Denise stepped upon it, they ascended into the main cabin, and the hatch sealed below them.

"Welcome aboard, Ms. Walker," a female voice chimed.

Denise looked around, confused. "Who's that?"

"That's *Gwen*," Will replied. "She's the ship."

Denise's eyes widened and she looked up to the ceiling. "Good to meet you, *Gwen*," she replied, smiling. "You can just call me Denise."

"Very well, Denise," *Gwen* said. "Would you like something to drink before we take off?"

Will laughed.

"What?" Denise asked with a confused look.

"She's messing with you," he replied. "She's acting like a flight attendant. You must be in first class."

"Oh," Denise said and laughed. Her eyes remained wide as she looked around.

"*Gwen*, can you reconfigure the cockpit for a copilot?" he asked.

"Sure thing," she responded as the pilot seat shifted to the left and another seat popped up next to it.

"Shall we?" Will said and pointed Denise to the seat on the right.

"I can't believe this is happening," she said as she sat down. Straps wrapped around her waist and crisscrossed her chest. "Where are we going?"

Will grinned. "You'll see."

"Are we going into space?" she asked with an expression of excitement.

"Eventually," he said as he took his seat and strapped in. "But we have to go somewhere else first."

As the beamer lifted silently from the pines, Denise grabbed his forearm in a panic. "You know how to fly this thing?"

"As it turns out, I do," he replied and then elevated to a thousand feet.

"What does that mean?" she asked as she looked to the ground with a panicked expression.

He accelerated the beamer forward and brought it up to 5,000 feet.

"Oh my God!" Denise yelped. "It's beautiful!"

Indeed it was, he thought as he admired the wide view of the pale landscape.

Moonlight glittered on a span of open water as they passed over it.

"That's Milford Lake," Denise said. "My family used to go there when we were kids."

Will slowed the ship and brought it down to 30 feet. They glided over the water and patches of ice for a few hundred yards and, before they came to the shore, he pulled up on the control rings, and then pressed forward.

Denise gasped.

In an instant, they were at 10,000 feet and heading west at a speed that made it difficult to focus on the features of the landscape below.

A minute later, although he didn't have to, he slowed to weave about the peaks of the Sangre de Cristo Mountain Range, in Colorado.

"That was incredible," Denise said as they exited the mountains and accelerated.

"I'd like to take credit for the flying," he said, "but *Gwen* is the one correcting my maneuvers."

"Don't let him fool you, Denise," *Gwen* said. "Will is an ace beamer pilot."

"What does she mean?" Denise asked.

Will just shook his head. "I have so much to explain," he replied. "We'll have time for that later."

A minute later they were flying over desert.

"Where are we going?" Denise asked.

"There are some people who will want to see you," he replied. "But we'll have to make ourselves a little easier to spot."

He turned off all cloaking and slowed to a speed that would have them arriving in 30 minutes. It would give those at their destination time to prepare.

"We'll be there in half an hour," he said. "In the meantime, maybe we can have a glass of wine in the cabin."

"You can do that?" Denise asked. "The ship – *Gwen* – will fly herself?"

Will laughed. "*Gwen* flies herself far better than I do," he said as he unstrapped his harness and stood. "Let's go."

"IS IT THE SAME SHIP?" Daniel asked as he joined the others in the elevator.

"Don't know," Thackett said, "but it's taking a similar trajectory – but from the east this time."

Five minutes later, they were all standing and shivering at the mouth of the tunnel.

"There it is!" Jacob said and pointed to faint red and green lights in the distance.

"I see it, too," Jonathan added.

The craft landed in the same spot as last time, and the underbelly dropped down. Daniel saw two figures this time, one smaller, one larger.

"Looks like he brought a friend," Sylvia said as she squinted.

"Will?" Daniel called.

The larger of the two figures waved, but Daniel couldn't make out either of their faces in the dark.

Suddenly, Sylvia gasped, grabbed Daniel's arm, and fell to one knee.

"What's wrong?" Daniel asked as he crouched and clutched her upper body.

Sylvia pointed toward the visitors. "It's Denise," she said in a hoarse voice. Her eyes were tearing.

"What?" Daniel said and looked up to the approaching figures.

Then it was Jonathan who staggered, and Thackett and Jacob steadied him as he squinted and pointed at the approaching pair.

"My God. How is this possible?" Jonathan said, his voice gravelly.

The smaller figure suddenly ran toward the group. "Jonathan!" she yelled as she approached, and then lunged into him and hugged him before he had time to react.

"Is it really you?" Jonathan asked, looking to Will over Denise's head.

Will kept a few feet away, smiling, and seeming to enjoy what he was seeing. "I told you she was alive," he said.

Jonathan gently cradled Denise's head between his hands and looked at her face. "You look like a teenager," he said as tears ran down his face. "You cut off your hair."

"I tried to call you," Denise said to Jonathan, and then looked to Sylvia who was still wobbling with Daniel maintaining his grip on her upper arm. "And I tried to call you, too, Sylvia. Both of your phones went directly to voicemail."

"We don't have access to our phones here," Daniel said. "And we can only call out using the in-house system."

Jonathan looked to Will. "You told me to call her, but I didn't – I couldn't," he explained. "I was going to stop at her parents' place on my way back to Chicago, when all of this was over." His eyes went back to Denise. "Is that where you've been?"

"All I know is that it was like I fell asleep here – at this place – and then woke up at my childhood home," Denise replied. "I don't know where I was in between."

Sylvia edged her way to Denise and the two women embraced and cried.

"Don't you think it might be time for you all to go home now?" Will said, looking to Thackett and then to Daniel. "The war and the pandemics are over."

"We're all going home next week," Thackett said.

It was news to Daniel. "Back to Space Systems?" he asked.

Thackett nodded.

Daniel knew that life would never be the same, but he looked forward to getting back to Space Systems. "And what about you, Will?" he asked.

"My situation is complicated, but I'll be back from time to time," he explained and looked to Denise.

"Where will you be in the meantime?" Sylvia asked.

Will pointed to the sky.

"Oh," Sylvia said. "And you, Denise?"

Denise looked to Will and slowly pointed to the sky.

Will smiled and nodded.

"Can I see that notebook you carry around?" Will asked Daniel, who then pulled it, and a pen, out of the inner pocket of his jacket and handed them to him.

Will wrote something and gave them back.

Daniel looked at the notebook. It read: *Lux@Exodus9.delta.kn.* "An email address?"

Will laughed and nodded. "You'll all get one through the Knowledge Network as well," he explained. "There might be some delays in my responses, depending on where I am at the time."

They chatted for another 15 minutes and everyone seemed to be happy – elated – for the moment. Daniel thought it was as if the dark shadow of a storm had moved on, allowing the bright sunshine to break through and warm their faces and soothe their minds.

Will was alive. Denise was alive. The pandemic was over. The war had stopped.

These were all inexplicable miracles.

It was time for the world to move into the next phase of existence. Daniel felt privileged to have been alive to witness the transformation – to be a part of it, in some way at least.

Everyone said their goodbyes, and they watched the two space travelers – their friends – ascend into the belly of their sleek craft.

As they watched the ship lift off, Daniel put his arm around Sylvia's shoulders and squeezed her tightly.

"Do you think they'll come back?" Sylvia asked.

"I do," Daniel said.

When the craft was at about 1,000 feet, it flashed its lights a few times and then darted upward and to the west, out of sight in an instant.

As they all turned to the tunnel entrance, Thackett said, "It will be nice to get home."

Sylvia smiled, looked to Daniel, and said, "Home is being with the people you love."

WILL GUIDED the beamer toward the moon, where the *Exodus 9* was orbiting.

Although it was obvious that she was exhausted, as was he, it seemed that Denise could hardly contain herself as they skimmed along the lunar surface.

"At some point, we'll land on it if you want," he said.

"My God, really?" she asked.

"Sure," he replied. "I've done it once already."

As they approached the dark side, Will pulled up and headed for the *Exodus 9*. Denise's eyes seemed to get larger and larger as they closed in on the ship and, just as the bay doors started to open, she exclaimed, "It's enormous!"

"The *Exodus 9* welcomes you aboard, Denise," *Gwen* said as they pulled into the hangar and landed.

Denise smiled and looked at Will with the wide eyes of a child. "Thanks, *Gwen*," she said and looked to the ceiling. "And thanks, *Exodus 9*."

As they unstrapped from their seats, Will said, "Well done today, *Gwen*. Thanks."

"Aye aye," *Gwen* replied. "Good night to you both."

"Good night," Denise replied as they descended from the hovering craft.

She stepped off the lift and onto the floor, and then turned in a circle and looked around the massive hangar. "I can't believe I'm here," she said.

"Me either," Will said and grabbed her hand and started walking. "There's a lot to see, but I need some sleep. I'd guess you do, too. It's going on 3:00 a.m."

They exited the hangar and entered the main mall.

"It's like a city," Denise gasped.

"Very much so," he said. To him, he realized, it was home.

"We'll explore tomorrow," he said as they entered a Tube portal.

During the five-minute ride, Will thought Denise might have asked 100 questions.

As they walked down the hall to his quarters, she said, "It looks like a fancy, futuristic hotel."

"Actually, the *Exodus 9* is from the distant past," he said as he opened the door to his quarters and led her inside.

The first thing that seemed to draw her attention was the large floor-to-ceiling window on the far end. Earth was in view.

"That's the strangest thing I've ever seen," she said. "It's beautiful."

They both probably could have used a shower before bed, but they grabbed pillows from the couch and lay on the floor with a good view of the window.

Denise put her head on his chest, and he hugged her close.

"I'm in a different world now, aren't I?" she asked.

"We all are," he replied. "But it's a better one."

"I love you, William Thompson," she said.

"I love you, Denise Walker," he replied.

As Denise's breathing became heavy and his own eyelids slowly lowered, Will tried to think of a happier time in his life – or in any of his lives. He was asleep before anything came to mind.

19

A NEW AGE

WILL WOKE UP ON THE FLOOR WITH DENISE IN HIS ARMS, STILL ASLEEP.

He separated, took a look around, and returned. It was all real.

Before making his critically timed reappearance at Denise's childhood home, he'd made an appeal to the Regenerators. After some negotiating, supported by Landau, the Regenerators' representative, Ratha, had made some compromises on his restrictions. In the end, with their permission, he was allowed to occasionally come back to Earth to see Denise and to visit his family. A Delta ship was to be in low orbit at all times and set on alert to regenerate him immediately in the case he was somehow killed. And he had to promise not to reincarnate. He thought he'd be able to control that now, knowing what to expect after his recent excursion with death.

There were other strict rules that he also promised to follow. First, he was not allowed to regenerate anyone, other than Denise who, of course, had already been regenerated once. The human race had to figure these things out for themselves, albeit with the guidance of the Deltas' structured, illumination program. Other than the beamer, he was not allowed to reveal Delta technology – no visits to the *Exodus 9*, and no taking people on excursions into deep space in the beamer. Again, Denise was exempt from all of these rules.

In the end, he was convinced that the Regenerators were reasonable curators of developing life. As it turned out, new races and civilizations could go badly wrong, and in many ways. The most likely source of a downturn, however, was rooted in power or, rather, the imbalance of it. Disproportion could emerge in various ways, from monopolies of resources, such as food, to economic disparities, to differences in technological development.

Will understood now why the Regenerators couldn't allow someone like him to exist on the planet before the human race as a whole naturally transformed into evanescent beings. Had he been evil enough to want to, he could have put the entire world into chaos. He was too powerful. To start, as just a lone evanescent being, he could have killed every major leader in the world, and no one would even have known what had happened to them. He could simply scramble their brains from a long distance away, or tear holes in their hearts. If the Nazis' Red Falcon project or China's Red Dragon had succeeded, the world would have been immediately dominated by them. Just one evanescent being might have been enough.

Another imbalance of power could come from technology. Disregarding his evanescent abilities, with only his beamer Will could outmatch the collective military might on Earth. It was just one tiny ship.

He was reminded again of the ant analogy. Compared to other civilizations throughout the universe, humans, and the planet on which they resided, were nothing but a pile of ants on a desert island. They weren't in danger of being attacked because no one felt threatened by them, and no one wanted their island. That the ants fought amongst themselves made no difference to anyone on the outside.

To carry it one step further, however, suppose those ants somehow developed a poison that could kill a human with a single sting. And suppose that these ants were known to float on dead wood that could carry them to different places. The prudent recourse would be to exterminate them on their own island before they had a chance to spread.

The other option, however, was to make sure that they never became poisonous.

Will was the reason that the Regenerators had judged humanity as "poisonous." And his removal from the planet was to ensure that they didn't become poisonous before a time when they could be trusted not to sting.

Denise opened her eyes, sat up abruptly, and looked out the window.

"Thank God," she said, breathing heavily. "I thought I was dreaming all of this."

Will sat up next to her. "Me too," he said.

"Where's Earth?" she asked and nodded toward the view of radiant celestial objects.

"Far away now," he replied. "We're on our way to another system. It will take a couple of weeks to get there. But we can go back to Earth whenever you want."

She seemed to contemplate his words, but he wasn't sure she was appreciating the magnitude of what he'd said – they were outside the solar system and her world was far behind. He figured it would take some time to sink in.

"What are we going to do now?" she asked.

"Anything you want," he replied. "And I mean this in the most literal sense."

She looked at him for a few seconds. "I'm not sure I understand."

He realized that there was no way he could explain it all in a reasonable amount of time. "I'll have to show you," he said. "In the meantime, you hungry?"

A tear streamed down her face.

"What's wrong?" he asked.

"You saved me," she said. "You dug me out of my grave and brought me back to life."

"You were never really dead," he said. "And you never will be. I just had your body regenerated so that you could return to your current life."

She stared at him with a confused expression.

"I know," he said and smiled. "You'll understand in time. Do you remember anything from when you were out there – maybe a memory of having been someone else?"

"No, I don't think so," she said. "I only remember going through a tunnel and then emerging in a vast open space. There was a sort of a conduit of light with bright, filamentary structures emerging from it – they were moving."

Will nodded. He thought perhaps Denise was a young soul – living her very first life.

"I saw it, too," he said.

"You did?" she asked. "How? Were you – "

"Dead?" Will cut her off. "Yes. Well, like I said, I needed a new body, like you."

"What happened?"

"I did it on purpose," he replied.

"Suicide?" she asked. "Why?"

"I had to," he replied. "It's a long story that I'll explain later. The point is, we're both alive right now. What do you want to do?"

"You choose something," she said.

"Okay," he said. "Food. I think I have the perfect thing to get us started."

Twenty minutes later, after a shower and getting Denise some clean clothes – something she marveled at – they went to a Tube station and were on their way.

DENISE FOLLOWED Will out of the Tube, and they walked hand-in-hand down the mall. They were on the 22nd level, and she pulled him to the railing on her right and looked over.

She could see the other levels across the mall, and the main "street" below. There were trees and fountains and waterfalls on the ground level, and the ceiling was a night sky glittering with stars.

"It's stunning," she said.

Will tugged her back on track.

After another few minutes of walking, they entered one of the storefronts on the left that had an illuminated sign in the window that read "Relaxing Ventures."

"Where are we going?" she asked.

"You'll see," he replied as they walked to the front desk. His watch vibrated and he glanced at it. "We're in Room 8."

"Nice watch," she said.

"Oh, right," he said. "You're going to get one of these, too."

They found Room 8 and entered a small foyer with another door.

He looked to her and asked, "You ready?"

"I ... I have no idea," she replied as she hooked her arm around his and clenched it with some force.

He laughed. "Don't be so nervous," he said. "It's just a gentle warmup for what you can find here."

He opened the door and intense light spilled over them.

Denise squinted as what seemed to be sunlight bathed her face in a gentle warmth.

They stepped through the door, and a mild breeze of cool air infused with the scents of sea and flowers soughed through her short hair. When her eyes adjusted to the light, she could barely speak.

They were standing on a sidewalk next to a narrow, cobblestone street. Directly in front of her was a short railing next to a steep cliff that dropped a few hundred feet into blue water – a bay scattered with anchored sailboats and yachts. The sky was a fierce blue with high, delicate clouds.

"Where are we?" she asked.

"This is Italy, the village of Positano," Will replied and then pointed to the water. "And that's the Tyrrhenian Sea, which is just a part of the Mediterranean."

"How is this possible?" she asked as she turned around and gasped. A tapestry of pastel-colored buildings climbed the hill hundreds of feet above them.

"That will take some time to explain," he said. "Why don't we get some breakfast, and then explore the place?"

"Okay," she said. "Where do we go?"

Will grabbed her hand and, as they walked uphill, a tiny car that looked like it was from the 1950s drove down the street, toward them. Denise stopped and watched as it passed by, its tires making a clacking noise on the cobblestone road and the engine grumbling like a lawnmower.

"Oh, and we're currently in the early 1960s," he said.

"There was a person in that car!" Denise said.

Will pointed down the hill to one of the storefronts where two children were kicking a soccer ball. "They're all around us," he explained. "But they're not people from Earth."

"You mean they're aliens?" Denise asked. "Or that they're not real?"

"I have come to think of them as real," he said. "It's just that they're not human – so, yes, maybe aliens. They're artificially intelligent."

"Why are they here?"

"Because they're a part of this program."

"Can you talk with them?"

"We're about to," he replied as they crossed the street and entered a coffeehouse that was all windows on the outside.

When they entered, Denise's senses saturated with the aromas of coffee and toasted bread. Directly across from the entrance was a counter with a glass case that contained an assortment of bakery items. The room to the right was cluttered with tables, and there were people sitting at them. Some were talking and many were reading books, and a few were reading newspapers. The chatter seemed to be in both English and Italian.

Will stepped up to the counter.

"Hello, Will," a young woman behind the counter said in a slight Italian accent. She had long, dark hair pulled back in a ponytail, and she was smiling. Denise thought she was beautiful.

"Good morning, Sabrina," he said as he approached the counter, and then turned to Denise and winked. "They know me here."

Denise laughed as Will ordered coffee and a brioche with cheese.

Next, Denise stepped up to the counter.

"What's your name?" Sabrina asked.

"I'm Denise," she replied. "Good morning."

Sabrina took her order, coffee and a panino, and then Denise followed Will to a seat with a window overlooking the street, and the ocean far below.

Will grabbed her hand and pointed up and away from the window, back into the café.

She turned her head and was immediately awestruck. The room expanded in that direction and the ceiling was at least 40 feet high. Three floors of bookshelves made up the far wall and people were perusing the tomes on the narrow walks between tiers.

"Is this a library?" she asked.

"Sort of, but it has more of a used bookstore feel," he replied. "You can find any book ever published in those stacks, no matter how rare. And you can take it with you if you want to."

Denise looked around at all the people. They varied in age from teenagers to pensioners. Two older men played chess at a table in a corner, both smoking cigars that Denise could barely smell but she thought the aroma was pleasant. A college-aged woman who looked to be studying sat at a nearby table. All were elegantly dressed in 60s attire. Denise thought the scene would look like an old photo if it were in black and white.

"Will, what is this place?" she asked. "I mean, why is it here – the ship, and all of this?"

He looked over Denise's shoulder and she turned just as Sabrina delivered their coffee and breakfasts.

"I'll be back later with coffee refills," Sabrina said and left.

As Will stirred cream into his coffee he said, "This ship was meant to transport a million people from Earth before the Regenerators destroyed it," he explained. "The Deltas had thousands of these *Exodus*-class ships ready for us when the time came for us to escape."

"Where were they going to take us?" she asked.

"To habitable planets that they had ready for us, far from Earth," he replied. "The *Exodus 9,* and the others, were designed to keep us all sane and occupied during the long trip."

"How long was the trip supposed to be?"

"Many years," he replied. "But I'm not exactly sure."

"But now it's only you," she said. "Are you supposed to go there by yourself?"

He shook his head. "My task is to make sure that our generation still gets there when the time comes."

"What does that mean?" she asked. "When will that happen?"

"When humans make the transformation on their own," he replied.

"You mean, when they're able to separate?"

"Yes, that, but also when they figure out how to, well, overcome death," he said.

"Is that what the Deltas have done?"

"Your being here now is a testament to that," he replied. "And the same for me."

"You brought me back to life," she said.

"No," Will argued. "You came back on your own. For that to happen, you had to have a body to which to return, and that's where the Deltas' technology came in. All I did was to provide your old body so that it could be accurately replicated."

"So, if I die again?"

"Your body info is on file," he replied. "They'd just make another one, and you could return if that's what you wanted to do."

"What would I do instead?"

"For one, you could reincarnate," he replied. "That's what humans have been doing up to this point, for the most part."

"For the most part?" she asked. "What else is there?"

He shrugged. "The phrase is that they go 'beyond the horizon,'" he explained. "And no one really knows what that means, although most think it's an elevation to another level of existence."

"How long before humans make the transformation?" she asked.

"A few thousand years, probably," Will replied. "Although, it could be quicker, depending on how well the Knowledge Network plan works out."

It was too much for Denise to mull in her head all at once and, after Sabrina refilled their coffee mugs, she asked, "What's next on our agenda?"

"First, you have an appointment for a medical checkup," he replied. "And then a meeting with a counselor."

"What?" she asked, eyes wide. "Are you trying to have me committed as well?"

"I already know you're crazy," he said. "You're with me, aren't you?"

She laughed and then looked into his eyes. "Thanks," she said.

"For what?"

She felt her eyes starting to burn and wiped them with the back of her hand. "For keeping your promise."

DANIEL PARSONS POURED hot water into his cup as he stared out the window of his Space Systems office on the seventh floor. The twilit but darkening skies above the pines that swayed in the mild, late spring breeze had a new meaning to him. The stars he saw now were the same as those he'd seen as a child from the pier at his parents' summer cottage, but they now carried a new meaning to him. At that time, they'd been untouchable. But now, he knew someone who was among them.

It had been over a month since they'd returned from the underground facility in the Nevada desert. At that time, they'd been at war, and on the verge of total destruction by a mysterious enemy. But the outcome was the opposite of what he'd expected. Now, the world was at peace, and working feverishly on advancing society and technology toward a common good – an improvement of life. Everyone's life.

As he dipped a tea ball into his cup, he caught motion out of the corner of his eye and turned his head just in time to see a bat flutter above the treetops, in the light of the rising moon. He wondered if it could be the same bat that he'd seen on multiple occasions – perhaps the one that Sylvia had photographed. He smiled. If so, he was happy it was still alive. That bat had been oblivious to recent events. It made him wonder what he, himself, still didn't know about the world – the universe.

He flinched at a reflection in the window and turned around.

"In your socks again, huh?" Daniel said and glanced at Sylvia's feet.

"Best way to sneak up on you," she said as she leaned against the doorframe and dangled a cup by her finger. "Teatime?"

They'd been spending a lot of time working together on their joint project. It was going to be a set of monographs that told the full story of William Thompson: everything that had led to his transformation and to the transformation of the world. It would now be a series of four books, rather than the three they'd originally planned, and, unlike their usual monographs, they'd eventually be made available to the public over the course of a decade.

As Sylvia extracted tea leaves out of a can on the shelf, Daniel recognized how fortunate he was. They'd been a part of something that had profoundly changed the world for the better. It was the reason he had become an Omni, and why he'd dedicated his life to his work.

He poured hot water into Sylvia's cup, and then followed her out to the main room and sat next to her on the couch.

"Are you happy with the way things turned out?" she asked.

"What do you mean?"

"Do we have a place in this world anymore?"

Daniel immediately understood her line of thinking. "Save the pandemic, we haven't solved any problems yet," he said. "There are still bad characters in the world – and there always will be. And there will still be mysteries to solve. Our focus may change, but we'll still be needed."

She smiled and kissed him on the cheek. "Just this once, why don't we knock off early and have a glass of wine?" she said. "What do you say?"

It took him no time to answer. "Your place, or mine?"

"It will have to be mine, since I know you don't have any wine."

On their way to the elevator, it struck him that there might come a day when all of the world's problems were gone. There'd be no disease, no wars, and no crime or violence. There'd be ample energy, food, and shelter, and everyone would be free of all the responsibilities that were presently the norm. No one would need a job, and their every desire would be satisfied.

It sounded great, but what would happen after that? Would people get bored? Would they turn to learning new things? Would they turn to exploration? It seemed to him that humans were driven by needs, those which kept them alive in this world, and curiosity. The question was, what happened when both need and curiosity were gone – when one didn't need anything, and knew everything. Perhaps that's when they'd find that their current existence had no meaning. And maybe that's when they'd need to move on to a new world – to that new existence, beyond the horizon.

JACOB HALE POPPED OPEN an ice-cold can of Pepsi and brought it up to the loft. He'd been back at his flat at 17 Swann since returning from the desert facility, and he had no immediate plans to move out. Pauli would be back from London in August and resume her job in DC. Perhaps he'd consider a change at that time.

He'd just gotten an email from Daniel that contained a recent photo of Mars, taken from one of the Chinese space telescopes – by a Chinese astronomer. When he opened the file, he was shocked. Mars was no longer the "Red Planet." It was as blue as the "big blue marble" – Earth. It was stunning. Mars had an atmosphere, oceans, and a magnetic field – something needed to protect the surface from radiation. It had been terraformed – regenerated – and, Jacob speculated, seeded with life. The Regenerator ships had completed their task, and they were now gone.

He figured that, when this was officially released to the public, people would see it as an inspiration. Perhaps it would serve as an example of what was possible.

It certainly inspired him, and he knew his job would become more fascinating than ever. He'd spend time in the Knowledge Network and learn about energy technologies, and probably reverse engineer devices others created along the way. But he knew that the future wasn't going to be as bright as people were saying – at least not for a while. There would still be conflicts, but they'd be fought in different ways. And he knew he'd be in the middle of it. For the moment, he'd try to enjoy the calm in the eye of the storm.

His thoughts then turned to Uncle Theo, or Horace, as his Omni colleagues had known him. Theo had funneled him into his current state of existence – working for the CIA as an Omni and living at 17 Swann Street. And Theo had been right: everything he'd done had existential consequences. Perhaps William Thompson never would have gotten off the planet without Jacob's help, in which case the world would have been destroyed. And Jacob would not have been there to help him but for Uncle Theo.

He took a swig of soda and tilted his head back to look at the stars through the skylight. His perspective was different than it had been just a year ago. There were things out there that were beyond the imagination – and he didn't mean giant celestial objects or feats of nature. He meant life, intelligence, and magical technologies, but it went beyond that.

There was something else hidden in the black between those stars. Something that gave him hope for what came after this existence. It gave him a sense of peace that made him feel like he was just biding his time until he moved on to that new place, beyond the horizon.

LENNY BUTROLSKY PULLED his rental car to the side of the street, turned off the engine, and took a deep breath of warm, spring air, scented with the fragrance of the blooming magnolia trees that lined the boulevard.

When he'd received the email from James Thackett, he'd assumed it was about another job. But it wasn't. The first thing it had said was that Lenny was now free from his obligations with the CIA, and that he was officially retired, for the second time. The second thing, however, had been most unexpected, and was something that frightened Lenny almost as much as dying and facing judgement for his life.

It was a file on his daughter that contained information on her location and her family. Lenny was a grandfather.

There was a postscript in Thackett's email that read, "This is intended to save you some time, in case you want to pursue it. My thanks for all you've done, and best wishes for a peaceful future. –James"

Lenny had the impression that Thackett may have had some experience in his line of work. Thackett had come up through the CIA ranks, and seemed to have an appreciation for someone like Lenny. Perhaps the director had been like him – someone who did the dirty work that had to be done, but which no one else had the stomach to do.

But that was over for Lenny now. By his estimate, the number of people he'd saved exceeded the number he'd killed – by a great amount. He hoped that meant something. But there was no way to know for certain. He supposed he might find out when he died, but he'd lead a clean life until then, however short that might be.

Lenny got out of the car, stepped onto the sidewalk, and took a deep breath as he looked over the premises. It was a modest, two-story house with white siding and brown trim. The garage door was open, revealing the back ends of a minivan and late-model Honda sedan. A small bicycle and a tricycle were in the driveway, and a soccer ball was nestled in the grass near the front stoop.

As he stepped onto the porch, the sounds of voices and the giggling of kids came through the screen door.

He pushed the doorbell button and chimes sounded throughout the house. The voices inside went silent, and then the slapping sounds of approaching bare feet on wooden floors came from somewhere inside.

Lenny wasn't sure what he was going to say to his daughter. She wouldn't recognize him. He had a picture in his wallet of her with him and her mother from when they were in Russia.

There was little he could tell her about why he'd left, and why he'd returned. The world had changed. His purpose in life had been fulfilled. It was time for him to resume his life, or to salvage it, and, perhaps, make someone else's life a little easier.

JONATHAN McDOUGAL SAT at the breakfast table with his wife and their daughter's family, who had flown in from California a few days prior.

The kids tapped around on their cell phones, the oldest already exploring the "Knowledge Network for Kids," and learning about math, biology, chemistry, and physics. People around the world were learning the language of the Deltas – both verbal and written. Jonathan thought their language sounded like a cross between French and Portuguese. It was a little strange, although somewhat comforting, that the online Delta avatars who tutored the classes referred to the language as "our" language, all-inclusive – as if we were all Deltas. From what Will had told them, he knew that, deep down, we all were.

Jonathan didn't know what the future held for him, or anyone, but he felt good for the time being. Everyone was alive – Denise was alive – there were no wars for now, and there was no threat from the outside. The world was safer than it had ever been, and lives were going to improve quickly based on medical advances alone, not to mention everything else the Deltas were in the process of teaching them.

Jonathan had also spent some time on the Network, primarily in the "Thought" module. His first impression was that it was going to have to do with psychology, and the workings of the mind. But there was only a small amount of brain function discussed. The rest was of a more philosophical nature, such as exploring one's existence, and our place in the universe. Our physical bodies were but an incomplete and temporary manifestation of our existence. Our souls, however, were inextinguishable entities that were as much a part of existence as was the universe itself. And there were other worlds in which they could exist, and might have existed in the past.

He'd followed some visualization exercises and found himself trying to exit his body and look at it from the outside. On other occasions, he'd tried to extend beyond his fingertips and slide a glass across a table, or flip a page of a book. It never worked, but he was starting to believe that it was possible. He knew it was possible for William Thompson, who had been forced to develop such skills through fear and pain.

Jonathan didn't know how much "Delta blood" he had in him, but it was generally accepted that everyone had at least some. Maybe he'd be one of the first to accomplish separation the right way. *Probably not,* he thought, but he'd have fun trying while expanding his mind in ways he'd never before considered.

Jonathan's life would go back to relative normal for a while. There were still people who had been wrongly convicted of crimes who needed to be freed. But his overall outlook on life would be forever changed for the better, and for that he credited William Thompson, who he hoped he would see again.

DURING THE PAST WEEKS, Denise had experienced things beyond her imagination. She'd played volleyball matches in her old high-school gymnasium, visited her mother's hometown in Colombia in her own era of the 1960s, and taken classes on biology and biochemistry to get a start on her new passion, genetics. While on Earth, during her time away from Will, she would work with Jonathan at the foundation, and learn what she could through the Knowledge Network.

Some of her drive now came from something originally unforeseen. It was a kind of precursory, survivor's remorse: she'd probably outlive everyone she loved on Earth. Even though she was as likely as anyone to get killed in an accident, she'd be regenerated. It didn't mean, however, that she'd take that option, but she probably would as long as Will was still around.

Denise's Delta counselor helped her to overcome some of the underlying guilt in two ways. First, he convinced her that, with Delta assistance, humans would develop regeneration capabilities at an accelerated rate. Second, he helped her to understand that death was just a construct of the mind. It was a speculation – something she knew the Omnis abhorred in their work because it led to false conclusions. What she understood now, partially from firsthand experience, was that the soul was an eternal entity that evolved and transformed. Her loved ones might have already lived hundreds of other lives, but the memories and experiences of those lives would be with them forever.

There would be a time when she'd have to make a choice. She'd be in the void, and would have to decide, once again, whether to regenerate, reincarnate, or head for the horizon. But she chose to not contemplate that dilemma at this point. She was going to live in the present and do whatever good she could in this life.

WILL FOUND Landau at his usual spot in the whiskey bar.

"William," Landau said loudly as he stood and held out his hand. "I was hoping I'd see you tonight."

"I've been checking in here regularly looking for you," Will said. "It's been a while – I haven't seen you since our last negotiations with the Regenerators."

"How is Denise faring?" Landau asked.

"I think she was overwhelmed at first, but happy now," Will replied. "A lot has happened."

Landau nodded and chuckled. "That's an understatement."

"We both have our tasks," Will explained. "She'll be trying to contribute to development on Earth, while I'll secure the places for the next generation's relocation, when that time arrives."

Landau nodded. "And after that?"

"After they leave Earth? – that's a long time from now," Will replied.

Landau grinned. "You think ten thousand years is a long time?"

"It is to me," Will replied. "Right now, anyway."

"Do you remember how long a year felt to you when you were a child compared to how fast they go by now?" Landau asked.

"Years now pass like weeks," Will admitted.

"Time is relative, and it means nothing without a point of reference," Landau explained. "Until recently, your point of reference was the expiration time of your aging body. But that is gone now. Time will be of no concern."

Something suddenly came to Will's mind. "By conquering death, one also conquers time," he said.

Landau smiled. "Precisely," he said. "And removing the constraint of time opens you to a new existence."

"Like yours?" Will asked.

"Like the one I'll be going to soon," Landau replied. "I've accomplished what I'd intended here, and soon you will have done all that you can do as well. When you're ready, you shouldn't hesitate."

A server came with a tray of drinks. "A *Hennessy Paradise Imperial* for you," the man said and set a snifter in front of Will. He then pivoted to Landau and set a cognac before him. "And a *Seraphim Hors d'Âge* for you."

Will looked to Landau with concern.

"It's more of a symbolic gesture, really," Landau explained. "It marks a celebration of sorts."

"What do you mean?" Will asked.

"I'm not going to a place to rest," Landau explained. "On the contrary, I'm going to a place filled with marvels that have no analogies in this world. And I am content with the current state of things here, as should you be."

"Don't I have more work to do?" Will asked. "Don't I have a responsibility to see things through?"

"Humanity will flourish or perish by its own making," Landau explained. "And you were not the sole reason they were in their predicament. But now they will either embrace their second chance, or they will burn it. You will not be able to control that."

"Should I not go forward and explore the new worlds that the Deltas prepared for them?" Will asked.

"By all means, you should," Landau replied. "But it is beyond your influence to determine whether they will ever make it there. Although the Regenerators' condemnation has been withdrawn, humans may still choose to condemn themselves, despite being given an opportunity not afforded to anyone else in this existence."

Will's gut seemed to twist in knots. "So it all could have been for naught."

"No," Landau said. "They have been given a chance and the means to save themselves. That is the most precious of gifts."

"You saved them from extermination," Will said.

Landau shook his head. "No. We saved them from being exterminated for the wrong reason," he corrected. "And the Deltas' fallen angel was recovered in the process. My task is complete."

Landau lifted his glass. "Drink with me," he said.

"Before you go, can you answer one question?" Will asked.

"Sure, my friend," Landau said and set his glass back on the table.

Will looked him in the eyes. "Who are you?"

Landau grinned. "Who is it that you think I am?"

"I don't know," Will said. "For a while, when I was in the Exoskeleton, I thought you might have been an angel. Later, I thought you were the Devil. And then I thought you might be God himself."

"The Devil?" Landau laughed loudly, bringing his cognac up to his lips, and then setting it down again. "Oh, better hold off on that for the moment."

Will laughed. "Yeah."

Landau continued. "That part of the soul that resides in the isolated mind senses something beyond itself that is concealed," he explained. "It is not wrong. However, the images it conjures to answer its questions are inaccurate."

"You still haven't answered my question," Will said, grinning.

"I am who I told you I was, but I am also a bit more," Landau replied. "This universe in which you currently reside is not a mere spontaneous occurrence of nature. Just as the Regenerators are responsible for cultivating life on worlds in this galaxy, there are others who maintain galaxies, and others who maintain this universe. And there are other universes with their own curators."

"And which are you?" Will asked.

"I oversee them all," Landau replied.

Will shuddered and stared back at him for a few seconds, his mind spinning. "What does that mean?"

"I think you know," Landau replied. "Before I go, I'll let you in on one more secret."

Will felt lightheaded. "What's that?"

"I knew where you were the entire time, just as I know where every soul is," Landau said. "I wasn't going to deprive you of your journey. In fact, I rather enjoyed sharing it with you."

"I don't understand," Will said.

"One day, you will," Landau said and picked up his drink and gestured to Will's.

Will lifted his glass.

"We will meet again," Landau said as he winked and tapped Will's glass with his.

Landau swallowed his sweet cognac in one gulp, and Will followed.

And then Landau was gone.

Will didn't feel sad. He believed him.

WILL GLANCED over the top of his book at Denise, who was buried in one of her own, completely oblivious to her surroundings. The café had just the right amount of background noise to allow them to concentrate on their work. It was approaching 11:00 p.m. and, when they were done for the night, they'd head to a pub on the cliffs for a nightcap. They were in Positano again, an excursion that Denise requested often, probably because it was the first place she'd visited when she'd arrived, over a month ago now.

The *Exodus 9*'s destination was an enormous space station constructed by the Deltas as a rendezvous point after the next generation's escape from Earth. The trip that originally was to take four months would now only take five weeks due to the ship's recent propulsion upgrades, making it just the right duration, round trip, to get Denise back to her family in the promised amount of time.

Communications with Earth – mostly emails – were delayed by just a few days despite the *Exodus 9* being thousands of light-years from Earth. The reason for this was that communications were not sent using electromagnetic waves – radio waves – but instead were relayed through extradimensional means from the Delta ships in Earth orbit.

The Deltas had constructed more than 20 of these enormous outposts whose purpose was to facilitate repairs to both the *Exodus*-class ships and warships to be used in humanity's escape from the Regenerators. Will knew that there would be no "escaping" from the Regenerators now. They had a deal, and he trusted them, but humans would eventually have to leave Earth – there was a time limit. He had no idea what would happen if the 10,000-year lease expired, and humans hadn't yet vacated the planet. He'd do all he could to help but, as Landau had told him, it was mostly out of his hands.

Will's first task was to make sure that the stations were still functional, and to start waking them up. It would take some time to visit them all, and he'd take Denise with him on many of those missions. After that, he was to check out the planets that were supposedly ready for settlement. Those were much farther away, and he didn't yet know how that was going to be handled. He wasn't going to worry about it now.

Will found it odd, but also somewhat relieving, that, after all that had happened, he still didn't have answers to the most fundamental questions. From where did he originate? Where was he before his first life? Where would he go after he lived his last? And, finally, why did he exist at all? They were questions that, in one form or another, every self-aware being asked themselves often, either consciously or subconsciously.

One thing he had learned, however, was that this life wasn't the end. There was something beyond and, although it was complicated, that knowledge was a wellspring of hope.

Denise grabbed Will's hand and squeezed, pulling him out of his meditations.

"What are you thinking about?" she asked. "Your face looks so serious."

He huffed and laughed. "I'm just happy you're here," he said. "Happy that things worked out."

"Me too."

Many things had changed in Will's worldview since his life before the Exoskeleton. One fundamental change was the evolution of his meaning of the word "believe." It was too strong for most things. To him, more appropriate words to use in its stead were "hope" and "faith," and, perhaps, "trust." Without seeing something for oneself, a person could only hope something were true, or assume it were true based on faith or trust. Belief, however, was something else.

After everything he'd witnessed and experienced in 400 lives, Will had found the answer to only one difficult question, perhaps the most important one, and he *believed* the answer he had found.

Indeed, there was something magnificent beyond this life.

THE END

MEMORIUM

In loving memory of my mother

Elissa Jean Stadler

September 21, 1948 – November 12, 2021

ACKNOWLEDGMENTS

The author would like to express his deepest gratitude to Jessica Fiorillo for her irreplaceable editing talents and her encouragement and feedback throughout the long-term development of this novel. She made this a better book. Thanks are also due to Shanan Schatzle for her detailed proofreading and to Nayeli Zúñiga-Hansen for her final reading of the manuscript.

ABOUT THE AUTHOR

Shane Stadler is an experimental physicist and university professor. He spent his early career at the US Naval Research Laboratory researching artificially-structured magnetic materials, and his current research is funded by the US Department of Energy. He has written five novels, including the four-book, sci-fi *Exoskeleton* series, and *The Peregrine Conjecture*, an Orwellian sci-fi novel. He is the coauthor of a well-known college physics textbook, and has published over 250 scientific papers on topics that range from magnetic cooling to spin-tronics to superconductivity.

You can contact Shane at www.ShaneStadler.com

ALSO BY SHANE STADLER

Printed in Great Britain
by Amazon

45448900R00381